ALL SINS REMEMBERED

ALL SINS REMEMBERED

A Novel by

PHIL RYAN

San Francisco
CITY PRESS
SAN FRANCISCO, CALIFORNIA

All Sins Remembered

Published by
San Francisco City Press
An imprint of Andarin Publishing

944 Union Street
San Francisco, California 94133
Visit our website www.sanfranciscocitypress.com

First Edition Spring 2008

The characters and events in this book are fictitious.
Any similarity to real persons, living
or dead, is coincidental and not intended by the author.

Art Direction & Cover
By Phillip Tommey

Printed & bound in
The United States of America

Library of Congress Cataloging-in-Publication Data
ISBN 978-0-9802018-0-2

To my wife, Dina Bitton,
as an awkward and delicate recognition that
her faith in this story made the telling possible
and to my daughter, Kelly, and son, Padraic,
who keep believing in me in spite of
all evidence to the contrary.

ACKNOWLEDGEMENTS

With special thanks to the following:

Patricia Klauer, my friend and soul healer.

Zoe Ann Nicholson, author of books, mentor to many and my personal Marine drill instructor.

Dan Dillon, publisher, writer, political guru and underage member of the Washbag senior center.

James Kavanaugh, America's best selling poet and dear old friend who gave me faith in my words.

Naprisha, Demetrius and Dante Ryan, my grandchildren, who taught me the importance of finishing what you start.

Jessica Ryan, my daughter-in-law, whose personal story would make a great novel except that it is true.

Linda Chester, my brilliant and lovely literary agent, without whose nurturing my stories would be still born.

Rev. Tony Sauer, S.J. former President of my alma mater, St. Ignatius College Preparatory, for giving me a literary dispensation for my novel's heresy.

I had assumed that my debut novel, after more than three decades in trial courts, would be a solitary affair. My assumption has proven wrong. Many friends, fellow authors and family supported and encouraged me to persist. I mention a few here, but space prohibits the inclusion of all. My thanks to my sisters, Camille Pulsoni and Suzanne Ryan and my brother-in-law, Bill McLean and my new family Dr. Andrea Cervenka, Dr. Shai Friedland and Mirit Friedland. Thanks also to my author and publishing colleagues Warren Hinkle. Robert Blair Kaiser, Wendy Werris, Christine Philpot and Al Baccari. Finally my gratitude to loyal friends who held my hand on this long journey: Judge Alfred Chiantelli and Cuppy Chiantelli, Wilkes Bashford, Willie L. Brown, Terry Berman, Anne Blue, Arnold Johnson, Shuli Dichter, Leland and Susan Faust, Tim Leonoudakis, Michael McCourt, Chris Stone. As for others not named just buy the book and I'll make it up to you in my second novel, *Bella Cora*.

Thus conscience does make cowards of us all;
And thus the native hue of resolution
Is sicklied o'er with the pale cast of thought,
And enterprises of great pith and moment
With this regard their currents turn awry,
And lose the name of action.

Hamlet, IIII, i, 56

Nymph, in thy orisons
Be all my sins remembered.

Hamlet, III, i, 89

"A courtroom is a place where
people say things they do not mean
and mean things they dare not say."

Joe Desmond, Court Reporter,
from *All Sins Remembered.*

ALL SINS REMEMBERED

PROLOGUE

Old Timers claimed that San Francisco's first century was a two-act play. Act I was her birth, sired by a rush to riches that created a bizarre, intercontinental migration unique in recorded history. Act II was her resurrection from entombment in rubble and ashes by which the City defied the life cycle of dust to dust. Patrick John Kelley and his beautiful wife Maria had both been born in 1906, Pat on the fourth day of that year and Maria a month later. Earthquake lore had it that when the first shocks were felt all San Francisco infants clenched their tiny fists as though defying Nature's whim. Native San Franciscans often defined their histories by their relationship to or involvement in The Great Earthquake and Fire, even more than the two ghastly world wars that shaped the 20th Century and sculpted the entire globe. And though citizen and soldier alike had battled that earth trembling inferno with furious futility, they never seemed to adopt the blank disillusion and numbing guilt of survivors. Rather they threw themselves into the task of restoring a fabled City and erected on a catastrophe of cinder and ash their City by the Bay - even grander than the one that had been obliterated. And they inculcated in their kids, these *Little Shakers*, as they were called, these fist trembling infants, a sense that the *San Andreas Fault* was more oracle than wrathful God. For from this groaning subterranean error, Nature had proclaimed the death of the 19th century and the birth of 20th century San Franciscans. Perhaps it was the fear they saw in their parents' eyes on that April day, as their wooden homes went up in flames, that taught them the fundamental lesson of their century: tranquility was but a waiting period between disasters; security conquerable by whim; and life itself ephemeral. They would grow to live their century to the fullest, for in the recesses of the subconscious lingered the central truism of their generation: You could lose everything, even your own family, in an instant.

Pat Kelley - no one ever called him Patrick; it was just Pat or "Pat-kelley," pronounced as if it were a single word – knew his own father but briefly. Jack Kelley had been a San Francisco fireman, a slight, hot-tempered Irishman with a sardonic wit, backed up with flashing fists that often dispatched men twice his size in Mission District saloons. He was something of a legend in firefighters' lore because of his incredible speed afoot. He'd married Pat's mother, Kate, when she was a provocatively mature sixteen-year-old and Pat was born eighteen months later. With the arrival of his son, Jack Kelley no longer boarded at the Valencia Street firehouse when on duty. Instead, he slept with the windows of his 17th Street apartment open so he could easily hear the fire alarm bells. He'd bolt into his boots and sprint down 17th Street, leaping onto the rear running board of the horse-drawn fire wagon to the cheers of his mates, who often wagered that Jack Kelley could outrun any fire-horse in the City for a half city block, His quickness afoot was matched by his decisiveness in emergency and peril. In the four days that he'd battled *The Great Fire of '06*, he'd single-handedly carried five children and a just-made widow from burning buildings.

Pat Kelley adored his father, who took him to the firehouse where he put on a fireman's helmet that covered his eyes and gleefully slid down the gold brass pole. His father taught him to bridle horses and then to drive the fire-wagon, never, of course, allowing the boy to exceed the speed limit of a gentle canter. He trained the boy to box. He'd told Pat, "In a fight, lad, it's all about the speed of feet and hands and what's in the head and heart. Go to the mid-section, attack the stomach and his feet and heart will quit. Then ya' finish him off with combinations!"

When Pat was thirteen, he came home from his first day at Lowell High School, but his father didn't. Kate, sobbing, told him his father was dead. Jack Kelley had died a hero's death. Fighting a blaze on Castro Street, he had charged into a burning Victorian and carried a mother and her son from their doomed home. Then he raced back into the flames to save the kid's dog! But the roof, all flame and cinder, collapsed on him. Kate Kelley was a widow at twenty-nine, and Pat a fatherless teenager.

Kate took a job as a telephone operator and worked overtime as much as she could to keep them afloat. For a while, Pat was subjected to the taunts of his teenage peers. "Where's your old man? You some kind a bastard or something?" was followed by guffaws and sneering. Pat, although small in stature, had his father's hands and feet. To hecklers' barbs, he bloodied their noses and split their lips. In athletics, he sprinted ahead of the track field and, on the diamond, slid spikes high, breaking up double plays, and in the gym launched two-handed set shots through sighing nets. Whether on Mission District street corners or the playing fields of Lowell High School, punk and prep alike quickly learned that there was a price to pay to insult Jack Kelley's heir.

Kate, afraid of a replication of her husband's fearlessness in her son and certain that daring in an adolescent was dangerous and reckless, intervened. In the summer following his freshman year she managed to get him a job as a porter at the wholesale produce and poultry market. It was hard physical labor and his work hours were from four in the morning until noon. The demands of Pat's first job and the odd hours assured that he'd be off the streets at night. But Kate's greatest gift to her son was language. She piled their apartment with books and required him to read every afternoon and report to her over their evening meal. First she gave him poetry, and then drama. She had him recite the verses of Shelley, Byron, Blake and Shakespeare and the sheer magic of their words forever seduced him as a life-long reader. After poetry she added Swift, Wilde, Pope, and then Defoe, Dickens and Austin. She climaxed his summer with the theater. A week before school reopened Pat escorted his Mom to a performance of *Hamlet*. By the summer of his fourteenth year his mother had taught him the value of honest labor and the power of the printed page. He had learned that language was more frightful than his clenched fists, more compelling than the allegory of athletic competition. His mother's army of literary masters had taught him to think critically, and in so doing, a boy's rage surrendered to a life of rational inquiry.

In his first summer as "the man of the house," the orthodoxy of his generation burst, and in its wake his vision of manhood was formed. His mother was a suffragette and wage earner by necessity. He was a student and homemaker by her insistence. So his vision of adulthood and his future paternity were at odds with the culture of his day. He felt that a man should protect and teach his family; a woman nurture and teach hers. In such a union, neither was required to sacrifice their individual intellectual pursuits. It was also that summer, laboring at The Market, as it was called, that he met her. He was wheeling a hand-truck down chaotic Davis Street, loaded with four one hundred pound sacks of potatoes, when he saw a voluptuous, raven-haired girl going over some papers with a tall, middle-aged man in a white smock and brown fedora in front of Western Poultry Company. From the man's attire Pat knew he must be the owner of Western Poultry, but who was she, he asked himself. What's such a beautiful girl doing in this entirely male world, he wondered. He didn't realize he was staring at her, his eyes running over her white cotton dress, with its pink and red roses as though to sniff her dress' decorative buds. Suddenly the steel wheels of his hand-truck bounced over a cobblestone and crashed into the curb of the sidewalk and all four potato sacks rolled out onto Davis Street. The swarming mass of porters and teamsters laughed at the clumsy boy and needled him mercilessly, knowing full well that the lovely girl had caused his navigational incompetence. He scrambled to lift the sacks back onto his hand-truck, his face flushed pink more from embarrassment than exertion. The tall man besides the girl asked in a stern voice, "Young man, what's your name?"

"Pat, sir. Pat Kelley."

"You Irish lads always seem to have trouble with your potatoes," the tall man said, with a half smile and a faint Italian accent.

"I guess so," Pat mumbled, lifting the last sack chest high and topping off the load.

"Keep your eyes on the road, Kelley," the tall man admonished. Pat nodded nervously.

"Ah, this is my daughter, Maria." Palm up, the poultry house owner gestured toward his daughter and said, "Maria, this is Mr. Patrick Kelley." To Pat he said in an authoritative baritone that frightened the lad, "I'm Bartolemeo Bertolli."

She smiled and flicked her fingertips at him. Pat half bowed, "Pleased to meet you, sir. And ah…" he stuttered on her name.

"Maria," she said with a smile that made Pat's knees tremble as he stared into the darkest, deepest eyes he'd ever seen.

"Is this a summer job or are you a career potato pusher?" Mr. Bertolli asked. "Yes…ah…no. I mean yes it's a summer job. I go to Lowell High, so I guess that's my career," Pat said.

"Me too," Maria said excitedly.

"*I also*," her father corrected. Maria scrunched her shoulders, said something to her father in Italian. He smiled at her benevolently and she said to Pat, "I'm going to Cal when I graduate. I'll be the first in our family to go to college. Are you going to college?"

There was something about her that reminded Pat of his Mom. Perhaps it was her confidence that there was nothing remarkable about a girl going to college any more than his Mom thinking it natural for a woman to join the work force. For the first and probably last time in his life Pat Kelley felt tongue-tied. "I don't know. I just started high school."

Her father intervened, "You'd best get back to work, young man."

"Yes sir," Pat said and wheeled his potatoes toward the Oregon Café.

The Indictment

On a fog shrouded June evening in 1949, 43 year-old Pat Kelley, Chief Clerk of the San Francisco Superior Court, placed a court file alongside a thick pile of papers, yellowing with age, on the roll top desk in his small study. The Kelleys lived in southwestern San Francisco, about a dozen blocks from Ocean Beach and the San Francisco Zoo. Pat and Maria Bertolli Kelley, their two daughters and only son, lived in a two-story, Spanish-style house on the upper perimeter of a forest of pines, eucalyptus and cypress overlooking Pine Lake. To the surprise of just about everyone Kate, Pat's mother, had risen quickly from telephone operator to a junior executive in the phone company. But when she was in line for and had earned a vice-presidency in the company, management regretfully informed her that it would be inappropriate for a woman to hold so senior a position. Although furious at the insult, Kate calmly negotiated a severance package and began playing the stock market at the height of *The Roaring '20's*. And she did quite well. She was shrewd enough to get out of the stock market before *The Crash*, saying, "When something's too good to be true, it ain't. So I got out of the market." She invested her winnings in real estate, and shortly before her son married Maria Bertolli had engineered a deal with developers by selling them a large stretch of arid sand dunes in exchange for this pastoral forest lot and a small percentage of their future development fees. She gave the lot to Pat and Maria as a wedding gift and Bertolli, Maria's Dad, designed their house.

Pat was fond of his small study, particularly at this time of night. He was soothed by the melodious virtuosity of his fourteen-year-old daughter, Kathleen, intently practicing on the ebony grand piano in their living room. "She even moves me when she practices her scales," he thought. Sometimes, when she'd pause to rearrange her musical scores or pencil notations on them, he'd hear the roar of the lions at the zoo or the bluesy groans of the foghorn beyond the Golden Gate. These were the rare moments of peace in the hectic life of the Kelleys of Crestlake Drive. The youngest, ten-year-old Megan, was all tucked in by now and Maria was correcting the papers of her elementary school students.

As for his only son, twelve-year-old Terry, who knew what the boy was up to? "He's probably smuggled his radio under his bed covers to listen to the Seals baseball broadcast," Pat thought. He rubbed his chin with his thick hand and thought about his boy. He was a bright, no, a truly brilliant lad, whose I.Q. and aptitude scores stressed the comprehension of his testers. As an athlete, he had already drawn the attention of baseball scouts, and high school basketball coaches were feverishly recruiting him for their teams. Yet since transferring Terry from public to parochial school four years early, his classroom performance had been modest and the teaching nuns seemed unable to reign in his loquacious mischief. To their no doubt sincere pedagogy, Terry seemed impervious. When Terry's third grade nun tried to tap into his sports interest by saying that all he talked about was Babe Ruth, Terry shot back: "Sister, all you talk about is Jesus Christ, and he never hit sixty homeruns!"

It troubled Pat that his son was indifferent in the classroom, even though an avid reader at home and a vigorous participant in family debates and discussions at the dinner table. Pat felt that the intellectual conversations around their family table were remarkable and unique for a middle-American household and well beyond the scholarship of teaching nuns. But he remained mystified that Terry did not transfer his home learning to the classroom, as his sisters had. Pat could not ascribe his son's academic indifference to the emerging hormonal changes of imminent puberty since the effortless report cards of *B's* and *C's* began when Terry was eight-years old. Pat suspected that something traumatic and lasting had happened to Terry on the night he'd witnessed a violent outburst on the steps of Saints Peter and Paul Church. It was a common street fight turned ugly when Pat, for one of the rare times in his adult life, lost control of himself.

Pat thought back to a few years earlier, when the boys were returning from the war. He and Maria, Terry and their oldest daughter, Kathleen, were attending a church bazaar. The festivities of what most referred to as "the Italian Church" were taking place in the gymnasium of the Salesian Boys' Club adjacent to the church, and in the basement auditorium. Maria had stepped out of the chaotic room filled with happily shouting kids and gaming adults for a cigarette break. She didn't notice a tall Marine captain who had followed her outside; he had been watching her intently for almost an hour as she operated the roulette wheel from a booth near the stage. As she put a cigarette to her provocative Latin lips, the Marine, now beside her, flicked his lighter and lit her cigarette. "Thanks," she smiled.

"It must be pretty hot in that booth," he said.

"It's okay." She looked at his chest full of ribbons proclaiming his experiences island-hopping under fire in the South Pacific. "Are you on leave?"

"No, it's all over for me. I'm due to be discharged in ten days."

She dragged on her cigarette. As she exhaled into the coolness of the night, he suddenly grabbed her shoulders and roughly pulled her to him. His mouth covered her startled lips, and his tongue foraged in her mouth. His large hard body crushed against her softness. When she felt his hand kneading her buttocks she stabbed her cigarette into his ear. As he reached for his burning ear, she jerked her knee violently into his groin. He stumbled backwards, and she fled into the sanctuary of the church bazaar.

Pat had been standing at the bar with Joe Desmond, a young, highly decorated veteran of the 101st Airborne, and was suggesting that Desmond enroll in court reporting school and that he could arrange his appointment to a court. Suddenly Maria, her pace quick and agile, headed directly for her husband. She didn't have to pause to locate him with her eyes. It seemed some primal feminine instinct told her precisely where he was. When Kelley saw his wife's ashen face, he ran to her. Young Desmond followed tentatively and saw him holding her shoulders as they spoke. The only words of hers that Desmond could decipher were "Marine" and "touched me." Kelley's handsome, round Irish face turned grotesque with rage. He bolted from the auditorium, Desmond following a few yards behind.

Once outside, Kelley assumed a boxer's defensive position a few feet in front of the Marine, who towered over him and must have outweighed him by a good fifty pounds. The size disparity between the combat Marine and the court clerk startled the battle-tested Desmond, but didn't seem to faze Kelley at all. "Go back inside to your hot little dago wife before you get yourself hurt," the Marine mocked. As the two men circled, Kelley said, "Soldier boy, I'm a little Mick. To the Irish, irony is everything. *Requiescat in pacem*, punk!"

"I ain't no soldier, shit head! I'm a goddamn Marine!" he screamed as he began his advance on the little man twenty years his senior.

"A dead Marine," spat out Kelley, dancing ballet-like as he flicked three stinging left jabs into the big man's startled face. It was either the speed of Kelley's blows, the Marine's taste of his own blood from his cut upper lip, or Kelley's verbal ridicule that compelled him to charge Kelley and unleash a fearsome right to Kelley's head. The blow was certain to render Kelley senseless. But just as the Marine's bone crushing fist was about to re-arrange Kelley's face, Kelley tilted his head ever so slightly, and the blow whistled harmlessly into the foggy night air. Even before the missed punch could complete its arc, Kelley fired a vicious left hook, catching the Marine above his right eye. It seemed to travel no more than six inches, landing at the moment the full weight of his missed right hand was leaning into Kelley. The impact of the blow stopped the Marine in his tracks. His hands dropped to his sides. His mouth gurgled blood, and more blood flooded down his face from a cut above his right eye. His expression was one of disbelief. Before he could sort out what his tiny tormentor was doing to him, Kelley delivered a combination of lefts and rights to the Marine's unprotected mid-section, with such force and speed the larger man couldn't even collapse to the ground, as each punch burrowed into his gut.

Kelley took a step back from the bigger man who dropped to one knee. He was positioning himself to deliver a blow born in his thick, coiled legs. Pushing off his back foot, Kelley unleashed a right cross that smashed against the Marine's ear, forcing him to collapse backwards onto the church's granite steps. He was finished. But Kelley wasn't. Kelley stood momentarily at the feet of the unconscious Marine. Then he pounced on his prostrate body, grabbing both sides of his head and began pounding it against the unyielding granite stairs of The Italian Church. "Jesus Christ, Pat! You'll kill the sonofabitch!" Desmond yelled. Then he ran to the church steps and grabbed Kelley, attempting to pull him off the Marine. But the madness that possessed Kelley infused him with such furious strength that Desmond's efforts at restraint only resulted in the three men rolling down the church steps. Desmond disengaged from the two men and raced back into the bazaar for help. He spotted Ed O'Day, San Francisco's Chief Homicide Inspector, playing roulette at Maria Kelley's booth.

"Inspector, you gotta do something! Pat Kelley's in a fight with a goddamn Marine outside!" Maria's expression was one of proud contentment, as though she already knew her husband had vindicated her. O'Day instantly bolted for the door, Desmond at his heels. They ran outside and found Kelley dragging the bleeding Marine back to the church steps to resume bashing his head. O'Day and Desmond finally pulled Kelley off of him. O'Day, a bulky six-foot-two veteran of twenty years on the force, held Kelley in a strong but soothing grip. "Easy now Pat. It's over."

"The sonofabitch, I'll kill the bastard! He'll never put his grubby hands on my wife or anyone else again!"

"Pat, Maria's fine. But she won't be if her husband kills this asshole." Then O'Day barked: "Desmond, go get my partner! He's in the bingo hall. And don't let anyone leave 'til I tell you!"

Desmond got Inspector Mike Murphy, and told the pastor to position himself at the vestibule door to make sure that no one came outside. "We've had a bit of an incident involving Pat Kelley," he lied without remorse.

"I understand," the padre said, no doubt grateful that he didn't. Desmond took his post outside the double door that opened to the vestibule. O'Day continued talking to Kelley, calming him as Murphy attended the wounded Marine. "Jeezus Pat, you really kicked the shit outta this jarhead!" Murphy said, placing his coat under the bloodied head of the Marine, slightly elevating his battered skull. Murphy went to his car and radioed for emergency medics. "Don't sweat it, Pat. They'll sew this prick back together at SF General. Hell, it's Friday night. That's all they do out there – bashed heads and bullet holes," Murphy grunted.

"Better call Robbery, Mike," his partner directed. "You got the story?"

"No problem," Murphy replied. Then he radioed the police department's Robbery Detail to avoid police assistance from General Dispatch. This way he could insure that police inspectors would respond rather than patrol officers, who might ask too many of the wrong questions of the right people. Moreover, by reporting the incident as a robbery, Murphy defined the nature of any subsequent investigation

"This is Murphy with O'Day of Homicide. Let me have Landucci. Ted?" Murphy barked into the transmitter.

"Yeah, what's up, Mike?"

"We're in North Beach when all hell breaks loose at the church bazaar. Looks like a couple of Chinese punks jumped a Marine, kicked the shit outta the poor bastard. We figure they're after his severance pay. They didn't take his wallet, but his money's gone. He told me he had a hundred and twenty bucks. I'll write up the report so you guys don't have to talk to him." Not only had Murphy relieved the Robbery Detail of dreaded paper work, he had assured that the Marine's version of events would be written by Murphy himself and accepted without question. The professionalism and integrity of homicide inspectors was beyond challenge within the department. Murphy glanced over to his partner and Kelley. O'Day nodded. Murphy resumed his report to Inspector Landucci: "Actually, the guy's damn lucky those Chinamen didn't kill him. Apparently, Pat Kelley stepped outside for a smoke, saw these punks pounding the Marine's head on the church steps and he belted one of 'em. They took off toward Chinatown and Kelley goes after 'em."

"Kelley, the Chief Clerk?" Landucci asked incredulously over the radio.

"One and the same. He chased 'em to the edge of Chinatown and figured he didn't want to mess with the Tongs. By the time we got on the street, Kelley was huffing and puffing like he'd just finished a ten rounder. We sent him home before he had a fucking heart attack. I'll write up his statement for you."

Inspector Murphy signed off, walked over to the unconscious Marine and removed his wallet. He took all the cash, scattered some of the contents onto the sidewalk and then laid the wallet five feet from its owner. Waving the cash to O'Day, he said, "I'll dump this in the poor box." After providing alms for the church's needy, Murphy joined O'Day and Kelley. O'Day said something to Kelley and then approached Desmond. "You've seen a lot in a few short years, Joe. But you didn't see shit tonight. You never left the bazaar. Got it?"

He could see that he didn't, and proceeded to give him his first lesson in street justice. "Look, Joe, Kelley's the Chief Clerk. He runs the damn courts. The judges, the damn lawyers, even we rely on him to do our jobs. We don't need a gang of reporters snooping around and writing stories about court personnel beating the shit out of war heroes 'cause they copped a feel off a guy's wife. Only Kelley and this hero actually know what happened. You don't know shit 'cause you're not really here. Because of his head injuries, this guy won't remember jack shit after the first good punch Kelley popped him with. We'll talk to him tomorrow. He doesn't want an attempted rape charge laid on top of the headache he'll wake up with. Now go back inside, Joe." O'Day put his beefy hand on Desmond's shoulder and added, "You did good, kid. A few more blows to the head and it's *Taps* for that Marine."

As Joe Desmond turned to leave the crime scene created by the pride of the police department, he saw the boy. Behind a cyclone fence in the parking lot adjacent to the church, appearing hypnotized by such a shocking moment stood little Terry Kelley. The lad had generous hazel eyes – almost too large for his face. His wide-eyed stare was riveted on his father as his Dad conversed with the two bulky cops.

"Jeezus!" Desmond thought, "The kid saw everything!"

He saw a strange man kissing his mother on the mouth and holding her like only his Daddy did. He felt the shame at perceiving adult intimacy, but a deeper, more insidious shame at his fear of the big, strange man; shame that he was afraid to rescue his mother from the man's lewd, clutching hands. Then his father appeared, and the bad man and his father cursed each other, and he knew they were going to fight. The boy's self-debasement grew stronger. Surely, this giant – for that is how he appeared to the boy – would kill his father. Yet he remained crippled by fear. He saw his father's flashing fists, the big, bad man reeling in pain and confusion and his heart soared with pride. His Daddy was tougher than a Marine, more courageous than a soldier who had defied death on the islands of the Pacific. Now that the violence had ended as quickly as it had erupted, he just stared at his father through the wire fence and saw a man he had never known. He knew the soft-spoken father who tousled his hair and played catch with him for endless hours in their backyard as he dreamed he was in Yankee Stadium. He knew the father whose magic storytelling each night sent him to sleep dreaming of far-off places and fabled peoples. But on this night, from his hidden vantage point in a church parking lot, he had learned that his gentle, laughing, loving father could surely kill.

Pat Kelley's dazed expression evaporated when his eyes met those of his only son. The sight of the boy instantaneously restored the natural warmth to his expressive face. It was as though the mere sight of his boy exorcised the demons that compelled so explosive a fury. He jogged over to the cyclone fence and knelt in front of his son. Their fingers snaked through the fence, as though by touching their filial bond in a moment of terror would be restored. The father spoke, his voice tender, yet resolute, "Did you see it?" His son nodded. "What did you feel?" Pat softly asked.

"I was scared," his son answered.

"Tell me what you feared."

"I was scared the man would do something bad to Mommy. And I was scared he'd kill you," Terry sobbed. He didn't want to cry. Men weren't supposed to cry, he felt.

"It's okay, Terry. Mommy and Daddy are fine. And it's okay to be scared. Only the brave truly understand fear. Did you feel anything else?"

Terry's tears dried up and his little fingers tightened on his father's. "I wanted you to kill him! I wanted to pee in his face when he was dead on the church steps." Sadness darkened Pat's brown eyes as he rose to his full five-foot-six inch height. He walked along the outside of the fence until he reached the gate. He entered the parking lot, and his son ran to him. He reached down and swept the boy up into his arms. He kissed him feverishly as the child wrapped his arms around Pat's thick neck. Terry snuggled into his father's shoulder as Pat carried the boy back into the church bazaar, a tear sliding down a father's flushed cheek.

Now, in the quiet of his study, Pat thought he could mark Terry's loss of self-discipline in the classroom to that street brawl. But it wasn't all that simple. He understood what the boy had witnessed, but couldn't be certain what and how an eight-year old processed such violence. It had taken Pat, who, at the time was thirty-nine years old, weeks of reflection while walking the family dog, Clio, along Ocean Beach to come to grips with his own behavior on the steps of the Italian Church. He'd accepted that had it not been for the intervention of Chief Inspector O'Day and Inspector Murphy, he would have killed that Marine captain. He'd imagined the headlines in Hearst's *Examiner*: "High Court Attaché Slays War Hero." Perhaps *The Chronicle's* headline would be more restrained: "Marine Slain on Church Steps."

Of course, he had no doubt that he'd beat the rap if ever charged and, given his position and the Marine's assault on his wife, the D.A. would no doubt rule it justifiable homicide, an act in defense of others. A husband rushing to the defense of his wife's virtue was not the stuff of criminal prosecution any more than a husband walking in on his wife *in flagrante delicto* with the plumber was. In places like Texas, when an aggrieved husband killed his adulteress wife, the courtroom boys called it "Summary Divorce." Pat's lucid and searching mind rebelled at legal fictions rationalizing male/female relations with the same vehemence that he rejected celibate papal bromides that sought to dictate which days of the month that he and Maria could explore the infinite intimacies of their bodies. Raised by and married to liberated women before that notion had insinuated itself into the American consciousness, Pat was not burdened with the faux chivalry of mid-twentieth century men. Yet he was not the least bit self-delusional and he knew that how he had reacted to another man touching his wife and what he had done to him was a perversion of the protective love that he believed was man's best nature.

In the solitude of his study Pat analyzed his actions at the Italian Church as though he had actually beaten the Marine Captain's brains out. Superficially it appeared that he was guilty of manslaughter at worst. This mid-range homicide was an intentional killing in the heat of passion upon sufficient provocation. Few would contest that a stranger sexually assaulting his wife in the shadow of her church's spires wasn't intensely provocative. But Pat, unlike a mythical jury, didn't require legal principles and factual inferences to determine his intent. Indeed he was enraged when Maria told him what had happened to her, and it was fury that drove him to confront the offending Marine. But once outside the church bazaar he cleared his mind and calmed his heart the moment he realized the size and age disparity between the war veteran and him. His father had taught him to box and drilled into him that anger in the ring was an enemy more dangerous than any opponent of any size or skill. "Never fight yourself, lad. Be as cold in your heart as a block of ice," he had taught Pat.

His Dad had been like a spiritual corner-man when Pat had fought a couple of dozen Golden Glove fights at Kezar Pavilion without a defeat. So when Pat started dancing, bobbing and weaving under the Romanesque towers of Saints Peter and Paul, he was as cool as the North Beach night fog that caressed his face. He replayed the scene in his memory and, at once, he knew that even if some remnant of provoked passion had caused the battle, it was icy malice that motivated him to bash the fallen Marine's head against the granite stairs of the Italian Church. When he had decked the man, the fight was over and Maria vindicated. But he, not she, wanted more. He wanted to kill and, when he'd first grasped the man's unconscious head and slammed it against the stairs, he knew that he could. Although no judge or jury would ever be called to determine his intent, Pat accepted that, on that North Beach night, he had attempted an act of premeditated murder. Worst of all, his only son had witnessed it and he feared that his boy was the jury sitting in judgment of his momentary malignancy. How could he now teach his son that self-control is the first, perhaps most difficult step, to fulfilling manhood?

1

Pat opened the court file folder on his desktop to learn what manner of homicide brought the Panforte family to the Hall of Justice. He read the Indictment out loud:

"The Grand Jury, in and for the City and County of San Francisco, hereby charges Robert Agnello Panforte, with a felony, to wit, a violation of Section 187 of the Penal Code, in that said, Robert Agnello Panforte, on or about the fifth day of June, in the year of Our Lord, nineteen hundred and forty-nine, in the City and County of San Francisco, State of California, did willfully, unlawfully, feloniously and with malice aforethought murder Paula Brady Panforte, a human being, contrary to the form, force and effect of the statute and against the peace and dignity of the People of the State of California."

"Returned by the Grand Jury on June 13, 1949."

"Jeezus!" Pat thought. "The Legislature's prose is so damn tortured and unrevealing." His criticism of lawyer language was not merely based on his voracious appetite for literature, but his position as Chief Clerk of the Superior Court – the top administrator of San Francisco's courts. His position gave him intimate familiarity with every aspect of trials over life, liberty and property. Kelley was no ordinary civil servant, nor has there ever been, or ever will be a Chief Clerk like him. The Great Depression and his marriage to Maria Bertolli required that he forego a scholarship to the University of California at Berkeley and quickly find a secure job not subject to the savagery of economic cycles. Although his civil service rank was that of a court clerk, he was appointed Chief Clerk by vote of the members of the Superior Court bench and served at their pleasure.

He had a photographic memory and could call forth a passage of literature or a moment in history that he'd recite with easy eloquence. His Irish wit, combined with an uncanny instinct to fathom every nuance of courthouse politics assured him a lifetime position as Chief Clerk and the loyalty of all who labored in the San Francisco courts. Because he was the Chief Clerk – or "The Chief" as the lawyers, cops and even judges often called him – he was the first person to receive the Grand Jury's secret Indictment. Because he managed the court system with such anonymous efficiency and had the absolute trust of all who worked in the Hall of Justice, he thought nothing of taking sealed and secret Grand Jury materials home with him. But he had another reason to study the transcript of Grand Jury proceedings before the defense, the press and even the judges learned of its secret story. He knew the families of both accused and victim. One he knew historically and anecdotally; the other personally. Tomorrow morning all of San Francisco would learn what was said about them in secret. Pat braced himself for the impact this might have on his own family. He would read it cover to cover, like a narrative. Then he would re-read it with a detective's eye.

The accused murderer was Robert Panforte, the thirty-year old son of the City's wholesale poultry king, Fabrizio "Fred" Panforte. The Panforte family story read like the triumphant synthesis of the American and California dreams. The fable began with Fabrizio Panforte's arrival from Italy at the Port of San Francisco in 1908. According to Panforte lore, young Fabrizio hired out as a ranch hand on a poultry ranch in Petaluma, thirty miles north of San Francisco. As Kelley read the Grand Jury Q&A, he mentally inserted what he knew about the Panforte family from his own personal knowledge. The poultry ranch that hired the young immigrant had belonged to Bartolemeo Bertolli, who had founded California's poultry industry in Petaluma before the turn of the century. It was Pat's father-in-law who gave Panforte his first job in America. Panforte quickly learned to read, write and, most importantly, to count in English. A few months after his arrival, he Anglicized his Christian name to *Fred*. His extraordinary skill with numbers facilitated his graduation from anonymous ranch hand to trusted bookkeeper for the largest poultry operation in California in a few years. By his early 30's he was the controlling shareholder and president of the largest poultry business in the West. Great Western Poultry Company provided the Panforte family with a Seacliff mansion at Land's End, from which he viewed the building of the Golden Gate Bridge; five ranches in Sonoma County, America's topographical simile of his native Tuscany; a summer home on the north shore of Lake Tahoe, a hunting lodge in the shadow of Mt. Tamalpais and a Stanford education for his only child, Robert. By the time Panforte's son went on trial for the murder of his wife, Petaluma was called "The Egg Basket of the World."

The generosity of the New World to the Panfortes seemed inexhaustible when they stood proudly in St. Mary's Cathedral as the Archbishop married his son to a lovely socialite, Paula Brady. The glamorous wedding couple had met when Paula was a Stanford coed and her handsome groom a Stanford football star, playing blocking quarterback on offense and linebacker on defense. Paula, a debutante, was the daughter of Paul Brady, one of San Francisco's most powerful trial lawyers. Because of his professional prominence and Kelley's court position, the lawyer and the clerk respected each other and had become social friends as well. Brady's formidable courtroom talents were offered in the service of insurance companies and financial institutions. Since San Francisco was then the financial capitol of the West, Brady's influence in the circle of the City's elite was considerable. With the marriage of his son into so eminent a family, Fred Panforte was, at last, admitted into the ruling establishment.

Tomorrow, Pat reflected, five years and ten days after the Panfortes' triumphant moment in St. Mary's Cathedral, the City will be stunned to learn that Paula Brady Panforte's battered body had been unearthed in the woods of Mt. Tamalpais in Marin County. And the collective shock of this news may ascend to frenzy when they read that District Attorney Michael Moore is seeking the gas chamber, accusing Robert Panforte of murdering his lovely, wealthy bride, the mother of their seven-month-old son.

Pat closed the transcript and went to the kitchen for a glass of port. The kids were all asleep by now and Maria was lounging in her nightly bath. He returned to his study, glanced at the pile of ancient papers next to the Grand Jury transcript and sighed. He picked up the transcript and thumbed through the pages quickly. The homicide investigation had been conducted by his pals, Chief Inspector Ed O'Day and Inspector Mike Murphy – the two cops who had covered-up Pat's crime scene when he'd almost murdered a Marine. And Fred Panforte's money had retained Daniel David Loeb to defend his son. "Jeezus!" he whispered aloud, as he realized how close and personal this murder case was to his own family. He rose from his chair, turned off the green Tiffany desk lamp and resolved that he must tell his wife of the Panforte murder case. He could not permit her to discover it in the headlines of the morning paper. He took a deep breadth and trudged, slump-shouldered, up the staircase to their master bedroom.

Pat thought that the term *master bedroom* was chauvinist. If anything it should be called *mistress bedroom* for it had been entirely designed and furnished by his wife. The room was a feminine world, which delighted him. A large bay window gave them a view of patches of lake-water through the dense eucalyptus forest and a smattering of cypress trees surrounding Pine Lake. From their bay window they could see Pat's major contribution to their bedroom, a lovely terraced backyard that he had planted and tended. His father-in-law had helped him layer his spacious backyard in the Tuscan mode to accommodate the dramatic slope of their forest property and insure proper irrigation. Their garden within Pine Lake forest burst with spring colors from rhododendron, fuchsia and camellia shrubs and rows of multi-colored rose bushes, scattered among swaying sword ferns and overseen by an old Monterey cypress in which their two oldest kids had built a tree house. Pat took pride in providing his wife with fresh vegetables and herbs from his fecund vegetable garden for her culinary artistry. Maria delighted watching Pat garden on the weekends. She saw that he lacked the natural facility with tools and manual labor that her father possessed from his childhood farming in Italy, but what Pat lacked in dexterity he compensated for with enthusiastic vigor. He read everything he could on plant life from nurseries and the public library. Although he never achieved his father-in-law's level of understanding soil, climate and ecosystem of plant life, his garden flourished. Even Maria conceded that he grew better, riper tomatoes than her dad ever had.

A four-poster bed centered the room and Maria had colored their bedroom in soft pastels and off-whites to elicit a feminine hint. On the wall opposite their bay window she'd placed a comfortable, dark tan cushioned chair that provided weightiness to the airy room and suggested a mood of reflective masculinity. As the only masculine piece in her design she had nominated it, "Pat's Chair." A beige hardwood floor outlined a sky-blue area rug that was the pallet upon which all the other colors in the room played. In the corner near their bay window she'd placed a Victorian lounge with an arching back, which one imagined a French impressionist would use to paint a reclining woman in languid meditation. To the side of the lounge was a French antique, mirrored dressing table complete with perfumes and the other potions of beauty enhancement.

When Pat arrived in their bedroom he heard Maria's bath water gurgling down the drain and saw that she had slipped on one of his silk pajama tops. She was primping her jet-black hair with her long, graceful fingers in front of her bathroom wall mirror. Her slender raised arms, fluffing her wavy hair, caused the pajama top to rise almost to the small of her back, exposing the two opulent half-moons of her rump. As she fiddled with her hair, the unbuttoned pajama top parted and the mirror's reflection of her light tan nipple, exclaiming her flawless full breast, winked at Pat. "Nice view," he said with a not entirely innocent leer. Turning her head quickly, looking over her arched shoulder and, seeing that he was clad only in his silk pajama bottoms, she said, "Yours or mine?"

"Beholder's choice," he said. They smiled. She propped up two feather pillows to support her back for reading and slipped under the down comforter. Pat took a seat in his chair with matching ottoman. "We need to talk," he said.

"I gather," she said, putting down Joyce's *Ulysses* on the end table. Pat and Maria had but a few rules in their marriage. One of them was that they would never discuss problems, finances, the kids, careers and the like in their bed. Their bed was theirs and theirs alone. It was their respite from the hectic activities of their lives, their lustful playground, their pacific retreat from everyone and everything. So their rule was that discussions of matters other than foreplay could never take place when they were in bed together. Thus, Pat's selection of the chair and Maria's acknowledgment of it.

Pat told her that Fred Panforte's son had been indicted for the murder of his wife. He narrated what he knew about the case. More accurately, he told her what he wanted her to hear. She listened without interruption or question. Her eyes widened when Pat told her that Mike Murphy had led the investigation. When he told her that the District Attorney himself would try the case and was seeking the death penalty, she crossed her arms across her chest in a gesture of adamant approval. Only when Pat mentioned that Daniel David Loeb was the defense attorney did her luminous eyes squint in rage or fear. Perhaps both, Pat thought. When he'd finished, she said with an edge in her voice, "Is that all?"

"For now it is. Tomorrow all hell's gonna break loose! I just wanted you to hear it from me first," Pat said softly.

"Thank you, darling. You're such a dear! But before you come to bed, I want you to do something for me," she said.

"Sure. Anything, honey."

"I want to go to the trial. I want to be there everyday, every tedious hour!" Maria said.

"Honey, it's gonna be standing room only. All four papers will be covering the trial. You can read everything about it, every day."

"No! I have to be there! You've always said that homicide is personal. Well, this is personal for me. I want to see that bastard suffer! Is it too much to ask the Chief Clerk to get his wife a seat in your hallowed courtroom?"

Pat shook his head, "No love, it's not too much to ask. But what about you? Are you sure that courtroom suffering is reserved exclusively for them?"

"I'm a big girl. Just get me a seat!"

"Consider it done," Pat said, rising from his chair. Maria rolled onto her side and turned off the bedroom lamp. Pat slid into bed beside her. She was on her side, her back to him. It was the universal female statement: "Not tonight, dear." Pat lay on his back, his hands pillowed his head, staring at an unseen ceiling. Then Maria whispered into the bed sheet at her lips, "Hold me! Hold me close…" He rolled onto his side and slipped his arm under hers and cupped her breast, her nipple hardening in his palm. She backed into him, spoon-like, and the full length of their bodies melded in a sentient coalition searching for sleep; blessed, blessed rest.

2

The morning newspapers on June 6, 1949 informed San Franciscans that A.P. Giannini, founder of the Bank of America, the world's largest bank, had died. But thirty-year-old Robert A. Panforte hadn't had time to read his morning *Chronicle*. At 5:40 a.m., he had called San Francisco's Central Police Station and reported his wife missing. Patrolman Ed Cragen responded to the Panforte Marina home in ten minutes. When Cragen was admitted into Panforte's home, he immediately recognized Bob Panforte as an ex-Stanford football star. Cragen noted that Panforte appeared to be in football-playing shape, about six-foot and a well-muscled hundred and ninety pounds. Patrolman Cragen asked him for a general description of his wife. Panforte's indolent blue eyes surveyed the cop as he contemplated the words to describe his bride. He was surprised that the officer had never seen his wife's lovely face in the society pages, but then realized cops probably didn't read the society section of the newspapers as he and Paula always did. Cragen looked into Panforte's eyes and their deep blue, circled thinly with a gray, almost silver-like lining, revealed nothing of Panforte's emotions as he calmly discussed his truant wife. Somehow the blue of Panforte's eyes seemed dissonant with the warm tan of his skin, the pure onyx color of his hair and his graceful, aquiline nose.

"She's twenty-six, five foot six, about a hundred and twenty pounds. Her hair is reddish brown – more red than brown. Very light complexion. Green eyes. She's in good condition, she plays tennis three times a week at the California Club. We've been married five years now. We met at Stanford. She went to St. Vincent de Paul grammar school and the Convent of the Sacred Heart. Would you like to see a picture of her?" Panforte said. Patrolman Cragen nodded, but was startled when Panforte handed him a snapshot of Paula taken shortly after she delivered their baby. To Cragen, she'd didn't look at all like a woman exhausted by labor. If anything, she looked younger than her wedding picture atop a baby grand piano in the living room. The only indication of her labor was her wildly splayed hair that covered the hospital pillow and framed her beaming face like a halo. "She sure doesn't look like she's just had a baby!" Cragen said.

Panforte shrugged. "It was an easy birth. Only took about an hour. That's Paula. Her life's always been effortless. Tennis, dancing, playing the piano comes easy for her. Making babies too," Panforte said. Cragen asked, "Do you remember how she was dressed last night?"

"She had her wedding band on, a green coat, a green and brown skirt with white around the waist and silk stockings. She always wears silk stockings," Panforte replied crisply.

"Her shoes?" the Patrolman asked. "I didn't notice," Panforte shrugged. After Patrolman Cragen left to file his report, Robert Panforte called his father at work. He calmly told his father that his wife was missing and he'd notified the police.

"Jesus Bob! Whadda ya mean she's missing? How can your wife be missing?" Fred Panforte shouted into the phone. Then his father said knowingly, "You were drinking again?" Bob Panforte wondered how his father knew he had fallen off the wagon last night. He hadn't been drinking hard booze – just wine with meals - since a month before his baby son had arrived. He didn't ask his father why he suspected he'd lost a battle with whiskey. Instead he simply said, "Yeah, we had a bit too much to drink."

"So, tell me what happened at your place last night," Fred said, his tone affecting paternal empathy. His son told him they had been drinking, he'd grilled some lamp chops and they fooled around in their bedroom. He had told his wife he wanted to go out dancing and she had refused. They briefly argued. Then Paula got dressed and told him she was going downtown to a show. Bob Panforte concluded his evening summary saying, "I guess I must've passed out on the couch. When I woke up this morning she wasn't here. I was so loaded I don't even know if she came back from the show and went somewhere else this morning."

Fred said decisively: "Now listen up, kid! I want ya to stick to the story you just told me. Ya didn't do nothing wrong. It's no crime to get drunk and have a spat with your wife. I'll call Paul. With his cop connections, maybe he can get some action and find her without the goddamn press getting wind of this. Now it's really important when the inspectors come to see you that you're straight with 'em. Just tell it like you told it to *me*. But remember this: only answer the questions they ask! Don't volunteer nothing! These guys are pros, they know what to ask."

"But Dad, don't you think they'll think something's fishy about letting my wife go downtown alone?" Bob replied, panic creeping into his voice.

"Don't worry about it. She's been going downtown since she was a teenager. Used to meet her Dad all the time at the movies. They can check that out with Paul. Her girlfriends can tell the cops she always goes to the opening of new movies at the Fox and you can't always go because of your work hours. So she goes with them or by herself. By the way, have you called any of her friends? Maybe she's with one of them."

"No Dad, it's too early. And I feel like a fool calling her girlfriends asking 'em where the hell my own wife is!" Bob Panforte replied.

"You can start calling them in an hour. But call Paula's mother right now! And for Chrissake, don't sound so damn detached. Ya call the cops on your wife and you make it sound like you're reciting the grain prices from Petaluma. Remember, Eileen adores you. Maybe ya outta get Aunt Lil to take the baby," Fred said.

"Okay, Dad," Robert said, hanging up. Then he phoned his mother-in-law as her sister, Aunt Lil, entered his son's room.

When Chief Homicide Inspector Ed O'Day learned that Paul Brady's daughter had been reported missing by her husband, he didn't suspect any foul play. Chief Inspector O'Day was personally acquainted not only with the victim, Paula Panforte, but her husband Robert. The Chief Inspector had first met Robert Panforte at his wedding reception at the Olympic Country Club, where he'd been a guest of Panforte's father-in-law, Paul Brady. O'Day had, of course, worked with Paul Brady years ago when Brady was earning his bones as an aggressive, brawling homicide prosecutor. Chief Inspector O'Day was second in command only to the Chief of Police in the respect and reverence of the men of the SFPD. In some circles, including the courts, he surpassed the Chief of Police with his reputation for intelligence and integrity. As Pat Kelley had put it: "Ed O'Day has committed far fewer sins than the Archbishop himself." Once he became Chief Homicide Inspector, O'Day personally selected every detective on his detail. He made no secret that he intended to become Chief of Police, yet he disdained the Byzantine police politics that led to such an appointment. He refused to climb the civil service ladder to a captaincy, the normal prerequisite for the Chief's job, saying, "I'm a cop, not a paper pusher." In the City, there were three unwritten requirements to be the top cop – you had to be Irish, have the support of the Mayor and the approval of the Archbishop. O'Day only needed a Mayor's support to meet the job specifications.

He was a big man, about 6'2 and 200 pounds. He had thick, dark brown hair and a complexion swarthier than usual for a man of Irish descent. It was perhaps his only concession to ambiguity that he concealed that his mother, who lived in the East Bay, was a full-blooded Genovesi. Only his partner, Mike Murphy, and Pat Kelley knew of his secret. In fact, it was the annual San Francisco visit with his mother at the Italian Church bizarre that made him available to prevent Kelley from bashing a horny Marine's brains. He had a photographic memory with which he recorded witness statements and suspects' as accurately as any court reporter did with pen or machine. As a homicide inspector, he spurned making notes of his interviews, relying entirely on his remarkable abilities of recall – a practice that infuriated defense attorneys accustomed to cops with much more modest minds. O'Day's manner on the witness stand was relaxed and confident, but not arrogant, as is often the case with professional witnesses. He spoke in a mellow baritone that belied that he was the toughest, most incorruptible cop on the force. His dark brown suit hung on his solid frame evenly, save for a slight bulge under his left breast where he holstered his .38 Police Special.

A little under fourteen hours after Robert Panforte had first reported his wife missing, San Francisco's preeminent homicide inspectors were buzzed into his Marina home. "Mr. Panforte, I'm Chief Inspector Ed O'Day and this is my partner, Mike Murphy. We're conducting an investigation about your missing wife. May we come in?" Panforte nodded. "Do you mind if I look around the flat?" O'Day asked.

"Of course not. I'd be happy to give you a tour."

"Maybe later as we talk through this. I'd like to get a feel for the place before we talk." O'Day began a walk through the flat while Murphy engaged Panforte in idle but intentionally disarming conversation. "I saw you play in The Big Game in your senior year. You had a helluva game. Looks like you're still in good shape," Murphy said warmly.

"I'm about five pounds over my playing weight. I watch what I eat and I'm thinking about playing a little semi-pro ball this year."

"Ya gonna play both ways, like college?"

"I don't think so. I don't think my body can handle both offense and defense anymore. I'll stick to playing linebacker."

"No more quarterbacking?"

"In football it's better to give than receive. I'd rather be hitting guys than getting hit."

Murphy mentally noted Panforte's appetite for aggression over glamour in a game of sanctioned violence. O'Day returned from his brief house tour. "Talking football again, Mike? Every Monday all I ever hear about are the goddamned Chicago Bears." O'Day said.

Panforte and Murphy smiled and Panforte said, "So you're a Bears fan?"

"I was born in Chicago. I guess it's a requirement of citizenship to root for Papa Bear's team," Murphy replied.

"I assumed you're from Ireland," Panforte said.

"When I was two years old my father moved us back to Ireland. By the time I got back to the states, I'd been infected with this damn brogue."

"I see." Panforte thought Murphy's accent pleasant and the young man was comforted by the melodic quality of the Irish inspector's speech.

"Let's drop the pigskin for a moment. Let's see if we can do something to find Mr. Panforte's wife," O'Day suggested.

"Please, Chief Inspector, it's Bob."

Murphy removed Patrolman Cragen's police report from the inside pocket of his gray suit. Neither detective revealed to Panforte that they'd been briefed on his prior statements to his mother-in-law and her sister, Lillian Foley. "According to the patrolman's report, you and your wife and baby were here last night during the evening hours. Did you go to work yesterday?" Murphy asked.

"Yes."

"What time did you get home from work?"

"About four, four-thirty in the afternoon. We work crazy hours in the poultry and produce business. What with refrigeration and mechanized transportation, it's really not necessary to open The Market in the middle of the night. It's more a cultural thing. My Dad says half The Market men would drop dead if they didn't go to work before dawn."

"I guess you've been working at The Market since you graduated from Stanford?" Murphy asked innocently.

"Well actually, I'm in charge of our Petaluma ranch operations. So Monday through Thursday, I'm up there. I work The Market on Fridays," Panforte explained.

"So you were up in Petaluma yesterday?" Murphy said.

"No I wasn't. My Dad had decided to reorganize our ranch operations. Starting yesterday, I'd be working at The Market and we'd send a new guy up to the ranches," Panforte said.

"Was this a recent management decision?" Murphy pressed. Panforte remembered his father's admonition not to volunteer more than was directly asked. He was uncomfortable that his father had unilaterally told him of this work change the Sunday before Paula disappeared, but didn't want to reveal that he had little voice in his company's management decisions. So he answered, "It's sorta been coming down the line for a while, I'd say. The good thing about it is, I get home in the afternoon and get a lot of time with the baby."

"When do you usually sleep?" Murphy asked.

"When I was going to Sonoma, I'd spend Monday and Wednesday night up there. Now I'll be in the City all week. So when we go out at night I'll take a nap. If we're not going out I'll hit the sack around nine. I remember one time, when Paula and I were dating, we went to the Cotillion Ball and I didn't take a nap. I ended up going to work at four in the morning in my tux! Everybody at The Market had a big laugh, except my father, who was really pissed. I didn't even take a lunch for fear I'd pass out in my soup."

"I gather you didn't take a nap yesterday?" Murphy asked. Panforte nodded. "I see. Did you and your wife have dinner together?"

"Yeah. I barbecued some lamb chops."

"Approximately what time did you finish dinner?"

"After six."

"You indicated to Patrolman Cragen that your wife left around seven last night. What did she do between the time you finished dinner and the time she left?" Murphy pressed.

"We did the dishes and then started to fool around. We started to make-out."

"In the living room?"

"Yeah. We were kinda rolling around on the floor, kissing and feeling each other up and then Paula says she wants to have intercourse in our bedroom."

O'Day noted the clinical detachment Panforte projected as he discussed with strangers a moment of marital intimacy. Murphy asked, "Bob, I know this is very personal, but we need to get a sense of your wife's mood last night. Can you tell us what she said when you were in the living room?"

Again his father's admonition that he be completely forthright with the inspectors and his Dad's assurance that he'd done nothing wrong came to mind. "Just answer their questions and don't volunteer," his father had said. After all, Bob thought, these two cops were his father-in-law's pals. It was just that he had not anticipated that their questions would be so specific. So he answered, "Well, we were on the floor and she was lying on top of me. We still had our clothes on, but I'd unbuttoned her blouse and unhooked her brassiere. She pulled her face up from mine and sorta lifted her upper body off me. She kinda crawled up me and presented her breasts and said, 'Your Bunny's in the bedroom.' Bunny was ah…a nickname we used. On our honeymoon she said we were gonna screw our way through Ireland and Italy like a couple of rabbits. So I started calling her Bunny. Then she went into the bedroom and I went after her." Both homicide inspectors found Panforte's explicit description of their love play jarring, but they maintained the poker faces that were the mask of their trade. O'Day interrupted his partner's interrogation: "Do you mind if we continue this in your bedroom? It'll be easier for us to get the picture."

"Sure," Panforte agreed and led the detectives to the master bedroom. He sat on the edge of the bed and Murphy took a seat on a pastel ottoman across from Panforte. O'Day remained standing near a clothes closet, out of Panforte's line of sight, in an effort to go unnoticed, so Murphy and Panforte could converse like young men sharing their sexual conquests. "Go ahead, Bob," Murphy encouraged.

"So I came in here, she's lying on the bed with only her pink silk panties on. So I undressed and she says: 'Come here Rabbit, take Bunny's panties.' I sat on the edge of the bed and slid her panties off and saw she was having her period. I said we shouldn't go through with it, 'cause of her period. She kinda challenged me, so we did it. Afterwards, I told her I didn't approve of what we'd just done and we had a short argument. She says she loves to make love when she's menstruating. She said her skin's incredibly sensitive when she has her period. Then we just dropped the subject and were just lying on the bed."

"Is that when she left?" Murphy asked.

"No. We started to fool around again. She was like wrestling with me. You know, all in fun. She's trying to pin my shoulders and I'm resisting, just enough to make it a contest. Of course I let her pin me, so she can win. Anyway, while we're wrestling, I accidentally hit her nose with my elbow. It was a pretty severe blow 'cause her head was bobbing down. Her nose started bleeding profusely. We went into the bathroom and put a wet towel on her face. I made an ice pack for the back of her neck. That's what our football trainer did to stop nosebleeds. She was real upset. She accused me of doing it on purpose. I told it was nonsense to think I'd hit her intentionally and if she was gonna get angry, she shouldn't fool around. When the bleeding stopped, she said: 'I'm going downtown to a show.' I said that'd be a good idea 'cause there'd be no more arguments. Then she got dressed."

"Could you describe what she put on?" Murphy asked.

"It was a print dress and her green coat with matching scarf. She asked for some money, so I gave her ten bucks."

"Bob, when she left for the show, was she angry with you?"

"Not really. She's a very passionate woman. You know how the Irish are. She can be mad as hell one minute and laughing the next. I guess she was sufficiently upset she didn't kiss me goodbye." Murphy pointed to brownish stains on the bedspread, "Are those blood stains?"

"Yeah and it's Paula's blood."

"It appears the bedspread has been washed recently and, from the color of the stains, it looks like it was washed after Paula's blood got on there," Murphy said.

"Right. After she left, I tried to get the stains off. But they didn't come all the way off."

"Where'd you wash it?" Murphy asked.

"Downstairs, in the garage."

"Mind if we take a look," O'Day suggested. Panforte nodded, thinking how much more thorough these cops were than the patrolman he'd met earlier in the morning. It was like the crime magazines he liked to read. The detectives always asked their questions in the scene where the events under discussion took place. As Panforte led the detectives down a two-story, switchback wooden stairway to his basement, he wished that his father was with them. If his Dad were here, he'd have some idea of how he was doing. A Westinghouse washing machine was located under a window looking out to the Panforte's backyard. An eight-foot wooden fence enclosed a patio, the only vegetation a small plot of grass surrounded by orange brick masonry and two potted plants at the far corners of the yard. Next to a homemade barbecue pit O'Day noticed a hand carved wooden stick with fresh rosemary tied to it by twine. From his memory of childhood picnics with his mother at Searsville Lake, he knew this basting brush was a sign of a Tuscan barbecue and it confirmed Panforte's story of mesquite grilling lamb chops.

While Murphy and Panforte continued their conversation, O'Day inspected the east side of the garage. On his right was a black 1947 Chevrolet coupe. In the laundry room Murphy noticed a box of Ivory detergent. He thought of the radio jingle. "Ivory Snow, 99/100% pure."

"So this is where you washed the spread. I guess you hung it up to dry over there?" Murphy pointed to a clothesline that shadowed his partner on his search of Panforte's basement.

"Right. It's so damn foggy this time of year, I figured it would dry better in here."

O'Day walked up the west side of the garage toward Murphy and Panforte. He called out to Panforte, "Mind if I check your car?"

"Not at all. You don't have to ask my permission. I just wanna find my wife."

Murphy said, "He's that way, Bob. Its awkward for him looking for clues in someone's house." Panforte assured, "Well, my father-in-law says he's the finest cop on the force. So he can snoop all day as far as I'm concerned."

"We'll find her, Bob. It may take a little time, but we'll find her. By the way, I understand you didn't leave the house last night after your wife left?"

"I got that one wrong, Mike. That's what I told the patrolman, but I forgot my trip to the grocery store. I misunderstood the patrolman. I forgot that when I came down here to wash the spread, we were out of detergent. So I went to the store."

"Did you walk or drive to the store?"

"I drove."

"Do you remember what time it was when you went to the store?"

"After Paula left for the show."

"What store did you go to?"

"It was on Chestnut Street, a store that's open after six. It may have been the Milani Market. I'm not sure."

The Chief Inspector joined the two men in the laundry room and O'Day said, "I see the car's registered to Great Western Poultry Co. But it's a two-car garage?"

"Our company provides me and my father with cars. It's a tax thing. My Dad picked a Cadillac, but I think my Chevy's the best car on the road."

"So other employees of your company don't use the Chevy?" O'Day said.

"Right - and they sure as hell don't touch my father's Caddy!"

"Does your wife use the Chevy?" O'Day asked.

"Occasionally on weekends. Now that I won't be using it to go to Petaluma, she'll get to use it more." O'Day ran a hand through his curly hair and said, "I assume the other parking space is for your tenant. What kind of car does your tenant drive?"

"My wife's aunt is our tenant, but she doesn't drive. My car's the only one we have." O'Day said, "Bob, you've been very helpful. We'll get back to you. If you think of anything else, just call Mike on his private number. Our other inspectors won't bother you."

"Thanks, I'll let you guys out through the garage door."

Panforte watched the inspectors drive west on Francisco Street and then turn left. He closed the garage door. He briskly ran up the stairs to his upper flat and called his father. He reported the details of his interview with Paul Brady's inspector friends, editing out of his summary all of the sexual play that he'd revealed to the cops. He was hoping for his father's approval that he'd done well. All his father said was: "They ask ya anything more about our Petaluma operations?"

"Just what I told you, Dad," Bob Panforte said.

Driving up Baker Street, Inspector Murphy radioed the Homicide Detail and instructed Homicide Inspectors Jack Berman and Peter Mitchell to meet them at the Hall of Justice. Murphy put down the transmitter and asked, "Ya find anything in the car?"

O'Day let pedestrians pass in front of his gaze before answering. "Blood. There was a smear of blood in the trunk of his car. I used my pen flashlight. You know, the one you gave me for my birthday. Without a light, you couldn't detect it. But it's what I didn't find in the trunk that bothers me. The tire jack was there, next to the spare tire. But there was no jack handle. Not in the trunk, not anywhere, and the car's perfectly maintained. Real neat and tidy. Blood in the trunk and no jack handle. Makes you wonder..." The Chief Inspector's voice trailed off as he parked across the street from Marina Joe's Restaurant, directly in front of a grocery market, whose red neon lights blinked: "The Milani Market."

"Did you notice that Army entrenching tool near the garbage can in his garage?" Inspector Murphy asked.

"Yeah, I saw it all right. It had remnants of damp clay and a pine needle stuck in the clay on the face of it," The Chief Inspector said.

3

The following morning, June 7, 1949, Inspectors O'Day and Murphy began checking out Panforte's neighbors. They'd learned from inquires at Lake Tahoe that there was no sign of Paula Panforte up there. There was no sign of her on trains, buses and planes between seven Monday night and this morning. She had no contact with relatives in Nevada or Southern California. They checked the Tahoe casino scene, and apparently Paula was a high roller who liked to hang out at the Cal-Neva Casino. According to the casino manager she had dropped a couple of grand over the Memorial Day weekend. He said she got into a shouting match with her husband. Seems Panforte's pretty tight with a buck. He said it was pretty ugly. "But the next night they were dancing at the club and were all lovey-dovey," the casino manager had said, "They were making out on the dance floor." That's the last time she had been seen at Tahoe.

"Interesting," Murphy said to O'Day. "Panforte described the fight and make-up routine taking place Monday night. Sounds like a volatile relationship."

"Sounds like a typical Irish/Italian love affair to me," O'Day said. Murphy shrugged in deference to his partner's expertise in Irish/Italian relations. Since the detectives had learned that no relatives or friends in two states had seen or heard from Paula in two days, they figured it was because the dead don't speak. Assuming that she was dead, rather than missing, focused their investigation. They decided not to go downtown to the Fox or the other Market Street theaters because they figured Panforte wanted them to look there. If something went terribly wrong in their home Monday night, it'd be natural for him to deflect them as far away as possible. First they interviewed Harold Pierce, who lived next door to the west of Panforte on Francisco Street. Pierce owned an auto mechanic shop on Fillmore and Filbert Streets. He told the Homicide Inspectors that he got home about seven-thirty the night before Paula was reported missing. He told them he had noticed "dog shit" on the sidewalk in front of his house, so he cleaned it off with a garden hose. There's a thin planter box between Pierce's house and Panforte's. It looked like it was on the property line, but Pierce said it was Panforte's. The plants looked pretty dry, so good neighbor Pierce sprinkled 'em. As he was watering them, Panforte's Chevy drove out of his garage, and drove away. Presumably this was when Panforte went out to buy detergent.

But this was not the only time Panforte had left his house the night in question. O'Day and Murphy talked to the neighbor on the other side of Panforte's house. He was a fourteen-year-old a kid named Damon Busby. He attended Marina Junior High. He got home Monday around six-thirty, tired from baseball practice at Funston Field. His mother, who's divorced, was out for the evening with a friend. Busby went to his room, turned on the radio and got into bed. No dinner, no homework. At seven-thirty, he was listening to *The Lone Ranger* on his radio. Halfway into the show he heard loud voices coming from Panforte's home. He got up and put his ear against the wall. It seems Brady's daughter was quite loud and graphic in her lovemaking and young Damon had been getting sex education with his ear to the wall and his dick in his hand, the inspectors surmised. Busby couldn't make out any words, just lots of yelling. Then he heard Panforte's garage door opening, so he went to the window. O'Day reasoned that the kid likes to look at Paula's boobs when she's decked out in her fleshy formals for society parties they go to. The kid saw the Chevy back out. No Paula, no tits, the kid thinks.

Busby told them he fell asleep after *The Lone Ranger* rode off into the sunset. His mother came home around ten thirty and checked his room. Typical teenager, now he's hungry. He goes down to the kitchen to get something to eat. He's eating a mortadella, cheese and peanut butter sandwich when he hears Panforte's garage door opening. So the inspectors figured that they had Panforte *backing* his car out of his garage while Tonto and the Lone Rancher are chasing bandits across the plains. But neighbor Pierce said that he saw the car driving *hood-end first* while he was watering the plants.

Now they had Panforte backing the car out around seven-forty-five. Fifteen minutes later Pierce sees the car drive out *hood-end first*. Their theory was that the shouting the kid had heard was a fight between the Panfortes in their bedroom. When it was over, Panforte backed his car out of the garage and then he backed it back in, so the trunk was near the stairway, down which he would carry her body. Then he loaded her into the trunk, which explained the bloodstain

O'Day had found, and drove out hood-end first to dispose her body. But they reasoned that Panforte could still maintain that the only trip he took on the night in question was to buy the Ivory soap. So they went to the only grocery store on Chestnut Street that was open after 7:00 p.m. It was the Milani Market and they talked to the owner and a clerk at Milani's. The owner, Gary Milani had known Panforte all his life. The clerk, who was working that night, was a football fan and knew Panforte from his Stanford days. Not only did Panforte not go to Milani's, he never shops there. It seems Milani buys his poultry and eggs from Washington Poultry Co., a competitor of Panforte's, so he doesn't even buy cigarettes there. But there was a Panforte in Milani's on Monday, June 5, 1949. Bobby, Jr., Panforte's baby, was wheeled into Milani's in his baby carriage, shortly before noon by old Aunt Lil! She bought a half-pint of Old Crow, six jars of baby food and a box of Ivory soap.

Chief Inspector O'Day concluded, "So we have a homicide without a body!" His partner replied, "No body, no case."

They decided that their only hope to find Paula Panforte's body was through her husband. They would revisit Robert Panforte's home and Inspector Mike Murphy would lead the interrogation of him. Perhaps Murphy's greatest detective skill was his ability to draw out information from reluctant witnesses and wary suspects. To them, Robert Panforte was now both a witness to his wife's last living hours and a suspect in her presumed death. Murphy was an inch or so under six feet, barrel-chested, with thick, flaming red wavy hair. Although born in Chicago, Murphy had spent his childhood in Ireland as his father's carpenter apprentice until he returned to America in his late teens. Pat and he were fast friends. Murphy was a closet poet and he and Kelley shared a love of jazz and blues music. Kelley and Murphy had attended Billie Holiday's show at the *Say When*, a notorious after-hours club. After her show, she'd been busted on a heroin beef. With Pat's help, Murphy leaked police information to her lawyer, Jake Erhlich that proved she had been set up by her manager. She was promptly acquitted of all charges. Murphy was fluent and often eloquent in both English and Gaelic and his reedy tenor voice was laced with a soft brogue. "At least I could speak English," he'd told Pat while giving him a lift home after Billie Holiday's performance. "The others, like the Italians and Chinese, they really had it hard. You really have to admire 'em." Perhaps it was Murphy's sensitivity to an immigrant's feeling of difference and distance that made him the perfect interrogator of Fred Panforte's son.

At 11:00 a.m., Wednesday, June 7, 1949, O'Day and Murphy were joined by Inspectors Jack Berman and Pete Mitchell at Panforte's Francisco Street home. The addition of these homicide inspectors meant that Paul Brady's clout had secured the four top cops in the city in search of his daughter. Inspector Murphy explained to Panforte that Berman and Mitchell would be searching the entire house for evidence. Sitting at the dining room table, Inspector Murphy again took Panforte through his story while Mitchell searched the flat, including the baby's diaper drawer, and Berman searched the basement and backyard. Panforte stuck to his story. Murphy studied him, looking for telltale signs of deception. There was no tremor in his tenor voice nor any hint of guilt in the blueness of his eyes. "Let me ask you something, Bob," Murphy said, resting his elbows on the table, his eyes intent on Panforte: "When you talked to the patrolman on Tuesday morning and when you first spoke to family members, why didn't you tell them that you'd accidentally bloodied your wife's nose?"

"When I woke up at five o'clock and found she wasn't home, I became a very scared rabbit. I thought about the Black Widow sex killings I'd been reading about that night. If something happened to my wife like the Black Widow case, and the police found blood on the bed, they'd be suspicious of me. That's why I tried to wash the bloodstain." Inspector Murphy had already learned that Bob Panforte liked to read detective stories. The Black Widow case was in one of the detective magazines he'd been reading the night before. The story was about a serial killer who believed she was capable of committing perfect crimes. She was a wealthy, attractive woman who seduced men and then murdered them and disposed of their remains at secret locations. The writer named this fictional lady-killer after the black widow spider, which purportedly devours her mate after breeding. Murphy asked, "So you washed the bedspread in the morning, before calling Central Station, and that's why it was still damp when Lillian Foley and your mother-in-law touched it?"

"Yeah."

Inspectors Berman and Mitchell searched Panforte's house for the Chevy's jack handle, bloodstained fabrics, shovels, gloves and weapons. All they found and seized was an Army entrenching tool with the clay residue and pine needle on its face. Murphy reasoned that if the tool had been used to bury Paula Panforte, the burial site couldn't be in Robert Panforte's backyard or anywhere in the Marina. Before being populated in mid - 19ᵗʰ Century, San Francisco's topography was arid, desert like sand dunes with sparse vegetation and few trees. Its forests and parks were all man made. As such, quick growing eucalyptus trees predominated at Sutro Forest and Pine Lake. Conifers that could produce a pine needle, such as the one on the tool, and Monterey cypress trees could be found in Golden Gate Park and the Presidio. Secreting a body in Golden Gate Park was unlikely because it was so heavily trafficked. As for the Presidio, it was Sixth Army Headquarters and was intensely patrolled by M.P.'s, highly security conscious and strictly enforcing federal law against offending civilians. The seizure of the entrenching tool and its earthly remnants was sufficient to cause Inspector Murphy to invite Robert Panforte to the Hall of Justice for further questioning.

At two in the afternoon the four homicide inspectors and Panforte arrived at the Hall of Justice. Panforte sat alone in a cramped interrogation room smoking. For four hours they were unable to shake Panforte from his version of his wife's disappearance. Finally O'Day said: "Bob, we know you left the house Monday night. First you said you hadn't, then you claimed you drove to the store to buy detergent. We know that's not true. Lillian Foley bought the box of Ivory earlier that day. Around eight, we know you drove your car out of the garage and spoke with your next-door neighbor. Do you remember that? He was watering your plants for you?"

Panforte nodded, "Yeah, I shouted down from upstairs that I was going to the show to pick up my wife."

"Where did you go, Bob?" O'Day asked.

"I started to drive to The Fox, but almost hit a fuckin' bus on the Fillmore Street hill. I was pretty shook up, so I came home," Panforte insisted.

"Wait a minute!" Murphy interrupted. "Would you fellas step outside for a moment. I'd like to speak with Bob alone. It's getting confusing with so many people asking so many questions. Is that okay with you, Bob?"

"Sure. Whatever you want."

The three detectives left Murphy and Panforte alone. Murphy closed the door behind his colleagues, turned to Panforte and said, "Bob, your stories don't make sense. You're changing it each time we confront you with a new fact. First you say you went to the store, now you say you went to get your wife. Are you sure you don't know what happened to her?"

"I'm positive," Panforte professed, his blue eyes dauntless. Murphy sat across from him, elbows on the table, his hands folded under his decisive chin. "Bob, sometimes there's a clash of personalities between men. If for some reason I make you uncomfortable, please say so. If there's anybody in this detail you wish to tell a different story to, I'll get him."

"That's not necessary, Mike. I've got no problems with you. Inspector O'Day gets under my skin a little bit though."

"Okay. Now Bob, put yourself in my shoes. You like detective stories. Would you believe the stories you've told us?"

"What can I do? I've told you all I can remember."

Murphy stood up and walked slowly to the door. He reached for the door knob, then half turned and said, "Bob, if that's all you can tell us, I don't know what else to ask. Let me tell you one thing. We're gonna find your wife or her body. You haven't been home tonight and, if it takes a week or a month from now 'til we find her, you won't go home."

Panforte remained silent in the face of Murphy's ominous threat to hold him hostage to the inspector's vision of the truth, his face a mask of sincerity. He tried to think of a point in his lengthy interrogation by the police where he hadn't followed his father's advice to answer truthfully but not to volunteer. "It must have been when I told 'em about going to the store for detergent," he thought to himself. "Christ, it was just a little white lie. Shit, I told Harry I was going to get my wife and it's true. If I hadn't almost hit that bus I wouldn't have turned back home. I didn't want 'em to know how fucking drunk I was! Jeezus! What would they think of me if they knew I'd left my kid home alone? If they'd asked me about booze, I'd have told 'em. But I sure as hell wasn't volunteering anything!" Robert Panforte thought of asking Inspector Murphy for permission to call his father, then figured that Murphy – who up to this moment had been very friendly – would think him unmanly.

Murphy started to turn the doorknob when a fresh new line of questions came to him. There were ten hours of darkness in Panforte's story. They'd all failed to penetrate Panforte's mind during these hours. But the detectives had approached these crucial moments with direct questions, and Murphy realized that Panforte was fearful of becoming a suspect in the mystery of his missing wife. He decided to take an indirect approach, one that didn't frighten the former football star, one that would permit him to answer truthfully, or at least with a partial truth, thereby illuminating the darkness that enveloped the Panforte home. He needed to find a body, not an errant wife. He released the doorknob, faced Panforte and asked with warmth, "Bob, have you ever blacked-out?"

"No."

"Never had any blackouts from say...a football injury?"

"No," Panforte answered after a pause.

"And you say you're not a heavy drinker?"

"Right."

"Ever drink to the extent that you couldn't remember what you did?" For the first time in the grilling of Panforte, whether by relatives or cops, he hesitated. His luxuriant blue eyes ran from Murphy to the floor. Murphy knew he had his man. "Let me ask you again, Bob. Have you ever had so much to drink that you can't remember what you did or where you may have been?"

Panforte bowed his head into his hands and sighed as though relieved of an enormous burden. "I'll tell you what I think happened."

Murphy took a seat alongside Panforte, who stared at the table-top. Murphy's manner was that of a confessor, assuring a sinner that no deed of man was incapable of forgiveness if but admitted. Panforte said, "I arrived home Monday around four. I'd stopped by the Paragon Bar and had several drinks before going home. At home, I had some more drinks before barbecuing. After dinner, we started to make-out in the living room, like I said. We ended up in the bedroom. Everything's hazy, like in a dream. We argued about her period and then were fooling around again, and I bloodied her nose. After we stopped the bleeding, I remember leaving the bedroom and fixing myself a couple more drinks. When I returned to the bedroom, she was dressed and I said, 'Great, let's go out.'

"She yelled: 'You're shit-face drunk and you don't love me if you expect me to go out with you in your condition! It would humiliate me to be seen in your company!' Something like that. I got goddamn mad that she refused to go with me when I wanted her to. Then she stormed down the hallway and left. Everything's so vague. We both seemed so angry. I can't remember everything. I must've passed out on the sofa...it was five o'clock in the morning when I felt something terrible must've happened to my wife." Inspector Michael Murphy had finally touched Panforte's marrow and illuminated a moment of terror. But he knew that even as his interrogation had brightened the dimness of Panforte's memory, it also contained the germ of a defense to the charge that he'd murdered his wife. The remaining investigation must be rigidly disciplined to prevent the defense his questions had implied and which he was certain Panforte would seek to construct. Without her body, they had no case. Inspector Murphy believed that Panforte's statements to him, coupled with the physical evidence, had expanded the crime scene. Murphy knew that Fred and Robert Panforte were hunters who maintained a hunting lodge in the woods of Mt. Tamalpais in Marin County. The clay residue and pine needle they had found on the Army entrenching tool could be found over at Mt. Tamalpais. Before going to Marin County, the inspectors needed to exhaust the evidentiary value of Robert and Paula Panforte's home.

They drove to the Marina in a two-car caravan. O'Day pulled into the driveway of Panforte's house and he, Murphy and Panforte got out of O'Day's unmarked car. Inspectors Mitchell and Berman parked behind them and they all stood for a moment on the sidewalk in front of Panforte's home. A gentle Marina breeze caressed their faces. It was 8:00 p.m. and for hours these men had been confined within smoke filled walls, trapped in the combustible embrace of Paula Brady Panforte's mystery. All of them had spent close to a full day contemplating life and death, learning of love in its majesty and madness, mutually seeking to deceive yet searching for some truth, each aware that human life hung in the balance – not Paula's, but Robert's. The naturally air-conditioned city caused them to pause on a soundless Marina night. They breathed in the damp air that prophesied the morning fog. They smelled the swelling sea and listened to the *basso profundo* of a lonely foghorn wailing disconsolately beyond the Golden Gate, its solo of the night drifting on the nocturnal breeze over the sleeping, sleepless city. For a speck of insignificant, unnoticed time, these intense, powerful men paused and let the dank air seduce their skin, the darkness of the night calming the tumult in their guts. It was Panforte who broke the spell of a June night, who terminated a sober instant when men feel no compulsion to act and experience that uneasy masculine feeling that silence is redemptive. "Let's go," the former quarterback called and the cops followed him into his home.

Once inside his home Panforte he led them down to the basement. He pointed to the laundry room. "My clothes are in there, behind the laundry chute." Murphy, the carpenter's son, entered the room, the walls and ceilings of which were knotty pine, the floor the same uncovered concrete as the basement. It was obvious to Murphy that the room had been recently added and was not part of the original floor plan. He looked behind the laundry chute and found a narrow shelf-like board held in place by brackets on each side. Upon closer inspection Murphy determined it was a piece of oak, added to the room after the carpenters had installed the knotty pine. He called to Panforte, "Looks like the cupboard's bare. I don't see any clothes."

"Reach around the two-by-four on the left," Panforte said.

Murphy's searching fingers returned to the secret compartment and removed a pair of freshly laundered trousers. Murphy said, "No gloves, Bob."

"They're in the alleyway," Panforte said listlessly. He led them out the backyard door to the eastern boundary of his lot. "The gloves are under there," Panforte said, pointing to the stair in the narrow alleyway. Murphy grunted as he got down on all fours. He again attired his hand in his handkerchief and probed under the stair. He felt a two-by-four blocking his hand, which he assumed, was part of the foundation. He shook his head, "Nothing there."

"Can you feel a two-by-four?" Panforte asked. "Yeah," Murphy grunted.

"Push on the right corner, it'll open for you." Murphy and the two-by-four and, like a revolving door, it spun open. He retrieved a pair of badly soiled garden gloves.

Panforte was mystified by their searches. He couldn't fathom what bearing his clothes and their compartments had on finding Paula. He had understood their interest in the Army entrenching tool they had seized from his garage, but did not mention to them that he was surprised by its presence in his garage. He had no recollection of bringing it over from their hunting cabin at Mt. Tam and he would have absolutely no use for it at his Marina home. Panforte looked out the window at mid-span on the Golden Gate Bridge, and his lucent, blue eyes captured the revolving spotlight from the federal penitentiary on Alcatraz Island. He'd always been fascinated by this dismal rock that housed the nation's most dangerous felons. As a boy, accompanying his father to their Marin hunting cabin, he'd asked his father about this rock of shame. It was when his father told him that the island was a prison that his appetite for detective and crime stories was born. He feared that in some incomprehensible way he might be implicating his father with these true-life detectives and he shivered at the thought. As they sped across the Bay, he wondered if he might soon join this island population of despair. His Stanford educated mind had not informed him that Alcatraz was a federal, not state, penitentiary.

Emerging from the tunnel at the summit of Waldo Grade, Panforte saw the regal yachts in Sausalito Harbor bobbing on tides drawn by a vigilant moon. At the bottom of Waldo Grade, Panforte said to O'Day, "Don't take the Richardson Bridge. Take the Mill Valley Road under the bridge." O'Day picked up his radio transmitter and, through a previously agreed radio frequency, conveyed Panforte's directions to Inspectors Berman and Mitchell. Berman wrote down Panforte's instructions, thereby memorializing each detail in the search for Paula Panforte.

At the Stinson Beach intersection, Panforte instructed O'Day to turn left. The road narrowed dramatically, barely tolerating two cars traveling in opposite directions. The road evolved into a series of twists and turns, and they entered a dense forest of towering pines and fragrant eucalyptus, shielding the road from moonlight. With only the headlights from the crawling police cars, the road seemed to O'Day like some giant, prehistoric, flat-back snake slithering through a primeval forest. "Around the next turn, take a right," Panforte said. O'Day radioed the directions and Berman copied them down, along with the mileage and time between each of Panforte's instructions.

"We're here," Panforte said. "Our cabin's about 50 yards down that path. You'll see it's not really a lodge. We call it that as sort of a joke." The inspectors examined the premises. It was a small shack for shelter and storing supplies. There was an outhouse toilet fifteen yards from the shack. Although it had running water, there was no electricity. Panforte lit a kerosene lamp once they were inside the cabin. There was no sign of Paula or any tampering with the environment. But Chief Inspector O'Day pointed out to Murphy some Army supplies that seemed foreign to a sportsmen's shelter. There were a number of canteens, wrapped in olive drab covers, attached to infantry belts. There were two metal green tanks that could be used for transporting liquids by K.P. details or as fuel tanks for jeeps. And there we two Army issue, olive-drab entrenching tools, folded into their locked position. O'Day examined them and they were clean. Murphy casually asked Panforte about his military experience. He confirmed that Panforte was exempt from military service during the war because agriculture, especially poultry, was vital to the war effort. "Did ya get this stuff at Army Surplus?" Murphy asked.

"No, the Army left it here when they used our place for training during the war," Panforte said. Murphy remembered that Paul Brady had mentioned something about Panforte volunteering to assist an army-training project in Marin County. So he asked him about it.

Panforte told him: "I was real familiar with the Mt. Tam area and the Army brass at Fort Cronkite was looking for training aides, sort of guides, I guess you'd say. They had this training course. I think they called it something like 'escape and evasion.' I guess the idea was that the troops are behind enemy lines, without weapons, and they gotta escape through a dense forest without detection. I was practically raised over here, hunting with my Dad and everything. I know the area like the back of my hand, so they asked me to teach the guys how to escape through the forest, with no compass or anything. So I taught 'em about how you find North by the moss on the trees and stuff like that. They used our cabin as sort of a headquarters. The GI's were supposed to escape from here into the forest and infiltrate or something up to right under the summit, where they'd find friendly troops. It was my job to figure out a route and then teach 'em how to make it through."

"Do you recall how many troops you trained and how many times you guided 'em up to the summit?" Murphy asked.

"Well, originally they told us it'd be an infantry company. But I don't know how many guys are in a company. I figure I did about a half dozen trips. First I had to map out the route, which I did by myself. Then I took a few groups of about ten guys and then they were supposed to do it without me. That was the test, I guess. Anyway, they canceled the program after the first test. They never told us why, but they let us keep this Army stuff you see."

"Could you take us through that route where the friendly troops were supposed to be?" Murphy asked.

"Sure, but it'd be a helluva lot easier to drive up there," Panforte said.

Back in their cars, Panforte directed them to turn right onto a badly worn, one-lane road leading up Mt. Tamalpais. Panforte cautioned O'Day, "Take it easy, Inspector. There's a lot of chuckholes and boulders on this road. It's not maintained by the county." Three times, while climbing up the mountain face, they came to forks that branched off into three distinct directions. There were no road signs. At each fork, O'Day stopped until Panforte told him which road to take. Once they had to re-trace their steps, Panforte having made the wrong directional decision. Three quarters of the way up Mt. Tamalpais, Panforte instructed O'Day to go left onto Ridgecrest Road that led to the summit. They drove cautiously toward the peak while Panforte pointed out landmarks learned from his years of forest explorations –

first with his father and later with friends. Then he said, "Pull over. This is it."

They got out of their cars and Panforte led them to the east edge of the roadside. They looked down the steep, densely forested embankment on the grandest mountain by the Bay. Elegant pines and redwoods reached for the predawn sky and were fondled by a faint mountain breeze that dislodged fatigued needles, falling soundless to the ground. In the stately shadow of conifers, receptive rhododendrons and giant sword ferns nursed fertile acids from expiring pine needles. Panforte pointed down the rugged slope and said, "The rendezvous point's down there."

O'Day glanced at his watch. It was 5:15 a.m., June 8th. "Anybody know what time the sun rises?" he asked.

"My guess is about five-forty, five-fifty," Murphy answered.

"We'll wait a half hour, then we'll go down," O'Day decided. Panforte lit a Lucky Strike.

They got out of their cars and Panforte led them to the east edge of the roadside. The peeping sun bathed the summit at 5:48 a.m., announcing a glorious Marin day. It had been almost forty-eight hours since Panforte had reported his wife missing. "Now, point it out to me again, Bob." Murphy said. Panforte pointed down slope and said, "See that wire fence about a hundred feet down hill? Ya see where the wires are sagging from the posts?" Murphy nodded. "About another hundred feet, you'll find two fallen pines. That's where the GI's destination was."

"Let's go," O'Day commanded. As he and Murphy descended the steep slope toward the forest, Murphy slipped twice. "Slow down Mike. We got all day," cautioned O'Day. When they reached the tired barbed-wire fence, O'Day instructed Murphy to go on and locate the fallen pines, while he remained at the fence so that he could communicate with Panforte. At the two fallen pines, Murphy inspected the immediate surroundings. The trees had fallen from the higher elevations of the slope. Between them was a lush sword fern shadowing a petrified log. He estimated the log to be about five-foot long and six-inches wide. His trained eyes studied it. Clay did not smear its surface nor were there any disturbances on the soil that inferred the hands of man. He concluded he'd found the wrong fallen trees. He pressed on down the damp wooded hill until he heard Panforte yell to O'Day: "Tell Mike he's gone too far." Murphy stopped in his tracks and shouted back, "Ed, come on down and give me a hand."

O'Day joined his partner who was sitting on one of the prostrate pines, his feet resting on the petrified log. Together they lifted the petrified log and placed it on one of the pine trunks. Murphy crawled between the fallen trees. He estimated that they were approximately five feet apart. He examined the ground between them, and it appeared undisturbed. On hands and knees, he crept to the southern fallen tree. He discovered that the trunk didn't touch the ground, creating two feet of crawl space. He gently probed the ground with a stick. "Loose dirt," he called up to O'Day. "Give me a shovel." O'Day tossed him an entrenching tool they'd borrowed from Panforte's hunting cabin, the twin of the one they'd found in Panforte's home. "Take it real easy now," O'Day said.

"There's no other way to take it. It's so cramped I can barely move," Murphy complained. Using the blade in a scraping, rather than digging, motion, Murphy removed a shovel full of clay and soil from under the tree. He put the tool aside and, with his fingers, probed the soil. His sightless fingers searched the damp earth for the feel of fabric or skin. He felt nothing but mountain dirt. He skimmed another shovel full of terrain and piled it neatly with his initial digging. He pawed the earth again, but only felt twigs, sand and leaves of the subsoil. After his fifth shovel full, his fingers spoke to him of fabric. He kept his fingers on it and his right hand pawed furiously at the ground until he'd burrowed an oval opening in the earth. Beads of sweat slid from under his thick red hair, ran down his pale forehead and fell onto the earth he was rearranging. He pulled out his flashlight and shined it into the hole, his left hand still in contact with the fabric. His eyes translated what his fingers had unearthed. He saw the luxurious left hip of a young woman, clad in a green, brown and white print dress – the dress Panforte had described his wife wearing when last seen.

"We've found her," Murphy reported flatly to the Chief Inspector. When he removed the remaining soil Paula Brady Panforte was lying peacefully on her right side, her radiant auburn hair swept back from her ear and revealing her stunning profile. Her head leaned forward and her knees were pulled up against her opulent breasts. She lay fetal-like in a pit in the Marin woods, yet her wondrous beauty struck Murphy. Her skin had a lambent glow, her cheeks rosy as though she was sleeping contentedly after having made earthy love. The tint and tone of her skin startled Murphy. "Christ Almighty! She's still alive!" he muttered to himself. He touched her face, his finger's kissing her blushing cheek and her frigid skin repelled the policeman's touch. She looked so vibrant that she'd fooled Murphy's eyes. But his fingers on her chilling, lifeless skin told the awful truth. Paula Panforte, mature daughter and new mother, was dead.

Then Inspector Murphy noticed blood near her nose and mouth. He saw that the green coat, described in Patrolman Cragen's report, lay underneath her body, as though her gravedigger had sought to shelter her from the dankness of her mountain tomb. She was shoeless, but Murphy observed a pair of white loafers laid neatly by her delicate feet. Sweating, he muttered, "Thank God that patrolman got her clothing details down in writing before we found her. Some damn lawyer won't be able to claim we made up Panforte's description after digging her up."

O'Day and Murphy commenced the intimate inspection of the corpse essential to any homicide investigation. They removed Paula's dress and saw she was wearing a pink silk slip with matching brassiere. When Murphy pulled her slip from her shoulders and removed her bra, they saw that her prideful breasts were severely black and blue. Murphy examined her pink silk panties and noted a single word was stitched on the back, inside panty band. The word was Lucca. When they'd completed their examination they redressed her. Murphy slipped her white loafers onto her petite feet and noticed an anklet on her right ankle. It was gold and inscribed with the name *Bunny*. He thought of Ireland. Not the Ireland of his youth, but the Ireland of Paula's honeymoon. A faint touch of nausea hit his gut as he remembered Robert Panforte's description of his bride's sexual plans. He thought of the dead girl's father and how he'd break the news to him. He dreaded the paucity of his vocabulary.

4

Pat Kelley jumped off the L streetcar's running board at Market and Kearny Streets. Just as he had expected, the headlines of the morning papers screamed, *"SOCIALITE SLAIN AT MT. TAM!"* as the newsboy hawked tragedy from his corner newsstand. Kelley had thoroughly studied the Grand Jury transcript and nowhere in the record had it been definitively established that Paula Panforte had met her death over at Mt. Tamalpais. As he walked up Kearny Street toward his office at the Hall of Justice, Pat made the first of a series of decisions that would dramatically affect his family and the family of the accused. Pat had been the chief executive officer of the Superior Court for five years and he had offices at City Hall, where civil trials were held, and the Hall of Justice, where criminal cases were adjudicated. He preferred working at the Hall of Justice because of its location and the intriguing cast of characters that populated the criminal courts. The Hall of Justice, along with Bartolemeo Bertolli's wholesale poultry building, were the only buildings to survive The Great Earthquake and Fire. The Kearny Street location of the old Hall of Justice cast history's varied shadow from San Francisco's first plaza – Portsmith Square. You could imagine the fervor of 19th century labor organizers calling for the City's first labor strikes, or Dennis Kearney's strident racist crusade against Chinese workers, or the lynchings of the Vigilance Committee momentarily silencing political discourse with a coarse noose. The Hall of Justice in which Pat worked was a grand building of exterior granite, it's Doric columns creating the intended feeling of a temple. Pat thought that the interior marble of the echoing corridors and rich luster of the mahogany fixtures created a sense that the pursuit of justice was a sacred rite, that court combat might be deadly, but not mindlessly violent.

The City, as all Californians referred to San Francisco, was a vibrant, often wild town. Always a strong labor town, wages were high and work plentiful. The war industry had forever changed labor demographics in the state, bringing women into the workplace and a great black migration from Texas, Arkansas, and Louisiana. The public schools taught the kids and sent a generation on to higher education in such numbers as to create the best-educated generation the country had ever produced. Stockbrokers on Montgomery Street, which locals provincially called "The Wall Street of the West," bought and sold scraps of paper in a profit frenzy that perceived no end. The Irish ran the courts and the police department with brilliant efficiency and only as much graft as was prudent.

The location of the old Hall of Justice placed the temple in the very heart of The City. To the west, Pat could walk the streets of Chinatown to a chorus of singsong dialects and the aroma of exotic foods. To the east, he strolled by the ramshackle huts of the wholesale produce and poultry center. In this commission market, Italians and a handful of Jews that spoke English with Italian rather than Yiddish accents, fed the growing state and amassed their fortunes. "The Market," as it was called, opened at three in the morning in order to assure that retail outlets had fresh produce and poultry. When the stockbrokers, bankers, insurance men and leggy secretaries began to fill the modest skyscrapers of the financial district, they walked on streets teeming with hand trucks bearing crates of tomatoes and cantaloupes and an army of push carts carrying five hundred pounds of potatoes piloted by swearing, sweating Italian laborers. It was here that his father-in-law had made and lost his fortune. And it was here that Robert Panforte's father had waged his stock battle to take over Bertolli's business and building.

To the north of the Hall of Justice was the infamous Barbary Coast, the night-lights of Broadway and storied North Beach. On Pacific Avenue the International Settlement sign, arching over the street, enticed the lonely to the erotic. Strippers and B-Girls whispered behind curtained doorways to which sailors and old men flocked in search of a moment of warmth, rarely found on a foggy San Francisco night. Watered drinks sold at premium prices were anxiously paid as a tax on yearning. Above Pacific Avenue was the nightlife of Broadway. The Broadway of the middle years of the Truman era was a street of light and an avenue of gaiety. Sweating chefs behind the counters at New Joe's and Vanessi's sent flames up exhaust fans as they sautéed Italian meals cooked to order. Family French, Italian, Basque and Chinese restaurants presented sumptuous feasts at prices a pauper could afford. The Jazz Workshop brought an American art form to the street and Pat first heard Miles and Oscar and Dizzy and Brubeck in its smoky confines. There were nightclubs and cabarets all along the street. Aspiring singers at the Bocci Ball bar performed grand opera, and every night Broadway's sidewalks were packed with people. It was a street of food and drink and song and dance and laughter where, for an evening, you could be forever young.

Around the corner of Broadway and Columbus, in the shadow of Coit Tower and the Romanesque spires of The Italian Church, was North Beach. The fragrance of freshly brewed cappuccino and the daily and infinite variety of breads from Tuscan bakeries were the first intoxicant seducing the stroller. Fresh fish, drawn each morning from the Pacific, was displayed open-air at storefronts as the fishermen of Genoa, Venice, Florence and Lucca had done for centuries. At Molinari's Delicatessen, prosciutto hovered like a guardian angel above counters filled with fresh pasta and varied rich cheeses. Along Grant Avenue poetry was recited in coffee houses, while art and sculpture and avant-garde bookstores offered lavish culture, the soul of even the most humble Italian. Women bargained vigorously with butchers while old men sat, dressed in full business suits and fedoras, in Washington Square Park, conversing in their native tongue of the land they'd left, still arguing about Garibaldi and the Church, forgetting why they had left their homeland.

Pat felt that "The Hall," as the cops called it, was a stoic island in the swelling sea of contradictions that had always been San Francisco. Now his wife would be coming to The Hall for Robert Panforte's murder trial. But Pat knew that her witness at the Panforte trial would not be in pursuit of elusive justice. Her mission was vengeance. Perhaps her only flaw, Pat thought, was the rage that simmered in her soul for what she believed Fred Panforte had done to her father. She would take her seat at the trial, prayerful that she would observe the debasement of Fred Panforte through his only child. So Pat decided to assign himself as the court clerk for the Panforte murder case. From the clerk's desk, he could monitor Maria's emotions and perhaps temper her volatility by his calming presence. He would explain to the Presiding Judge that with all four daily newspapers covering the trial and the families of victim and defendant so prominent, the trial court should be staffed by the most able court personnel. He would also suggest that his young friend Joe Desmond be assigned as the court reporter. He would point out to the P.J. that Desmond already had reported the Grand Jury testimony and that the lawyers would no doubt demand a daily transcript, so Desmond's familiarity with the case would be useful.

Unspoken to the Presiding Judge was Kelley's comprehension of courtroom roles. It is in the nature of a court reporter's job that they become the most trusted confidante of their judges.

Judges often involve them in their reasoning process that leads to their decisions. They share their family and career frustrations, their infidelities and their kids' delinquencies, their petty prejudices and injudicious appetites. Judges do so because they know that their reporters are record makers by profession, and they would never reveal off-the-record confidences entrusted to their sworn silence. And the smart cops and truly talented trial lawyers selectively shared their secrets with court reporters. Sometimes they wanted the reporter's critiques of their performances or they'd use them as trial balloons for some tactical coupe they'd planned. Occasionally, comforted with a few too many drinks, judges would tell reporters things they had no business talking about. Court reporters had these moments because they knew that the only offense that would cost them their lifetime jobs was uttering a single secret that had been filed with them off-the-record. With Danny Loeb leading Panforte's defense, Pat needed a loyal court reporter to penetrate Loeb's confidences. Joe Desmond had demonstrated his courage one Christmas in a place called Bastogne and his discretion of never mentioning Kelley's curbside lobotomy on that groping Marine was certain. Because of Pat's relationship to Bertolli and Maria's presence at the trial, Loeb would be wary and unlikely to confide in the Chief Clerk. So Desmond, under the cover of his court reporter's position, would be Pat's agent in the defense camp.

In his morning meeting with the Presiding Judge, Kelley pulled another trick from his bureaucratic bag. He casually mentioned to the judge that with the intense press coverage of the trial, involving as it did prominent families, it might be wise to bring in an out-of-town jurist to preside. The Presiding Judge frowned at Pat's suggestion. He was certain that bringing in a judge from another county would not sit well with his colleagues on the bench and he was equally concerned that the press might criticize him no matter which local judge he assigned the Panforte case. After he expressed his dilemma, Pat said, "Perhaps you could use the jury wheel. I'll put all the criminal court judges in the wheel, give it a quick spin and pull out a name. The press can't make anything outta that. It's picking a judge the same way we pick jurors."

"Excellent idea, Pat!" the Presiding Judge said. Pat went into the vacant courtroom. He placed a dozen scraps of paper in the jury wheel, spun it and called out to the Presiding Judge who was standing in his chambers doorway: "You wanna do the honors, Judge?"

"Naw, you go ahead. I never win at Bingo!" Pat reached into the jury wheel and removed a single paper scrap. He read the name, looked over to the Presiding Judge and said: "It's Judge Grant's case if she wants it."

"Pat, you'll explain to the press boys how we did this, right?" the Presiding Judge said somewhat tensely.

"Of course," Pat said. "That's why I'm clerking this damn case."

When the Presiding Judge had returned to his chambers, Pat emptied the jury wheel and dumped all the paper scraps into his briefcase. When he got home he would burn the scraps and no one would ever know that all twelve pieces of paper had the same name – Judge Lucille Grant, San Francisco's first and only female judge! And in Pat Kelley's mind the finest jurist he had ever known. Pat pranced down a flight of marble stairs to Joe Desmond's cubicle in chambers. He informed Desmond that Judge Grant would try the Panforte case, he would clerk it and Desmond would produce a daily transcript. "Sweet Jesus!" Desmond exclaimed. "I just struck it rich!"

"Yeah, but you'll be working night and day, so you won't have much time for your lovely girlfriend." Pat was referring to Mary Healy, a voluptuous redhead who was the first female clerk hired by the Superior Court. Kelley, well ahead of the times, had wisely assigned her to the court's only female judge and Desmond and she had fallen in love a few months after Mary had integrated the "Boy's Club" of court attaches. Pat invited Desmond to attend Paula Brady Panforte's funeral along with Maria and her father. On their way to St. Mary's Cathedral, Pat said, "How about joining me for dinner? I'd like to go over some details we're likely to face in the Panforte trial."

"Sure. Where do you want to eat?"

"Fior d'Italia."

"Of course," Desmond smiled. One of the perks of being a close friend of Pat Kelley was that he could get a table at any restaurant in town without reservations or greasing the maitre d's palm. As Chief Clerk of the Superior Court, Kelley personally picked the eating places for all serving jurors. He believed that civic duties were best performed when jurors dined in the finest San Francisco tradition. Court bailiffs joked that no jury ever reached a verdict during Kelley's administration without sampling at least one elegant meal with wine, courtesy of the city treasury. When it came to North Beach restaurants, Kelley's clout was even more formidable. As Bertolli's son-in-law, some of the reverence in which the old man was held in the Italian community naturally rubbed off on Kelley. And everyone knew the story of how Pat had enrolled in Galileo Adult School, with recently arrived immigrants, to learn Italian so that he could ask for Maria's hand in her father's native tongue. When Bertolli asked Kelley why he was speaking Italian, Kelley said, "I feel Dante's tongue conveys passion better than English."

Bertolli smiled wryly and said, "But *your* Italian accent doesn't. No matter, your eyes convey all the passion a father could hope for his daughter."

Although Pat's Italian didn't quite measure up to Tuscan standards, he was much more an Italian Catholic than Irish Catholic. Like his father-in-law who came of age when Garibaldi's republican armies toppled the Papal States, Pat's searching intellect rebelled at the notion of papal infallibility. Indeed he believed that the very history of the papacy was a sorry chronicle of errors, some of monstrously immoral dimensions. "No thinking person can study the Crusades and The Inquisition without being sickened by the moral depravity of the Church!" he had told his son's Godfather. But he didn't have to search back into the centuries for the events that drove Catholicism from his soul. When Pope Pius XII made alliance with Hitler and ordered Christian Democrats, the Nazis' only remaining political opposition, to refrain from politics so that the Church could continue to operate her schools, Pat Kelley left the Church. Other than weddings and funerals, a couple of Jesuit friends and his kids' parochial schools, he was catholic only in the breadth of his intellect.

Yet at Paula Panforte's funeral he felt that the rite of Christian grieving seemed the only Catholic tradition that spoke poignantly to the living through the dead. Perhaps it was his distant Celtic genes so nurtured in historic tragedy and unending pathos that penetrated his Renaissance soul. Or maybe it was that this was the only Catholic Church service conducted mostly in English that rendered young, violent death marginally expressible. He thought of the murdered girl's father and glanced at his oldest daughter beside her grandfather. He thought, "She's maturing into a beauty like her mom. And so talented and assured without any of her brother's arrogance." He coughed to suppress a sob in his chest at the thought of losing his first daughter.

He glanced at his wife standing for the Gospel, flanked on one side by her father, a head taller than she and the other by him, an inch shorter than Maria. She was dressed appropriately in mourning black, a hat with a spidery veil webbing her elegant cheekbones. In an era when women were required to cover their heads whenever out of their homes, Maria hated hats. Because of her father she'd been a tomboy as a child. In her youth she had broken and trained horses on their Sonoma ranch, was taught to throw a ball whip-like as any boy, had been a high ranking junior tennis player and a fearsome field hockey player in her undergraduate years at Berkeley. She loved the feel of a foggy breeze rippling through her raven wavy hair, whether on the athletic field or stepping out onto breezy Van Ness Avenue after a performance of the San Francisco Opera Company. Pat felt that her dignified composure at this memorial service was authored by the fact that he and her father anchored her. She was flanked by unconditional love and it soothed her and tempered her anguish. Pat couldn't help but compare his wife to the dead girl. Both were beautiful, desirable women with strong and unquestionably loving fathers. But Maria had a mind that matched his. And Paula, well, she was glamorous all right, but Pat thought glamour was simply frivolous beauty.

Paula Brady Panforte, a shapely, auburn haired Irish lass who had laughed and danced her way through life, was dead in the full flower of her beauty at the age of twenty-six. Her seven month-old son was in the temporary custody of his maternal grandmother. It was too early to speculate on how the Brady and Panforte genes would paint the little boy's features, but he had his father's piercing blue/gray eyes and his mother's careless smile. Paula was born when her father, Paul Brady, was a young Deputy District Attorney, whose aggressive court-room manner frequently ended up in courthouse fisticuffs in which he dispatched defense lawyers with the same vehemence that he sent their clients to prison. Honing his natural skills in the brawling criminal courts, Brady quickly attracted the attention of insurance companies who lured him into private practice where he quickly established a reputation as a brilliant, resourceful and ruthless insurance defense attorney. Large financial institutions, noting his constant and well-publicized courtroom triumphs, retained him whenever they feared their decorous Montgomery Street lawyers might lack the fortitude to protect their prodigious assets from the graspings of private litigants.

Three things centered Paul Brady's life – the courtroom, his leadership of the Irish community and his daughter. So focused was his life on this trinity of devotion that it ultimately fractured his marriage to his wife, Eileen. Divorce was out of the question for an Irish Catholic of Brady's stature, so a separation was arranged in which Brady generously supported his estranged wife and enthusiastically helped raise his lovely daughter. He'd sent her as a teen to the Convent of the Sacred Heart, the Catholic girls' finishing school for the wealthy and from which she had graduated and matriculated to Stanford University in search of a spouse. Paul Brady's Broadway Street penthouse, with its panoramic view of the Golden Gate, was only a block from the convent school. During Paula's high school years she'd walk to her father's apartment. Girlfriends and boyfriends tagged along and they hung out until her father came home in the evening. Then he'd take her out to dinner or the movies or the theater. He delighted in acting as a chaperon at school dances and laughed to himself at the hungry, almost terrified expressions of St. Ignatius or Stuart Hall school boys as they ogled his daughter from across the dance floor. When the boys finally worked up the courage to ask her to dance, he loved the way she played with them, feline-like, elusive. And her wit, like his, was tart and sarcastic, but tempered by her shining smile. It was said of Paul Brady that the only time he relied on his Catholic faith was during her high school tennis matches, when he would cross himself before her every serve. Brady had been an intercollegiate boxing champion and she rewarded his innate competitiveness with an enthusiastic junior tennis game. Like most fathers, he failed to note that her tennis ardor was not matched by her athletic skills. By her senior year she was spending more and more time under her father's roof than with her mother. She had complete sets of clothes both in her mother's Vallejo Street mansion and her father's apartment. If you studied the contents of both her closets, the dangling apparel proclaimed the closet in her mother's house was that of a girl, while the closet in her father's home was the habitat of a glamorous woman.

Pat felt that the similarities between his wife and the dead girl were superficial. True, both were beautiful women. But Paula worked at her beauty and Maria didn't have to. There was only so much time in her day and Maria thought it a chronic waste and absurd vanity to spend it looking at herself in her mirror. Paula, on the other hand, constantly shopped for the latest Paris fashions, treated her skin to a sun lamp, and applied all the potions of make-up that had come into vogue in post-war America. Both women had college degrees. Maria had worked for hers, Paula's father had purchased hers. Both women had played tennis. For Paula, it was a social occasion, a chance to exercise and keep her body firm. She played a dainty baseline game, as though it was unfeminine to sweat or be seen sprawling on the court flagging down a passing shot. For Maria tennis was competition, and fierce competition at that. The goal was to conquer your opponent by defeating them first mentally and then physically. She used a power game, serving and rushing the net with dazzling speed and choreographed footwork. She loved the feel of sweat cascading over her body, the salty taste of her own perspiration on her lips. Even when tennis was supposed to be social, she couldn't restrain her tomboy nature. Pat always chuckled when he recalled Maria's exhibition match with the great Helen Wills. The many-times Wimbledon champion had come to dedicate the playground at Larkin and Broadway, a couple of blocks down from Bertolli's Russian Hill apartment. The City had named the playground after her and picked teenage Maria Bertolli, then the top ranked junior player in the City, to play an exhibition with San Francisco's greatest tennis champion. As an exhibition, no score was kept except secretly by Maria. She would tell Pat and her kids that she lost to the world's finest tennis player six games to three. Then she added, absolutely convinced it was true: "If I'd gotten 70% of my first serves in, I'd have beaten her!" Her family indulged her fantasy with smiles.

At the consecration of the Requiem Mass for Paul Brady's dead daughter, Pat Kelley studied the tall, broad shouldered trial lawyer. He stood erect alongside his softly sobbing, estranged wife, Eileen. When the first plaintiff chords of *Ave Maria* sighed from the great pipes of the church organ and the haunting tenor of Sean McCormick filled the sepulchral church, Pat saw Brady's shoulders sag under the burden of the loss of the only love he ever allowed himself to accept without reservation. Archbishop Malloy, who last saw Brady in church the day he gave his daughter to Bob Panforte in Holy Matrimony, delivered the eulogy. It was compassionately brief, designed to subdue what it could never heal. Unlike the spring wedding day five years earlier, there were no Panforte family members present at this June mourning. The Governor, the Mayor, all members of the Board of Supervisors, the Superior Court bench, the cadre of lawyers with whom Brady had fought so many battles, and hundreds of anonymous Irishmen paid hush homage to the grieving family. Bob Panforte was in jail awaiting trial. His father had escaped to his turkey ranch in Sonoma to avoid the press hordes that clamored for interviews. His wife, Angelina, had sealed herself in their Sea Cliff mansion, staring vacantly out at the Golden Gate.

The truancy of the Panfortes from this ritual of departure was understandable. Pat noticed that absent from the Cathedral were the leaders of the Italian community that had joyously attended the glamorous couple's wedding. He speculated that there might be a sense of collective guilt that one of their own was suspected of so foul a deed or that North Beach Italians might be apprehensive of the possible reaction of the Irish to Paula's murder. But he quickly dismissed such notions. After all, San Francisco was born with a Gold Rush population speaking every tongue, practicing every faith and representing every color on the globe. Unlike the east coast, the City's nationalities had not been ghettoized. They didn't vote in ethnic blocks but made easy alliances of principle and opportunism. Irish-Italian relations in the City had always been, like his marriage to Maria, intense, intimate and operatic. The Italian Church had been funded by a Spanish bishop, designed by an Irish architect and built on land sold by a French Jew. And St. Patrick, after whom Kelley was named, was Italian. Or as Pat's father-in-law had said, "St. Patrick was a Roman and that's certainly not Italian!"

Of the fifteen hundred mourners assembled, there were only two Italian Americans – Maria Bertolli Kelley and her father, Bartolomeo Bertolli. For Bertolli, this was the second large funeral he'd attended in the first weeks of June 1949. On the very day Robert Panforte had reported his wife missing, Bertolli's old friend and banker, A.P. Giannini, the founder of the Bank of America, had died. Pat recalled Bertolli's eulogy for Giannini. His father-in-law had commented that Gianni had a peculiar habit of speaking in the third person when emphasizing a point. Bertolli concluded his eulogy saying: "Giannini says: No man owns a fortune. The fortune owns the man." Pat thought that his father-in-law's presence at Paula's memorial service was as sort of a representative of the Italian community. After all, he was probably the only Italian-American in the City who had been close to both the victim's family and the defendant's family. Pat wondered if Bertolli's quote of Giannini was intended for Fred Panforte, his protégé who had turned on his mentor and seized his business from him decades earlier. Was this somehow a curse or prophecy that demanded Panforte's only child stand trial for his life? And was the Panforte murder trial, bringing so many prominent families into the courtroom, somehow ordained - the inevitable offspring of past sins – unforgiving and unrepentant?

5

After Paula Panforte's funeral, her parents invited Bartolomeo Bertolli, Pat and Maria Kelley to Eileen Brady's home in Pacific Heights on Vallejo Street for refreshments. It was a ritual of Irish Catholic grieving that family members and close friends gathered for drinks and food at the home of the bereaved. As a twenty-seven year-old housewife with a baby daughter, Eileen Brady had been recruited by Bertolli to manage the San Francisco Opera Company's ticket operations during the company's first year of performances at Stanford Stadium in 1922. Like most of the volunteers who gave their time and effort to establish and develop Bertolli's vision of a world-class opera company, Eileen still volunteered at the ticket office at the War Memorial Opera House. As for her husband, Paul, he was one of the two thousand San Franciscans who contributed a thousand dollars to fund the development and construction of the War Memorial Opera House. The Bradys had known Bertolli longer than the Kelleys and, like most of the show business world, referred to him as "Mr. B." Paul's friendship with Pat Kelley had blossomed when Pat became the Chief Clerk of the Superior Court.

Across Eileen Brady's living room Maria Kelley stood alongside her father near the keyboard of a dark mahogany baby grand piano. It was odd in that it seemed like Bertolli was the center of a reception line as most of the guests approached him, shook his hand and said a few words to him. He appeared quite different at this ritual of passing, as he also had at Giannini's funeral. He was eighty-three years old and usually appeared every bit his age. He had an old man's slump to his shoulders, and his movements suggested brittle, aged bones. There was a deep sadness in his gray eyes that only seemed to evaporate whenever his grandchildren shared their latest discoveries with him. He was bald with a semi-circle of white hair above his ears and a few wisps of random gray and black hairs on the top of his head, behind his prominent forehead. He had a strong Roman nose, and you imagined that he could have posed for a Roman sculptor chiseling the bust of a Caesar. He was always formally attired in suit and tie, even at his grandchildren's birthday parties and holiday celebrations. It was as though he was attending a perpetual wake, perhaps even his own. His spell of sadness was broken, however, on his grandchildren's birthdays and Holidays. The Kelley family did not exchange gifts in the traditional and commercial sense of the season. Each child would create something as a gift to the extended family. From a stick drawing of a little girl riding a stick-horse with a huge head to a sophisticated painting of fog shrouded Ocean Beach, the Kelley children celebrated their day as the birth of creativity. When Terry dramatically recited a poem he'd composed, Bertolli broke into a broad grin and said to Pat, "I think we've got a little Dante here!"

"More like a struggling Yeats," Pat replied. When fourteen-year-old Kathleen Kelley played her piano arrangement of Puccini's music, which she'd called, "To Nonno From Lucca," her grandfather burst into a chorus of "Bravas" as tears of joy slid down his cheeks.

Pat Kelley had noticed that at Giannini's funeral, and here in Eileen Brady's home of mourning, his broad shoulders were erect and thrown back and his movements graceful and sure. It was as though in moments of the tragedy and loss of others he summoned from his Renaissance soul a reservoir of compassionate vigor that was palpable throughout the room. Pat was sitting in the glass enclosed sun porch with Eileen Brady and her older, spinster sister, Lillian Foley. The porch was furnished with a rust colored cushioned sofa and matching love seat, a round rosewood coffee table and two large, thickly pillowed reading chairs. Two floor lamps rose from the bay blue carpet, their shades hovering over the armrests of each chair. In the center of the porch was a vacant baby's playpen. Eileen's grandson, Robert Panforte, Jr. was napping in what had once his mother's bedroom. Eileen reached into her grandson's playpen and picked up a tiny cotton ball. She fiddled with it as Pat Kelley gently probed her big sister Lillian about her morning visit to her niece's home on June 6th.

This was the beginning of Pat Kelley's unauthorized investigation into the death of Paula Brady Panforte. He had thoroughly studied the transcript of the Grand Jury proceedings and concluded that there were holes in the prosecution's case against Robert Panforte. He felt that the homicide investigation had placed too much importance on Paula's grave, high atop Mt. Tamalpais. He intuited that young Panforte's guilt or innocence would be discovered only by deciphering the intricacies and intimacies of his family life. Pat was particularly focused on a more expanded time frame than the police investigation had accepted. The homicide detail had framed Paula's mystery from Monday, June 5th to the discovery of her body on Mt. Tamalpais. They had posited that domestic violence had erupted in the couple's Marina home on Monday evening and that this was the motive for Paula's slaying. Not only did this theory seem too orthodox for Pat, the momentary passions in the young couple's home implied something less than first-degree murder. The very suddenness of a husband's alleged attack on his wife was an obvious defense to the capital charge. It seemed to Pat that the frame of suspicion had to be moved backwards to include the weekend prior to Paula's disappearance to find motive and premeditation. And he felt that he, as the possessor of the history of the Tuscans who thrived in California, was more qualified than the City's top homicide cops to uncover family secrets that might render this tragedy comprehensible.

From pure physical appearance, you wouldn't suspect that Lillian and Eileen were sisters, nor for that matter, even distantly related. Eileen was a petite woman, with thinly penciled arched eyebrows. Though diminutive in stature she carried herself with an almost patrician air, her page-boy blonde hair, tinged with red, was swept back from her finely sculpted face, commenting on her highly defined cheekbones. Lillian, sixteen years her senior, was a large boned woman, plump in face and body, whose naturally curly white hair implied that she gave little attention to her appearance in contrast with her impeccably groomed baby sister. Although they came from the same parents, their rearing reflected the different coasts of their childhood years. Lillian started life in a cold water Boston tenement, while her sister was born in a Pasadena, California mansion, their gambler father having struck an oil vein on an arid piece of real estate in the Pico area of Los Angeles. As a gangly teenager Lillian Foley felt that she was homely and culturally conflicted in the nouveau riche milieu of Southern California. She bore a thick Boston accent and somehow could not dress the scars of her impoverished childhood in the home of a hard drinking, hostile Irishman. Convinced that marriage was unlikely for her, she devoted herself to her infant sister, Eileen. Lillian, much more than their own mother, nurtured and taught and raised Eileen until she met and married Paul Brady. With the arrival of Eileen's grandson, Lillian moved into the lower flat of the Panforte duplex on Francisco Street in the Marina District so that she could nurse and nanny Paula and Robert's son. The Marina duplex had been purchased by the Bradys and Fred and Angelina Panforte and then given to their kids as a wedding present. Aunt Lil, as everyone but her sister called her, rose early every morning to wash and feed the baby, while her niece slept late, recovering from her frantic social whirl. Bob Panforte was usually long gone to work when Aunt Lil let herself in.

On the June 6th morning that Paula had been reported missing, Aunt Lil was surprised to find Panforte still home. She heard him talking on the phone in the den as she stepped into the baby's bedroom. She lifted the kicking infant from his crib. She felt his damp diapers. He was sopping wet, but his beaming blue eyes were lustrous at the sight of Lil's familiar, wrinkled face and the soothing sound of her voice. "Boy, you must be drinking beer to pee this much!" she admonished the baby. "You're showing your Irish already. Wet all over and a twinkle in your eyes. As though nothing in the world matters but your next pint!"

She removed the baby's soiled diapers and then bathed him in the tiny tub across from his crib. She dried him, then powdered his delicate pink skin as he kicked his chubby little legs wildly. She pinned clean diapers on him and then lifted him up and snuggled him against her small shoulder. As she carried Bobbie, Jr. to the kitchen for his morning feeding, she noticed that her niece's bedroom door was wide open. She was mystified because Paula and Bob Panforte always kept their bedroom door closed when Aunt Lil was in their home. Lil had assumed that Paula's husband was a typically over-sexed Italian. But she also knew that her niece possessed an equally greedy libido and that the closed bedroom door accommodated the couple doing to each other what no one had ever done with or to Lillian Foley. She stood for a moment in the doorway and saw that Paula wasn't there. But it was the condition of her niece's bedroom that startled Lil. It was immaculately clean. No negligee hanging listlessly on Paula's beige chair. No silk stockings strewn across the dressing table. No full-length formal dress in a pile at the foot of her bed. No generous bra on one side of the marital bed and abandoned silk panties on the other. Something was drawing Lil into their bedroom. It was their bed. The bed, in which the infant she cradled in her arms had been conceived, was neatly made. Paula Panforte did not make beds. Aunt Lil, Paula's maid, her mother and, perhaps even her father, made beds. But Paula slept in beds, read in beds, made love in beds. She did not make them. Her bed was her pleasure, Tucking in sheets, smoothing bedspreads was work. And Paula did not work. She played.

Aunt Lil entered the bedroom and absently touched the bed-spread. It was warm and slightly damp. It had recently been washed and ironed. On the spread, she saw a small spot – not really red, more like brown. She knew that machine-washing transforms blood spots into telltale brown. Her heart began to pound against her chest and it was making the baby restless, as though he somehow sensed that something terrible had happened to his mommy.

She briskly walked to the kitchen and quickly fixed Bobbie, Junior's formula. While she fed the baby Bob Panforte came in and told her that Paula had gone downtown to a show and hadn't returned. Aunt Lil was struck by his calm manner, his almost matter of fact recitation. Knowing her niece so well, the notion that her niece would go downtown alone did not surprise her. Lillian tried to imitate his detachment by suggesting that she take the baby up to her sister's house while he tried to find his wife. Bob agreed and Aunt Lil bundled the baby up and got out of the Francisco Street duplex as fast as her old lady legs could carry her.

Pat Kelley remained on the sofa across from the sisters as Lillian Foley finished her story. Eileen sipped a cup of tea and Kelley and Lillian drank their second round of Coffee Royales. Through the bay window Pat could see the Spanish tiled roof of Central Station, which was the police station Robert Panforte had called at 5:40 a.m. June 6, 1949 to report his wife missing. This police station was misnamed Central Station when it was in fact located on Greenwich Street in the northern most section of San Francisco. To the rear of Central Station, the mansions of Pacific Heights, like Eileen Brady's, clung to the steep, dramatic hills as though suspended by their opulence. Her estranged husband lived a few blocks away, but they'd held the post-funeral gathering in Eileen's house so as to accommodate the large collection of appropriately subdued guests. Both of their residences shared one of the most dramatic views in the world through expansive bay windows that framed the Golden Gate Bridge, the green hills of Marin County and white-masted sailboats circling Alcatraz and Angel Islands. As the crow flies, Eileen Brady's home was located almost directly above her daughter and son-in-law's Marina District duplex, constructed on landfill from the 1906 Earthquake.

Pat commented to Eileen that he could see her kid's residence on Francisco Street. Eileen said that she cherished the residential proximity to her child. It was as though Paula had not really moved out of her mother's house to take up her life with her husband, she told Pat.

She thought of the couple's flat as like a daughter's room, downstairs, and she felt a more secure sense of her daughter's life than when Paula had lived with her – single and swept up in the dazzling social whirl so intoxicating to the idle rich and so corrupting of indiscriminate youth.

Pat gently questioned Eileen about how and when she first learned that there was something wrong at her daughter's home. She said, "Bob phoned me sometime after six and told me that Paula had gone to the show the night before and hadn't come home. He told me he'd called the police and reported her missing. He said his father was calling my husband to see if he could get special police attention. After we hung up, my sister arrived with the baby." Lillian Foley nodded, established eye contact with Kelley, who nodded back.

"Lillian told me she'd noticed blood on their bedspread when she was feeding the baby," Eileen continued. "When she touched the bedspread it was damp and warm as though it had recently been washed and steam ironed. So I decided to go down to their flat to talk to Bob.

"We sat at the kitchen table and had coffee. I told him I needed to know everything that happened last night before Paula left, and he repeated what he'd previously said. He was unshaven and he apologized for his appearance. I was struck by his calmness. As we spoke, he looked me straight in the eye, with his sincere blue eyes. He seemed so...I don't know, confused.

"I told him in order to find Paula, we had to recreate her last hours at home. If we could, we might find a clue as to where she'd gone. Then I said: 'Bob, you said Paula wanted to go to the show. Did you want to go with her?'

"He said: 'No, she made it clear she wanted to be alone.' I asked him why and he said: 'Mom – that's what he calls me when his mother's not around - she was kinda mad at me. We were fooling around in the living room. She wanted to make love and I wasn't in the mood. She made some flippant comments. You know how she can be. Then she said she was going to the show.'

"I thought it possible Paula was having her period; some men are repelled by a menstruating woman. Perhaps Bob was. And it also explained the blood spots Lillian saw.

"I told him I understood how difficult it was to tell me these things and that he was a very brave young man. He didn't say anything, but he had a grateful look in his eyes, as though he'd been waiting for someone to say this.

"Then I told him we needed to understand what was on Paula's mind last night. I remembered when Paula was a teenager and she got upset with me, she'd bolt out of the house without telling me where she was going. I suggested we look in her personal affects.

"When I entered their bedroom, I noticed that the bedspread wasn't there. I looked in Paula's walk-in closet and I saw the bedspread folded in the rear corner of the closet. I picked it up and put it on the bed, still folded. One corner was damp. Then I went into the bathroom and…" Eileen's sobs interrupted her narrative.

Suddenly, Maria Kelley appeared on the sun porch, carrying a sterling silver serving tray. Almost from the moment they'd arrived, Maria had assumed the role of hostess, as though to liberate Eileen Brady from the social duties of this Irish wake. "Drink this," Maria said, handing Eileen a glass of ice water. Then she added, "You're with friends, Eileen. We'll help you get through this." Pat Kelley patted Eileen's knee and said gently, "Try breathing deeply, Eileen."

Eileen reached up with her thin fingers and rubbed her delicate neck. Her pert breasts rose and fell with her labored breathing. She resumed, "I opened the medicine cabinet and I saw Paula's engagement ring on the bottom shelf. I looked all over for her wedding ring, but it wasn't there. Just her engagement ring, with its huge expensive diamond. I think Bob paid more for the diamond than we paid for their duplex. But I couldn't find her wedding band. Oh, how I wanted that ring to be there!" Pat said, "What significance did you attach to Paula's wearing her wedding band?"

"I wanted to believe that Paula's rage had driven her out of the house. Maybe she was looking for a man to give her what Bob hadn't. I don't know, it was all so confusing. Maybe she'd gone bar hopping on Market Street and spent the night with a sailor in a cheap hotel where no one would recognize her. I figured she'd have taken off her ring to hide her marriage from some hungry stranger. But going out with her wedding band on made no sense."

"So I called Bob into the bedroom and told him the spread was damp. I said, "Bob, you must tell me the truth.'"

"He said, 'I can't tell you, it's personal.'"

"I said: 'Bob, this isn't the moment for anything personal. Now matter how hurtful it is, you must tell me the truth!' He told me that he'd accidentally bumped Paula's nose during love play and that she'd bled a lot. He said: 'I helped put ice packs on the back of her neck. She accused me of doing it deliberately. She was in a very bad humor when she left.'"

Pat mentally noted that Bob Panforte had acknowledged blooding his wife's nose to her mother long before the indelicate prying of the homicide detail. Kelley put his Coffee Royale on the coffee table and rubbed his chin thoughtfully. "Eileen, I'm afraid you're in for a long and awful ordeal with this trial of your son-in-law. Perhaps if you share some of your personal thoughts with old friends, the indelicate probing of prosecutors, cops and defense lawyers will be a bit more tolerable." Eileen Brady nodded and her sister's fierce eyes urged Pat on. "You indicated that Bob said something about Paula making flippant remarks. Did he tell you what she actually said?" Kelley asked. Eileen detested profanity, even when uttered by her cranky oldest sister. She closed her eyes, bit down on her lower lip and said, "Bob said: 'She pointed at me and yelled that the most overrated fucks in the world are football players and Italians!'"

Pat didn't have to ask if Paula was capable of such graphically foul language. She was, after all, her father's daughter. To ease Eileen away from her daughter's profanity, Pat said softly, "Eileen, I gather that you and the Panfortes were very close?"

She nodded, "Oh yes! The kids would dine at my home and I'd dine at theirs. We usually spent the holidays at Bob's parent's place at Lake Tahoe. We were even closer, warmer after the baby arrived." Eileen's eyes welled up with tears.

"So you had a strong affection for your son-in-law?" Kelley pressed.

"It was more than affection. I greatly appreciated him. I felt that Bob was responsible for bringing my daughter and I closer. As you know, Paul and I separated when Paula was ten. During her teens and at Stanford, I felt we'd grown apart. I felt I wasn't part of her life anymore. But when she married Bob, he had this very strong sense of family. I suppose it's his Italian heritage, but he went out of his way to include me in their lives. In a way, I felt like he'd given my daughter back to me. That's why I just don't understand any of this..." Her shoulders shook with her sobbing and she dabbed her eyes with a wrinkled hankie crumbled in her tiny hands. Pat sensed that this was the moment to ask Eileen Brady about the weekend prior to her daughter's disappearance. He had avoided the crude question of when was the last time you saw your only child alive and Eileen was obviously less strained talking about her family in the past tense as though it had not been so cruelly shattered. More conversationalist than interrogator, Pat absently asked: "Did you have any kind of family get together or outing that first weekend of June?" Eileen Brady shook her head and told Pat that she and her sister had taken the train to visit family in Pasadena over the weekend and hadn't returned to the City until Monday evening. Pat concluded that neither Paula's mother nor aunt could shed any light on the two days preceding the tragedy. That left Paula's father and her in-laws to account for. Eileen took a deep breath and said, "Oh Pat! You don't really think he could do it, do you?" Kelley rose from the couch and placed his thick hand on her shoulder, squeezing for reassurance. "Eileen, I don't know enough to answer your question. I do know that men who beat their wives do it habitually, over an extended period of time. More often they themselves are the victims of abuse. Bob Panforte's never shown anything but love for Paula, and his childhood was certainly privileged.

"But your intuition that Paula may have left their home enraged is sound mother wit and solid investigative theory. Perhaps that downtown stranger that you feared is responsible. So much time elapsed since Paula was last seen alive that we don't even know where she was first harmed, much less by whom. All I know for certain is that you mustn't agonize over such a dreadful mystery. You'll need all of your strength to manage your grief and loss. Perhaps in mothering your baby grandson, in somehow shielding him from the loss of his mom, you'll lighten the terrible burden that will always weigh on you."

Maria looked at her husband and felt a surge of love and pride for the easy compassion her husband was sharing with this bereaved grandmother. Eileen Brady nodded and sighed as though to thank Pat for his kindness and care. Aunt Lil's furious eyes, however, were unrelenting, as though her spinster's vision beheld secrets about men that neither Pat nor her baby sister could perceive.

6

Pat Kelley was already seated at what everyone considered his family's booth at Fior d'Italia Restaurant when young Joe Desmond arrived for their dinner date. Fior d'Italia, located on a corner across from Washington Square Park, boasted that it was the oldest Italian restaurant in America, established in 1896. It seems a dubious claim, but it had long been a favorite haunt of Kelley's father-in-law. San Francisco lore had it that Bertolli conceived the San Francisco Opera Company while dinning at Fior d'Italia a year or so before The Great Earthquake and Fire at its original location on Broadway. Although Kelley could get a table at any restaurant in town, he generally selected Fior d'Italia when his dining had something to do with his family. Since returning from the war, Pat and Maria had made Joe Desmond sort of a quasi-family member. Pat had nominated him as his kids' "uncle." Pat was an only child and Maria's older brother had been killed in World War I. Their son, Terry, was, as any American boy, mightily impressed by flickering movie images of GI's battling around the globe. His real uncle had died a hero's death in France, so he enthusiastically embraced Desmond as his uncle because he believed Joe had lived a hero's life. And Maria felt that her son's warrior hero worship would be tempered by brotherly intimacy with the ambiguity of a survivor.

Pat greeted Desmond with a raised martini glass: "Joe, here's to your maiden murder trial. There's nothing like a trial about death. The implications of designed killing seem to penetrate the core of our souls." Their waiter appeared before Desmond could ask Kelley what the hell he was talking about. They ordered and Kelley said, "I'm in the mood for French wine. You must've learned something more than shooting Germans and wenching in France. Pick something on the dry side."

"Number 72, the Poully-Fuisse. Jadot," Desmond ordered.

"Excellent, Signore," the waiter conceded. When he was gone Joe said, "Pat, what can I expect in this trial?"

"Mike Moore will try it."

"The District Attorney himself?"

"You bet. He's eyeing a run for Attorney General and he needs Paul Brady's clout. Even if he wasn't looking to move to the capitol, Brady was his mentor in the DA's office years ago. So he not only knew the victim as a little girl, he's the avenger for Brady's kid's murder."

"Sounds kinda personal and political to me."

"Joe, everything in this murder trial's gonna be personal and intensely so," Pat said pensively. Then he ran down the lineup of courtroom players for Desmond. Lucille Grant, the trial judge, was a close personal friend of the murdered girl's father and, during Paula's turbulent teens, she was closer to Lucy Grant than her own mother. Judge Grant was also on intimate terms with Paula's husband. Lucy and Paula had attended Bob Panforte's last Big Game in which he'd played a starring role for Stanford. Paula had told Lucy she thought he was cute and that one of her sorority sisters was going to introduce him to her at a victory party. And it was Judge Grant who had called the homicide boys into the case. "Jeezus Pat, our courtroom's gonna be like one big unhappy family!" Desmond interjected. "Do think Loeb'll move to disqualify her? If he does, do I get screwed out of my daily?" Pat shrugged indicating he didn't know what Loeb would do. He explained that Daniel David Loeb had successfully represented the defendant's father decades earlier in a stock proxy battle by which Fred Panforte had taken control of Bertolli's business empire and for which the Panforte name had earned Maria Kelley's limitless contempt. He said that Judge Grant might chose to recuse herself on her own motion. Pat told Joe that he had guaranteed his wife a daily seat at the trial. "Is that why you're clerking it?" Desmond asked.

"Partly. But I've got other issues. We'll talk about it later," Pat said dismissively.

"What's Moore like in court? He seemed pretty subdued in the Grand Jury."

"You can't compare Grand Jury proceedings to a jury trial. Joe, some men are born to be almost perfect in one thing, no matter how inadequate they may be as persons. I don't know if it's genes or rearing. Maybe God designs some men to be flawless in what they do. Don't you think if God were creating a baseball player, it'd have to be DiMaggio? Well, if you were making a natural prosecutor, it'd have to be Michael Moore.

"That good?" Pat nodded as he bit off a chunk of melon wrapped in

prosciutto. "What about Loeb?" Desmond asked.

Kelley sipped his wine. "Joe, this is excellent. The first words you'll take down from him will be: 'Danny Loeb, appearing for young Bob Panforte. Good morning Judge, Mr. Prosecutor.' He'll never refer to Panforte as the Defendant or his client. He'll attempt to humanize him. He'll never refer to Moore as the People's lawyer. It's as though repeated references to Moore as the prosecutor will transform him into The Persecutor. His cross-examinations are classics and his speech so rapid, he's a reporter's worst nightmare. Although reputed to have high ethics, I know his foot has slipped over the line on occasion. Not the least of which was when he represented old man Panforte against my father-in-law in the stock battle for control of the poultry empire."

"You don't think clerking a case where Panforte's kid is on trial is ah... a little touchy?"

"Perhaps," Kelley said, spearing an anchovy fillet. "What I'd like to do now is play a little forensic game with you. I want you to make the case that Panforte did it and that it's murder one. I'll play sort of a poor man's Socrates, asking some questions, looking for contradictions or nuances that may shed light on this case."

Joe knew Pat Kelley well enough to know that he was a master at the Socratic method. It was his tutorial style at the family dinner table by which he educated his bright kids. His many silent years in court studying the great cross-examiners of the day, and his grasp of philosophy and literature, allowed him to draw from others truths they were unaware of until they heard their own answers to Kelley's clever, often profound questions. Dinner dialogue with Pat and Maria Kelley was most often an intellectual feast and the hearty portions of controversy they served up breached the era's most accepted bromide – that you never spoke of religion, sex or politics in polite company. Terry Kelley had once remarked to Desmond: "Hell, that's all we ever talk about. My dad says what else is there?" Joe had often wondered of the career heights to which Kelley might have ascended had not economic circumstances and an early marriage sidetracked his ambitions for a career in law or politics. Yet he never expressed the slightest regret that his innate gifts found so little expression in the career of a civil servant. The court system that he managed with such effectiveness, combined with his wife and three children, provided him all the treasures he required. He was a most balanced man, rarely displaying annoyance or anger no matter how justifiably provoked. But when

something touched or threatened his family, his passion was fearful.

Desmond told Pat that he thought the keys to the prosecution's case had three important elements. The first were the contradictory statements Panforte gave to his relatives and the cops. Then there was the time-line established by his two neighbors and, finally, his alteration of the crime scene by washing the bedspread and secreting his clothes in secret compartments in the utility room in his basement.

"Let's take your so-called contradictory statements first," Pat said, sipping his wine.

Desmond replied: "First he claims that his wife went downtown to a movie and that he accidentally bloodied her nose at love play. Then he says he got pissed that she wouldn't go out with him. So maybe he belted her and gave her a nosebleed…"

Kelley interrupted Desmond's Sherlock Holmes impression, saying, "Hold on! Let's take this one step at a time. As for his statements to his relatives and the cops, we know that he was drunk on the night in question, and probably hung over, and terribly confused when he discovered his wife missing and called the police. As for Paula going downtown, we don't know that she didn't. The homicide boys never checked out the box office at the Fox or any other Market Street theaters and joints. Isn't it just as likely that she was pissed off at him and split for downtown? And if she did, not only is the crime scene enlarged, but so is the suspect pool. A gorgeous broad like her out by herself, think about it, Joe!

"As for bloodying her nose accidentally or intentionally, Panforte's obviously having a tough time with his memory due to all the booze. But he does admit that *he caused* her nosebleed. If he wanted to lie, he could've said the blood on the bedspread was caused by her menstruating or shaving her legs or who knows what." Then Pat asked, "You ever heard of temporary traumatic amnesia? In intense emotional moments, our minds blank stuff out. Our memories are sponges, but terrible trauma can squeeze the drops of recollection out of our psychic sponge so that we can forget what hurts or shames."

Joe's eyes dropped to his tortellini as he spooned more pesto on his pasta. Pat asked softly, "Do you still have your nightmares, those flashbacks?"

"Yeah. Only they're not really flashbacks. They're always the same. I'm freezing all the time and there's nothing but frozen corpses, frozen limbs with no bodies, bodies with no heads, and the winter sky is blood red. And my nightmares seem to come in thirty-day cycles, like

my mind's waiting for my paycheck or it's on the rag or something. So yeah, I know about that amnesia shit. But I don't think a bedroom brawl with a guy's wife amounts to a pile of shit compared to what I lived through," Joe said bitterly.

"Of course it doesn't, Joe! But events that induce trauma are unique to the person who experiences them. Nothing in your life could have prepared you for the carnage you saw, much less caused. Only rarely do we learn what prepares men and women for their bedroom lives. Didn't it seem odd the way he talked about his sex play to Paula's mother and even to Murphy? It's the girl's mother for Chrissake and Murphy's an absolute stranger! Murphy found his comments jarring and, frankly, so did I. Eileen Brady speculated to me that Bob's sexual comments sounded to her like he'd had a problem getting or sustaining an erection. It makes sense. Big football star unable to get it up, gotta be quite traumatic. Guys rarely cop to virility problems. Joe, the only thing I'm certain of is that sex is the key to this riddle and that the sexuality of that glamorous, tragic couple was formed, as all of our sexuality is, by whom and how they were raised." Desmond started to protest, but Kelley waved him off and continued, "But the most important thing is that he ultimately tells Murphy that they were both pissed, arguing and drunk! If he'd coolly planned to kill his wife, why tell Murphy about this domestic turmoil? Why implicate himself when there's no way the cops will ever find her if he just sticks to his original story that she's missing? There are no witnesses or physical evidence to contradict him!"

"What about his altering the scene?" Desmond protested. He was animated when he told Pat, "The guy's supposed to be so fucking drunk he doesn't remember if he fought her or fucked her! Yet he methodically washes the bedspread, the clothes he was wearing and hides his clothes and gloves in secret little compartments he'd built just for that purpose."

Pat smiled wryly and said: "First of all, anything done *after* Paula's death is inadmissible to prove premeditation. Cold homicidal planning must occur *prior* to a lethal attack. As far as washing the bedspread, he gave a very plausible explanation and admitted that it was Paula's blood. You don't know *when* he built the compartments that he put his clothes and gloves in, and whether they have a legitimate utilitarian purpose. Besides, if her blood had gotten on his clothes while he's slaying or carrying her, he couldn't have washed if off any better than the bedspread. And remember, Paula was probably wrapped in her green coat, which was spread under her in her grave. So it's unlikely any of her blood would have stained his clothes."

"Yeah, but the soil and clay at Mt. Tam would have gotten on his clothes. Maybe that's what he washed off," Joe rebutted.

"Excellent point!" Pat admitted. "Dessert?" Pat asked. Desmond shook his head and they ordered espresso and a round of Hennessey cognacs. Kelley twisted a lemon peel and dropped it in his espresso. "So, tell me about your time-line," the Chief Clerk said.

Desmond related that the horny teenager heard an argument in Panforte's home during the commercial break of *The Lone Ranger* radio program. He said, "That makes it 7:45 p.m. A little later the kid sees Panforte *backing* his '47 Chevy *out* of the garage. Then Panforte must have *backed* it back *into* the garage since his other neighbor, watering off the dog shit, sees him drive outta the garage hood-end first fifteen minutes later. Panforte must have backed it in so he can get the trunk close to the back stairway. Then he stuffs her in the trunk and that explains the blood spot O'Day found in the trunk…"

"It was a blood *speck*, Joe, not a bloodspot or stain," Pat corrected. "And it was so small that they couldn't test it for blood-type. So there's no way of knowing whose blood it is, much less *when* it got there."

"So anyway," Desmond plodded on. "His neighbor, Pierce, sees him drive out of his garage around eight and that's when he drives her body over to Mt. Tamalpais. He knows the area like the back of his hand, and he buries her where no one will find her in our lifetimes. Then he leads the cops right to her grave! Pat, I don't see how you get around that."

"You know what you've just done?" Pat said, waving at the waiter for their check. "You've described the perfect crime! As for the friendly neighbor cleaning dog shit off the sidewalk, Panforte told Pierce he was going to pick up his wife from the show! That makes a lotta sense. They've had a beef, and she's taken off angry. Isn't it natural that he'd go after her? And it's important that only neighbor Pierce actually saw Panforte driving his Chevy that night! The Busby kid claims he saw the car, but never said who was driving it!

"Then there's her grave. As of now, that's the heart of Moore's case. Bob Panforte, the expert woodsman, detached and methodical, takes her to his secret forest, digs her grave and dumps her in it. Now, you insist that he led the cops to her grave. But he didn't! He led them to his father's hunting cabin, where they found not a shred of evidence implicating Panforte. Remember, Panforte had been out of communication with his father for almost two days and that's when he told the cops about his volunteer work with Army training, and Murphy asked him to show them the training destination. If this guy knew that he'd buried his wife in that grave, do you think he'd have shown it to O'Day and Murphy?

"Don't you see, Joe? All Panforte had to do was stick with his original story and they never would have found her. There's not a scintilla of physical evidence that contradicts his original story about her going downtown. It all comes out of his own mouth! You gotta ask why? Why would he implicate himself to Murphy?"

"What about their baby?" Desmond asked pointedly. "Panforte sure as hell couldn't ask Aunt Lil to baby sit while he buried her niece over at Mt. Tam!"

"That's a crucial point, Joe! Abandoning his kid for a couple of hours is precisely why the DA thinks such a callous sonofabitch deserves to be gassed!"

"I figure that's why he came up with the bullshit story that he drove to the market for detergent," Joe added.

"Perhaps," Kelley seemed to concede. "But it's also plausible that he figured a five minute trip for groceries wasn't a serious breach of parent duties." Pat didn't tell Joe that Aunt Lil wouldn't have been available for nanny duty since she had not yet returned from her trip to Pasadena with her sister. "Ultimately, Panforte cops to leaving the baby alone to get his wife."

Joe grimly asked, "So what's an Army entrenching tool with Tamalpais clay and pine needles doing in his garage?"

Animated, Pat replied, "That's the key. It links Panforte to Mt. Tam. That's why O'Day and Murphy checked out their hunting cabin. That entrenching tool is the bridge between San Francisco and Marin County.

"Here's what I'm thinking. Right after Panforte called Central Station, he called his father at Great Western Poultry. Old man Panforte tells him to call Eileen Brady immediately and then he tells him to start calling Paula's friends. After that, the homicide boys have him in virtual custody for forty-eight hours. Two full days without his daddy! The last words he'd heard from his father were to find his wife! That's why he told the cops what he did. He was doing just what his daddy told him, like he probably always does! That means his state of mind was focused on finding his errant wife. And that means he *believed* she was still alive!"

Kelley paid the check and then abruptly changed the subject, "Joe, do you know anything about this Army training course Panforte talked about? What did he call it? *Escape and evasion*?" At last they were on a subject Desmond knew something about. "Well, in airborne training, in the sweaty south before D-Day, we had intensive training in what the Army called, 'Survival, escape and evasion.' But remember, *our* training was unique. Our mission was to drop in behind enemy lines and raise hell. Lines of communication and supply were expected to be cut. We were trained to survive what no regular infantry soldier was likely to experience. And the odds of being captured by the krauts were far greater. So avoiding or escaping capture was drilled into us. The only fucking normal infantry battle I ever engaged in was the Bulge. Being trapped and surrounded was *S.O.P.* for the 101st," Joe said.

"But isn't it possible that, after your success at Normandy, the Army came up with a similar training program for regular infantry?" Pat asked.

"That's easy enough to find out if ya know somebody over at Sixth Army Headquarters," Desmond said. Kelley nodded and said, "I was hoping you'd say that."

Pat got up from the table and said, "Joe, in a murder case, you've got to be able to pull back from the facts and look at them through a prism of opportunity and motive. No question Bob Panforte had the opportunity. At this point, we don't know where the killing actually took place. Was it their bedroom? If it was, where is the premeditation necessary for murder one? Did she die in the trunk of his car or the trunk of someone else's car? Or did she die at the gravesite or in the grave itself? There's no question that Panforte had the opportunity, but it's unknown whether anyone else had the opportunity outside the Panforte home.

"But what's his motive? Everyone says he played Prince Charming to her Cinderella. There's no evidence that he's a wife-beater. If he'd ever laid a hand on her before, Paul Brady would've killed the kid with his bare hands. Guys who beat on women show a history of it. They've often themselves been victims of abuse. It's frequently a generational thing, like-father-like-son, or there's something screwy in their sex lives. I need to know more about Robert Panforte, other than he's handsome, rich without working a day in his life, has an over protective mother and a miserable sonofabitch for a father!"

This was the moment that Pat had given Desmond his first hint that the Panforte murder trial would be much more than a homicide case. It would involve a number of prominent San Francisco families in ways no one could foresee, with consequences to their children both lasting and damaging.

"You think there's something in his family that's kinda weird?" Desmond asked.

"I don't know. Let's go for a walk and get a nightcap at the Oregon Café. I have a proposition for you," Pat said.

"I can't think of a better place to be propositioned in," Desmond laughed.

7

The cool damp breeze of the San Francisco night kissed their faces as they walked from Fior d'Italia along Columbus Avenue toward the financial district and then to the wholesale food distribution center where the Oregon Café was located. The Oregon Café was a full purpose establishment in every sense of the word. It served meals twenty-four hours a day. It was breakfast for the Market men and, at lunchtime, the pinstripes of the financial district dropped in for hearty Italian food and the best minestrone in the City. In the evenings the hard drinkers took over and gamblers assembled in the back room around oval card tables. On the second floor was one of San Francisco's numerous and great whorehouses, and, before falling in love with Mary Healy, Joe Desmond confessed to having been an occasional client. San Francisco's great columnist, Herb Caen, once wrote that: "The test of a great city is where you can get a good hamburger and a bad woman at three o'clock in the morning." The Oregon Café contributed mightily to San Francisco passing Caen's test for urban greatness.

San Francisco, perhaps because of the century of new immigrants washing up on her shores, is the ever changing pearl of the Pacific. Some things are unchangeable. The evening breeze carrying moist wisps of fog still greets the night stroller when he steps from a smoke-filled bar, a clammy theater or a crowded restaurant. It is San Franciscans eternally caressing, refreshing companion on almost any San Francisco night. The City's skyline during the Panforte trial proudly emphasized her swelling, sensuous hills that plunged suddenly, without warning, into the Bay is now dominated by bland, contemporary glass-masked, high-rise buildings that seem to phallically erupt from the flatlands of the financial district. The old, colorful clap-trap produce and poultry market that Kelley and Desmond were about to walk through is gone, banished to sterile, but admittedly efficient industrial parks – one faction of The Market, the Genovese, in southern San Francisco, the other, the Lucchese, on the northern border of

San Mateo County. From its unseen footprints sterile office buildings and overpriced hotels have blossomed, creating wind canyons, hiding the sun from the sidewalks, and contriving to render San Francisco's downtown indistinguishable from Houston's. Sadly, the Oregon Café and its hookers are gone, replaced by urban development that has given the City the Hyatt Regency Hotel. But somehow room service sex is not quite as sinful as a second story brothel with slowly simmering Bolognese sauce wafting up from an all day kitchen. The streetcars, called Iron Monsters, no longer rumble up and down Market Street on thick tracks, replaced by sleek subway cars carrying sullen, sightless passengers through an antiseptic underground tube. And vanished is the symphony of neon lights winking from the grand Market Street movie marques, like the Fox Theater, that Bob Panforte had claimed his wife had gone to on the last night of her life. Market Street is dark now. It's a boulevard of fast food, panhandlers, porno shows and shady merchandising, where store after store proclaims "going-out-of-business" bargains. Of course the City's contemporary politicians don't steal like some of their predecessors. But it's likely that the absence of graft owes more to the paucity of their imaginations than the integrity of their characters.

But some things have not changed over the years. The silver sliver of fog that slides under the Golden Gate Bridge just before a Sunday sunset, announcing the playful weekend's end, hasn't abandoned San Franciscans and never will. The little cable cars still scramble up Nob Hill and Russian Hill, packed with excited tourist and Japanese cameras while native males strain to look up the skirts of lady passengers, sitting unwittingly on open-air cable car benches. The Tadich Grill still takes no reservations, and the restaurant's brusque white-jacketed waiters still serve the best fish in town. And yes, the cool, damp breeze of the San Francisco night still caresses her people's multi-hued faces.

On their way to the Oregon Café, Kelley and Desmond stopped for a moment at the corner of Washington and Davis Streets. In the soft illumination of a corner streetlight and a half moon that filtered through the high diaphanous night fog stood the Great Western Poultry Building. Fred Panforte's concrete building was the largest building in the wholesale produce district, extending a half block up Washington Street toward the Hall of Justice and a half block up Davis Street toward North Beach. Had the building been used for office space, it would have comfortably housed four stories. Its design and use as a wholesale poultry distribution center required a configuration in which it was divided into two floors and a sub-basement for storage and heavy equipment. The ceiling of the street level floor rose to a height of three-quarters of the building. Sliding metal screen doors secured the ground level. Joe saw cage-like wooden crates populated with live, sleeping chickens, clucking in their cramped captivity when another chicken stepped or shit on their heads. Along the back wall, Desmond saw the massive refrigeration system that preserved their plucked and slaughtered brethren. The top quarter of the building's interior was the second floor, which housed bookkeeping offices and Fred Panforte's executive suite. Kelley knew that the management suite was composed of numbers crunchers and old man Panforte's office. Although Fred's son was a Vice-president of the company, he did not have his own office in the City.

The building was bannered with large, green wooden signage on both Washington and Davis Street that announced in gold lettering: Great Western Poultry Co. In smaller gold letters beneath the company trade name the sign read: *F. Panforte, Proprietor*. Desmond mentioned to Pat that he thought it odd that old man Panforte used 19th century nomenclature to proclaim his proprietary interest. It was as though the sign reassured him that this poultry empire was truly his. But Pat thought that this dated nomenclature said something about Fred Panforte more than his vision of his commercial self. If the sign were truly 19th century vintage, it would read: *F. Panforte & Son, Proprietors*. Fred Panforte, formerly a poor Tuscan peasant, had given his son enormous wealth, a Stanford education and the Vice-presidency of the largest poultry operation in the West. Yet he had not allowed his boy's name or his relationship to share this sign of ownership. He had assigned his son to oversee his Petaluma poultry and egg ranch operations, limiting his work-time at the chaotic and often ruthless wholesale market and distribution center. Great Western Poultry Company's Petaluma operation were the simplest and most basic to manage. Non-English speaking Italians and Yiddish-speaking Jews, financed by A.P. Giannini's Bank of Italy and tutored by Bartolemeo Bertolli's Western Poultry Company, had mastered the rapid grow cycles for massive poultry production for forty years.

Little had changed in Petaluma's poultry production industry until World War II, a war that Bob Panforte had avoided because his employment was deemed vital to home front industry, if not essential to his father's commercial empire. Other than sensitivity to grain prices, poultry ranches pretty much ran themselves and did so with backbreaking, filthy labor. Fred Panforte had commenced his American quest with just such work. His only child's manicured nails had never plucked or slaughtered a single chicken or purged feed bins of chicken shit. He wore well-pressed slacks to work, instead of Levi's, the uniform of a chicken rancher. More significantly, Pat reflected, Fred allowed his son no role in day-to-day operations at The Market. It was a turbulent, often brutal commodities exchange. But Bob Panforte had mentioned to Inspector Murphy that his dad had transferred him from Petaluma to The Market.

Perhaps the greatest difference between the expansive poultry business centered in this building was what it said about the two men who had owned it. Bartolemeo Bertolli never personalized his business, never advertised his own name, never promoted his own business acumen. Indeed, he was more acknowledged for his contributions to the arts, his financing of the Italian variety theater at the turn of the century and his dogged pursuit of his dream to create an opera company for the city that had welcomed him as a raw Italian teenager. When this concrete survivor of The Great Earthquake was Bertolli's it had been incorporated, as had been all of Bertolli's holdings. Closely held, non-publicly traded corporations were commonly formed by entrepreneurs to limit their personal legal liabilities. But Bertolli saw the corporate form of business as more than a family run business. He believed that stock ownership was a sort of democratic capitalism, and that men who had an equitable interest in their jobs would be more productive than mere wage slaves and their loyalty to the enterprise insured by their ownership of it. Long before it was a common business practice, he granted his employees, laborers, executives and salesmen alike stocks and profit sharing in his company's gains.

Ironically, it was Bertolli's visionary approach to labor and management that proved his downfall at the hands of his protégé, Fred Panforte. It was through a stock proxy battle, unheard of in the world of closely held corporations, that Panforte senior had seized control of Bertolli's company. Over the years and through a series of national economic crises, Panforte had subtlety reorganized the company. His employees, shaken by the Great Depression, eagerly sold their stock back to the corporation for ready cash at devalued prices. In very short order Fred Panforte, his wife, Angelina and his only son, Robert, owned all the capital stock of Great Western Poultry. But Pat knew that it wasn't truly a family owned business. For Fred Panforte had his lawyer, Daniel David Loeb, draw up voting trust documents for his wife and son's signature. These empowered Fred to vote their shares of stock, leaving them with only a beneficial interest in the company. He truly was *F. Panforte, Proprietor.*

Pat thought of his first summer job as a porter at The Market, when he'd first met Maria and her father. Although the work was physically demanding there was an aura of family that seemed to prevail in this competitive chaos. Owners, salesmen, porters, lumpers, and teamsters seemed to pass on their positions and experiences to their sons or sons-in-law, like ancient clans or mythical kingdoms. But not Fred Panforte. His signage seemed to proclaim to Pat the supremacy of ego, of one immigrant's triumph in America, as though his only child was a mere trophy to his virility. To second generation Americans much is given and little required. Robert Panforte was a handsomer, less crude, quieter, more shallow, and yes classier, man than his father. Such is the price of unearned wealth, Pat reflected.

But he felt that there was another distinction between the man who had designed and constructed this defiant building and the man who now owned it. It was perhaps the difference between the first and second Italian immigration waves to San Francisco. Bartolemeo Bertolli, the leader of the first wave, navigated his American triumph with unflinching loyalty - Fabrizio Panforte's oars sliced through the tides of opportunity.

Kelley and Desmond resumed their walk toward the Oregon Café, passing L. Scatena & Co., the wholesale produce house founded by A.P. Giannini's stepfather. It was while Giannini was a partner at L. Scatena & Co. that he and Bartolemeo Bertolli had met and become fast friends and lucrative business collaborators at the turn of the century. More to himself than to Joe, Pat said softly, "This is where it all begins. Or maybe ends."

"The earthquake and fire?" Joe said. Kelley nodded grimly.

Forty-three-year old Bartolemeo Bertolli stood in front of his whole-sale poultry building that he'd designed and built three years earlier. He wore a neatly pressed, starched white smock — emblematic of produce and poultry business owners — over his brown three piece suit. Across the street Al Levy, a young produce man, and Police Sergeant Jesse Cook were chatting. They waved to Bertolli and he acknowledged them with a tip of his brown fedora. He heard the sweet song of St. Mary's bell tower ring out from Chinatown announcing the fifth hour of Wednesday April 18, 1906. The air was unusually still, he thought, as though in sympathy with the sleeping city. The Market, which had already been open for business for two hours, was its usual chaotic scene, with sweating, shouting men, powerful draw horses, sacks of potatoes, onions, turnips, carrots and crates of tomatoes, melons and lettuce, cages of live chickens, cartons of slaughtered poultry and fresh eggs, clogged the streets and sidewalks. The cool morning air was filled with earthy pungent commerce. Along Front, Davis, Washington and Jackson Streets, two, three, and four story brick wholesale food markets presided over this normal pre-dawn bedlam. Bertolli's Western Poultry building was the only concrete building at The Market. He had constructed it following models of his native Tuscany. In place of the bound wood supporting pillars of Italy, he'd employed re-enforced steel.

Bertolli had not slept since he had taken a midday nap the previous day, in preparation for attending a touring Metropolitan Opera Company performance of "Carmen." He had a low regard for Metropolitan Opera productions, but the opportunity to hear Enrico Caruso in a live performance overcame his disdain for America's leading opera company. After Caruso's thrilling performance before a capacity crowd of three thousand at the Majestic Theater on Mission Street, he had driven one of his company's four automobiles, which he'd recently purchased for his distribution system, to North Beach to count and bank the box office receipts from the variety theater he had financed and helped found. But on this April morning, he felt no fatigue at all. He was exhilarated that his twenty-four years in America seemed an unending saga of challenge and resounding fulfillment. His invention and installation of the first refrigeration system in the wholesale food market had revolutionized product distribution. From a successful business in a frantically competitive market Bertolli's Western Poultry Company now completely dominated the California marketplace. Soon he would utilize railroad refrigeration to extend his empire to Nevada, Oregon and Washington.

He was the first man in San Francisco to appreciate that the combustion engine would soon replace horsepower, and was already integrating four rickety gas propelled vehicles into his distribution system. He reflected on his friend, Giannini, and felt a sense of wonder that Giannini's bank had been so successful and gratitude that the Bank of Italy had been so beneficial to his enterprise. When Giannini sold his interest in the L. Scatena & Co, produce house he purchased a saloon on Columbus Avenue and opened his Bank of Italy. He convinced Bertolli not only to invest in the bank but to become the bank's first prominent commercial account. Then he advertised Bertolli's name and quickly signed up other major Italian and Irish businesses. Together Bertolli and Giannini scoured farm and ranch *lands north and south of San Francisco. They advised growers on the best times to bring their product to market. Giannini made loans to "the little people," as he called them that no commercial banker would even talk to. Bertolli cut exclusive distribution deals with them that no competitor could match without his refrigeration capacity. In an incredibly short period of time they had wedded the point of food origin to the point of distribution that would transform farming into the industry of agribusiness. It was Giannini who had financed Bertolli's refrigeration system with a $17,000 loan and only Bertolli's handshake as a promissory note and security.*

From the previous night's box office receipts at his theater, competing head-to-head with the great Caruso, Bertolli was confident that the theatrical business he'd funded would also succeed. Most importantly his Italian variety theater had sold out in the first performance in which his star soprano and artistic director did not herself star in the production. Two hours earlier at Antonietta's apartment on Green Street off Dupont Avenue she'd said to him, "Our show's got legs! I don't have to carry it anymore." But now they carried something heavier, yet not burdensome, Bertolli thought. After two years of resisting Antonietta's arms and honoring his marital vows, he had finally surrendered to her. For the first time in his life, he'd dishonored his word, failed to keep a promise long ago made. Yet he didn't feel at all dishonorable nor did guilt stain his soul. He closed his eyes and the vision of her played movie-like on the screen of his memory. Her dark brown hair splayed against feather pillows in rivulets of abundant curls, her hazel eyes wandered over his naked body like sparks. She saw his arousal and her pink tongue tip wetted her full lips, inviting him to her. He knelt on the end of her bed, her arms reached out for him, her thighs parted and drew him to her. When his lips surrounded her nipple, he moaned, almost in pain. Her fingers cupped his ears and gently, insistently guided his moist kisses down the swelling waves of her body…

On this April morning he had walked to work without shaving. He had taken her scent and taste with him to The Market. He rubbed his palm across his mouth as though to imprison the remnants of illicit love and glanced at the clock on the Ferry Building. It was 5:15 a.m. His thoughts of her were rudely interrupted by the horses on the street. They nervously shifted their hooves on the cobblestone and whinnied and began spooking. Then his caged chickens panicked, squawking and flapping their wings, straining to escape their premonition. "Oh no!" Bertolli said aloud, realizing that animals react to Nature's whim moments before catastrophe. And then a terrible groan erupted from the bowels of the earth. The sidewalk on which he was standing trembled and then convulsed with such force that Bertolli was thrown to the ground in the doorway of Western Poultry Co. He heard a profound distant rumbling, like thundering artillery, and he reached up with his hand to the door jams to brace himself from the shocks that seemed to be turning the ground to liquid. He glanced up Washington Street, and he actually saw the earthquake coming for him. The street was undulating, like waves at Ocean Beach, billowing and relentless. Then the tortured cobblestone of Washington Street surrendered to the rapine force of Nature's fault and split apart, a jagged, waterless creek twisting in the middle of the street. And then the street seemed to explode as though a bomb had struck The Market. In seconds, men and animals were crushed by tons of fallen bricks. Whole buildings collapsed as though they had no foundations at all. The few produce buildings that remained standing were but facades, looking like a theater set of an Old West town. The roar of the outraged earth and the crumbling of The Market were joined by a cacophony of church bells clanging madly in the sway of their steeples. The shock was over in little more than a minute. For Bertolli and the men of The Market, it seemed that they'd witnessed the end of the world.

Bertolli pulled himself to his feet but remained standing in the doorway. His building had defied the trembling earth and he knew that a doorway was the safest place for the after-shocks that were inevitable. Other than the loss of electric power, his building appeared unscathed. But he knew that it still must face the flames that were sure to come. He quickly surveyed his work force and equipment. He ordered one of his drivers to drive to his Russian Hill home and pick up his wife, children and servants. He directed him to take them to the Port and board them on one of Western Poultry's ferries to sail immediately to his ranch in Sonoma. Then he thought of his theater director at her home in North Beach. He started to send a driver for her, then scanned Davis Street and saw that it was all carnage and chaos. No motor vehicle could make it through. So he ordered his three remaining motor vehicles to be driven to the Port and await further directions from him and only him. He ordered the rest of his men to clear out every piece of wood in the building. They removed furniture, chicken crates, tore off wood fixtures and dumped them on Washington Street, providing an improvised burial for six dead horses lying on their sides, still fully clothed in their tack. When the building had been cleared of as much flammable material as possible he ordered his men to douse the entire building with water. They broke open a fire hydrant and hooked their houses to it. There was very little water pressure. They ran to Bertolli and told him. "Oh Dio!" he said through clenched teeth realizing, as firefighters would soon discover, that the water mains had burst. "Use our well!" he directed. Bertolli had dug a well that he used exclusively for refrigeration experimentation, not wanting to be dependent on the water supply of San Francisco's corrupt private water company.

His men responded without hesitation or doubt. They trusted him. He paid them well and generously granted them stock in the company, believing as he did that a man's loyalty to an enterprise was insured by his equitable interest in it. When they'd completed watering down the premises he ordered them to bring the large wrought iron safe from the bookkeeping office on the second floor and place it in the largest refrigeration unit. The men shuffled the safe into the refrigerator, while Bertolli stuffed the day's receipts and the previous night's box office into canvas bank pouches. He placed them in the black safe, closed it and spun the combination locked.

When The Great Earthquake had struck A.P. Giannini was already at his desk in the Bank of Italy on Columbus Avenue. Although he was now a banker and not a produce man, he still kept the pre-dawn hours of The Market. He disdained conventional bankers and their delicate hours and felt that working from dawn to dusk gave him an edge on his competition. When the first shock abated he ran outside. He saw terrorized men, women and children fleeing from their wooden North Beach homes into the streets. He was certain that the quake must have ruptured some gas mains and that fire was inevitable. From a garbage dump he retrieved an orange crate and raced back into his bank. In the walk-in vault he quickly stuffed as much cash, gold and papers as he could, filling the orange crate. He slid the orange crate onto the bed of his wagon, jumped on and whipped his dapple mare toward the Port, toward blessed water.

It was slow going as he maneuvered his skittish mare around debris and frightened, frantic people. He glanced over his shoulder and saw that the northern sky was turning pink He knew it was not the rising sun, but the beginning of the conflagration that would quickly race through the wood frame structures of North Beach before its fiery assault on the financial district and The Market.

At Davis Street he saw that the route was impassable. Then he saw his friend Bertolli directing his men like a combat field officer. He tied his mare to the spoke of an upright wagon wheel mired in a pile of fallen bricks, the wagon having been crushed by the falling façade of a building. He ran over to Bertolli and told him that the bank's treasure was in an orange crate and that he needed help to get it to the Port. Bertolli shook his head and told Giannini to get the crate and bring it to his building. In Italian, Giannini expressed his puzzlement. In English, Bertolli said, "I've got an idea." A Bertolli idea was good enough for the Genovesi banker. He ran to his wagon and returned with the orange crate with the Bank of Italy's assets. Bertolli led him to his huge refrigerator in which he'd already stored his cache of cash. Other than Bertolli's safe the freezing walk-in unit had only a series of palates with plucked, dead chickens piled about six feet high. "What the hell is this?" Giannini asked.

"Frozen chickens," Bertolli said, allowing himself a small smile in this moment of madness. The banker cried, "Oh Dio, what good are frozen chickens?"

"It's an experiment. I'll tell you later," Bertolli said. "Let's get to work."

Bertolli opened his black safe and Giannini removed the Bank of Italy's cash and papers from the orange crate, placed it in canvas bank pouches and Bertolli put it in his safe. Under Bertolli's direction, the two men scraped the frozen chickens off their palates and piled 1,000 of them on top of the safe. Then they carried the empty orange crate and palates out to the street and dumped them on the refuse on Washington Street. Their hands stung from the freezing temperature in which they'd labored. They rubbed and clapped their hands to stimulate circulation. Then Bertolli slammed and bolted the freezers' large, metal door. Giannini's eyes scanned the freezing unit that reached halfway to the ceiling. "Will it work?" he asked.

"I don't know. I know how to freeze poultry, but I've never frozen assets before," Bertolli said. Both men chuckled and Giannini said, "Let's get the hell outta here!"

"I'll meet you at the Port. I've got one more job to do," Bertolli said somberly.

Bertolli jogged through the Davis Street debris to Broadway. Then he ran west faster toward Grant Avenue. He had to find Antonietta. Broadway was filled with people milling about aimlessly, as though in a trance of shock. What struck Bertolli as bizarre was that all the men were dressed in well-pressed business suits, wearing handsome derbies and fedoras. And the women wore their ankle length dresses and dramatic bonnets. Even the children were scrubbed and dressed. It was as though the earth's furious ringing of church bells had summoned North Beach residents to Sunday services.

In front of Tony Delmonico's Fior d'Italia Restaurant Bertolli slowed to a walk. And then he saw her. She had just turned the corner of Dupont onto Broadway. She calmly walked toward him. She was wearing slacks covering riding boots, a blue blouse, waistcoat and was carrying a handbag. She was hatless, her long, wavy hair swept up in a high bun. In the madness that surrounded them on Broadway she walked with the poised grace of an actress making her stage entrance. And then she was in his arms, her cheek crushed against his hard, broad chest. His body trembled. Hers did not. She seemed to melt through his pores and they enveloped each other, breathless and oblivious to the pandemonium around them. For a moment, Bertolli recalled the initial moments of the quake and his vision of Washington Street rising and falling like a breaching whale, as though it were coming for him, the agent of a wrathful God, intent on smiting his moment of sublime intimacy. She lifted her cheek from his chest, looked into his gray, bloodshot, eyes and read his thoughts. She whispered vehemently, "Don't you dare think that!" Then they walked purposefully hand in hand down Broadway to the Bay and momentary safety.

For the next forty-eight hours Bertolli, his employees and his lover Antonietta battled along with firemen, police, the U.S. Army and the men and women of San Francisco to save their city. In chaos there was no gender, no color, no accent. There was only defiance overcoming fear. They were brave, but their adamant wills were no match for the inferno that engulfed the City by the Bay. Without adequate waterpower, with both telephone and telegraph down, the City was defenseless and devoid of the communications necessary to coordinate a counter-attack against the delirious fires. In one of those curious historical ironies the automobile, in its infancy, played a starring role in the defense of the City. All motor vehicles were turned over to the command of the Army including Bertolli's four vehicles. Bertolli himself volunteered as a driver, and for two days without sleep he and Antonietta delivered orders and responses to soldiers and firemen. It was the automobile that provided the means of communications on Nature's battlefield. Nonetheless, San Francisco was destroyed. All that was left were her people. And that was all that was necessary.

By Saturday rain aided the firefighters and the inferno at The Market had run its course. North Beach was little more than smoldering black ruins. Antonietta, her face blackened by smoke and soot, her beautiful hair singed by the intense temperature of the fires they had battled, was exhausted and finally collapsed on a bench on The Embarcadero and slept.

Only the Hall of Justice on Kearny Street and Bertolli's Western Poultry Building remained standing. Since the fire had struck The Market in the first hours of the disaster Bertolli believed that his refrigeration system had cooled sufficiently to open the freezer without blowing up his building from the intense temperatures created by the fire. The odor of water damage, burnt human and animal flesh, rotting fruits and vegetables, singed brick and concrete was overwhelming. When Bertolli and Giannini opened the massive freezer door, a novel scent rushed into the air. It was the smell of charred meat! The thousand formerly frozen chickens blanketing Bertolli's safe had been baked crispy black! When the two men started to remove the chickens, they disintegrated into ashes. They simply brushed the chickens to the floor.

Bertolli touched the safe and found that it was only lukewarm. He opened it and removed the money pouches. He handed one to Giannini. They opened the pouches and the cash and papers had been safely preserved. "It worked!" Bertolli said with amazement.

"Yeah, but you overcooked the chickens," Giannini laughed, clapping his friend on the back.

By Monday, four days past doom, A.P. Gianinni had set up a table at the Port and was lending Bank of Italy money to San Franciscans to survive so that they could rebuild. His bank looked more like a kid's lemonade stand than a serious financial institution. Perhaps it was this make-shift shore-side bank that gave Giannini the idea of branch banking that would make his Bank of America the largest financial institution in the world. As for Western Poultry Company, the building would have to await the restoration of electrical power. So Bertolli employed his barges and ferried foodstuffs from Sonoma farms and ranches. He paid his food producers with the money he'd saved in his refrigerator and then gave the food to his fellow San Franciscans free. Six weeks after the disaster a messenger arrived at Western Poultry with an envelope for him. Bertolli opened it and found an official looking document from the Bank of Italy. It was a promissory note for the $17,000 loan to finance his refrigeration experiments and systems. The document confused him, for he and Giannini had never before signed papers, relying instead on their word alone. Then he read at the bottom of the page, in Giannini's bold script: "Paid in full. Signed: Amadeus Peter Giannini, President. Banco d'Italia."

8

At the Oregon Café, Pat and Joe took a booth and ordered a round of cognacs. Joe Desmond now understood that his remarkable friend was invested in the Panforte murder case far beyond the bounds of his clerical duties. And he suspected that Kelley was about to involve him in whatever plans Pat had for the trial. For his part Kelley realized that he'd engendered curiosity in his young friend, and that Joe would be a willing participant in his scheme. Pat recalled Oliver Wendell Holmes' comment, "Law is life and life is not logic." He felt that there were at least two explanations for why Bob Panforte blew his perfect cover. His father wasn't around to tell him that he'd done well, or he wasn't bright enough to realize how well he'd actually done. Perhaps both, Kelley thought.

After a shapely waitress returned with their drinks, Desmond said, "So ya figure there's some holes in the prosecution's case?" Spinning the stem of his snifter with his thumb and forefinger, Kelley said, "It's not so much holes as perspectives. Murder prosecutions necessarily rely on macro-vision while the defense looks through a micro-lens. You've got two evenly matched lawyers at the peak of their careers. It's an O'Day/Murphy investigation with Murphy in the lead, and Loeb got old man Panforte to finance David London as his investigator. So you've got the three best detective minds in the state. But London's job is easier than Murphy's. All he's gotta do is unravel a few strings and the prosecution's ball of circumstantial evidence gets unwound. Panforte's wealth can match the D.A.'s public purse dollar for dollar and then some. The evidence is circumstantial, and both sides will try mightily to force the jury to look through *their* version of the window of death. My gut tells me something unexpected will come up during the trial that'll tip the scale."

Joe hadn't picked up on Kelley's phrase: *the window of death* when he asked, "Like what? If these guys are so good, won't they anticipate every move?"

"Probably. But I think of murder trials as forensic warfare. More often than not battles are decided by accident, fate or some freakish incident that no one anticipates. That's what I think will happen in the Panforte case." Pat accepted Joe's puzzled expression as an invitation to elaborate. "I think there'll come a moment in the trial when some procedural or evidentiary quirk will suddenly predominate. When that happens, the search for the truth will get lost while the peculiar brains of lawyers wrestle with their arcane theories. That's when the judge will make a ruling or a seemingly insignificant decision that will gut one side's case or the other."

Joe asked, "What the hell kind of ruling could have that effect?"

"I don't know. But there's nobody better to make it than Lucy Grant. She the gutsiest, fairest judge I've ever seen, and I've seen 'em all!"

"Jeezus Pat, how can she try this case? You've as much as implied she's in love with Paul Brady and was kind of a surrogate mom for his kid during her troubling teens. What's the fuckin' P.J. thinking of when he assigned it to her?" Desmond protested.

Pat didn't tell him how he'd secretly gerrymandered the Panforte case by rigging the Presiding Judge's Bingo wheel. Kelley sighed heavily, bracing himself. He told Joe that the P.J. had planned to assign the case to Judge Francis X. McLain, the junior jurist on the bench, until Pat confidentially informed him that Judge McLain had been a guest of the Oregon Café the previous night. "Well, not here really, he was upstairs. The girl's name is Regina. I suggested to the P.J. that we didn't want to see an item in Caen's column reading: 'Who was the tall, handsome, white-haired jurist sampling the non-culinary delights at the Oregon Café? The Shadow knows.'"

Desmond thought it a bit disingenuous of Pat to be worried about San Francisco's witty columnist, since he was Herb Caen's best confidential item source at the Hall of Justice. Pat rubbed his chin with his thick hand and said, "Look kid, I know you and Mary Healy have a strong thing going. That's part of the reason for me to clerk the case. It'll take the heat off her. But I really think you and Mary ought to cool it while the trial's going on. There'll be more than enough sex and passions coming from the witness stand to keep old man Hearst salivating."

Desmond nodded that he understood. Then Kelley said, "Joe, we need a judge with brains and confidence without arrogance. Lucy's tried more homicide cases as a prosecutor and judge than anyone in town. And she's got the biggest set of balls on the bench. It's really gonna be up to Danny Loeb. If he doesn't want her trying the case, she'll step down immediately and the P.J. will probably call in an out-of-county judge. But Loeb's gotta think twice about dumping her. He's known her for twenty years and he respects her as much as Danny Loeb can respect any judge. And what he gets for a replacement, he doesn't know. A redneck from Alameda or a hick from Yolo County? With his guy's life at stake, he's gonna have to think long and hard on this one.

"I'll level with you. I've got a personal investment in this damn trial. My wife and kid will be in that courtroom every trial day and I don't want them hurt."

Joe incredulous, "Maria and Terry? For Chrissake Pat! How can you clerk the goddamn trial with you wife and kid there and all that history with your father-in-law and Panforte?"

"How can I not, Joe? How can I not?" Pat said, sniffing his cognac. Then he added, "The thing that gets to you in any murder case is the familiarity of it all. Usually the victim knows the killer. In the Panforte case every member of the court knows the victim and her parents and the accused and his parents. And they all know Maria and me. Maybe they don't know a helluva lot about my father-in-law, but Danny Loeb and old man Panforte do. Loeb was old man Panforte's lawyer in the proxy battle and Loeb's now rescuing his kid from the clutches of the law, just like he used the law to steal Maria's Dad's business."

The waitress announced last call and Kelley ordered another round and the check.

"I don't know, man," Joe said softly. "It's such a strange case. I mean here's a guy with plenty of money, a gorgeous wife, a new baby, and not a worry in life. It just doesn't make sense. It's one thing if he comes home and she's fucking the plumber. Like you said, she played Cinderella to his Prince Charming. Why would he do it?"

Kelley put his cognac snifter down. "We don't know that he *did do it*. We don't know if she went downtown to a show and something terrible happened. But you've asked the right question. We can't understand killing unless we answer the *why* question. You're a combat veteran, so you know why men kill. You saw me try to kill a man because he touched my wife. Unless we get into young Panforte's mind, and Paula's, we'll never understand what happened to her or what he had to do with it."

Joe shook his head. "You really think this is the kind of trial your kid should sit through?"

"He's twelve, almost a teen and bright enough to handle it. I want him to see topflight lawyers and learn about the discipline it takes to become a major player. I want him to realize the self-control you have to have when you're in combat, when you're competing against the best. I don't want my madness on the steps of the Italian Church to be his image of manliness."

"Still haunted by that, Pat?" Joe said gently. "Let it go, man. It happened. It's over."

"Like your war, Joe? Like freezing Bastogne?" Kelley nodded, accepting his young friend's advice even though he new he couldn't follow it. Trying to shift the conversation away from their violent ghosts, Joe remarked, "He's a smart little shit, but do you really think he'll follow everything?"

"I suppose," Pat sighed and a slight frown marred his round face. "Terry's very bright. All our kids are, but his is a really brilliant mind. It's almost scary. Unlike his sisters, he's all over the lot. He has his mother's temperament, which is where he gets his compassion and competitiveness."

"Yeah, but I think he gets his wit from you. What father wouldn't love a son who's compassionate, competitive and funny? And he just idolizes you, Pat."

"That's the problem. It's one of the reasons I'm having him sit through the trial."

"What's wrong with a son looking up to his father? I sure as hell wish I had a father to look up to. Maybe I wouldn't be so fucked up if I had a heroic father."

"Bullshit! You're not fucked up. You're free-spirited because your father was trapped in his own mediocrity. You're sexually liberated because you saw your father repress his feelings into a bottle. You found your manhood on a fearsome battlefield where you learned there are no heroes except the petrified ones inside ourselves."

"I still think it's normal for a kid to look up to his dad."

"Sure it's normal. But it's also an illusion. Boys look at their fathers and see a giant. A son sees that hair grows on his father's face and body, his father's voice is deep and foreboding, while a boy sounds just like his sisters. Fathers are so culturally vested with authority and wisdom they're more likely to suffocate the man that springs from them. And there's the matter of Terry witnessing what I did to that Marine. I don't want him making me his hero 'cause I'm handy with my fists. I don't want him to think a man's protective love only finds expression in violence and danger. My father died when I was only thirteen, so I never went through the teenage years with him. These are the years when the man emerging from the boy begins to look and feel and lust like his father. It's when a son discovers his father's flaws, when his hero's mantle begins to crack. My Dad was a fireman who died a hero's death saving a mother and her child from their burning home. But the feisty bastard ran back into the blaze to save the kid's goddamn dog! Then the roof, all flame and cinder, collapsed on him. The kid lost his dog and I lost the years in which I might have discovered my Dad's blemishes. He's still my hero 'cause I never learned his weaknesses, never saw him stumble, never discovered an infirmity or two. I have no map to chart my own journey to surpass him. All I can do is try to equal him. Like him, I have a loving wife and a wonderful son and I get a modest but secure paycheck from the city. But I'll never try to rescue a dog from a burning building," Pat said with uncharacteristic bitterness.

"I don't see how this trial's gonna somehow diminish you. I mean, how's he gonna feel when you arraign a big football star? You'll be charging him with murder one in a packed courtroom. Terry will be bursting with pride!"

"That's the illusion. Think about what'll happen during the rest of the trial. After Panforte enters his plea, we pick a jury. Then we have a three-week trial and Terry will be there every day. He'll hear clever arguments, scathing cross-examinations. From the witness stand he'll see pathos and perfidy. But he'll not hear a word from me in our courtroom. I'll be required to be as silent as he. Sure, I'll be center stage, but he'll realize that I'm not central to the play, no more so than the chair I sit in. In this magnificent war of words, he'll see I'm sitting out the battle, just as I missed out on the two wars that shaped the century. He'll discover my storytelling eloquence at his bedtime has no place in the Hall of Justice. He'll see that my playful Socratic method at home is but a feeble imitation of courtroom warriors to whose skills human life is entrusted. He'll see the only contribution his father makes to the fulfillment of human justice is to take papers out of a folder and then put them back in."

After the two court attaches had closed the Oregon Café's bar, if not its upstairs and back rooms, they headed for their streetcars. A block before Market Street Joe asked, "So what's the other reason you're bringing Terry to court?"

Kelley didn't tell his friend that the idea had come to him at St.

Mary's Cathedral during the singing of *Ave Maria* at Paula's funeral. Maria had seemed so poised and strong with the two men in her life at her sides, as though their unspoken but unconditional love barricaded the memorial grief of a mother losing her daughter and a son losing his mother. At that funereal moment Pat was certain that it took the combined love of Maria's father and husband to brace her to resist a tragedy so searing to the feminine soul. And he knew that Bertolli, after his experiences with American law as handed down by Fred Panforte and Danny Loeb, would never walk into an American courtroom, even as his daughter's escort. He also realized that, as the trial court clerk, he'd be immobilized behind his court desk, cut off from her by court railings, separating spectators from participants, unable to reach her when the words from the witness stand ignited her memory and her memories drowned her soul in a girl's first unearned sorrow.

He had not been with Maria when her teenage world came crashing down with her father's fall from commercial grace. It was 1923 and Pat, having graduated from Lowell high, was off in Mobile, Alabama for his cup of coffee as a professional baseball player. Maria was in her freshman year at Cal when Bertolli and Fred Panforte settled their litigation and stock battle. Pat didn't really know what she went through then. Even now, after almost twenty years of marriage, he still didn't fully comprehend the scars inflicted on a daughter by her father's failures. He still carried a great deal of guilt that he wasn't with her when she needed him most. They were in love, of course, they had been sweethearts from the moment that he'd looked into her dark, pool-like eyes that summer that he'd labored at The Market. Even when he'd finished his two-year stint as a pro ballplayer and returned to the City for a few months, he'd failed to sense both the depth and nature of her emotions. Oh, he intuited that she was different from when he'd gone off to play ball and she to college. He'd felt that she laughed less at his jokes and her ebony eyes seem to mist over more. At parties she was less than her vivacious self, and Pat felt that her social graces were more those of a skilled actress than the laughing, dancing girl he'd fallen in love with. He was her lover, and unwilling to suspend disbelief that there was nothing wrong with his girl.

Only she was no longer a girl and he was a boy no more. What troubled Pat deeply during this period of their relationship was his sense that she wasn't confiding in him fully. From their first high school date they'd shared their secrets, their dreams, their doubts. Maria had always said that Pat was a unique man because he was such a good listener, even better than her own father. But in her summer of discontent she had closed herself off from his tender probing as though revealing her darkest thoughts would drive her lover away. All she told him about *The Troubles*, as they called her father's business problems, was that her beloved Sonoma ranch and its hot, idyllic summers were gone, seized by Fred Panforte along with Western Poultry, which Panforte had renamed Great Western Poultry Company. When she told him that Panforte now owned all of the patents on her father's inventions, her lips curled down, weighted by unspeakable bitterness, making her beautiful face seem ugly and old, as though the lad her father had succored to grow into an American had stolen Bertolli's very intellect. Her father still owned their Russian Hill apartment building and a few acres of undeveloped property in Fairfax. However Maria's pain was most evident to Pat when she told him that her father's theatrical business partner, Antonietta Pompa, had sold their theater at Washington Square and fled to New York City. When Pat asked if old man Panforte had gotten their theater in the settlement Maria replied with more bitterness and anger than he'd ever seen in her: "No! Antonietta would never give in to that bastard!"

Being young and in love, Pat figured it must be the expected changes and challenges of college life and the burdens of a young woman who had matriculated to Berkeley to become a scholar and not find a football player for a husband. But Pat also noted that her academic approach had also changed dramatically. She had always been a gifted student, nurtured by her profoundly thoughtful father. But now she threw herself into her college life with a furious intensity. In athletics her competitive nature, so rare in women of her era, seemed almost obsessive, as though each tennis match or field hockey game won, was a retaliatory blow against the demons that were haunting her. In university lecture halls and seminars she became a glutton for scholarship. She took a double major in Philosophy and English Literature. Her predominately male classmates thought she was beautiful and sexy until she opened her mouth and silenced their sophomoric observations with a withering intellectual quip or a direct quote from Plato or Descartes or Spinoza. Her professors, on the other hand, were intrigued by this lovely co-ed. A few, after reading her research papers, invited her to audit their graduate seminars. Participating in advanced courses, in an intimate academic setting, so close to learned faculty and surrounded by men students who had longed passed the frivolous, beer drinking, panty raiding stage of college life, Maria told Pat that she would pursue a post-graduate degree. She wanted to teach. She felt that her father and professors had shared their wisdom with her. That's what education was to her. It was sharing the knowledge of centuries with others.

Given her academic obsession, Maria had little social life at Berkeley. But she didn't care. She had found her life companion in Pat. As a man Pat had assumed that her frequent blue moods and dramatic mood swings attacked her because they had to await marriage until after she'd graduated. Unable to recklessly consume their passions for each other without living together, Pat took a job as an assistant purser on the Matson Lines and sailed for China. They corresponded almost daily, their letters epistles of love across the sea. Pat wrote of the wonders of Asia and Maria of the thrill of higher learning. But she never wrote of that dark place in her heart. Pat wrote of his *want* for her and she wrote of hers for him. But she never wrote of her *need*.

As her father and Pat had escorted her down the aisle of St. Mary's, both guiding her with their hands on her arms on the way to internment of Paula at Holy Cross Cemetery, Pat felt that, at a terrible moment in her life, one that he still did not fully understand, he'd abandoned her for a kid's game and a sailor's adventure. This time he would be there for her. This time, no matter what the risks to his career, he would not abandon her to face her demons alone. Pat Kelley was forty-three years old on the day Paula Brady Panforte was buried for the second time. At Holy Cross Cemetery when the priest sprinkled holy water on the dead girl's silver casket, he decided to have his almost thirteen-year-old son escort his Mom to the Panforte murder trial. He prayed that his and his son's presence in the courtroom would have the same soothing affect that her male escorts had had at Paula's funeral. Pat answered Desmond's question, simply saying: "His mother. The moment I told her Panforte's son had been indicted, she demanded a seat at the trial."

"Did you discourage her?"

"Not at all. It would have been pointless. She's waited since she was a teenager to see old man Panforte suffer."

"Jeezus Pat, that seems so unlike her. I mean she's so openly loving and warm and generous. It's not old man Panforte on trial; it's his kid. And Bob Panforte was just a kid when his father took over Maria's father's business."

"I don't think there's a poet whose pen could capture Maria's loving nature. I'm the luckiest guy in the world that she chose me. But I fear her hatred for the Panfortes would embarrass the Devil himself."

Joe remarked, "It's so strange to believe Maria feels so deeply about this. It's just a business and a building with a bunch of stinking chickens. It's not like her Dad's in the poorhouse."

"For my wife it's not about business or money. And that leads me to my proposition for you." Pat reached into his briefcase and pulled out a Dictaphone cylinder and a poorly typed letter. He explained to Joe that, beginning with Bartolemeo Bertolli and ending with Fabrizio Panforte, a priest named Father Giovanni Agnello had educated and trained peasant boys from the Tuscan village of Farneta for their journey to America. These boys had all become commercial and cultural leaders in the Bay Area and among its most prominent citizens. During the course of his teaching Father Agnello had kept a journal or manuscript charting the journey of his students and their growing, prospering families in California. San Francisco's immigration records had perished in the 1906 Fire. Pat explained that the priest's manuscript was the only record of the migration of his students to San Francisco and their liberation from peasantry. Father Agnello called his boys his *Precious Ones*. "His last student and the only one for whom San Francisco immigration records exist is Fabrizio Panforte," Pat adamantly said. He continued: "When Father Agnello sent Panforte from Lucca to San Francisco in 1908, he gave him a sealed letter of introduction to Bertolli. Father Agnello knew that he wouldn't live much longer and that Panforte would be his last student. He knew his life's work was over, so he gave Panforte his manuscript and told him to give it to Bertolli. He knew Bertolli would understand its importance. The old priest told Panforte, 'Other than you personally, there's no more important cargo on the ship from Genoa to America than our manuscript. Guard it with your life!'

"Fabrizio replied: 'You call it *our* manuscript. Is it not *your* writing?'

"Father Agnello taught his final lesson when he told him: 'I've only preserved the story. Bertolli, Sebastiani, Milani, Bricca, Simi, the other Lucchesi boys and now you, Fabrizio, have authored it. There's no more important story than the triumph of common men over uncommon barriers.'

"Even then Panforte displayed his skeptical nature by saying: 'If what we've done is really so important, why not send it to the library in Lucca?'

"The old priest answered: 'It's important we never again let other men make us anonymous. We did live. We did struggle. We did grow. I, an old teacher, taught as best I could and my students taught me my faith in human potential was surely correct. If you remember nothing of what I've taught you here in the church of San Lorenzo, outside the great wall of Lucca, remember this, a man will never know where he is if he forgets where he came from.'

"On Maria's second birthday, her father met eighteen-year old Fabrizio Panforte on the second floor of Western Poultry, the building we just walked by. Bertolli told Panforte that he'd be staying at his Sonoma ranch until he was accustomed to American ways and could speak passable English. My father-in-law had sent his family to Sonoma after The Earthquake, while the city was being rebuilt. Before ferrying over to the security of Bertolli's ranch, Panforte presented him with Father Agnello's chronicle of the men from Lucca."

"What did Bertolli do with it?" Desmond asked.

"He gave it to me and now I want to give it to you."

"To me? What the hell would I do with it?"

"Joe, here's my proposition. My father-in-law believes that in their rush to become Americans, succeeding generations will shed their native language and lose the richness of their culture. Even though his own grandchildren presently speak fluent Italian, he's not certain their kids will. So he gave me the manuscript and asked me to translate it into English. With an English version the children of the men and women from Lucca will know where they are because they'll have learned where they came from.

"But I'm really a shitty typist and it would take forever for me to translate and type this stuff. This typed letter is my translation of Father Agnello's letter introducing old man Panforte to my father-in-law. So I borrowed one of those Dictaphone machines from the reporter's pool. The kind you talk into a microphone and it has a cylinder that a needle cuts into. Then, by a miracle of technology beyond my grasp, you put earphones on and there's your voice. I dictated my English translation into the machine. I'd like you to take the cylinders and type up my translations."

Joe smiled and said, "I use wire recorders, Pat. That's what J. Edgar Hoover's boys use. They're a whole lot better than Dictaphones." A look of disappointment came over Pat's face that Joe quickly erased by saying, "I think I've got an old Dictaphone at my apartment."

"Of course I'll pay you at your expedited rates."

"Don't insult me Pat. I'd pay you to hear the old priest's story."

Pat handed him a cylinder and said, "I've never dictated before, so you may have some trouble on this first one. I've heard you guys dictating for your transcribers and I noticed you say the words *coma* or *period* or *question mark*. I didn't do that. I found it distracted me. I just recited it, like an oral reading. Is that okay?"

Joe laughed at Kelley's modesty for his gift of language and his candid confession of incompetence in matters of technology. "Pat, whadda ya think I do for a living? The reason we dictate punctuation is the dumb, underpaid transcribers we exploit don't understand English any better than the waiters at Fior d'Italia. If I can take down lawyers in a pissing contest, I sure as hell can get the words of an Italian scholar recited by an Irish storyteller!"

"Great! Let's go home."

The green light at Market Street invited them to the safety zone to catch their different streetcars. While they waited for the electric iron monsters that patrolled Market Street, Joe remarked, "You were saying Terry's attending the trial partly because of Maria. Does he know her feelings about Panforte? Or that his grandfather and Panforte have such a bad history?"

"No, he has no idea of the source of his mother's feelings. He realizes she's rooting for the D.A. to gas Panforte, but he doesn't know that his grandfather and the ex-football player's Dad are from the same village. He thinks his grandfather was a drinking buddy of Puccini, hanging out with him at the Café di Simo in Lucca, pinching firm-butted girls. To Maria's credit she's never burdened our kids with her rage." Misty melancholy glazed over Pat's rich, brown eyes, but all he said was: "Goodnight, Joe. Thanks for listening to Father Agnello and me." He disappeared into the mouth of an iron monster, as it lurched forward to transport him from the safety zone to his family home.

At his Mission District apartment on 17th and Church Streets, Joe read Kelley's typed translation of Fred Panforte's priestly introduction to San Francisco and Bartolemeo Bertolli.

My dearest Bartolemeo,

The young man bearing this letter is my final student. I had not planned to train any more Precious Ones to journey to California after completing young Samuele Sebastiani's education in the vintner's art in the year of Our Lord Nineteen Hundred and Two. My days are much shorter now and my old man's mind is surely dimming. And I felt that you, my first and finest student, and the eleven other boys from Farneta, had accomplished so much in so short a time in America that teaching further Lucchesi youth to make the voyage to freedom was but the self-indulgence of an old teacher whose time had past.

But then the news of San Francisco's calamity reached Lucca. I wept when I saw the newspaper photographs of your city in desolation. I saw nothing but smoldering rubble and I despaired for my American sons. I tried to imagine the tribulations that you and Milani and Bricca, Simi, Sebastiani, the others and your families are compelled to suffer. To think that God could allow such a desecration of your triumphs as new Americans shakes the foundations of my faith with all the force that reduced your homes and businesses to ruins.

From your lately infrequent letters I have learned of your mighty efforts to restore "The Pearl of the Pacific" and rebuild the great commercial enterprises that all of you founded. Alas, I have come to believe that perhaps one more Precious One from Tuscany might help the children of my celibacy in this decisive moment in your journey.

I urge you to accept Fabrizio Panforte under your beneficent care, as you have done for all my students. I confess I am not the teacher I once was, and I hurried his training to speed him to your aid. He is very strong in mathematics, less so in philosophy and even less so in literature and linguistics. He lost his mother when she gave him life, and the unearned guilt he carries in his young soul no doubt explains his too somber demeanor. But it also explains why he burns with ambition. I implore you to complete his training in the code my Precious Ones.

I have also commissioned Fabrizio to deliver my sealed satchel to you. It contains my diary of the emigration from Tuscany to California. Perhaps I am guilty of the sin of pride when I refer to it as our manuscript of the transformation of Northern Italians to Northern Californians. The satchel also contains our personal correspondence over all these years. These papers I leave to your good graces.

As always, my fervent prayers are with all my sons and their families,
Giovanni Agnello
16 April 1908

Joe Desmond searched his hall closet for the old Dictaphone machine that he'd used for a while in court reporter's school. He slipped Pat Kelley's cylinder onto the spool, pored himself a glass of port and listened to his finest friend's narration of the journey of *Precious Ones*.

9

Sunday mornings for the Kelleys of Crestlake Drive were the only moments of respite from the hectic pace of a family with two working parents and three school-age kids. In appearance the Christian day of rest seemed to center around mandatory Sunday Mass for Catholics. But Pat Kelley had made an art of appearing what he wasn't. The family ritual started off with the Kelley kids rising by 8:00 a.m. without any parental prompting. They scrubbed and dressed themselves in their Sunday clothes, and because the Church required fasting before receiving Holy Communion their Mom was relieved of her breakfast duties. Not altogether bursting with Christian fervor and with grumbling empty stomachs, the three Kelley kids trudged fifteen or so city blocks to St. Cecelia's Church for Children's Mass. To his big sister Terry remarked, "I know why they call it The Holy Sacrifice of The Mass. *We're the sacrifice* 'cause we gotta go to it, while Mom and Dad stay in bed!"

"Oh, shut up, Terry! Don't be such a selfish brat! They're entitled to some time alone. Besides, they go to The Twelve-Fifteen Mass," Kathleen Kelley admonished. A few years earlier, Kathleen would have undoubtedly punched her little brother, but he wasn't so little anymore. In the last year he'd sprouted so many inches that he was two inches taller than his dad, an inch above his mom, and now even with his full-bodied teenage, older sister. But even before reaching height parity with her, Kathleen had that girlish intuition to recognize the very moment when her younger brother's body and coordination asserted male superiority in brawling matters. In matters of the brain, however, Kathleen was certain that a boy brain had not and could never match hers. Of course she never let on to him that she knew he could now whip her. In their final sibling confrontation, she'd shrugged and told him that she couldn't risk her priceless piano playing hands just to bloody his nose. Then she turned and walked away, her long, naturally curly brown hair, her father's gift, dancing on her shoulders, mocking her brother's pugilistic skills. On Terry's part he actually believed her, and, moreover dared not risk injury to the Kelley family's musical prodigy and face the wrath of both mom and dad simultaneously!

Pat and Maria, for their part, delighted that Monsignor Harold Collins had created Mass times for kids and adults. "He knows his flock," Pat would always say. And he surely did. The monsignor was a portly, balding chap – more charming than charismatic. First economic depression, then World War had transformed the barren sand dunes that bordered his church and parochial school into the final colonization of the western most point of San Francisco. Thousands of carpenter's hammers had built row houses for thirty blocks, all the way from his church above 19th Avenue to the beige sands of Ocean Beach. From the western border of Golden Gate Park to Vicente Avenue, on the edge of Pine Lake, four blocks from the Kelleys of Crestlake Drive, a city within a city had been built overnight – which was San Francisco's way. The Sunset and Parkside Districts were a bourgeoisie promised land for returning GI's and young middle-class families. Pat believed that Monsignor Harold Collins was a marketing genius! For his emerging middle class flock he'd ordered his priests to make their confessionals fast, simple and all penances extremely modest. Rumor had it that adultery only got the sinner three *Hail Marys*, three *Our Fathers* and a sincere *Act of Contrition*. But Pat thought Monsignor's nine o'clock Mass for kids and a noon Mass for their parents was a stroke of liturgical genius. *The Adult Mass*, as Pat called it, accommodated Saturday night partying Catholics time to recover sufficiently so that their hangovers would not cause them to miss the Second Collection, even though they might have missed the risen Christ. It also allowed the pastor's married couples to loll in their beds while there kids' spiritual needs were attended, thereby assuring new brothers and sisters for them and new Baptisms for St. Cecilia's. Pat had re-named his parish after Reno's most highly promoted gambling casino. In mirthful respect to Monsignor Harold Collins he called it *Harold's Club* and it stuck for the next twenty years.

For Pat and Maria, these weekly Sunday morning hours were the mandatory Mass of their marriage. Instead of a Solemn High Mass and the monotone of Gregorian chant, Pat had declared, "This is *our* High Mass - The Mass of the Holy Union!"

Maria had giggled, "Do I need to know how you're spelling *holy*?" She crawled on top of him, smoothing his face and mouth with kisses, silencing her garrulous husband. So for them, Sunday mornings became celebrations of sensuality and silliness, intimacy and passion and most of all the only certain time that they were completely alone with each other.

Pat was in the kitchen cooking Maria's Sunday morning break-fast-in-bed. It was their Lord's Day ritual that, after making leisurely morning love, Pat would cook her a breakfast of scrambled eggs, juice, a slice of cantaloupe and, by all accounts, the most dreadfully scalded coffee ever brewed. Maria never commented on his coffee making failures because she thought it was so sweet that he devoted his entire day to her. After breakfast in bed, they'd walk along Pine Lake, trudge up the lake's steep eucalyptus forest embankment to St. Cecilia's, ar-riving just as *Twelve Fifteen Mass* let out, in time to be duly noticed by their pastor and neighbors, all of whom had assumed that the Kelleys, like they, had fulfilled their Sunday duty. "In a way, we have," Maria had said, as they walked holding hands down 19th Avenue to Sloat Boulevard and then down the blacktop path to Sigmund Stern Grove on the east tip of Pine Lake.

To be fair, his scrambled eggs were excellent – not too dry, not too runny, Maria thought, as she searched under her covers for her black silk negligee that had been discarded during their intensely loving night. She found it in a wrinkled lump at the foot of her bed. She slipped the full-length sleeping-garment over her head, tugged at the string-like shoulder straps. She ran her hands over her body, absently attempting to massage the wrinkles out of her negligee. She propped two large feather pillows up against the headboard, got back into their queen-size bed and, half sitting, waited for her husband's first gift of the day. "Well actually, it's his second gift," she thought contentedly. She closed her eyes, drew a deep breath and spread her arms wide, stretching her morning muscles, her skin still tingling from her lover's touch.

When Pat returned with her breakfast she was sitting with her back against her pillows, their down-comforter at her waist cover-ing her legs. He noted that her stark black negligee emphasized that her skin this time of year was almost white, her rich olive complex-ion grown faint during the foggy Parkside District spring. But once school was out, she'd be off with the kids to their small, cabin-like summer place in Fairfax in Marin County. In a matter of just days, the Marin summer sun would transform her complexion to its natural dramatic darkness. As a girl who had spent her childhood summers on her Dad's Sonoma ranch, Maria's father had always kidded her that she was so dark of skin and eyes that she must be part Sicilian!

He'd nicknamed her *Moretta*, Italian for *Blackie*. Bertolli had reverted to her little girl nickname on what for him was the proudest day of his life, in one of the darkest hours of the century. Maria handed him her Master's Degree in Education from the University of California at Berkeley in 1929, his eyes filled with tears and all he could say was: *"Bene Moretta, molto bene!"*

Pat had told her it was like being married to three distinct women at the same time. In the summer he bedded a southern Mediterranean or perhaps a North African girl. In the fall and early winter she would turn into a golden Tuscan woman. This time of year she was clearly an American woman – beige, suggesting mysterious mulatto blood, perhaps, from licentious, cosmopolitan New Orleans. When Maria had asked him which of these three women he loved the most, he'd laughed and said, "The one I'm with, of course!"

Pat walked over to the side of their bed and rested the tray on her lap. She reached up and touched his cheek with her fingertips. He smiled down at her, then took his coffee over to his chair. When he sat in his chair instead of beside her, Maria arched a challenging eyebrow. In answer, Pat said, "Honey, we need to talk a bit about this trial." Maria chewed on piece of melon and nodded apprehensively.

"Some things I can control, some things I can influence and some I can do neither," Pat began. "You'll have your seat at the trial everyday. It will be in the Brady family row and the Panforte family will be across the aisle. If you're comfortable with that."

"That's fine," she said, smiling but wary.

"I've also assigned myself to clerk the trial and Joe Desmond will report it," he said.

"That's very thoughtful, Pat. Being there with you will make it easier for me. And Joe's such a sweetie."

He never referred to it as the Panforte case. He didn't have to. The only case at the Hall of Justice that Maria Kelley would ever attend during her husband's tenure as Chief Clerk would be the Panforte murder trial. He told her that the case had been assigned to Judge Grant. Her eyes brightened and cheeks flushed at the prospect of a woman having Panforte's life in her hands. Maria suspected that Judge Grant's assignment to the case might be one of those things Pat had influenced, but knew enough not to inquire. As the Chief Clerk's wife she was privy to many courthouse confidences that not even spouses – particularly judges' wives – would ever learn. Because of Pat's position, her attendance at Bench and Bar social functions was mandatory. While she carried off her wifely social duties with charm and grace, she secretly detested most of the members of the legal profession. Perhaps detested is too strong a word, but she didn't respect them. She found them boring, one-dimensional conversationalists with an excess of in-joke sarcasm at the expense of the people who populated their courtrooms in search of justice. Because of her father, Maria's childhood and teens had been spent in the company of show business people, beginning with a transcontinental train trip with her Dad to New York City in 1910 to attend a notable theatrical premiere. Her first job after graduating from Cal and before obtaining her initial teaching position was as Executive Assistant to the General Director of the San Francisco Opera Company. There was but a handful of members of the legal profession that Maria liked or respected - Lucille Grant was one of them. Maria thought Lucy, as the judge insisted everyone call her when she wasn't wearing her judicial robe, an irreverent woman with a self-deprecating wit and an adamant aversion to "talking shop" outside the Hall of Justice. Lucy even had a hilarious routine about being the only woman on the Bench. At a State Bar Convention, she'd opened her address on judicial ethics by asking the distinguished audience: "Fellas, what do you *really* think about a woman who works in her robe with nothing but guys around her?" She'd concluded her speech saying: "Looking around this entirely male room, perhaps now you'll appreciate why the goddess of justice wears a blindfold!"

Pat saw that Maria was pleased; no, excited at the prospect that the Panforte trial would be presided over by an independent career woman like herself, both of them flanked by her darling husband and the Kelley's good young friend, Joe Desmond. But it was time to dampen Maria's enthusiasm. So he told her, "Among the many things I have no power over, is whether Lucy stays on the case or sends it back to the P.J. for reassignment. That's Loeb's call."

"How can that be? You mean Panforte's lawyer gets to pick the judge?" Maria asked, anger simmering in her widening eyes.

Pat, at his soothing best, explained the Superior Court process of judge selection, without reference to his own manipulation of it, and Judge Grant's relationships to the courtroom players. Maria calmed, but Pat could see that she wasn't entirely mollified. He put his coffee cup down on the end table, rubbed his chin and said, "Maria, I'd like Terry to escort you to the trial. I'd like him to be there with you, with us."

Maria was incredulous. "You want our son in that courtroom!"

Pat started to rise from his chair, thought better of it and said evenly, "Honey, just listen for a moment. Have you thought about Fred and Angelina Panforte's reactions when they see you in the courtroom? They've known you since you were a little girl. But they don't know me. I've never met them and from all I've heard I haven't missed a damn thing. So they won't know that the court clerk is your husband.

"But what are they gonna do when they see Bertolli's daughter, his special child, unescorted at their son's murder trial? They're gonna ask their lawyer, what the hell's going on! Then Loeb will have to tell 'em, I'm your husband! That's the last thing Loeb wants. The less the Panfortes know about our incestuous little courthouse the better for Loeb to control them and his own case. If Terry's there with you, nobody will think twice about a son escorting his mom."

"Is that all?" Maria asked, knowing that it wasn't. Pat took a deep breath, like an opera singer girding for an exacting aria: "There's more. I want this for Terry, even more than misleading old man Panforte. Honey, all are kids are gifted. But the girls are so much more focused. Terry's gift of language is extraordinary for a boy his age." Maria nodded in agreement. Her husband continued: "But Terry, well, he doesn't appreciate that the power of language derives from work and damn hard work at that. Like any smart kid he knows what it takes to get by in school. So his gift for language becomes glibness and the poor, under-educated teaching nuns coo and cluck over his essays, as though they had a young Jonathan Swift in their classrooms. I want Terry to sit through this trial, where he'll have to be absolutely silent, and do nothing but listen and watch. I want his mind entirely engaged by the spoken words of Moore and Loeb. I want him to experience the awesome power of words in action!"

"Oh please!" Maria shook her head. "Lawyer's language bears only faint similarity to English. They speak and write in convoluted sentences, reveling in adjectives, disdaining verbs. They repeat judicial clichés as though redundancy creates profundity, and they constantly display a momentary lust for a comma when a lasting relationship with a period would suffice!" Then Maria smiled shyly and said, "Like that last sentence of mine."

"You're right, honey," Pat seemed to concede. "But you've never witnessed a murder trial. There are only a handful of lawyers capable of trying a capital case. Lawyer prose, in the shadow of the gallows, is not the language of law! Both Moore and Loeb are among the best in matters of homicide. They understand that the power of persuasion derives from an economy of words, and that the clarity of conflict is more readily perceived when presented in its starkest form."

"Is that where you get your notion that a trial is performance art – from murder cases?" Maria asked skeptically. Pat nodded and then she said, "So what's our part in your little drama? Who do you and Terry and me play? Are we the Greek chorus?" Pat seemed to resign, "Perhaps." He went to her bedside, removed the tray from her lap and took the dishes downstairs to the kitchen. When he returned, he sat in his chair again, his gesture that there was still more to discuss. Pat said, "We've always been candid with each other, Maria. Especially when it comes to our kids. We've always shared our doubts about ourselves as parents and teachers. You've been blessed with a terrific father, and I lost mine when I was about Terry's age."

"Yes, but you have a terrific mother, darling, and I don't," Maria softly interjected.

"I know," Pat said. "And I'm not getting Freudian with you. What I'm getting at is that Terry's going through changes that I've already been through, that I understand. I didn't have my Dad to guide me when my teenage hormones took over. I think I can help Terry get through this confusing stage. At least I've got to try.

"Sometimes I think Nature is so bizarre. I mean, here's our darling daughter with a body fully capable of conceiving and giving life to a child! But she's still just a girl and yet every component of maternity, save mature judgment and mother wit, is in place. Love, you're the one who has to be her soul's surrogate until her mind grows into her lovely body." Pat shook his head at the mystery of his maturing daughter and said, "I don't know, but when Kathleen started growing breasts and had her first period last summer at Fairfax, it was so strange for me. It was like I'd just gotten *another* daughter to love. For me, even now, there's like two Kathleens – the young woman she's become and the joyous little girl that I can't let go…"

Maria, her eyes Athena-bright, gently said: "Then don't, darling. Don't ever let that little girl go! That's what fathers are for. To keep the girl alive in their daughter's grownup soul," Then she reminded him, "I thought we were talking about Terry and the trial."

"We are," Pat said. "But we're also talking about us. Or maybe we're talking about me. When our daughter came of age it made me think that girls and women are cyclical creatures, while boys and men are so linear. I was struck that female and male physiology are almost perfect metaphors for the *telos* of the sexes. A vagina is oval, capable of extraordinary reformations and total transformations of function, without ever breaking the infinite continuity of a circle. A penis, on the other hand, is a straight line. Well, guys like to think of it like that. It has only two forms – turgid and limp, and only two purposes – peeing and planting..."

Smiling, Maria held up her hand to stop Pat's monologue. She loved it when he lectured on his latest theories or shared his unique speculations with her. She had told him that he was never boring, but sometimes a bit tangential, given to analogies and metaphors that tempted incredulity. So she said, "Darling, I have a vagina and, because of you, love, more than a casual familiarity with a penis. Get back to Terry."

"Of course. It's just that the maturation of girls, while internally complex, is so clear and simple. One day they're girls and a day later they're women. On the other hand, a boy seems to have a hiatus, sort of a teenage time-out, when he's neither boy nor man. If I know one thing about teenage boys, it's this: there is no human creature potentially more violent than one who is no longer a boy and not quite a man! I'm afraid I've given Terry a terrible example of manhood when I attacked that Marine at the Italian Church..."

"Oh darling, you mustn't feel guilty about that bastard!" Maria cried, her eyes watering.

"Not guilt about him. No! The appalling thing is that I'd do it all over again to the sonofabitch, only I'd do it better," Pat said, for the first time an edge in his voice. "Maria, do you ever think about what our son feels about his maleness."

She shook her head, "Pat, I've no idea what you're talking about."

Pat explained, "All his young life men have been presented to him as warriors, as athletic competitors. Combat and competition, we tell our boys are what make a man. Then he sees his Daddy triumphant in both! Only he sees more than that. He sees his father defending his mother. Unfortunately, what he sees reinforces the very worst in masculine mythology - that damnable chivalrous legend of a knight coming to the rescue of a damsel in distress! Let's face it, Maria! You weren't helpless, but that Marine sure as hell was when you stuck a cigarette in his ear and kneed him in the balls!" Maria smiled wryly at the image but said: "So what's it got to do with Terry taking me to the trial?"

"For two, maybe three weeks, he'll be in a packed courtroom where his father's silence puts bread on our family table. All of his senses, all of his emotions, all of his thoughts will be authored by the spoken words of others, words in horrible conflict. I just want to help him become a man. In our courtroom, I want him to learn that a man's words are far more lethal than his clenched fists."

Maria started to reply, but he waved her off, saying: "More than anything, I don't want you to go through this alone. Your father will never set foot in the Hall of Justice. I want the other two men in your life with you ever minute of this trial. Is that so terribly wrong?"

Her face softened and she said, "No, it's not wrong at all. It's...it's terribly right."

She flicked her fingertips at him, mutely calling him to her bed. He sat beside her on the edge of their bed. She reached up and ran her hand through his thick curly hair. She loved to play with his rich brown hair. His full head of hair, that aging never shed, was Pat Kelley's only vanity and she knew this. Pat looked into her liquid eyes and saw sorrow and pain and hope. She touched his lips with her fingertips to silence him. "No more words," she whispered hoarsely. He nodded and together they collapsed back onto their Sunday morning bed.

When Pat was certain that Maria was dozing contentedly after their love-making he slipped out of bed, showered and shaved. His morning toilette was a regretful moment for him. He hated to wash her taste and scent off, as though it might erase his memory of their intimacies. He dressed and took the serving tray downstairs and washed their breakfast dishes. When he returned to their bedroom Maria was dressed in the black mourning two-piece suit she had worn at Paula Panforte's funeral. Pat realized immediately that she was standing him up for their Sunday stroll from Pine Lake to Sigmund Stern Grove. She was primping her hair at her antique French dressing table. Without looking at Pat, she asked, "When do you expect the trial to begin? Will we have to cut short our stay in Fairfax?"

"Not likely," Pat replied. "In a death penalty case both sides need time to prepare. Then there's August, when we pretty much shut down The Hall for vacation. My guess is it won't go out 'til September, maybe October."

As though she was talking to herself in her mirror, Maria asked, "What about Terry's school? Have you thought about that?"

"Actually, I have. I figure we can get Sister Beatrice's lesson plan for that month and you could tutor him. That way he'll keep up with his classmates," Pat said.

"If I tutor him it will be to surpass his classmates!" she said to her mirror.

Pat sensed anger in his wife's tone. He said, "I suspected as much. I'm going to bargain with him. Terry and I will make a deal. He comes home with a single C and it's outta the courtroom and back to the classroom!"

Maria turned to face her husband and said, "I don't teach kids to get letter grades! I help them grow to their potential. And when they do I raise their bar still higher. The most enduring lesson I give them is that there is no final grade to learning. Education is growth, and while their young bodies will one day stop growing their minds must not. So you make whatever deal you want with Terry. Just leave me out of it!" A chastened Pat nodded, "Okay."

Maria rose, walked briskly to her clothes closet, picked out a hat and put it on. She said, "I'm going to Mass. I'll meet you at Stern Grove later." She walked past Pat to the hallway without kissing him and then down the stairs to the front door. When Pat heard the door close behind her, he went downstairs and called out for their dog, Clio. Their black part-retriever, part- shepherd bounded clumsily up to Pat's leg, panting, her tale wagging furiously in anticipation of a walk around Pine Lake. "Come on, mutt. It's just you and me."

As soon as Clio was let out the side door she sprinted down the steep slope to water's edge. She took a couple of laps of tepid water, shook her head disapproving of the water's taste. Once Pat was lakeside, Clio ran about fifty yards ahead of him. But she'd periodically look back at Pat to make sure her master was following her or that she hadn't gotten into any dog mischief. Pat would give her a hand wave of reassurance and off she'd happily prance. He laughed to himself at Clio's futility in making bumble bees busily darting over berry blossoms her playmates or when she chased sparrows and wrens, utterly mystified by the phenomena of flight. Clio's play caused him to think of his own kids playing at Pine Lake before they'd hit double digits, as they had described their ages. Kathleen and Terry, and later Megan, would rummage in the berry bushes that surrounded Pine Lake armed with empty mayonnaise jars with nail holes puncturing the tin lid, hunting black bees marked with a single yellow stripe. They avoided yellow jackets because they could sting you at least once before expiring and the bumblebees couldn't. Or so they believed. When they'd captured enough bees – or a *herd* as they described their prey – they'd scramble up the hill to their mom and ask her to make honey. Maria and the kids studied the buzzing, panicky insects bumping into the clear glass walls of their prison and falling momentarily dazed from the impact to the bottom of the mayonnaise jar, landing on a piece of lettuce. Maria smiled and asked, "What's the lettuce for?"

"It's in case the bees get hungry," Terry replied, implying to his mom that it was his idea. Maria suggested that rabbits would find lettuce more appetizing than bees. She gently told them these were not honey bees and that she wasn't a queen bee – except in the metaphorical sense. "What's the point of being a bee if you can't make honey or sting?" Terry mumbled.

To temper their disappointment at their failed nature excursion, she suggested they go back to the lake and pick black berries and she'd teach them how to prepare jam preserves. They happily slid down the steep Pine Lake slope, liberated their honey-less bees to the damp spring fog and set about harvesting berries for Mom's kitchen. They stuffed their mayonnaise jars and pockets with ripe black berries, eating every third or fourth plucked berry, and then raced back up the hill to show their mom their harvest. When Maria saw their berry stained faces and hands, her kids looked like they'd escaped from the clutches of a primeval forest monster only after bloody combat. She sent her kids to wash up, and after they did she taught them how to put up preserves, which they did without her help for the next few years. When Pat happened into the kids' bathroom, the stained sink and bath tub looked like a particularly gruesome homicide scene without a dead body.

On this Sunday walk with Clio Pat reflected that you didn't immediately notice the growth changes in your kids. He wondered if Maria did. Probably, he thought. He hadn't noticed the subtle changes in their neighborhood either, as row houses crept closer and closer to the Kelley's private rustic preserve on Crestlake Drive. San Francisco's final migration had brought an army of middle class kids to their neighborhood. It seemed to Pat that almost as soon as his kids had abundant playmates other than bees and berries they ran off on iron monster streetcars and cable cars all the way across the City to their French grammar school. They were becoming city kids, like New York City children, freely roaming the urban landscape even as their neighborhood peers became San Francisco's first suburbanites. He liked the notion that his kids were seeking a world beyond Crestlake Drive, even beyond his control. This was why, it seemed to him, Terry escorting his Mom to the Panforte murder trial made sense.

Pat had to admit to himself that it had gone poorly with Maria this morning. He had anticipated that Maria would experience mood swings when told her of his plan to have Terry escort her to the trial. But he'd not foreseen the intensity or rapidity of the moods that had so overwhelmed her. He had thought that the setting and timing was just about perfect to tell her of his plans for their son. With the kids gone, alone in their bedroom after making morning love and serving her breakfast in bed, Pat had figured that she'd feel pampered and this would cushion the emotional blows she was likely to receive from their dialogue. For a while his strategy seemed to have worked. But then he remembered that there was an almost desperate quality to Maria's lovemaking after he'd revealed his plans. It was as though she had panicked that she was somehow losing her beloved. When they'd climaxed she had told Pat not to move, and then she had clamped her thighs together, trapping him inside her, her body implying that if he withdrew from her she feared he would never return. As he strolled to Stern Grove to meet Maria and his family a sin of Fred Panforte that he hadn't understood as a young man in love with Maria came to him. He had come to believe that the fervor of his wife's college scholarship was compelled by old man Panforte's seizure of her father's patents. Pat realized that, to Maria, this was like seizing her father's intellect, violating his creative Muse and pimping Her like a Tenderloin hooker. Bertolli, even more than the saintly Father Agnello, had been Fred Panforte's greatest teacher. Yet Panforte had repaid the life scholarship he had been given by Bertolli with betrayal.

As he reached the eastern tip of Pine Lake Pat thought it was Maria's sense that Terry's attendance at the Panforte trial would occasion their son's loss of innocence. She must fear that Terry will learn more than the cruelty of murder. He may discover the brutality of human betrayal, the sheer horror his mother experienced whenever the Panforte and Bertolli names were linked. For Maria, soon to become her son's substitute teacher because of her husband's plan, he now realized that Fred Panforte's most grievous sin against Bertolli was as a student turning against and destroying his mentor.

Pat delighted that Maria was a truly remarkable teacher, particularly with boys. It seemed to him that she was always able to find a boy's hidden spot of vulnerability and gently show it to him so that he could marshal his weakness into an essential strength. After the war, she'd insisted on a teaching position at All Hallows parochial school in the Bayview/Hunter's Point District of the City. What had once been a working class Irish/Italian neighborhood known as "Butchertown" because of its slaughterhouses and meat packing plants had been transformed by the Hunter's Point Naval Shipyard during the war. "Rosie the Riveter" and a mass migration of Negro defense industry workers coming from Texas, Arkansas and Louisiana overnight rebuilt the United States Navy and launched her fire power at imperial Japan. The parish school, therefore, became populated with kids whose parents had been raised in the segregated, Jim Crow South, where public education's principle mission was to teach their darling black babies that they were not entirely human. But in post-war San Francisco this new immigrant wave was earning wages they had never dared dream of. So they enrolled their kids in their neighborhood Catholic school and Maria Kelley rushed to southeastern San Francisco to brighten the eyes of their kids, to give them a bar to reach for and then to raise that bar again and again.

Unlike the teaching nuns, she didn't feel answerable to bishop or pastor, only to her kids. She took over the 7th grade class and when the first boy who spoke had called her *Missy Kelley* she told her class, "I'm Mrs. Kelley. I'm married and have three children. Married women are called *Mrs.*, unmarried women *Miss*. There are no *Missies* or *Massas* in California. Children, I have very few rules, but you'd best remember them. None of this master/servant nonsense, and when you speak to me keep you heads up and look right into my eyes. And boys, no shuffling feet!" Maria's girl students giggled until she said to them, "And girls, no swaying hips. Save that for your husbands!" Then the boys guffawed, until Maria said, "It wasn't *that* funny!"

She asked her class if any of them played basketball. Most of the boys nodded with enthusiasm and a few boasted of their court prowess. Then Maria announced another of her rules, saying, "Let's get this straight! None of you talk in my classroom unless you raise your hand and I recognize you."

Jonathan Powell, the tallest boy in the class, raised his long bony arm. Maria recognized him and he asked, "What happens if we don't follow your rules?" Maria walked over to his desk and told him to stand up. He was about her son's height, so they were eyeball to eyeball. His skin was semi-sweet chocolate and he had big, lovely brown eyes; like Pat's she thought. Her classroom was absolutely still as she starred intently into his eyes. Then she said deliberately, but without anger, "Oh Jonathan, you don't *really* want to know what will happen to you if you break my rules, do you?"

For a moment, he held her fierce black stare in silence. Then he whispered, "No ma'am."

"No, Mrs. Kelley," she corrected. Jonathan repented:

" No, Mrs. Kelley"

Then Maria Kelley took her entire class out to the school-yard. She challenged Jonathan to a game of horse and soundly trounced him by sinking two-handed set shots from beyond the key. She organized her class into co-educational basketball teams and held an impromptu tournament to the delight of the children. In her first moments as their teacher, she had used child's play to subvert the dour pedagogy of the Sisters of St. Joseph of Orange. For Maria, however, coaching athletics was a fundamental component of her educational program. Her father had raised her in the ancient Hellenic tradition of sound mind, sound body. Using team sports as a metaphor she taught her kids that success requires cooperation, self-discipline and striving. Within days Maria Kelley was the talk of the neighborhood, the pretty dark-haired schoolteacher who could shoot the eyes out of the basket.

As he walked his dog Pat realized he had made a terrible mistake. He had brought the Panforte ghost into the sanctuary of their bedroom, the room that she had designed for them to love without fear or condition. He had imposed upon her tutoring duties for their son. For Maria, all her students were *Precious Ones* and Pat knew that he was manipulating his wife in the hope that she would pass on to Terry the educational code an unknown Italian peasant priest, even as Terry might learn of the sole Tuscan student who had dishonored his teachers' gifts.

Of course the Panforte case was front-page news, and the victim and accused so prominent that the whole town was engaged in wild speculations. But Pat was a courthouse insider, admittedly an anonymous one. Because of his position and reputation for discretion judges, lawyers, cops and public officials freely confided in him. So he had full access to the homicide inspectors' investigation. But he had no way of penetrating defense counsel's theory of the case, which Daniel Loeb and his private eye, David London, guarded with rigid secrecy, other than striking out on his own. He had already mastered the details of the prosecution's case, somewhat anticipated the defense's response, namely that this glamorous loving couple had too much to drink that caused an uncharacteristic domestic spat. Loeb didn't have to prove that Paula had in fact gone to the movies, but the DA had to prove that she hadn't. Pat was certain that there was more to the Panforte defense, and he had to discover what it was before his wife and son did. What struck him most was that both sides seemed to have confined the scope of their inquiry to the Panforte's Francisco Street home and the days following Paula's reported disappearance. Kelley was confident that the seeds of this tragedy had been planted in the folds of family. He felt that his anonymity would provide sufficient cover to moonlight on his own into Paula Panforte's death.

There were too many missing pieces or ambiguous ones for Kelley's fertile mind. Why didn't the homicide detail check out the Fox Theater? Bob Panforte's statement that his wife had gone to a show alone was inherently plausible, and even the dead girl's mother thought so. Shouldn't the homicide boys have expanded the scope of their investigation beyond a Marina bedroom and a Marin mountain to exclude all others with homicidal opportunity? And what was the true nature of the couple's marital relationship? Based upon his conversation with Eileen Brady and her sister Pat had no doubt that Paula had a healthy sexual appetite. Indeed, the girl's own mother had actually prayed that Paula's infidelity had driven her from her home.

And what could he make of her husband's expressed disapproval of sexual intercourse during her time of the month? If he was in fact repelled by her menstruation, why did he have sex with her and complain after the fact? Did they actually have sex on the last night of Paula's life? Pat must also look with the Coroner through the window of death to determine the time she'd expired. If Pat discovered *when* she'd died, he'd be able to establish *where* she died and the location of her death might tell him *how* she died.

On his Sunday morning stroll Pat Kelley decided to undertake a surreptitious personal investigation of Paula's mysterious death. He would not re-trace Inspector Murphy's investigation. He would go to places and sources that the homicide investigators had not probed either because they thought these places unimportant or they were unaware of these sources. *Where, when* and *how* had always been homicide's mantra that sang *why*. He had to get into Robert and Paula Panforte's minds to determine the *who* and *why* of it all. To do this he must back track to the last weekend of Paula's life and beyond. Somehow he had to penetrate the natural family shield of the Bradys and Panfortes that obscured tragedy's truth. Pat had to escape the all encompassing shadow of young Panforte's father. But where was there a place that Fred Panforte didn't psychically hover over his only child,

Pat asked himself. Well, there was their Petaluma poultry operations that were so self-managing that Fred had entrusted his son to run them, Pat answered. And there was Bob Panforte's exemption from military service during the war and that Army training program over at Mt. Tamalpais. Since the incriminatory Army entrenching tool in Bob Panforte's garage had linked him to Paula's burial site, perhaps this was the place to start. Maybe Pat's pal, F.B.I. Special Agent Bill Moriarity, might know something about it. Moriarity was Terry's Godfather. The Kelleys were driving to Moriarity's home in San Rafael later to celebrate Terry Kelley's Confirmation. Terry's marginal religious training caused Pat to think of Bob Panforte's high school years at St. Ignatius. Perhaps his four years with the Jesuits might have revealed some inclination or aptitude that he was something other than a good-looking rich kid. Pat decided to have a chat Rev. Louis Barnett, S.J., the principal of the Jesuit college preparatory that Bob Panforte had graduated from.

Pat also realized that he had a source of information about Panforte men that no one else had. He had Father Giovanni Agnello's papers that told the story of the boys from Lucca. Perhaps in this old teacher's pages Pat would find the key to Fred Panforte's paternity. Pat believed that the sins of a father were visited on his son – whether his own father or his own son's father - and that he might find in Father Agnello's papers clues about Fabrizio Panforte that predicted the American that he'd become and the father that he was. There was one fact, one terrible similarity that only Pat Kelley, knowing the history of his father-in-law and his protégé, was aware of. If Fred Panforte's son had indeed turned against his wife, was it some kind of an emotional replication of something his father had done at about the same age. Fred Panforte had turned against the most important person in his life and seized Bertolli's creations. As Maria had said, "If it wasn't for my father, that bastard would still be grubbing porcini mushrooms in a Tuscan forest!" Had Bob Panforte repeated his father's sin? Had he attacked the most important person in his life, his own wife - the mother of their baby? These were the questions that Pat would investigate, and the answers, though he had no premonition of their consequences, would determine the outcome of the Panforte murder trial and forever change his family and all of the families who would assemble in the Hall of Justice.

Pat had decided to employ Joe Desmond for record making purposes and as a credible witness in case anyone challenged the orthodoxy or propriety of a court attaché investigating a murder case while the trial was pending. He knew that any hint that court attaches were moonlighting as private eyes would cost both of them their jobs. But he also believed that Joe Desmond, tempered in horrific combat, was as loyal and tough a young man as he'd ever known. He'd use Joe to perform tasks that his relationship with old man Bertolli disqualified him from performing, particularly if they involved Danny Loeb.

10

When Pat arrived at Sigmund Stern Grove for the San Francisco Opera Company's free performance of Puccini's *Madama Butterfly*, the grass amphitheater was packed with 10,000 spectators. He immediately spotted his wife, father-in-law and mother-in-law and his youngest child, Megan, sitting at a green picnic table on the grassy knoll that allowed them an elevated view of the stage. There were only about a couple of dozen picnic tables at Stern Grove for the summer free concert season, and you had to take dawn possession of them since there were no reservations. Unless, of course, you were Pat Kelley and your doubles tennis partner was the Director of Parks and Recreation, which owned and operated Sigmund Stern Grove. Thus this center picnic table was effectively a Kelley family possession. Most of the crowd was packed into the bowl, many with blankets to ward off the dampness from the lush fog drenched lawn. Other thousands sat on lawn chairs or used eucalyptus trees as back-rests row upon row up the slope of Pine Lake forest.

When Pat arrived at their table, his father-in-law, dressed in a gray suit with vest and a gray fedora with a green pheasant feather peeking from the hatband, rose to greet him. The two men embraced and kissed cheeks in the European fashion. Renee, Maria's mother with her perpetual frown, pecked Pat coldly on the cheek. She was a petite woman with thick long black hair striped with gray that she always wore pinned up in a bun, accenting her dour demeanor. She dressed in dark colors in fashions that concealed her full, but drooping body. And her wardrobe was at least twenty years old. It was as though she was in perpetual mourning, her wardrobe a relic of her days as the wealthy wife of Bartolemeo Bertolli before Fred Panforte's seizure of his empire. Maria's mother still hadn't accepted Pat as the proper spouse for her youngest child. True, he had given her adorable grandchildren, but she thought he's so...well, so *common*. Given her daughter's college degree and the Bertolli's social position, Renee felt that Maria had married below her station. Initially, her attitude hurt Pat when he was younger and infuriated Maria, who had threatened to exile her from her grandchildren's lives if she so much as mentioned a critical word to Pat or the children. So locked into her life, or more accurately her memory as the wife of a wealthy man was she, that Renee never understood that at the time of her daughter's marriage Pat's Mom could have bought and sold her a couple of times without diminishing her own net worth. Kate had dismissed Renee's rejection of her son, telling Pat, "She's just a peasant with airs!"

Unlike her daughter, Renee did not harbor hatred for the Panforte clan nor did she blame Fred for the loss of the business. She blamed the family fall on "that showgirl your father spent so much time with!" Maria was so outraged by her mother she threatened: "Mom, if you ever so much as mention Antonietta again, so help me God, I'll slap your face!" Mrs. Bertolli got the message and never again did. Except for free summer performances in Sigmund Stern Grove she'd never accompanied her husband to the theater. Then again, her husband's theatrical life had been one from which she had always been excluded and Maria, as a little girl, intimately included. Renee's segregation from her husband's show business world was not, however, unilateral. She was uncomfortable in crowds, a bit mystified by rarified literary conversations and, frankly, perplexed that her husband was so attracted to a business that he had to put money into rather than his chicken business that he took so much money out of.

Even the Kelley children sensed the tensions between their parents and their *Grandmere*, as she required them to call her. Renee had emigrated from Brittany, France and was a Francophobe, devoted to the French Hospital in which her grandchildren were born and the French school which all three now attended. In the early days of Pat's marriage, she used her native tongue whenever she wished to criticize Pat to Maria. However when Maria cautioned her that her grandchildren were fluent in French and would repeat every word she'd uttered, Renee was at last silenced. For his part Pat diplomatically refrained from telling his mother-in-law that her ancestors in Brittany were, in fact, Celts and not Franks!

Maria glided around the picnic table and hugged Pat tightly and kissed him full on his lips, her message that she had risen from the despair with which she had left their home for church. Maria was a *toucher*, a woman whose greetings and departures seemed to always require a tactile message from her heart. Her elongated kiss of her husband was her message to her mother as well. Pat was relieved that she seemed in fine spirits, and credited her father's presence rather than any divine inspiration available at St. Cecilia's. That was the strangest thing about Maria Kelley, how quickly and unpredictably she could shed her skins and paint for others an untroubled face. From a quiet distressed moment alone with her father or Pat or others she'd emerge reborn, with a serving tray of food delicacies and laughing, engaging chatter as though food and charm allied to rescue her from her shadows. At their picnic table in Stern Grove, she was in constant motion, arranging the anti pasta, smearing sardines and anchovy fillets on slices of baguette, refilling wine cups, all the while seeming to chat with everyone at their table and a few at neighboring tables simultaneously. Pat marveled but was a bit frightened at the celerity of her mood swings. She could, as she had in their morning bedroom, dive so deeply into her waters of despondency and now had risen so quickly to the surface of social normalcy. She was like a deep-sea diver rising too rapidly from the ocean floor but not becoming delirious from the bends, recapturing her breath by tending to the supper of all who came to her table. But then he hadn't gone with her into her depths and so her speedy rise to light was hers, not his.

Pat sat down across from Bertolli and Megan. Maria served him a plate of prosciutto and melon and Bertolli poured him a Dixie cup of red wine from a jug. "Where's Kathleen and Terry?" Pat asked.

"Kathleen's warming up the singers," Bertolli replied. Then shaking his head and smiling he added, "Terry's backstage with her. He's trying to convince Gaetano that he's her agent and he's exploiting his client by not paying her!" Maria grinned at the thought of her bold, precocious son negotiating on his big sister's behalf with the founder and General Director of the San Francisco Opera Company.

Bertolli offered Pat the libretto, which he declined, saying he had the story line down by now. In truth, Pat's mind was not on an American naval officer who shirked his paternal responsibilities with such tragic consequences for a lovely and loving Japanese girl. In two days he would formally arraign Robert Panforte on the charge that he'd murdered his wife, making his own son as motherless as his own father had been as a child in Tuscany. More and more, Pat was beginning to feel that this upcoming trial had a sub-text of strong men's paternities. He had speculated that Robert Panforte's blandness, his lack of accomplishment other than on the gridiron, might be generational in nature. He had observed that the second generation of immigrant stock, the first American born, often did not measure up to their fathers and only rarely surpassed them. But his wife was a marvelous, living refutation of such a notion. She had a dazzling intellect, refined cultural tastes and a frenetic energy level that would have exhausted a lesser man than her husband. Thinking about Maria as the first chords of *Madama Butterfly* floated with the breeze through the scented eucalyptus leaves, Pat realized that it was not purely vengeance that compelled her to attend the Panforte trial. She was doing it for her father. She knew that he would never set foot in an American courtroom because of what Fred Panforte and his lawyer, Daniel David Loeb, had done to him twenty-seven years earlier. Maria felt there had to be a Bertolli presence in the Hall of Justice, and she was the only Bertolli strong enough to confront Fred Panforte's paternity.

Studying American immigrants, you observe that their characters are molded by both the leaving country and the receiving country. For both Bartolomeo Bertolli and Fred Panforte, their leaving country was Italy – more particularly Lucca, Italy. In most ways, their Italian backgrounds and experiences were similar. Both were contadini, whose families had farmed fertile Tuscany for centuries. They were shaped by hard, physical labor, but captives of an economic structure that promised meager advancement and little security. Both had been advised and trained to journey to San Francisco by the same village priest who concealed his scholar's mind with a cassock of humility. It was, therefore, the receiving country that would mature their characters, if not assure their ultimate conflict. But the reception of migrants to America is as varied and distinct as the generations, even the decades, in which it occurs.

Bertolli was sixteen years old when he sailed from Genoa to San Francisco in 1882. He had no relatives or acquaintances when he arrived. He was a strapping lad of six-feet, well-muscled from his young life of demanding physical labor. He had a full head of curly, jet-black hair that accented his fog gray eyes and senatorial Roman nose. It took him six months to become fluent in English, indeed quite eloquent, but only one month to start his first business hauling other men's products with his horse and wagon – his first American capital investment. His arrival in San Francisco coincided with a wave of Northern Italian immigrants from Genoa, Lucca and Piedmont. They all blended well with the dominant American Puritan ethic of prudence and industry. But Bertolli, like his countrymen, possessed that genius for innovation so natural to Italians. As a driver for truck farmers he was introduced to the wholesale produce commission market, and by 1890 had founded Western Poultry. Although Nativism still persisted in California, ethnic discrimination against Italian-speaking laborers was neither as brutal as it was for the Chinese nor as pervasive as it was for their Southern Italian brothers in the cities of the eastern United States. These new arrivals, Bertolli noted, understood neither the nature nor the purpose of labor unions and had a peasant's suspicion of savings banks, preferring to hide or bury their paltry savings. Well before A.P. Giannini created his bank for just such a class, Bertolli came up with a plan to assure the stability of his workforce.

Although his Western Poultry Co. was incorporated it was really a family business in fact, if not in form. In an era and locale that knew nothing of stock options or profit sharing plans, Bertolli decided to offer his employees stock in his company along with their salaries. A similar concept had been tried by the Italian Swiss Agricultural Association at its vineyards in Asti, California. The vineyard workers, however, were given a choice between room, board and stock in Italian Swiss-Colony Wine, or salaries. Knowing little of equity ownership, they opted for cash salaries. So Bertolli offered his employees – executives and laborers alike - both wages and equity, and was rewarded by never having a work stoppage or serious labor dispute. His was a closely held corporation so there was never any intent to declare dividends. Nonetheless Bertolli granted generous year-end bonuses based on productivity and company performance. He never paid much attention to the requirements of legal forms of business entities. Although he'd been raised a Roman Catholic, he had been educated as a renaissance man and thus rejected legalisms as little more than coerced morality. His only teacher had taught him that the beauty of the Hebrew bible was its revelatory literature; its terrible flaw, the failed codification of divine sentiment. He was taught that the splendor of the Christian gospels was in its parables, each a metaphor of mercy. The Scripture, he believed, in the hands of pontiffs, pundits and prelates, was as draconian as the Napoleonic Code or English common law and not nearly as socially relevant. So it was not out of character that his contractual relations were governed by his word, no matter how ill advised it may have been given. For Bertolli, lawyers were superfluous. He considered his business an extension of his person. He had never considered the legal consequences of holding his real property, including his Russian Hill home, in the company name.

The San Francisco to which eighteen-year-old Fabrizio Panforte had arrived two years after The Great Earthquake and Fire was of a different century and a distinct ethos. It would prove a century of unimaginable scientific discovery and inconceivable genocide, a hundred years of stunning human progress achieved in a milieu of the most appalling human

*debasement. Young Panforte was dazzled by his first sights of San Fran-
cisco. The only images of the City he had seen before his arrival in April
1908 were news photos that his teacher in Italy, Father Giovanni Agnello,
had shown him. They pictured a city of rubble shaded by dense clouds of
smoke and lonely skeletons of tall burnt-out concrete buildings. Father Agnello had told him that he had trained and sent a dozen boys from Lucca
to San Francisco where they and their families grew and prospered until
their city and businesses were devastated by trembling earth and searing
flames. He had told Fabrizio that his mission was to join the Precious Ones,
as he called them, and help them re-build their city, their homes and their
enterprises. When Fabrizio stepped down the gangplank of the S.S. Santa
Clara he was shocked by the city that greeted him. In the two years since her
destruction, while Panforte studied under Bertolli's teacher in Italy, San
Francisco had risen, phoenix-like, grander than she had ever been. Of the
28,000 buildings destroyed in 1906, 22,000 had risen to replace them —
taller, more ornate, and structurally stronger.*

*At the Embarcadero he saw mobs of people squeezing into locomotive-
less trains, not powered by steam but by a single trolley on the car's roof
attached to a black wire. Up Market Street for as far as his eyes could see,
slim, tall buildings – much taller than even the duomo in Lucca - stretched
for the sky on both sides of the street, creating a concrete canyon. The air was
filled with the raucous sounds of carpenters' hammers, steam shovels and
mechanical cranes competing with draw horses and wagons as thousands
of cursing construction workers raised even more and higher buildings. He
saw his first horseless carriage jugging by right in front of him!*

*Fabrizio set his single suitcase and Father Agnello's satchel on the dock
and removed an envelope from his inside coat pocket. Signor Bertolli had
mailed Father Agnello a map he'd drawn for Fabrizio with directions to
Western Poultry Company. He precisely followed the written directions,
stopping at each street corner to verify that he was on course. He was in
the wholesale produce and poultry center and the fragrances of lettuce and
herbs, caged live chickens and citrus fruits reminded him of his trips with
his father to Lucca's Roman amphitheater where they bartered their meager
farm products. But this market was astonishing to him. It was so huge and
the wholesale outlets were housed in buildings, not open air stalls like Lucca.
Not even Father Agnello's lessons on the richness of California's soil and the
enormity of her population could have prepared Fabrizio for what he was
seeing. At Davis and Washington streets, he saw a large concrete building
with a sign reading: WESTERN POULTRY COMPANY. He checked his
map to make sure the English words on the building matched those on his*

map. On the sidewalk piled four and five-feet high were crates of canta-
loupe, casaba melons, butter and romaine lettuce. Water gurgled like a small
stream down the Washington Street gutter until it cascaded like a waterfall
through the wrought iron grates of a sewer. Inside Western Poultry, Fab-
rizio walked down a corridor formed by tomato crates stacked eight-feet
high and cartons of grapefruits and oranges about the same height. He
walked directly to a glass-enclosed stall that was lettered with the English
word: CASHIER. As he had been instructed by Father Angello he talked
into the round hole in the glass window to a red-faced Irishman who was
stuffing a large quantity of American currency into cash drawers. In Ital-
ian, Fabrizio said, "I am Fabrizio Panforte, from Lucca. Father Agnello
has sent me for Signor Bertolli."

In Italian with an accent unfamiliar to Fabrizio, the Irish cashier said,
"Oh, he has, has he?" Then in English, he yelled out to a Chinese porter, "Oh
Louie, take this Lucchessi lad to the boss!" Fabrizio had never seen an Asian
face before. The porter parked his hand truck under a tier of tomatoes and
gestured with his head for Fabrizio to follow him. They found Bartolo-
meo Bertolli in what Fabrizio thought was a large storage facility. He was
working with tools and wires at the far end of a refrigeration unit. Fab-
rizio shivered in the cold. He had never seen, much less heard of electrical
refrigeration. Bertolli looked up from his work, smiled wryly and said in
Italian, "You must be Fabrizio. I've been expecting you. You had a pleasant
voyage?"

"Si, Signore."

"Well, let us get out of the cold and go to my office where you can tell me
all about Farneta," Bertolli said, placing his arm around the young man's
shoulder.

In his second floor office Bertolli invited Fabrizio to talk about his fam-
ily and life in Tuscany. His comments about his father and brothers were
brief and unenlightening. He talked almost exclusively about his two years
studying under Father Agnello as though his very existence was limited
to these years. Bertolli understood his shyness and believed his reticence to
talk about himself natural for a lad in his first days in a new land. As the
first of Father Agnello's students to reach the Bay shore, Bertolli's first days
in America had been unique from all who followed from Lucca. He was
completely alone in a foreign land, not yet able to converse in English. Yet
he didn't feel alone or abandoned in a strange land. His education had
been so profoundly thorough that he was able to make ideas his companion.
He bought a horse with money Father Agnello had loaned him and then
constructed a wagon and hired out as a teamster. He studied placards that

advertised services, eavesdropped on bartering conversations to learn pricing for his drayage services. Each evening in his small rooming house quarters, he'd write Father Agnello and report on what he'd learned. As subsequent Precious Ones and other Lucchese arrived in San Francisco Bertolli made it a point to greet them and show them around the City. Although he had been comfortable in the solitude of his first American days, he realized the value for new immigrants having a friend welcoming them in their mother tongue. So greeting and providing an urban orientation to his mentor's final student was by now a ritual for Bertolli and one that he enjoyed. He felt that it was his job to minimize the fear these brand new Americans understandably felt and maximize their wide-eyed wonder at this sparkling city by the Bay. Remembering that Father Agnello had praised Fabrizio's mathematical aptitude Bertolli tried to draw him out by propounding mathematical problems to him. Fabrizio handled the problems easily and quickly. Bertolli nodded approvingly, "Bene, molto bene!"

Fabrizio presented Bertolli with his letter of introduction from Father Agnello and Father Agnello's satchel with his manuscript and correspondence. Bertolli quickly read the letter, then said, "So you want to become an American?"

"Si, Signore." Bertolli leaned back in his desk chair, "We can help you, but to become an American, you must have it here," Bertolli said tapping his finger to his heart. "And here," tapping his forefinger on his forehead. Fabrizio nodded and Bertolli continued, "You will be a guest in our home tonight. Tomorrow, we will sail over to our ranch in Sonoma. You will be quite comfortable there. The land is much like our native Tuscany, although the climate is much better for vintners and farmers."

"Yes, Father Agnello told me you had written to Signor Sebastiani and told him about Sonoma. You wrote: 'I have found our country, but here, we can own the land,'" Fabrizio said.

Bertolli smiled, "So you know that story. Did our Father also tell you what would be required of you in your first days here?" Fabrizio shook his head, noting that this was the second time Bertolli had referred to their teacher as our father. He had never thought of Father Agnello as paternal figure because he was a celibate priest and he hadn't thought of his own father at all during his voyage. Father Agnello's priestly humility and his father's meekness did not measure up to Fabrizio's image of paternal authority. On board the Santa Clara his thoughts focused on Bartolomeo Bertolli, as he tried to imagine what the man in whose hands his American destiny rested would be like. Now, in Bertolli's presence at the center of his commercial empire, he felt the first stirrings of a son's awe of a father. Of course, he kept such thoughts to himself for fear that Signor Bertolli might think him disrespectful. It didn't occur to Fabrizio that his thoughts implicitly disrespected the man who had bred and raised him without a wife and the teacher who had educated him for his journey to this land of unimaginable opportunity.

In a deep fatherly tone, Bertolli said, "Your first job as a Western Poultry employee will be to attend the Sonoma school. There Mrs. Calderon will teach you to read, write and count in English. Mrs. Calderon teaches the first eight grades of elementary children at the little schoolhouse a meter or so from the piazza. It's a short walk from the bunkhouse where you will be staying."

"You are sending me to a school for little children?" Fabrizio frowned.

"Young man, you will find that playful children are the best teachers of your new language. And you can help the children with their mathematics. Think of it as a trade – they teach you English words, you teach them numbers. Many of the men you see working in this great marketplace stayed with us in Sonoma and learned the language and American ways in that little red schoolhouse. Also, while you are at the ranch you are not to speak any Italian. After today all my family members and ranch hands will speak only English with you. If you are as diligent as our father has written, you should be speaking passable English in a few months. It will take somewhat longer for you to write well. If you agree to these terms, you will have a job that you are suited for at Western Poultry."

Before Fabrizio could verbalize his assent, a black, odd-looking instrument on Bertolli's desk began ringing like church altar bell. Fabrizio had never seen a telephone before, so he was mystified when his new boss began speaking into a cone while holding a fat tube to his ear. Bertolli was speaking English into this odd equipment, so Fabrizio was utterly baffled. When Bertolli replaced the tube in a cradle-like device sticking out of the long black cylinder he explained to Fabrizio that he had just spoken to the pastor of the Italian Church and had to meet with a man about purchasing some North Beach property. He invited Fabrizio to join him.

As they walked up Columbus Avenue on the way to Bertolli's meeting with Father Raffaele Piperni he told Fabrizio that the Italian church pastor had grown up with Father Agnello in Genoa, and that Father Agnello had advised his boyhood friend to enlist with Don Bosco's Salesian Order because he wanted to be a missionary. The Archbishop had requested that the Salesians come to San Francisco to solve the Church's Italian Problem. Fabrizio asked what the Italian Problem was and Bertolli explained: "When the first big wave of Italians came over, most of us were Republican followers of Garibaldi. Some were monarchists, adhering to the House of Savoy. But all of us were anti-clerical and rejected the Church's opposition to unification. Many of the most prominent men in our community are free masons, running large enterprises such as Fontana's California Fruit Canners Association and Ghirardelli's Chocolate Factory. The Archbishop thought that all these free thinking Italians were a threat to orthodoxy."

Fabrizio asked, *"Are you a free mason?"*

Bertolli laughed, *"No. The only religion I practice is the one I learned from our teacher in Farneta."* Fabrizio asked him if he attended Mass regularly. Bertolli smiled coyly and told him that he'd received sort of a dispensation from Father Piperni. Bertolli told him that he financially supported the Salesian's educational work with North Beach children and attended a monthly seminar in classics conducted by Father Piperni in Greek or Latin, depending on which of these ancient cultures was the discussion subject. Bertolli explained that one of the brightest members of their classical seminar was a very powerful man politically by the name of Abe Ruef. Ruef, the son of a French Jewish merchant, had graduated from the University of California at the age of eighteen in the year Bertolli had arrived in San Francisco. Over the years he had been a strong supporter of the Salesians education of young Italian immigrants, and deeply respected the ingenuity and hard-working ethic of the North Beach community. He was thrilled to learn from Bertolli that Father Piperni was fluent in Hebrew, having directed an orphanage years earlier in Palestine. The pastor and the ambitious lawyer added the Hebrew bible to their classical curriculum. So elated was Ruef by the addition of Hebrew to their studies that he doubled his annual contribution to the Italian parish to $1,000. By the turn of the century Ruef was the political boss of San Francisco, having elected a handsome musician, Eugene Schmitz, as Mayor. During Mayor Schmitz's first two administrations Ruef, the unofficial legal advisor to the Mayor, had made a fortune by charging legal fees to businesses needing licenses or municipal contracts to fatten their bottom line. Railway companies paid six figure fees to convert from cable cars to electric trolley carriers, a phone company retained Ruef for a quarter of a million dollars to secure their monopoly, and he represented all of the notorious French restaurants, where a gentleman's meal was sweetened by the amorous professional services of a lovely prostitute. If you operated a French restaurant you had to hire Ruef to obtain and renew your liquor license. The City's tolerance for graft, however, did not survive The Great Earthquake and Fire, Bertolli informed Fabrizio. Ruef had long been the lawyer who had preserved the Spring Valley Water Company's monopoly on San Francisco's water supply. When the Great Quake struck, the antiquated and miserably maintained water mains burst, denying firefighters any chance to combat the flames of 1906. "A month before you arrived, Abe was indicted on corruption charges and now faces prison if he's convicted by a jury," Bertolli concluded.

Across from Washington Square Park, Bertolli realized that Fabrizio had no idea what a jury was, so he explained: "In America we, the people, pick our rulers and when a citizen is charged with a crime his judges are his fellow citizens. Only a man's twelve neighbors can take his liberty away."

Bertolli interrupted Fabrizio's civics lesson by inviting the lad to step into a small Tuscan bakery across the street from Saints Peter and Paul's small wood-frame church on Filbert and Dupont Streets. The baker and his wife greeted Bertolli warmly and he introduced Fabrizio to them. The chubby baker's wife giggled and said in English, "I just took it out of the oven, so it's nice and warm." From the back shelf she slipped a dark, crusty loaf of bread into a white paper bag. She handed the bread to Fabrizio and said in Italian, "Panforte for Signor Panforte, just like they make in Siena!"

Fabrizio thanked her and she told him the thanks was due to Signor Bertolli who had specially ordered this loaf of panforte in honor of the young man's arrival. As they walked out of the bakery, Bertolli turned to Fabrizio and said, "It's only flour, eggs and seasonings, but it bears your name. Your name now lives in two countries. Never forget the one you came from, and never disrespect the one that welcomed you."

They crossed the street to Washington Square Park for Bertolli's meeting with Father Raffaele Piperni. The pastor was sitting on a green park bench in the shade of a Monterey cypress tree, studying architect Frank T. Shea's initial design drawings of the Italian cathedral. Father Piperni was a small man, with receding black hair, large ears and wire-rimmed eyeglasses anchored to his face by his long, hooked nose. Bertolli introduced Fabrizio to the priest who said, shaking the immigrant's hand, "Another of Agnello's boys, welcome!"

Father Piperni handed the architect's drawing to Bertolli and asked him what he thought of the design. Bertolli studied it for a moment and said, "Very interesting! But I think twin Romanesque towers would provide more dramatic balance with a simple unadorned crucifix between them. I'm not sure I like the façade. It's too ornate. Perhaps a stark façade would emphasize the grace of the towers and grand dome. It's a good start. Frank has done a nice job."

Since these were his first American hours, Fabrizio thought it impudent to join in the conversation about the construction of the Italian cathedral.

But his facile mathematical mind did agree that Signor Bertolli's design suggestions had a purer geometry to them than the drawing displayed. Since the pastor and his boss were speaking Italian as a courtesy to him, Fabrizio thought it might be their invitation to contribute to the dialogue. And surely Signor Bertolli would be pleased that his newest employee agreed with his architectural judgment. But he didn't know how Father Piperni felt about the architect's creation or Bertolli's critique of it. These were important men and he was just a contadini. From observing his poor father he'd learned that a peasant's silence was the safest method to avoid opprobrium. He had learned much from Father Agnello and would learn even more from Signor Bertolli. But he dared not expose that timorous feeling in his gut whenever in the presence of men more accomplished than his father, which was just about every man he'd ever met beyond the boundaries of his pathetic family farm. So he just listened and occasionally nodded as Father Piperni explained to Bertolli his purpose for their meeting.

Father Piperni had decided that lots on the six hundred block of Filbert Street were the perfect location for the Italian cathedral. These lots belonged to Abe Ruef, and when Father Piperni had told Archbishop Riordan that he thought he could make a good deal with Ruef the Archbishop was apoplectic at the thought of his diocese doing business with a Jewish crook under indictment. Father Piperni had suggested that the purchase of Ruef's property could be brokered by his most distinguished parishioner, thereby insulating the Church from any hint of scandal. Bertolli chuckled, "So I'm your most distinguished parishioner?" His pastor laughed, "Of course!"

Bertolli accepted the assignment and told Fabrizio that they were going to Abe Ruef's office to buy the land from which the Italian cathedral would spring. They walked a few blocks to the corner of Columbus Avenue and Kearny Streets and entered a spanking new, triangular shaped office building taller than any building Fabrizio had ever seen. A brass engraved nameplate identified the structure as the Sentinel Building. Fabrizio was wide-eyed when Bertolli led him into a black, wrought iron steel cage that was pulled by thick cables up to the fourth floor of the building. This was Fabrizio's introduction to an elevator. On the fourth floor, the flying steel cage stopped, Bertolli slid open the metal gate and Fabrizio followed him down a marble corridor. They reached a door, the upper half of which was frosted glass with gold printing. Bertolli translated the English words for him, informing him that the sign said: A. Ruef, Ideas, Investment, Real Estate. The young immigrant knew what ideas were, but investment and real estate were mysteries to him.

As they sat silently in the reception room waiting to be ushered into

Ruef's office, Fabrizio began cataloguing the remarkable things he'd witnessed in his first hours in San Francisco. He had seen more tall buildings – and was now sitting in one – than in Lucca and Genoa combined. The streets had been filled with horseless carriages and there was that huge storage room at Western Poultry where, by some Bertolli magic it was kept as cold as a winter night in Tuscany. Fabrizio had been dazzled when he saw Signor Bertolli talking into a black gadget, and he had just taken a ride in a moving cage. He wondered if Father Agnello had any idea of the strange and wonderful things that seemed so common to San Franciscans, and he knew that his father and brothers would never believe him if he wrote to them about his first day in America.

Abe Ruef waved Bertolli into his office and Bertolli introduced Fabrizio to San Francisco's deposed political boss as his "associate." He explained that it was Fabrizio's first day in America and requested that Ruef speak Italian so that the young man might learn about real estate negotiations from a successful businessman. Ruef smiled modestly and said in perfect Italian, "I'm afraid Signor Panforte will only learn that 'the meek will not inherit the earth.' With lawyers' fees, the bail premium, and disbarment likely, how can I refuse the Archbishop?"

Bertolli assured his fellow classicist that Father Piperni would never take advantage of his recent misfortunes, for to do so would be contrary to the paramount Christian virtue of mercy. Ruef rolled his eyes and said, "So, I'm to be treated like the Good Thief at Calvary. That's most reassuring, Bartolemeo. But he did, after all, end up hanged!"

"Don't be silly, Abe. You have nothing but goodwill in North Beach. Your present legal troubles are relevant only as they create necessity for you and opportunity for an Italian cathedral," Bertolli said.

"Precisely!" Ruef replied. "So let's dispense with any notion of mercy. In matters of business, for Jew and gentile alike, 'the quality of mercy' is indeed strained. I'm honored that our old friend wants to build his church on my property and will happily deed both lots for the modest sum of $60,000."

Although Fabrizio had no idea of American currency, his fine mathematical mind easily grasped the numerical values as the two older men bargained vigorously. After discussing comparable land values, Bertolli countered with an offer of $40,000 for both of Ruef's lots.

To Fabrizio, Ruef seemed gravely insulted by Bertolli's counter-proposal as he said, "My friend, enough of this hondling. You know that I can beat your price on the open market. Out of loyalty to Father Piperni, let's shake hands on $50,000 and not a penny less!" Fabrizio watched Bertolli slowly shake his head. It was a gesture of neither rejection nor acceptance.

It was more like he was contemplating that they had struck a good deal and he was forming the words to close the deal in his mind. Moreover, Fabrizio had overheard Father Piperni tell Signor Bertolli earlier, at the park, that he was willing to purchase the property for as high as $55,000 and that anything below that figure would be, in the priest's words, "a steal."

Bertolli said heavily, "I'm afraid we're at an impasse. I only have authority for forty-seven-five." Ruef shrugged, his palms outstretched, as if to say: "So be it." Then Bertolli said that he had an idea that might break the impasse. He proposed that Ruef agree to sell the lots to the Archdiocese for the construction of the Italian national church for $47,500. In addition, Bertolli suggested that Ruef act as a broker for Antonietta Pompa who wished to purchase the Russian Orthodox Church on Powell Street between Union and Filbert, across from Washington Square, for her variety theater. He urged Ruef that the commission for what Antonietta would rename the Washington Square Theater would more than make up for the discount he was giving the Salesians, particularly if he could convince the Russians to pay his commission. As the two men shook hands, Bertolli said, "All in all, it's a good deal for everybody. You make a nice profit and contribute to the religious and cultural life of North Beach. As for the Russians, well, they were the first Europeans in California. They didn't appreciate the value of their holdings then and they don't now. They won't even know the difference." Ruef smiled generously in complete agreement.

As Fabrizio and Bertolli rode in the elevator silently down to the ground floor, Fabrizio mentally processed the first American business deal he had just witnessed. Of course, he was too new to the land to appreciate the historic importance of the moment or the ecumenical irony of an Italian basilica designed by an Irish architect, to be constructed for an Italian flock on the consecrated grounds of a Jewish crook.

Outside the Sentinel Building, Bertolli led his young student back to Washington Square where he introduced him to Antonietta Pompa, the artistic director and star soprano of Teatro Italiano, for whom the political boss of San Francisco had just agreed to act as her real estate broker. Bertolli quickly explained to Fabrizio that he and others, including Abe Ruef, had been financing the internationally acclaimed performing artist who was producing a rich menu of Italian variety-theater in North Beach. Bertolli's words were like a whisper to Fabrizio as he tried not to gawk at the stunning Neapolitan actress. He thought of the lovely soprano, Angelina, who he had met in the duomo in Genoa days before sailing for America and that his first sighting of her had had the same affect on him. But the loveliness of the young church soprano and this American stage star were complete opposites.

Signora Pompa answered the Genovesi teenager's Carrara-white skin with a faint olive complexion and Angelina's startling aqua-blue eyes with flashing her hazel ones that she seemed able to transform into different hues as easily as she changed the tone of her voice. And the girl in Genoa was petite, with pears for breasts, a delicate frame, almost like a fragile doll. This American woman, whose hand Fabrizio had clasped in greeting, was tall, full-breasted, the geometry of her body an intricate and infinite interplay of circle and plain. As they conversed, Fabrizio felt that she seemed to use every part of her body to form and emphasize her words, whereas Angelina had often lowered her eyes and head as though her brain had ordered the rest of her body to remain motionless, fearing somehow that feminine fluidity might betray her. It didn't occur to him that this classically trained actress was required to master body movements before she could utter a single stage word or sing a single note, nor did he realize the girl in Genoa suffered from a teenager's insecurity at the recent arrival of a woman's body in her convent environment, where feminine forms were but stealthily acknowledged. Fabrizio was quite shocked at Signora Pompa's attire. She wore beige slacks – Fabrizio had never before seen a woman in trousers – with a white silk blouse open at her neck, the swell of her breasts peeking out above the pearl-like third button. Her light brown hair was piled high on her head, a few random streams of curls dangling over her ears. But it was the gracefulness of her long neck that he couldn't help staring at. He had assumed that Antonietta was his boss' mistress and his admiration for Bertolli soared even higher.

Later, alone in a guest bedroom in Bertolli's Russian Hill home, Fabrizio reviewed his first American hours and tried to formulate the subtle meanings in his day of passage, perhaps even transformation. He looked out his bedroom window at the Golden Gate that he'd sailed through at dawn and saw, from the peak of the highest populated hill in San Francisco, the jagged green arms of land's end in Marin and San Francisco reaching toward each other across the bay. It was as though the earth itself had embraced his ship as it had calmly slid toward harbor. But it was the incredible warmth that Bartolemeo Bertolli had exuded from his first moments at Western Poultry Company that touched him. Now he had taken him into the very bosom of his family.

Signor Bertolli's lovely wife, Renee, had prepared a sumptuous French meal with the delectable accent of her native Brittany. Signora Bertolli was not as gracious and vivacious as Signora Pompa, but that might simply be the difference between a Frenchwoman and a southern Italian one, thought this lad who had known no women in his life. He wondered if

Signora Bertolli had any hint of her husband's gorgeous lady friend. The dinner conversation in Italian, out of deference to their young guest, was genial and Fabrizio was surprised that Signor Bertolli's two oldest children, twelve-year-old, Michael, and eleven-year-old, Clare, were allowed, actually encouraged, to participate in the conversation. It was in cold contrast to his family dinners, where his older brothers ate in silence and anger that their father seemed to pay attention only to Fabrizio. But it was his baby girl, Maria, age two, who was clearly the center of Signor Bertolli's affectionate attention. He spoke with her more maturely than Fabrizio had expected, and surprisingly she was mischievously articulate for a two-year-old. Her older siblings didn't seem to resent her at all, but at this family table you had to be aggressive and even a bit quick to stay in the dialogue. Although Signora Bertolli contributed sparsely to the conversation, Fabrizio was grateful for the loquaciousness of his other hosts because he didn't have much to say, and there was that ubiquitous pinch of shame in his heart that had been with him since his earliest conscious recollections, which cautioned verbal reticence.

As he gazed out his window at the firefly lights of the city, he couldn't help but think of his derisory Farneta household. It seemed so devoid of useful possessions and warmth, so wealthy in anguish. Yet on Russian Hill, he was enveloped by an opulence of things and filial affections. It did not occur to him that Bertolli and all of the Precious Ones came from the same impoverished roots from which he had sprung. Perhaps this was the greatest lesson Father Agnello had failed to teach or he had not learned. His welcoming dinner ended with little Maria crawling onto his lap and looking up at him with her wide, black eyes and saying, "Are you coming to our ranch? I'll let you ride my pony, if you want."

"Grazia, mia piccina," he said, and her father's smile beamed at him.

He got into bed and courted sleep, but the images of the people he'd met in his first day off the ship danced in his imagination. His new boss had referred to him as his associate, as though they were long time partners with that unspoken intimacy born of successful collaboration. What was it that he had witnessed or maybe even participated in, he asked himself. He had been part of a deal unlike any of the bartering he'd learned with his father in the marketplace in Lucca. It seemed to be a contract with the Church, a crook, a capitalist and a singer. Accustomed to the rigidity of caste and class in Italy, he was confused by the ease with which so many different and contradictory worlds interacted in San Francisco. He calculated the mathematics of the bargain that he'd witnessed, but they seemed incapable of numerical computation. It was as though the men and woman who had bargained before him had placed a value on appearances. Abe Ruef wanted to appear an Italian Church benefactor and patron of the arts for the jury that would judge him. Fabrizio suspected that one or two of these neighbors who apparently picked America's rulers and decided men's freedom would likely be of Italian descent. Therefore he concluded that Ruef's sale of his property to the Salesians must be like the tax his father had to pay to pass through the Wall of Lucca to sell their produce. Then there was the Archbishop who wanted Ruef's land without the scandalous encumbrance of his name and reputation. So the transaction had been made to appear Bertolli's business deal. But Bertolli had received nothing, not a single lira for his efforts. To Fabrizio this made no sense. Numbers were pure logic and Bertolli's efforts without profit was illogical. But Fabrizio didn't and would never understand that goodwill is its own value and can never be quantified.

Finally, there was that woman. That she shared her bed with his boss, Fabrizio assumed. But the notion that Bertolli was in business with a woman seemed bizarre or worse, perverse. But even she seemed at ease with the creation of appearances. As an actress, he thought, that's what she does. In her little play she wanted the Russian Orthodox Church purchased from straight-laced clerics to transform an altar of holiness to a stage of secular or even blasphemous fantasy. In the sheer illogic of San Francisco, it seemed to make sense that the Russians – so long oppressive of Jews – would be more pliant with a beautiful gentile woman than Ruef.

Fabrizio couldn't help but think of his father in Farneta. He contrasted his Papa to the first American men he'd met. He twisted his head on his pillow in an attempt to banish this polarity from his mind, to purge his vision of paternal pathos of Italy combating American masculine refinement from his thoughts. In his pre-dreams, he saw his father's unsmiling, sunken face. And then Signor Bertolli's sculpted cheekbones, gray eyes and Roman nose appeared. At last, Fabrizio drifted off to sleep and, never again, remembered his own father.

11

The first sixteen anonymous years of Fabrizio Panforte's life were lived with his father and his two older brothers in the small village of Farneta on the outskirts of the Tuscan city of Lucca. Fabrizio's mother had died bringing him to life, and there lingered in the boy's subconscious the feeling that he was somehow responsible for her death. When the priest spoke of original sin at Mass, the boy failed to grasp the mystery that an infant was accountable to God for the sins of Adam and Eve. Yet he accepted that his own young soul had been stained by his mother's death, and he prayed to the Blessed Virgin that the waters of Baptism had cleansed his soul of his original sin.

Fabrizio's father, Carlo, and his brothers worked a meager plot of land on which they raised chickens and grew carrots and tomatoes. Every Friday Carlo transported their humble bounty on an oxen-drawn wagon to the walled city of Lucca, where he bartered meekly with the merchants and servants who fed the ancient city. Carlo was a simple peasant and yet, like most who barely subsist from the land, possessed an intuitive sense of Nature's ways and the unwritten moral code which circumstance proscribed for the poor. Like many Tuscan peasants, his family name was taken from something that came from nature but was molded by man. Panforte is the name of bread made in Siena, the city of Carlo's birth. It's a dark, crusty bread with a hint of bitter aftertaste. As he grieved at his wife's grave, cradling his infant son, he accepted that he was well named.

His wife's premature death was more than a terrible family tragedy for Carlo and his sons. It threatened this peasant family's very existence. The survival of peasant families of that time required that the entire family work the land and a peasant wife and mother was the essential component of the collective farm. She worked in the fields tending crops as well as maintaining their humble house. She was the "family physician" and the only teacher her children would ever have. As Carlo tucked Fabrizio into his crib, it was the loss of the infant's nurse and teacher that tormented him most. As if his baby son could sense his father's painful musings, Fabrizio started to fuss and then began crying. Carlo walked quickly to the sink and picked up a piece of linen Gina Bertolli, his baby's wet nurse, had left for him with instructions that, if Fabrizio cried for a night feeding, linen dipped in goat's milk would pacify him until she arrived at dawn for his morning feeding. Carlo wrapped the delicate linen around his left thumb and dipped it in a pot of fresh goat's milk. When it was fully soaked, he took Fabrizio in his arms and pressed the fraudulent nipple to his baby's lips. Carlo cradled his baby in his right arm and pressed his tiny body against his flat, barren chest. As Fabrizio sucked greedily on the man made nipple, tears filled Carlo's eyes at the realization that his boy's lips would never find the contentment and intimacy of his mother's breasts, never experience the nurture of a human's first and enduring love. It was at this moment that Carlo Panforte realized that the Tuscan ethos of primo genitor was a heresy for a motherless child. He anointed Fabrizio Panforte, over his oldest brother, as his family's sole heir. The two older boys, Riccardo and Fillippo, would be little more than unpaid hired hands. Carlo decided to take Fabrizio with him to the marketplace in Lucca. Although he could never replace Fabrizio's mother, he believed that the ancient city might become his son's teacher.

Indeed, Fabrizio's happiest times were his weekly trips with his father to Lucca. Their expeditions from the lush valley of Farneta to Porto San Pietro through which they entered the walled city was a few miles, and when the dirt road was dry, the oxen labored for about an hour to pull their cargo to the gate. Lucca's a compact, Roman, walled city not far from Pisa to the south and Florence to the east. Like most cities in Northern Italy, Lucca tells her long, often turbulent and fascinating history through her architecture, sculpture, paintings and music. She flavors her epic tale with the expansive propensity of the Lucchese for legend, often stretching the limits of hyperbole. To hear Pat Kelley speak of the Lucchese, they sounded much like his Irish ancestors given to loquacious fables, frequent foibles, but ardent in their laughter or their sorrow.

Fabrizio's trips with his father to Lucca were in a very real sense school days. When he was ten, he asked his father why he had to pay a toll at Porto San Pietro to enter the city. Carlo explained to him that until Napoleon led the French into Italy, one could not be a citizen of Lucca unless he was born within the city's walls. Before Napoleon, the Church and merchants ruled Lucca. Napoleon crushed this ruling class and gave Lucca as a gift to his sister, Elisa. Carlo had told his son, "Princess Elisa was married to a Lucchesi businessman named Baciocchi. She was good for Lucca. She fostered education, built the road system we use today and insisted that we contadini have a chance to sell our goods in the marketplace. So paying a toll is a fair *price for this opportunity." Young Fabrizio took from his father's story that important men lived in cities; poor men, like his father, lived in villages like Farneta. He dreamed of one day living in this city, but realized to do so he'd have to learn how to make money. So he never made friends with other Lucchese boys who darted in and out of the city's portals and caverns and kicked balls on her cobblestone streets. Instead he eavesdropped on the bargaining and squabbling of merchants, bankers, even bakers. He avoided watching his father barter because Carlo wasn't very good at it. Fabrizio thought he was too timid and awkward at raising motherless children to compete in the aggressive Lucchese marketplace. But Fabrizio was always thrilled by his sessions in the riotous Roman amphitheater that was the distribution center for Tuscan farm products. The symphony of barter echoed off the four-story houses built into the sustaining walls in the Middle Ages. While his father seemed to get lost in this sea of commerce, Fabrizio was free to roam the city's cobblestone streets and explore its narrow treasure filled corridors.*

On Fabrizio's twelfth birthday he made a pilgrimage to the duomo di San Martino, the Mother Church of Lucca. On the eve of his manhood Fabrizio's birthday celebrations were tempered, as they always had been, by honoring the anniversary of his mother's death. Inside the cathedral, he studied the magnificent paintings decorating the side chapels along the naves. At the third chapel altar he discovered Tintoretto's masterpiece of The Last Supper. The brilliance of color seemed to erupt from the wall, and Fabrizio was drawn to the painting by its vivid realism. It was though he could actually hear the clinking of wine glasses, and the breaking of bread. In the right foreground of the painting, below the two-tiered platform upon which Christ and his apostles shared their final Seder, Fabrizio saw a beautiful woman depicted. Her white blouse was opened, revealing her beautiful right breast at which a baby boy suckled vigorously. As Fabrizio gazed at the sensuous beauty of renaissance art, he thought of his mother and wondered if her breasts were as lovely and yielding and warm as this mother in the painting.

He shuffled up the aisle toward the main altar, which was larger than the entire church in Farneta. Before reaching the altar he came upon a figure so brilliantly pure white that it startled him. He stared at the sculpture of a sleeping woman of such feline beauty that he gasped for air. Fabrizio had discovered the sarcophagus known as "Illaria del carpetto," sculpted by Jacopo della Quercia in 1405. His eyes trailed down from the woman's sleeping face, so peaceful that it brought dryness to his throat. He saw the graceful swell of her breasts, covered in a silken sleeping dress of Carrara marble, and saw the lush undulations of a young woman's body and felt the first stirrings of his adolescence in the cathedral of San Martino. When his gaze reached her tiny feet dressed in delicate slippers he noticed a small, pet dog quietly tending to his mistress in her slumber through eternity. When he returned to her peaceful face, it seemed to him almost fragile. Yet he felt that the sheer whiteness of her countenance exuded flawless purity. To Fabrizio this was not simply stone shaped by man. In her repose of death he sensed life and wanted to touch the statue, to feel if marble felt like flesh. As he studied her sublime sleeping face, he imagined that this was the face of his mother. His hand reached tentatively for Illaria's face, his fingers trembling as they approached her cheek. He touched her cheek and felt the coolness of her skin, but his body felt warm and his fingers no longer shivered as they moved to her lips. He traced the pout of her thin lips and then rested three fingers on the line between her upper and lower lips where a woman's smile is born. His fingers on her lips, he waited for her kiss and whispered, "Momma." From that day forward Quercia's lovely Illaria was the portrait Fabrizio carried of the mother he had never known.

Fabrizio's trips to Lucca provided him with those quiet talks so essential to the father/son relationship. Carlo was a subdued man, and meals were mostly spent in silence or discussing work. But on the trips to and from Lucca Carlo became expansive with his son. On a trip to Lucca in the spring of Fabrizio's fifteenth year Carlo said, "Fabrizio, do you ever look at the tombstones in the cemetery other than your momma's?"

"No, Papa. I don't know anyone in the cemetery but momma."

"When we next visit her I want you to look at the other graves." Fabrizio steadied his gaze on his father who held the reins easily in his callused hands. Carlo continued, "For centuries families like ours scratch out our existence, raise our chickens and children and then we're buried in the cemetery with our names carved in stone, the only evidence we lived at all. But the gravestones in our cemetery tell a different story for some men. Look for the stones carrying the names Bertolli, Bricca, Milani, Sebastiani, for they are great men!"

"I don't remember any of them living in Farneta," the boy said.

"That's because they've all left. You see my son, these families, whose ancestors repose in our cemetery, have lived and worked in our village before Columbus discovered the New World – America. Before you were born their sons, not much older than you, went to America. Though they didn't speak the language of America they worked as only a peasant can, and they saved and they learned. They took small land holdings and planted vineyards and *created a wine industry. They started great commission produce markets and poultry businesses that provide more food in a single day than is sold in Lucca in a month. As they succeeded they sent for other members of their families until all had left our village and become Americans. In America they found the dignity Tuscany denied them."*

"Do you know any of these families, these Americans?"

"Only Gina Bertolli, who was the youngest sister of Bartolemeo Bertolli. Gina nursed you when you were a baby. After you and her daughter were weaned her brother brought her to America. The others left before we arrived from Siena."

"How do you know so much about them if they're so far away?"

"I've been talking with Father Agnello. He keeps records on them and he writes to them in America, in a place called California."

From this initial conversation of a world grander than even the city of Lucca, Fabrizio questioned his father relentlessly. When his father's knowledge of these emigrants was exhausted, the boy approached Father Agnello after Sunday Mass. He asked the village priest about these Americans, and his probing revealed to the priest the fervor unique to a young, acquisitive mind. In Father Agnello, Fabrizio Panforte found the teacher for whom he was to be the final student.

Father Giovanni Agnello, his impoverished parish notwithstanding, was not of peasant stock. He was the youngest son of a wealthy banker from Genoa, the city in which banking originated. He'd spent the early years of his priesthood in Rome as a professor, a scholar of emerging note. His Church career seemed destined for a Bishop's throne until his clerical ambitions conflicted with his nature as a scholar. Father Agnello's search for the truth led him to side intellectually with Garibaldi on the unification of Italy, and therefore he was at odds with the Pope. The teacher in Father Agnello was incapable of the silence required by papal indignation at his political heresy. But for the wealth of his father, generously shared with a powerful Cardinal in Rome, Father Agnello would undoubtedly have been expelled from the Church for his support of the creation of the nation of Italy. Of course his father understood that no amount of money could save his son's professorship, and accepted his banishment to minister to the peasants of the parish of San Lorenzo rather than educating the men of Rome.

Denied the brilliant students of Rome or Florence, Father Agnello studied the young boys of his parish so that he might find those with the character and imagination necessary to liberate themselves from the generations of poverty into which the accident of birth had consigned them. He selected boys he thought possessed the qualities to cut themselves from their caste, and then taught them of a new land in which work, not birth, measured a man. He taught his boys to read and write and count. When they had mastered these basic skills he taught them to think. Once they learned to think, they began to dream. And then Father Agnello told them, "When a peasant learns to dream, he is a peasant no more." He called them, "Miei Prezioi. My Precious Ones." It was these Precious Ones, who from the moment they accepted his tutelage, Father Agnello trained to leave Italy. Their graduation from his school was a brutal and dangerous voyage over angry oceans. Their diploma was their name, often misspelled, pinned to their lapels by indifferent immigration officials. But it was these Precious Ones who brought modern commerce and everlasting culture to Northern California.

While the libraries of the Vatican no longer welcomed Father Agnello's research he maintained correspondence with his flock in America. Over the years as their families grew they wrote to him, telling of their lives as Americans. It was the first of his students, Bartolemeo Bertolli, with whom Father Agnello maintained the most intimate relationship. The priest and his student exchanged letters monthly from Bertolli's arrival in San Francisco in 1882 until the 1906 Earthquake and Fire. More than any of his students Bertolli was special to Father Agnello. His primacy in his teacher's heart arose from the completeness of the man he'd become. His business thrived in California, and his family and fortune were growing. The classical education Father Agnello provided him was reaping its harvest in Bertolli's passionate immersion in San Francisco's rich cultural life – particularly the performing arts, where Bertolli had become a prominent theatrical producer.

Father Agnello not only tracked the lives of his Precious Ones, he also studied the evolution of the Italian community in Northern California. Armed with data from across the seas he wrote an unpublished history of Lucca's colonialists and shared their story with young Fabrizio each Sunday evening for two years until Fabrizio embarked on his pilgrimage. It promised that his name would never be carved on a tombstone in a silent, country graveyard.

Having matriculated to Father Agnello's academy of the Precious Ones Fabrizio's life changed dramatically. Though he continued to accompany his father to Lucca to sell the product of family labor, he no longer contributed his toil to the family farm. His sessions with Father Agnello consumed the entire working day, so his siblings assumed his workload. Neither he nor his father hinted to his brothers that America was his destiny. To temper his brothers' jealousy Fabrizio led them to believe that his time with Father

Agnello was in preparation for his entry into the seminary on his eighteenth birthday.

Father Agnello found the boy a hungry student and diligent in his studies. Although he struggled with literature he displayed a remarkable capacity for math, a disarming glibness in oral expression and an absorbing curiosity to learn all he could about Bartolomeo Bertolli's poultry empire. "Papa says Lucchese sell more produce and poultry in one day in San Francisco than is sold in Lucca in a month. Is this possible?" he inquired of the priest one evening after dinner.

"It's true such quantities are sold by Italians, but not only Lucchese. Signor Bertolli owns the largest poultry business, but the food business from farm to market is dominated by men from Liguria, Tuscany and Piedmont."

Father Agnello opened a black iron safe. He removed a thick, leather bound manuscript in which he'd chronicled the emigration of his flock to the California. He handed the boy his manuscript. "Read this while I read my breviary."

The last of Father Agnello's students became the first to read his teacher's story, begun in 1882 and completed when Fabrizio sailed off for San Francisco in 1908. Neither the wise old priest nor the ambitious boy could have realized that all of the records of the Italian migration to San Francisco had perished in the earthquake and fire. And that this history of the fifty-six-year emigration to Northern California from Northern Italy, composed in the elegant hand of a scholar/priest, was the only written record of the Italians who forever changed California and the nation which adopted them.

From Father Agnello's manuscript Fabrizio learned that Bartolemeo Bertolli was only twelve years old when selected as the first from the village to settle in California. Bertolli was not only the first chosen; he was the youngest ever nominated for so speculative a venture. His training by Father Agnello took four years, during which the priest added one young man each year to his academy of adventure. In selecting Bertolli, Father Agnello relied on the boy's creative aptitude. He'd observed that Bertolli was constantly inventing gadgets to facilitate the operation of the family farm. His faculty for invention revealed to the renegade scholar that Bertolli's mind was capable of focused analysis of phenomena, isolation of a problem and creative resolution of it. Father Agnello believed that Bertolli's intellectual disposition was to see not only that which is, but to comprehend what might be. It was this aspect of his personality which, when fully developed, made Bertolli the ideal first candidate for his American experiment.

The morning after Fabrizio had read his teacher's manuscript Father

Agnello found the boy at the grave of Bertolli's father. By this time Fabrizio had grown to his full six-foot height. He was a handsome lad with a sharply chiseled face, a prominent nose and jet black hair. "Good morning, Fabrizio. What brings you here?"

"In your writings you say Bertolli had three brothers and two sisters, but there are only the graves of his parents."

"You must finish reading the manuscript. You'll find that Bartolemeo, as he succeeded, gradually brought his brothers and sisters to San Francisco so that only his parents remained with us until their deaths."

"Why didn't he send for his parents?"

"He did, but they were too set in their ways. The old are cautious because they sense the fragility of life. The young only see life's promise." Teacher and student walked through the cemetery, stopping briefly at graves with the names of Bricca, Sebastiani and Milani. Father Agnello explained that these were the family names of his students who had followed Bertolli to San Francisco and to enormous success in science and business. He told him his reasons for selecting each boy. When they arrived at Fabrizio's mother's grave Father Agnello blessed the tombstone, and Fabrizio crossed himself saying, "It appears all the boys you selected had very special skills. Why did you pick me, a motherless farm boy?"

Father Agnello sighed, "Fabrizio, you must not condemn yourself for your mother's death. She was too poor to have assistance bringing you into the world, too poor to nourish herself and you in her womb. Poverty, next to ignorance, is the most deadly disease of mankind. Though both are readily curable if only our hearts were not so burdened with greed. Your anger at the loss of your mother should not be directed at yourself but at a social order which sentenced her to death and all peasant women to a life of silent agony and unrewarding toil."

In the shade of a birch tree, Father Agnello wiped his sweating brow and said, "All of my Precious Ones had special qualities. You have a gift for numbers, and your mind is at ease with pure logic. In America the inexorable logic of profits and losses rules the nation, not hereditary fortunes and a corrupt clergy. Your facility with numbers will allow you to perceive financial opportunities others fail to grasp."

"So you picked Bertolli because he was inventive, Bricca for science, Sebastiani, the vintner, Milani the salesman and me, a mathematician?"

"No! These are merely individual gifts the development of which promises success. What you and the others have in common is ardent ambition. None of you is capable of accepting the life designed for you by sorry custom, and each of you is driven by a woeful childhood. Bertolli's father ridiculed his

inventions. Bricca's older sister died in his arms when he was but ten years old. Sebastiani's father drank and was given to frequent rages. Milani fell in love with a Lucchesi merchant's daughter and was forbidden from seeing her. In your first moment of life you lost your mother. All of you are bonded in a child's pain, psychically united in lost innocence. From these boyhood wounds springs your ferocious initiative and your unspoken faith that there is more to life than dull, omnipresent sorrow."

Fabrizio studied the face of the old priest with its deep circles under his penetrating eyes. He was a tall man, a bit over six-feet, but noticeably shrinking as he approached his ninth decade. His white hair receded gracefully and his thick eyebrows, which retained their rich black color, accented his gray eyes. Fabrizio said, "I don't understand how such goodness can grow from foulness."

"My son, man only comprehends good when he's confronted by evil. Aquinas was wrong when he defined evil as the absence of good. Good is the negation of evil, and therefore evil must exist in order for us to know what is good. Don't you see that Bertolli was creative precisely because his father was not? Don't you understand that Bricca's devotion to healing is his penance for his dead sister? Surely you understand that Sebastiani's tender care of the grape is his search for a spirit which calms man rather than unleashing his fury. Isn't it obvious that Milani's humor springs from the deep well of sadness of lost love?"

"And me, Father?"

"You, my Precious One, denied the love of a mother, will seek the love of a woman with your vulnerability fully revealed. In so doing, you will liberate her to love you as a man, not master. When you are loved for your weakness, you will have truly been caressed by God."

"How can you be certain that men from such poor backgrounds will be good and succeed in America? Why are you sure I'll be like them?"

"There's no certainty for any of you. The only thing that's certain is none of you would be allowed to choose between good and evil, success or failure if you remain in Italy. A peasant has no choices. He accepts what nature accords him and submits his life to a patch of soil that makes all his decisions for him. But America admits no peasants to her shores. Fabrizio, every man and woman in America made a choice to go there. Once a man makes his first choice his life becomes an endless process of choosing. America is a New World because its people are choosers. It matters only to God whether we choose good or evil. But God insists that we must at least exercise choice."

"So it's really our willingness to go to America that's your basis for selecting us?"

"Yes. By this decision, each of you performed your first act as free men. It's the moment when each of you slayed the peasant in your soul and became in that instant Americans!"

Fabrizio was silent for a moment, wondering what it felt like to be an American. Then he said, "So I'm to go directly to Signor Bertolli and he'll help me find work?"

"Yes. I've written him about you. He'll do much more than give you a job. He'll teach you far more than I've taught you. And for this you must honor him with your loyalty."

12

Unlike Bertolli, Fred Panforte was not a lonely pioneer. He was welcomed by an Italian-American social and economic infrastructure that was protective and nurturing. He didn't start a business like Bertolli had, but he went to work for Bertolli. He was bright and ambitious. He wanted to be important and respected like his boss, Signor Bertolli. He rose more quickly in the ranks of Western Poultry than any immigrant or native ever had. He mastered the intricacies of the wholesale food market, and his mathematical aptitude made him Bertolli's chief bookkeeper – the equivalent of today's CFO - within five years of his arrival. Whereas Bertolli moved easily in political and cultural circles, Panforte seemed one dimensional, devoted, some thought, obsessed with Western Poultry's bottom line. Bertolli spoke and wrote fluent English, Italian, French and read the classics in Greek and Latin. Panforte struggled with heavily accented English and except in the marketplace seemed too reserved for an Italian, perhaps a bit shy, Bertolli thought.

Bertolli was delighted when Panforte asked him to help him bring a bride, Angelina, to San Francisco from Genoa. They were married in 1918, and Bertolli delegated almost complete operational responsibility of his business to Panforte. After restoring his business and rebuilding the City from the ruins of 1906's catastrophe, Bertolli was intensely involved in his theater and on the verge of realizing his long-held dream of creating an opera company in San Francisco. It was the Roaring 20's and entrepreneurs and show business folks saw no end to bubbly contraband champagne successes. More and more of the day-to-day operations of Western Poultry were assumed by Panforte.

By 1920 Bertolli was spending most of his working hours on the formation of a resident opera company for the city. His appearances at Western Poultry were limited to the informal meetings of the Board of Directors. Frankly he was pleased with Panforte's executive efforts, although other board members complained of his dictatorial, humorless methods. Since Panforte's marriage he seemed to them more driven and more secretive. At a private lunch after a Board meeting even Giannini cautioned Bertolli to keep an eye on Panforte. He suggested that Panforte seemed somehow different since his marriage than the bright, eager teenager who Bertolli originally took under his wing. Bertolli brushed him off saying, "Of course he's different. He's got a wife and kid to take care of. We all change when we start a family."

"I don't know, Bartolomeo. I built my bank on instincts about people, not their balance sheets. There's something funny about that fellow," Giannini said, shaking his head.

"I built my business on instincts and I haven't done so badly," Bertolli shrugged. Giannini knew enough about his stubborn friend to drop the subject.

But the banker's vague instincts had been prescient. For a year Panforte poured over company financial records at night. He composed columns of figures, made sophisticated calculations, ostensibly according to sound accounting principles. Then he began secretly meeting with Western Poultry's laborers who held shares of stock. These were the porters, lumpers, teamsters - the beasts of burden of the enterprise. He explained what the numbers meant and how stock dividends were earned. He implied that Bertolli's absence from The Market, pursuing his theatrical dreams, made it unlikely that these physical laborers' stock would ever be more valuable than the paper they were written on. He explained the company's profit and loss statement that clearly showed that profits were on a downward trend. He didn't explain, however, that the company's bottom line was diminished because of the generous salaries and benefits the company paid to its employees at Bertolli's insistence. During his campaign he never shared his concerns with fellow board members, company executives or the sales force – all of whom understood financial reports.

Panforte explained to the laborers that while their stock was worthless their stock voting power was not. He told them that if they joined their stock in a voting block they could elect some of their own to the board of directors. Because the men revered Bertolli, he never directly criticized his leadership. But he did imply that Bertolli's theatrical venture had distracted him and then playfully suggested that the beautiful star and artistic director of Bertolli's theater would distract any full-blooded Italian man. It made sense to these workers, and they didn't feel there was any disloyalty to the company founder. After all, they figured, hadn't Bertolli put Panforte in charge, and wasn't he just taking care of business while the boss played with the lovely Neapolitan soprano? Besides, the idea of a workingman or two on the board of directors seemed very American, very democratic. So they gave Fred Panforte their proxies, confident that his financial wizardry would return Western Poultry to its rightful place of market dominance. At the annual shareholder's meeting of 1921 Panforte made his move.

Western Poultry Company's annual shareholder meeting was not exactly a Wall Street-like affair. It was held at Bertolli's Sonoma ranch on Independence Day weekend. The meeting itself was held in the morning and it was quite informal, reviewing the year's progress, commending individual productivity and ratifying previous actions by the board. Once completed, the real purpose of the gathering began. Western Poultry's employees, their wives and children were ferried over to Sonoma on the company fleet. It was an all-day picnic where the children played hide and seek in Bertolli's vineyard, swam in his pond or rode horseback in the ring under the expert equestrian direction of teenage Maria Bertolli. At midday, on her favorite quarter horse, Maria led the older children on a two-hour trail ride that she called "Trails of Tuscany." Along the ride Maria explained to the city kids the similarities in the topography of Tuscany and Sonoma as she had learned it from her father. The men played horseshoes and bocci ball, and wine was plentiful. It culminated in a huge Tuscan barbecue, and ended with the men sipping grappa and smoking cigars while exhausted kids napped in their mothers' laps. When Western Poultry's senior teamster nominated a porter for the board of directors and Panforte's proxy votes elected him, Bertolli thought nothing unusual was happening. He rather liked the idea of common workers gaining fuller participation in company management, and he was confident that they would support his executive team, led by Panforte, enthusiastically.

When Panforte elected two more board members with his proxies, Bertolli was oblivious to the fact that Panforte had just engineered a bloodless coup by which he was now in control of the Board of Directors of Western Poultry Company. Even Panforte's wife Angelina had failed to grasp the significance of her husband's corporate political maneuverings. He had never shared his career ambitions or business activities with her. Indeed her only association with Western Poultry operations was the annual shareholder meeting which, like most spouses, she considered a happy family picnic more than a serious business conference. She greatly admired Bartolemeo Bertolli, and was profoundly grateful for all he had done for her and her husband. She felt that without Bertolli's intervention, she would be still trapped in a convent choir in Genoa. So she attended these annual affairs both happily and out of respect for the man who had helped her become an American wife. She hadn't paid much attention to the business part of the Sonoma meeting, and the only difference she'd noticed from past meetings was that her husband played a more active role. She just assumed that he was doing *so at Signor Bertolli's direction.*

Within a few months of Panforte's Declaration of Independence from the man who made him an American, Bertolli realized the import of Panforte's scheme. Bertolli had never really needed board votes to run the company any more than Caesar ultimately needed senate votes to run his empire. But now it was different. Panforte made the decisions and he had the votes to enforce them. For the first and only time in his life Bartolomeo Bertolli turned to the law to recapture his company.

For a year the two men fought through their lawyers. Bertolli retained a prominent Montgomery Street law firm. A.P. Giannini dissented from his friend's choice of counsel. "They're WASP," he told Bertolli. "You need a street-fighter to beat Panforte. You outta get Vin Hallinan. He's got the brains and guts ya need." Once again Bertolli failed to heed his friend's advice. Panforte retained a sharp-tongued, hungry, young Jewish attorney – Daniel David Loeb. The tedium of endless depositions, production and exchange of documents, the squabbling between the lawyers all gravely offended Bertolli. What did any of this have to do with fairness or ethics, he asked his lawyers. They tried to explain that it was a matter of process. Bertolli replied angrily, "I thought it was a matter of justice." They assured him that it was. But he sensed that what he had done and what Panforte had done would remain unfathomable as long as it was in the grasp of this utterly alien lawyer language. His lawyers painstakingly explained what was at stake. "It's not just the poultry company," they told him. "It's every asset you've got! Everything is in the company's name! We understand how that happened, but in a trial we may not be able to prove it. Mr. Bertolli, we know how you feel, but we must try to settle this case, to compromise it. It's the only way we can save some of your assets."

Bertolli's gray eyes burned. "What kind of compromise do you have in mind?"

"We think if you concede control of the business to Panforte and surrender your stock in the company to him, we can save some of your real estate holdings, like the Russian Hill apartment building," the senior partner said as his associate scribbled on yellow legal pad.

"The Russian Hill apartment building, as you call it, is my family home. I designed it and built it!" Bertolli's voice revealed rare anger.

"Of course. We understand," mollified the senior partner. Now Bertolli realized that Giannini had been right about his attorneys. "These guys are so frigid!" he thought. Then he softly said, "Tell me again, what's really at stake here?"

The prissy junior associate read the assets at risk from his yellow legal pad: "Control of Western Poultry Company and all it assets. And those assets are: all patents, five Sonoma poultry ranches, including the one you use for your family's summer home, all of the San Francisco real property, including the income units and the Russian Hill apartment ... I mean your residence, and the unimproved lots in Marin, Mendocino and Sonoma Counties."

"You say it doesn't matter that each of those patents is a personal invention of mine?" Bertolli said evenly.

"I'm afraid not, Mr. Bertolli," the senior man said.

"If Panforte's position is so strong, why would he entertain compromise?" Bertolli said.

"Well, we don't know that he will, Mr. Bertolli. But our long experience in these matters requires that we at least try," the senior partner said.

Bertolli rubbed his chin, "I see. What about the Chinatown properties?"

"We've included them in the income properties list," junior replied proudly.

"Interesting," Bertolli said. "I'll think about it and let you know." They shook hands and Bertolli decided to walk to Washington Square Park and reflect on what he must now do. He walked north on Montgomery Street. In his blue three-piece suit and gray bowler with a black hatband, he mingled comfortably with stockbrokers and bankers rushing to and from the stock exchange, whispering conspiratorial secrets about "bears" and "bulls." At the corner of California Street he watched a cable car chug up Nob Hill. From the sidewalk he followed the clang of its bell as far as Grant Avenue and Chinatown. He turned right on Grant and walked into the heart of Chinatown, toward North Beach. Chinese women and men – some still clad with pig-tailed queues – shuffled by him in both directions. Shop owners and grocers recognized him and nodded respectfully. Women selected ducks hanging in storefront windows, pinched fruits, sifted through crates of fresh green beans and bartered in vehement sing song Mandarin – both merchant and customer accusing the other of theft. For forty years Bertolli had witnessed and participated in the daily ritual of buying and selling, of mock suggestions of unconscionable pricing and consumer breast-beating. It was the same in every language and every culture – east or west. It was endless millennia of planting and harvesting, selling and buying, peeling, cooking and eating. Barter was what his lawyers were telling him he had to do. "Barter with Fabrizio Panforte, barter with my morals. That's what this legal business seems to be," he thought.

At the corner of Washington and Grant he tipped his hat to Ho Chung, who was standing in front of Won Duck Company,, his import/export establishment. "Good morning, Mr. B. You in Chinatown on business?"

Chung greeted. Bertolli's intimates called him Bartolomeo and only cops and politicians called him "Bart." To everyone else he was "Mr. B."

"Just out for a walk and doing some thinking," Bertolli said.

"Ah...yes. You have much to think about these days, my good friend," Chung said. He looked up to the taller man's grim expression and added, "If there's anything we can do, just give us the word. You have the loyalty of all the Five Companies."

"Thanks Ho. That means a lot to me. But right now, I've got to figure this out for myself." They shook hands warmly and Bertolli resumed his walk to Washington Square Park. He'd planned to sit for a while on a park bench and reflect on his meeting with his lawyers, but he was continually interrupted by men and women coming up to him and asking questions or commenting on the Washington Square Theater across from the park. "Thank God, its not in the company name," he thought, grateful that Antonietta Pompa held title to the property.

In search of solitude he trekked up Union Street to his Russian Hill apartment building. He took the lift up to his fifth floor flat and then the staircase to the rooftop. He'd built what looked like a crown, topping the building that was his study. The interior of the room was modeled after a clipper ship's captain's cabin. It was furnished with a narrow cot, a rolltop oak desk with a lamp and a gold-framed portrait of Bertolli's wife, Renee, hung on the rosewood wall panel. Bertolli removed the portrait and laid it on his cot. He twisted the portrait hanger and it unlocked a wall panel that concealed a combination safe. From his wall-safe, he removed a leather-bound handwritten Italian manuscript and placed it on his desk. Then he removed a thick accordion file filled with correspondence. The author of the manuscript and the letters was Father Giovanni Agnello - the man who had trained and sent both Bertolli and Panforte to America. Perhaps in his mentor's writings he might find some insight as to how to resolve the conflict with Panforte.

Years later when his son-in-law was translating his papers, what Bartolemeo Bertolli had found in his village priest's papers provided Pat Kelley with a clue that implied that Robert Panforte's compelled attendance in the dock was ordained, somehow the inevitable product of a conspiracy of genes.

When Bartolemeo Bertolli finished reading his teacher's papers he returned them to his wall-safe. Then he took another file from his safe and placed it on his desk. This file contained a complete listing of all the real property in Chinatown to which Western Poultry held title. He removed his Last Will and Testament from the safe and placed it on top of the Chinatown real estate inventory. Then Bertolli removed a pistol from his safe. He placed the Chinatown real estate inventory and his Will in a brown leather briefcase. He flipped open the revolver's chamber, confirmed that it was fully loaded, then placed his pistol in the briefcase. He closed the wall panel and re-hung his wife's portrait. Briefcase in hand he left his home resolved that his decision was the only course of action open to him.

Bartolemeo Bertolli jumped on a cable car at Hyde and Greenwich Streets for his ride down Russian Hill and up and down Nob Hill to the turntable at Market Street. In the marble lobby of the Flood Building he checked the tenant directory. He took the elevator up to the eighth floor and walked down the corridor until he reached Suite 825. He read the black signage on the frosted glass door: "Daniel D. Loeb, Counselor." He opened the door and was greeted by a matronly secretary who was talking on the phone, a cigarette dangling from the corner of her mouth. When she saw Bertolli she extinguished her cigarette and wrapped up her phone conversation. Bertolli mentally compared the modest law office of Loeb, which consisted of the reception area and a single attorney office to the rear and right of his secretary's desk, to the two floors of lawyers that populated the law firm representing him. Despite the apparent legal brain-power disparity between Bertolli's prestigious Montgomery Street law firm and young Daniel D. Loeb's solo practice it was Loeb who had dictated the terms of the legal battle. Bertolli accepted that Loeb had a brilliant analytical mind and was gifted with the ability to express himself cogently and forcefully.

"Can I help you?" Loeb's secretary asked.

"I'm here to see Mr. Loeb. I'm Bartolemeo Bertolli." The secretary's raised eyebrow informed Bertolli that she realized the enemy had just walked into the office. "Mr. Bertolli, I'm afraid Mr. Loeb only sees those who have an appointment." Bertolli sat down on a brown leather couch, put his briefcase in his lap and said, "I can wait. Patience is a virtue of a man my age."

"Oh, dear!" she half whispered as she left her desk to enter Loeb's office, closing the door behind her. After a few moments the door opened and five-foot five-inch Danny Loeb was framed in the doorway. He wore no suit jacket but his charcoal vest matched his wiry hair, and his gold cuff-links emphasized his perfectly manicured hands. "Mr. Bertolli, do your lawyers know you're here?" Loeb asked. Bertolli shook his head. "Then I'm afraid I can't confer with you. It's unethical for a lawyer to speak with an adverse party without the knowledge and consent of his counsel," Loeb said.

"Your ethical concerns are quite touching, Mr. Loeb. But I have a proposal for your client. It's a business proposal. Since Fabrizio refuses to meet with me, I'd like to use your good offices to communicate it to him. I've come

here on a business matter, not a legal one."

"But sir, can't you see that it's totally inappropriate for me to be meeting with you? I could be accused of taking advantage of you," Loeb said.

"Young man, you overestimate my vulnerability. I have some materials that you should see if for no other reason than wisely advising your client," Bertolli said, walking to the doorway in front of the smaller man. Looking down on Loeb, Bertolli firmly said, "I insist."

Loeb relented, instructed his secretary that they were not to be disturbed and led Bertolli into his office. Seated in front of Loeb's desk Bertolli opened his briefcase and removed his Last Will and Testament and the list of Chinatown real estate. He handed them to Loeb across his desk and said, "I'd like you to read these documents carefully. Then you will listen quietly while I explain what they mean and how they afford the basis for settling this 'legal business' with Fabrizio." Loeb began reading the documents, aware that a subtle transformation had occurred in his office. Bertolli, not he, was controlling the dynamics of their meeting, and he felt powerless to resist Bertolli's directions. When Loeb had finished reading the documents, he looked up and Bertolli explained: "You no doubt recognize the Chinatown properties from the complete listing of the assets in controversy. The property list you have just read is the only copy by which the Chinatown properties are segregated from all other assets. Now I'll tell you why.

"When your client was just a boy in our common ancestral village before the turn of the century I, along with eleven other men from Farneta, had already established successful businesses in California. One of our number, Michael Milani, had established a retail poultry and fish market on Polk Street. Of course he purchased all of his poultry product from my company. Milani was a master at marketing. He solicited the Chinese houseboys who worked for the railroad barons of Nob Hill to buy fish and poultry from his market. These Chinese servants did all the buying and food preparation for the likes of Crocker and Stanford. Milani got me to sell him product at a discount based upon the volume of his sales. Or at least that's what he told me.

"Years later I learned that he was discounting his sales to the Chinese boys. He'd verbally cut ten per cent off the price and gave them a receipts for the full retail price. I guess you could call it a kick-back for the servants. Milani figured that the Nob Hill fellows wouldn't notice the difference, he'd have a steady stream of business and the Chinese guys would be getting a commission to do business with him. And he was right, it was a good deal for everyone.

"But Milani also knew that I didn't do business that way, so he never told me until years later. I don't know how much you know about our

Oriental brothers in California, but they've been subjected to humiliation after humiliation. During the Gold Rush a tax on foreign miners was imposed on them. There were the Chinese exclusion acts, there were laws forbidding them from bringing wives from China to America. They couldn't testify in your so-called courts of justice nor could they vote or own real property in their own names. Yet in the face of such appalling indignities they persisted. They labored hard and they saved frugally. They stitched our nation together with the railroad tracks of the trans-continental railroad and telegraph wires. They bled and died boring tunnels through the sheer granite of the Sierra. But in the eyes of your profession, Mr. Loeb, they were not white men, so they must be less than fully human.

"Some years ago Milani came to me and told me the truth about his marketing practices. He apologized for misleading me, but knew that I wouldn't have gone along had I known the truth. Then he told me of another plan that he had, and he begged me to help him execute it. He gave me the names of 12 Chinese buyers to whom he had been paying commissions. If you look at that list of Chinatown properties that I gave you you'll see the names of each of those former houseboys."

Loeb picked up the list and read the names. He recognized the first name on the list as Ho Chung, owner of Won Duck Co. He nodded, and Bertolli resumed: "Milani explained that the twelve men had saved their commission money and wanted to buy real property. They needed a front man, a white man, to hold title for them. I told Milani to have the most respected man among them to meet with me at my office. The next day I met with Ho Chung. We talked for more than an hour. Ho was an extremely cultured man, and I marveled that a man from a civilization that existed when European men were barely out of their trees could speak so calmly and without apparent pain that our nation had denied him the right to own property simply because of the accident of his ancestry.

"'But why me,' I finally asked him. 'Because,' Ho said, 'Your word is sacred to you, it is therefore security for us.' So I agreed to do it. Every penny used to purchase those Chinatown properties is from those twelve Orientals. They were each granted a life estate on the properties, and I promised to grant them a fee simple absolute in my Will. Upon my death the properties will be in their names. You will note that beginning on page five of my Will each of the twelve men and their heirs are listed, and the legal description of all properties is set forth.

"Not a single penny of Western Poultry's money or my money has gone into these properties. My only contribution has been my word. Mr. Loeb, neither you nor Fabrizio Panforte nor your sanctimonious courts will ever

force me to violate my word! I will gladly die before I'll ever breach the trust these fine men have placed in me!"

The diminutive lawyer rubbed the back of his neck and said, "That's quite a story, Mr. Bertolli. But I don't see how it changes Mr. Panforte's legal position."

"I don't give a damn about anyone's legal position!" Bertolli's baritone deepened in rage. "I no longer even entertain that a semblance of justice will come out of all of this! Stop thinking like a goddamn lawyer! Think like a man, even if your client doesn't know how to. I'm here to deal, Loeb! And even greedy bastards like you and Panforte will find my offer generous."

Danny Loeb thrived on confrontation and was fearless in the face of other men's threats. But old man Bertolli was not like anyone he'd ever squared-off with. "With a fortune at stake, all he's focused on is his word given to a bunch of Chinamen years ago," Loeb thought. Throughout the litigation struggle, Panforte had anticipated Bertolli's every move as though he'd read the man's mind. So Loeb had out-maneuvered Bertolli's lawyers time and again. But the man he now confronted in his own office was nothing like the man Panforte had described to him and it greatly unsettled the young lawyer. He sighed heavily. "So what's your proposal, Mr. Bertolli?"

"It's quite simple. All of the Chinatown properties immediately go to the men on my list. I'll take the Russian Hill apartment building and the unimproved lots in Marin and Mendocino. You can have everything else — the patents, the business, the ranches, the income properties. Everything. I'll just keep my home and a couple of lots for my daughters and grandchildren, if I ever have any."

"So that's it, that's all there is?" Loeb said, trying not to look startled.

"Well, there is one more thing. My offer has a life of only thirty minutes. You will phone your client right now and get his approval of the deal. Then you will draft a letter agreement for your signature, Fred Panforte's and mine and you will messenger it to my lawyers."

Loeb thought the deal was more than generous. It was more than he expected to win at trial or in settlement negotiations with Bertolli's lawyers. It was in fact a complete capitulation by Bertolli. But he deeply resented Bertolli dictating the terms of his own surrender, so he foolishly said, "And if I refuse?"

Bertolli sat back in his chair and said very evenly, "That would be a tragic mistake, Mr. Loeb. For then your young bride would become a premature widow and my middle-age wife a mature one." Bertolli reached into his briefcase and slowly withdrew his pistol. He placed it between folded hands in his lap and fixed Loeb with an icy gray-eyed stare. Loeb's face paled and he started to say something, then thought better of it. He reached for his phone with a trembling hand and phoned Fred Panforte. He recited the terms of the deal quickly and breathlessly demanded Panforte's agreement. He got it, and Panforte agreed to come to his office in an hour and sign the paperwork. He placed the phone back on the hook and slumped back into his black leather swivel chair. Bertolli's expression had not changed at all. Loeb felt the rapid beat of his heart and felt as though it was audible to Bertolli. Then Bertolli whispered, "Finito."

13

After Sunday night dinner at Terry Kelley's godfather's San Rafael home Pat drove his powder blue 1948 DeSoto sedan cautiously toward the Golden Gate Bridge while his wife and kids dozed. As he drove on the Richardson Bay Bridge Pat glanced to his right and scanned the verdant slopes and summit of Mt. Tamalpais, the Bay's grandest mountain. This was the focal point of the Panforte murder case. But was it really, Pat asked himself, as he reflected on what he'd learned from his friend, F.B.I. Special Agent Bill Moriarity. The mountain was clothed in deep, dark green from summit to base, and its forest garment was like a woman's formal gown, graceful, billowing at her hem. Out of the corner of Pat's left eye he saw the pastel walls, red-orange tile roof and stark steel gun towers of San Quentin State Prison resting on a point of the Bay, tiny tides lapping against its dull, gray rock foundation. The mountain summit to his right had been Paula's final destination in life. Would the prison to his left be her husband's, Pat wondered. Inside of San Quentin's ominous walls was *The Green Room*, as it was called – the gas chamber. It was not the rich green tone of Mt. Tam. This room's décor was pale green, faint, as though sickly commenting on the dimming hours of remaining life for the occupant of the straight-backed, heavily strapped chair that was the chamber's soul. If Robert Panforte were required to take a seat in that terminal chair it would be in the shadow of Mount Tamalpais. In a way, Pat thought, Paula Panforte, from her mountain grave, would be a witness to her husband's execution.

On Moriarity's porch, Pat had gently probed the F.B.I. agent about wartime activities in Petaluma's poultry industry. Moriarity had given Pat this Petaluma opening when he told him that the Bureau was looking into Communist Party activities in the area in preparation for the upcoming perjury trial of left-wing Longshoremen's Union leader Harry Bridges. It seems Hoover's Boys were up in arms over a benefit for Bridges Defense Fund, starring Negro actor and singer Paul Robeson. Pat began to think of Robert Panforte's Petaluma job as the likely locale where he could study him out from under his father's shadow. And there was that vague Army training program that young Panforte had worked for during the war. Pat had always been bothered by Robert Panforte's exemption from military service during the war. As an employee in what the War Department considered a vital home industry Panforte was of course legally entitled to his exemption. But most young men Panforte's age at the outbreak of the war rushed to get into the fray whether they were exempt or not. Some men, like his friend, Joe Desmond, enlisted when they were underage, so compelling did their generation respond to the worldwide fascist threat. Indeed Pat had always regretted that when Terry had asked him why he didn't fight in the war he had to feebly reply: "I was too young for the first war and too old for the second." As a college graduate and noted athlete Bob Panforte would have been a cinch for a commission. As the heir to a family fortune, why had Panforte not followed the path that almost all of his peers had taken, Pat wondered. So he'd asked Agent Moriarity if he'd ever worked on investigations in Petaluma before the Robeson concert for Bridges' Defense Fund, and was rewarded when his son's Godfather told him that he'd investigated a black market operation on Petaluma chicken ranches during the war.

Pat had elected not to question his friend too closely about an F.B.I. investigation that resulted in a federal indictment and conviction of a number of chicken ranchers, among whom the Panfortes were not included. Pat could ferret out specifics later and without compromising his friend. When Pat had asked whether old man Panforte and his kid had been suspects Moriarity had replied: "Originally everybody was. They were running the biggest operation up there, so naturally we looked at 'em real close. But we couldn't make 'em. Right before the indictments came down young Panforte volunteered to help with infantry training in Marin, so the U.S. Attorney felt that would be screwing with the home effort. So a bunch Jewish ranchers and a Chinaman cut a deal for probation and a fine and took the fall." Then Pat had asked if Moriarity knew anything about the Army training program Bob Panforte had worked for. Moriarity shook his head and suggested Pat check with Sixth Army Headquarters at the Presidio. Finally Pat had asked, "You know who defended those Jewish ranchers?" Moriarity said blandly, "Yeah. Daniel Loeb."

Back at Crestlake Drive, after his kids were in bed and while Maria bathed, Pat phoned Joe Desmond and told him to meet him at six-thirty in the morning at the Oregon Café for breakfast.

When Pat Kelley arrived at The Market early Monday morning it was at the peak of its working day. White smocked salesmen, under handsome fedoras barked prices for bananas in front of Milani's Sunset Produce. At Levy Zetner's a salesman bargained in pidgin English with a Chinese grocer. "Snow peas. Four dolla for you!"

"Tree fifty. No more."

"Four dolla. Big, big bargain."

"Booshit. Tree seventy-five."

"I bling down, tree-ninety. Deal?"

"Deal! Five crates."

In the alley behind the Oregon Café, four abandoned hand trucks were parked while the porters who manned them took an unauthorized coffee break in the very restaurant where their bosses would be dining. Pat loved The Market morning chaos and sensed that Fred Panforte was no fool to protect his son from it. While Pat marveled at his mom's acumen playing with the big boys of Wall Street, even she stayed out of this wild and brutal commodities exchange. Just like its Hall of Justice neighbor the wholesale market wasn't what it seemed. At The Market, you'd swear that nothing was planned and every price fluctuation a demand performance for capitalist improvisation or your fortune would be nothing more than a wilted, soggy butter lettuce leaf swimming in the gutter. In the Hall of Justice you were certain that every word was scripted, the courtroom itself blocked off by a brilliant stage director so that every actor's line echoed with its most dramatic impact. But Pat knew it wasn't that way at all. Both The Market and murder trials were tediously staged events. Improvisations were the adjustments of the players to the facts or the illusion of facts.

Pat pushed open the swinging glass door where Frank Cavaretta, the owner, presided over a sizzling greasy griddle talking to Joe Desmond at a counter seat. "Kelley, what the hell are you doing here this early?" smiling Cavaretta greeted.

"Joe and I have go over a few things before we open the courthouse," Pat smiled.

The smile evaporated from Cavaretta's face. "I figure ya got the Panforte case," he said to Desmond more than Pat. At the mention of the Panforte name the dice cups stopped beating on the bar, the porters glanced over at Joe and Pat and murmured stealthily in Italian. Even the Chinese busboys, conveniently claiming to comprehend no

English or Italian, looked in their direction. Cavaretta asked Joe, "Did the kid do it?"

"How the hell do I know?" Desmond shrugged

"Don't bullshit a bullshitter, Desmond. You goddamn court reporters know everything that goes down at the Hall. That's what my fuckin' bail bondsman says." Given the second floor activities of the Oregon Café Cavaretta relied heavily on the skill of his bail bondsman to assure that the arrest of one of his girls didn't result in her missing a shift. Therefore the bondsman's description of a court reporter's prescience was accepted as a matter of faith and morals by the proprietor of so varied an enterprise. Pat Kelley suggested they take a booth, then turned to Cavaretta and said, "Frank, why don't you stick to your griddle. Joe reported the Grand Jury testimony. They're secret proceedings and if Joe utters a word that he heard in there, it's a felony and he's liable to end up in a cell with young Panforte as his roommate!"

"Justa asking, *mi amici.* What'll ya have?" Cavaretta backed off.

"Italian sausage and eggs."

"Eggs basted, right? Got some great fried polenta. Want some?"

"Sure," Pat said. Desmond said he'd have the same.

In the relative privacy of their breakfast booth Pat Kelley briefed the young court reporter on some, but not all, of his the homicide investigation. Pat said, "We've got Panforte's arraignment on Wednesday, so that gives us a couple of days to check out some leads."

Desmond gave Pat a puzzled look as if to say who's *we* and *us* and what *leads* was he talking about. Pat informed Joe that he was going to investigate beyond the four corners of the prosecution's homicide investigation, and he could use Joe's help. He explained that homicide investigations are partnership affairs, and that pairs are essential for back up, corroborating data and witnessing statements and scenes. In addition he told Desmond that they might have to go undercover, playacting roles to acquire leads and information from unsuspecting sources. Finally he added, "Joe, this is all off-the-record and I'll understand if you don't want to get involved. You know it's damn near impossible to get fired from a civil service job in this town. But if anyone gets wind of this, we'll both be shit canned in a minute! You volunteered for the paratroopers, so I've got no problem if you wanna pass on this."

Desmond half-grinned and said, "It doesn't sound as crazy as jumping out of an airplane hanging onto an exaggerated bed sheet!

Let's go for it!"

"Good man!" Kelley said, clapping Joe's arm. Kelley related what he'd learned about the Petaluma black market during the war from his kid's godfather the night before. He explained to Joe his theory that old man Panforte had assigned his son to Petaluma ranches because he didn't believe his kid was man enough to make it in the rough and tumble of The Market. Pat asked Desmond to confirm his suspicion that college boys made up the bulk of the junior officer corps during the war. Desmond replied, "Yeah, all of our second lieutenants were college boys." Desmond shook his head and added, "They didn't last long in combat. After a while, ya felt sorry for the poor bastards. Our NCO's were career guys and high school guys like me. I don't know, maybe we were just more streetwise. The guys who got battlefield commissions did a little better. But I wasn't about to take one of those goddamned officer bars! Seemed to me they came with a kraut bullet not far behind."

Pat nodded sympathetically and said, "Joe, there's one more thing. I don't know of a single American born son of a foreign immigrant in San Francisco who didn't enlist! It was true in the first war as well. Look at Maria's brother! American warrior sons' blood makes their fathers' citizenship no longer tentative! Yet Bob Panforte takes a military exemption!"

Pat dropped a sugar cube in his coffee and explained that the Panforte poultry exemption was based on national security needs to feed our armies and people. Bob Panforte was classified as vital to the war effort. Yet it was also the greatest expansion of profits for Great Western Poultry since it had been founded by Bartolemeo Bertolli a half-century earlier, and Bertolli's son had gone off to war and was now buried in France. Moreover, Great Western Poultry, during the war years and currently, was entirely owned by the Panforte family. "If Bob Panforte's Petaluma ranch duties were vital to the war effort, his volunteering to train infantry personnel takes him away from his vital home front job!" Pat argued. "Then you look at when he suddenly gets patriotic and it's when his company is under federal investigation for profiteering! I wanna find out if this black market business may have been young Panforte's first business venture beyond his father's knowledge and control."

"So what's this all got to do with the case?" Desmond asked.

"I don't know," Kelley admitted. He rubbed his chin and said, "I've gotta find leads that will tell me more about this kid maybe even more about his father. I wanna go to the Presidio and find out everything I can about that Mt. Tam Army program. That's where you come in." Pat explained that he would pose as a freelance author who was Desmond's ghostwriter for a book on the specialized training of Joe's unit, the 101st Airborne. "You'll play your shy warrior role, so I'll do most of the talking," Kelley said.

"Great! I appreciate your vote of confidence," Desmond said. Then he laughed, "Ya better approach this at the officer level, since no NCO's gonna fall for such a scam."

"How 'bout more coffee," Cavaretta interrupted their plotting. They waved off his uplifted coffeepot. The owner of the Oregon Café asked: "You guys see what the poor girl's father said in the paper?"

"Brady? He talked about the case?" Desmond said startled.

"Sure did. He was out at the cemetery the day the D.A. says he's gonna gas Panforte. Seems Brady goes there everyday. Fuckin reporter follows him and just watches. Brady stays there about an hour, always by himself. He never kneels or anything, just stands there staring at her name on the tombstone. He never cries, but he brings flowers every visit. I know that's not bullshit 'cause my brother Vinnie is a gardener out there, and he tells me the girl's got so many fuckin' flowers, after Brady leaves they put 'em on the graves nobody visits."

Pat Kelley looked down into his coffee cup as if to avoid eye contact with Caverretta. Desmond said, "I thought you said Brady said something about the case."

"Right, it's in the morning paper. This reporter who's following him goes up to Brady yesterday as he's about to get into his car and says: 'Excuse me, Mr. Brady. I don't mean to impose on you, but District Attorney Moore has said he'll ask for the death penalty for Robert Panforte for what he did to your daughter. Are you satisfied with his decision?'"

"You mean this asshole reporter goes up to this pain- burdened man and asks him about his old buddy in the D.A.'s office gassing his son-in-law?" Desmond said angrily.

"Yeah, it's pretty chickenshit," Caverretta conceded.

"The bastards'll do anything to get a byline. But what did Brady say?" Desmond pressed.

Cavaretta's finger traveled down the page of the *San Francisco Chronicle*. He took off his glasses. "Here it is. He told the reporter: *'I can't see what would be served by executing Bob. There are no recriminations.'*"

"No shit!" Desmond exclaimed, looking over to Pat Kelley who was still contemplating his half-empty coffee cup. Joe Desmond thought that in two simple sentences Paul Brady had announced to the city that vengeance was a father's right and he relinquished his parental privilege to the courts in which he had so long and brilliantly labored. A disconsolate father insured his son-in-law a fair trial in which he would battle furiously for his life, confident that the political power of Brady would not penetrate the forbidding granite walls of the Hall of Justice. The first blow in the battle over Panforte's endangered life had been struck by the defense, delivered with numbing power by a victim-father before the prosecution had even walked into the court-room. "Let's get to work," Pat said, knowing what *The Chronicle* reporter didn't. Namely, that each morning after his gravesite visit, Paul Brady dropped by a Pacific Heights liquor store, purchased a bottle of Irish pain killer and then drove to Fort Point under the graceful span of the Golden Gate Bridge and drank until he passed from grief to oblivion.

That afternoon Pat Kelley arranged an appointment with a Sixth Army Information Officer, one Captain Jeff Woodward. Captain Woodward was a West Point graduate who had fortunately missed the war. As an officer and a gentleman in the peacetime Army he was the perfect sucker for Kelley's yarn. Pat told the gullible captain that their research must remain absolutely confidential since the press would have a field day if word got out that a San Francisco war hero was writing a book. Desmond played his reticent warrior role to the hilt, contributing a litany of "Yes sirs" and "No sirs" to punctuate Kelley's fraud. Pat told Captain Woodward that Sergeant Desmond – which was how both men referred to him during the meeting – would provide all the necessary information about airborne training, but that they needed the captain's help to compare it with the standard infantry training experienced by most recruits. Kelley explained: "Since Sgt. Desmond's from California we want to look into infantry training in the Bay Area. In particular we're interested in training programs run out of Fort Cronkite in Marin."

Deeply impressed that he was making a major contribution to military history, Captain Woodward ordered his First Sergeant to fetch the files for all training programs in Marin County during the war. Then he led the Chief Clerk and court reporter to a conference room where they could rummage through the files. He decisively declared the conference room "Off Limits" to all other military personnel. As he was leaving them to their historical search, he said "Have you got a title for your book yet?"

"We're thinking of *Screaming Eagles*, sir," Joe volunteered.

"Excellent, Sergeant! Excellent!" he said enthusiastically, closing the door and leaving them to their research. Pat and Joe cracked up that the pompous captain had been such an easy con.

After three hours of research Kelley found the files on the Army training program with its headquarters at Panforte's hunting cabin in the shadow of Mt. Tamalpais. It confirmed Bob Panforte's statements to O'Day and Murphy completely. More importantly, however, it revealed the reasons that the military brass had terminated this program. It appeared to be modeled after Desmond's airborne training, although it was not as intense and elaborate as the one he had been put through. In the first squad that Bob Panforte had trained, only three GI's made it to the escape point that would later become Paula's burial site. The others got lost in the forest, and Panforte had led search parties to round them up. Within ten hours all but one soldier was accounted for. The missing infantryman was a Jack Hill, a twenty-year-old draftee from Houston, Texas who would give missing-in-action a new meaning. After three days of searching the Army concluded that Hill wasn't lost but had gone AWOL. This military suspicion was confirmed a day later when a dairyman near Stinson Beach discovered Hill screwing his fifteen-year-old daughter in his barn. Military police immediately arrested Hill, roughing him up sufficiently to abate a Marin father's outrage. The last sentence of the Army report revealed that Hill was booked in the stockade and court martialed for statutory rape and AWOL.

Kelley and Desmond then paid a visit Judge Advocate General's Corps. They dropped their phony personas and Pat handed the Sergeant Major his business card identifying him as the Chief Clerk of the Superior Court. Joe flashed his gold Grand Jury badge, emphasizing the official nature of their business. Kelley inquired if there was an official court reporter's transcript of the court martial of Private Jack Hill. The Sergeant Major sent his clerk to check their files, and he returned with the trial transcript. Pat scanned a few pages, handed it back to the Sergeant Major and asked that he keep it available for further study. "Of course," said Sergeant Major.

As they drove through the east gate of the Presidio onto Lyon Street and back to civilian life, Pat told Desmond what he had found in his brief examination of the court martial transcript. Jack Hill had been convicted on both counts, sentenced to Leavenworth Prison, dishonorably discharged and required to register in California as a sex offender. Hill's criminal prosecutor had been a volunteer to the Judge Advocate General's Corps. His name was Paul Brady!

On the eve of Robert Panforte's arraignment for the murder of his wife, Pat Kelley had one more lead that he wanted to check out before reciting the words of the Indictment – the only words he would utter in the trial – before his wife and son. He dropped by the campus of the University of San Francisco, where the Jesuit rectory was located behind St. Ignatius Basilica, high atop the blustery Fulton Street Hill. Kelley asked to see Rev. Louis W. Barnett, S.J. Father Barnett was the Principal of St. Ignatius High School, the Jesuit college preparatory. Pat was in the process of picking a high school for Terry and the Jesuits were vigorously recruiting the boy. Although their promise of a classical education tempted Pat he realized that the ardor with which they courted his son was heavily influenced by Terry's athletic prowess. Terry was one of the best grade school basketball players in the City, but he was a phenomenon as a baseball player, who dreamed he'd one day play shortstop for the New York Yankees. Father Barnett believed in the "sound mind, sound body" educational approach of the ancient Greeks, but he also had a Jesuit's competitive fire that his St. Ignatius Wildcat teams be winners. So remarkable was Terry's ball playing skills that he was granted an exemption to play in the American Legion Summer League even though the other boys were two to four years older. Of course Pat had himself been a good ball player and one of his minor league teammates had been his boyhood pal, Pete Conroy. Following their brief baseball careers Pat had married Maria and Conroy had enlisted with the Jesuits and was currently Retreat Master at El Retiro Retreat House. He periodically spent weekends with the Kelleys and introduced the St. Ignatius principal to the Kelley family.

Pat shook hands with Father Barnett, a short, bulky fellow, with a bald pate and small pot belly hanging over his trademark Jesuit black cincture. He greeted Kelley warmly. They walked from the rectory across the modest hilltop campus of the University of San Francisco. In the shadow of the basilica's grand dome, second only to City Hall in its magnificence, most of the campus buildings were Quonset huts except for the administration and classroom buildings and the Jesuit residence for their high school and university faculty. On the down slope of Stanyan Hill was the baseball field of the U.S.F. Dons, bordered by Masonic Avenue. They took seats on the temporary metal bleachers along the third base foul line. Predictably the two men began talking about the S.I. sports, Father Barnett hoping to close the deal for Terry's enrollment in his school. Uncharacteristically, Pat dispensed with subtly and said, "I'm here to talk about a past S.I. athlete, not a possible future one. What can you tell me about Bob Panforte?"

"Oh dear!" the Jesuit mumbled, running his palm over his baldhead in search of a strand of hair. "It's just awful! It's so terribly tragic!" Pat's silence encouraged the Jesuit to say what was really on his mind. Father Barnett apologetically said, "Pat, I think you should know that young Panforte's father is a generous contributor to our Jesuit mission. He has been for years, long before his son came to S.I."

"I understand," Pat said. "I'm not interested in old man Panforte. What can you tell me about his kid? What was he like in high school?"

"Well, he wasn't a very good student. He wasn't lazy like some of our kids. He just didn't have the aptitude. He even struggled with Latin, which surprised us since his parents are fluent in Italian. He wasn't shy, but he wasn't gregarious either. His clique was all jocks, although even with them there was this vague sense of distinction, distance, you might say. He never seemed to go through the gawky stage most boys experience. He was very powerfully built, yet graceful in a primitive sort of way. For such an outstanding football player he wasn't particularly athletic, although he was quite fast and a ferocious hitter. I speculated that behind his cool blue eyes and almost passive demeanor there was that teenage rage that you can't put your finger on. He was a perfect Stanford man – intellectually modest, loving and thoughtful of his mother and the heir to a fortune."

"So he was no trouble for your Prefect of Discipline?" Pat pressed.

"Not really," Father Barnett said. "Oh, there was one incident that didn't amount to much. In his senior year, after the football season, he got caught drinking in Golden Gate Park, in the bushes around the Polo Grounds. You know how these kids are."

Kelley nodded. "How did you learn of it?"

"We always learn these things," Father Barnett smiled impishly. "When the cops see an S.I. student body card, they bring 'em to us instead of their fathers. We have a better record in youth discipline than most parents, and the boys are so grateful that we keep their indiscretions secret from their parents that the recidivist is rare. Bob was lucky that Gil Dowd caught him and brought him straight to the rectory."

"Inspector Gil Dowd?" Kelley asked. Father Barnett nodded. The two men walked back to the rectory. Pat thanked S.I.'s principal and as he was leaving asked, "By the way Lou, did Dowd tell you what side of the Polo Grounds young Panforte was caught drinking in? Was it the paddock side or the Sunset District side?"

"The paddock side, if I recall. The Richmond side of the park," Father Barnett said.

Kelley walked through Haight Asbury and entered Golden Gate Park at Kezar Stadium. The sixty-thousand seat stadium was the home of Catholic intercollegiate football, the new home of San Francisco's first major league team, the San Francisco 49ers, and the gridiron on which Bob Panforte first came to football prominence as a prep star. He strolled leisurely through the Park past the De Young Museum, the Japanese Tea Garden, a redwood forest, stitched together with equestrian trails. The early afternoon sun caressed families picnicking in the meadows and cyclist peddling to Playland Amusement Park at Ocean Beach. At the Polo Grounds in western Golden Gate Park a few blocks from the Pacific Ocean, Kelley sat in the concrete spectator stands for a few moments watching powerful thoroughbreds speeding around the racetrack that surrounded the polo field. He noticed a jet-black Tennessee walker with high prancing fore hoofs and a long main flowing in the breeze, trotting around the track in the dusty wake of racehorses. He walked through the paddock area and saw a mounted San Francisco Policeman chatting amiably with a few teenage girls on their way to workout their horses in the show ring. He thought it odd that young Panforte had selected the Richmond District side of the Polo Grounds for sipping contraband booze. Although teenagers, including Kelley himself when he was a high school student at Lowell, had long used the eucalyptus forest surrounding the Polo Grounds as a secret drinking site, they normally chose the Sunset District or southern side of Polo Grounds. The northern side, bordered by the row houses of the Richmond District, was not only a more open area, but the Park Mounted Police Station was located about three hundred yards to the west and green-tiled, faux adobe public restrooms were situated on the flat grasslands below the down sloping forest. The proximity of this police station was enough to discourage underage revelers, but the presence of park public restrooms, known by every high school boy as a place of homosexual assignations, was an obvious magnet for vice squad scrutiny. Kelley thought it was also peculiar that a police inspector rather than a patrolman mounted or on foot had been the one to bring the teenager's misbehavior to the principal's attention. Because this had been a "Church" matter, he knew that there was no police report of the incident, and Father Barnett had made it clear that he would volunteer no further information about it. As for Inspector Gil Dowd, Kelley knew that he had died in a shoot-out in the Mission District three years earlier. A dead end, he thought as he headed for Fort Funston Boulevard at his walk to his lakeside home.

14

Bailiff Dan McCann slid open one of the huge, wooden doors of the courtroom and stepped out into the corridor of the fourth floor of the Hall of Justice. A sea of spectators that had packed the hallway hoping to secure a priceless seat at the Panforte trial greeted him. "Any members of the Defendant's family and the Bradys, please step forward," McCann announced. There was shuffling ten yards down the marble corridor and an opening appeared in the crowd. Daniel D. Loeb led Mr. and Mrs. Fred Panforte through the human aisle formed by the parting crowd. Loeb, shorter than Mrs. Panforte by a generous inch and slight of build in his three-piece charcoal suit, looked more like the family valet than the protector of their son's life and liberty. Armed only with a small ebony briefcase initialed in fourteen-carat gold letters *D.D.L.,* the attorney led the couple to the courtroom. Fred Panforte held his gray fedora in one hand and clutched his wife's arm above her elbow with the other. His gray pin-stripe suit accented the light olive tone of his handsome, mature face and deferred to the vivid black of his hair, which was combed straight back from his brow, emphasizing his decisive nose. His well-muscled body moved in rigid discipline toward the courtroom, his receding hairline and graying sideburns his only concession to his almost six decade journey from peasantry to power.

When they reached the portal to the courtroom flash bulbs exploded. Mrs. Panforte winced at the brash eruption of light. She wore a net-like black veil, which hung vulnerably from a black pillbox hat too frugal to cover her rich charcoal hair caressing her slender neck. As the flashbulbs subsided, she waved her hand in front of her eyes, as though sweep away their luminous intrusion. Her trim, almost boyish body was dressed entirely in black. Her only accommodation to color was her deep-set blue eyes hiding behind her veil of shame, which she lifted after entering the courtroom. Her face, once liberated from her transparent shroud, was not the face of a new grandmother but seemed that of a woman half her years. Her features were refined, almost brittle.

Her thin lips, giving the illusion of fullness by the design of her lip-stick, were drawn in a straight line below her slightly upturned little nose. But it was her eyes that were so alluring. Their blue shade was touched with a hint of green, and in their well-like roundness, one sensed the affliction of a stolen youth. Robert Panforte's parents, in appearance and attire, validated the law of physics that avows that opposites attract. She, draped entirely in black, stressed her exquisite, Carrara-white complexion. He, clad in gray, his skin singing of his Mediterranean roots, implied darkness, some ethereal shadow obscur-ing an unsuspected truth.

"Right this way, madam," McCann guided Angelina Panforte. To Loeb he said, "We've reserved the first row on the right side of the courtroom for 'em.'" Mr. and Mrs. Panforte took their seats. Both glanced at the vacant jury box. Then their eyes traveled to the elevated bench that dominated the courtroom. Pat Kelley, the only other per-son in the courtroom, was seated at his desk. "Is he the judge?" whis-pered Angelina to her son's defense counsel.

"No, he's just the clerk. The judge sits behind him. We got a lady judge. You can always tell who the judge is by who the lawyers fawn all over," Loeb said. Mrs. Panforte frowned at Loeb's cynicism. She didn't care for her son's attorney and was offended by his disdain for judges, particularly since the life of her only child might be abridged by one. She couldn't imagine that a woman could be a judge, much less preside over such an awful case as this one. She worried that, be-ing a woman, the judge might think her football playing son was an aggressive, violent male who could actually do such a thing to Paula. She found Loeb's manner brusque and was put off by his aggressive-ness. Even as a girl, assertive men had frightened her. Indeed, it was Fabrizio Panforte's – she still called her husband by his Italian name – shyness, his vulnerable, hesitant bearing that had first attracted her forty-one years earlier when she met him at the *duomo* in Genoa. Even his letters to her while she was in a convent school in Italy and he was making his way in San Francisco were gentle and encouraging. Like any man, he wrote about himself and his job and how well he was do-ing. He told her what a wonderful man his boss, Signor Bertolli, was and how he'd made Fabrizio feel almost a part of his family. When Fabrizio had proposed to her he'd written that Signor Bertolli had just elevated him to a high position of great responsibility in the company, and that his boss had volunteered to assist her in emigrating from Genoa to San Francisco. He would also arrange a singing audition for her, as Fabrizio had written: "Signor Bertolli is a very important man of the theater." Angelina Panforte reached into her black purse and removed her rosary beads. "It was all so long ago," she thought, "As though another life. Her wedding night, her baby and now this…"

But she also recognized that Loeb was a brilliant lawyer and he had, after all, extricated her husband from that unpleasantness with Bartolomeo Bertolli almost three decades ago. She tolerated Loeb's abrasive personality and affected warmth toward him in the frantic hope that his persuasive powers might save her son's life, as his cunning had preserved her husband's career three years after their son was born. She accepted that her husband, a shrewd though secretive man, was so different from the boy she'd met in Genoa and fallen in love with from his letters to her from America, understood lawyers better than she did. When she'd expressed her reservations about Loeb, he dismissed her concerns, telling her: "*Non ti deve piacere per usarlo.* You don't have to like 'em to use 'em." Still, she had never truly understood what had happened between her husband and Signor Bertolli. Fabrizio only confided that he had done what he had to do for the good of the company. He'd vaguely mentioned that Signor Bertolli was spending so much time in his theater that the men of Western Poultry were being short-changed for "that soprano of his." Angelina didn't understand the slang expression "short-changed," but she knew "that soprano of his" was Antonietta Pompa, who she felt was a lovely, talented woman. If it was true that Signor Bertolli was having an affair with Antonietta, what business was that of her husband – particularly *her* husband, she'd thought. Antonietta had tried diligently to teach Angelina the ways of the stage, but she struggled to overcome her freight at singing to men while they looked at her. In the *duomo* in Genoa, from high in the choir loft, the audience's back to her, it was only her voice that mattered. As a girl, she believed her soprano instrument was the only beautiful part of her being and that her trills and fortissimo masked from others the ugliness that she felt inside. And then her son was born, and she needed a mask no longer. In his beautiful aqua eyes, she had discovered her certain beauty.

The defense lawyer pushed through the swinging mahogany gate and joined Pat Kelley in the well of the courtroom. Loeb was a bit shorter than Kelley and their appearances attested to their divergent heritage and distinct stations in life. Loeb's face was tautly chiseled, climaxing in a finely sculpted Semitic nose. Pat was a round-faced man whose soft features seemed a comment on the ambiguities of life.

The defense attorney had a full head of black kinky hair, dotted with curly strings of gray, each a trophy of a courtroom triumph. The Chief Clerk's unruly brown hair was the only thing he seemed unable to influence, and it was the only vanity to which he succumbed. He prided himself that his hair neither thinned nor grayed until the eve of his eightieth year. Loeb's green eyes were fox-like narrow slits, searching for a weakness, a flaw, that he could exploit. Pat's fulsome, brown eyes were an invitation to candor, drawing from others whatever essential goodness they possessed no matter how meager their offering.

While Mr. and Mrs. Panforte waited for the arrival of their son from the holding tank Loeb and Kelley exchanged pleasantries in the courtroom area lawyers called "the Pit." Joe Desmond thought it an apt appellation. He envisioned a striking resemblance to an arena in which he'd once viewed a cockfight. In Tijuana, you get a couple of animals – roosters or lawyers, it makes little difference – surround them with spectators with an appetite for combat or a lust for blood and let 'em got at it. You're guaranteed the greatest spectator sport – compelled fury. What he never figured out was whether the roosters loved the battle and he knew the trial lawyers did. But you have to wonder about a breed of men who enthusiastically jump into the Pit to abuse and be abused in pursuit of real or imagined justice. To Joe, the most bewildering mystery about the psyches of these paid advocates was their ability to step out of the Pit and transform themselves back into persons again. Once out of the Pit, you'll likely find two guys who have just spent hours trying to humiliate each other, sipping drinks at a corner bar or conducting a joint seminar for awed law students on the art of cross-examination. Once out of The Pit, these beasts of battle are husbands, fathers, lovers and laughers. He thought that this is what makes them different than fighting roosters. A rooster is forced to battle for his life to pleasure man. Danny Loeb freely chose to fight for another man's life. And that, in Joe's mind, made him a truly noble cock.

"Whadda ya doing here, Pat?" Loeb asked.

"Trying to justify my exorbitant pay check," the Chief replied. Loeb's first question had unearthed considerable data for the defense lawyer to evaluate. Every great criminal lawyer is always looking for conspiracies hatched in or out of the courthouse, designed to snare his client or him and sometimes both. That the Chief Clerk had demoted himself to a courtroom clerk perplexed Loeb. He wondered if Kelley, whom he knew to be Bartolomeo Bertolli's son-in-law, had a hidden agenda that motivated his participation in the Panforte trial. Was his presence somehow connected with Loeb's representation of Fred Panforte in his legal battle with old man Bertolli for control of the poultry empire? The Irish never forget a past abuse, Loeb feared. As for Kelley's wife, Italians take their vendettas as seriously as their operas. Loeb worried that Kelley's presence might be a plot to tilt the playing field toward his opponent. Loeb's years of trial experience had taught him that Kelley possessed one of the best minds in the courthouse, and he was the most influential non-jurist in the courts. Perhaps he'd have his private investigator keep an eye on Kelley just to make sure nothing from Panforte past inculcated itself into Panforte present. Then there was Paul Brady's close relationship with Judge Lucille Grant and their years together as young prosecutors. His investigator, David London, had uncovered the fact that Brady had sought Judge Grant's counsel when he'd learned that his daughter was missing, and it was Judge Grant who had summoned the homicide detectives into the case. Combining Brady's relationship with the trial judge with Kelley's family's ancient conflict with the defendant's father, agitated the criminal lawyer's paranoia gland. But he decided not to mention Kelley's relationship with Bertolli to his client or his client's parents. "No sense stirring up old rivalries and past shames," Loeb thought, just as Pat Kelley had anticipated.

"Is the judge in yet?" Loeb asked Kelley.

"Yeah, she's been here for more than an hour. She wants you and Moore in chambers as soon as our fearless prosecutor arrives," Kelley said.

There was a stirring out in the hallway as District Attorney Michael Moore entered the rear of the courtroom, followed closely by Homicide Inspector Michael Murphy, past patron of the poor of the Italian Church. They walked up the center aisle toward the Pit. Moore, lanky with dark, slicked back hair, moved with the resolute elegance of a man who considered the courtroom his kingdom. The top of his skull, when he was still, which was rarely, seemed a bit too large for his spindly body, and the orbit of his face tapered markedly to form a sharp chin, punctuated by a dramatic dimple. He looked more Mediterranean than Irish, especially in contrast to the chunky Murphy who labored up the aisle like a tackle-busting fullback for the Chicago Bears. A touch under six-foot, Murphy had a rich bushel of wavy, red hair and his commanding tenor voice was faintly laced with a County Cork brogue. He was irrefutably Irish and obviously a cop, yet when he interrogated suspects or testified on the stand the rhythm of his speech had the gentle lyric quality of a poet. Joe Desmond had learned, after reporting a Police Commission hearing at which he'd testified, that he was indeed a closet poet, who shared his poetry only with his wife and children and non-cops with whom he occasionally drank. Desmond couldn't recall any of his poems, but that may say more about the sobriety of Murphy's audience than the splendor of his verse.

As the D.A. parted the gateway into the Pit, he bowed to the parents of the man whose death he was designing. Fred Panforte nodded, as if to say, *"Ya gotta come through me to get my boy."* Mrs. Panforte looked down at her hands fingering her rosary; the steady movement of the gold links joining the tiny beads verified that she was speaking to the Mother of God. "Morning, Danny, Pat," greeted Moore, as he reached for the outstretched hand of Loeb, over whom he towered. Fred Panforte frowned at the affability Loeb displayed toward the man he considered the deadliest enemy in his life. He didn't understand that this veneer of civility was but a quiet prelude before the storm of words with which both lawyers would seek to destroy the other.

"What's Murphy doing here? The case isn't important enough for O'Day to carry your briefcase? Or is our venerable Chief Inspector so embarrassed by his detective handiwork that he sends junior here to clean up his mess?" Loeb taunted.

The D.A. smiled condescendingly down at Loeb and said, "I thought you wanted to try a murder case, counsel. I even feared you might succumb to originality for a change. I guess you're just too old. Try the cops, try the D.A., try anybody but your client. Vintage Daniel David Loeb. Anyway, I thought you'd prefer having Inspector Murphy here since your client seems to consider him something of a personal confidant, if not his private confessor."

"Fifteen hours of uninterrupted police interrogation of my man without an attorney, or the courtesy of a telephone call, or a lousy tuna fish sandwich!" Turning to Murphy, "Whadda ya call that, Murph? *An Ode To The Spanish Inquisition?*" quipped Loeb, revealing that his private investigator had exposed Murphy's secret poems to defense counsel's immodest scrutiny.

"Gentlemen, if I may abuse the term," interrupted the Chief Clerk. "The judge would like to see both of you in chambers."

Loeb opened his briefcase, removed a thick set of papers and handed them to the D.A. "Here's some bedtime reading." He handed the originals to Kelley for filing. The Clerk's file stamp tattooed the *Defendant's Motion to Dismiss the Indictment of Robert A. Panforte*. Then both lawyers headed for Judge Grant's chambers.

Kelley rose from his desk and walked to the rail separating the Pit from the spectator section. He placed his thick hands on the mahogany rail and softly addressed the Defendant's parents. "Mrs. Panforte, Mr. Panforte, I'm Pat Kelley and I'll be the clerk during your son's trial. We've reserved this row for you and anyone you wish to have with you during this difficult time. If you have any problems with the press or court personnel, just bring it to my attention. Under our law, when your son walks into this courtroom, he does so as an innocent man, and therefore he and you deserve to be treated with respect. I'm going to admit the public now. Try not to let their curiosity offend you. They mean no harm. It's just that witnessing human sadness is easier that living through it, as you must."

"Will we be able to speak with our son?" asked Fred Panforte in an Italian accent more pronounced than the Chief Clerk had expected.

"I'll arrange it with the bailiff," Kelley promised. Fred Panforte rose and extended his hand to the Chief Clerk saying, "Thank you, Mr. Kelley." He turned to his wife and said to Kelley, "This is all very ah… difficult. Especially for my wife." Kelley gripped Panforte's hand, nodded and said, "*Prego*." Panforte was surprised that an Irish bureaucrat used the Italian phrase for "*You're welcome*." Mrs. Panforte saw the gentleness in Kelley's eyes and heard the warmth in his voice and, for the first time since arriving at the Hall of Justice, felt she was not an alien in the court of her adopted land. Neither she nor her husband suspected that the man who was comforting them was married to the daughter of Bartolomeo Bertolli.

And Pat Kelley wasn't about to tell them.

Inside her chambers Judge Lucille Grant waited for the trial lawyers. She appeared calm, but she continually rubbed her hands together to relieve the tenseness in her stomach. When she noticed her nervous hand gestures, she reminded herself that the first lesson she'd taught herself in law school was: "Never let 'em see that you're scared." She closed her eyes and breathed deeply and calmed herself. She had been San Francisco's first woman prosecutor. In her time law schools discouraged women from a career at the Bar. There were barely a couple of hands full of women lawyers practicing in the City, and almost all of them were restricted to domestic relations practices. At Hastings Law School, as the only female in the class, she challenged restrictive chauvinism with an irreverent wit and a bottomless reservoir of off-color jokes that her classmates found shocking coming from a woman's mouth. But they laughed nonetheless, and discovered that she was neither an intrusion in nor a challenge to their masculine world. In classroom debate she was tenacious and anxious to attack any judicial precedent if it compelled an unjust result or promoted perverse public policy. When she graduated first in her class old Dean Arnold Johnson summed her up best at a graduation party when he inelegantly toasted: "Lucy doesn't take any crap!"

It was no surprise to Dean Johnson or her classmates that Lucille Grant became San Francisco's first female prosecutor. On her first day as a prosecutor she was assigned to share an office with another rookie Deputy D.A, Paul Brady. The office was little more than a cubicle with one desk and two chairs. Lucy laughed when she arrived at their closet-size office on their second day on the job and saw that Brady had pasted *His* and *Hers* signs on their chairs. There was nothing modest or tentative about these two young attorneys. Brady had been a championship boxer in college, and Lucy had to batter every door that barred her from her unlikely ambitions. They instantly established a personal and professional rapport.

They shared the secrets of their cases, counseled each other on strategy and tactics and hit the streets at night with the cops serving arrest and search warrants that they'd scrupulously drafted. Lucy charmed the street-wise cops with her ribald humor and her ability to drink everyone, even Brady, under the table. Old time cops still claim that she was the best damn pocket billiards player in the City.

After Brady had left the DA's office to start his own law firm and bank his first million, the lady lawyer and brawling barrister maintained their abiding friendship. Brady, a boxing aficionado who sparred at Newman's Gym into his middle years, made Lucy his date at ringside. His wife, Eileen, was repelled by everything about the sport of boxing. The savagery of it all, the animal lust for blood and pain roaring from the hoarse throats off over-weight men and over-dressed women she found revolting. She was very comfortable with her husband's relationship with Lucy. She knew how closely and capably Lucy had worked with Paul professionally, and she greatly admired Lucy's remarkable accomplishments in a man's world against enormous, unflattering odds. Although her estranged husband had always been an unfaithful husband, Eileen Brady realized that Lucille Grant was the best friend he'd ever had.

During the many years of this most unconventional friendship between an accomplished man and woman the chaste nature of their relationship was never spoiled. Although they shared the most private details of their personal lives, they never extended their warm intimacy to explore the secrets of each other's bodies. Not that Lucy wanted it this way. On the contrary, she would have preferred Paul Brady in the yielding warmth of her bed to the countless smoke-filled boxing arenas where their physical contact was limited to her hand resting on his jacketed arm.

There was another secret yearning that Lucille Grant shared with her dear friend. After fifteen years as a successful prosecutor Lucy told Brady that she wanted to be a judge. As an advocate, she told him, she felt incomplete. "I've faced unfairness all my life because of the accident of a chromosome. When you're treated fairly by someone, like you've always treated me since we packed ourselves into that tiny office, well…it feels so good, so special. I want to touch people's lives more intimately. I want them to know fairness. Paul, do you think a woman's electable in the City?"

"We don't have to find out. We just have to make you appointable," Brady said. Brady delivered for Lucille Grant with boxes of Irish votes and campaign money for the Governor's race. Upon his inauguration the grateful Governor appointed Chief Assistant District Attorney Lucille Grant as the first woman on California's Superior Court.

"Morning judge," both lawyers chorused. Judge Lucille Grant, clad in a beige skirt and jacket with a green silk scarf was a small, compact woman with dark brown, closely cut hair. A few strands of gray had insinuated themselves into her bangs which she brushed back with her fingers as if to cast the evidence of her aging out of sight. "Mike, Danny, it's good to see you," she said warmly. Judge Grant sipped her coffee and then said, "Fellas, I think we need to have a little talk off-the-record. You both know that I served in the DA's office with Paul Brady. You probably know that Paul and I are dear personal friends." Loeb nodded, encouraging her candor. "I've also known Paula her entire life. I'm even acquainted with the Defendant and his parents, although not as intimately as the victim and her father. If either of you feel that my personal relationships might cause harm to your case, just say so and I'll immediately recuse myself."

Loeb started to respond, but Judge Grant waved him off. "There's more," she said. "On the day that Paul learned his daughter was missing he came to my chambers. Obviously he was distraught, almost terrified. We talked for quite a while and he shared with me all that he knew about her disappearance including his conversations with his son-in-law - your client, Danny.

"I tried to get Paul to think like the fine lawyer that he is, not a frightened father. But it was all just too much for him. Danny, it was I who called O'Day. That's how Homicide got in the picture. I think you and your client have every right to have me step down from hearing this case. Just say the word and it'll be done."

Loeb, of course knew from his private investigator, London, that it was the judge who'd called in Homicide. But he needed to hear it from her. This was Loeb's first test as to whether he should require her to step down from the case. If, like most judges, she'd simply neglected to mention her contact with Homicide Loeb would conclude such a lack of candor as a bias against his cause. But her forthright admission of her extra-judicial participation in the case was a strong indication that the evenhandedness that had marked her judicial career would assert itself in this celebrated case. Like most defense lawyers Danny Loeb didn't expect much from trial judges. He thought of them as occupationally pro-prosecution and didn't expect to get the close calls. All he required was that they listen and that his logic occasionally penetrates their lofty impressions of their impartiality. But he expected and needed more from Judge Grant. This woman didn't have a pretentious bone in her body and had never shied from a controversy. He leaned forward in his chair and said, "Judge, I've been in this business for more than thirty years. And I've never heard a more honest and sincere statement than what you've just told us. I pray that you won't consider me intrusive if I ask you a question or two."

"Of course not," she said.

"Can you tell us why you decided to involve the homicide boys in the investigation? Did you or Paul have any suspicions that my client might be involved in his wife's disappearance?" Loeb probed.

"No, we had no such suspicions," she said. "Paul was very fond of his son-in-law, and I had no reason to doubt your client's story. I was trying to get Paul to analyze the facts as he knew them, like the fine prosecutor he'd been. But he was too emotional."

"That's understandable," Loeb said softly. Judge Grant continued: "As I thought about our years in the DA's office I couldn't help but think about the rarely spoken dread of every cop and prosecutor who's put someone in jail. We have to learn to live with the fact that the men we send to prison are bitter and hateful and frequently blame their predicament on cops or prosecutors, perhaps both. It's odd that they rarely personalize their anger at the judges who actually sentence them. Perhaps it's the aura of the robe.

"If you're a cop or DA, you learn to watch your back, you sort of monitor the cons you've sent away to do hard time. These are bad and bitter people, Danny. You don't often lose, so you may not know this. They've got nothing but time to think about sweet revenge against their persecutors or their families. I don't know if you've ever tried a case with Paul, but Mike was trained by him. He's a force, an almost furious force in the courtroom."

"He's the toughest, meanest s.o.b. who's every stepped into the Pit," the DA said.

Judge Grant sighed, "Paul seemed to arouse more intense hatred in criminal defendants than most of us did. A year after he'd left the DA's office for private practice, we cracked a conspiracy in San Quentin to snatch Paula from grammar school. A jailhouse snitch tipped us off and I personally sent the vicious bastards away for life.

"When I brought up the subject of convict revenge and retaliation Paul shrugged it off. 'I haven't been a prosecutor for years,' he said. 'Most of the cons I nailed are dead or feeble by now.' That's when I decided to call Ed O'Day.

"Paul was correct about the staleness of his criminal convictions from his DA days. But in his emotional state he wasn't thinking about what he did during the war. He'd volunteered for the Army Judge Advocate Corps and was given an honorary commission to prosecute courts martial cases. He never talked about his wartime prosecutions, but the proximity in time to his daughter's disappearance was enough for me to call the smartest cop I know."

"Did you mention your fears of retaliation by a military miscreant to Chief Inspector O'Day?" Loeb asked.

"No, I didn't have to," Judge Grant said. "He knew that he was looking for a suspect or suspects with a motive to harm Paul. What crueler way than to snatch his only child?"

Pat Kelley sat in his leather chair in chambers phlegmatic, knowing. He'd always known that Paula's killer would be discovered through the prism of opportunity and motive. Judge Grant's first suspicions were not of Loeb's client, but some anonymous, bitter soldier Paul might have prosecuted. Pat's Presidio investigation had put a face on such a soldier, and he was certain that Danny Loeb knew that face and probably a great deal more.

"So that's it. I'll gladly step down if either of you wish," Judge Grant said.

"One more question, Judge," Loeb said sitting back in his chair as though to brace himself for her answer. "Can you be fair?"

"Danny, I'm afraid I've never learned how not to be fair," she said.

Loeb turned to the District Attorney and said, "Mike, let's try this sonofabitch right now!" The DA said, "Amen!"

"What's your time estimate for the trial?" Judge Grant asked as though nothing unusual had happened in her chambers.

"The People estimate two weeks to put in our case," replied Moore.

"That assumes the prosecution's got a case to put on," shot back Loeb.

"Meaning?" she said.

"The indictment's no good. We've moved to dismiss," Loeb said. The judge turned to the D.A. "Mike?"

"The indictment's fine. It's in the verbatim language of the statute. Last time I looked 187's murder. I haven't read Danny's motion but it looks like a standard 995 motion."

"I like to think that none of my motions are standard, particularly in death penalty cases," Loeb said.

"Danny, why don't you give me an outline of your motion and Mike may wish to comment," the judge suggested.

"It's quite simple, Judge. There's no evidence before the Grand Jury of premeditation or deliberation. An indictment must be based on material evidence, and premeditation is the essential element for first-degree murder. Without evidence my guy deliberated killing his wife, there's no death penalty," Loeb confidently.

"Mike?" Judge Grant said.

"A hundred and ninety pound former Stanford football star beating his wife to death is as much malice as you can get in a marital bedroom, Judge," the D.A. replied.

"Pat, let me have the Panforte Grand Jury transcript," Judge Grant directed. Kelley handed it to her and she thumbed the pages contemplating her reading time. "Mike, how much time do you need to file a written reply to Danny's motion?" the judge asked, disappointed that the DA's rebuttal of Loeb was no more enlightening than the morning headlines.

"We don't need to file anything. Oral argument will suffice," Moore blandly.

"Here's what we'll do," Judge Grant said. "I'll re-read the Grand Jury transcript and Danny's motion. Then we'll arraign the Defendant and you can both argue the motion." Both lawyers agreed and rose to return to the courtroom. At the chambers door, Loeb said: "One more thing, Judge. I want Bob seated in the courtroom before the families and public are admitted. I don't want him led in and out of the holding tank looking like Jack the Ripper to the jury."

"Mike?" Judge Grant said.

"That's agreeable, Your Honor," Moore conceded to the special treatment to which the Panforte family's wealth entitled their seriously errant offspring. The attorneys took their seats at counsel table, awaiting Judge Grant's study of the record.

While Judge Grant was reading Loeb's motion to dismiss, Fred Panforte was stunned to see Maria Kelley walk into the courtroom accompanied by a lanky boy. He watched her tug her snug skirt over flaring hips as she took her first row seat. He expected the Bradys to be seated in the family row, but he didn't expect her. Not here, not now. Maria did not look over to the Panforte family pew. She peered straight ahead, waiting for her husband's appearance in the Pit. Panforte studied her elegant cheekbones and her pouting, crimson lips and whispered to his wife: "That's Bertolli's daughter! What's she doing here?"

Angelina glanced furtively at the younger woman across the aisle. She shook her head. She had not seen Maria in years. She remembered Maria at the annual company picnic that Maria's father hosted for the employees of Western Poultry at his Sonoma Ranch. Angelina was still nursing her son then, and she remembered how gentle and benevolent her husband's boss had been on that warm July so long ago. She recalled Bertolli's laughing preteen daughter so playful on her father's lap and he beaming and prideful. After dinner, when the men drank their grappa and smoked and pontificated as only satiated men can, young Maria sat with Angelina as her son nursed at her small breasts. The girl asked, "What does it feel like? Does it hurt? Does he bite you there?"

Angelina smiled, "No, it doesn't hurt. It's wonderful. Sometimes he bites, but he has soft gums and he doesn't mean to hurt me. It's just that little boys get anxious when they're hungry."

On the day her grown son stepped into the dock that curious girl of summers past had become a beautiful, mature woman. Angelina felt instinctively that Maria's presence at the trial had something to do with the ancient enmity between her father and Angelina's husband. She thought of her first days in San Francisco before she was married, when she was singing in the chorus of Antonietta Pompa's theater. It seemed that young Maria Bertolli spent almost as much time in the theater as she did. She attended rehearsals and followed Antonietta around like a loyal pet as she blocked out the stage or directed set changes. Sometimes Antonietta let her accompany the singers in rehearsal when the particular song was a popular Tin Pan Alley tune. It was obvious that the girl adored the Washington Square Theater's artistic director and that Antonietta reciprocated her affections with an almost maternal intensity. It was this patently intimate relationship between a mature, extraordinarily accomplished woman and a growing bright-eyed girl that Angelina felt refuted her husband's assertion that his boss and the actress were having a torrid love affair. Infidelity seemed so unlike Signor Bertolli and, she just couldn't believe that Antonietta could be so nurturing to his daughter after sharing his bed. "No," she thought, "my husband must be wrong. He just doesn't understand women. Since he lost his own mother at birth he probably never has. He sees a woman only in relation to a man. He sees Signor Bertolli as a rich and powerful man and Antonietta as a beautiful plaything to which such men are entitled. Even when he first saw me, singing a requiem in Genoa, I'm sure he saw a pretty little virgin, my purity protected by incense-scented priests. Oh, my husband is so blind!"

Angelina never understood how the bad blood between her husband and Signor Bertolli had arisen. Her husband had never confided his career ambitions or business dealings in her and Angelina accepted that it was probably not a wife's business anyway. She was intrigued, however, that Signor Bertolli and Antonietta Pompa seemed so comfortable sharing their vocations with no apparent regard for traditional gender roles. And she could never forget that it was this couple who had made it possible for her to become an American. After all it was Signor Bertolli who had used his influence with Washington politicians to secure her passage to San Francisco so she could marry Fabrizio. And it was Antonietta Pompa who had given her work in the theater as a singer, which was the only profession for which she had received any training. When Angelina had auditioned for her she had done very well Antonietta had told her. "You have a delicate instrument, my dear. But it has a mournful quality that superbly suits you for tragic soprano arias," Antonietta had said.

For Angelina it was one thing to sing in an empty theater with only a piano accompanist and the artistic director present and quite another to sing before a full audience. In her first chorus performance she became frozen with stage freight and couldn't utter a single note. But Signora Pompa did not scold or criticize her after her maiden performance in San Francisco. Instead, she invited her for espressos after the performance and gently questioned her about her musical training in Genoa. For an hour Angelina told Antonietta everything about her musical schooling in the convent school from the age of six on. Antonietta smiled her luminous smile, patted her on the hand and said, "Little Angel, I think I know your problem. Meet me tomorrow at noon in the choir loft of Saints Peter and Paul."

When Angelina arrived at the choir loft, Antonietta handed her the score for Mimi's aria *sensor rancor* from *La Boheme*. Accompanying Angelina on the church organ, Antonietta directed her to sing the aria at full voice. She did so, and according to Signora Pompa sang beautifully. Then the Neapolitan singing star told Angelina something she never forgot. She said: "You were terrified last night because your whole singing life has been singing in church with your audience's backs to you. This allowed your instrument to become a disembodied voice. And that is fine and natural for church music. Indeed it is the very purpose of liturgical composition to affect pure spirit.

"Last night the audience faced you, and you were terrified that they could see you. You silenced your lovely voice because they *saw* you as a woman and didn't just *hear* the sound of an angel. When you sing in church your body must not exist if you are to lift the spirits of the congregation. In the theater it is precisely your physical body that projects the divinity of your song! In church you sing to the faithful, to believers. In the theater you must suspend the disbelief of your audience. You do so by not singing to the audience, but *to* your lover or *of* your character! You've just sung Puccini's aria of parting lovers, separating without bitterness. Because the passion is in your soul and not in the eyes of spectators, the beauty and pathos of that dramatic moment you completely captured.

"Angelina, when you go on stage tonight remember that there are no eyes on you. You are completely concealed in the character you're playing." She threw her head back in laughter, saying: "As actors, we practice the craft of deceit. As women, we raise it to an art form!"

For a while, Angelina thrived at the Washington Square Theater. But her fiancée began to complain that her hours in the theater and his at The Market were incompatible and she, of course, had come to San Francisco to marry Fabrizio. So in exchange for a wedding date Angelina gave up what many thought was a promising career. At the time she didn't regret her decision. Indeed she was certain that life with her handsome American husband would diminish the mournful music of her youth in Genoa.

On this, her first day in court, Angelina Panforte had no idea that the courteous courtroom clerk was Maria's husband, but she was certain the handsome lad sitting at her side was her son. He had her penetrating eyes, though they were lighter in color. She thought it odd that a mother would bring a child to a place such as this. He would be required to be quiet and not fidget which was unnatural for a boy his age, and she could not imagine her own son at the same age having the self-discipline to do so. This fearful trial was after all about death and misery, and what mother allows a child to learn such terrible things at so tender an age? The answer came to her in the biblical admonition she feared Maria, by her presence, was defying. "Vengeance is mine, sayeth the Lord!" Angelina tried not to shudder at her thoughts and resumed fingering her rosary.

When Joe Desmond entered the courtroom the press became silent. District Attorney Moore and Inspector Murphy snapped to attention at counsel table. Robert Panforte removed his elbows from the defense table and folded his hands together as if to pray. The court reporter's entrance is the dimming of the house lights before the curtain's rise, the signal that a robed conductor will assume the elevated podium and the opera will begin. The door of the judge's chambers opened and Judge Grant, her black robe swirling around her legs, bounded up three steps to assume her presiding position. As her foot hit the first step, Bailiff McCann leapt to attention and bellowed, "All rise!" and all in the courtroom save Pat Kelley and Desmond jumped from their seats. "The Superior Court of the State of California in and for the City and County of San Francisco is now in session, the Honorable Lucille Grant presiding." Judge Grant assumed her seat in the high back leather chair and, when she was secure upon the bench the bailiff commanded: "Please be seated."

Judge Grant said, "Will the clerk arraign the Defendant." Kelley opened the file folder on his desk, remained seated and spoke up to the tall handsome Defendant: "Robert Agnello Panforte, you are charged in an indictment, returned by the Grand Jury on June 13, 1949, in and for the City and County of San Francisco, State of California with a felony, to wit, a violation of section 187 of the Penal Code. The Grand Jury alleges that you, Robert Agnello Panforte," Kelley spoke with deliberation, and pronounced the Defendant's name in a perfect Tuscan accent, even rolling the *r* in Panforte's family name. The accused's father appreciated the correct annunciation of his name and felt he was being accorded the respect that his name had earned as he listened to Kelley advise his son that: "On or about the fifth day of June, in the year of Our Lord, nineteen hundred and forty-nine, in the City and County of San Francisco, State of California, did willfully, unlawfully, feloniously and with malice aforethought murder Paula Brady Panforte, a human being, contrary to the form, force and effect of the statute and against the peace and dignity of the People of the State of California. Robert Agnello Panforte, is that your true name?"

Panforte nodded. Kelley admonished, "You'll have to reply audibly. The court reporter can't take down nods or gestures."

"Yes, that's my name."

Loeb interrupted the Chief's intended remarks, "We'll waive formal instruction and advisement of rights."

"For the record," Judge Grant said, "the Court has read the defense motion to dismiss and has read the Grand Jury record. Anything further, gentlemen?"

Loeb directed Panforte to take his seat. He stood directly in front of Kelley, center stage, and began his defense: "The Grand Jury proceedings reveal not a hint of premeditation or deliberation on the part of Bob Panforte. Premeditation is the essential element that distinguishes first-degree murder from all other homicides. Since there is absolutely no evidence of deliberation before the Grand Jury, the prosecution may not proceed with this Indictment charging first degree nor may they seek the death penalty!" As Kelley had warned Joe, Loeb spoke rapidly. Yet his sentences were concise and his rhetoric pedantic, and Desmond quickly grasped the rhythm of his speech and found his argument easy to take down.

Loeb continued, "Accepting for the purposes of argument *only*, the evidence presented to the Grand Jury shows that they were both drunk. She had a nosebleed and they argued about it *after* blood flowed. In fact their quarrel was whether the blow that caused the blood was purposeful or accidental. But there's no evidence of Bob Panforte plotting his wife's death, no brooding in the afternoon and evening hours, deliberating methods and means to slay his wife, nor is there even a hint of malice displayed in the record."

Loeb paused, walked from the gold bar of justice in front of Kelley and positioned himself behind his client. Fred and Angelina Panforte were seated to his back and to the right. He was forcing the entire Panforte family into Judge Grant's line of sight. He was compelling her to look into the tremulous, aqua blue eyes of a mother and their perfect replication, the eyes of her son. By doing so, Loeb brought the Panfortes to life, even as his practiced words diluted designed death to a mere abstraction. "What must be proven to the Grand Jury to sustain a capital murder charge is that the killer is thoughtful, deliberate, his intent sculpted by thorough premeditation. It is precisely the coldness that is manifest, the frigid deliberation to terminate human life which is revealed that is said to justify the state, with comparable aloofness, imposing the ultimate penalty. So offended is society at the icy indifference to human life displayed by such a killer, that the law declares: 'An eye for an eye. A life for a life.'" Loeb argued.

"What do we have here? A domestic squabble, a taunting wife. No icy deliberation, no mulling meditation. A fleeting second of drunken, angry spouses. No deliberation. No premeditation. Therefore under the implacable rules of logic we must say: 'No Murder One, no death penalty.'" Loeb slipped into his chair at counsel table.

As Loeb concluded his argument Pat Kelley studied his wife's face. He was pleased that she displayed no emotional reaction to Danny Loeb's words reducing the issue to a drunken, petulant bedroom brawl. She was sitting ramrod straight, focused but not tense, like a tennis player eyeing her opponent across the net before smashing her serve into play. Over their morning coffee Pat had cautioned his wife as to what to expect on her first day in court. He'd said, "Honey, pretrial proceedings are like foreplay, so don't get your hopes up for something dramatic today."

Maria had pouted her lips and replied, "Darling, foreplay is a hope for you and drama for me."

Pat had tried to explain to her that Loeb's sole purpose in this opening skirmish was to chase the shadow of the gallows out of the courtroom. To eliminate the death penalty from the case he would accept as substantially true the prosecution's evidence before the Grand Jury. He told Maria that Loeb would argue, as he just had, that the prosecution's evidence viewed in its most favorable light established that this was not a first degree murder case. Anything less than murder one eliminated San Quentin's gas chamber from Robert Panforte's future. However, Pat could not have prepared Maria for Loeb's brilliantly surgical excising of premeditation from his client's brain on his first day in the dock. He was therefore quite surprised that his wife studied the diminutive lawyer with the expression of a teacher reacting to her brightest student's dissertation – she was not surprised but somewhat amazed.

Judge Grant turned to the District Attorney, "Mr. Moore?"

District Attorney Michael Moore fluidly pushed his chair back and rose to speak. "Mr. Loeb has attempted to reduce the words 'premeditation' and 'deliberation' to static concepts. He seeks to require the People to prove that all murderers are like contemplative monks, pinning away their solitude, ruminating on the death of others while a mournful requiem plays in the background. Murder doesn't work that way, Your Honor. A killer can premeditate his evil in an instant. The violent dispatch of human life can take but a second of deliberation, of thought, of consideration. How much thought does it take to pull a trigger? How much reflection does it take to strike at a defenseless woman?

"The Defendant is a man who played varsity football at Stanford. Don't tell me a great athlete like Mr. Panforte escaped the attention of the grand jurors. This is a man whose recreational life was crafted to controlled violence, structured to organized mayhem, playful though it may have been. His athletic exploits have been reported in the press…"

Judge Grant interrupted, "Counsel, I'm loath to interrupt lawyers when they're arguing. But Mr. Panforte is not on trial for playing football at Stanford. Although as a Cal graduate I think it probably should be a crime. Let's get off the gridiron and back to the Grand Jury." From the spectators, titters of laughter and both Moore and Loeb, as Berkeley graduates, smiled. Robert Panforte remained impassive.

Moore resumed: "Very well, Your Honor. I'm willing to give the Defendant the benefit of the doubt. Let's accept that he was angry. Let's even agree that his wife provoked him. But we're not talking about a simple nosebleed here. You have to look, as the Grand Jury did, on what he does *after* his initial anger. In their bedroom, he beats her unconscious, then carries her down to the trunk of his '47 Chevy and dumps her limp body in the trunk! Then he drives almost to the summit of Mt. Tamalpais, to a secret hiding place that only someone who knew the area well enough to be hired by the United States Army…"

Judge Grant barked: "Hold on, Mr. Moore! Precisely what evidence was presented to the Grand Jury that Paula Panforte was alive when she was placed in that mountain grave?"

Picking up the Grand Jury transcript and waving it at the judge, Moore argued, "the Coroner's Report, was presented to the Grand Jury. The autopsy revealed that Paula Brady Panforte had a twelve percent saturation of carbon monoxide, meaning that she'd inhaled exhaust fumes while in the trunk of the Defendant's car!"

"Just a minute, counsel," Judge Grant again intervened. "You chose not to call the Coroner to the witness stand. Therefore the Grand Jury then and this Court now have no expert testimony on how carbon monoxide got into her blood stream. I am striking all your references to burying her alive since no competent evidence of this allegation was presented to the Grand Jury. You've got your headline, now please give me a legal argument!"

Loeb was expressionless and concealed his delight that Judge Lucille Grant was living up to her reputation for being tough on prosecutors. It may have been an unconscious remnant from her own extraordinary District Attorney days, but Judge Grant was a stickler for prosecutorial precision and she adamantly believed that, as a judge and not an advocate, she was duty-bound to grant defendants every sacred right proclaimed by the Constitution and engraved in criminal jurisprudence. It was equally true that, having been given a fair trial, once convicted, criminal defendants in her court would expect that she'd invariably sentence them to the maximum proscribed by law. For Judge Lucille Grant it was all about fairness. She conducted her criminal trials by bestowing fairness on the individual citizen, the defendant, in conflict with the state. Once convicted she showered her fairness on an aggrieved people, the collective citizen, by expelling the guilty from this collectivity and stripping him of the very individuality she had so assiduously protected during his trial.

District Attorney Moore continued: "Let's look at all the detailed and specific things the Defendant did upon his return to their Marina home on the night in question..."

"Let's not!" Judge Grant firmly. "The prefix *pre* means *before*. Meditation means to reflect, to think. The only facts presented to the Grand Jury and now being reviewed by the Court are the Defendant's thoughts prior to his wife's death. Anything after she'd expired could not have legally been considered by the Grand Jury and must not be considered by this Court."

The D.A. said pleadingly: "What about the multiple injuries the Coroner discovered on this young woman's head? What about her two black eyes? What about the large gaping wound in the back of her head that went down to the very bone? What about her lovely auburn hair turned crimson from this wound? What about the bruise in the muscle of her right temple? Judge, premeditation is here, deliberation is here! There was no one else who could have administered this frightful beating. Only the Defendant was with his wife on the night she was murdered, and no amount of sophistic rhetoric can conceal this fact. He pounded a defenseless woman. He beat her and beat and beat her. Every powerful blow was deliberate and propelled by the mind of this man, a mind utterly committed to kill!" a frustrated District Attorney concluded.

Judge Grant allowed a moment of silence as she looked down at her notes. Then she ruled: "The Court finds that while the evidence of premeditation and deliberation presented to the Grand Jury is sketchy at best, there appears some indication the Grand Jury did consider this issue. Let me caution both counsel, the Court is not finding that the evidence of premeditation and deliberation is weighty enough to support a trial jury's verdict of first degree murder. Indeed, were the evidence presented to the Grand Jury the totality of evidence presented to a trial jury, the Court has severe doubts that I would allow the jury to consider first degree murder. But since the standard of proof used by the Grand Jury only requires a suspicion based in reason, I cannot say that there is no rational basis for the Indictment.

"I call counsels' attention to page twenty-one of the Official Transcript. You'll recall, Mr. Moore, that you had concluded your presentation of evidence and invited members of the Grand Jury to ask questions. The Foreman accepted your invitation. The record reads as follows: 'The Foreman: *Inspector Murphy, would you be inclined to think that it was prearranged or premeditated affair, rather than out of a drunken stupor, that he may have arranged to commit the murder before?*'

"Inspector Murphy answered as follows: '*I don't believe he was intoxicated to the extent that he told us he was intoxicated, sir.*'

"While Inspector Murphy's answer to the question is not very responsive nor a expansive as one might have hoped, the question clearly reveals that the issue of premeditation was considered by the grand jurors and they considered the possibility that the murder of Paula Panforte was prearranged. Because they considered, however fleeting, this issue of planned killing, I cannot and must not substitute my judgment for theirs. Accordingly Mr. Loeb, your motion is denied."

Loeb was not easily nor gracefully denied. "Judge, I move for a stay of these proceedings pending a petition to the Court of Appeal for a Writ of Prohibition." Normally in a criminal trial an appeal is allowed the defense only after conviction. However in California intermediate appeals during trial proceedings, are infrequently permitted by way of extraordinary writs. Loeb was challenging Judge Grant in the higher court with a direct attack on her exercise of discretion and a militant claim that the judge had abrogated Panforte's constitutional rights.

"Do the People object to a stay?" Judge Grant, confident that her ruling would be sustained and that Loeb was properly exhausting all his remedies to keep Robert Panforte from visiting San Quentin's *Green Room.*"

"The People take no position on that, Your Honor. I don't imagine it will take much time for Mr. Loeb to get a postcard from the appellate court denying his writ."

"How much time do you need to prepare your petition, Mr. Loeb?" the judge asked.

"Two days, after I receive the reporter's transcript."

"Joe, how long will it take to print up today's record?" the judge asked Desmond.

Joe fiddled with the paper in his stenographic machine as though the machine had the answer. He looked up at her and said, "On an expedited basis I can have it ready tomorrow morning by ten." He turned his head to the spectator section. He saw Pat Kelley turn to the empty jury box to his right. Kelley rubbed his fingers against his temple obscuring from the audience the tiny crack of a smile as he immediately realized that, for an expedited transcript, his young friend's per page fees were doubled!

"Very well," Judge Grant announced. "The Court will stay the proceedings until Friday, July second. Upon filing and serving the petition, the stay will automatically be continued until further notice from the Court of Appeal. If there's nothing further we'll stand in recess."

15

After Judge Grant had repulsed the defense's first assault on the prosecution, Maria and Terry Kelley agreed to meet Pat on the Kearny Street steps of the Hall of Justice. They had all accepted that their courthouse contacts should be minimal in order to avoid Fred Panforte's detection of their relationships. To Moore and Loeb, Kelley said: "You fellas got any objection to my pre-marking the Coroner's exhibits?" Both lawyers shook their heads and asked for an index so that they could conform their discovery documents. After they'd left Pat skipped down the marble stairs to meet with his wife and kid. He told them that he had an appointment with the Coroner to go over trial exhibits, so they should go to lunch without him. A low, broth-like fog enshrouded the granite Hall of Justice like an ominous veil both hiding and inviting Pat to the mysteries of death in a forensic laboratory in the bowels of the building. The purely legal arguments by the prosecution and defense had revealed to him the reason District Attorney Moore had charged a capital crime and why Loeb insisted that, even viewed in its most favorable light, the death penalty was grossly unjust.

Moore's theory of the case was that Robert Panforte had brutally beaten his wife in their bedroom while their infant son slept sucking his thumb. So severe was the ex-football player's assault that Paula was knocked unconscious. It was likely Moore would argue that the Defendant actually believed that she was dead when she was sprawled on their bedroom floor. Having previously prepared her grave at Mt. Tamalpais, probably on the weekend preceding his attack, Bob Panforte methodically goes about disposing her body and the evidence of his cruel criminality. He backs his '47 Chevy out of his garage and then backs it back in, with the trunk next to the stairs. He carries his wife's limp, battered, and bloody body down the stairs and dumps her in the trunk. He blithely drives to his beloved Mt. Tamalpais and carries her down a steep slope. When he places her in the grave, he notices her breasts rising and falling and realizes that she's still alive.

He takes the Chevy's jack handle and fractures her skull. With his Army entrenching tool that he'd used a day or so before to prepare her grave he shovels dirt to cover her.

Given the prosecution, Pat was certain that the DA's first witness would be Dr. Ernest A. Rosenberg, the Coroner for the City and County of San Francisco. It was standard practice to commence a murder prosecution with the Coroner on the stand. It was also a moment of defense lawyers' dread. The learned physician of death would explain to the jury that forensic pathology was the application of the art of medicine to medical-legal issues involving both living and dead persons. It included issues of battered children, sexual assault, spousal abuse, homicide and injuries caused by a person or persons on another. For deceased individuals forensic pathology included investigation and evidence collection at the scene, reconstruction and interpretation, including a medical-legal autopsy and laboratory testing to determine the cause and circumstances of death. In relation to the live or the deceased, medical examiners attempted to determine how the injuries occurred or did not occur, the presence or absence of poisons and what part, if any, they may have played. Finally the Coroner would attempt to develop information about how something could or could not have happened based on physical injuries, body trauma and the like. After the jury was comfortable with the expertise of the Coroner out would come the inevitable series of gruesome morgue photographs. It was during this early moment of any murder trial that every juror learned that their civic duties were as repugnant as they were awesome. The was the trial moment when photography and medical science taught jurors that homicide was no legal abstraction and when District Attorney Moore would bring Paula Brady Panforte to life by displaying her nude, battered body in death.

Kelley not only wanted a private preview of these photos, he wanted to probe Dr. Rosenberg on how his medical opinion supported Moore's theory that the missing jack handle was the murder weapon and whether the presence of twelve per cent carbon monoxide in Paula's system established conclusively that she had expired at Mt. Tamalpais.

Pat also understood the nature and scope of Loeb's defense. It had two essential prongs, either of which blocked Robert Panforte's path to the gas chamber. In his technical argument before Judge Grant, Loeb had insisted that at worst Paula's death was the result of domestic strife that might support a manslaughter conviction. It was therefore crucial that Loeb's cross-examination of the Coroner cast doubt on the carbon monoxide content in her blood and the Chevy jack handle as the murder weapon. The second prong of Loeb's defense was that Robert Panforte was innocent, and someone else had murdered his wife. His ally in this attack was the length of time between her disappearance and discovery of her body and the compelling evidence that Bob Panforte had cooperated with the police fully, believing that they were looking for a missing person not a dead body. How else could you explain Panforte leading the cops to the Army training rendezvous other than he had no idea his wife was buried there?

At his office in the morgue Dr. Rosenberg greeted Kelley cordially. The Coroner was a short man, mostly bald save for a horseshoe of black/gray strands from ear to ear. He wore wire-rim glasses that emphasized his sharp, rodent-like face. Like almost everyone involved in the Panforte case, Dr. Rosenberg was personally acquainted with the Defendant and his parents and the victim and hers. He had worked closely with Paul Brady when Brady was the City's top homicide prosecutor and knew Paula as a little girl. He had been Paul Brady's guest at his daughter's wedding. Dr. Rosenberg told Pat that he had set up the medical records in the conference room where Pat could work as long as he liked. When Pat was finished with his study, Dr. Rosenberg invited him to ask any questions about the autopsy. As the Coroner ushered Pat into the conference room Pat said, "Ernie, I noticed from the Grand Jury transcript that you performed the autopsy surgery. Any particular reason that you did the procedure rather than one of your assistants?"

"Yes, there was. Mike Murphy had called me to say her body was on the way by ambulance. He indicated that her body had been recovered from the woods at Mt. Tam and that she'd been buried there for a number of days. I concluded immediately that the body's signs of life and dying would be greatly diminished by the passage of time and circumstances. So I decided that the most experienced physician in our office should conduct the inquiry."

Sitting at the conference table, Pat said, "Ernie, I'm sure Loeb's going to ask you if any part of your decision to personally conduct the autopsy was your professional and personal relationship with Paula's dad?" The Coroner sighed, removed his glasses and rubbed the bridge of his nose with thumb and forefinger. He said, "No, it wasn't. But it should have been."

"How so?" Pat asked.

"After the my Inquest when Paul came for his daughter's remains, he thanked me for the thoroughness of our investigation. I realized then that what he was really expressing was his appreciation that his late daughter had not been examined by a complete stranger, and it comforted him to think of me as his daughter's surgeon, even though he was devastated by my discoveries."

"Thanks, Ernie. I'll check in with you in about an hour," Pat said, and the Coroner left him alone to study the forensic evidence.

In Pat's review of Dr. Rosenberg's superficial analysis of Paula's body on arrival at the morgue the Coroner found: "The subject to be a well-developed, well nourished, adult white female, appearing twenty-five years of age. There was no rigor. Hypostasis of blood was present, in a mild degree, on the dorsal aspect of the body." Pat mentally translated Dr. Rosenberg's medical terms to laymen's language. He'd meant: that Paula's blood was settling in the back of her body when she appeared at the morgue lying face up. It was a technical way of saying: When the heart fails as a pump, gravity takes over.

Pat reviewed the surgery on Paula and made notes on a yellow legal pad. Dr. Rosenberg had opened Paula's cranial cavity and found no fracture, but her brain was slightly softened. He entered her cervical spinal canal and found nothing remarkable. When he cut into her heart, he found it was normal, as was her liver. Deep in her trachea and bronchi, he found a mushy liquid material with tiny food particles, similar to what he later found when he slit into her stomach. "These food particles confirm Panforte's story that they ate around six that evening," Kelley noted on his legal pad.

Dr. Rosenberg took a vaginal smear that showed no evidence of sperm or blood, ruling out sexual assault. Kelley noted a slight abnormality in her anus indicating some tearing of tissue, and made a note to ask the Coroner about it. He studied the toxicological report, which had tested specimens of Paula's blood, stomach and contents, and sections of her liver and kidney. He read that spectroscopic analysis revealed a twelve per cent saturation of carbon monoxide in Paula's system and that she had a blood alcohol content of point-one-five. Her blood alcohol level confirmed her husband's story that they had been drinking heavily.

Pat commenced his examination of the graphically grotesque series of black and white morgue photos depicting the dead woman's body trauma. The first photo showed Paula fully clothed. As the Coroner had removed each item of her clothing another photo was taken to memorialize the process. Pat saw that Paula was dressed in a print dress, silk stockings, pink slip with matching brassiere and panties. Her panties were a particularly fine quality of silk from Lucca. When Paula's body was completely nude on the gray marbled slab in the morgue, the photo depicted a frontal view of her voluptuous, lifeless body with lacerations, contusions, abrasions and other evident trauma. Her left cheek was dark and evidenced swelling. There were numerous injuries about her head and she had two black eyes. Pat noted a dark area of her hair. Her head wound had bled profusely. He noted the matting effect of blood and hair. He set the photo aside to question Dr. Rosenberg about it.

The next photo Pat put aside was a frontal shot of Paula's torso from her lower neck to the pelvic region. It was a still life study of her pendulous breasts. Her breasts were badly bruised and Pat noticed that the bruises formed an almost perfect circle of trauma, slightly smaller than the circumference of a baseball, just above her nipples, creating the impression of a ball-like tattoo on her breasts. He would ask the Coroner about her breast trauma. Pat picked a photo of Paula lying on her stomach in the morgue. She didn't seem dead in this photo. Rather, she looked like a woman faintly napping under a sun lamp. But photo depicted a large, gaping wound to the back of the head. "This must be it," Kelley said to himself.

Finally, he examined a comprehensive series of twenty-five photos of Paula's gravesite and the environment on Mt. Tamalpais. The first photo portrayed Paula immediately after she'd been exhumed by Inspector Murphy. She was lying on her side, fully dressed, in a fetal position, a pair of white loafers a few inches from her silk stocking covered feet. Kelley examined three photographs that depicted the grave after Paula's body had been removed. The grave was four-feet deep at one end and two-and-a-half feet at the other. It was three-feet wide and five-feet long. Kelley studied the yawning hole. It was a very precise rectangle, with the interior walls smooth and neatly sculpted. He thought that this was not a hole in the ground someone in a hurry or excited had dug to hide a body. Except for its depth it was very much like a grave that you'd find out at Holy Cross Cemetery – thoughtfully designed for its eternal function.

Once in Dr. Rosenberg's office they had coffee brought in. Pat went directly to sexuality, which he felt was at the heart of Paula's tragic death. He needed to include or exclude some aberrant sexual aspect of her death. "Your necropsy report indicates that you took a vaginal smear. I assume your purpose was to determine if sexual assault was involved," Pat asked.

"Actually it was a smear of vaginal exudate. This was to determine whether sexual assault was involved and also whether she'd had recent sexual intercourse. There was no evidence of sperm nor any other evidence of sexual intercourse," the Coroner answered.

"Were you able to determine if she was menstruating at the time of her death and if she was still nursing her baby?" Pat asked.

"Yes, she had been menstruating and no, she had weaned her child more than a month before her death. Her mother had informed us that she stopped breast feeding sometime in May and our examination confirmed this."

"I noticed that you observed a 'slight abnormality in her anus,' some tearing of tissue. Did your autopsy rule out anal intercourse?" Pat asked.

"Frankly Pat, we didn't rule it in or out. She's a mature, married woman who's born a child, so I didn't think these observations particularly significant."

Pat Kelley, however, did think this was significant. Bob Panforte had expressed revulsion at the notion of making love to his wife while she was having her period. Then he'd said their quarrel started when he'd remonstrated with her about love making during her bleeding cycle. Had the couple adjusted to her monthly moment with an act of anal intercourse, and was this a comment on Bob Panforte's sexual preference or a sense of shame that he'd engaged in such an act? We may never know, Pat thought.

Then he handed a photo to the Coroner and asked what was the cause of death. Dr. Rosenberg said, "Her brain showed significant changes and hemorrhaging, which caused death. These hemorrhages were due to brain concussion, resulting from repeated and powerful blows to her head. The large gaping wound in that photo is the wound that killed her."

Kelley asked if Dr. Rosenberg had examined the Mt. Tamalpais burial scene. He said that he had not, that he'd relied on the comprehensive package of photos taken by the homicide detail. He did indicate, however, that he'd examined the Panforte home and photographed all of the rooms and furnishings with particular emphasis on the couple's bedroom. Kelley handed a series of photos of the Panforte's bedroom to Dr. Rosenberg. Pat was focused on the prosecution theory that the missing jack handle was the murder weapon and certain that Loeb would question the Coroner closely on this. "As I understand it," Pat said. "The large, gaping wound in Paula's skull caused her death and that you do not believe her fatal wound could have been caused by a human fist?"

Shaking his head, Dr. Rosenberg said, "That's right, Pat. It's my view that this wound was caused by a long instrument with a narrow, but not sharp edge."

"Does that rule out the handle of an Army entrenching tool?"

"No, but Panforte's entrenching tool handle had so sign of blood, hair or fibers."

"Have you seen an instrument whose shape and dimensions are consistent with what Moore asserts is the murder weapon?"

"I have. Mike presented me with a jack handle from General Motors in Detroit. It's standard issue with all '47 Chevrolets. The shape, size, length and width of the replica Mike provided me is entirely consistent with the fatal wound to her head."

Pat slid a series of photos of the Panforte's bedroom across the physician's desk that the Coroner's staff had taken and asked, "Looking at these photos of the Panforte bedroom and recalling your personal inspection of it, could the large gaping wound to the back of Paula's head have been caused by her falling backwards onto any objects in her bedroom and, if so, which ones?" Dr. Rosenberg didn't need to study the photos to reply. "The were various furniture pieces, such as the four-poster bed and night stands could do the job, but I'm afraid that doesn't help young Panforte. He's no less culpable if he carted her dead body over to Mt. Tam than if he buried her alive!"

"How about a blackjack or a standard piece of water pipe or the barrel of a pistol?" Kelley pressed.

"All of them are consistent with the gaping, fatal wound," Dr. Rosenberg answered with his legendary scientific candor.

Pat zeroed in on the carbon monoxide concentration in Paula's system as the linchpin of the prosecution's theory that Panforte had buried his wife alive. The Coroner said, "The fact that we discovered twelve per cent saturation of carbon monoxide during the autopsy allows the inference that she was still alive when placed in the car trunk and that she inhaled gas fumes on the drive to Marin."

Pat remarked, "The carbon monoxide also explains Murphy's observation of her flushed cheeks, misleading him to believe that she was still alive when they found her,"

"Precisely!" Dr. Rosenberg agreed.

Then Pat said, "Let's get to the heart of the theory. It's that Paula died over at Mt. Tamalpais, as opposed to in her bedroom, downtown or anywhere else. Since Paula wasn't a smoker, twelve per cent carbon monoxide in her system must have come from breathing in exhaust fumes on the ride over to Marin." Dr. Rosenberg nodded in agreement, and Pat continued, "Now, we know Bob Panforte barbecued lamp chops that evening, the couple had cocktails while he grilled the chops. They were both drunk and he was a smoker. Might not the barbecue smoke and Panforte's secondary cigarette smoke be inhaled by Paula while she sipped her wine?"

"Obviously, if smoke was in the air she was breathing, she'd inhale it. And your theory would explain the modest amount of carbon monoxide we found in her."

"Ernie, how does the prosecution integrate your forensic findings into a theory that Bob Panforte was exclusively responsible for his wife's death?" Dr. Rosenberg packed his pipe with fresh tobacco, lit it and said, "As I understand it there was some kind of domestic conflict in the Panforte home. Both were intoxicated, Panforte by his own admission and Paula by virtue of her .15 blood alcohol. The prosecution theorizes that young Panforte beat her unconscious. They theorize it's what happened *after* the initial conflict in their bedroom that defines the crime. Pat, did you notice her severe chest trauma?"

Pat nodded and pulled out Paula's morgue torso shots. Dr. Rosenberg continued: "Her breasts injuries seem to evidence a rather defined pattern. If we assume Paula was undergoing a violent assault and resisting as best she could, she would have been a moving target. The bruises to her breasts would be in random places as a result of her movements, her assailant's movements and, indeed, the motion of her breasts themselves – particularly such pendulous breasts as hers. If you'll look closely at the darkest bruises on both breasts, you'll note that they form an almost perfect circle. Both of these circles of trauma begin just above her nipples. What's unusual is that these bruises are very similar in appearance and location and not the least bit random, as one would expect in an assault or fighting situation. The only difference in her breast trauma is that the wound on her left breast is somewhat deeper, suggesting that greater force was exerted against her it. This in turn suggests that her assailant was right-handed." Bob Panforte was right handed. Pat didn't know yet whether Jack Hill was right or left-handed.

The Coroner continued: "Now if you assume that multiple blows to the head and face rendered Mrs. Panforte unconscious and, if you assume further, that she was lying on her back, there's an explanation for these quite defined breast wounds. Imagine her assailant making fists as I'm now doing." Dr. Rosenberg formed his hands into fists. He had his elbows on his desk. His fists were upraised so that his little fingers were the lowest point of his fist, closest to the desk-top, with the thumbs and index fingers forming the top point. Then he slowly and with pounding force brought his fists down upon the desktop, striking it with the bottom portion of his clenched fists. He explained his demonstration, "If the assailant were pounding on Paula's breasts, while she was unconscious, like I'm doing, and striking these simultaneous blows while she was stationery, that would explain her breast trauma."

Dr. Rosenberg's demonstration of an assailant pounding on Paula's breasts was analogous to a Congo drummer pounding on two drums with his fist balled-up, rather than using his fingertips and palms. But it was a subtle change of reference that arrested Pat's facile mind. Their dialogue had been amended from the universal to the particular, from neuter to a contemplation of sex. The asexual word *chest* had been replaced by *breasts* – a woman's breasts, the love obsession of men, the sustaining nurture of a child. Pat almost shuddered at the thought of Paul and Eileen Brady's reactions to these lurid photos of their daughter and Dr. Rosenberg's demonstration of unfathomable male perversity. And he thought of his own son, whom he'd commissioned to care for his mother at the trial, and what his young eyes would see in the morgue photo shoot and the Coroner's rational recitation of what they depicted. He had been confident that bringing Terry to the trial to watch masterful advocates would prove educational and stimulating. But he hadn't thought of the Coroner's photomontage of death and the indelicate probing of his scalpel. There was no way he could prepare his son for such a graphic display of the desecration of a woman's body as he sat beside his mother, on the eve of puberty and was lectured by a learned physician on twisted maleness.

"Is it the DA's theory that this bizarre mammary attack occurred in their bedroom?" Kelley asked softly.

"Either there or over at the gravesite," Dr. Rosenberg said. Kelley urged the physician to continue. The Coroner said, "So Panforte carries her downstairs and places her in the trunk of his '47 Chevy. He drives over to Mt. Tamalpais to a spot he'd previously selected…"

Kelley interrupted, "What's the forensic evidence that Panforte pre-selected her grave?"

"None, Pat. Absolutely none."

Kelley rubbed his chin and said, "Ernie, let's just stick with the forensic evidence. It seems to have three essential elements. First, that the missing jack handle caused her fatal wound. Second, that Paula's ball-like breast wounds were caused by her husband playing like a perverse drummer on her breasts. We've covered the missing jack handle and carbon monoxide. Let's address Paula's breast wounds - her dramatic chest trauma. Ernie, assume that Paula, obviously drunk, fell. Might not the impact on her breasts from such a fall cause the ball-like bruises?"

"Certainly there would be some bruising, but I doubt that such a fall as you've described would account for the depth of the trauma we found."

"How about if she fell in a drunken stupor? Her falling body would, pardon the expression, be dead weight, wouldn't it?"

"Yes, her breast wounds are consistent with such a theory. More coffee?" Pat waved his offer off. "And add to that," Pat insisted, "that she was driven by someone in the trunk of a car over Mt. Tam chuckhole filled roads and partially dragged down a mountain slope some two hundred feet. Might that not account for her breast trauma?"

"Of course it could!"

Pat paused, then said: "One other thing, Ernie. Is her breast trauma consistent or inconsistent with more than one assailant?"

"It's entirely consistent with multiple assailants, as are her other wounds."

"Ernie, let's take a peak through the window of death," Kelley said.

"I thought you'd never suggest it," Dr. Rosenberg grinned.

In preparation for of this meeting Pat knew that Dr. Rosenberg was devoted to the theory of the window of death as a forensic pathologist's surest method to determine the nature of unexplained death. They focused their inquiry on an imaginary window, framed on one side by the last known moment someone was alive. The opposite frame of that window was when the body was discovered. This was the initial window into which they peered to determine how the person had died. If they could establish an estimated time of death the window of death was smaller, their focus more disciplined, the view of death clearer and the likelihood of determining how someone had died greater. The only truly accurate determination of the time of death was to be present when death occurred and to have an accurate clock. Beyond that, they could only make educated guesses. The most universally accepted test was a body temperature analysis. Pathologists attempted to calculate the rate at which the body cools. If they could determine the rate of cooling then they could infer an approximate time of death. So they'd take the body temperature at the time of discovery and the ambient temperature where the body was located. They'd continue taking a series of body and ambient temperatures over a period of time to find the cooling rate.

There were numerous variables factored in. If a body's discovered in a bedroom, let's say, where the room temperature was seventy degrees, that would affect the cooling rate. Or suppose the body was discovered in a garage where the temperature was thirty degrees, the cooling rate would be quicker. If a dead person had been involved in a vigorous struggle before death, the body temperature would be higher because of his exertions. The variables of what was happening to the body immediately before death and the environment at and after death dramatically effected these measurements. Dr. Rosenberg said, "Pat, what do those perceptive Irish eyes of yours see through the window?"

"Not a helluva lot, Ernie," Pat replied.

"What I see are the limitations of science in establishing the time of death," the Coroner explained, "If we could constrict the window of death by establishing the approximate time of Paula's death we might have a better idea of *how* she died, since it would reveal *where* she died. But in her case there are numerous possible places of death. There's her home, the trunk of the car, a hill in Marin and a hole in the ground. Perhaps even downtown near the Fox. It's difficult to conceive of more contrasting environments with radically different ambient temperatures. If we'd discovered her body within ten or twenty hours of burial, we might have had something to work with. Finding her days after her death makes it impossible to shrink the window of death."

"So you're saying that science cannot tell us *when* Paula died?" Pat said.

"That's exactly what I'm saying. And because we don't know when she died, medical science can't tell us *where* she died. Since we don't know when or where she died, we're unable to tell *how* she died."

Most importantly, Pat thought, medical science can't tell us *why* she died.

16

In his study after his wife and kids had gone to bed Pat Kelley wrote some notes of the first day of the Panforte trial and Maria's and Terry's reaction to it. He noted that Maria seemed worried during District Attorney Moore's argument and startled by Judge Grant's frequent interruptions. She seemed confused and unable to grasp the incisiveness of the judge's comments and their vital relationship to the capital case before her. Terry, on the other hand, leaned forward in his seat as though he didn't want to miss a single word of the colloquy between the jurist and the advocates. Pat hoped that both his wife and son realized on their maiden day in court what he had long known. His court career had taught him that what distinguishes great trial lawyers from litigators was their seemingly pedestrian ability to form simple sentences. Both Moore and Loeb understood the power of persuasion derives from an economy of words, and that the clarity of conflict is more readily perceived when presented in its starkest form. Of course neither his wife nor kid had the benefit of Pat's studies with the Coroner. What the forensic evidence established was that suspects other than Bob Panforte could not be excluded nor could the possibility of multiple attackers. At this point there was no empirical evidence that Paula did *not* go to the Fox and her breasts mutilation – purportedly portraying her husband's depravity – had an equally non-incriminatory explanation that Danny Loeb was sure to exploit.

Pat closed his spiral notebook, sipped from his glass of port and picked up the typed transcript of his translation of Father Giovanni Agnello's papers that Joe Desmond had prepared for him.

In 1850, the year before my ordination, the Word arrived in Rome. And the Word became God and the Word was Gold. Gold in quantities unheard of in man's history had been discovered in the foothills and mountains of the Sierra Nevada in Northern California. Unlettered men armed with only a shovel or pan and the eternal lust for a better life scoured the Mother Lode in search of instant wealth. They left their homes and jobs in the east and

Midwest of America and flooded into San Francisco. From distant China, packed in grimy steerage, men who were forbidden by American law to bring their wives, sailed to what they called "Golden Mountain," dreaming of their return to their families as men of affluence. From Europe waves of New Americans swelled from across the seas, their faith devout that the Promise Land awaited them.

The emigration from Northern Italy was significantly different in destination and composition from the migrations of Southern Italians. Shortly after Californians discovered gold, my father's bank financed a Genoa steamship company that established a route from Genoa to San Francisco. The steamship's advertisements implied that for the mere price of passage and a shovel a man could mine gold and return to Italy rich beyond measure. The steamship line offered to provide the shovel for the price of a ticket. Of course, these commercial exaggerations gave no hint of the danger of the journey, the barriers of language or the unlikelihood of extracting a fortune from the dirt of a foreign continent. But men have always been lured to obtain something for apparently nothing. I suspect that even if the steamship line had disclosed the peril that awaited the voyagers, like Adam they would have devoured the forbidden fruit precisely because it was proscribed.

Somehow poor peasants from rural villages in the hills and valleys of Liguria, Tuscany and Piedmont found the funds to sail to San Francisco. Unlike the emigration from Southern Italy, countrymen of accomplishment joined them. Men of commerce and education from the port city of Genoa joined these peasants in the great venture. Like those who formed the original thirteen states of America, these new colonials brought with them an ancient proficiency with land and an educated and commercially seasoned class of men. The gold they found in America proved not to be the metal of her mountains but the soil of Northern California from which these Italians created California's first and greatest industry – agriculture. Their Southern Italian brothers, possessing few skills and no commercial acumen, chose to journey to the East Coast of America. Without land, education or capital these immigrants were forced by circumstances to live in the squalid ghettos of teeming eastern cities, laboring under oppressive conditions at paltry wages or sadly descending into criminal enterprises.

Northern Italians returning to San Francisco from the Sierra without the promised treasure explored the land in Northern California. The Lucchese sailed across the bay and discovered sweeping hills that cradled the lush, sun-drenched valleys of Marin, Sonoma and Napa. They felt they were once again in Tuscany. They quickly realized that the soil of their new home was richer than that of their native land and they discerned a climate more moderate than Italy. They noted that crops would be caressed softly by summer fog and knew this land could be farmed year round. They shared their discoveries with the Genovese businessmen. On horseback the Lucchese and Genovese rode south, finding San Mateo's golden hills, plentiful rainfall and tranquil climate. It was on the lands around The Bay, not the Sierra Nevada, where Northern Italians staked their claims and drew their fortunes from the ground by giving it life.

Initially the Lucchese worked as farm laborers on farms owned by the Irish and Germans who had migrated earlier. The Genovese, with their resources, started businesses to support the farms with equipment and supplies. My interest in the evolution of California began when the Holy Father banished me to Farneta for the impudence of advocating that the descendants of the ancient Roman Republic were fully capable of ruling themselves through democratic institutions. As we traveled from Rome to Lucca in April of 1876 my father told me of the emigration to California of which I have written. Once I settled into the life of a village priest I read the letters from America that my priestly predecessor left behind. From this correspondence I perceived that the land to which these poor Tuscans had gone had an abundance unimaginable even in fertile Tuscany. And I thought that the nature of the peasant farmer, so oppressed in Italy, could liberate the land in California and plant the seeds of their own emancipation from the caste into which they had been born.

A number of events conspired to cause me to begin selecting young men from our village as prospective Americans. First, the colonization of San Francisco was unique in world history. Eight months following the cry of gold, 832 vessels – a third with foreign registry – deposited more than 39,000 searchers on her sandy shores. They came from every continent on the globe, speaking every tongue known to mankind. They were every color and hue, every religion and culture. San Francisco was therefore the first city in the world to be multi-tribal at birth. Freed from Anglo-Saxon orthodoxy, California's promise accepted no limit. Scores of Italians worked as farm laborers, harvesting hay on coastal ranches and picking potatoes on Irish farms. Alas, the Irish and their cursed potatoes again proved the engine for great social change. Just as the potato famine in Ireland had driven millions of Irish men and women from their island country to America, so a potato blight south of San Francisco freed the soil for the seasoned ministrations of the Lucchese farmers.

When the potato crop failed the Irish abandoned their farms in Colma and Half Moon Bay, south of San Francisco, just as they had deserted their starving, desperate island earlier. The Lucchese simply assumed possession of the land and began developing the diverse crops that would make California the greatest food producer the world has ever known. Modern California agriculture owes its development to the Lucchese peasants' collective approach to farming. In the Old World, the entire family worked the farm. In their New World they expanded their collectivity beyond family members. They created farming partnerships in which each peasant was a partner and all shared in the work and profits equally. Depending upon acreage or the variety of crops, these agricultural partnerships ranged from a minimum of four to as many as twenty-six partners. Occasionally the Irish would return to their lands and discover that cabbage, artichokes, spinach, lettuce, cauliflower, sprouts and radishes grew in place of their sorry potatoes. Often the Irish sold their land to the Italians. Sometimes they charged rent. More often they never returned, so the Italians acquired title to the land by simply enriching it.

Pat put the translation down and walked to the kitchen to refill his wine glass. He thought of the opening words of an anonymous Italian priest translated into English by an anonymous civil servant and was struck by the ancient relationship of the Irish and Italians of which his marriage seemed an inevitable and wonderful consequence. After all, St. Patrick was the son of a Roman diplomat in England, kidnapped by Irish raiders and made a slave. Irish monks converted by him, sailed to Lucca in the Dark Ages and brought with them the writings of the Hebrews, Greeks and Romans, planting the seeds from which the Italian Renaissance bloomed. An Irish bishop presided over medieval Lucca and earned sainthood from his adoring Italian flock. San Francisco's Irish proposed and then designed Saints Peter and Paul Church, and Italians provided the votes by which the Irish ruled the city.

Back in his study Pat read the conclusion of the first chapter of Father Agnello's story.

Just as Italian peasants traveled with their produce and poultry to sell it in Lucca, the Bay Area Italian farmers hauled the generosity of their new land on horse drawn trucks or sailed on barges across the bay to the swarming Port of San Francisco. From wagons and barges they sold their produce to housewives, innkeepers, restaurateurs and Chinese houseboys in the service of gold and railroad barons. San Franciscans, unaware the Lucchese had always farmed in this manner, called them "Truck Farmers."

So effective were these Truck Farmers that they created a massive traffic jam. This resulted in the spoiling for fresh produce because the delivery system collapsed from the burden of plenty. In 1876 the Lucchese farmers combined with the Genovese businessmen to form California's first commission produce market. The Colombo Market occupied a square block in downtown San Francisco. With its concrete floors and many stalls it diminished the traffic congestion and disciplined the food distribution chain. The clever, commission-bred Genovese sold and shipped the produce of the truck farmers, assuring them of a more dependable market and more predictable profits.

I believed that young peasants of character and imagination from our village were ideal candidates to explore the fertile soil of Northern California. I felt that the peasant family ethos, so singularly devoted to vigorous family labor, created a natural sense of collaboration in these boys. They matured in a collegial milieu rather than the hierarchical structure of more affluent families such as my own. These lads were therefore frugal by upbringing. Yet their proximity to Lucca and the sale of their farm products so close to the point of origin exposed these boys to the barter essential to commerce. By the time they were teenagers they had a well-developed sense of economic practices and commercial conspiracies which, it seemed to me, would prepare them to act decisively, if not dominantly, in the emerging California economy. All they lacked was education, and that would be my gift to the boys of Farneta.

I also perceived that the skills of the lads selected to leave the Old World for the New required that the receiving country afford them opportunity for growth. The failure of the Southern Italians on the eastern seaboard resulted not merely from the poverty of their education and aptitudes but from a paucity of available land on which to employ the few skills they brought to America. California was not only larger than all of Italy, it was composed of mostly unsettled land. The normal passing of title from generation to generation had not yet taken hold in California. The Spanish land grants were effectively voided by California's admittance to the Union. Furthermore the frantic population explosion resulting from the construction of the transcontinental railroad created a huge market for agricultural products. It was clear to me, and proved to be the case, that ownership of California land would not pass by heredity but to those who possessed it with passion and fully exploited its fecundity. The San Francisco Bay Area had the land, the Genovese the commercial experience and the young men from Lucca the farming genius to feed the grand market created by California's population explosion. I was certain that selected youth from our village would find *freedom in the bay city and determined to mold them to become Italians so their children would one day be Americans. In the Year of Our Lord, 1878 I selected Bartolomeo Bertolli, then age twelve, as the first of our village to be educated for the expedition to freedom.*

As Pat finished reading his translation he heard the distant wail of a foghorn. It sounded like a baritone moan and Pat imagined that it was the voice of Bartolemeo Bertolli. But he couldn't discern whether the foghorn's song was a manly groan of pleasure or pain. Something not expressly written by Father Agnello was insinuating itself into Pat's reflections. In the maze of his imagination the dreams and aspirations of Father Agnello for his *Precious Ones*, these sons of his celibacy, began to suggest the thematic core of the Panforte trial as a story about fathers and their children. One father stood accused of killing his own son's mother. It was this heinous charge that brought other fathers to the Hall of Justice. Pat fantasized that the stories of the first and last *Precious Ones* was admissible evidence at the Panforte murder trial. In such a mythical trial the jury would learn the different natures of two proud fathers and perhaps understand how their respective paternities compelled their children's attendance at the bar of justice.

In the earliest pages of Father Agnello's tract there was a line that kept echoing in Pat's mind. It was about land and heredity and what Father Agnello had envisioned for his students. In his own hand the old priest had written that California would belong to those who possessed it with passion and fully exploited its fecundity. And that was precisely what Bertolli had done and Fred Panforte had not. If you were to characterize Bertolli's greatest strength and most apparent flaw it would be the passion that ruled every aspect of his life's journey. If you studied Fred Panforte's life you'd discern that calculation was the engine that motored his soul. In a bizarrely ironic way, the debate about Robert Panforte's right to continue living, in the first day of his trial, had been about whether he had been ruled by passion, like his Tuscan predecessors, or calculation derived from his father's seed. Pat Kelley believed that Father Agnello's prescience was vivid when he wrote of the peasant boys he'd educated and their relation to California's soil and climate, its vastness and virginal anxiety. Bertolli and his wave of immigrants planted and harvested, nurtured and grew. They procreated with Nature and their offspring was abundance. This was another striking difference between a village priest's first and

last students, Pat thought. American citizen Fred Panforte had created nothing in California. Although he owned things of enormous
value, he'd acquired them. Whether through cunning or the missteps
of others there was nothing that he had created. He was a man who
possessed nothing and owned everything. How could Panforte's son
learn that a man's possessions are only precious when they are not
owned, Pat asked himself. Preciousness and love, Father Agnello had
taught, must be earned and therefore can never be owned.

Pat tidied up his study and washed the kitchen dishes. It had been
a long, tiring day and he was relieved that Maria would be deeply
asleep when he slipped into bed. Unlike his wife, Pat didn't hate Fred
Panforte. He pitied him. He felt that old man Panforte carried within
a deep reservoir of shame from his mother's death that was far more
insidious than a boy's guilt that Father Agnello had diagnosed. It was
as though everything in Panforte's Tuscan family life had been purged
by his journey to America. Fred Panforte's sins were becoming clearer
to Pat Kelley. Panforte had breached the ethics of his two greatest and
only teachers – Father Agnello and Bartolemeo Bertolli. He'd effectively stolen the creations of his American benefactor and dishonored
the code of the *Precious Ones*, who were dedicated to being renaissance men and raising their children to surpass themselves.

In bed, his arms around his wife as he drifted of to sleep, Pat was
still mystified by the sins of Fred Panforte that had brought so many
powerful men to the courthouse and placed their paternity, along with
Robert Panforte's life, on trial.

17

At 8:30 a.m. in the Chief Clerk's office Joe Desmond handed Pat Kelley the official transcript of the first day of the Panforte trial. "Here's the first installment of Father Agnello's manuscript," he said, giving Kelley his typed translation.

"That was fast. I didn't expect it for a week or so. Were you up all night?"

"Naw, I hit the sack around four. It was real easy. It's not like a couple of lawyers squabbling, and the old priest writes so fluidly. At least your translation comes out that way."

"It's the priest. He writes beautiful Italian," Kelley said.

"You do a pretty good job making English sing, and I'm fascinated by his story. It's like an epic novel or something. I can't wait to hear more."

"Terrific! I have more cylinders I dictated last night." Kelley's eyes brightened as he reached into a weary briefcase and pulled out four cylinders. "These two are more of Father Agnello's manuscript. The others are my translation of the letters between my father-in-law and Father Agnello. They wrote monthly from Bertolli's arrival in the City in 1882 until the priest's death. By the time he died Panforte was my father-in-law's bookkeeper," Pat said.

"How did you get hold of the letters Father Agnello got in Lucca?" Joe asked.

"When Father Agnello gave Panforte the manuscript and a letter of recommendation, he also gave him a sealed satchel with all of Bertolli's letters. He told Panforte to return Bertolli's correspondence when he met him in San Francisco."

"Jesus Pat! You gotta big chunk of San Francisco history on your hands!"

"It's more than that, lad. There's more than three hundred letters between a couple of visionaries. It's like a complete biography of Bertolli until Panforte arrived in the City in 1908."

"What do you want me to type first?"

"The manuscript should have priority because it will be shared with others. The letters were written in confidence and should remain in our family, at least for now."

"Well, I gotta meet Loeb and give him the transcript. See ya tomorrow." Desmond started to leave but Kelley stopped him. "Joe, don't mention the correspondence to Loeb."

"Of course not," Joe said, feeling a bit indignant that Kelley felt it necessary to warn him about trafficking in his family's secrets.

"Oh, I know you're discreet, but be on your guard. I suspect Loeb wants to probe more deeply about the Bertolli family presence at the trial."

"Don't worry, Pat, he won't get shit from me."

"Maybe you can get some from him."

"Whadda ya mean?"

"My guess is that Loeb has two reasons for meeting with you. First, he'll confide in you some tidbits of his defense, figuring you'll share it with the Judge. It'll be like a trial balloon. Maybe London's found something at the Fox or over in Marin. It's likely that he knows as much as we do about that fella Hill. London may be trailing you, so they know about our visit to the Presidio. When he figures you feel like his confidante he'll probe my family's connection to the case. That's when I want you to get some information from him."

"Like what?" I asked.

"Joe, when Loeb represented Fred Panforte in his legal battle with my father-in-law he seemed to know more about Bertolli's nature than even his own family. Somehow he was able to push all the right buttons. His comprehension of Bertolli's strengths and weaknesses was so complete that he anticipated every strategic move he made to keep his business. The only thing he didn't anticipate was Bertolli packing a pistol to his office. Perhaps Loeb got hold of my father-in-laws letters."

"I thought you said Panforte brought the letters from Italy in a sealed satchel."

Kelley pulled open the bottom drawer of a cabinet behind his chair. He removed a light brown satchel and dropped it onto his desk. "He did. Ya see Joe, when Panforte first learned of Bertolli from his father he began to study him. He learned much from Father Agnello, and he read the priest's manuscript. But it was the man's correspondence that revealed every flaw of Bertolli's personality, his dispositions, including his stubborn trust that those to whom he gave opportunity would never fail or betray him. Armed with the intimacies of his soul, penned in his own hand, Panforte had the key to take over his business. Only planning and time remained."

"You're saying old man Panforte rifled though his letters before he gave 'em to Bertolli?"

Kelley leaned forward, elbows on his desk, his hand locked together: "He read every damn one of them on the boat over from Italy!"

"How do you know?"

"First of all, he displayed a complete understanding of the poultry business as soon as he arrived. He rose up the ranks of Western Poultry faster than any immigrant or native before or since. He was in charge of the company books after a few years. Bertolli figured he was just a brilliant kid, like Sebastiani in the vintners' art."

"None of that proves he broke Agnello's seal of confidentiality."

"But this does," Kelley said, pointing to the old leather satchel. "Look here. See this broken wax seal over the latch? That seal was on the satchel when Panforte gave it to Bertolli in April, 1908 at Western Poultry. It's one of those seals they used in the old days. The wax is yellow. But look under the latch and you'll see a small piece of red wax – cardinal red."

Desmond examined the latch and saw a speck of cardinal red wax. "I don't know shit about wax seals. For all I know, they used feathers for pens in those days."

"Joe, the churches in Italy are the first repository of any family history. They have the birth and death records, baptisms and confirmations. At San Lorenzo, Father Agnello and his predecessors even recorded when any of their congregation emigrated to San Francisco. The Church's seal is cardinal red. I deduced the speck of red wax is the remnants of the seal Father Agnello placed on the satchel, and the yellow wax seal was placed while Panforte was at sea after he'd read the letters."

"Where would he get a seal that looks so official? I mean its even got a saint's imprimatur on it. Looks like it's the seal of *Santa Clara*."

"So it does," Kelley grinned as Desmond stepped into his Socratic trap. "That's precisely why I know Panforte broke Father Agnello's seal, read the letters and then affixed a new seal so Bertolli would think his correspondence retained its confidentiality. Agnello's seal would have been cardinal red and have the name of his church on it – San Lorenzo. Panforte sailed from Genoa on the steamship named the *Santa Clara*. It's obvious he removed Father Agnello's seal, but missed that little piece of damning red wax under the latch. After he read the letters he obviously prevailed on the ship's captain to re-seal the satchel with the seal of the vessel. Bertolli, who'd been an American businessman for more than a quarter century, would have known nothing of Old World seals. His seal was his handshake. The yellow seal had no more significance to him than a used postage stamp."

"Christ, Pat! So Panforte didn't win control of a big enterprise with his business skills, but by stealing a man's private correspondence!"

"If you know a man's thoughts at unguarded moments you can predict his actions and dictate his reactions. What I need to know is whether Loeb knows these secrets also. I want to know if Panforte copied the letters. And if he did, did he give them to Loeb?"

"But all this happened almost thirty years ago. What difference does it make if Loeb had the letters?"

"If Panforte didn't copy the letters he conveyed their content orally to Loeb and probably didn't disclose the source of his information. Having used the letters to accomplish his purposes, he'll never use them again. He's probably already erased them from his memory so he can live out the lie that his brilliance in the proxy battle won him the company. But if he copied the letters and gave them to Loeb, then Loeb knowingly used stolen documents and may pull something funny in this trial."

"Like what?" Desmond asked. Pat ran his hand through his hair. "I don't know. What I do know is that old man Panforte hasn't got a semblance of scruples. Pilfering a man's letters to his priest is like eavesdropping on the confessional box. The sonofabitch is capable of anything to get what he wants. If Loeb read my father-in-law's letters then his ethics are no better than Fred Panforte's, and I'll have to watch both of them like a hawk.

"But what I really need to know is who's running their show. It's obvious that Fred dominates his kid's life, and I have to figure out if he – not Loeb – is running the defense. I've been thinking about that Army entrenching tool they found in young Panforte's garage. It's odd when you think about the kid washing the bedspread, folding his clothes in those compartments and making everything is his house neat and tidy. Yet he leaves the entrenching tool on the floor of his garage in plain view for the cops. It makes no sense that a guy who's just allegedly buried his wife with that tool in Marin County would bring it back to his home. He'd have thrown it in the Bay along with the jack handle.

"What's intriguing is that both Fred and Bob Panforte have access to and own the '47 Chevy, the Marina garage, their hunter's cabin at Mt. Tam and that Army entrenching tool!"

Desmond, stunned said, "Jeezus Pat! You're not saying old man Panforte planted the tool in his kid's garage, are you? And what about the neighbors who saw Bob Panforte driving in and out of his garage?"

Kelley leaned back in his chair and said, "Plant it, no way. Forget it, leave it, who the hell knows? As for the Chevy driving in and out, neighbor Pierce was the only one who positively identified young Panforte on a single occasion and Panforte admits it. No one claims to have seen the car's driver on the other trips. If Loeb doesn't cross examine them to establish that they couldn't actually see the driver, what does that tell you?"

"It tells me I'm in way over my head hanging out with guys like you and Loeb," Desmond said as he left for his meeting with Danny Loeb at the Oregon Café.

When he arrived at the Oregon Café it was packed with salesmen in white smocks, teamsters and porters in Levi's. The dice cups drummed a discordant chorus on the grand oak bar while management and labor dined together, momentarily oblivious to class and position. Frank Cavaretta greeted him from behind his cash register: "Hey Desmond, you're spending enough time in my joint to be considered a boarder!"

"I just have a taste for greasy food and loose women."

"Taste, my ass! You're Irish, ya got no taste. And don't be insulting my food," Cavaretta wagged a finger at him, defending the honor of his kitchen if not the virtue of his girls. He pointed to a booth across the room and half whispered, "Panforte's lawyer's waiting for you. What would our D.A. think if he knew you were consorting with the enemy?"

"He knows I'm meeting Loeb. But what would he think if he knew what goes on upstairs?"

"Who says he doesn't?" Cavaretta grinned.

"Did Loeb order yet?"

"Yeah, but he said not to fire it up until you got here. Whadda ya want?"

"Coffee and buttermilk pancakes," Joe ordered on his way to join Danny Loeb.

"Morning, Joe," Loeb greeted, looking up from the sports page. "Morning counselor." Joe handed Loeb his transcript. He rapidly thumbed through the pages, stopping when he found Judge Grant's characterization of the apparent weakness of the prosecution's case. "Good," he muttered as he scanned his own spirited words in defense of Robert Panforte. He closed the booklet, buttered a piece of toast and asked, "Were you up all night transcribing?"

"No, I finished around midnight. Transcribing oral argument's easy. It's not like Q and A. That's tougher 'cause ya got two or more people talking and jumping from subject to subject. But you guys maintained a stream of logic, so it just sorta flows. How long will it take to draft your writ?"

"I'll file it Friday. My motion's already got all the law I need. I just need to weave in what was said yesterday." Cavaretta interrupted their conversation to personally serve breakfast in an attempt to eavesdrop. When Loeb noticed him, he immediately changed the subject. All Cavaretta overheard was Loeb's complaints about the baseball mind of Lefty O'Doul, the beleaguered manager of the San Francisco Seals. After Cavaretta returned to his grill, Loeb said, "So this is your first murder case. Was it just another day in court?"

Desmond poured maple syrup on his pancakes. "I suppose. Lawyers bitching and the judge trying to control everything like a second grade teacher presiding over a class of unruly brats. But it did have a different feel. There's a presence I felt. I dunno. Maybe it's just a first time thing. Maybe the next murder trial will be just another day in court."

"I think not. You'll feel that presence in every murder case. I know I still do."

"How many murder cases have you tried?"

"This is my twelfth," Loeb shrugged. "Probably my last. As you get up in years it's harder to get it up in the bedroom and the courtroom. I almost didn't take this one on, but old man Panforte's money is very persuasive."

"Have you lost any murder cases?"

"Just one, but I've never lost a capital case. Knock wood," Loeb rapped on the tabletop. "I don't know if I can get the fruits of London's investigation before the jury. Judge Grant was right on the mark when she suspected there might be a bitter convict from Brady's courts-martial prosecutions. He sent a guy to Leavenworth. We don't know for what yet, but it had something to do with that training program over at Mt. Tam that my client volunteered for. Right now it's too tenuous and it's real sticky given her relationship with Brady."

So Pat Kelley's suspicion that Loeb was onto the stalker angle was right, Desmond thought. Kelley had figured that Loeb might have London tail Joe when he joined Kelley on his investigation. Apparently Loeb's private dick had followed them to the Presidio.

Cavaretta returned to their booth and asked if they were satisfied. "Another coffee, Loeb ordered. "And put a splash of brandy in it. I need an eye opener."

"Just coffee for me. You don't trust Moore, do you?" Joe said.

"A criminal defense attorney doesn't trust anybody, not even his own client. The client's just as likely to put a banana peel under your heel as the cops."

"What about the kid's father? Do you trust him?" Desmond decided to steer the conversation away from the trial and attempt to explore Loeb's relationship with Fred Panforte. Loeb smiled wryly and said, "Fred Panforte's not on trial. So what's to trust?"

"He's paying your tab, and I figure the guy who pays the bills calls the shots."

"He's paying your tab also, Joe. By the way, what do we owe you for the transcript?"

"I haven't calculated it yet," Joe lied. "I'll get a bill together and send it to your office." Loeb sniffed his Coffee Royal and asked, "Do you know much about Fred Panforte?"

"Some, maybe a little more than most. There's the American success story of an Italian teenager who comes here and becomes a captain of commerce. I've heard some courthouse gossip. I know you represented him years ago in some kinda stock dispute involving the poultry business. That's about it." Of course Loeb realized the gossip to which Desmond alluded was information gleaned from the Chief Clerk and it was therefore both reliable and considerably more detailed than Joe had implied. Joe wasn't about to tell him that he knew Bertolli had threatened to shoot him if he didn't settle the case with Panforte.

"Well, since you know I was Fred's lawyer you know I can't discuss attorney/client confidences," Loeb smiled.

"Who asked anything about your lawyer secrets? I only asked if you trusted the guy."

"I said a criminal defense attorney can't afford to trust anyone. Fred's case was a civil matter. There's a world of difference between civil and criminal law."

"I figure a civil lawyer is a contradiction in terms, and criminal lawyer is redundant."

Loeb chuckled, "Such cynicism is rare in a young man."

"I guess I picked it up in the war along with some other dubious habits."

Loeb's green eyes darkened at the mention of Desmond's military service. "Right, I read about you. You were a paratrooper, right?" Joe nodded. Loeb was quiet for a moment as he struggled to find the words of appreciation he felt for the soldiers who crushed the Nazis, although not before they'd annihilated European Jewry. Joe was always uncomfortable when others acknowledged his combat record. Loeb cleared the bubble in his throat and called out, "Frank, bring me another Coffee Royal." Desmond declined more coffee in an effort to temper the mounting stimulation of the breakfast conversation.

"You haven't told me whether you trust Fred Panforte," Joe recast his bait.

"You're certainly persistent." Loeb reached into his coat pocket, pulled out a pack of Chesterfields, lit one and puffed. "Yeah, I trust him. We go back a lot of years. We went through a lot together, so I feel I owe his kid the best defense I can give him." He dragged on his cigarette. "I guess it's a trust based on our common experience. I'm a bit older than Panforte, so when he came to me with his problems at Western Poultry we were both in our early thirties. We were at that point in our careers where we'd either take off or just languish in middle class mediocrity. Handling his case was a great challenge and a great opportunity for me.

"In those days, I represented a lot of Jewish retailers in slip and fall cases. The only gentiles who retained me were criminals whose threatened loss of freedom overcame their anti-Semitism. I'd just defended Ed Montgomery, the biggest bookie in town, and won his federal tax fraud case. I got a lot of press. A *Chronicle* reporter wrote that I was a wizard with numbers and documentary evidence.

"Panforte read about the case and he was brilliant mathematically. He figured his fight with old man Bertolli would be waged on a mountain of papers, so he called me up." As Loeb recounted his fateful meeting with Fred Panforte, Joe realized that he'd never thought this famous trial lawyer had once scrambled for clients and causes just like all the others with a ticket and some talent. He tried to imagine what he was like as a young lawyer. The specks of gray hair wouldn't have been there, and he doubted judges and opposing counsel held the little man in the awe they presently exhibited. He wondered if in his youth he spoke even more rapidly. Joe suspected he'd have been the same dapper dresser, and that tough arrogance was his natural demeanor - except for that moment of humility when he confronted the barrel of Bertolli's pistol.

He crushed his cigarette in the ashtray and continued, "You gotta understand, in those days the successful Italians only hired Irish attorneys. Occasionally they gave the WASPS on Montgomery Street some estate work. Western Poultry was a huge business, and I was thrilled that an Italian businessman, claiming stock control of the company, would pick a Jew for his lawyer. If I won Panforte's case I figured it would break the invisible cultural barrier that restricted my practice to marginal Jewish merchants and grandiose gentile crooks. Some say Panforte's case against Bertolli made my career."

"Sounds like an exaggerated sense of gratitude more than trust to me."

"Sure there's some gratitude, but I won for the guy and that pays off the account. I think trust arose from a mutual sense of isolation, of social exclusion that Panforte and I shared. I was limited to my Jewish circle and he felt distant from his own Italian community. Bertolli was a big man. And all The Market sided with him. Even Giannini and the bankers shunned Panforte."

"That shouldn't surprise anyone. Bertolli and A.P. Giannini were pals before he started his bank. Bertolli was one of the original investors in the Bank of Italy and its first commercial account. Didn't you know the two of them revolutionized the food distribution system in California?"

Loeb shrugged and Joe told him what he'd learned from Pat Kelley: "Before the turn of the century Bertolli took a trolley from the Embarcadero all the way out to Colma and back. He was fascinated by the possibilities of electricity. He sought out the Jesuit physicist Father Neri, who'd devised an electrical lighting system a decade before Edison invented the incandescent lamp. Then Bertolli designed the first electrical refrigeration system for his poultry business. Giannini financed it. Where the hell do you think frozen food comes from? Together those guys created modern banking and agriculture in this state. You didn't expect Giannini to be as disloyal as Panforte, did you?"

Of course Loeb knew that Fred Panforte had taken over all of Western Poultry Company's patents in the settlement of his first big lawsuit, but until this moment he didn't know that Bartolomeo Bertolli was the sole inventor of them. And Fred Panforte had never confided to him that Bertolli's refrigeration experiments around the turn of the century led him to package the first frozen foods in California. Since Bertolli had placed his most valued creations in the company name it meant that all of the assets that Loeb had negotiated over to the control of Fred Panforte were de facto personal and not corporate. No wonder Bertolli was so enraged that he packed a pistol to the diminutive lawyer's office, Loeb thought uncomfortably. He tried to banish the most terrifying moment in his life and said: "I'm not saying that. I'm just trying to tell you how isolated Panforte was back then. But he was a tough bastard. He had to be. He was damn near an orphan when he came here from Italy. His mother died at birth, and, from what he told me his father was a poor dumb peasant. His only education was in the streets of Lucca. He studied the merchants and realized how limited his own father was. He felt ashamed of his father because the other peasants and merchants always took advantage of him. He didn't want to end up like his old man, so he did what millions have done. He came to America.

"It took a lotta guts to take on Bertolli and all North Beach. And he had this unerring sense of how Bertolli would attack or counterattack. Of course he'd worked for him for years, so he had plenty of opportunity to study the man, to know his petty blindness. But he was absolutely uncanny in his ability to predict how Bertolli would respond to every parry and thrust of the litigation."

Loeb drained his Coffee Royal and shook his head as he recalled Panforte's clairvoyance in matters of the heart and mind of Bartolomeo Bertolli. It was now obvious to Joe Desmond that Danny Loeb had never seen Bertolli's letters to Father Agnello. For if he had, he'd know that Fred Panforte had been a *Precious One*, educated by a classicist in Farneta and nurtured to maturity and position by Bertolli from his first moments in San Francisco. It was obvious that Loeb had accepted Fred Panforte's fraudulent autobiography that erased the two most important men in his life from its pages. Still, Joe didn't know how Panforte had used the letters. "Sounds like Panforte was a pretty active client," Desmond said.

"I don't usually tolerate active clients. It's their own foolishness that requires a lawyer in the first place. I need to control every aspect of the case. It's the only way I know how to do it. With Panforte it was different. We'd meet every Friday for dinner. We stayed clear of North Beach joints, only ate at French restaurants. I love French cuisine and do a little recreational French cooking myself. By sticking to French restaurants we avoided eavesdroppers and the gossip of the Italian community. Panforte had this thing about Fridays. He said everything he learned about life he learned going to town with his father to sell their chickens. What the hell, we all make up our own folklore to rationalize what we've become.

"Anyway, it was during these wonderful meals that he'd tell me about Bertolli, about how he thought or had responded to some past crisis, how he did business and who his confidantes were."

"How do ya know it wasn't the French wine talking? Did he back up his stories with documents or anything?" Joe probed for Bertolli's letters.

"He provided me no physical evidence. Given some of what he told me – little of which I remember and none of which I'll share with you – documentary evidence was the last thing I wanted to see. 'Cause then I'd have to ask how he got the material and I sure as hell didn't want to know that. We kept it strictly verbal. As far as the truth was concerned everything he told me checked out. Only one time, right before we settled, did he fail to predict Bertolli's actions." Loeb twitched slightly as he ambiguously alluded to Bertolli's pistol packing visit to his Flood Building law office.

Joe would report to Pat Kelley that Panforte had not copied Bertolli's letters, and Loeb never knew of their existence. Both men had banished another man's secrets from their memories – Loeb because they were no longer any use to him, Panforte because his exploitation of them had satisfied his ambition. But the enormity of Fred Panforte's betrayal struck Joe Desmond like a sucker punch in his stomach. In the confidential secrecy of his attorney's office Fred Panforte had portrayed himself as a motherless orphan shamed by his ignorant peasant father. This was the father who had literally discarded his two older sons to make Fabrizio the sole beneficiary of his paternity. This was the father who took his boy to Lucca so that he might learn the ways of the city and dream beyond their small shack in Farneta. This was the father who had told Fabrizio about the Lucchese in San Francisco and how their village priest had educated them for liberation from poverty. What perversity of a young man's soul could tarnish such a father with shame, Desmond wondered. He accepted that Fred Panforte had lied to his lawyer by deleting Father Agnello's and Bertolli's influence on his life because he wanted to present himself as the underdog in his battle for Bertolli's business. But he had been truthful, and painfully so, when he'd told Loeb that he was ashamed of his father. So Fabrizio wedded shame to ambition to destroy his American father.

Cavaretta suddenly reappeared at their booth, a pot of fresh coffee in hand, a white towel draped over his beefy shoulder. "More coffee?" he asked.

"Not for me," Loeb said. Joe shook his head. "Some dessert? A cannoli maybe?" Cavaretta suggested. Looking up at their grinning host, Loeb said, "Frank, let me ask you something. Suppose you took me on a tour of your kitchen, introduced me to your chef and I repaid your hospitality by stealing your recipe for minestrone and opened a joint next store. You'd be pissed, right? Don't ya think it's obvious that you're trying to pick up on our conversation so you can pop off from behind your bar on the Panforte trial? Why don't you take of couple of your cannolies and stick 'em in your ears!"

"Fuck you, counselor! I'm no goddamned gossip! I don't give a rat's ass about Panforte or his kid," Cavaretta huffed back to his grill.

"You better have a taster the next time your order minestrone here," Joe said.

"Frank'll be all right. Ya just have to tell the nosy bastard to bug off once in a while."

"So haute cuisine, Panforte's ability to predict Bertolli's actions and your photographic memory brought Bertolli down?" Joe said.

"I prefer to think we brought Panforte up. Anyway, when we settled, Bertolli was still a substantial man with considerable real property holdings."

"But he never went back to The Market again."

Loeb shrugged. "Maybe he didn't have to work anymore. Anyway, no one stopped him from opening a new shop."

What about his pride? What about the humiliation of having the business he'd created stolen from him by the very one he entrusted its preservation? What about stabbing him in the heart with the dagger of his own generosity? What about taking title to his inventive genius? What about shadowing his renaissance soul in the dogma of deceit? Joe thought, but didn't say.

Loeb waved for the check, placed a ten spot on the plate and dispatched the waiter, telling him to keep the change. "Speaking of old man Bertolli," Loeb said. "I'd like to talk to you about his daughter. Now I know you're very close to the Kelleys. My guess is Pat got you the job, and I know you and his son go out to the movies and dinners regularly."

"You got David London tailing me or something?" Joe interrupted. "That fuckin voyeur you've got for a private investigator probably has a list of who I sleep with so he can whack off with it!"

Loeb, at his soothing best said, "Joe, the courthouse is like a tiny village, everybody knows everybody else's business. No one needs a private eye to discover your considerable appetite for female companionship. If London had a list he probably would jerk of with it. Some of the judges might also. I know how close your are to the Kelleys and I'd never ask you to compromise that relationship. Just let me share my concerns and ask you a few things. If you don't want to answer, it's okay. Just hear me out."

"So go ahead and ask," Joe said blandly, trying to conceal the butterflies whirling around in his gut. Loeb leaned across the table and in his best rabbinical manner said, "Joe, I don't have to tell you what's at stake in this trial. I want ya to think about what our courtroom will be like. We're gonna live together for three weeks, maybe more. All of us, the judge, Kelley and his wife and kid, you, me, Moore, the cops, the Panfortes, the Bradys and those asshole reporters. And there's that presence you felt yesterday. It's in every murder case, only it intensifies every day of the trial. It seems like the walls start to press in on you and you feel like you're in a boiling cauldron of human emotions. Sometimes you can't tell whether it's your emotions burning or someone else's. It's the closeness that gets you. God never designed us to feel such brutal human intimacy – so raw, so close." Danny Loeb's eyes were on fire. He paused and leaned back in his chair. Joe leaned forward in his, his peripheral vision was lost and all he saw was Loeb's burning green eyes. In a stage whisper he said, " I love it! I goddamn love it! Every friggin' minute of it. So does Moore. I don't know what it is about guys like us. We seem to find ourselves in the maelstrom of a murder trial. Freud could have made a bundle off people like us."

Suddenly Loeb terminated his analysis of his adversary and himself. It was as though he realized he'd crossed some invisible line, an advocate's psychic border that cloisters how these men truly feel in the Pit, in conflict, in danger. Or maybe it was just a clever lawyer's ruse, a cross-examiner's set up to make Joe feel he'd shared a part of his soul so that Desmond might expose his own to him.

"Joe, let's assume the appeal boys deny my writ. So we've got a jury trial – three weeks, three families."

"Three families?" Joe interjected to break the spell the little lawyer was casting on him. "You've got the Panfortes and the Bradys. Unless you or Moore bring your mothers, who's the third family in our boiling cauldron?"

He lit another cigarette and through a haze of smoke said, "You've got Fred Panforte, a powerful man, with his kid on trial for his life. Brady, another powerful man, lost his daughter. And there's Pat Kelley, also a powerful man. No, Joe! Don't shake your head. Kelley's no common clerk. He's as fine a mind as I've met in court and a powerful force in the Hall. Fred Panforte's the linchpin who ties all three families, Brady's because of his son-in-law, Kelley's because of his father-in-law."

"I don't see Brady as a problem. Hell, his comments to the press at his daughter's grave look like the best part of your defense."

Loeb frowned, "What happens outside the courtroom isn't what necessarily happens inside. What's said today may not be what's felt tomorrow. Joe, let me tell how I think this case will play out. This is in the strictest confidence, any problem with that?"

"No problem. As for as I'm concerned all we talked about was Lefty O'Doul mismanaging the Seals."

"Good! I'm gonna have to put Bob Panforte on the stand. Sometimes you put the defendant on the stand so the jury gets to see him. You just want to humanize him for the jury so they don't think he has horns. But in this case Bob Panforte, more than me, will have to win it. What he says, how he says it, whether he can withstand Moore's cross-examination may determine whether he lives or dies."

"I told you I require complete control of my cases. I have to be the producer, director, playwright and star. But there's one frightful moment when I have no control, no influence at all. That's when my guy takes the stand. All I can do is sit and disguise my panic from the jury."

"I've never thought of it quite that way," Joe confessed. "But surely you can prepare him well. After all, he's a college boy, handsome, well-spoken. If you have enough women on the jury they'll take one look at his beautiful blue eyes and probably want to bed him."

"You're right. He's presentable and educable. The question's whether he's strong enough, hard enough inside. If it were his father on trial we'd be okay. Sometimes there's a loss or a diminution of talent in the American born generation. That's what I've got here with Fred and Bob. Whatever you think of Fred Panforte, the man's fought for everything he's gotten out of life. His son's just the opposite. He has a doting mother, the best schools, travel, an adoring public when he was a football hero and a partnership in a thriving business built by other men. When he puts his hand on the Bible he'll be alone in the courtroom and, for a rare time in his life, he'll have to do something by himself. And that scares the hell out of me!"

Joe would report to Pat Kelley that Loeb would use Bob Panforte's father to control his kid. Kelley would have to figure out if old man Panforte already controlled Loeb. Joe casually remarked, "I guess it goes with your job. At least the pay's good. What's all this got to do with Kelley's wife?"

"It's not so much Kelley's wife as it is her father. I accept Maria Kelley will attend the trial to keep their kid in line. Frankly I was touched that Kelley thinks his boy might learn something from Moore and me. But what I've got to do to get Panforte through his testimony is surround him with a comfortable environment. I have to construct a milieu in which he feels unthreatened and protected. I can only do this through his father.

"Joe, look closely at this case and you'll realize Bob talked himself into this murder beef. If his father had been with him on those days when the homicide boys questioned him he'd never have taken them over to their hunting cabin. Fred would have realized that the cops considered his kid a suspect, and he'd have shut him up and gotten my old ass over there in a minute! They'd have never found the poor girl if Bob hadn't stupidly taken them on a guided tour of Mt. Tam.

"I don't think I'm outta line telling you Fred Panforte's the most dominant force in his son's life. Even though Bob's a grown man he's still awed by his father. Everything he's accomplished in his young life he's done to please his father. It was his father who urged him to play football because he thought it would teach him the toughness old man Panforte thinks life requires. I doubt Bob ever played a game where he wasn't proving his grit to his dad. He's always known he's not as smart or shrewd as his dad, so he earned a Stanford degree and gave it to his father to hang on Fred Panforte's office wall. It's a proclamation the Panfortes are no longer shoeless, ignorant peasants."

"The only flaw Bob ever saw in his father was Fred's exclusion from the social circle to which Fred believed he should be invited because of his wealth. Bob felt that his father was excluded from the society scene because of his thick Italian accent. When he married Paula Brady the barriers to The Establishment collapsed. He felt his marriage was his gift to his father. Now he's accused of killing the very woman who gave the Panfortes entree into the City's elite. He feels an overpowering sense of guilt that what happened to his wife will get his father expelled from membership in the ruling gentility. And if Bob Panforte displays a son's guilt on the witness stand, he's a dead man!"

Joe remarked, "You sound more like a shrink than a criminal lawyer. You're talking about putting your guy on the stand, not a couch."

"True. But unless I anticipate Bob's emotions, I'll not be able to control them. That's where his father comes into the picture. Fred will be at his son's side every minute of the trial. His role is to constantly remind his boy that he approves of him, they're in this together and that he's not afraid. Yesterday I had Fred with me when we went over the Coroner's autopsy photos in Bob's jail cell. I always show my homicide clients the morgue shots well before trial so they won't react inappropriately in front of the jury. I make 'em look at the photos enough so they get inured to such shocking pictures. If Bob's dad wasn't in that jail cell looking at that poor girl's dead body, Bob would have puked his guts! See, if Bob feels his dad is fearless, he'll perform for him, he'll imitate his defiance. If every word he utters on the stand, if every gesture of his body plays to his father's vision of a man, he'll survive his moment in the dock and I'll have a chance to win for him.

"That's where Bertolli is crucial. Joe, Fred Panforte is like a courage transfusion for my client. If Bob senses his father fears anything or anyone his whole ideal of him will be shattered. It's obvious, from what I've told you about the Bertolli/Panforte dispute, that Fred was obsessed with Bertolli. No man could know another man so well without a lifetime studying him." Or stealing and reading his private correspondence, Joe thought to himself.

"Not once during the year long-struggle with Bertolli would Fred meet with him to try to work out their differences. The most compelling reason for me to settle the case out of court was Panforte would have to confront Bertolli at trial. I knew he feared Bertolli. Not anything Bertolli or his lawyers could do to him. Just fear, blatant terror in Bertolli's presence. I don't know why he felt this way. There must have been something in their past. I knew that Fred, for all his cunning, for all his Italian bravado, could never face-off Bartolomeo Bertolli in a courtroom!" Joe silently accepted Loeb's reason for settling the Bertolli case even though he knew it had been Bertolli's murder threat that resolved the dispute. Loeb said: "If Bertolli shows up in our courtroom while Panforte's kid is on trial for his life Fred will be unable to conceal the terror he's so long hidden. When that happens his son, who knows nothing of his father's ancient enmities, will see for the first time a fearful father's face. And his heart will turn to jelly, for he'll have lost the anchor to his own courage."

Loeb sighed heavily before asking Joe the question for which he'd designed their meeting. "I need to know, and I think you can tell me: will Bartolomeo Bertolli join his daughter and grandson at the trial?" Joe shrugged his shoulders in feigned indifference and determined to add to the defense lawyer's discomfort. He said, "Why don't you two go to a nice French restaurant Friday, drink some good Bordeaux and you can ask old man Panforte himself?" Loeb groaned, "Come on Joe, that shit was years ago. Panforte's long since purged it from his mind."

"What was more difficult for him, counselor? Purging Bertolli from his mind or purging him from the industry he'd created? And did he need your dexterous lawyer reasoning to erase Bertolli from his memory with the same ease he erased the man's name from Western Poultry?"

"For Crissake, Joe! I'm just the guy's lawyer, not his priest. I spill my guts and you shit all over me. If you don't know if Bertolli will show up, just say so. If you don't wanna tell me, that's fine. But don't try to make me feel guilty for doing my job."

"I didn't mean any criticism of you, Danny," Joe repented with little sincerity. "It's just that as I listened to you talk about Fred and Bob Panforte it seems these guys hurt the very people they're closest to. Fred Panforte turns on the guy who gave him a job in America, and his son's accused of killing his wife. But I *can* tell you whether Bertolli will attend the trial."

"And?"

"I'll tell you, but I want you to hear the reasons. And you may not like what you hear."

"Fair enough. Will he come to court?"

"No. Not a chance." The pained expression on Loeb's face evaporated, but Joe was determined to restore it. "Bartolomeo Bertolli will never attend the trial of Panforte's son. Unlike his daughter he doesn't transfer his anger to Panforte's kid. I don't know if he's really angry with Panforte anymore. It's more like sadness. I sometimes think he's the saddest man I've ever met. But there's another reason you won't have to worry about Panforte's old nemesis. Bertolli will never walk into an American courtroom as long as he lives!

"You see, Danny, Bertolli's come to believe the law, as much as

Panforte, stole his business from him. He's a wise old man. He was a true California pioneer. He can even reconcile that Panforte's avarice drove him to disloyalty and deceit, for he's long known that flawed men do bad things to good people. But he's never understood how the law tolerated the awful things Panforte did to him. He feels the law and lawyers were accomplices in Panforte's theft of his life's work."

Loeb's eyes were riveted on Joe as he spoke of a man who had been the only opposing party in his lawyer's life to threaten him with a gun. Joe detected a softening in his stare. He felt that he was Pat Kelley's surrogate, and prayed that Kelley's easy eloquence would fashion his words about Pat's father-in-law. "I think Bertolli's a man from another era and Panforte's a man of our time. Bertolli was a 19th century man in a 20th century world. His business was a world of tough bargaining and honored promises. He knew nothing of lawyer-drafted contracts or that fancy stock certificates could give you ownership of land you failed to enrich. His handshake was his contract, the fertility of the land his equity.

"Counselor, we're talking about a man who made a handshake deal when he sold his small Sonoma winery after the turn of the century, to his raw, young cousin from the same village he and Panforte came from. The moment Bertolli and Sebastiani clasped hands, the wine industry in California was born. They didn't need title searches and layers of lawyers to create in a matter of years what took Europe centuries to refine.

"Bertolli finds the law incomprehensible. He can't fathom why one man must pay another to speak for him. Nor can he understand how a man's signature on a piece of paper adds any honor to his word. To Bertolli a courtroom is a foreign place and those who populate it, aliens from some unworldly planet where basic morality is unknown and where people say things they do not mean and mean things they dare not say.

"So you needn't trouble yourself about Bertolli. Panforte's secret foreboding will remain hidden, and your client will have all the courage transfusions he needs to sit in a chair and tell the world what he did or didn't do to his wife. And Bertolli? Well, while you and Moore savage each other, he'll be playing bocci ball at Aquatic Park or sitting in the sun on a park bench in Washington Square reminiscing with old friends on the times they understood. Or maybe he'll take one of his frequent walks in North Beach and smell the scent fresh bread floating out from Tuscan bakeries and remember that day, so very long ago, when he bought of loaf of fresh bread for a teenager just off the boat from the Old Country.

"Do you know that story, Mr. Loeb? Did Fred Panforte tell you of his first day in our city? Do you know the significance of your first important client's name? Let me tell ya. Panforte is the name of bread made in Siena, the city of Fred Panforte's father's birth. The day Panforte first put his lowly peasant feet on the dock of San Francisco, Bertolli gave him a job at Western Poultry. Then he took him for a walk through North Beach. He told one of the Tuscan bakers to bake of loaf of bread, bread like they made in Siena, called *panforte*. He gave it to your first important client as a symbol. He told Fabrizio Panforte – that was his name, not this Fred shit he invented later – he said: 'It's only flour, eggs and seasonings, but it bears your name. Your name now lives in two countries. Never forget the one you came from, and never disrespect the one that welcomed you.'"

Loeb cleared his throat and softly said, "Joe, I appreciate what you've told me. I, uh, I...I know you don't care much for Panforte, and I understand. You may not think much of me. But I want you to know, for whatever it's worth, I don't believe Bob Panforte murdered his wife."

Desmond pushed up from his chair to signal their morning meeting was over. He picked up his stenograph case with the cylinders of Father Agnello's manuscript and Bertolli's letters, stolen by Loeb's first big time client. He reminded Loeb, "I didn't know lawyers had beliefs. As for me, I don't believe anything. I just take down the words."

"Bullshit, Desmond! You wouldn't have even met with me if you're just a recorder of other men's thoughts, with none of your own."

They walked past Frank Cavaretta and waved goodbye to their officious host. He flipped them the finger. Outside the Oregon Café, Joe hailed a cab. "Wanna lift?" he invited.

"No thanks. I gotta go to Great Western Poultry and then up to jail to see my client." Joe started to enter the cab and Loeb grabbed his arm. "Joe, Pat Kelley's got one helluva friend."

"See you in court, counselor." Joe closed the cab door, gave the driver his address and told him, "Step on it, man. I'm late for an important appointment."

An appointment with Father Agnello's manuscript and Bartolomeo Bertolli's letters to his priest.

18

Maria Bertolli, born two weeks before The Great Earthquake and Fire, was the youngest of Bertolli's children. Eight years separated her from her closest sibling, her sister Clara, and the differences in Maria's upbringing were more than simply age disparity. From the moment her father brought her home from the French Hospital she was the center of his life. Raising Clara and Michael, Bertolli's first born, had been largely the responsibility of their mother, Renee. With the arrival of Maria the founder and driving force of Western Poultry assumed a dominating role in her parenting. Perhaps Bertolli, who had scaled to the peak of his remarkable business career, felt secure enough to adoringly raise his youngest child. Or it may have been that he felt that his paternal province with his older children had been stolen by the exigencies of building an enterprise with only his burning ambition and inventive mind. Whatever impelled his lavish affections it was obvious, from his faithful attendance at her night feedings to the June day when he escorted her up the aisle of the Italian Church to marry Pat Kelley, Maria was Bertolli's *Precious One*.

Bertolli broke the traditional mold of Italian/American fathers. His experience in America and his vision of his adopted country had taught him the only limits on human growth were a lack of learning and a hesitant will. He passionately wanted to give Maria what his teacher had given him. He refused to allow the restrictions of sex to circumscribe their relationship. He drew her into his world, a world of life-long learning, fierce but fair competition, social responsibility and show business.

As early as she could remember, Maria was his date at the theater. She loved seeing her tall, balding father formally attired, his powerful shoulders draped in his black tuxedo and, what he called his "Roman nose," made more distinguished by his black tie. He lavished her with a fancy new dress for each performance. This was the only aspect of her nights at the theater that she didn't like. She was a quintessential San Francisco tomboy, more comfortable playing basketball with boys at the playground than decked out in the female frills of the day. But an evening in North Beach, or at the Civic Auditorium, or the Tivoli Theater with her father and the swelling music of Rossini, Puccini, Verdi, Donizetti, Bellini, Mozart, and even the somber darkness of Wagner, was worth the sacrifice of getting dressed up. It was from these glittering nights at the theater that Maria's life-long passion for music was born – a passion she inculcated in her own children. With her father she discovered the power of mature love to liberate the spirit and she learned from a remarkable woman that such love is at once mighty and fragile.

Bertolli was among a crowd of buzzing San Franciscans at the Apollo Theater on a Saturday evening a year and two months before The Great Earthquake and Fire. The hall had been renamed for the evening "Teatro Apollo," in honor of the internationally acclaimed Neapolitan singer and actress, Antonietta Pompa. Signora Pompa presented the elated audience a program of songs and dramatic sketches in the format of an Italian variety show. She displayed a full range of dramatic skills in her portrayal of the character Santuzza from the opera Cavalleria Rusticana, which she contrasted in a one-act farce called, Presami Tua Moglie Per Dieci Minuit, which Kelley translated: "Lend Me Your Wife For Ten Minutes." When she took her curtain calls the audience leapt to their feet and the hall reverberated with shattering shouts of "Brava! Brava!" as flowers rained down upon the stage.

The San Francisco press raved about Signora Pompa's stunning performance for days. Bertolli hosted a reception for the soprano in his Russian Hill home on Larkin Street. Toward the end of the party Bertolli's wife Renee conversed vacuously with a handful of stragglers, none of whom had sense enough to realize Bertolli had arranged the reception so that he might spend some private moments with the actress. Sensing Renee's banter was engaging the remaining guests Bertolli asked Antonietta, "Would you like a glass of grappa, Signora? I make it myself at our ranch in Sonoma."

"That would be delightful, Signore. Grazie."

"Prego. May I show you our garden? I've planted a garden on the roof, as is a custom in Lucca, where I'm from. It will also afford you an impressive view of the city whose heart you captured tonight."

"Ah, another Lucchesi! Since I arrived, I've met so many Lucchese I doubt there are any left in Lucca." They smiled and Bertolli led her up a narrow wooden stairway to the roof. When he'd first read Signora Pompa would be performing in San Francisco he researched her performing life. He inquired

of theater managers, producers and newspaper reporters to learn as much about her as possible. He sent for old news stories and magazine articles from New York, Chicago and Philadelphia that recorded her theatrical triumphs. He learned that she'd come to America as a gifted child and that she was much more than a singing actress. She was a talented theatrical producer who had organized and operated four theaters in New York City. Her career demonstrated her competence both in front or behind the footlights. He also knew that in a cruelly short span of time she'd been devastated by the loss of her mother and husband. He hoped a change in environment and career emphasis might be a welcome respite from the sad burdens she'd been prematurely required to bear. The locale he had in mind was San Francisco, and the career change was to take his conception of the musical theater and bring it to life in his adopted city.

Bertolli pushed open the roof door, turned on the exterior gaslights and the night burst into color. "Oh, how lovely!" Antonietta gasped, as her eyes surveyed a four-quadrant rose garden, three stories above the earth. "I never imagined roses in so many colors!" she gushed.

"We can grow anything in the Bay Area," Bertolli said as they walked along a center pathway of travertine marble to a water pond in the center of the garden. "Did you know we've created a park, three miles long on sterile, ocean sand dunes? It's quite remarkable! Thousands of flowers and soaring pines, cypress, eucalyptus, even redwood trees! Have you been to Golden Gate Park, Signora?"

She shook her head, her luxuriant, cascading brown hair waving at him. "I'd be honored to show it to you. I think you'll see we're a bit more civilized than eastern writers suggest."

"That would be wonderful! This is so unlike New York. We hang out our wash on roofs."

Bertolli led her to the northeast corner of the roof. They placed their glasses on the chest-high ledge of the roof and looked out over the lamp-lit city. A cable car bell sang out as it was pulled up Hyde Street from the Ghiradelli Chocolate Factory. The cable car stopped atop Russian Hill, and for a moment the only sound was the murmur of the underground cables. Antonietta surveyed the breathtaking view from the Golden Gate to Alcatraz Island and then to Fisherman's Wharf and over North Beach to the wooden houses crawling up Telegraph Hill. The cable car bell rang in the night and her hazel eyes followed the bantam car as it slid down Hyde Street, gathering speed for its strenuous climb up Nob Hill to the baronial mansions of Stanford, Hopkins and Crocker. "I like to come up here at night and listen to the moaning cables and whispering of the sea," Bertolli broke their silence.

"And think?"

"I'm not certain my meditations rise to the dignity of thought. More like dreams, I suppose. When you see so much of what the City is from here, it makes you imagine what she might become."

"In my profession dreaming is the highest level of thinking."

"In your profession you give life to dreams every time you step on a stage. I'm just a businessman. That's such an American word – businessman. I'm a peddler. I peddle chickens and eggs, but in America I'm a businessman."

Antonietta studied Bertolli's profile as he gazed out on Telegraph Hill. It's a handsome face, she thought. His black hair was beginning to thin and slowly recede from his broad, strong forehead. The high cheekbones of his clean-shaven face seemed in perfect symmetry with his prominent nose, as though his face was always aimed in a forward-looking direction. His large, gray eyes implied a constant peering into a future unseen by others. The black jacket of his tuxedo failed to hide his muscular upper body that culminated in a decisive set of broad shoulders. The only incongruity she noticed in her host's towering, dignified appearance was his hands. It was not their large size or the long, thick fingers, perfectly proportioned to his powerful body that struck her. It was his calluses. The movement of his hands to accent his speech was graceful and subtle, like a maestro luring a song for her singer's soul. But the roughness of his sun-stained hands testified they'd labored long and hard and were still an essential part of his life's work.

She turned from her host and joined him viewing the winking gas-lit city. She smiled, *"Five ranches, a market building that covers half a city block, and this mansion overlooking your charming city hardly sounds like a humble Lucchesi peddler to me."*

"I see you've been talking to my wife." She detected irritation in his warm baritone voice. *"I'm afraid Renee suffers from the French tendency of counting other people's money and talking too much about their own. I'm more like the Genovese when it comes to finances."*

"The Genovese are so secretive. I can never figure out what they're really thinking. For Italians, they're so reserved," she said.

"Perhaps that's why they've been masters of commerce for centuries. If Columbus had been Lucchesi instead of from Genoa, he'd probably have regaled his cronies with stories of the New World without ever having set sail!" She laughed at his self-deprecating wit. Through her laugher he added, *"Those Genovese in the theater tonight, throwing roses at your feet and bellowing 'Brava' like drunken Irish seamen on leave were not very reserved."*

She raised her glass acknowledging his compliment. *"I noticed you spoke only English with your guests during the reception. Yet here, in your garden with me, we converse in Italian."*

"Up here I like to talk to my plants when I'm gardening. Of course flowers can't hear, but I like to imagine that all God's creations can somehow communicate. I feel Dante's tongue is more soothing than English. Tonight, with so beautiful and brilliant a flower of the stage, Italian seems the more expressive language."

Antonietta looked into his gray eyes and saw earnestness, an almost boyish sincerity. She sensed the reception in her honor was but a gracious artifice of a married gentleman's design to find a moment of intimacy with her. She didn't rule out the possibility that his intent was romantic in nature. She did not retreat from this encounter nor did she encourage, by word or gesture, the likelihood such an advance would be accepted with enthusiasm or coldly rejected. She tilted her head and ran her fingers through her lovely, cascading brown hair conveying to Bertolli that she found him interesting and was curious where their garden conversation might lead. He sipped his grappa, admiring her Mediterranean beauty. She tied her red silk scarf across her sleek neck and then crossed her arms across her chest, her hands softly caressing her thin, tender biceps, the swell of voluptuous breasts straining above her bodice. Bertolli saw her shiver. "Are you cold? Perhaps we should go back inside."

She shook her head. "No, not at all. The air is so exhilarating! My skin feels like I've just dried off from a leisurely bath. But let's speak English. Tell me Bartolomeo, were you educated here or in the Old Country?"

"My formal education was at the University of Farneta," a crooked half smile appeared on his face and a look of puzzlement on Antonietta's. "Farneta? Is that here in California?"

Bertolli's smile broadened. "Farneta is the village I come from. It's a few miles outside Lucca, little more than a small church, a Chartreuse Monastery, an insane asylum and peasant farms. But a great man made it into an academy for me and provided me with an education worthy of a Medici."

Antonietta implored him with her melodious eyes to reveal more of himself and he told her how Father Agnello had educated him. When he finished his story, she asked, "How old were you when you got here?"

"Sixteen."

"My God! You were just a child!" she exclaimed, her fingertips touching her lips.

"No Signora. I don't think I was ever really a child," he said without bitterness.

"Did Father Agnello teach you to speak English so well?"

"No. English was one of the few Western languages he couldn't master.

He told me: 'To be fluent in a foreign language, you must think like the people whose tongue you seek to use. It was difficult enough for me to think like a German. To think like an Englishman is impossible, perhaps even sinful!'"

Shaking her head slowly she said, "So you got off the boat a teenage boy, with a few dollars in your pocket, unable to speak a word of English, and tonight we chat on the roof of your mansion, overlooking all of San Francisco, like a hilltop Tuscan villa! You're remarkable, Signore. But how did you lean such fine English and how long did it take?"

"I was able to converse adequately within two months of my arrival. It took about six months before I could write passably. Speaking the language was easier than writing it. Probably because I learned English in the theater."

"In the theater?" she gasped.

"Yes. You see, Father Agnello was a great lover of Shakespeare and, under his tutelage I read all of *The Bard's* plays - in Italian, of course. He told me that Shakespeare had written not only the greatest drama in literature, but also the finest librettos for opera. He predicted Verdi would put those magical words to music. Remember I told you Father Agnello made me a loan with which I purchased a horse so I could support myself transporting the products of others?" She nodded, encouraging him to continue. "Well, I used some of the loan to buy tickets to the theater. In my first year here, I attended every production of Shakespeare's plays. I even saw Booth in Othello. I knew the plays in Italian by memory. By hearing the beautiful English on the stage, I taught myself the language. The wonderful actors taught me how to think in English. So my love for the theater is not merely for the truths it reveals, but I feel deep gratitude to the plays and players who taught me the language."

"That's just fascinating!" Antonietta threw her head back in warm laughter. "No wonder I couldn't put my finger on your accent. My ears are trained to detect every dialect imaginable, but I couldn't figure yours out. I heard the remnants of your Tuscan upbringing, but the rest of it I couldn't place. Now I understand. You speak Elizabethan English with a San Francisco-Tuscan accent! How delightful!" They both smiled.

"We really should be getting back to the reception," Bertolli cautioned. "Otherwise the imaginations of my guests may descend to low levels of speculation about what went on between the beautiful actress and the peddler in the rose garden."

"Such speculations might make for good opera, Bartolomeo," she smiled provocatively.

"I quite agree. But such speculations also make for troubled marriages. Andiamo." She took Bertolli's proffered arm and they walked through the rose garden to the head of the stairs. Before descending, Bertolli turned to her and said, *"May I drive you to the Palace?"*

"Of course. What actress could pass up a conversation with the world's only Italian Elizabethan?"

Bertolli's guests were gone and his youngest sister, Gina Bertolli Copertini, formerly the infant Fabrizio Panforte's wet nurse in Farneta, was helping Bertolli's Chinese housekeeper, Liu Chen, with the dishes. *"Renee's gone to bed,"* Gina informed her brother. *"I'll help Liu tidy up."*

"I'll give Signora Pompa a lift to her hotel. Don't wait up for me, Liu. I'll lock up."

"Okay. I finish dishes," the housekeeper said. *"You want blekfist tomollo?"*

"No thanks. I'll be going to The Market early. I'll eat there."

Outside his home, Bertolli easily lifted Antonietta onto the black hooded, single horse drawn surrey. He tightened the tack of the sorrel, quarter horse. The surrey listed left accepting his 190-pound frame. His thick, laborer's hands snapped the reins twice on the horse's back and he made a clucking sound with his tongue. He guided his horse south on Larkin Street to Broadway and then reigned right toward Van Ness Avenue and right again toward The Bay. *"Aren't we going in the opposite direction of the Palace?"* asked the actress.

"Momentarily we are, but it's best to avoid Russian and Nob Hills. Cable cars conquer them easily, but horses struggle."

At the end of Van Ness Avenue, Antonietta heard the groan of a foghorn crying beyond the Golden Gate. She tightened her black, wool shawl around her shoulders and said, *"It's eerie. It sounds like a lonely baritone."* Bertolli nodded as he reined his horse toward Fisherman's Wharf. At the wharf he told her about Tom Maguire, an illiterate Gold Rush Irish gambler and saloonkeeper who parlayed his vice profits into a chain of legitimate theaters throughout California and Nevada. *"It was Maguire who made San Francisco a world class theatrical city,"* he said. *"His greatest love was Italian opera. Frequently he had to fill out the chorus with locals."* Pointing to Fisherman's Wharf, he smiled: *"So he'd come down here. It was called Italy Harbor in those days. He'd audition Neapolitan fishermen right here at the wharf. Maguire once remarked: 'The greatest butters-in of opera are Eye-talian fishermen. They didn't have the price of a ticket, but they knew their music. When we were short in the chorus, we'd go to the wharf. They all knew their scores, singing Ernani or Traviata. We could only use some of 'em, but they'd all show up banging on the stage door and shouting they were in the chorus. We knew they wasn't, but what the hell. We let 'em in anyway."*

Antonietta laughed at the thought of her countrymen standing in their fishing boats, bobbing on the water and belting out La donna e mobile. "Will I have a chance to see one of these seaside auditions?"

"I'm afraid those days are gone. Shortly before I arrived here, Maguire went bust trying to finance opera. Now we don't have a full opera season, so we have to rely on touring companies. The Met's been sending a company for the last few years, but we're appalled by their productions. Opera produced by a real estate holding company for the tastes of heiresses doesn't play well in San Francisco."

"But your city has a wonderful reputation as an opera loving town. What about the Tivoli Opera house? I've heard they produce fine theater."

Bertolli nodded. "The Tivoli's productions are excellent! I saw Cavalleria Rusticana there a couple of years ago." Peering into Antonietta's eyes, he said, "She was no match for your Santuzza tonight."

"You're too kind, Bartolomeo."

"Their opera productions are modest. The orchestra is smaller than it should be, but it's competent. There are rare prima donnas to excite the audiences, but the Tivoli's been a faithful teacher of opera. But without a full season, with full orchestra and renowned artists, I fear the public appetite will be diminished or even lost."

"But if Maguire went broke producing full seasons, doesn't that indicate a weak market?"

Bertolli reined his horse up Columbus Avenue. "Maguire proved there's a great opera audience in San Francisco. His financial difficulties were more a function of the economics of scale than the lack of an audience," he said, his eyes peering over his horse's perked ears down the gas-lit street. In this moment of silence, broken only by the clip-clop of hooves on cobblestone and the creaking of his wooden surrey, Antonietta studied his profile. It seemed to her that his forward stare peered into a future unseen by most, but he was somehow bound to a past that had been forgotten by all. So she said, "Tell me more about this unlettered Irishman."

Bertolli sighed deeply, "I think it was his illiteracy and poverty that made him feel like he was a nobody. Artists were somebody. For Maguire actors and singers personified a magical power that transcended class and wealth. In the theater, language was not just symbols but action and therefore universally comprehensible. Most believe that he had a great eye for talent and completely understood the instability of public taste. Although his greatest love was Italian opera, he presented Gold Rush pioneers with the whole gamut of performing arts in his theaters. He created a minstrel company, presented tragedy and comedy, trapeze artists, vaudeville, novelty programs, even burlesque of grand operas like his production of Ill Treated Il Trovatore, or The Mother, The Maiden and the Musicianer.

"But I think Maguire's true genius was his understanding that those who pioneered the American West had transformed themselves into a new people. Fifty years ago San Francisco was little more than a shanty town with an overwhelmingly male population. The water, plumbing and lighting were primitive, and the streets, rivers of mud in winter and a dust bowl in summer. So gambling and saloon halls, bordellos and theaters became the social soul of a largely rootless, childless population. The City had a dozen theaters before we even had a City Hall. Maguire's Opera House was the first concrete building constructed in San Francisco. In fact he sold it to the city fathers as the first City Hall!

"Maguire had operated the bar concession at the Park Theater in New York City and that's where he found the two great loves of his life – his wife, Emma, and Italian opera. But on the east coast, opera has become the private plaything of the wealthy, J.P. Morgan and Mrs. Vanderbilt. Maguire felt show business must serve a mass audience, diverse culturally and economically. That was the audience he played to. All Westerners were immigrants and pioneers not restricted by the conventions of the giant trusts and Social Register.

"The west and California, from the beginning to the present, have always been in harmony. Italian opera, with its themes of murders, duels, adulteries, slavery, massacres and madness, is more than a metaphor for the American West. It speaks directly to our history, to what we were and what we became. The greed of gold fever, the vigilante lynchings, the flagrancy of vice, the Indian massacres, the Chinese conquering the Sierra and the Irish the plains, the slaughter over slavery is California! Our audiences don't exercise a willing suspension of disbelief in the theater. They see their history, and themselves on the stage as though in a mirror. The massed choral power of voices and instruments, the explosive, soaring vocalization of violent passions, the staging of a driven people struggling for an unknowable destiny, these are the elements of Italian opera! Opera provides music to the libretto of our California life!

"Maguire understood as do I that opera is not an art form for evening gowned matrons and top-hated capitalists. It is the washed and unwashed masses to whom opera sings. That is the audience Maguire discovered in San Francisco and that is the audience that adored you tonight!"

Bertolli paused to glance at Antonietta. Her wealthy eyes were rapt on him. "Scusi," he said. "I got a bit excited. By the way, we're in North Beach. You can tell when you're in the Italian Colony from the aroma of the bakeries."

"The sea and baking bread, salt air and sourdough! Are your nights always so intoxicating? Oh! Il giardino? Look at that lovely garden across from that Russian Church," Antonietta exclaimed.

"That's Washington Square. In San Francisco, our piazzas are parks. I think they soften city living."

Antonietta nodded, thinking there was something seductive about this city. During her performance, she had felt authentic warmth emanate from her audience, and it seemed more spontaneous, less layered with critical analysis, than the appreciation of her eastern audiences. She felt San Franciscans had embraced her with their applause, and it was a caress laced with gratitude for her rare gifts. Perhaps it was the mild, damp night air that massaged her delicate skin and made her feel open and receptive to the novel and different. Or maybe she felt it was this enormously successful man escorting her to her hotel and speaking of tempering urban life with flowers, enriching its people with theater and music, which intrigued her most. He was not at all like New York City's capitalists, whose generosity to the arts was the tariff they paid for their ascendancy into American aristocracy. Bartolomeo was a man indebted to the city that had liberated him from an impoverished past. She sensed he was intent on repaying all that San Francisco had given him and with generous interest at that. In some undetermined way she was part of his repayment plan. She shivered under her shawl, anxious to learn his designs for her.

Bertolli guided his carriage into the courtyard of the Palace Hotel. It was a massive seven-story structure, its footprint covering an entire block. The courtyard was surrounded by six rows of opulently pillared balconies, topped by a penthouse level. He parked the surrey, handed the reins to an uniformed doorman and then lifted Antonietta down to the sidewalk. "Would you care for a glass of port before retiring? I'd like to speak to you about your stay here," he said.

Inside the Palace, Bertolli checked his top hat and black cape and the handsome couple took a corner table in The Garden Court Restaurant. Over a glass of port, Bertolli described the state of performing arts in the large Italian colony. While crediting the social clubs and fraternal societies with creation of the Italian Variety Theater, he emphasized the amateur quality of the productions. Italian audiences thirsted to hear great operatic arias and folk songs sung in their melodious mother tongue, but the performers were inconsistent and untrained. "What's needed," he told her, "is a professional artistic director who can form these eager amateurs with talent into a competent theatrical company. I can help with the initial financing and finding an adequate theater. But the creative side of the venture requires an impresario and a truly gifted artist. We need someone who's vivacious, shrewd, fully versed in the varieties of performing arts. Someone who sings like an angel but can also direct others. Someone like you, Signora."

Antonietta sipped her port though full lips and said, "You're proposing I abandon my career, move to San Francisco and start a theater company from scratch with a bunch of amateurs!"

"Why not? Maguire did it. Besides, you'll get to audition those Neapolitan fishermen." He grinned mischievously, adding, "I've told you about our audiences. All that's needed to earn their applause is talent and will – qualities you possess in abundance."

She studied his frank gray eyes and shook her head slowly, "You're a dreamer Bartolomeo." She waved the waiter over to the table and ordered, "Please arrange with the concierge to extend my stay. I'll not be checking out tomorrow."

"How long will be staying with us Signora?" the waiter asked.

Raising her glass to Bertolli, "Until Signor Bertolli finds me a place to live." Thus was born Teatro Italiano, which Antonietta Pompa founded and directed for the next fifteen years. Italian opera was preserved in San Francisco, and an artistic talent pool created from which the San Francisco Opera Company would be formed by another Neapolitan musician a year after Fred Panforte seized control of Bartolomeo Bertolli's business empire.

Two months after Bertolli persuaded Antonietta Pompa to professionalize Teatro Italiano she was producing nightly shows from a repertory of opera gems, comedy, tragedy, one act character sketches and her own performances of operatic arias and evocative Neapolitan folk songs. On the opening night of Pompa's first production she sang arias from Tosca, Madama Butterfly and La Boheme, dedicating her performance to Bartolomeo Bertolli and "all of San Francisco's Lucchese!" For the first time since the boy Bertolli heard the melody of a Puccini composition from a humble church organ in Farneta, the music of the most passionate composer he'd ever heard erupted from the brilliant soprano voice of Antonietta Pompa. Her music engulfed him in a whirlpool of emotions which he'd tempered for his almost three decade journey from an anonymous Italian village to a vibrant American city. From the stage Antonietta saw him standing with the rest of the wildly applauding crowd as she bowed gratefully. He didn't clap or *shout his approval. He stood amid the pandemonium and gaped at her on center stage. She saw his powerful body trembling with emotions her performance had unleashed. She'd sung Puccini's songs of women's doomed loves, and he'd become an unpublished poet living on the damp Left Bank of Paris, an American naval officer returning to Japan, an artist painting a fresco behind a Roman cathedral's alter. He was her lover whose passion inexorably culminated in denial or death. As the affection of the audience washed over her she feared she would never hold him in her arms, never be able to release the boy he'd never been permitted to be, never make him quiver in her tenderness and warmth. He tossed a bouquet of his rooftop roses onto the stage. She curtsied, picked them up, clutched them to her breasts and her tears flowed. The audience roared, certain their plaudits were the author of this singing angel's obvious emotions. But hers were bittersweet tears. She sensed at this, their triumphant moment, footlights would barricade Bartolomeo from her bed and their love would always be no more than her marvelously lyric voice and his utterly expressive heart. Like Mimi and Tosca and Cio-Cio-San she grasped that love without touching is cursed. All could she could do was sing for, to, and of him. All he could do was watch and listen and yearn for what his nature decreed he must never have.*

To celebrate Antonietta's stunning success — the suddenness of which even astonished the always-optimistic Bertolli — he'd invited her to the Tivoli Theater for the American debut of soprano Luisa Tetrazzini, who would perform in La Boheme. Antonietta sat in front of her mirror backstage removing her stage make-up, "What about your wife?" she asked.

"Renee never attends the theater with me. She finds the crowds oppressive."

"Isn't she upset about all the time you're spending with me?"

"No. She has her social circle and is quite active in the Vittoria Colonna Club. And there's our children." Antonietta detected strain in Bertolli's voice.

"She has no suspicions about us? After all, we spend four or five nights a week together," she pressed.

"What's to be suspicious about? We're always in public. Besides, she knows me."

Antonietta pursed her lips, painted them with lipstick and said, "Really? What could a wife know about her handsome, wealthy husband that would make her feel comfortable with him spending his nights with an actress some men find attractive? Do you think I'm attractive, Bartolomeo?"

"You're beautiful! I suspect every man in North Beach wants to make love to you. But I see beyond your loveliness. It's the beauty inside you that fascinates me. I watch you working with young actors and marvel at your

ability to decipher where their talents dwell and pull the best they have to offer from them. It's the beauty beneath your skin, the capacity to draw from others the best that's in them, that amazes me."

She dabbed powder on her face to hide the blush his words had painted on her cheeks. "Bartolomeo, that's the kindest, most touching thing anyone's ever said to me. I think your wife's a fool to let a man like you to freely consort with an unattached woman."

He smiled, "On that you're wrong. Antonietta if you understand how I do business I think you'll appreciate why Renee doesn't worry that I'll stray from our vows. You and I made an agreement at the Palace. We signed no papers nor will we ever. I gave you my word of financial assistance and have honored it." She nodded and he continued, "In my business, I drive hard bargains with ranchers and retailers. When we shake hands, whatever promises I've made will be performed. Sometimes I make poor bargains. Sometimes deals go sour, but I'll never break my promise. Surely the promise I made before God when we married is as important as the word of a chicken peddler." He paused and removed a photograph from his wallet. He handed the picture to her. It was his wedding picture on the sun-drenched steps of Saints Peter and Paul. "She's very beautiful," Antonietta said. He nodded and sighed, "I was a young man who thought he was in love, so we married. I promised I'd be faithful to her as long as we lived. I'm older now and know more of what love is and what it's not. Like a bad business deal, I can't break my vow. My word has always been my bond. If it binds me to a bad deal or a sad marriage it's dishonor will neither make the deal good or the marriage happy. But it would destroy the man I am, the man I seek to be."

Antonietta lips trembled. She thought of his description of her inner beauty and reflected that he'd told her she drew from others the best they had to offer. In her dressing room, she had just drawn the very best that Bertolli had to offer her – the unexpressed love of an uncompromisingly moral man. A knowing smile lit up her face, "Bartolomeo, I'd love to go to the opera with you!" He returned her smile and offered her his arm.

In his study at home Pat Kelley switched off the Dictaphone machine into which he'd dictated the latest of his father-in-law's papers. He now realized that Bertolli's decision to rear Maria differently than her siblings was driven by a loveless marriage and an unconsummated love affair. Pat had originally assumed that Bertolli introduced Maria to the theater to infuse her young life with the richness of performing arts. But his letters revealed his dominant motive was so the girl might study and, ultimately, know Antonietta Pompa. In Antonietta, Bertolli had found a woman who defined herself and refused to be defined by the men in her life. He saw her as a woman of passion and intellect, compassion and competitiveness, a woman who insisted on the essential interdependence of love and yet saw no conflict with the natural independence of self. She was, in short, all Bertolli's wife and Maria's mother was not. Bertolli desperately wanted his special child to learn from this woman he dared not love, that the measure of any person is the extent to which they drew the best from others. And Maria Bertolli Kelley learned her lessons well. But discerning the best in another inevitably exposes the worst in them. For Maria there was no best to be found in Fred Panforte. Therefore the boundless love that she so constantly displayed enunciated its inherent antithesis, unveiled its other side – pure and absorbing hatred.

Pat also thought that it was Fred Panforte's outrage of the code of the *Precious Ones* that chorused in the background of the Agnello/Bertolli correspondence. He believed that Panforte's theft of the sealed letters was far more than the tactical impropriety of an ambitious young man. It went beyond spying on the secrets of a future adversary. In Bertolli's letter to his priest in which he'd written of his pretentious wife and his passion for a beautiful actress Panforte had acquired the key to defeat his benefactor. When Fabrizio Panforte had sat in Bertolli's office at Western Poultry and accepted a generously offered job he already knew the soul of his new employer. He had learned from Bertolli's own words that not even the fervid love of a brilliant woman could induce him to break his word. He perceived that the tragic flaw of the man who had bought him a loaf of bread on his first day in America was his absolute inability to compromise his integrity, even for a truly remarkable woman's love.

19

On the holiday before the start of the Panforte trial Pat Kelley drove to Petaluma to meet with Isador Poplack. At their Columbus Day celebration in Washington Square Park, Pat had secretly probed his father-in-law about Petaluma politics and practices during the war. Bertolli advised Pat to meet with his old friend Poplack, who was a wealthy grain provider to Petaluma's poultry industry. Pat had mentioned rumors about black market operations during the war and that it was run by Jews. "Nonsense!" Bertolli had said angrily. "You want to know about that business, you go see Izzy Poplack!"

Pat drove down Western Avenue in Petaluma and saw the twin spires of St. Vincent's. As he drove toward the edge of downtown, he passed the granite gothic corner building of The Bank of America amid 19th century two story commercial buildings. He parked in front of a nondescript little stucco building distinguished only by a modest Star of David above the doorway. His sense of Irish irony was pricked by a bulky corner building two blocks away that dominated the avenue. It was the Hermann Sons Hall where Nazis met in the 1930's. Izzy Poplack greeted him in the entryway of the Jewish Community Center. He was a short, chubby-faced man, with balding gray black hair and a white walrus mustache. He smiled easily, and there was a sense of charming whimsy when he greeted Pat Kelley. They shook hands in front of a large dramatic photograph of the banquet celebrating the opening of the building in 1925. It depicted immigrant chicken ranchers and their kids sitting at long banquet tables, dignified in their best suits and dresses, posing with evident pride in their new community center. "It's good to meet you. My father-in-law speaks very highly of you. But I thought you'd been banished from this place," Kelley said.

"I have," Izzy Poplack shrugged. "But the reactionaries ignore my leftist politics because they need my grain and credit. We're practical folks here in Petaluma. A theoretical communist with a capitalist's net worth is not a threat to the Republic. Besides, I like to come here as an act of defiance. Perhaps even arrogance. How's Mr. B? His health is good, yes? He's okay with this Panforte business?"

"He's fine, Izzy. He's leaving it to the courts. The family stuff, I'm kinda looking after. That's why I wanted to talk to you."

Poplack suggested they take a walk and get a cup of coffee. "I'm trying to get a grip on what kinda guy young Panforte is. I don't know much about their Petaluma operations other than Panforte's kid runs it. I'm particularly interested in the poultry industry during the war years. From what I've learned, Great Western Poultry had enormous profits during the war."

"We all did. You have to understand, Pat, old man Panforte's poultry business, like all war related businesses, literally exploded with profits during the war. But it was a totally different operation than it had been in Bertolli's day. Panforte's a vicious bastard, but you gotta give him credit, he's a wizard at playing stock games!"

Of course Pat already knew about his father-in-law's fatal mistake in granting his employees equity in Western Poultry Co. and Fred Panforte's exploitation of his mentor's progressive generosity. Panforte had conned Western Poultry's laborers into giving him their proxies by showing them phony financial statements and alleging that Bertolli's absence from The Market was because he was keeping late hours sleeping with a pretty showgirl. In truth Bertolli's devotion to the theater and creating an opera company was fully discussed with Panforte, who Bertolli had considered his brightest and most valuable executive. In the very office in which Bertolli had first welcomed Panforte to America thirteen years earlier the first *Precious One* sought the last *Precious One's* counsel. He explained to Fabrizio that he believed they were within a year or so of putting on an opera season with the City's own company. He'd asked Panforte if he thought the business could get along without him working on a full-time basis. He proposed to take a sabbatical from commerce until the new San Francisco Opera's maiden season was completed and asked Panforte if he'd be willing to run the company in his absence. Bertolli said, "I simply can't develop the theater and run this company at the same time. To continue to do so is fair to neither. If you believe a sabbatical is bad business and you're unwilling to take over the reins of leadership, then I have no choice but to resign my interest in the theater. After all, I owe it to our employees and their families."

Fred Panforte immediately assured his boss that he would be honored to run Western Poultry and that Bertolli's contribution to the

City's cultural life was much too vital to be inhibited by any commercial enterprise. When the two men shook hands on the deal that made Fabrizio Panforte's future coup possible Panforte said, "I have only one condition. The company's first production must be a Puccini opera, since we're all Lucchese boys!" Bertolli laughed, clapped the younger man on the shoulder and walked out of the building that he'd built, confident that Father Agnello's youngest son would do an outstanding job running his company.

Pat also knew that Bertolli's settlement, arrived by at gun point, required his father-in-law to transfer all of his stock back to the corporation. What he didn't know and what Izzy Poplack now told him was that most of Western Poultry's executives and sales force remained loyal to Bertolli and left for other jobs in other wholesale houses. They figured that without Bartolemeo Bertolli at the helm of the company, their stockholdings would never amount to much. "So they sold their stock to Panforte dirt cheap! With the retirement of your father-in-law's stock and Panforte's purchase of the Bertolli loyalists' paper, Panforte packed the Board of Directors with his own cronies," Izzy related.

Izzy Poplack explained to Kelley that while business expansion was universal during the war, Fred Panforte's was the only wholesale house that expanded during the Great Depression. When the panic first hit the nation, Panforte began importing Mexican labor to work on his poultry ranches. "Employing scab labor at the point of production gave him a helluva competitive edge," Poplack said. At the wholesale market in the City, Panforte executed a modified stock scam Izzy explained, "With so many union laborers facing layoffs, Panforte offered to buy their stock to give them a hedge against long-term unemployment. By the time the Depression was receding and they got their jobs back, the last thing they wanted to have anything to do with was stock and the stock market, which they figured caused them to loss their jobs in the first place! By '39, Panforte's family owned Western Poultry lock, stock and barrel. That's when he changed the name to add *Great*."

He told Pat that Fred Panforte, with absolute control of Great Western Poultry, no longer responsible to shareholders, with a greatly diminished payroll because he hired Mexican labor, was perfectly positioned to exploit the darkest days of the Depression. During FDR's first term in office, growers were losing their ranches left and right. Izzy recounted: "If the bank didn't foreclose, the feed suppliers did.

And that's when old man Panforte started buying up foreclosures. That's also when I gave up the chickens and started my feed supply business."

Poplack told Pat that sometime after Pearl Harbor, but before D-Day, Fred Panforte sent his son to Petaluma to manage their operations. Since Great Western Poultry was now an entirely family owned corporation, Bob Panforte was exempt from military service as vital to the home front war effort.

Pat said, "My kid's godfather's an F.B.I. agent and he tipped me off that there was a black market scandal here during the war. You know anything about it?"

Izzy Poplack laughed and skeptically said, "No offense to your kid's spiritual mentor, but the F.B.I. didn't know shit about the black market. You wanna talk about it, we go for a little walk. These walls got ears."

They walked on Western Avenue, the main street in the town that hens and roosters had built. "You say your dad-in-law's leaving this Panforte business to the courts? And you work in the courts, right?" Izzy said. "Right," Pat nodded.

"Well, tell Mr. B I love him, but good fuckin' luck with the courts!" Poplack said.

As they strolled down Western Avenue in the dry hot Petaluma sun, Isador Poplack gave Kelley a brief oral history of the Jewish chicken ranchers of Petaluma. They had migrated from the pogroms, revolutions and oppressions that had swept Eastern Europe. Many were Zionist, some revolutionaries, some socialists and others orthodox Ashkenazi. Many came to America believing that they would learn farming in Petaluma and then journey to Palestine to become farmers. Indeed some did found kibbutzim in the Holy Land, but most succeeded so well in America that they stayed in Petaluma. Bertolli had already told Pat of the vitality of the Jewish Community Center in Petaluma. He had emphasized its cultural richness and demonstrated it when he took Pat and Maria and his granddaughter Kathleen to a concert at the War Memorial Opera House, starring violin prodigy Yehudi Menuhin, the son of Petaluma chicken ranchers. Poplack, a wealthy capitalist with socialist politics was telling him that the only thing the Jewish right and left had ever agreed on was constructing the center in the first place so they'd have a place to debate and squabble over everything from the Bolshevik Revolution to FDR's New Deal. But Pat could sense Poplack's bitterness that the Jewish right had kicked their leftist brothers out of the very center that they'd built and maintained together. Pat appreciated that Izzy was furious that American courts did nothing to prevent this social expulsion.

Izzy told Pat about Ben Hochman, chicken rancher, scholar and socialist who was the last man in California to be tarred and feathered by Santa Rosa right-wing vigilantes in the 30's. Hochman's sin was supporting Oakie apple pickers whose struggle was immortalized in John Steinbeck's *The Grapes of Wrath*. Poplack complained that the upcoming criminal trial of longshore labor leader Harry Bridges was more of this reactionary strain in American politics that reared its ugly head whenever labor leaders refused to sell out working stiffs. Pat tried to steer Poplack's history lesson back to World War II and the rumored Petaluma black market. Izzy said, "Ya wanna know about Petaluma war profiteers? So listen, kid. Maybe you'll learn that justice is no blind goddess. She's a whore like the rest of us."

"So teach," Kelley said smiling. Poplack told Pat that the Petaluma wartime scandal was a damn good illustration of the flaws in the American justice system. "It's a system where money talks and bullshit walks!" Izzy said. To give Pat a sense of context he told him that when the war broke out, their Petaluma youth, like the rest of the nation, ran off to Europe and Asia to fight fascism. "In war everybody but the kids who fight it makes money," Izzy said. He admitted that Petaluma Jews were no different from the goyim who had sent their sons to bleed and die across the seas. But he'd seen their womenfolk – women who had worked the ranches alongside their men, who'd nursed diseased chickens like of their own babies, who'd shoveled chicken shit just like the men – cry when they saw news photos of the Russian Front with its frozen corpses and dead horses and over-turned carts.

"At home, war's a business. Don't kid yourself, all the chicken ranchers made money during the War. They all paid off their mortgages," Izzy said. He explained that that the OPA set the price of birds. At the height of poultry war production, the OPA set the price of chickens at thirty cents a pound. Petaluma operated in a ten-week raise cycle in which a rancher could raise 20,000 birds at roughly two and a half pounds each. Then wholesale dealers would pay the ranchers the OPA price in check. They would then pay the ranchers in cash under the table from ten to fifteen cents a bird. So chicken ranchers increased their net profit by two to three grand for each raise cycle – all of it tax free! According to Poplack the wholesalers would in turn sell to retailers, grocers and restaurants at 50-60 cents per pound, with the ten or fifteen cent under the table payment likewise in cash.

Kelley asked how Panforte's business fit into this black market scam. "It's simple," Izzy answered. "It's simply a matter of scale. The guys who really cleaned up were the wholesalers and slaughterhouses. Panforte's was the only outfit vertically integrated from chicken coop to grocery store shelf. As I told you, during the Depression he'd bought up foreclosures on lots of ranches and processing plants to add to his distribution center in the City. So he could and did mark up prices at all points in the food chain."

"So how did the Feds miss an operation as big and obvious?" Kelley asked. Izzy scratched his head and said, "Who says they missed it? Like I was telling you, J. Edgar Hoover's boys are thought police. They see what he tells 'em to see." Poplack explained that at the outbreak of world war all the chicken ranchers in Petaluma and Sonoma played around in the black market. Even militant Communist Party members who owned chicken ranches set aside their socialist ethics to cash in on this under the table scam. But as the war stories began reaching Petaluma a growing discontent was felt at the Jewish community by both left and right. These Eastern European immigrants intuited before most others that Hitler's plans for European Jewry was to purge their people from the face of the earth. And their feelings grew more personal as they lost their boys in Europe and the Pacific Islands. "It seemed to come to a head when we learned that Hochman's kid was in a German POW camp," Izzy said glumly.

Hochman, with Poplack's support, pointed out to party members that the Communist Party line was to keep food prices as low as possible for the workers. Party functionaries from San Francisco got the message and put some party members who were ranchers on *trial*, charging them with "crimes against the working class." Izzy shook his head, smiled and said: "Anyway, both the left and right got the message that gouging housewives while our boys were fighting fascists abroad wasn't kosher. So the left came to me to organize a poultry cooperative. I helped set up the organization, built a processing plant in Petaluma and rented retail outlets in the City. The *co-op* kept all the Jewish ranchers outta the black-market for the duration of the war, and frankly it was a windfall for my grain business."

Izzy told Pat that right after V-E Day, a couple of OPA investigators showed up at Morry Finklestein's wanting to look at his books. Morry was a *co-op* man with nothing to hide, so he cooperated. "The next thing you know, the F.B.I.'s all over Petaluma going over all the co-op guys' books and records!" Izzy said.

According to the Army training records at the Presidio that Pat Kelley and Joe Desmond had examined, Bob Panforte had volunteer to lead the Mt. Tamalpais infantry training the day after Hitler surrendered and while the Pacific war still raged. Pat was struck by the inherent contradiction that the military would deem Bob Panforte's poultry work vital to the war effort and then take him away to lead a training program of dubious military value to the Pacific war now completely dominated by American air and sea power. It was obvious to Pat that Bob Panforte's military volunteerism was transparent device no doubt conceived by his father to deflect federal scrutiny from his Petaluma operations.

Poplack continued, "What happened was the Feds came across receipts of Ho Chung, who was a big chicken dealer in Chinatown during the war…"

"Isn't he a Chinatown importer? I think my father-in-law and he did business years ago," Kelley interjected.

"It's his son," Poplack said. "Anyway, Ho had some special book-keeping, this odd way of figuring prices. He always bought choice stuff for Chinatown and paid premium prices. Hell, we don't know shit about abacuses. He's one of the most responsible men in China-town, so everyone trusted him even though nobody could figure out how he computed prices.

"Then United Press breaks a story that the government broke up a huge black-market ring in Petaluma. It was all bullshit. They arrested twenty-nine chicken ranchers. All of them were left-wingers. All of them were members of the poultry co-op and all of 'em were Jewish! They were probably the only chicken ranchers in the industry who *weren't* cheating! I think their real crime was their politics and belief that co-ops could thrive in a capitalist system.

"The real proof that it was all politics came when the government took a dive on the case. At first the ranchers wanted to fight it in court. But their lawyer warned 'em that irate housewives on the jury would throw the book at 'em."

"And their lawyer was Daniel Loeb?" Kelley asked.

"Yeah, that's right. Fred Panforte picked up the tab for Loeb's attorney fees, and Ho paid their five hundred dollar fines. The guys figured, what the hell? Let's get back to work. But the public humiliation of this phony prosecution still sticks in our craws. And it always will!"

At Kelley's parked car in front of the Jewish Community Center,

Pat warmly thanked Poplack for his time and help understanding Petaluma poultry politics. "It's nothing," Izzy waved his hand. "You're Bertolli's family and we've never forgotten him. Besides, there's all kinds of folks poking into Panforte's kid." Izzy had an impish grin on his face, and his dark eyes sparkled with mischief. Pat realized that he'd been saving this morsel of information all along. "Who's doing the poking? You know what they found?" Kelley said.

"I heard they were insurance investigators. My guess is the murdered girl's dad sent 'em up here. They got an interpreter from the Sheriff's Office and talked to a Mexican kid who works on a Panforte chicken ranch. The interpreter wouldn't say what they talked about."

"What do you know about this Mexican ranch hand?" Pat pressed.

"Nothing, really. He's a truck driver for the Panfortes, so he's got the softest job on the ranch. It's odd for a Mexican laborer to be driving a truck. Most of 'em are here illegally, so they got no license. His name's Manual Abascal. The only other thing I know is that he's non-union. That means young Panforte must've paid off somebody in the Teamster's local."

"Interesting," Kelley said. "And thanks again, Izzy. You've been a big help."

Izzy shrugged, "No big thing. Give my best to Mr. B and a hug and kiss for Maria. I know her since she's a baby. She married you, so I figure you're a real *mensch*."

Pat said, "That I am, Izzy. That I am." The two men shook hands and then embraced. Kelley pulled his car from the curb and headed back to the City and saw Izzy Poplack in his rear-view mirror waving goodbye.

Pat Kelley decided to drive over to Sonoma before returning home. When he drove in the country alone, which was rare, he liked to let his mind wander, almost engaging himself in a Socratic dialogue. He had no question that Fred Panforte had a bright mind and his Stanford graduate son didn't. Fred Panforte's strategy and tactics to seize control of Bertolli's creations had been brilliantly conceived and flawlessly executed. And every aspect of it was legal. After all, it was Bertolli himself who had asked Panforte to run the company while he and Antonietta Pompa pursued their theatrical dreams. As for obtaining the proxy votes of Western Poultry's laborers to take over the Board of Directors, that also was legitimate corporate maneuvering, admittedly rarely seen in closely held, non-publicly traded companies. Izzy

Poplack's recitation of Panforte's purchase of the shares of desperate Depression-era, laid-off employees to gain complete ownership of the company was likewise perfectly legal. What Panforte's plan revealed to Pat was a complete understanding of Bertolli's nature and what Maria considered his two greatest strengths. Father Agnello's classical education of Bartolemeo Bertolli was devoted to creating a Medici, a man who believed that commerce was a means and wealth not an end. To pursue riches and nothing more was, Father Agnello had taught, America's greatest sin. Father Agnello, born to great wealth himself, believed and taught his first *Precious One* that affluence without the arts and scholarship and literature was the very definition of primitive, the negation of the Greek concept of the whole man. So it was Bertolli's very nature to seek avenues of self-expression beyond his business world, to civilize the city that had so graciously adopted the poor boys from Farneta.

Fabrizio Panforte, whose soul never lost the sting of grinding, motherless Tuscan poverty nor the humiliation he felt about his father's barter ineptitude in Lucca's marketplace, had a mathematician's love of pure logic and, it seemed, little more. He was therefore cut of a different cloth than the dozen Farneta boys who had preceded him to San Francisco. Perhaps because he was sort of a last minute addition to their number or because they were already so well established in America, Fred Panforte never felt fully included in their fraternity of new Americans. So it was quite natural that he adopted the ethics of the receiving country rather than those he had learned from Father Agnello. After all, Father Agnello was from the Old World, a world of largely pre-ordained limits. In this New World, it seemed to Fabrizio, that the only limits on ambition were the proscriptions of American law. From his first days in his benefactor's care Panforte noticed that Bertolli paid little attention to legal documents or the norms of the law. His handshake and his word were not only his bond, but were readily accepted by everyone with whom he did business. But Fabrizio felt that the law, written by men certainly as wise as his only teacher and Bertolli, was America's ruler. Fabrizio therefore designed his actions to be faithful to the law and, since the law was made by wise men he came to believe that the failure to use it would be unwise. As Kelley pulled into the town of Sonoma and parked across from the park-like piazza that was the town's civic center he concluded that his wife's detestation of Panforte began by how they viewed her father's principle moral notions. For Maria her father's faith that law was irrelevant to the behavior of a moral man was one of his greatest virtues. To Fred Panforte, it was Bertolli's tragic flaw.

Bartolemeo Bertolli's abiding sense of personal loyalty was to his daughter his greatest virtue and therefore Fred Panforte's betrayal of that loyalty a sacrilege. Maria could not accept that Panforte's notion of loyalty was whatever was required by law. Pat understood that as a company officer he had a fiduciary relationship to the Western Poultry and its shareholders. He had reasoned that his actions, while Bertolli had taken a sabbatical from the business to pursue his theatrical dreams, was consistent with his fiduciary obligations and in the best interest of the company. Clearly, Panforte had thought, Bertolli's obvious sexual affair with the actress was an act of disloyalty to his wife. Therefore he and his associates should not be heard to complain that he had wrested control of the business by devious methods. Again, Pat Kelley thought, what Maria saw as strength in her father, Fred Panforte perceived as a weakness in his boss.

Pat decided to take a walk in Sonoma to sort out what he'd learned about the Panfortes that he hadn't already known or suspected and how Isador Poplack's revelations factored into the Panforte murder trial. Pat walked from the center of the small town about a quarter of a mile to the Sebastiani winery. He entered the tasting room and queued up for a glass of Sebastiani's cabernet sauvignon. The cool room temperature was a welcome respite from the dry, searing Sonoma heat. He wiped the sweat from his brow with the back of his hand. There was a tourist couple in front of him and about a half dozen others taking a docent tour of the winery. Pat sipped his wine and walked over to an enlarged black and white photograph that covered the entire wall to the right of the winery's entrance. It was like the camera had created a photo fresco. It was an expansive shot of Farneta, the Sebastiani family's ancestral village. In the foreground was the Chartreuse Monastery, behind whose thick ivory walls, tonsured, silent monks, followers of San Bruno, observed thousand year-old contemplative rituals. It was here that Samuele Sebastiani, one of Father Agnello's *Precious Ones* and the founder of the Sebastiani California wine empire, had learned the vintners' art. Overlooking the Monastery from a bluff stood the church of San Lorenzo, Father Agnello's pastorate, its modest campanile presiding over verdant fertile lands worked by the *contadini* from whom the priest had selected his California pioneers. In the distant background, only partially visible in the panoramic photograph, stood a Tuscan insane asylum. Bartolemeo

Bertolli had remarked that the first sounds he heard every morning in Farneta were the morning crow of roosters until he got old enough to realize that you could not distinguish the cry of a morning cock from the bleating screams of human madness. Other than the un-pictured peasant farms this was all there was to Farneta – a mute monastery, a humble church that seated not more than fifty congregants, and a large mental institution. Pat couldn't help but think of Father Agnello's admonition to young Fabrizio when he'd sent him off to aid his San Francisco *Precious Ones* in the reconstruction of San Francisco. He'd told Fabrizio, as he had told the twelve before him: "Never forget the land you came from and never disrespect the land that welcomed you." Bartolemeo Bertolli's steady correspondence with Father Agnello over the years demonstrated that he had followed his mentor's counsel. The poignant wall photograph at the Sebastiani Winery in Sonoma testified that this remarkable American family had never forgotten their roots nor disrespected the land from which they had harvested their fortune. Of all the *Precious Ones* only Fabrizio Panforte seemed to have purged Farneta from his memory. He had written only one letter to his hometown and that was to Father Agnello to advise him of his safe arrival and that he was learning English at Bertolli's Sonoma ranch. He never wrote to his own father to tell him of the wonders he had seen in America or that Sonoma's rolling hills and fertile soil was so like Tuscany turned golden in the summer sun.

Pat left the cool of the winery, walked past the Sebastiani villa across the way and headed for what was once his father-in-law's Sonoma ranch, his wife's childhood summer playground. It was now a turkey farm owned by Great Western Poultry. Pat walked east on Milani Road and noted that all of the roads in this area that bordered the little town of Sonoma were named after Father Agnello's first twelve students. Only the thirteenth, Panforte's name, was missing from the green and white street signs. The awful irony, Pat reflected, was that Bertolli Road dissected the center of Panforte's turkey farm. He needed to somehow integrate the history of these lads from Farneta that he'd learned by virtue of his relationship with Bertolli with the more current data that Isador Poplack had provided him. The most obvious difference between Fred Panforte as an aspiring capitalist and as a dominant one was that his seizure of Bertolli's business was legal, if not ethical, and his participation in the war-time black market illegal. But such a notion seemed to contradict the normal immigrant path to American success. Frequently, new immigrants resorted to criminality to get their American start and if they were clever or lucky enough to avoid arrest graduated to respectability around middle age. Why would Fred Panforte take the risk of criminal conviction and scandal as a war profiteer when he owned the only vertically integrated poultry operation in Northern California, Kelley asked himself. Besides, the cash profits described by Izzy Poplack, while lucrative for most Petaluma chicken ranchers, would be mere pocket money to Panforte's vast operations. A man as facile with numbers as Fred Panforte would surely calculate that the risk – jail – reward ratio simply wasn't worth it.

Moreover Pat was certain that Fred had assigned his son to manage the production plant in Petaluma in order to secure his exemption from military service. Poultry employees working at The Market were not exempt, since these were largely sales jobs and commodities speculation. Fred was well past military serving age, so he could remain at The Market while his son qualified as vital to war-time food production. Perhaps, Kelley thought, it was Bob Panforte, in his first management position after graduating from Stanford, who had fallen in with black marketers. Being the boss' son and impressionable and apparently working beyond the reach of his father's formidable shadow, it would be easy for young Panforte to get swept up in these under-the-table deals that seemed par for the Petaluma course. Naturally when the Feds started snooping around Fred Panforte would come to the defense of his son. He had funded Danny Loeb's defense of the accused chicken ranchers. It was undoubtedly old man Panforte and Danny Loeb's idea to offer the Panforte hunting cabin at Mt. Tam to the U.S. Army and volunteer Bob Panforte as a training guide. And Loeb had put together a deal where no one did time, and an enormous public scandal was avoided for the poultry industry in general and Panforte's family in particular.

But there were subtle flaws in this theoretical scenario, Pat felt. There was nothing in Fred Panforte's business history to suggest that he would allow his management team sufficient autonomy where they could personally profit without his knowledge, consent and likely participation. In addition, the decisiveness with which Fred acted when he got word of federal investigators strongly suggested prior and thorough knowledge of the Petaluma chicken scam. If the old man was wise to and a participant in the illegal scheme, he had effectively allowed his kid to ride the beef. Pat thought of successful high level smugglers and how they always avoided touching and possessing the contraband. Their underlings and mules packaged and carted their illegal product while the kingpins remained out of sight. It was axiomatic that the kingpin never got caught *holding* the goods. All a clever smuggler left for prosecutors was the uncorroborated testimony of their hirelings, who had been busted red-handed. As for these unfortunates, a top-flight criminal defense lawyer was provided to guarantee that their Constitutional rights were protected and their lips sealed. The analogy to smugglers and mules between Fred and Bob Panforte's roles as black marketers was intriguing, Pat felt. Did it suggest a father and son modus operandi that might be applicable to this murder mystery, Pat speculated. And what about this Mexican truck driver and the special status the Panfortes had granted him? Why was Paul Brady sending private investigators from his firm to nose around Petaluma ranch operations and what, if anything had they learned? Kelley would have normally disregarded the vague information about this ranch hand except that Brady's interest in him could only mean he thought he had something to do with Paula's death. But it seemed so remote and obscure to Pat.

As he headed back to his car at the Sebastiani Winery, the invisibility of Fred Panforte in a war-profiteering scheme stimulated Paula Panforte's window of death. But Pat expanded her imaginary pane by pushing the frame back to the weekend before she met her fate. Presumably this must have been the period of time her killer dug her grave. But Kelley's expanded view did not reveal Fred Panforte's whereabouts on the weekend before Paula's disappearance. He thought of Angelina Panforte. He realized that his compassion and graciousness to her on the day of her son's arraignment had touched her deeply. Pat had sincerely offered it because he felt that she was also a victim in this tragedy. "Perhaps," he thought as he switched on the ignition, "there might be a moment during the trial when we're alone and she can tell me about her husband's relationship with Paula and where *he* was during these crucial days."

20

On the opening day of the Panforte jury trial Pat Kelley was at his desk in the Pit culling through the jury list. Bailiff McCann had gone upstairs to fetch the Defendant. Judge Grant was at her desk studying the file and scribbling on a yellow legal pad. In the courtroom, as Joe Desmond was feeding fresh paper into his stenograph machine, his damp hands fumbled the roll. "Damn! I'm sweating like a goddamn longshoreman," he muttered to himself.

"Here," Kelley said, tossing him what looked like a beanbag. Desmond caught the bag and a powdery puff exploded like smoke. "What is it?" he asked.

"A rosin bag," Pat grinned. "I borrowed it from Terry. He uses it when he's pitching. When your hands sweat, just give it a squeeze. That'll do the trick."

Joe laughed, "Jeezus, Kelley, you think of everything. If my forehead starts to sweat, you've probably got some of Maria's make-up for me." Pat just grinned. Then he briefed Desmond on the latest discoveries of his moonlighting, unauthorized investigation. Pat edited out his Petaluma meeting with Izzy Poplack and all of the speculations it had aroused in him. It was too remote, he felt, too premature to share with his young court reporter friend. Instead he related to Joe only those facts known by the defense. He explained that he had acquired more information on the dishonorable soldier, Jack Hill. Of course Joe already knew that Hill had shacked up with the dairyman's daughter, had been busted by M.P.'s and convicted by Paul Brady for jailbait rape. Pat explained that such a sex offense required that Hill be registered in California as a sex offender. This registration allowed the Vice Squad to keeps tabs on him. "Not surprisingly," Pat said, "He acquired an appetite for buggery in the pen."

Pat reported that two weeks *after* Panforte was indicted, Vice busted Hill for soliciting an undercover cop. "When the cops searched his North Beach studio, they found a stash of homosexual pornography and – get this – all four newspapers' accounts of Paula's murder!" Pat said to a puzzled Joe Desmond. "I don't get it. What's it got to do with this case?"

"Maybe nothing," Pat replied. "Maybe everything." Pat told Desmond that he'd gone over the search and seizure inventory from Hill's apartment. Among the items discovered was sort of a scrap book of society page news photos of Paula Panforte at charity affairs and the Cotillion Ball. One of her news photos found in Hill's apartment was framed so that you wouldn't easily notice that it was a newspaper photo. "Obviously any public records that I can get my hands on, Loeb can also," Kelley said softly as though to prevent eavesdropping on their conversation. "As required by law, the search and seizure inventory was filed with the court. After Danny Loeb saw it he sent his investigator to the Fox to ask some questions. London talked to the manager at the Fox who told him Paula was one of their best customers. He said she almost always attends the first showing of new releases on Monday nights. Like a real movie buff, she often attends the Fox alone, the manager tells London. The Monday night that she disappeared was the premiere of *Home of the Brave*."

"Did the manager confirm that Paula had been at the Fox that night?" Joe asked.

Pat replied, "He didn't confirm or deny it. He was in his office, so he wouldn't have noticed if she was there or not. But the manager did confirm that ex-con Hill was at the Fox!" He related to Joe that London had shown the manager Hill's mug shot and asked him if he'd ever seen him at the Fox. The manager told London that Hill showed up at the box office a few days *before* he read about Paula's murder in the papers. Pat concluded, "Hill claimed to be her out-of-town brother! He wanted to know if she was in the theater, said he had a surprise for her."

"Sweet Jesus! Is this guy stalking her or something?" Desmond asked.

"Maybe. Let's wait and see how Loeb plays this one. We'll talk about it later," Pat said. "Here come the lawyers." Kelley sent them into chambers. Desmond squeezed his rosin bag and followed Pat into chambers.

Judge Lucille Grant questioned the lawyers on their proposed witnesses and order of proof. She directed them to submit their first set of proposed jury instructions by the following week and asked Danny Loeb if he'd be making an opening statement or reserving it until the close of the prosecution's case-in-chief. He told her that it was his practice to always give an opening statement immediately follow-ing the prosecution's. "It's important to let the jury know something about the defense. It makes it easier for them to follow our cross-examinations."

Judge Grant asked, "Danny, can you give me an idea of what you intend to say in your opening statement? Think of it as an offer of proof."

"Sure," Loeb said. "As we see it, Your Honor, the prosecution's case in one in which my guy had the opportunity to kill his wife, but no conceivable motive. We think our investigation has discovered a sus-pect who has a compelling, if debased, motive *and* the opportunity." Loeb identified the ex-Houston soldier and ex-con Jack Hill as his suspect. He explained to the Judge Hill's dishonorable discharge and conviction of statutory rape at the hands of Paul Brady. He pointed out that because of his Army training he was very familiar with the topography at Mt. Tamalpais and particularly Paula's gravesite since he'd trained there under Bob Panforte. He showed Judge Grant an inventory of newspaper clippings and photos about Paula Brady Pan-forte that vice squad officers had seized from his apartment after his arrest.

"His animus toward Paul Brady was obsessive!" Loeb claimed. And Judge Grant was certain that it was, that her terrible fears of con-vict revenge that she'd expressed to Brady and revealed to Moore and Loeb might well prove true.

"Granted this fella Hill has a motive, but Danny, what evidence do you have of opportunity? It seems like the case against Hill is the converse of Mike's case. Hill's got motive, but no opportunity," Judge Grant said.

"We can establish that Hill went to the Fox box office with a photo of Paula a few days before she was reported in the press dead!" Loeb asserted.

"But how do you get Paula to the Fox on the night in question?" Judge Grant asked, combing her fingers once through her hair. When she uttered Paula's name there was an intimacy in her tone, a sense of personal history that she couldn't conceal. "That's where her husband said she was," Loeb answered.

The DA interjected, "For chrissake Danny, your client told so many stories about what happened that night no one's gonna believe him when he says his wife went to the show!"

Judge Grant nodded at Loeb, inviting him to elaborate. He said that all Bob Panforte's statements could be true no matter how apparently contradictory. There could have been love play that descended into discord. Indeed it made sense for Paula to leave the house after he'd bloodied her nose and she'd angered him about his drinking. They were both drunk and Paula was known to frequently go out by herself at night, often to the Fox. "Remember," Loeb urged, "Bob works those crazy hours that require him to go to bed when most folks are just starting their social evening. In fact, four days a week he works out of their ranch in Petaluma. Now I don't want to get personal here, but Paula's family and friends will confirm that it's not unusual for her to go out alone."

Judge Grant suppressed grimacing when Loeb remarked that Paula went out by herself in the evenings. She of course knew Paula's social habits probably better than Paula's mother. *"Why in God's name is he letting me sit on this case?"* she asked herself. As Loeb spoke, she thought back on her meeting with Paul Brady in her chambers when he'd come to her to help find his daughter. She had questioned him more thoroughly than any homicide inspector had or could. Their friendship and her closeness to his daughter gave her insights into Paula that no stranger could know. She knew that Paula had admired her perhaps even more than her own mother. In a way, she'd been a big sister to Paula during her teen years. She knew that Paula had not been a virgin when she married Bob Panforte, and she'd told Paul this in her chambers. She told him that Paula had come to her for birth control advice and she'd sent her to her own gynecologist. She had grasped his hand and told him that she wasn't judging Paula or his paternal example. She was just looking for a lover or lovers who might help find her.

In her chambers, where she'd shared such intimacy with the murdered girl's father, she was hearing Daniel David Loeb describe Paula's social life more knowledgably than the girl's own father. She shouldn't be trying this case, she thought. When both lawyers had so graciously waived any suggestion of her conflict of interest, she was certain that her passion for fairness would direct her conduct of the trial, as it always had. But none of them had thought about her conflict of emotions. Loeb had even told Pat Kelley that both he and Moore dreaded the thought of an out-of-county judge trying the case. Loeb had said to Kelley, "Lucy's the only goddamn judge in this town who can give both of us a fair trial."

Yet as she listened to Loeb outlining his defense it was clear that he intended to put his client's dead wife and her father on trial as well. She couldn't let that happen. But if she tried to stop Loeb, would she be denying his client a fair trial, would she unilaterally be dooming him to the gallows? That was wrong, she knew. And she also knew that Loeb had said nothing untruthful about Paula, and that sullying a voiceless homicide victim's character is a classic criminal defense. "*You're the judge*," she thought, as Loeb finished speaking. "*You wanted this job and you get paid to make decisions. So make one!*"

She stood up and lifted her judicial robe off the hanger and draped it over her shoulders. She remained standing and said, "Danny, I'd like you to clarify a couple of points. You're relying on your client's statements and the hearsay statements of the box office people to place Paula and this guy Hill at the Fox, right?"

"That's right, Your Honor," Loeb said.

Judge Grant said, "But none of them place Paula and Hill at the Fox on that precise Monday evening when she disappeared. Assuming Paula was at the Fox on Monday, the witnesses place Hill there 'a few days before' the newspapers ran the story of the discovery of her body. They found her on Thursday. So Hill could have been seen at the Fox on Saturday or Sunday *before* she disappeared, or Tuesday *after* your client reported her missing. Without direct evidence that Hill was there on Monday your notion of his opportunity is highly speculative."

Loeb said arrogantly, "If Hill testifies that he was there on Monday, is that direct enough?"

"Come off it, Danny! The guy's got a rap sheet a mile long, and he's got a pending pimping and pandering felony for his latest beef. No way he's gonna implicate himself in a capital case!" Moore said.

Judge Grant squinted when she asked Loeb: "Danny, you've talked to Hill?"

"My investigator interviewed him in City Jail," Loeb said blandly.

"Was he represented by counsel," the Judge pressed.

"He is now," Loeb replied.

Pat Kelley thought, "*Counsel no doubt selected by Loeb and paid by old man Panforte. Petaluma black market déjà vu.*"

"I see," Judge Grant said. She half sat back on the edge of her large mahogany desk, her toes on the carpet. Then she said firmly but without anger, "If Mr. Hill's attorney represents to the Court, on the record and in the presence of his client, that Hill will not assert his Fifth Amendment rights and freely implicate himself in a capital crime, I'll allow you to make the opening statement you've just described. What I will not tolerate is an opening statement in which you discuss Hill's proposed testimony and then he takes the Fifth in front of the jury. If that happens Danny you and Mr. Hill's attorney will be sharing a jail cell with him for contempt of court, and I'll declare an immediate mistrial! Do I make myself clear?"

"Very!" an apparently chastened but undeterred Danny Loeb said. Judge Grant then turned to the DA and asked for an overview of his opening statement. When District Attorney Moore began discussing Robert Panforte's housecleaning efforts, Judge Grant interrupted, "Just a minute, Mike. What's your theory of when and where Paula died?"

"Your Honor, we intend to prove that she was alive when the Defendant placed her in the grave he had previously dug for her. She was unconscious after he'd severely beaten her, but he noticed that she was still breathing. So he bashed her brains out with the Chevy jack handled and, in effect, buried her alive!"

Judge Grant had been listening to Moore's proffer with her hands clasped together prayer-like over her mouth. She dropped her hands to her desktop, folded them and asked, "So, you're restricting the scene of her demise to Mt. Tamalpais as opposed to her bedroom or some other local? Are you quite sure that's what you want to do?"

Moore shrugged casually, "It's what the evidence shows, Judge."

"Very well," Judge Grant remarked as though she thought the DA was making a tactical mistake. She added, "In light of your theory of the case, you are not tell the jury that any acts of the Defendant that alleged occurred after Paula's burial are evidence of premeditation."

"What about covering up evidence as an indication of consciousness of guilt?" the DA protested.

"That's a jury instruction, Mike. I'll decide if it's appropriate after all the evidence is in. What I don't want is any characterization by you in your opening statement as to what may be inferred from this *housecleaning*. The Defendant's activities in his house may have an entirely innocent meaning. I remind both of you an opening statement is not argument! Gentlemen, I trust you understand me," Judge Grant cautioned. Both lawyers nodded, implicitly acknowledging that the trial judge they both had wanted was willing to use tight but fair reins.

The lawyers returned to the courtroom and Judge Grant reached for her judicial robe. Joe Desmond slipped the rosin bag into his coat pocket and followed Kelley into a courtroom sea of expectant faces.

In the first row sat Fred Panforte and his wife, her black gloved hands rubbing her rosary. Across the ten-foot center aisle sat a hatless Maria Bertolli Kelley accompanied by her son, who gave Joe a thumbs-up sign. On the black keys of Joe's stenograph machine, with bone-dry fingers, he punched in the date and time of the commencement of the trial of Robert Agnello Panforte. Jury selection took a half a day. Then District Attorney Michael Moore rose to give his opening statement to a jury of eight men and four women.

The DA paced leisurely from one end of the jury box to the other, and in a calm voice told the jury what he expected to prove. He began with Robert Panforte's phone call to the police, reporting his wife missing. Reading from Officer Cragen's report, he told the jury that Panforte had denied any quarrel with his wife. He emphasized to the jury that Panforte described to the responding officer the clothes his wife was wearing when he claimed she'd left home for the show, and that this was the exact apparel she was wearing when the homicide detail dug up her body on Mt. Tamalpais days later. District Attorney Moore told the jury: "The essential elements of first-degree murder will come from three primary sources. The first source will be the Defendant's own words and the second source will be the Defendant's next-door neighbors who will testify as to his activities on the night Paula Brady Panforte was murdered. The third source will be a silent witness. This silent witness will be the ghastly wounds on Paula's body!

"The Defendant and his late wife, the mother of their then seven-month-old son, finished dinner on Monday, June 5, 1949 around seven o'clock. They had been drinking, and in their bedroom they quarreled. The Defendant wanted to go out with his wife who was clad only in her panties and she refused, telling him she would be ashamed to be seen in public with a drunk! Enraged because he felt his wife was mocking him the Defendant, a former intercollegiate football star, struck her with his fist, knocking her the floor! While Paula Panforte was prostrate on the floor of their bedroom, her husband brutally beat on her head, neck and chest rendering her unconscious! The violence of the attack was sufficient to be heard by the Defendant's next door neighbor, fourteen year-old Damon Busby, who was listening to a radio program in his bedroom, the wall of which is adjacent to the Panforte flat.

"Certain that she was dead, the Defendant then began pounding on her breasts with his fists in some perverse ritual that escapes my powers of articulation…"

Judge Grant interrupted the District Attorney, "If it escapes your ability to articulate it, then it necessarily cannot be proven. Your last comment may be proper for closing argument, but not an opening statement. The jury is instructed to disregard your comments on perversity."

"Very well, Your Honor," the D.A. replied. Turning to the jury, Moore resumed, "The Defendant's brutal assault on his wife in their home was now complete, so he methodically went about the task of disposing of her body. He went downstairs to their garage and backed his 1947 Chevrolet Coupe out of the garage, trunk end first. The Busby boy next store was very fond of the Defendant's car, volunteering to wash it frequently. He saw the Chevy back out of the Panforte garage during the commercial break of *The Lone Ranger* radio program, which would have been about seven-forty-five.

"The Defendant then backed his car back into his garage so that the trunk would be closest to the back stairs down which he would carry his wife's body. He returned to their bedroom and dressed his unconscious wife. When he reported his wife missing the next morning, the Defendant described the clothes she was wearing perfectly. It was this wardrobe that clothed Paula Panforte's dead body when the homicide detail dug up her remains on Mt. Tamalpais.

"After wrapping her body in her green coat to minimize her bleeding all over him and the trunk of his car, the Defendant carried her down the back stairs and dumped her in the car trunk. When the Defendant drove his car out of his garage his other next-door neighbor, Harold Pierce, was cleaning his sidewalk with a garden hose. The Defendant had told Mr. Pierce that he was going downtown to pick up his wife from a movie. Mr. Pierce will testify that the Chevy exited the garage hood-end first!

"Then he drove up a torturous, obscure, little-used road in Marin to bury her. The People ask you to pay particular attention to the route that he took to just below the summit of Mt. Tam and the location and nature of the deceased's grave. Only a man with his full faculties, with minute knowledge of the terrain, could have decided on this burial sight and found it."

The D.A. paused and turned to look at Bob Panforte, and the jury's collective eyes followed his stare. Turning back to the jury he said softly: "Ladies and gentlemen, the evidence will show that Paula Brady Panforte was still alive in the cramped trunk of her husband's car on her journey to Marin County! She had inhaled carbon monoxide from the vehicle's exhaust fumes. The Coroner's spectroscopic examination revealed 12% carbon monoxide in her system. When Inspector Murphy exhumed her body days later, her cheeks were flushed, leading the Inspector to momentarily believe she was still alive! The Coroner will testify that the coloration of her cheeks was caused by carbon monoxide, the gaseous waste from the Defendant's Chevy!

"When the Defendant arrived at the spot on Mt. Tamalpais that he'd previously selected for her burial, he opened the trunk. He carried her limp body down a steep slope to the grave he had prepared for her. When he placed her in her crude tomb, he was startled to realize she's still alive! He raced back up the hill and retrieved his Army entrenching tool and the Chevy's jack handle. Back at her grave, he used the full weight of his one hundred and ninety pound athletic body, and smashed her skull with the jack handle!

"Ladies and gentlemen, you will be provided with Paula Panforte's autopsy photos and an exact replica of the standard jack handle for 1947 Chevrolets. You will see with your own eyes the jack handle is a perfect fit for the length and width of her fatal head wound. We will prove that long after the initial bedroom attack, Robert Panforte's powerful right arm wielded his jack handle and cracked his wife's skull on a mountain in Marin! Then he calmly covered her grave using his Army entrenching tool. This grave-digging instrument was found by Homicide Inspectors in the Defendant's garage. It had a residue of clay identical to the terrain of the gravesite and utterly foreign to The Defendant's Marina neighborhood. After disposing of the murder weapon, the Defendant returned to his Francisco Street home and began fabricating a story for his family and the police that his lovely wife, the mother of his infant son, had mysteriously disappeared."

The DA returned to his seat at counsel table and the spectators stirred in their seats at the sudden coldness in the courtroom. Judge Grant declared a recess. The recess couldn't have come too soon for Danny Loeb and his beleaguered cause. He spent a good ten minutes in the holding tank with his client. From Pat Kelley's desk in the anteroom of chambers, he could hear him screaming at Panforte. He couldn't make out his words, but he had no doubt he was telling the young man that the murderous, cold-eyed stare he was fixing on District Attorney Moore was not the image Loeb wanted him to convey to the jury. Loeb came out of the holding tank followed by his client, and walked briskly over to Fred and Angelina Panforte. Loeb's head bobbed emphatically as he huddled with Panforte's parents.

He seemed to calm down when he began speaking with Angelina, who barely nodded her head. Loeb abruptly ended the conversation, walked over to the water cooler and poured himself a paper cup of water. Angelina summoned her son with a tiny wave of her gloved hand. He stepped over to the rail separating the Pit from the spectator section. He rested both hands on the rail, hunched his shoulders, his head bowed into the air space of the spectator section.

His father leaned forward, looked up at his son and there was an indulgent expression on his face. His rugged features softened as he studied his clearly depressed son. While Bob stared down at the floor, the older Panforte seemed to be struggling with what he'd heard from Moore's opening statement. Angelina slid forward to the edge of her seat, her brilliant, aqua, tearless eyes never leaving her son's sadly handsome face. She reached up with her left hand toward her boy's troubled face and began delicately stroking his cheek. Her eyes spoke to him and told him that no matter what he'd done, no matter how awful the prosecution had made him sound, he was loved completely. His expression intimated a variety of deep emotions that he must have been experiencing. Was he feeling remorse for bloodying his wife's nose? Or was it sadness for the pain he was inflicting on his mother or the shame he'd brought to his father's name? Remorse, sadness, shame were all etched on that young man's face. But Pat Kelley also thought that his eyes darting back and forth between his Mom and Dad exposed confusion. He seemed bewildered by District Attorney Moore's recitation of what had happened in their bedroom and perplexed that anyone could believe that he'd killed Paula. Everything he'd told the cops he believed to be true and accurate. Only that damn entrenching tool he hadn't explained. But he couldn't explain it because he had no idea how it had gotten in his garage. Whatever the family catharsis during the recess had accomplished, one thing was immediately certain. A mother's touch had melted the ice in her son's eyes, and he now confronted his accusers, resolute in the knowledge he was not alone.

Joe Desmond joined Pat, Maria and Terry Kelley for an early dinner and post-mortem on the first day of the Panforte jury trial in a booth at Sam's Grill on Bush Street. They were already seated in an enclosed booth, and when Maria saw Joe she waved him over. The waiter handed Joe the daily printed menu and informed him that the Kelleys had already ordered. "What are you having, Maria," Desmond asked.

"I'm having the *tortellini in brodo* to start and broiled petrale sole," she said. Pat loved the way his wife's lips puckered when she pronounced the word "*brodo.*" It was as though she was kissing him from across the table. In her six weeks back from their summer cabin in Fairfax, her cocoa skin had lightened into a golden luster, giving her rich ebony eyes a stirring depth. Coatless, her beige satin blouse unbuttoned at the base of her long elegant neck, she lifted a Manhattan to her lips while the waiter stood over her, feigning interest in Desmond's order but more attentive to the swell of Maria's breasts and his search for a shadow of cleavage.

Joe ordered a Martini and sautéed calamari and risotto. Maria leaned forward toward Joe, her elbows on the white clothed table, rested her chin in her folded hands and said, "So, Joe, what did you think of Moore's opening statement and the Coroner's testimony?"

"You know me, Maria. Serious thinking isn't one of my strengths. I just take down the words," Desmond replied

"Oh, nonsense," she laughed, throwing back her head. "Once they excused that cute young juror you were eyeing, you were so intent, you looked like you were the one on trial."

"Yeah," Terry chimed in. "You looked like you were constipated or something." The boy's father grinned, but his mother shot him a single arched eyebrow of maternal disapproval. Terry happily kicked Uncle *Joe* under the table.

"Come on, I really want to know what you think," she pleaded in that irresistible Tuscan sing-song pout she used whenever she wanted something from a man. Pat felt that Maria was coaxing their young friend's reaction to the trial's opening in order to avoid his far more experienced analysis. "Well," Joe said, "I'd heard a lot of what he said when I reported the Grand Jury proceedings. So there were no surprises. But I felt the autopsy photos and Dr. Rosenberg's theory of Paula's beating and death was...was almost depraved. The Coroner's evidence seems to have really affected the jury. It looked like it got to young Panforte too."

"I know what you mean," Maria said. "How could what he did to the poor girl not affect everyone in the courtroom? The horror in their bedroom that night was so...so palpable!"

Neither Joe Desmond nor Maria Kelley had the advantage of the detailed preview and pretrial study of the autopsy evidence that Pat Kelley had. Perhaps this was the reason that they'd failed to grasp the significance of Danny Loeb's cross-examination of Dr. Ernest

Rosenberg, particularly his blurred vision through the window of death. Loeb, as Pat had expected, had completely neutralized Dr. Rosenberg's testimony about Paula's battered breasts because he knew that the Coroner would testify candidly on all of the possible forensic theories. Pat grasped his wife's hand. Her long fingers curled up into this thick ones and he said, "You're right, honey. But you must keep in mind that every piece of evidence in this case is subject to Loeb's questions. All he needs to do is raise doubts. It seems to me he did raise doubts when Ernie conceded that there were numerous objects that could have caused her fatal head wound!"

Maria shook her head vehemently, "Oh come on, darling! Your defense is so...so feeble. What difference does it make if he killed her in their bedroom or in Marin? Is it less murderous to beat her to death than burying her alive?"

"It's not my defense, honey. It's not even Loeb's. It's the prosecution's burden to prove young Panforte did it, and how he did it will determine whether he lives or dies. The D.A. has locked himself into the theory that he killed her on Mt. Tam. And he's trying to convince the jury Bob Panforte acted alone. Frankly her wounds are entirely consistent with multiple attackers as well as multiple weapons. As for what did or didn't take place in their bedroom, Loeb doesn't have to prove that Paula went to the Fox to see *Home of the Brave*, Moore has to prove that *she didn't*. Proving a negative is extremely difficult."

Maria slumped back against the backrest, folded her arms across her chest and glared at her husband's logic. Then Terry waded in. "But, Dad, the D.A. didn't say anything about motive. Is that because they don't know anything about Petaluma?"

"Not necessarily," the boy's father replied, stabbing a small squid with his fork. "If they've figured out the motive they wanna keep it from Loeb as long as they can. To mention it in the opening statement tips Loeb off, so he can adjust his defense accordingly."

"I wish my father's lawyers had kept Loeb in the dark. He's so damn shifty," Maria said. Then she leaned forward and said to her husband, "What's this Petaluma business?"

Pat explained that when he'd learned that Paul Brady had successfully prosecuted a GI who had been trained by Bob Panforte during the war, he had decided to check out Panforte's chicken ranch operations. Maria's mood swings were dramatic and sudden and they always first appeared in the darkening of her eyes, which spoke of emerging fury when she said to Pat, "So that's why you brought up the Panforte trial with my dad on Columbus Day! You know he doesn't want to have anything to do with Panforte and his kid! He won't even read the newspaper stories."

"Honey, I didn't say a word about the trial. I simply asked him about the Petaluma poultry industry during the war. Bill Moriarity tipped me off there was some kinda black market operation up there, so I asked your Dad to give me some leads on it, and he did," Pat protested.

Maria said that Moriarity's wife, Grace, had told her that Pat had questioned her husband about Robert Panforte's war-time service. "I suppose it's just a coincidence that you're interrogating an F.B.I. agent and my father about the same people in the same place at the same time!" Maria said, antagonistically running her fingers through her hair.

"Listen, Maria! This is a murder case. Forget for a minute the name of the accused. To find out who murdered Paula we've got to find someone with motive and opportunity. From what I've seen of the prosecution's case, young Panforte's got no motive to kill her..."

"He's Fred's son!" Maria interrupted.

"Evil seed is a literary convention, not a legal one," Pat said, miffed at Maria's sudden emotionalism. Pat sighed heavily and then told Maria about his undercover trip with Desmond to the Presidio and their discovery that Paula's father had successfully prosecuted and sent to prison a now registered sex offender who'd been lurking around the Fox. She listened intently to her husband, a look of incredulity in her eyes that he could be so convincing about this stranger, this suspect other than Panforte's son. Desmond tried to lighten the mood, "When are we gonna get our advance for our *Screaming Eagles* book. I could use some spare change," he said. Maria ignored him and Pat shot him a look that told him that sarcasm was no antidote to his wife's fury.

"My God, Pat! What do you think you're doing? Are you trying to prove Panforte is innocent? What if the press gets onto the fact that the Chief Clerk is leading a rogue investigation in a capital case? All those sanctimonious judges you work for would run you out of the courthouse if they found out what you're up to!"

Pat calmly said, "Honey, these walls have ears, so let's drop it. We can chat about it at home over a glass of port, if you'd like."

In an effort to deflect his Mom's anger from his father, Terry said: "How come Loeb didn't make an opening statement today? You've always told me the defense should give a statement right after the prosecution."

"Well, Terry, sometimes it's too risky for the defense. Loeb's not certain yet how Moore will attack. He doesn't want to pin himself down. He wants flexibility for his defense. It's a matter of tactics," Pat said calmly.

"What about the tactics of truth?" Maria sternly demanded. "Do you realize what you've just taught our son? You've taught him that in *your* hallowed halls of justice a lawyer can shield Panforte with silence in the face of an accusation that he murdered his own wife, the mother of their child. Then he can make up a justification for it, depending on what Moore can prove. Is this trial your idea of your son's first lesson in cynicism?"

The essence of Pat and Maria's marital debate was joined that evening at Sam's Grill, inspired by their precocious son. It was the clash between truth and justice. Maria was an educator, and so for her the search for truth was an abiding passion. But even she had to admit to herself that when she had observed young Panforte being solaced by his parents after District Attorney Moore's devastating opening she had intuited his vulnerability in his downcast eyes. It had seemed to Maria that at that moment there was some unspoken communication going on between father and son that burdened Robert Panforte's soul. His slumped shoulders confronting his father's stare implied that he had somehow failed his father's notion of manhood. It was only when his mother's fingers tenderly petted his cheek did resolve return to his athletic body. But Maria banished this thought from her mind, unwilling to empathize with the family she believed was the enemy.

For Pat Kelley the pursuit of elusive justice in human affairs absorbed his reflective mind. It may have been the mystifying unfairness of losing his father as a teenager to the flames of another boy's home, or the steadying compassion for a wife for whom the first man in her life seemed so disgraced, that ignited Pat's passion for justice. Or it may merely have been Kelley's romantic Irish heart that simply was unable to accept Maria's truth that life's not fair even as his formidable mind told him that she was probably correct. Pat loved to quote George Bernard Shaw, who said: "A reasonable man conforms to his environment. An unreasonable man seeks to conform his environment to himself. Therefore, all human progress is made by unreasonable men." Dining at Sam's this remarkable couple's philosophical clash was inadvertently shaping their son to be an *unreasonable man*.

A man who would resolve this parental controversy by pursuing, with equal vigor both truth and justice; a man who would unreasonably believe that the loftiest sentiments of mind and heart – truth and justice – need not be at war.

Accepting his wife's challenge, Pat said, "Honey, it's not cynical to insist on a sound method to find the truth. A scientist uses a microscope to discover truth. But the microscope's power to magnify the minute is itself a distortion of reality. Yet without this distortion we can't see the truth. Think of this trial as a sort of *moral microscope* through which Terry will study human behavior with the courtroom as a laboratory. We must view human behavior through a delusory focus if we are to discover its moral implications."

"But Terry's microscope has its lens covered," Maria retorted. "Panforte's silence is like a cloth blocking the microscope's light. And Loeb, by awaiting a view of the prosecution's specimen of guilt, is allowed to change the specimen on the slide. Although your laboratory metaphor is sound in one respect. The Panfortes are like the insects and rodents you'd expect to find in any decent lab!"

Terry kicked Desmond under the table, as if to say: "*Score one for Mom!*"

Pat persisted, "Don't you see, Maria, it's conflict our microscope studies. It's not Moore's specimen or Loeb's. It's their specimens in conflict, and how they contest that will identify the species of truth."

"That's where we differ. You think of truth as a species. To me, it's a genus," Maria said.

"But what if the truth is that Robert Panforte didn't do it? What if that pervert Hill killed her? Will that truth be generic for you? Will such a truth elevate Panforte's name up from a species of deceit and dishonor you've classified them as?" Pat challenged.

"Only a defective microscope could produce such a horrendous delusion. That's what your precious judicial system is – a flawed instrument," Maria said.

When he told her that Judge Grant would not allow Loeb to discuss Hill in his opening statement it didn't seem to register with her. Added to her dismay that Panforte might go unpunished was an even greater fear that her husband's conduct placed his job and their family security in jeopardy. Softly, Pat said, "Honey, it may be that later in the trial Lucy let's Loeb get into this Hill matter. It's about process. I want Terry to study *how* decisions on moral issues are made, not just the conclusions that are reached. I think it's important for him."

"Speaking of what's important, I need my rosin bag back," Terry said to Joe. "I'm pitching against Salesian's in the winter league Saturday."

Joe reached into his coat pocket and handed Terry his rosin back, saying, "I won't need it anymore. I've got my sea legs now."

Pat was certain that Terry's interruption of his parent's debate was intentional. By his father's design, he was his mother's emotional policeman for this troubling trial. So he blithely arrested his mother's emotional turmoil from his father's concession that the courtroom was an impaired laboratory for detecting truth. And he injected a child's game into a weighty and emotion-laden adult conversation. By doing so he'd banished the Panfortes and his parent's war between truth and justice from the dinner conversation, making himself the center of attention.

"Joe, you gonna come watch me play?" Terry said with a big grin.

"Where's the game?" Joe asked.

"Potrero Hill, at eleven o'clock," Terry said.

Joe told his nephew he'd be there. "I'll pick you up if you'd like," Pat volunteered.

"Great," Desmond accepted. Maria smiled warmly at Joe, grateful that he cared so much for her boy. And Pat thought that his wild kid was so easy to love.

21

The Panforte murder trial resumed to a blistering Indian summer day, transforming poet George Sterling's "cool, gray city of love" into the oppressive cauldron of emotions that Danny Loeb had predicted during his breakfast meeting with Joe Desmond. Pat Kelley thought that the remarkable thing about jury verdicts was that they almost always got it right, even when facts were kept from their consideration. Thus far the jury had been kept in the dark about a disgraced soldier, a punk who had the best of reasons to harm Paul Brady's daughter. Pat was sensing that there was some funny business on the chicken ranch that might have bearing on the mystery, or that something had happened on the first weekend in June that had bearing. But he had no choice but to let the story play itself out. It was a story authored by two lawyers, each contesting the mystery of a beautiful young woman's death. It seemed like a story being edited by Judge Grant. Somehow, Pat felt that the truth of Paula's death, the truth that Maria Kelley desperately yearned for, would only be discovered beyond court confines and that it would somehow be revealed to his searching, incisive mind.

Chief Inspector Ed O'Day took the witness stand. His eyes scanned the jury box as two floor fans labored futilely to temper the oppressively warm Indian summer courtroom. The DA took the Chief Inspector through the homicide investigation, starting with Judge Grant's call to him and the removal of Paula's body from her grave in Marin County. Then District Attorney Moore focused on the time-line. The Chief Inspector placed Mr. and Mrs. Robert Panforte in their flat at 7:00 p.m. when they finished dinner, according to what the Defendant had told the homicide inspectors. This Chief Inspector was not asked and did not relate to the jury the love play that Panforte had related to them. The only emotional moment at their home that night that he testified to was Paula mocking her husband's inebriation and his angry response to her. "We place the time of the initial assault at approximately 7:45 p.m.," O'Day told the jury.

"How did you determine this particular time as the moment of attack?" the D.A. asked.

Chief Inspector O'Day explained that Panforte's neighbor, teenager Damon Busby, whose bedroom was alongside the eastern side of Panforte's home, was listening to a radio program, and during the commercial break heard loud noises and shouting coming from the Panforte residence. Shortly thereafter the neighbor boy saw Panforte's Chevy coupe backing out of his garage. "The next time Panforte's vehicle was observed," the Chief Inspector said, "was approximately fifteen minutes later when the Defendant's other neighbor, Mr. Harold Pierce, saw it drive hood-end first out of the garage."

"Was that the extent of the reported activity at or around 2223 Francisco Street on the night of June 5, 1949?" District Attorney Moore asked.

"No. Young Busby told us that he heard the garage door at Panforte's opening and closing around 10:30 to 10:45 p.m."

Pat Kelley calculated that the prosecution was attempting to establish a two and a half-hour time frame in which the Defendant had to drive to Mt. Tamalpais, locate a gravesite, dig the grave, carry her body to it, cover the grave and return to Francisco Street.

O'Day testified that he and Murphy attempted to replicate the Defendant's actions. They drove from his residence to the burial site. It took an hour and a half to get from Francisco Street to almost the summit of Mt. Tamalpais. Then O'Day dug a grave the exact dimensions of Paula's grave, about eight feet away from it. It took fifty minutes to dig the mock grave. Then he filled it, and that took thirty minutes. Again, the drive back to the Panforte Marina duplex took an hour and a half.. They timed their activities with a stopwatch. It had taken the homicide inspectors almost two hours longer to replicate what they insisted were Bob Panforte's travels and excavations on June 5th.

"Do you have any explanation for this time disparity?" the DA asked.

"The Defendant had to have dug the grave *before* Monday night in order to arrive back home at 10:30 p.m. Subtracting the time it took to dig the grave makes it possible to get back to Francisco Street about when Damon Busby said he did."

"Are you telling this jury that the Defendant dug her grave before becoming enraged at her in their bedroom?"

"Obviously. The driving time each way is inflexible. As for digging and filling the grave, the digging took almost twice as long as filling it in."

The D.A. returned to the counsel table and said, "Your witness, counsel."

From the family row an inconsolable wail punctuated the Chief Inspector's answer. It was Robert Panforte's mother, Angelina. Little Angel. She'd lost her battle to mute her anguish. Her tears joined in chorus with her sobbing, and her husband's powerful arm around her small shoulders could no longer dam the torrent of grief and despair that a detective's time-line had painted. Judge Grant quickly recessed court to allow the restoration of a mother's composure. Her son called to Bailiff McCann, "Get me outta here!"

After a recess to allow Angelina to compose herself, Danny Loeb rose to cross-examine Chief Inspector O'Day. He thumbed through his investigative binder, prepared by David London. The defense lawyer and witness exchanged cordial morning greetings. Then Loeb asked: "Chief Inspector, your timeline and theory of this case have two huge, glaring assumptions. One is that Paula Panforte did *not* go downtown to a show; and, two, that what young Damon Busby claims he heard and saw and when he heard and saw it, are true.

"Let's explore the first assumption. At any time *prior* to the discovery of Paula's body, did you or your homicide investigators ever go to the Fox to determine whether she'd been there on June 5, 1949?"

"No, we didn't."

"But you had been told by Bob Panforte, on your first visit to their home, that his wife had gone to a show. And you had also been told on that first visit that Bob's neighbor had spoken to him when he drove his car out of his garage, and Bob said he was going to the show to pick up his wife. Isn't that correct"

"That's right," The Chief Inspector said.

"How about after Bob Panforte was indicted? Did you go to the Fox and investigate whether, in fact, Paula Panforte had gone to that theater on or about June 5, 1949?"

"Yes, we did." The jury's attention was riveted on the colloquy when Judge Grant cut in, "Counsel, that's enough on the Fox Theater. Should those issues crystallize or mature, you will be allowed to recall Chief Inspector O'Day or any other relevant witnesses to pursue it."

"Very well, Your Honor," Loeb said, satisfied that the jury's curiosity had been aroused. Then he flanked the judge's Jack Hill ruling by asking, "Chief Inspector, did your investigation at the Fox establish that

Paula Brady Panforte had *not* gone to the movies on June 5, 1949?"

O'Day glanced at the D.A., waiting for an objection. Hearing none, he shook his head and said, "We didn't establish that she'd gone there, and we couldn't excluded it either."

Loeb nodded knowingly and asked, "Now let's talk about your second assumption, namely the accuracy of Bob Panforte's teenage neighbor as to what he saw and heard and when he saw it and heard it. Chief Inspector, does it bother you that your timeline experiment accepts as its major premise the precise accuracy of this teenage boy?"

"No."

"Now, Busby lives with his mother in the apartment building immediately to the east of Bob Panforte's home, and Mr. Pierce lives in a duplex immediately to the west of the Panforte home. Are you aware that there are three garage doors identical to Bob Panforte's directly under young Busby's apartment building?"

"Yes, I'm aware of that."

"Did your experiment include listening from Busby's apartment to those three garage doors opening, as well as listening to Panforte's garage door opening, to determine *how* Damon Busby decided which door it was he claims he heard?"

"No."

Loeb slowly shook his head. "No further questions. Cross-examining such unscientific speculations is a waste of my energy, the Court's time and the jury's patience."

"Perhaps counsel will be energized by the first-hand testimony of his client's neighbors," the DA shot back.

"The Court's patience will not be taxed when both of you stop making editorial comments. So far your duel of wits employs very dull blades," Judge Grant ruled.

Pat Kelley was less impressed with conflicting time-line differences between Loeb and Moore than he was the timing of all that Bob Panforte's alleged task required him to do in either time-lines. There was something in District Attorney Moore's opening statement that troubled Pat. It was as though the prosecution was alleging too many specific acts that Panforte had performed to fit into any time-line. Clothing his wife after beating her unconscious seemed improbable to Pat, and he was certain that Loeb had grasped this fact and that he would spring it at the most dramatic moment.

Bailiff McCann had supplemented the floor fan near the jury box with an additional one across from the jury. The floor fans murmured along with the spectators as District Attorney Moore called Damon Busby, a fourteen year-old Marina Junior High student, to the stand. He was a lanky lad with angular features common to boys in their early teens. Questioned by the D.A., the jury was told that he had a passion for baseball and radio thrillers. On Monday, June 5, 1949, Busby came home from baseball practice at Funston Field at about 6 p.m. He was tired, ignored his homework, crawled into bed and turned on his radio at seven-thirty to listen to *The Lone Ranger*. During the commercial break at 7:45 p.m. he heard Mr. and Mrs. Panforte yelling. Then the boy testified that he saw the black '47 Chevy back out of the garage. He expressed a strong affection for Panforte's car, telling the jury: "It's a real cherry car. Sometimes he pays me a buck to wash it for him, but I'd wash that baby for nothing." After that, he fell asleep. His mother came home around ten-thirty, woke him up and bawled him out for playing his radio too loud. He was hungry, so he went to their kitchen and fixed himself a sandwich. That's when he said he heard Panforte's car re-entering his garage

"Ten-thirty o'clock, Monday night, June 5, 1949?" the District Attorney ominously repeated the prosecution's timeline.

"Yeah, right," the kid answered diffidently.

Busby saw Panforte's back his car out of the garage at 7:45 p.m. Pierce saw him drive out of the garage, hood-end first, around eight. The inference Moore wanted drawn from these two observations of his car was that he'd rearranged its parking position to facilitate carrying his wife's body down the back stairs to the trunk of his '47 Chevy. At 10:30 p.m. Busby said that Panforte returned in his car to their home, inferring that he'd disposed of Paula's body.

Pat Kelley noticed that defense counsel had received a manila envelope from his investigator, David London. He was certain that London had found something about Panforte's teenage neighbor that would muddy the clarity of the inferences the District Attorney wanted drawn from his testimony. Holding the manila envelope, Loeb asked the boy if he had any hobbies. Busby was confused and asked Loeb what he meant.

"Hobbies like photography, building model airplanes, things like that?" Loeb blandly.

"Oh, that kinda thing. Yeah, I fool around with photography a little."

"You needn't be so modest young man. You have a small dark room in your closet where you develop your own photos, don't you?"

"*Goddamn London!*" Pat thought. "*How does he dig this shit up, and where's Loeb going with it?*"

"Yeah," the lad said.

"Do you have any particular subjects that you like to photograph?" Loeb pressed.

"I don't know what you mean," Busby nervously.

"Well, some photographers specialize in mountains and others the sea, still others do portraits or *nature studies*. What's your specialty?"

"None, really. I just take pictures and develop 'em," he answered apprehensively.

"Isn't it a fact, young man, that you specialize in photographing beautiful women in various states of undress?"

Pat immediately realized that *nature studies* was a euphemism for nudist magazines sold at cigar stores, along with horse racing betting slips. Moore leapt to his feet. "Just a minute! What's the relevance of a teenage hobby got to do with what he observed at the Panforte residence on the night Paula Panforte was killed?"

"Counsel, approach the bench," Judge Grant ordered. They huddled at the side bar. "What's this all about, Danny?" the judge whispered.

"It's about a horny kid who specializes in taking pictures of shapely women sunbathing. His collection of photos reveals an inordinate interest in the shapely body of his neighbor, the late, lovely Mrs. Panforte," Loeb whispered intently, waving the envelope his investigator had given him. "I intend to show that this prosecution witness has surreptitiously taken more than twenty photos of Paula Panforte. He takes her picture from that fire escape outside his bedroom window. Most are of Paula sunbathing in her backyard or dressed formally for social events in gowns with plunging necklines. The camera angle the boy uses from the second story level is quite revealing. Obviously he couldn't get his pictures developed at the corner drug store for fear the pharmacist would tip off his mother that her son was creating a photo gallery of their sexy neighbor. It goes to the witness' bias to testify as he has."

"Oh, for chrissake Danny!" the DA moaned. Judge Grant shook her head, saying: "It goes to bias. But Danny, spare us the pornography."

"Of course, Your Honor," he assured.

In response to Loeb's questions about the late Mrs. Panforte, the crimson-faced boy admitted that he'd indeed photographed her and had done so without her knowledge or consent. Three of the photos showed her in two-piece sun suits, luxuriating under the Marina sun in her backyard. In one picture she was lying on her stomach on a towel, her halter untied to assure no tan line. The fourth picture, taken from the fire escape, showed her in a black formal, getting out of the '47 Chevy, bending over at her waist, her lovely, full breasts obeying gravity. Loeb passed the photos to the jurors, who studied Paula and then glared at the witness whom Loeb was portraying as a pimple faced teenage peeping Tom.

"Now, young man," Loeb resumed sternly. "You've said you heard the Panfortes yelling in their home about seven-forty-five on June 5th. Did you actually recognize Mr. and Mrs. Panforte's voices, or was all you heard just loud voices?"

The chastened boy retreated: "I can't say for certain it was them. But the voices came from their place, so I figured it must be them." Loeb pointed out that the Panforte flat had two units, and the boy's building had multiple units with windows all along the side of the building across the air space from Panforte's flat. Then he asked harshly, "How could you determine whether the loud voices were coming from the upper or lower flat of the Panforte's building or any of the many units in your mom's apartment building?"

The teenager scratched his head, perplexed at the rapid-fire questions, wanting to get out of the witness chair as quickly as possible. You could sense his adolescent mind telling him to give Loeb whatever he wanted as the surest way to escape the embarrassing exposure of his vicarious sex life to a room full of strangers. "I guess I couldn't tell where the voices came from," he answered lamely.

"Now, you've testified you saw the '47 Chevy back out of the garage during the commercial break in *The Lone Ranger* radio program. But you didn't see who was driving it, did you?"

"No, I just assumed..."

Loeb cut the boy off. "You just assumed it was Bob Panforte driving. That's okay, the cops made the same assumption, and they're a lot more experienced than you. Have you ever seen Mrs. Paula Panforte driving that Chevy?"

"Sure," Busby said with obvious discomfort.

"You've told us you heard Bob Panforte's garage door open around 10:30 p.m. Are you sure you didn't hear one of the three garage doors in your own apartment building open around 10:30 p.m.?" Loeb asked.

"I didn't...I don't...I guess I'm not sure what door it was," the boy said.

"Thank you, young man. I've no further questions."

Judge Grant excused the witness, who quickly left the courtroom with the dreadful anticipation that the newspapers would regale their readers with his collection of masturbatory photos. Happily for the lad the press didn't mention his youthful venture into soft core sin in any of their stories, discreetly preferring to allow the boy to continue on his turbulent trip through puberty, and sparing his hard working mother from learning what went on behind his teenage bedroom door other than the blaring sound of *The Lone Ranger* riding off into the sunset, crying a hearty: "Hi ho, Silver!"

Following the afternoon recess, District Attorney Moore announced that he had a quick witness that he wanted to sandwich in before calling Inspector Mike Murphy. Marjorie Peterson, a petite, pretty blonde housewife in her mid-twenties took the stand. Her thin blonde eyebrows, arched by artful tweezers, gave her pale blue eyes a wide-eyed look of amazement. Her free flowing blonde locks were framed by a navy blue lacy picture hat, and Pat felt that he'd seen her before. Then he realized that in the photo taken by the teen voyeur of sunbathing, topless Paula Panforte, there'd been another lovely young woman basking with her. And that woman was the fully clothed, full-bodied Mrs. Peterson.

From the D.A.'s questioning, the jury learned that she was married, the mother of two children and Paula's best friend since their giggling boy crazy teens at the Convent of the Sacred Heart. She and her husband Walter, or Wally as everyone called him, were social companions of Paula and Bob, including monthly card games of bridge in which they alternated as hosts at each couple's Marina homes. "When was the last time you and your husband played bridge with Paula and Bob Panforte?" Moore asked.

Her eyebrows assumed a higher arch; she bit down on her lower ruby lip and answered haltingly, "It was the Saturday before, at their house. It was their turn to host the bridge party."

"The Saturday before what, Mrs. Peterson?"

"The Saturday before she...before Paula...ah, disappeared." Her voice trembled, unable to mouth the words *before Paula died.*

"When did you learn Paula was missing?"

"Tuesday morning."

"I see. So you and your husband played cards with the Panfortes Saturday night, June 3, 1949, and you learned your friend was missing Tuesday morning, June 6, 1949, is that right?"

She nodded. "That's right."

"On the Saturday evening that you played cards at the Panfortes did you make any plans to get together the following day?"

"We were going to take a drive to the country. Bob and Paula wanted to look at houses in Marin, and they wanted us to join them. But Bob called us Sunday and canceled the trip."

Kelley realized that Moore was cutting off Bob Panforte's alibi that he hadn't dug Paula's grave on the Sunday before her disappearance. But what struck him as more significant was that Maria had speculated that something had happened in the Panforte home the weekend before her disappearance in which the motive of her killer would be found. Pat understood that Maria had assumed it was something between Bob and Paula. What was vital for Pat was that whatever had happened that caused the cancellation of the Marin County house hunting venture could only be discovered within the Panforte household. He thought of Angelina Panforte and wondered if he could somehow extend the borders of *household* to include her branch of the family.

"Mrs. Peterson, how did you learn on Tuesday that Paula was missing?" the D.A asked.

"Bob called me about 7:00 that morning and asked if Paula had spent the night at our house. I told him she hadn't. He said: 'She went to the Fox last night to see *Home of the Brave* and didn't come home.'"

"That's all, Mrs. Peterson. Thank you." The D.A. sat down.

Loeb paced behind his counsel table. "Good afternoon, Mrs. Peterson. I have just a few questions. You and your husband are close personal friends of the Panfortes, are you not?"

"Very close. Paula and I have been friends since high school and our husbands share a great interest in sports. We had lots of fun together, lots of good times."

"In fact, you and your husband spent the Memorial Day weekend with them at their Lake Tahoe summer home, did you not?"

"Yes, we did."

"Mrs. Peterson, how would you describe their relationship?"

"They were absolutely devoted to each other. They were so naturally affectionate. They'd always be holding hands or patting each other. After the baby came they seemed even more content. They always used terms of endearment. Paula called him *Darling* or *Rabbit* and he called her his *Bunny*."

"You mentioned their little baby. Were there any conversations about the baby when you were up at Lake Tahoe with them in May of this year?"

"Well, Paula was saying how she'd just stopped nursing little Bobby and how she kinda missed breast feeding. I told her I'd experienced the same thing with my kids. She and Bob talked about having another baby. I remember Bob said, 'This time I'd like a little girl.' Everything was so good then… and then… I just don't understand any of this…" Marjorie Peterson sobbed softly.

"Mrs. Peterson, you've indicated that Bob Panforte called you on Tuesday, June 6th and told you his wife had gone to the movies the previous night. Was it unusual for Paula to go to the movies alone at night?"

"No. Paula's crazy about movies ever since her dad took her to the show every week when we were in high school. Bob works up in Petaluma, so Paula often goes out without him. She always goes to the opening runs at the Fox, often by herself."

"Thank you Mrs. Peterson. I don't have any more questions," Loeb concluded, and Judge Grant excused Bob Panforte's former bridge partner.

22

Pat Kelley sat in his high-back, leather swivel chair at the court clerk's desk in Judge Lucille Grant's vacant after-hours courtroom. He had sent his wife and son home, telling them he had work to do before the next court session. The lights in the spectator section were off. Only the middle of three chandeliers illuminated Pat's desk in the Pit. It was as though the courtroom was a miniature theater after the audience, players and stage crews had left for the night. Kelley felt like the playwright contemplating a just completed performance of his work, alone on the set his imagination had created, disturbed that something was terribly flawed in his play, struggling to cure his script. His mahogany desktop was tidy, the Panforte file folder of exhibits on the right front corner of the desk. Pat's thick hands rested on the edge of the desk, framed on his left by Paula's silk stockings, bra and panties and on his right, the green cloth coat she'd been buried in. The shiny rectangle at the center of the desk was bare except for a tiny scrape of pasteboard. He reached for it and held it between his right thumb and forefinger and then dropped it in his left palm. It was a torn ticket stub. On the top of the stub was the bold-face letter *F*. The missing half of the ticket stub was undoubtedly topped with the bold-face letters, *OX*, having been torn by a Fox Theater usher and deposited as a box office receipt.

Pat thought of the fickleness of chance, the arbitrariness of accident. He had been storing the exhibits as he did every day after court adjourned. As he was about to put Paula's clothes away, something about her attire when her body was uncovered pricked his intuitive soul. On his desk he had segregated the green coat from all her other clothing. He studied her apparel, and there was something jarring about the articles. Her silk undergarments, imported from Lucca, were exquisite masterpieces of ancient artisans. In his fingertips the silk seemed possessed of the heat of a woman's skin, like the flush invitation of her inner thigh. He thought of how difficult it would have been for her husband to dress her while she was lying unconscious on the floor of their bedroom and the negating implications of carefully clothing Paula to the prosecution's time-line. He was confident that Danny Loeb would have much to say about the improbability that her husband had dressed her for entombment in his closing argument. But it was the green coat that had swaddled her opulent body in a damp grave that was so common, so unlike her sensuous elegance. It was the kind of coat you'd find on a child-burdened Sunset District mom carting her kids through a thick ocean fog to kindergarten. He had no conscious purpose when he absently reached into the coat pockets. It was as though tactile exploration of such contrasting fabrics might reveal something in Paula's final wardrobe that would testify to her last moments. When his fingertips touched the pasteboard he yanked his hand from her coat pocket as though stunned by an electric shock. "Oh my God!" he whispered to the vacant courtroom when he saw this theater ticket stub.

Pat thought of the crushing gravity of fate that *he* was the discoverer of physical evidence that Paula Brady Panforte had indeed gone to the Fox Theater as her husband had claimed. He thought of Maria and wondered how he could tell her that *his* rogue investigation had uncovered evidence that placed Paula and a vengeful pervert at the Fox Theater at the same time and the last time she'd been seen alive. Their marital tensions had intensified each time Pat had punctured a hole in the prosecution's case, and he had begun censoring his detective speculations from her to temper the withering rage she felt toward the Panfortes and keep it from scalding their intense intimacy. But this ticket stub was not theory, it was tangible, exculpatory evidence that supported Robert Panforte's claim of innocence. No matter what District Attorney Moore alleged about a bedroom altercation between husband and wife, if Loeb substantiated his client's claim that she'd left their home alive, Bob Panforte was innocent. To this point, Loeb only had his client's word that Paula had gone to the show and the dead girl's best friend indicating that it was not unusual for Paula to go downtown alone, particularly for premieres at the Fox. This ticket stub in Paula's coat pocket supplied compelling credence to her husband's story.

In the mute courtroom, Pat grappled with the consequences to his conscience. He reached down into the bottom left-hand drawer of his desk and pulled out a silver pint flask. He took a shot of Scotch, calmed himself and set his formidable mind to the task of determining what he'd actually discovered and defining what to do with it.

He needed to exhaust the possibilities as to how this Fox ticket stub got into Paula's coat pocket. His initial and obvious impression was that she'd put it there as she entered the Fox to see the opening of *Home of the Brave* on Monday, June 5, 1949. If the jury came to the same conclusion, they'd justly acquit young Panforte. But there were other possibilities, he thought. Dog- shit-watering neighbor Pierce said Panforte had told him he was going to the show to pick up his wife. Suppose Bob Panforte had driven to the Fox, purchased the ticket, torn it in half and planted it in her coat? It doesn't play, Pat said to himself. Bob Panforte's not bright enough to appreciate the persuasive force of exculpatory evidence much less conceive a plan to plant it on his wife. And if he did kill and bury her at Mt. Tam he never expected they'd ever find her body, so he'd never even think it important to manufacture evidence of her visit to the Fox. Besides he would have never so haplessly guided the cops to her hidden burial site. Most significantly, O'Day and Murphy never found the stub after they dug up her body. *Only now, months after they exhumed her, does it appear and I'm the one who finds it!* Pat mused without irony. Of course it's just a tiny scrap of paper, and it's possible the homicide boys could have missed it, but that's unlikely. They're legendary for their handling of crime scene evidence and they had checked her things numerous times. While homicide detectives have been known to suppress evidence that contradicts the theory of their case, leaving such a piece of evidence for later discovery was absurd. Prior to Panforte's indictment O'Day and Murphy were not the least bit invested in convicting him. Pat doubted that O'Day and Murphy would ever tarnish the integrity of their investigations, and if they had, they'd have destroyed the stub the moment they found it. It's unlikely they simply missed it, but then the Coroner would also have had to miss it. Unless....

Unless it wasn't in her pocket when they found her. What if it was planted *after* Paula's personal affects had come into the custody of the Homicide Detail? Pat thought. Box office stubs were not dated or numbered, so anonymously acquiring a Fox ticket at or around Panforte's indictment was simple. Pat took another swig of Scotch and played out another scenario in his mind. Panforte's defense team had access to all the evidence, including Paula's green coat, during pretrial discovery. However, the Homicide Detail maintained the chain of custody religiously and Danny Loeb would never risk the consequences of tampering with evidence in police custody in a capital case. Once the trial had commenced the court clerk took custody of the evidence. It had been years since Kelley had clerked a trial. He was the chief executive of the Superior Court, responsibly managing judges, hundreds of court attaches and thousands of litigants, and now he regretted that he'd appointed himself as a file clerk in order to become an intimate in the Panforte trial. He had successfully infiltrated the inner sanctum of the trial by attending in chambers meetings secreted from the press and public. While court reporters were expected to participate in these secret sessions, court clerks were charged with remaining in the courtroom tending to the evidence so as to assure its integrity. Because of his position and reputation no one questioned Kelley sitting in on confidential or off-the-record court sessions.

Pat concluded that the defense must have slipped the ticket stub into Paula's coat pocket at some point during the trial while the evidence was his clerical responsibility, but when he was in chambers. But who on the defense team would have had the opportunity and sufficiently degraded ethics to plant it, Pat asked himself. He doubted that Loeb had actually done the deed since he was in chambers with Kelley. Moreover, whatever the state of Danny Loeb's morals he wasn't about to tamper with evidence in a capital case since to do so would subject him to a seat in the gas chamber from which he was attempting to detour his client. As for the Defendant, he was under constant scrutiny by bailiff McCann, the press and public. One of the first lessons a defendant was taught by his lawyer was that he'd be under observation in court and his cell twenty-four hours a day. How he reacts, to whom he speaks, how he looks to others may have decisive consequences on his case. There was no chance Bob Panforte had anything to do with this stub and unlikely that he even knew about. For the moment, Pat ruled out Fred Panforte as the culprit, because as a spectator he did not have access to the Pit. That left Panforte's private investigator David London, who had ample opportunity and sufficiently degraded ethics to plant it while Pat attended in-chambers discussions with the court and counsel.

London had free access to the Pit and evidentiary items. It would have taken London but a second to plant the stub in Paula's coat pocket. It was one of the unwritten rules of private investigators to do the dirty work of criminal defense in such a manner that the defense lawyers who hired them always had deniability. It was standard courtroom procedure for the clerk to remain with the exhibits while the lawyers and judge discussed legal issues. To have done so would have defeated Kelley's secret purpose of getting as close to the trial participants as possible.

Perhaps this was the real reason the defense had not protested Kelley clerking the Panforte trial, even though Loeb and London knew that Bertolli was his father-in-law and that Kelley was conducting his own private investigation of the case. It was all so deviously simple, Pat thought. The defense knew there was a good chance that the ticket stub would not be discovered until the exhibits were brought into the jury room. In the jury's secret deliberations it would do its mischief, providing proof that Paula was alive at the Fox while her husband was at home with their baby. This tiny piece of refuse would establish in the jury's mind that Robert Panforte couldn't have killed his wife!

The problem with pinning this breach of legal ethics on David London alone was that a private investigator didn't undertake any action unless directed by defense counsel or the client himself. More significantly, a private eye's mercenary nature would require a bounty-like bonus for such an extraordinary risk. Since Pat had excluded Danny Loeb from the conspiracy, that left only the client. But really, who was the client? Bob Panforte possessed neither the intelligence nor guile to conceive such a scheme. His father on the other hand had the ruthlessness to carry it off. Viewing Fred Panforte as the *true client* in the case suggested to Pat that it was he who had conspired with David London to plant the evidence.

But London also must have anticipated that Kelley might discover the stub during the trial. If he did, the private detective was confident that Kelley would do or say nothing. It was in the nature of bureaucrats that they covered their mistakes with silence. Moreover, to call the Court's attention to this tainted evidence implicated Kelley in clerical incompetence. It was, after all, the clerk's most important responsibility to preserve the pristine veracity of items of evidence. Since only the defense and Pat knew of this liberating ticket stub, it was in Kelley's vital interest in keeping his job to do nothing about it. But doing nothing was not Pat Kelley's nature. To him it seemed obscene that the jury was in danger of being corrupted by this phony, though cleverly manufactured evidence. Unlike his wife he was not repelled by the thought that a jury might find Bob Panforte innocent. After all, his own investigation had raised serious doubts about the young man's guilt. What real harm occurred if the jury found the right and just result for the wrong reasons? Juries often did so, and Pat believed that this was the true genius of citizen judges. They almost always got it right. Perhaps just this one time he should step back and passively concede that Fred Panforte's legal team had trapped him just as they had ensnared Bertolli in a moral quandary more than two decades earlier.

He thought of Maria and her critique that he considered truth a species and she, a genus. What if he addressed the truth of the Fox ticket and his relation to it? If he told the truth, could his wife handle it? Would his son understand that moral implications often breed dire consequences? Alone in a dimly lit vacant courtroom, Pat searched for Maria's truth in the hope that in her deep wounded eyes he might find his own. He picked up the ticket stub from his desk and returned it to Paula's coat pocket. He plotted a meeting with Judge Lucille Grant and the lawyers in chambers before resuming the trial, at which he would tell the unvarnished truth about his discovery of the Fox ticket stub. In his mind he played out the full scenario with the judge and both lawyers. He would tell Judge Grant how he'd discovered the ticket stub. He would not say or even imply that the defense had been responsible for this surprise appearance of innocence proclaiming evidence. Both he and Loeb's investigator realized that the Chief Clerk could never prove that evidence had been tampered with, and that to accuse so distinguished a lawyer as Loeb would surely cost Kelley his job. So he would take full responsibility on himself. He would tell the judge and counsel that he had failed to completely inventory all the items of evidence received from Inspector Murphy. By admitting this clerical error the chain of physical custody of the ticket stub would remain at issue. Loeb would point out to the Judge that the clerk would have to take the witness stand and testify to his mishandling of the evidence.

Judge Grant would be faced with only two choices. She could order Kelley to take the stand, publicly admit his incompetence before his wife and kid, and send the stub and Loeb's Jack Hill stalker theory to the jury. She had properly forbidden Loeb from calling Hill to the stand, but now the Chief Clerk of the Superior Court would be this ex-con's surrogate! Judge Grant's other choice would be to bar Kelley, as a court employee, from testifying, refuse to admit the stub into evidence and declare a mistrial because of his mishandling of evidence. At Panforte's retrial the ticket stub and stalker theory would be fair game for the defense. Either decision by Judge Grant would put Pat Kelley's Irish face on the front pages of the four daily papers, along with an obligatory, innuendo-filled article about the Court's chief administrator appointing himself a filing clerk in a capital case. In either case, Pat Kelley's career as Chief Clerk was finished. He felt a touch of nausea that he would fall on his sword because he could not tolerate his beloved justice system being stained by indelible corruption.

Pat reached into Paula's coat pocket and removed the Fox stub and laid it on the desktop. He removed a small white envelope from the top desk drawer and placed it next to the stub. He shook his head and sighed deeply, accepting that he had been so brilliantly set up. He thought of Maria and the pain that she bore from Loeb's rescue of old man Panforte through the humiliation of her father. In a matter of hours her agony would become unbearable as Danny Loeb would redeem young Panforte by the debasement of her husband. Pat was confounded by Maria's truth - justice and truth were at war.

Pat's employment of the Socratic method was not merely a pedagogic device for stimulating his family and friends. He was a dialectical thinker who believed that the clash of thesis and anti-thesis conceived emerging truth as assuredly as conflicting courtroom advocates midwifed the peoples' justice. As he subjected the intellectual design of this plot to his rigorous dialectics, Pat appreciated the brilliance of the logic and the depth of comprehension of his fundamental nature. Of course, Fred Panforte knew little about Pat other than he had been kind to his wife and respectful of him. He probably considered Pat little more than a common laborer who wore a suit and tie to work. It was just such common men who Fred Panforte had enlisted in his stock coup against Bertolli. But David London, like everyone who worked at the Hall, knew Kelley well. It was this knowledge that made the plan failsafe. Once Panforte's investigator had secreted the ticket in Paula's burial coat there was only one person who could prevent it from getting into the jury room – the court clerk who controlled all the exhibits. But Kelley was a court clerk in name only. He was a handsomely paid political appointee who obtained and maintained his position by the discreet manipulation of other, more powerful politicians. Should he discover this tainted ticket during the course of the trial he would decide his course of action as a political man, not a bumbling bureaucrat, London had reasoned. It's why Kelley will probably do nothing, why he'll remain silent and keep the planted evidence a secret between the defense and himself, the investigator had figured. "It's the smart thing to do. God knows there's not a better mind in the courthouse than Kelley's. It's the right political move, not to move at all," Pat imagined London thinking. But should Kelley surrender to his sense of moral integrity, should he be afflicted with the same character flaw of unassailable honesty that infected his father-in-law, London would still have his way. It was at this moment that Pat perceived the sheer perfection of the scheme. Initially he'd thought that he was confronted with only two dreadful choices – one that challenged his character and the other that threatened his career. But through his dialectical microscope Pat now saw that London had created a single synthesis. Whatever Pat did or didn't do, the defense would get that ticket into the jury room and block Robert Panforte's path to the gallows.

A small smile crept over his face as he formulated his antithesis to this thesis. Intrinsic to its logic was the assumption that men like Kelley and Bertolli never change, that strong men like them always act in conformity with their natures. Pat decided to shatter these assumptions about him with one bold, undetectable move. The Fox ticket stub would never be seen by the jurors. Only he and part of the defense knew of its existence, and therefore he could destroy this devilish scrap of pasteboard with the same impunity Fred Panforte and London had sought to contaminate the jury with it. They could never protest that the court clerk had suppressed exculpatory evidence because they would be exposed as the planters of that evidence. Pat didn't rationalize his decision to confiscate the ticket on the basis that his deceit was necessary to combat defense dishonesty. Maria always told their kids that two wrongs don't make a right, and Pat accepted that his sin negating London's didn't make him a saint. The defense had attempted to foist phony evidence on the jury by using him as their tool. Now he returned the favor by stealing this key to the jury room without the spurious rationalization that his unethical act was righteous because of his morally superior motives.

Once he had decided to blunt this evidentiary trick, Pat Kelley realized that he had taken an irrevocable step down a path with no clear or certain ending. His doubts about Bob Panforte's guilt had been shaken by this attempt to pimp him to prostitute the jury. He now accepted that Panforte's father was in full play and that Fred's mercilessly calculating mind confronted Pat's thoughtfulness. But Pat Kelley wasn't Bertolli. Or was he, he asked himself. He picked up the envelope and the Fox ticket stub from the desk. He slipped the stub into the envelope and sealed it. He scribbled five words on the face of the envelope, signed and dated it. He put it in his inside suit coat pocket, turned off the courtroom light and headed for his wife's bed.

23

A thin wisp of morning fog floated past a courtroom window whispering a break in the Indian summer heat spell. Angelina Panforte was now applying make-up to her ivory skin to conceal the darkening circles under her dulling aqua eyes. Inspector Mike Murphy replaced his mentor/partner on the witness stand. His warm tenor voice embroidered with a Cork brogue inferred that his many hours with Bob Panforte were a trustworthy account and that he was not a severely judgmental man. While O'Day's credibility was projected by his inordinate self-discipline, Murphy engendered credence with his relaxed storyteller's air and a bright-eyed sense of whimsy, no matter how gruesome the subject of his comments. District Attorney Moore used Murphy to introduce twenty-five photographs of the burial scene. Each photograph was passed to the jurors for their individual inspection. As picture after picture passed the sight of the jurors, Panforte put his elbows on the defense table and rubbed his forehead. Somewhere down in an alley behind the Hall of Justice a mechanic was testing a police squad car siren. About a half dozen times the siren emitted a low groan, providing surrogate sobs for Eileen Brady and Angelina Panforte. When the jury completed their examination of the comprehensive photo display taken at Mt. Tamalpais, District Attorney Moore introduced a pair of dark gray slacks and a pair of heavily soiled garden gloves seized by Inspector Murphy from what the DA called "secret compartments" in Panforte's home. He asked Murphy if he'd had any experience in the building and construction trades, and Murphy told the jury he'd been apprenticed to his father, a journeyman carpenter in Ireland, until he was nineteen years-old.

He explained that he discovered Panforte's trousers in the area behind the laundry chute. They were located on a shelf-like board held in place by mounting brackets on each side. The board was oak, whereas the rest of the utility room was knotty pine. The shelf board could be slipped in and out, and Murphy concluded that it had been installed after the room's construction had been completed. Murphy said he found the soiled garden gloves in an enclosed alleyway running the length of the side of Panforte's house. Under a stair leading from the backyard to the alleyway, Panforte told him to feel for a two-by-four and push it on the right corner. He did and it turned out to be a false support. He described it as a swiveling device on which the plank rotated. Moore asked him if he could tell when these "secret compartments" had been constructed. Murphy testified that the remodeling of the utility room had been completed by February 3, 1949 and the building inspectors made no mention of these two building modifications. As for Panforte constructing these "hiding compartments" after he'd reported his wife missing, Murphy said he wouldn't have had enough time to complete the task.

"Thank you, Inspector," The DA said. "Your witness." Moore tendered the witness to Loeb without mentioning anything about Petaluma.

Terry Kelley patted his mother's hand, whispered something to her and she feebly smiled as Loeb rose to cross-examine the literate jazz loving cop. Loeb approached the witness stand, eyed Inspector Murphy respectfully and picked up the stack of photographs, studying each one. "Damned mad," Loeb said to no one in particular. "I believe you said Bob Panforte was damned mad at his wife that night in their bedroom, is that right, Inspector?"

"That's what he said, counselor." Loeb paced back and forth in front of the jury rail and asked, "Inspector Murphy, in your considerable experience as a homicide detective have you found that men who abuse their wives do so on a frequent and habitual basis?"

"That's invariably the case. It's also likely that the beatings only stop when one spouse kills the other," Murphy somberly.

"I gather, Inspector, that you thoroughly investigated Bob and Paula Panforte's marriage, including interviewing Brady and Panforte family members and all their acquaintances. Did you learn of a single incident in which Bob Panforte ever attacked his wife?"

Looking directly at the jury, Murphy replied, "No, sir, we didn't." Loeb picked up his client's gray trousers and garden gloves and plopped them on the witness table in front of Inspector Murphy. He said, "Now, if I understand your testimony, Inspector, you insist that the laundry chute addition and swivel device in the alleyway were designed by Bob Panforte as 'secret compartments,' that he built them before reporting his wife missing, and that their purpose was to conceal evidence of his planned murder of his wife. I gather, Inspector, that you never graduated beyond the rank of teenage apprentice to your Dad?"

Murphy smiled, "That's right."

"Let's talk about the compartment near the laundry chute where you found his trousers. It's located between the laundry chute down which dirty clothes are dropped and the washing machine itself. You fellas call it a 'secret compartment.' Aren't we talking about a simple shelf?"

"It is a shelf, but its location is obscured by the laundry chute. What purpose would a shelf serve at that location other than to conceal items?" Murphy gratuitously added.

"How 'bout being used to segregate items to be washed? You may have been an aspiring carpenter, Inspector, but are you claiming expertise as a maid or a housewife as well?"

To courtroom laughter, Murphy smiled: "When I was a boy in Ireland we didn't have washing machines, but that doesn't mean we lived in peat huts."

"I'm sure you didn't, Inspector. But surely you know that different fabrics require different detergents and different water temperatures. You wouldn't expect Bob Panforte's trousers to be washed with his wife's expensive, imported silk underwear, would you?"

"I suppose not."

"Nor would you expect to find a small utility shelf on home construction plans or referenced in a room remodeling, would you?"

"Probably not."

Waving the soiled garden gloves, Loeb asked, "Did you notice a large barbecue pit in the backyard near that alleyway stair?"

"Yes, we did."

"And you knew that Bob Panforte did most of the cooking for his family and considers himself an excellent barbecue chef. Did you also notice a fifty pound bag of mesquite a few feet from the barbecue pit?"

"Yeah."

Handing the gloves to Murphy, Loeb asked, "Inspector, look closely at these gloves. They're stained not only with the soils of gardening, but covered with mesquite and ashes from frequent barbecues as well, aren't they?"

"Obviously."

"What about barbecue tools? Did you find any long spatulas, prongs or forks utilized in barbecuing?"

"We did."

"Where, Inspector, where?

"After I found the gloves under the stair I pushed the rotating device and barbecue tools appeared on it."

"Were the tools clean, or dirty like these gloves?"

"Clean. They'd been washed."

"Inspector, did it occur to you that this rotating device under the stair, near the barbecue pit, was designed as a compartment to store washed barbecue tools and segregate them from filthy barbecue gloves?"

"Not until this moment," Murphy conceded.

"So both of these modest bits of home owner improvements have perfectly utilitarian functions, having nothing to do with creating secret places to hide evidence of terrible crimes, do they?"

"I suppose."

Loeb threw the soiled gloves on the prosecution's table, pulled his chair out and asked, "By the way, did you find any blood on these gloves?"

Murphy shook his head. "No, we didn't."

After the courtroom had emptied, Bailiff McCann came out of chambers and announced that one of the jurors had an illness in his family, so Judge Grant ordered the trial recessed for a day. In the court corridor spectators were filing to the elevators and the press boys were stuffing themselves into a bank of public telephone booths, calling in their version of the case against Robert Panforte. The Brady family and Panforte's parents had left in two different elevators, the Chief Clerk having briefed the elevator operators to segregate them. Maria and Terry Kelley and Joe Desmond were talking with Inspector Murphy in the middle of the corridor. Terry said something to Murphy and the burly cop laughed and ruffled his thick hand through Terry's hair. Maria quickly endorsed the quality of Murphy's work. "You did fine, Mike. You were so forthright, and the jury followed every word," she said, affectionately squeezing Murphy's arm. Murphy's face flushed, either from humility or a lovely woman's spontaneous touch. Maria's tactile proclivity was an absolutely innocent aspect of her personality, no more conscious than an Italian talking with his hands or an Irishmen talking too much. But her beauty was so classic and her movements so consistently, though vaguely sensuous, that her touch, however fleeting, had an effect of which she was unaware and which the recipient of her demonstrative grace was incapable of easily dismissing. Murphy said, "I just hope Joe got the words down. That damn Loeb's the fastest talker who's ever cross-examined me. And he's good, the best I've ever faced."

"He's a piece of cake," Joe assured. "It's that damn brogue of yours that's the problem."

Maria protested, "Oh, nonsense, Joe! Mike's a poet and you know it! You've been listening to lawyers too long. I think Loeb's manner of speaking so quickly is a device to confuse. And it didn't work at all with Mike."

"I don't know if the fast talking Mr. Loeb does it intentionally, but Mom's right. He didn't lay a glove on you," Terry Kelley chimed in.

"Maybe so, kid. But the real issue is whether we laid some gloves on his client. By the way, congratulations, Terry," Murphy said.

"For what?" the boy asked.

"Well, according to your dad, today you set a personal record for the longest period of sustained silence since you were eighteen months-old."

"Who's he to talk about being quiet?" Terry retorted. "He hasn't said word one since the first day of the trial. Besides, I talk to Danny..."

"Mr. Loeb," his mother corrected.

"I talk to Mr. Loeb and Mi...the D.A. and even the press guys all the time. That ought to count for something. All Dad does is put those little tags on pieces of evidence."

Pat Kelley had stepped out of chambers and overheard his son describing accurately his apparent role in the Panforte case. He detected boyish anger in the narrowing of Terry's expansive hazel eyes. Pat sensed his son's pique was not a reaction to being needled by Inspector Murphy about his natural loquaciousness. Rather, it arose from a frustration his boy did not then comprehend nor which his father anticipated when he decided to provide Terry the opportunity to witness his apparent irrelevance in a trial about life and death. Pat had planned that his son's daily presence at the Panforte trial would diminish the idolatry that often colored the vision young boys held of particularly brilliant fathers. He was certain Terry would compare the dramatic behavior of Moore and Loeb to his stationary silence as an obscure courtroom clerk. In such an unfavorable comparison, his son would discover that indigenous aptitudes without avenues of development would find no medium of expression. Once Terry discovered that his innate gifts of eloquence in speech and profundity of thought did not, of themselves, guarantee a forum of dissemination, he'd realize there's a price to pay if he wished to surpass his father. He didn't want

Terry to replicate his youthful decision to find security in civil service. He'd concluded that the Panforte trial would teach Terry that dues were required of those who aspire to a dominant place in the public arena. And he was confident his son's destiny was center stage; that the boy could never be just a necessary but rarely noticed prop in life's enduring drama.

But plans of parents, particularly fathers, often tap into unanticipated emotional wells within their children. He recalled Eileen Brady's remark to him after her daughter's funeral about her infant grandson. *"Who truly knows what a child understands or when they understand it? Their little hearts are a secret to us. We never know what they hear or how and when we scar them."* Terry, like his dad, couldn't speak in the courtroom. He couldn't contest with Loeb for the life of Panforte's son. He couldn't fight for his mom and conquer the man who had degraded her father and, by so doing, stained her loving soul. If he, like his father, couldn't be heard, if he was required to sit passively while his mother was torn by a ripe tide of emotions, was not his nature as a male negated before he even entered manhood? Perhaps it was this contradiction that engendered his anger at Murphy's comment on his polite courtroom deportment, Pat feared.

For a rare moment in his life Pat felt the pangs of guilt. Not only was his son displaying emotional disturbance, but for the first time in their marriage Pat was keeping secrets from his wife. For if he disclosed all that he had learned, he'd be required to tell her his deepest suspicion. He would be compelled to tell that he suspected that Robert Panforte was more pawn than perpetrator.

A suddenly calmed Terry asked his father how he thought the case was going. "So far it's a tie," Pat replied blandly.

"Really?" Maria challenged. Pat explained: "Well, you've got the Coroner unable to establish the time of death, so he has to concede that he doesn't know where Paula died. Obviously Moore wants the jury to believe that Panforte knocked her unconscious, stuffed her in the trunk of his Chevy and buried her alive over in Marin. The problem is *where* was she when the fatal blow was administered."

"*Administered?* Don't you mean *struck*, darling?" Maria interrupted, uncharacteristic sarcasm in her voice. Pat nodded, smiled sheepishly, "You're right, honey. Paula was struck a skull-crushing blow with an unknown instrument similar to a Chevy jack handle, a piece of pipe, a pistol barrel, and so on *ad infinitum*."

"So if Panforte struck her head *after* laying her body in the grave, while she was still breathing, you're not suggesting it's hyperbole that he buried her alive, are you?" Maria said.

"Of course not," Pat said. "But Dr. Rosenberg admits that there were numerous objects that could have caused the fatal wound. And remember, Maria, she was drunk! All I'm suggesting is that both sides' version of what happened is credible. To convict, the DA needs more than that."

"So what you're saying, Dad, is a tie base goes to the runner," Terry said.

"Precisely!" Pat said, accepting his son's baseball metaphor as an escape from his wife's perceptible wrath. "And that's all I'm saying, Maria. And what about Panforte's soiled gloves? They were the only items of clothing not washed, and there was no blood on them!"

"But Dad," Terry persisted. "What about Paula's bruised breasts? I'm not saying Panforte did it, but you gotta admit Dr. Rosenberg's theory that some guy pounded on her breasts is more logical than her falling flat on her face."

"Terry, logic knows no gradations. It's either logical or illogical," Pat said.

"But *truth* does recognize degrees," Maria said. Then she segued the dialogue away from Paula's anatomy, saying: "What about Ed O'Day's timeline experiment? If Ed's right, Panforte had to find and dig the grave over the weekend. And his bridge partner, that Peterson woman, said that he canceled their plans to go house hunting in Marin on Sunday. I'll bet something happened after the bridge game and that Panforte dug her grave that weekend, planning to kill her. Do you think that's a tie, darling?"

Pat mentally conceded Maria's point and he was actually pleased that she was theorizing beyond the borders of the courtroom. He was encouraged that she, like he, was searching for the motive of Paula's killer, and her intuition that something had happened in the Panforte household made sense to him. Thus far, however, he'd been unable to get Angelina Panforte alone to probe into the Panforte family weekend. Before Pat felt comfortable responding, Terry interjected, "But Mom, Inspector O'Day's whole timeline depends on that jerk, Busby! No one's gonna believe the testimony of a teenager who still listens to *The Lone Ranger!*"

"Besides," Pat added. "Mrs. Peterson, Paula's best friend, made it clear that the Panfortes were devoted to each other, talking about another baby and the like. Where's the motive for your speculation that something happened the weekend before Paula disappeared, Maria?"

Maria lit a cigarette, blew a blue stream of smoke and said softly, "Pat, you and your courts see motive as a cause of behavior. I see it as more. I see motive as an indication of character. To believe that Paula went to the movies after her husband bloodied her nose, even accidentally, you have to ask yourself: What kind of a mother would leave her baby home alone with her drunken, perhaps abusive, spouse? Conversely, to believe Bob Panforte that he drove downtown to pick up his wife you've got to ask this question: What kind of father leaves his seven-month-old son alone at home?"

"But Maria," Pat protested. "These kids are social animals and they've got Lillian Foley living downstairs as a twenty-four hour nanny."

"That's precisely my point," Maria purred. "Of course Paula would have asked Aunt Lil to sit with her baby. But she couldn't, because she was already dead or unconscious!"

"You gotta remember, honey, that Panforte had a big heat on. He even admitted to Mike Murphy that he was ashamed that he'd forgotten about his kid when he went to pick her up from the movies." Maria Bertolli Kelley crushed her cigarette into a floor ashtray. Her eyes were riveted on her husband. In a steady, soft voice she said: "Pat, have you ever in your life been so drunk that you forgot you had babies to care for?" Pat Kelley sighed deeply and shook his head.

24

A brilliant morning sun sweated the barely swaying palms of Mission Dolores Park, promising a relaxing day for Joe Desmond from the stress of taking down the conflicting words of the Panforte trial. He had decided to take the day off from transcribing Pat Kelley's translations of his father-in-law's papers. However his respite from Kelley family history and the trial was short-lived when Pat called his apartment and told him to meet him at Shanty Malone's saloon at noon. Joe asked what it was about and Pat said he couldn't talk about it on the phone. When he arrived at Shanty's, Pat was sipping a beer at a corner table. "What's up?" Joe asked.

"I need you to do an undercover job with me," Pat said. Joe asked him what he had in mind and Pat said, "I checked this fella Hill's bail records and found out Frank Cavaretta's bondsman posted his bail. Caverretta gave me the low-down on this guy. Cavaretta says Hill's got a show business front for a prostitution scam. I thought he'd been busted for solicitation of a vice cop, but the actual charges are felony pimping and pandering. Hill claims he's an artist's manager for an act at Finocchio's, a cabaret act who goes by the name of Contessa…"

"Wait a minute Pat! You're telling me this guy Hill's got a stable of female impersonators?" Joe said. Showing rare impatience, Pat said, "Just listen! He hasn't got a stable, just this one performer. Apparently she –he – it is a real looker. I talked to Rocco Casselli, the night manager at Finocchio's, and he says Hill's been pimping her on the side. Finocchio's management doesn't tolerate any of their queens moonlighting on the street. As Rocco put it: 'That's the surest way to blow off our liquor license.' So they canned Contessa and suggested she get out of town.

"Rocco said Hill's coming by the club this afternoon to pick up her stuff. He's arranged for us to meet with him. Rocco told him we had connections on the Sunset Strip nightclub scene, and we might be able to book Contessa down south."

"Jesus, Pat! Don't tell me I gotta wear a dress!"

Kelley grinned, "No, you're gonna be my muscle. I want Hill to think we're shady Sunset Strip thugs. Just act tough and dumb."

"Kinda type casting aren't you? I'm game, let's go," Joe said. From under his coat Pat removed a .38 snub nose revolver wrapped in a shoulder holster. He told Joe to go into the restroom and strap it on under his sport coat. Joe's eyes widened and Pat said, "It's just a prop."

They walked the few blocks up to Broadway, and Rocco Casselli took them backstage to the dressing rooms. He introduced Kelley to Jack Hill as "Jake" from L.A. Hill was a bit shorter than Pat with curly, unkempt brown hair and a pockmarked face. Pointing his thumb at Desmond he drawled, "So who's he?"

"My associate," Kelley answered. "He gotta name?" Hill asked.

"Yeah," Desmond said, giving him his best George Raft scowl. "First name's *My*. Family name's *Associate*."

"Ah'll just call ya' all *Mistah Ass*," Hill hissed.

"That's not very wise, Hill," Pat suggested. "My associate's not fond of your home state. He did stockade time in Fort Hood, so he's overly sensitive to your Texas accent." On cue, Joe unbuttoned his jacket to let the beady-eyed little prick see that he was packing. "No offense, suh," Hill said to Joe. "Actually, you a lot like that movie actor I saw in *Home of the Brave*. Frank Lovejoy, I think." Desmond grunted, deferring the dialogue to Pat.

"Your business is with me," Kelley said. Then he pointed to an eight-by-ten glossy taped to the dressing table mirror and said, "Is that your Contessa?" Hill lit a cigarette and nodded.

But it was two snapshots next to the glossy of Hill's drag queen that arrested Pat's attention. He knew that female impersonators selected pictures of real women as models to design their transformation of gender appearance. On the dressing room table was a white bust with Contessa's auburn wig on it. There was a padded bra that replicated the breasts form of the woman in the two snapshots pasted to the dressing room mirror. Pat had seen pictures like these before and the woman in them was unmistakably Paula Panforte! She had been Hill's model for designing Contessa's stage persona. Even more important was a photo of Paula in her backyard, lying on her back, bathing in the Marina sun - topless. It was obviously part of the series of photos teenager Damon Busby had taken of his sexy neighbor. That meant that Danny Loeb's investigator had been tipped of by Hill to Busby's voyeurism, and no doubt Hill was the source of the pictures Loeb had used in his cross examination of the teenager. Loeb had revealed on the opening day of the trial that David London had interviewed Hill in City Jail. Given the press clippings of Paula's murder the vice squad had found in Hill's apartment, it's likely that this ex-con, sometime pimp contacted the Panforte defense with a quid pro quid offer - Paula's photos in exchange for Danny Loeb's legal help extracting Hill from his most recent collar. It also meant that Hill must have had Paula under some kind of surveillance at her home to have acquired young Busby's peep shots. Perhaps Hill had been stalking her, Kelley thought.

Pat didn't confront Hill with what he'd discovered in Contessa's dressing room at Finocchio's. Instead he probed Hill's recent arrest. "Let's cut the bullshit, Hill," he said. "You and your *artist* got busted by Vice, so Rocco's kicked you out. You're not gonna work in this town anymore and who's gonna book your act with charges pending?"

"Don't worry about the charges, Jake," Hill said, crushing his cigarette out. "Really?" Pat said.

"The cops are gonna drop all charges. I guess they ah… are a little embarrassed that one of their finest tried to score a whore with a big ole dick," Hill grinned, showing yellow teeth.

Kelley stood up and Desmond immediately followed his lead. Pat said, "When you've straightened out your legal problems, let Rocco know. He'll know how to contact me. Maybe we can talk then."

Outside on Broadway Desmond didn't needed Pat's usual post-mortem on the significance of the facts they had just learned. There was no question that Jack Hill was obsessed with Brady's daughter, so much so that he'd created a male parody of her. As they walked back to the Hall of Justice, Pat commented on a fact that Joe had missed. Hill had said that Joe resembled movie star Frank Lovejoy in *Home of the Brave*. "That movie opened at the Fox on Monday, June 5th," Pat said. And that meant that the little cracker was hanging around Paula's home *and* her favorite movie house close to the time that Bob Panforte claimed she'd gone to the show.

What was even more interesting to Pat's speculative mind was the evolving nature of ex-con Hill's relationship with the Panforte defense. Pat had no doubt that Danny Loeb had retained Hill's defense lawyer and paid him with Fred Panforte's money in exchange for Hill cooperating with the defense investigator. Pat suspected that Hill provided more than a few covert photos of Paula sunbathing to London with which to impeach young Busby. By Jack Hill's own admission, he had seen *Home of the Brave* at the Fox at or about the same time Bob Panforte placed his wife at that movie. Perhaps Jack Hill was the original source of the Fox ticket stub that the defense had planted in Paula's coat. With Paula's slaying on the front pages, neither Fred Panforte nor David London was reckless enough to purchase a box office ticket after the fact. But if Hill had been at the show the night Paula disappeared, he could have offered *his stub* for David London's Panforte defense use!

Pat had no doubt that Jack Hill was a slimy opportunist. He had long recognized a class of criminals who are small time thugs who spend their lives in and out of jails, their street days scamming on the periphery of low level vice. Frequent arrests are an occupational hazard for such punks, and they work off their beefs informing on fellow conspirators or finking on cellmates by claiming they overheard a jailhouse confession. Both prosecution and defense knew these men were unreliable — many pathological liars — but they were as much a part of the criminal justice system as a bailiff or a court reporter. Some, presumably like Hill, were occasionally clever and sold their services to the defense. Pat was convinced that Jack Hill was the source of Paula's photos and the planted ticket stub. He had also realized that the more he explored Robert Panforte's persona beyond his father's control, the more curious he was about Fred Panforte's activities when father and son were not together at work or home.

Shortly before the trial resumed on Thursday at noon, Pat and Terry Kelley met Joe Desmond in chambers. Terry handed Joe a paper bag and said, "My mom got a sandwich for you at Molinari's. She says it's not good for you to skip lunch when you're under a lot of pressure.

"Thanks." Joe unwrapped a prosciutto sandwich on sourdough. "Where's your mom?" he asked.

"She went to school to pick up my homework and get the lesson plan from Sister Beatrice," Terry replied. Maria had arranged with his school principal to act as Terry's tutor during his absence from class to attend the Panforte trial. One of Pat Kelley's purposes for having Terry sit through the celebrated trial had been achieved. The boy threw himself into his schoolwork with a vigor he'd never before displayed. Every evening after court he completed his homework assignments before dinner, and after he and his sisters did the dishes, he'd spend two hours under his mother's expert tutelage quickly surpassing his classmates' academic performances. So creative were

Maria's pedagogic methods and so diligently did Terry work during the trial, that he brought home his first all *A's* report card, save for a *C* in deportment. More importantly for his father, however, was Terry's development of disciplined study habits during his parentally authorized truancy. In part, Terry's new appreciation for academics was motivated by his desire to remain out of the classroom and in the courtroom, and he knew his father would promptly exile him back to school if his academic performance slipped in the slightest. Pat also believed that having Maria as this teacher exposed him to the joy of intellectual pursuit. As the special child of the first *Precious One*, Maria molded her son's education as the third generation to follow Father Agnello's hunger for knowledge. She and Pat were intent on forming a Renaissance man out of their mischievous, brilliant son. From the Panforte trial through post-graduate studies, Terry's scholastic grades recognized only two letters in the alphabet. In matters academic he achieved straight *A's*. As for conduct, he was marginal.

The chambers door swung open and Bailiff McCann delivered Maria Kelley. "Joe, did you eat your lunch?" she asked.

"Sure did, and thanks. But next time have 'em put mayo on it," he said.

"Nonsense. Only a barbarian would put mayonnaise on prosciutto," she quipped.

"Or an Irishman," Pat said.

"That's redundant, darling," Maria grinned, as they all headed for the courtroom.

District Attorney Moore announced: "Your Honor, the People are prepared to rest, subject to the jury being taken out to view the scene of Paula Brady Panforte's grave on Mt. Tamalpais." A low collective gasp arose from the spectators. Angelina Panforte clamped her small hand over her mouth to still her groan and the press boys scribbled furiously on their notepads. Before Loeb could bellow an outraged objection, Judge Grant said firmly: "I'm sure that both sides want to discuss this with the Court. So here's what we'll do. I'll release the jury and instruct them to assemble at ten tomorrow morning to resume the trial. I'll meet with counsel in chambers to discuss the District Attorney's proposal. We'll take a short break to allow the bailiff to clear the courtroom."

As the final stragglers left the courtroom Inspector Mike Murphy said, "I gotta get upstairs and prepare for the jury visit to Tamalpais. See you guys later. Maria, have a wonderful night at the opera." She smiled and waved him away with fluttering fingers. Pat Kelley peeked out of chambers and said, "Joe, the judge wants you in chambers."

"Can I sit in on it?" Terry asked Desmond. Joe glanced at his father who was expressionless. "I'll tell you what," he said. "Why don't you sit at my desk. I'll leave the door open so you can hear the lawyers argue."

"That's cool," Terry nodded. "And Mom, why don't I spend the night at Joe's. I'll have more time for my homework and I can ride in with him tomorrow."

"Terry, it's customary to be invited to someone's home and rude to invite yourself," Maria said sternly.

"It's okay, Maria. He can do his homework in the courtroom while I dictate. Then we'll get a bite to eat. He's no trouble, and I could use some company," Joe said. Pat nodded and Maria relented. "Well, all right. I'm off to get my dad and Kathy," Maria said, bussing Joe and then her husband on the cheek. Terry kissed her and she held onto him longer than customary. Terry's arms snaked around her, and he held her gently in an embrace more mature than adolescent. When she pulled away, she was smiling shyly. She looked into his eyes, then over to her husband and she was radiant. "I'll pick you up in forty-five minutes on Kearny," she told Pat.

"What's the opera tonight?" Joe asked.

"*Aida*" she replied. "And Pat, please be on time. You know how my father is about being late for the theater." Terry said, "Don't be a nag, Mom. Dad's never been late for anything in his life. You're the one who's always fooling around in front of the mirror with your hair and stuff." Reflexively, Maria ran her fingers through her dark, thick hair. Her husband grinned and she pivoted on spiked heals and headed for the elevator her hips swaying in comfortable harmony with her brisk gate, her calf muscles winking back at them as her heels kissed marble.

Pat didn't join Desmond in chambers for the argument over taking the jury to the burial site. He went into the Pit and took his seat at his courtroom desk. Terry sat on the edge of Desmond's desk, close to the chambers' door. This allowed him a view of Loeb and, while Moore and Judge Grant were out of his sight, he'd be able to hear everyone. Joe sat to Loeb's right so his peripheral vision could monitor Terry. Loeb was scowling in a foul mood. Judge Grant said, "Danny, you gotta problem with a jury view at Mt. Tam?"

"When a jury views a scene they're taking evidence just like in the courtroom. So what's the relevance of this romp in the woods?" Loeb demanded. "Mike?" the judge inquired.

"Judge, the Defendant buried his wife on a mountain in Marin," Moore pushed back in his chair, implying he found the dialogue irritating. "He led the inspectors to the spot, and they recovered her body. It's a simple viewing of the crime scene by the jury. Judge, I want the jury to wind up that obscure, little traveled and less known mountain road. I want them to understand the complexity of the route to the grave and the difficulty digging it. When they see this with their own eyes, they'll draw the inescapable inference that the Defendant planned this location to dispose of her body and actually dug the grave days before killing her. According to the Coroner he may even have buried her alive! That's why we're asking for the death penalty!"

Danny Loeb insisted, "You're assuming my guy's the only person in the Bay Area who knew of the existence and route to that site. We know the goddamned Army used it for training during the war. And we've got an ex-convict pervert hanging around the movie house she loves who was sent to the slammer by her father! The site over in Marin is not a crime scene. And if it is, why shouldn't the jury be taken to Panforte's bedroom? Why shouldn't they inspect the trunk of his Chevy? How 'bout the box office at the Fox? That's your real problem. You haven't been able to establish the scene of the crime.

"Your Honor, you've ruled that we can't get into this Jack Hill evidence. I think you're wrong, but that's the call you've made." Loeb leaned forward in his chair and passionately argued: "Judge, it's a goddamned fraud on the jury to show 'em that gravesite without telling them about Hill! Judge, I move that you find a viewing of this dubious crime scene has little or no value, and that the prejudicial consequences far out weigh its probative value. But if you've got the slightest inkling to take the jury over there, then let us put Hill on the stand. Then the jury will have all the facts, all the geography and all the *suspects*!" the defense lawyer concluded.

"All right, gentlemen. I'll take the matter under submission and make my ruling tomorrow before we seat the jury." Both lawyers nodded, rose and left the chambers.Pat Kelley locked up the courtroom as Terry and Desmond entered it. "What did the judge decide?" the Chief asked.

"Nothing yet, she wants to sleep on it," Desmond said.

"Makes sense," Pat said. "Any idea what she's thinking?"

"Naw, she mostly listened. But it was pretty intense in there,"

Desmond said.

"That's for sure!" Terry interjected. "It was kinda like listening to a radio drama. It seems to me, this is the first time those guys have shown what they're really feeling."

"Joe, remember when we first discussed the case at Fiore d'Italia?" Pat said and Joe nodded. "I told you that the prosecution and defense are so evenly matched it might come down to a call the judge has to make. Well, I think this is *it*!" Joe recalled Pat's battlefield metaphor at Fiore d'Italia and the decisive impact on great events of what he'd called *accident, fate, the freakish incident*. Shaking his head, Pat added, "Loeb's leveraging the judge. If she gives Moore Paula's grave scene, he gets Hill in front of the jury. Jeezus! I gotta get outta here or I'll be late for the opera." He kissed Terry quickly and left to meet his wife in front of the Hall of Justice. Terry took his schoolbooks out and began his homework. Judge Grant, robe-less, peeked out of her chambers and said, "Joe, can you come in for a second? And bring those photos Inspector Berman took over at Mt. Tam."

"Do I need my machine?" he said.

"Not yet. I just want to go over a few things, talk a little bit," she said.

Inside her chambers she looked very tired. She played with an unlit cigar as though her fingertips were deciding whether she needed a smoke. A small, ironic smile formed on her lips and she said, "So, what do you think, Joe? Should we take a day trip to Marin?"

"Why not?" Joe said. "We can get Kelley to arrange picnic lunches from Molinari's. It'd be a nice break for everybody."

"I'm afraid Danny Loeb would suffer a bad case of heart burn," Judge Grant half smiled. She began leafing through the photos of Paula's gravesite and handed each one to Desmond. The last of the twenty-five photos was the first one taken after Paula's body had been uncovered. "What was O'Day's description of the photos?" she asked. Then she answered herself, "Comprehensive was the word he'd used." For a moment she just stared at the picture of Paula Brady Panforte - who she'd seen grow from a tart little girl to a lovely woman – lying in a fetal position in a hole in the ground. Incomprehensible was the adjective that came to Judge Lucille Grant's mind.

25

The J Streetcar rumbled to the passenger stop at Market Street and Van Ness Avenue. Terry Kelley, in Joe Desmond's charge for the evening, was scribbling a poem in his school binder. From the streetcar's rear window Joe saw the green and gold gilded dome of City Hall, its nightlights supplicant at its base. The crown of city government, grander even than the dome of the nation's Capital, presided over a buzzing parade of theater lovers filing into the War Memorial Opera House for the American debuts of soprano Renata Tebaldi as Aida and tenor, Mario del Monaco as her doomed lover. San Francisco Opera Company General Director, Gaetano Merola, had launched his offensive to elevate the company to rival La Scala and The Met by luring Toscanini protégé, Viennese conductor Kurt Herbert Adler, to become his chief deputy and bringing Europe's greatest stars to San Francisco for their American debuts. The Beaux-Arts Civic Center on Van Ness Avenue was the soul of performing arts in the City. Opera, ballet, symphony, legitimate stage, and San Francisco's longest running art form – politics - reigned in marble and granite splendor on a patch of land that made you think you were in Paris.

Some critics were offended that the rough and tumble politics of City Hall were practiced across the street from palaces of culture. But knowledgeable natives knew that the marriage of politics and performing arts was as old and as fruitful as the City itself. An illiterate gambler and saloonkeeper, Tom Maguire, used his vice profits to build the Jenny Lind Theater during the Gold Rush. His theater was twice destroyed by fire, and when it was re-built for a third time Maguire was broke. A former Tammany Hall pol, he convinced City Fathers that San Francisco's dignity as a world-class city required a City Hall befitting her public leaders. He convinced the Mayor to buy his Jenny Lind Theater for $200,000 for use as City Hall. Capitalized from the city treasury, Maguire built Maguire's Opera House and introduced opera to the city by the bay. Thus was born the merger of politics and show business in California, culminating in the election of a

Hollywood movie actor President of the United States a hundred and thirty years after Maguire first presented a Verdi opera in the City.

After World War I Bartolemeo Bertolli assumed the role of Maguire's show business/political heir. The American war victory produced a predictable wave of patriotic fervor to honor the American soldiers who had won the war. Veterans' organizations agitated for a memorial building for them, while other factions in the city argued for an opera house and art museum. Bertolli's years financing Antonietta Pompa's theaters and his dear war hero son gave him credibility in both factions. He believed that the project should embrace both ideas for a memorial. So he suggested to Major Charles Kendrick, the leader of the veterans, that the fund raising skills of both factions should be utilized to build a comprehensive War Memorial center, comprising a veterans building, art museum, theater, and a house for the ballet, symphony and opera. Shortly after Major Kendrick proposed the construction of a memorial hall for "veterans and for education, recreational, entertainment and other purposes," two million in pledges from San Franciscans came in, and ground breaking for America's first publicly financed and constructed opera house commenced.

No longer burdened with running his poultry business after Bertolli settled his lawsuit with Fred Panforte, he devoted his full and formidable energies to completing what he liked to call, "Democracy's Opera House." Behind the scenes he worked with architects, designers and theatrical directors to fashion an opera house as grand as any in Europe, but with state-of-the-art theatrical facilities. So the interior of the 3,200 seat house was wider than European houses, with only two tiers rising above the orchestra floor and only twenty-five boxes under the first tier. He recommended the subdued colors of cream and brown with gold gilding in homage to Maguire's Opera House and San Francisco's first City Hall.

Joe Desmond checked his watch, and it was seven-thirty. By now Bertolli, his granddaughter, Kathleen, Pat and Maria Kelley would have taken their seats in Box N, the center box. Bertolli strictly adhered to a ritual of seating his guest and himself a half-hour before curtain's rise. Joe thought about Bertolli's attendance at the premier performance in the War Memorial Opera House in 1932. He had four seats in the center box, which was shadowed by the signature of the house, a sky-blue oval shallow dome that housed not a chandelier in the classical sense but an Art-Deco starburst of stainless steel and aluminum. But only three of his seats were occupied for Claudia

Muzio's *Tosca*. He'd left one seat vacant, the only empty seat in the house on that historic night. Joe wondered if he'd find the reason for the vacant seat in Bertolli's papers. Once they reached Joe's apartment he told Terry Kelley he'd be transcribing in his rooftop office while Terry completed his homework. Actually, he wanted to read Bertolli's papers to find out what had happened at his date at the Tivoli Opera House with Antonietta Pompa in 1905.

A year before the earth shuddered and the sky burned, the theatrical producer, recently converted from a poultry merchant by the lovely Neapolitan actress, escorted her down the steps of The Tivoli Opera House to the wooden planks of a North Beach sidewalk. The mournful final chords of Puccini's La Boheme echoed in Bertolli's mind, and the vision of an unpublished poet clutching his dead lover to his heart remained with the business baron well after the final curtain severed the phantasm of anonymous young love on the Left Bank. They walked among the glamorously attired theater crowd flowing down a narrow corridor of Dupont Avenue, dispersing at intersections like small tributaries of a surging river. The theater throng was visibly excited and the night's mood manifestly gay as they boarded carriages or strolled happily to restaurants, ballrooms or coffeehouses. Antonietta slipped her dark blue-gloved hand around his gray-jacketed arm. He pulled his gold timepiece from his vest pocket and flipped it open with his callused thumb. "Supper?" he asked softly, putting on a dapper gray homburg. She smiled up at him, adjusted her blue bonnet and nodded. At the corner of Dupont Avenue and Green Street they paused, allowing a horse drawn carriage of laughing couples to prance by on their way to the Palace Hotel. A low vaporous fog swirled silently around corner street lanterns; gaslights flickered in the night, giving the moist fog the illusion of a flurry of darting moths. The steady clip-clop of horses' hooves drawing creaking carriages and surreys provided the beat to animated street conversations and the shrill buoyancy of ladies' laughter ringing in the air. Beyond the bridgeless Golden Gate a foghorn bellowed an incantation the night had just begun.

Antonietta squeezed his arm and whispered, "You're so quiet. What are you feeling, Bartolomeo?" He looked down into the deep well of her eyes and said, barely audibly, like a boy suddenly struck by shyness, "Much. Perhaps too much."

They stepped off the curb as she lifted her ankle length dress to accommodate the pitch of the street. She leaned slightly against him, as her high heels found cobblestones, her breast pressing against his arm. Glancing up at his profile she said, "You liked it, then? Your Lucchesi composer moved you?"

He stared straight ahead and shook his head in a gesture of wonder. "It was all so urgently unfeigned. I'm not sure what to make of it. This was not about warring kings or vengeful gods. You could find those kids so in love right here in North Beach."

"Or the Village in New York," she added.

"Or two adults walking arm in arm along Grant Avenue," Bertolli thought before saying, "Perhaps I'm just not used to so contemporary a drama."

"It's not the period of the piece, Bartolomeo. It's the piece. Period! That's what's so gripping about Puccini's work. It's a...what's the English word for it?"

"Verisimilitude," he said softly.

"That's it! I've sensed it in all his operas. They're populated with real people with real passions." Bertolli nodded. At Broadway he guided her toward Fior d'Italia Restaurant. She whispered, "Is it all too close? Are Rodolfo and Mimi, Marcello and Musetta and their doomed loves too immediate?" When he didn't answer, she smiled mischievously and softly sang a revised version of the first line of Mimi's opening aria. "Mi chimano Antonietta. My name is Antonietta." He turned to her, and his rich baritone sang through an emerging smile: "Non sono poeta, sono solo un venditore di gallina. I am no poet, just a chicken peddler." He pushed open the door of Fior d'Italia and followed the swirl of her dress into the restaurant. White jacketed waiters scurried with dedicated purpose, but little urgency, until they entered the kitchen and bellowed their orders to cursing chefs who managed to prepare an endless variety of Northern Italian dishes without a single written order. Tony Delmonico, the black-tied owner, greeted the couple, "Ah! Signor Bertolli and Signora Pompa, just the two of you?" Bertolli held up two fingers. "Perhaps you'll enjoy more intimate dining upstairs," their host invited, waving his hand toward the stairway to the second story of the restaurant.

"In your banquet room? That suggests all the intimacy of a vacant ballpark," Bertolli challenged.

"Signore, on weekends after the theater we rearrange the room. It's reserved for our most treasured patrons," Delmonico said. He led them through his restaurant amid a rising murmur when diners spotted the stunning star of Teatro Italiano. At the foot of the stairwa, a balding, fat mustachioed man elbowed his dinner companion, exclaiming: "Bella! Prima donna!"

Once in the second floor banquet room Bertolli saw that it had been partitioned off, shrunk to a fraction of its normal size. There were three round, candlelit tables, in each corner of the room. The tables were surrounded by flowers, plants and ferns, creating a booth-like ambiance, and providing the privacy that Delmonico had promised. The restaurateur slid a chair under Antonietta and Bertolli acknowledged his host's gracious treatment, saying, "Va bene!"

"It's more than good. Giovanni himself will be serving you!" Delmonico said, handing menus to the couple. Bertolli's thick eyebrows rose upon learning that the head Chef would be preparing and presenting their meal. Delmonico left to fetch their drinks, Bertolli put down his menu and said, "What did you think of Tetrazzini's Mimi?"

"Oh, Bartolomeo, she's absolutely marvelous! Her scales are dazzling, yet completely controlled and even. Her high notes sparkle like polished crystal, but are incomparably full. Her dramatic instincts are unerring, and she projects such warmth, almost a girlish softness. It's as though she refuses to be captive to her instrument, and that's rare for our breed."

"As rare as one soprano praising another?" Bertolli smiled wryly.

"We're alike only in our vocal register. I could never produce a sound like hers, and certainly not with the delicacy of her shadings. I don't think any diva could." Bertolli massaged his chin and said, "Such graciousness from one artist to another is quite rare, Antonietta."

"Don't you really mean graciousness between two women is the true rarity, Signore?" He shrugged and opened his palms in a gesture of peace. "Champagne?" he invited. They clinked their glasses and Bertolli toasted: "To a wonderful night at the opera!" The pout of her lips dissolved into a sensual smile when she said, "To our first date!" They sipped their champagne and he acknowledged her amendment to his toast. Antonietta removed her three-quarter length gloves and scanned the menu. Bertolli fiddled with the stem of his glass, studying her across the table. Her royal blue dress accented the faint gold of her Southern Italian skin. Her high collar, with a thin trim of delicate lace around her graceful neck, was embraced by a tiny string of pearls. A hand-sized, diamond-shaped cut-away below her pearls presented an inviting island of silken flesh. "Bella Antonietta," he said faintly.

"You're too kind, Signore," She smiled and her fingers brushed his hand. They were silent and their gaze sought to channel the hushed adjectives of deep and growing affection. Suddenly there was a burst of applause coming from the downstairs dining room. Antonietta leaned forward, asking: "What is it? What are they cheering about?" Bertolli shook his head. Busboys and waiters murmured excitedly at the head of the stairs. Delmonico burst through the door and, with a flick of his impervious wrist, scattered his curious employees back to their workstations. Bertolli and Antonietta saw a

handsomely dressed couple follow Delmonico into the private dinning area. "My God! It's Tetrazzini!" Bertolli blurted. The applause of Fior d'Italia's patrons was for Luisa Tetrazzini, who'd just made her American operatic debut at The Tivoli Opera House.

Antonietta ignored the sudden appearance of the star of La Boheme and called out excitedly, in Italian, to her escort. "Gaetano! Gaetano Merola! It's me. Antonietta Pompa!" Tetrazzini's escort's eyes widened and he smiled broadly in astonished recognition. He whispered to Tetrazzini in an animated fashion. She laughed and waved him off to Bertolli's table. He said, "Antonietta Pompa? I can't believe it's you! I haven't seen you since we were kids at the Naples Conservatory. What are you doing here?"

"I live here, Gaetano," she laughed. "Remember? I was thirteen when my parents moved from Italy to New York. But what are you doing in San Francisco? I assumed you'd have followed your father and become a violinist for the court, or more likely, the court conductor by now."

"Of course I remember when you left Naples. I had a terrible crush on you. My desire to become a conductor was born accompanying you in our music classes. I've been hopelessly attracted to sopranos ever since. My, how the flower of my youth has blossomed!" Merola said.

"And now you have a charming mustache, Gaetano. But you still haven't told us what you're doing here, much less in the company of the tragic Mimi," Antonietta said. Realizing that he'd left the brilliant diva cooling her high heels with the owner of Fior d'Italia, Merola raised his hands and said, "My goodness! Excuse me for a moment? Would you like to meet her?"

"Of course," Antonietta answered for Bertolli. Merola brought Luisa Tetrazzini over to their table and introduced her to his childhood crush. Both women nodded cordially. "May I introduce Bartolomeo Bertolli," Antonietta said as Bertolli rose. She added, "Signor Bertolli's one of our leading businessmen and my theatrical producer. Bertolli reached for Merola's hand, shook it and bowed humbly to Tetrazzini. She extended her right hand, palm down. He grasped it, raised it to his lips and kissed her hand reverentially. "Signora Tetrazzini, it is a supreme honor to meet you and an unanticipated opportunity to thank you for a splendid evening in the theater," Bertolli said.

"That's an extraordinary compliment, Signora Tetrazzini. My producer-friend has spent his lifetime in the theater. As a boy, he saw Verdi himself conduct Aida in Pisa. He's quite right, you were absolutely magnificent tonight!" Antonietta said.

Tetrazzini's cheeks flushed. "You're both so kind and your San Francisco audience so generous. But Puccini's genius is the true hero of the night."

"Signora, would you care to join us for supper? Of course, we understand if after so emotional a performance you may prefer to dine privately. Perhaps, like me, you may be curious to learn more of the young romance of these two Neapolitan artists," Bertolli invited, suppressing his momentary awe.

"Delightful! But if we're going to hear of scandalous love in Naples, it's Luisa," Tetrazzini relaxed Bertolli. Tony Delmonico eased a chair under the opera star, poured more champagne, ordered his staff to see that no other customers were to be admitted and then disappeared back into the kitchen.

The couples conversed in animated Italian throughout a five-course meal personally prepared and served by the head chef. They didn't order from the menu; rather they used it as a research resource for their individual culinary compositions. They negotiated directly with Chef Giovanni on such items as antipasto, what vegetables should compliment their entrees, and what were the best sauté wines. Luisa revealed a gourmet's aptitude comparable to her exquisite stage sense. Giovanni suggested a chicken dish, assuring Tetrazzini that they served only the finest poultry purchased exclusively from Bertolli. Good-humored bartering ensued between the diva and chef in which she amended the ingredients and presentation of her dish. It proved delectable, and Giovanni thereafter placed it on the regular menu. Later, when the chef at the Palace Hotel heard of the soprano's meal after her theatrical triumph, he added it to his menu, naming the dish, Chicken Tetrazzini.

Over grappa and coffee the artists and capitalist shared stories of Italy, their careers and their exuberant affection for the City. Merola's infatuation with Antonietta in Naples revealed he was so shy he never expressed his feelings, thereby disappointing any scandal anticipated by Tetrazzini and Bertolli. When Antonietta said she had a crush on the first violin, Merola exclaimed in mock horror, *"My God! That boy was Sicilian!"*

"A cute Sicilian," Antonietta teased.

Tetrazzini, in her early thirties, and Bertolli, about to turn forty, initially allowed the young Neapolitans to carry the conversation. Both artists spoke more of their older companions than themselves. Merola related that Luisa had been performing in Europe, South America and Mexico for fifteen years. While her musical brilliance had been critically acclaimed, she had not created audience frenzy over her artistry until her performance at the Tivoli. Indeed, her manager had been rebuffed by The Metropolitan Opera when he sought a booking in America's greatest house. *"I suggested she book San Francisco for her American debut,"* Merola said.

"Why here?" Bertolli asked. *"We don't even have our own opera company*

and most east coast critics think we're a barbarian town with little more than harlots, saloons and vigilantes with anxious ropes."

"Critics, what do they know?" Merola said disdainfully. "Anyone who knows anything about the theater knows San Francisco's always been a great show town. Every artist in Europe knows the story of your Irishman, Maguire, and how well he treated artists. During the Gold Rush you had more theaters than banks. As for being a crude frontier town, Maguire was a beguiling promoter. He convinced artists and managers that San Francisco was a Mediterranean city. He said it was Venetian in character because of your international flavor and maritime power. By God, he never broke his word to an artist. And that's unheard of for an impresario, then or now."

"But he went broke producing opera in the City," Antonietta said.

Merola shook his head. "That's what I never understood. From all I've heard, Maguire's productions always played to packed houses."

"Bartolomeo, tell them why Maguire failed," Antonietta urged. Bertolli explained, "I suspect it was his inability to control the costs of production while maintaining reasonable ticket prices. The popular myth is that his Irish extravagance was his tragic flaw. But I think it was the unique and somewhat bizarre population of San Francisco caused by the Gold Rush. You see, the city literally grew up overnight. Before gold was discovered, the entire population of California was only about 15,000. In less than a year, after gold was discovered, San Francisco's population mushroomed from 1,200 to more than 40,000. Most of them were men, under forty years of age and single. Only about 5,000 women lived in the city and I'm afraid many of these pioneer ladies practiced the oldest of professions. So there was a paucity of trained musicians for the orchestra and chorus. Indeed, Maguire's first production of Verdi's Il Trovatore had no women's chorus, and the men's chorus numbered only eight German locals. In those days, our German community was the most musical, since the Italian immigration had not yet begun in earnest. Anyway, the tenor and soprano were Italian imports, the mezzo and baritone, French, the conductor, English.

"You'll recall that this was a period of great technical advances with musical instruments. Composers like Verdi were writing much more complex scores, demanding virtuosity from cast and orchestra alike. Maguire had to import most of the talent if he was to be true to the composers. To his credit, he was an impresario unwilling to compromise artistic integrity. And he refused to price tickets so that only the nouveau riche could afford them. Sadly, this was a prescription for financial disaster."

Luisa asked, "Are you quite sure he failed? From what I observed tonight he certainly created an audience for opera. I've never experienced such enthusiasm and warmth from an audience before." Bertolli nodded. "You're right Signora. There's no question Maguire's legacy is San Francisco's appetite for great theater. And it takes performances like yours to fulfill that appetite. But I'm curious. Do you always blow kisses during your curtain calls?"

Luisa threw back her head and laughed, "Oh Bartolomeo, never! I've never done that before. During curtain calls, I try to remain in character. I'm sure the fragile Mimi would never behave as I did tonight. But the audience kept screaming and calling me back again and again. I was overcome by the most wondrous emotions, and it was so spontaneous. I wanted to embrace every person in the theater. So I just started blowing kisses. That seemed to inflame them even more." Suddenly she frowned and asked her host, "You don't think what I did was scandalous, do you? I realize it wasn't very diva-like."

Bertolli chuckled, "Spontaneous affection is never scandalous, Luisa."

Antonietta interjected, "Luisa, I've performed all over America, and there's something very special about San Francisco audiences. I think that's what you felt tonight. They have an openness, a willingness to embrace the new and different here. Bartolomeo convinced me to stay here because of it. He dreams of his city becoming a cradle of creativity, and that's what we're trying to do at our theater."

"Tell us about your Teatro Italiano, Antonietta," Luisa urged.

"It's really Bartolomeo's idea," Antonietta began. "He feels we can build on Maguire's achievements and, in our theater, create enough talent that will ultimately sustain an opera company! So we're producing everything from vaudeville to serious drama, operetta to farce, concerts and two locally cast operas a year. I feel more like a ringmaster for a Roman circus than a theatrical director. But we're definitely improving the numbers and skills of our local artists. In fact, two of the cellos and the clarinet who accompanied you are members of our orchestra."

Luisa nodded, "They're fine musicians. I feel the orchestra played with great passion."

Antonietta continued, "We believe that providing a wide variety of entertainment will broaden the base of our audience. We want to add to Maguire's audience, but we also want to appeal to the newly arrived immigrants. This is an immigrant town, always has been. And opera's the most popular form of theater here. By appealing to popular tastes, we're creating a talent pool of artists and keeping the Italian musical theater alive – both of which may form the foundation of a future opera company."

Merola, intrigued, said, "So you want to build an opera company, Bertolli? Doesn't an opera company usually start with an opera house?"

Bertolli dragged on his cigar and said, "That's certainly the way it's been done in America. But the cost of land acquisition and construction are so great that what begins as an artistic venture becomes a real estate investment. When this happens you have to rely on the wealthy to buy into Diamond Horseshoes or onto the board of directors. Take the Met, for example. That German fellow, Conried, who runs the Met, pays so much attention to J.P. Morgan that he missed a chance to book Luisa.

"A couple of months ago the Met's road company put on three operas here. Frankly, it was disappointing. They're planning to put on five operas next year and Caruso's performing in Carmen. Even I'll tolerate their poor productions for Caruso. I think talent makes the performance, not the house in which the performance is given. I dare say Luisa's Mimi would have been no less magnificent in a tent than in the Tivoli."

"My friend, I spent my first year in America as assistant conductor at the Met. One thing I learned is that opera in America is expensive. How can you compete for great singers and conductors without wealthy patrons?" Merola asked.

"If the Met gets 75 people to contribute $1,000 each, we'll get 750 to give $100, with a season ticket for each $50 contributed. We'll get small businesses, office workers and professionals. The wealthy will pay their ransom for culture just to be seen on opening night."

Merola conceded, "You may have something, Bartolomeo. It sounds like what Oscar Hammerstein's doing with his Manhattan Opera Company in New York. At the top end his ticket prices are as expensive as the Met. But the balcony and third tier are half what the Met charges. He's after a mass audience, not just rich folks. I hear he's going to sign Campanini as conductor and musical director now that he's left La Scala." To Luisa, Merola said, "You should consider working for Hammerstein, Luisa. His roster of women vocalists is thin. And though Campanini's a real tyrant, his artistic standards are the highest. Would you like me to contact Hammerstein and recommend you?"

Luisa said, "But certainly he's heard Signor Conried doesn't consider me good enough to sing at the Met. Why would Signor Hammerstein feel differently?"

Merola laughed, "Those two Germans despise each other. Oscar might hire you just to infuriate Conried. Hammerstein's a great showman and says Conried's got the artistic judgment of a stockbroker."

"It sounds irresistible," Antonietta purred. "The lovely Luisa singing in

the middle of a Prussian war!"

"I read somewhere The Met's indifferent to Hammerstein's house," Bertolli said.

"Of course, that's the official line," Merola said. "But don't believe it for a minute. The Met's got a monopoly on opera in America, and they'll try to crush Hammerstein to protect it. That's all J.P. Morgan knows, one monopoly after another. They just signed a deal with Puccini's publisher, Ricordi, giving them exclusive rights to all Puccini operas in America. No opera company in the world has ever gotten such rights." Turning to Luisa he cautioned, "Luisa, I must tell you, Conried's people are warning managers that to deal with Hammerstein will endanger their future relationships with the Met."

Luisa shrugged her shoulders. "Conried's made it clear I have no future with his Metropolitan Opera. It sounds like this fellow Hammerstein is playing to audiences like the one we had tonight. I'll take my chances with people like that anytime. So go ahead and tell him I'd love to sing for him."

"Va bene! I'll wire him first thing in the morning," Merola said as Delmonico appeared and announced that Bertolli's carriage was ready. Bertolli reached for the bill and Delmonico snapped it away. "No, Signore! I insist. You're the guest of Fior d'Italia, and you've dined with our compliments to la bella donna." Bertolli immediately realized that his meeting with Tetrazzini and Merola was not by chance, but orchestrated by the owner of Fior d'Italia.

"Grazie mille," murmured Luisa.

"May we give you a lift to the Palace, Luisa?" Bertolli offered.

"That would be nice," she accepted.

Outside Fior d'Italia a busboy attended Bertolli's carriage. He gawked wide-eyed at the two beautiful actresses. Merola lifted the sopranos up into the carriage, and Bertolli tipped the busboy with a silver dollar. The boy's hands trembled when he realized the gratuity equaled half a day's wages. Bertolli flipped the reins lightly and pulled away from the curb. During the five minute ride to the Palace, Luisa asked to no one in particular, "When do you San Franciscans ever sleep?" Antonietta laughed: "Not until the party's over,"

At the Palace, Bertolli and Antonietta escorted their new friends into the dramatic lobby. Word of Tetrazzini's triumph had spread rapidly and the hotel guests and staff milling in the lobby burst into spontaneous applause upon her entrance. She smiled brightly, touching her dainty fingers to her flushed cheek. Bertolli said, "Luisa, I was wondering if you would honor us at a reception in your honor on Sunday, at my home. My wife and

I would like you to meet some of our friends who are now undoubtedly your ardent admirers."

Luisa stole a glance at Antonietta at the mention of Bertolli's wife. Antonietta's smile revealed no discomfort that she was with a married man. "That would be wonderful," Luisa accepted.

Antonietta feigned caution. "Be careful, Luisa. He gave me a reception when I made my San Francisco debut, and in the intoxicating setting of his rooftop rose garden he convinced me to change the direction of my career and remain in San Francisco. These Tuscans have a way with sopranos."

"I'll be on my guard, Antonietta," Luisa said laughingly.

"Of course, Gaetano, we expect you to join us," Bertolli added.

"Delighted!" the young conductor accepted.

They bid their goodnights and Bertolli dropped Antonietta off at her Telegraph Hill apartment. At her door, her deep eyes invited him in. But he looked away and sighed, "It's late." She reached up, touched his cheek with her fingertips and whispered, "Buono notte, mio caro." She watched him from her window disengage his carriage hand brake and pull away from the curb. Her longing eyes followed him to Union Street where he reined his sorrel horse left. He disappeared from her view, on his way to his wife's bed.

Joe Desmond closed his black binder and placed Pat Kelley's typed translation on his rolltop desk. He tried to imagine what Bertolli was thinking as he rode down Telegraph Hill to Washington Square and up to his Russian Hill home on that April night. He'd experienced his first Puccini opera and perhaps reflected on how far these two sons of Lucca had come since the Sunday Puccini had played the organ at Mass in Bertolli's little church in Farneta. Possibly his mind dwelt on the overwhelming passion of Tetrazzini's performance or the tears she had drawn at the Tivoli – even from the stage-wise Antonietta. Most likely it was Antonietta who filled his thoughts on his short ride home. Joe suspected that he visualized her graceful fingers filtering unconsciously through her luxuriant curls or how she scrunched up her shoulders and closed her eyes when she stepped out into the cool San Francisco night as the fog gently kissed her skin. He must have questioned the soundness of his deeply felt sense of the value of his word, the loyalty of yesterday's promise so challenged by Antonietta's yearning eyes.

Was his resolve to live up to his unique moral code shaken by the coolness of her inviting touch, Joe wondered. Or was he so thoroughly principled that he had the will of a saint? Perhaps. But Joe thought, had Bertolli known that night that his city had only 365 days to live; that below the cobblestones over which his carriage rolled, the agony of the earth was mounting, simmering volcano-like until it would erupt in a spasm of violence and flame, he'd have spun his sorrel around and at a full gallop, sped to Antonietta's patient, open arms. For a man who sees catastrophe on the horizon will desperately seek a moment of nurturing and releasing warmth before he greets eternity. Even one so prescient as Bertolli was oblivious to the Armageddon that awaited San Francisco. But Joe also concluded from his correspondence with Father Agnello that Bertolli was unaware his dinner with Tetrazzini, Merola and Antonietta was the moment of conception of the San Francisco Opera Company. Neither the artists nor the businessman realized that the opera economics authored by Bertolli would be adopted by Gaetano Merola eighteen years later when Maestro Merola brought democratic opera to life in San Francisco.

26

After breakfast at the Oregon Café, Terry and Joe Desmond were greeted in chambers by the acrid fumes of Pat Kelley's coffee burning on the hot plate. "How was the opera?" Joe asked.

Pat replied, "Wonderful! Merola's a genius at discovering new artists. You should have seen the Met's Rudolph Bing after the show. Renata Tebaldi snubbed him and he's furious with envy that San Francisco's again the venue for the American debut of brilliant artists. And Adler was marvelous in the pit! My father-in-law thinks he'll succeed Merola as General Director. They say he's a tyrant, but every bit as visionary as Merola."

Indifferent to the machinations of opera directors, Terry asked where his mother was. "She's not coming to court today," Pat said.

"Why not?" the boy asked.

"She had to go out to All Hallows. Her fifth graders are giving the substitute teacher a rough time. Since we may be going over to Mt. Tam, I told her it would be a good opportunity to remind the kids she's still the boss."

Bailiff McCann signaled them to take their places in the courtroom. From the bench Judge Grant announced: "The Court's in session outside the presence of the jury. The District Attorney has moved to take the jury to the gravesite of the victim, and the defense has objected. Like all evidence, a jury viewing is a matter left to the discretion of the Court."

Here it is, Desmond thought, that moment of fate that Pat Kelley had predicted, the first time they spoke of the Panforte murder trial. Joe glanced at Paul Brady leaning forward in his seat, his face expectant, confident that his dearest friend would lead the jury to the mountaintop. Judge Grant caught Brady's eyes for a moment, then she looked down at Bob Panforte's downcast head. Then she authoritatively said: "I am going to deny the People's motion to take the jury to Mt. Tamalpais. At this time the Court believes such a viewing by the jury will lead to an overemphasis of the gravesite at the expense of what occurred at Francisco Street, in any motor vehicles or other locations in San Francisco on June 5, 1949. Because the evidence indicates possible multiple crime scenes, an inordinate amount of court time would be necessary for the jury to view them all. Moreover, these varied potential crime scenes can be and have been depicted by other physical evidence. Mr. Moore, will you be calling anymore witnesses or do the People rest?"

Moore said: "May I have a moment with Inspector Murphy?"

"Of course. We'll take a five minute recess and the Bailiff will bring in the jury," Judge Grant ruled. Then she stepped down from the Bench, trailed by the furious eyes of Paul Brady. Brady's face flushed pink, his hands in his lap formed into clenching fists so taut his knuckles turned white. His body was coiled. He wife whispered to him. He ignored her. He stood up and studied the vacant bench. He briskly pivoted and stormed out of the courtroom, the interior doors flailing in the wake of his rage.

When court resumed, the bailiff had turned off the floor fans. A cooling bay breeze had picked up, announcing the arrival of late afternoon fog. The prosecution rested, and Loeb announced that Fred Panforte would be the first witness for the defense. Fred Panforte rose from his front row seat, patted his wife's folded hands and walked in measured dignity into the Pit. As he raised his right hand to be sworn by Pat Kelley, Desmond stole a glance at Terry. Suddenly Joe was struck by the true reason for Maria Kelley's absence from the courtroom. It had nothing to do with disciplining her delinquent students and everything to do with her husband's manipulations of his family's environment. Pat had learned from Loeb that Fred Panforte would testify today, so he told Maria there was no point in coming to court since most of the proceedings would be taken up with a field trip to Marin. But he surely knew that had the judge allowed the trip it would only have consumed half the court day. Moore would rest and then Loeb would put old man Panforte on in the afternoon session. Pat realized he couldn't control his wife's emotional reactions to the perfidious *Precious One*. Not even Terry, so sensitive to her pain and attentive to her passions, could restrain her once Fabrizio Panforte told his family tale. Perhaps Pat felt even he was incapable of constraining himself in the face of his wife's certain agony. So he'd gerrymandered her day. He got her out of the courtroom at the moment her father's nemesis came to the defense of his son. The task of confronting Fabrizio Panforte with knowing silence he reserved for himself. And his only son.

Fred Panforte, courtly in a funereal black suit and solid silver tie, solemnly pledged to tell the truth, the whole truth and nothing but the truth. When Pat Kelley uttered, "So help you God!" he gave the impression that only divine intervention could draw the wholeness of truth from this *Precious One*. Had old man Panforte known that his oath was ordained by Bertolli's son-in-law, his confident bearing would have evaporated. Loeb commenced his direct examination with Panforte's family history. Pat immediately realized that Panforte's court version of his journey from Italy to America was an abridged and sanitized edition. As a result, Pat took copious notes.

Panforte described himself as an eighteen year-old farm boy who left his hometown of Lucca to seek his fortune in America. He didn't mention his teacher-priest who'd raised him from impoverished ignorance and directed him to a land in which his talent, not his meager birthright, would define his life. Nor did his testimony acknowledge his Lucchese predecessors whose journey from anonymous privation to freedom had been going on for more than a half century before he boarded a train bound for the port city of Genoa. He described the verdant Tuscan countryside fleeing past his window and the train plodding through the shadowy, lush hills of Liguria, finally coming out of a sharp turn where the brilliant, blue sun-drenched Mediterranean Sea kissed the thigh of the historic peninsula. In ancient Genoa he jumped off the train at *Principia Stazione*, carrying a brown suitcase with all of his worldly possessions. Pat Kelley noted that he didn't mention a sealed satchel bearing Father Agnello's chronicle of his *Precious Ones* and Bertolli's correspondence with their only teacher.

For a moment he stood between two of four travertine pillars supporting the archway of *Principia Stazione* and his teenage eyes studied the bustling piazza. Across the piazza he saw the outline of a white marble monument presiding from a small park, composed of pine, olive and oak tress, an eight-foot sword fern and a solitary and unlikely palm tree. He joked that the palm tree was a Genovesi boast that you could grow anything in Northern Italy. He crossed the piazza to examine the sculpture. From the base of the monument he saw Genoa's most famous son, Columbus, towering above him on a marble pedestal. Below the pedestal were figures of mature, shapely women, each representing a continent of the world. He saw Columbus' left hand resting on a waist high anchor, and above the other marble women, next to the explorer's feet, was the blanched statue of a vibrant, young woman representing the New World to which Panforte would embark in five days.

He wound his way through the *caruggi*, Genoa's narrow, alley-like ancient streets – which, even today are too cramped to allow vehicular traffic – to his destination, the *duomo* of San Lorenzo. His parish priest had arranged for him to stay as a guest of Monsignor Barbagelata at the rectory of Genoa's cathedral until he boarded his ship for San Francisco. As Pat had anticipated, he didn't tell the jury that his *parish priest* was the man who'd raised him or that Father Angello was such a pivotal figure in Panforte's life that he'd given his only son his teacher's name.

Panforte noted that San Lorenzo was not constructed with brick, marble, terra-cotta nor roofed with rich, rust colored tile typical of Tuscan churches. The Genovesi cathedral was built with chalk-like stones in alternating lines of black and well-aged gray. He pushed through a small portal within a heavy iron door under the right archway, dipped his fingers in tepid holy water and blessed himself. He spotted a frail, white-haired sexton replacing candles on the main altar. He walked up to the communion rail and gestured to the sexton with a sealed envelope. The sexton stiffly descended from the altar and Fabrizio whispered, "*Por monsignore.* For the Monsignor." The old man reached for the envelope but Panforte pulled it back, telling him it must be personally delivered. The sexton grunted, and with a twist of his head bade Panforte to follow him. He led Panforte through the sacristy, with its musky scent of the silks and satins of the Mass, and out to a granite stairway leading to the back entrance of the rectory.

Monsignor Barbagelata was seated at an expansive walnut table conversing with an elderly nun. The sexton whispered in Monsignor's ear, pointing to Panforte. Monsignor waved Fabrizio into his office. As Panforte approached, Monsignor offered his hand benignly to the old nun. She was a study in black, save for her lily-white breastplate and her ashen, well lined face. She bent arthritically and kissed his ring. That's odd, he thought. Bishops wore the kissing rings of the Disciples, not mere *monsignore*. The nun disappeared through a side door, her veils of ebony swirling, the rattle of her rosary cinched to her waist and dangling the full length of her gown punctuating the iron shudder of a door bolt that sealed Monsignor's chambers from the Convent.

Fabrizio bowed respectively from the waist and handed the envelope to the prelate. Under a pair of bushy eyebrows, through a pair of rimless glasses, Monsignor read the letter. When he finished it, he pushed his chair back exposing an abundant paunch and said, "So, you're going to America. Soon there will be no one left in Lucca. They'll all be in San Francisco." Then he rang a silver bell and a chubby woman dressed in the drab gray of a housekeeper appeared. He directed her to show Fabrizio to his room and informed him dinner would be served at nine. He also told him there would be a church service the following morning.

The housekeeper took Fabrizio's suitcase and led him up two flights of stairs to a small cell furnished with a single bed, a small night table with an oil lamp on it, a bed pan and a picture of the Blessed Virgin looking tenderly down from the wall. The housekeeper asked him if he needed anything. He shook his head, and she left him in his first home beyond his father's roof.

The jury was attentive to Panforte's story of his journey from the Old Country. A woman juror smiled when he apologized for his heavy accent and fractured grammar, saying: "I'm afraid my English is not too good. I had to learn fast when I got here. The ranch hands I worked with weren't the best teachers." Neither the lady juror nor any jurors were aware that marginally literate poultry workers did not administer Panforte's English lessons. Like all who'd come from Lucca to Bartolomeo Bertolli's employ, Panforte's initial education occurred at Bertolli's Sonoma ranch, a half mile from the Sebastiani Winery. Bertolli had taken Panforte to Sonoma's little red schoolhouse and commissioned the children's teacher to teach Panforte to read and write and count in English. Until he could do so, Bertolli forbade him from speaking Italian with his family and ranch hands. Bertolli was convinced that compelled English was the surest and quickest method of its mastery. During this period Panforte was not required to perform any labor in Bertolli's business. Bertolli told him: "Your job is to learn to be an American. When you have mastered this lesson, you'll work as an American. That means you'll work hard and long and with enthusiasm." But the jury learned nothing of Bertolli's welcome of Panforte to America. They were left with the impression of a teenager learning a foreign tongue in a strange land on his own, and their admiration of his achievements rendered his accent and awkward sentences charming.

Pat Kelley was relieved that his wife wasn't in court to hear Panforte's erasure of her father's beneficent role in the Americanization of young Fabrizio. Pat was satisfied that his manipulation of Maria's day had been a sound decision. To this day Maria Bertolli Kelley never had to pay for poultry or produce at The Market. So many of The Market men had been taught English and attended what they called "Mr. B's Little Red School House" that they wouldn't think of charging Bertolli's daughter, who they'd known as a girl, for a Thanksgiving turkey or a carton of citrus. Education was so central to Maria Kelley's life that Pat couldn't bear to think of the anguish she would feel if she would have heard Panforte deleting from his biography the only two men responsible for lifting him from ignorant peasantry.

On Panforte's second day outside the Wall of Lucca, there was a fateful moment during the cathedral services. Each of Father Agnello's *Precious Ones* had attended services in Genoa before their voyage. Father Agnello had explained to Bertolli: "Just as Columbus had his ships blessed, so you must seek God's guidance for your exploration." He directed him to a priest he'd met during his years in Rome. This Genovesi priest was Father Barbagelata, then an assistant pastor at the church of San Matteo. All subsequent *Precious Ones* spent a few days under Father Barbagelata's care. It was predictable, therefore, that, when these young men found their first success as truck farmers south of San Francisco, they gave the land of their triumph the name of Father Barbagelata's church. It's doubtful that the affluent citizens of San Mateo County have any idea the name of their affluent suburb was nominated by a handful of Lucchese farm boys. By the time Fabrizio arrived in Genoa, Father Barbagelata had been elevated to a monsignor and transferred from San Matteo to administer the cathedral of San Lorenzo.

Panforte recounted that the memorial service he'd attended was unlike any church service he'd ever experienced. Monsignor Barbagelata delivered a homily on the splendor of eternal life in the presence of an all-loving God. From the choir loft he heard the groan of bass violins elevated by the murmur of cellos, then led by the haunting strings of violins. The voices of the choir floated over the congregation, singing the biblical verses Brahms adopted as his lyrics for his German Requiem. Panforte was struck by regret at the passing of his homeland. He told the jury that for the first time since he'd contemplated leaving for America he experienced a deep sense of fear, a feeling that all he knew had prematurely died and all that was left for him was the unknown. He felt his San Francisco destination was as mysterious and incomprehensible as eternal life, promised as an essential article of his faith. Grief swelled in him, its undeniable tide drawn by Brahms immortal music of mortality.

Rising above the chorus, soaring like a gliding bird, he heard a soprano's sublimely soothing song. The German lyrics escaped him, but her melody massaged his sorrow, tempered his anxiety like a mother's breast pacifying an anxious infant. He didn't know the soprano's solo was inspired by Brahms' memory of his own mother, but the nurturing theme was unmistakable, even to a motherless child. The choir joined the soprano's plea for saddened souls to rejoice and he felt an airiness envelope him, urging him to drift with the buoyancy of a woman's orisons. His eyes glazed, and the altar hid behind a haze of novel emotions, the flickering candles the only image his mind could confidently discern. He turned slowly, hopeful that none in the congregation noticed his breach of Catholic etiquette when he turned his back on God's home in search of the angel whose voice was calling to him from the loft.

He saw the massive brass organ pipes shielding the backs of the musicians. Standing apart from the choir, her small white-gloved hand resting on the choir rail, was the soprano. The voice of the angel who had sung so intimately to him emanated from a petite teenage girl clad entirely in white, a transparent veil flickering in the breeze of her song. Behind her veil he detected a face of such extraordinary delicacy that he marveled it did not crack like a porcelain vase when she propelled her incandescent high notes. Where did all her power come from? How could so slight a child propel her sound to the church ceiling and beyond, he wondered. But it was her complexion that pierced his chest and caused him to breathe laboriously. Her skin was flawless, Carrara white. He thought of Quercia's *Illaria* and his birthday kiss in Lucca.

The service ended, and Fabrizio rushed from the church. He positioned himself in a corner of the vestibule and waited for the musicians to descend from the loft. As they filed down the stairway, he saw they were all mature adults. The bald, hawk-nosed choir director led the soprano from the choir. She was a child. Her movements were tentative, her steps shuffles, the pace of a girl not yet comfortable in the fluidity of a woman's gait. Her eyes were downcast not in piety, Fabrizio thought, but in awe of her divine instrument. She passed under the center archway of San Lorenzo to the shadow of the Tower of Ducal Palace. She paused briefly in front of Monsignor Barbagelata as he received his congregation. He smiled and patted her shoulder. Behind her veil her eyes avoided her pastor. At the base of the Tower of Ducal Palace she waited for two nuns to escort her back to the cloister of San Matteo.

Fabrizio studied her face though her veil, the translucent shroud merged with her complexion, blurring any definition of her features. Suddenly she looked up and her eyes caught Fabrizio's. She gifted him with her Mediterranean blue/green eyes and raven hair caressing her elegant neck. He felt blood rush to his cheeks and he wanted to speak to her, to tell her that her song had moved him, to somehow affirm the novel feelings she'd aroused in him. But he was just a farm boy undertaking an unlikely journey. He knew nothing of the words by which a man greets a woman. He took a half step toward her and stuttered: "*Scusi, signorina. La tua voce e'stata da Deo!* Excuse me, Miss. Your voice was kissed by God!" Startled, her cheeks flushed and Fabrizio's words rushed out with little thought and no gender tactics. "I was in church. I heard you sing. I had to tell you it was beautiful. My name is Fabrizio. Fabrizio Panforte from Lucca. I'm staying with Monsignor until my ship leaves for America. Please signorina, take no offense. I have only a few days in Genoa."

She shook her head, her veil swaying past her aqua blue eyes. She gently squeezed Fabrizio's arm and said: "*Mi chimano Angelina.* My name is Angelina. I live at the Convent of San Matteo, but sing with the choir of San Lorenzo. You are very kind, but I'm just one voice of many. And Brahms music...well, it's divine."

"Little Angel, you're well named," he smiled handsomely.

"And you, like Columbus, are going to America. Do you have family there?"

"No, signorina, my family is in Lucca. I'm going to San Francisco. There are many from Lucca already there. From Genoa also."

"You must be the oldest son in your family."

"No, the youngest. I have two brothers."

"Is not the oldest the one who should make such a voyage?"

"I suppose. But I've learned the ways of the marketplace in Lucca from my father. Maybe not as cleverly as the Genovese, but my brothers are just farmers."

They were silent for a moment, he seeming more vulnerable than she. Sensing this, Angelina asked, "Are you afraid?"

He nodded. "A little, but less since I heard you sing. I'm calmer now and realize others have made the journey to San Francisco and our faith will sustain me."

Two nuns who had been attending to Monsignor joined Angelina and Fabrizio. They were in their mid-twenties and had the air of upperclassmen. The shorter of the two said, "Angelina, we must return to San Matteo. Mother Superior expects us at vespers."

"I was just chatting with Signor Panforte. He's Monsignor's guest. He's from Lucca and he's going to America! Isn't that exciting, sister?"

"Quite. But we really must get back to the convent," the taller nun said, indifferent to Panforte's adventure.

He fidgeted his hat and said, "Sisters, I'd be honored to escort you to your convent. It's getting dark, and the streets are crowded. Allow me, please?"

"*Andiamo*," agreed the smaller nun, wrapping a black knit shawl around Angelina's fragile shoulders. The teenagers wound their way through the teaming *caruggi* flanked by the two nuns. They conversed haltingly, inhibited by the sisterly presence and their own adolescent shyness. Fabrizio learned that the soprano was fifteen and had been studying at the convent for three years. It was not clear whether she was simply a music student or a novice commencing her training as a nun. He chose not to press the point, fearing she might have already committed herself to the service of the Lord. What they learned of each other's past and dreams was obscure. But they sensed a commonality in each other. Perhaps it was that both had been separated from the protective circle of their families, Panforte speculated to the jury. Whatever it was, she revealed a generous curiosity about Fabrizio's distant destination.

They arrived at the ancient church of San Matteo, no larger than the modest church of the *Precious Ones* in Farneta, but bereft of a campanile. An undistinguished portal in the center of the facade pointed up to a loggia whose proportions appeared too large for the church, and when the door and loggia were viewed in context gave the impression of a sculpted, upside down exclamation mark. The shorter nun thanked Fabrizio for his escort and bade Angelina to come inside. The girl asked for more time and the nun granted, "*Una momento.*"

At the doorway, Fabrizio looked down on her shaded eyelids and asked, "May I write you from America? May I share my discoveries? Or are you not permitted to correspond outside the cloister?"

"What about your family? Surely they'll want to hear of your new life," she said, her brilliant blue eyes searching his handsome face.

"My mother died when I was born. And my father cannot read or write." Shame infected his voice.

"Oh, I'm sorry," her fingers played with her thin lips. She glanced over at the short nun, her eyes begging for a modest exemption from cloister's dictates. The smaller nun's eyelids dropped and she barely nodded her head twice, granting the girl's wish. Angelina smiled up at Fabrizio and accepted his invitation to converse across the seas. It was the first time he had seen her smile and the luster it brought to her stunning eyes. It was this image he carried with him, steaming out through the Mediterranean, across the Atlantic and around the Cape to the Pacific Ocean. He bowed to kiss her hand, and his lips trembled on the velvet cool of her skin.

"I didn't know at that moment I'd just met my future wife," Fred Panforte smiled warmly at the jury. He recounted that they corresponded for almost ten years until he felt sufficiently secure in his new country to propose marriage. He secured a salary advance from his employer to pay for Angelina's passage. He didn't tell the jury that his employer was Bartolomeo Bertolli or that Bertolli forgave his indebtedness as a wedding gift when the couple married at Saints Peter and Paul in 1918. The following year their son Robert was born.

As Panforte completed the story of his new American family Pat Kelley looked at Angelina in her first row seat. She looked up at her husband on the witness stand, voicelessly confirming their teenage meeting in Genoa. She was the petite picture of a faithful, loving wife. As Pat studied her eyes, the green shade predominating the blue, he sensed something detached about her gaze, something aloof from her husband's tale of their life-altering meeting in the cathedral of San Lorenzo. Pat had noted that throughout the trial Angelina Panforte seemed to have different masks. Her warmth and sensitivity toward her son during these terrible trial days was constantly evident. But when she looked at Maria Bertolli Kelley she seemed embarrassed, often tensely squeezing her gloved fingers. It seemed to Pat that she would always take a tiny step away from her husband whenever Maria's eyes meet hers, as though to distance herself from Maria's contempt. As her husband told their love story she had seemed to Pat almost taciturn. For Pat there was something fathomless about this couple who had been together for forty years. Other than brief exchanges of pleasantries Pat had been unable to get her alone. He had performed a number of services for her, such as arranging for her son to have a sun lamp in his jail cell and convincing the Sheriff to allow Mrs. Panforte to bring her son dinner meals from North Beach restaurants. She was as grateful for Pat's kindness and graciousness as she was unsuspecting that he was Maria's husband. Pat sensed that she wanted to talk to him privately, but her husband's presence prevented her from doing so.

On the morning of his last day in Italy, Fabrizio took his coffee in the kitchen with the housekeeper who reviewed the directions to *Stazione Maritima*, where he'd board the *SS Santa Clara* for San Francisco. After a ten-minute walk to the port he entered *Galleria Centrale*, passed through customs and boarded the steamer. He secured his belongings in a small berth that would be his buoyant home for the next two months. He didn't feel cramped in the tiny cabin, and not having to share his living quarters with his brothers, gave him a sense of privacy he'd never known. And a secure retreat in which to purloin the private correspondence of Bertolli, Pat scribbled down.

Fabrizio climbed up to the ship's deck, walked aft and studied Genoa's skyline, waiting for the ship to cast off. He tried to imagine what San Francisco looked like from the sea and whether it was anything like the twenty-five-centuries'-old city he was about to leave. He knew he was destined for one of the world's great port cities. Unlike Genoa, which had known Etruscans, Greeks, Phoenicians, Carthaginians and Romans, he found it impossible to conceptualize a city that was little more than a half-century old and yet had assumed so important a place in world commerce. His eyes scanned the dramatic slopes of this hillside city. Uniformly gray housetops seemed like glittering silver mirrors under the vivid Mediterranean sky. Higher and higher, crest upon crest, villas and palaces presided over the blue/green bay. Below the summit in the shadow of the Appenines, nature's inland fortress which had protected Genoa from Goths, Ostrogoths, Visigoths, Vandals and Huns, pure white monasteries meditated among cypress woods. He thought about San Francisco's hills and puzzled that the urban mountains of his destination seemed a topographical oddity. Unlike the hills of Tuscany they were not topped with fortress-like villas or compact walled cities by which elevation and masonry protected against the chaos and conflict of the migrating masses of the low lands. Nor did the San Bruno mountains to San Francisco's south or Twin Peaks at the city's heart provide, as did the Appenines for Genoa, a defensive barricade against the marauding tribes of time and the endless pursuit of conquest. It was California's absence of human history that perplexed the young man. Having grown up in a land in which the monuments of mankind speak in the tongues of thousands of years, he couldn't imagine a place populated with only its second generation. As a European, he felt that a country's or city's or even a village's history inculcated itself into one's soul from the earliest days of awareness. And this consciousness of a distant past created a definable order, a psychic structure by which one comprehends the unique expectancy of one's life. He felt the very lack of a past, the yet to be lived and written chronicle of California, was the very seductress that drew so many to her golden shores. Without the lessons of millennia, men were liberated of its burden, free to write their own writ, uninhibited by the echoing evolutions of antiquity. Panforte summed up to the jury his feelings as he waited for the *Santa Clara* to steam out to sea. "It wasn't so much what I was leaving behind. It was that there was so little to know about where I was going. I just believed my life would be better in America."

The bleating of the vessel's horn and the screams of straining iron drawing anchors from the water interrupted Fabrizio's shipboard speculations. The ship shuddered from the thrust of her powerful engines and the sea bubbled into white foam. A fleet of tireless tugs nudged the *Santa Clara* away from the pier. Once past the breakwater the tugs released the ship, and at three-quarters throttle she steamed out into the Gulf of Genoa, her white wake like a bride's cape trailing in effortless procession. Fabrizio remained at his observation post, intent on viewing Genoa until land was no longer in sight. He knew that once he passed through the Straits of Gibraltar it would be many weeks before he again sighted land and then it would be the shores of another continent. The city shrunk from his view, the sun slipped behind the Appenines and the wind whipped spray from the *Santa Clara*'s wake against his face. The Ligurian coast disappeared and he felt terribly alone, abandoned on an endless sea. The wind whistled at him as dusk descended on the Mediterranean. He imagined the wind was Angelina's voice singing Brahms' pacifying music. Above the choir of sea and gulls her soprano reached for the first star of the night and he heard her phrase Isaiah's reassuring lyric: "*Ich will euch trosten, we einen sein Mutter trostet.* As one whom his mother comforeth, so I will comfort you."

Danny Loeb walked from the jury rail to the defense table and asked the client who'd jump-started his legal career: "Mr. Panforte, your son married the late Paula Brady on Memorial Day, 1944. Will you tell the jury the circumstances regarding your son's marriage plans?"

"It was the month before Paula traveled to Mexico, so it must've been February of that year. We was working at The Market and Bob said he needed to talk to me. So we went to lunch at the Oregon Café and he told me Paula was pregnant," Panforte said, and the spectators suppressed a collective gasp. He continued: "Bob said he wanted to marry her. I asked him if he was sure that's what he wanted to do." A confused look glazed over Paul Brady's face, but his wife sat ramrod straight, her eyes slicing into Panforte like a deadly stiletto. Pat Kelley noticed that Angelina Panforte was staring at her husband on the stand, her rosary beads limp in her right hand, her face hard, almost contemptuous.

Panforte took a deep breath and said, "So I talked for a while to see if...you know...I asked if he was sure that's what he wanted, if this was the girl he wanted. I said somethin' about it was probably someone else who was responsible, but you'll get blamed anyway. We went down the line discussing things. He didn't like what I was saying."

"Did he say anything in response to your remarks to him?"

"He said: 'Dad, she's the girl I love, the girl I wanna marry. If you don't approve, we're gonna get married anyway.'"

Pat saw Angelina glance at the back of her son's head, her expression eased, the tension in her shoulders relaxed as though approving her son's unconditional expression of love for Paula.

"Mr. Panforte, did you feel your son married Paula Brady a few months later under the compulsion that she was pregnant?"

"No, no way! He was crazy about her! Anyway, she took care of her pregnancy when she went to Mexico in March."

Moore bellowed, "Good God, Your Honor! Do these people have no sense of decency? Are we gonna just sit here and listen to this poor dead woman being slandered?"

Judge Grant's cheeks flushed with fury. "Sit down, Mr. Loeb!" she ordered. Then she turned to the jury and firmly instructed: "Ladies and gentlemen, I'm instructing you that Mr. Panforte's purported conversation with his son is *not* evidence that the late Mrs. Paula Panforte was pregnant before her marriage or that she went to Mexico to terminate her pregnancy. This testimony is offered solely to show the Defendant's state of mind at the time these alleged statements were made. What relevance this issue has to a homicide five years later escapes me and may be a mystery to you as well. Proceed with your examination, Mr. Loeb. But I want no more of these father/son conversations. Limit yourself to this witness' personal knowledge!"

But Pat Kelley knew the damage had been done. Danny Loeb was employing a classic defense ploy, namely sullying the character of the dead victim to subtlety minimize the implications of designed death. The genius of his tactic was using the Defendant's father to brand Paula's character with the twin Roman Catholic taboos of pre-marital sex and abortion, the latter of which was a felony for both patient and physician. In Loeb's plan Fred Panforte was the preliminary bout to his son as the testimonial main event. Loeb was using a caring father to fling dirt, sparing his Defendant son from even a hint of marital discord.

"Very well, Your Honor," Loeb agreed to Judge Grant's admonishment with feigned sincerity. Through Fred Panforte, Loeb sketched a portrait of a close, enduring father/son relationship. As a boy, they'd bonded dear hunting in Marin. As for their "hunting lodge" which had been used by the Army as a P.O.W. training escape site, Panforte told the jury its designation as a *lodge* was their private joke – it was merely a hunting shelter and storage facility. He proudly admitted "his boy," as he called his son, was expert in navigating the forest of Mt. Tamalpais and Muir Woods, which was why the Army had selected him to guide their training mission. As for the locale of Paula's grave, Panforte dismissed it as a uniquely secret place, pointing out that it was well known not only by the Army but the army of recreational hunters. "*And,*" Kelley thought, "*completely familiar to you as well.*"

As soon as Fred learned of Paula's disappearance from his son on Tuesday morning of June 6th he called Paul Brady to use his influence with the SFPD to find his daughter-in-law. Panforte told the jury that Brady told him Chief Inspector O'Day was "the pick of the litter" and that he should cooperate fully with him. And he did. He consented to two searches of "the kids' house" and the Marin hunting lodge. But he claimed that O'Day did not reciprocate his cooperation and courtesy. "He wouldn't let me see my son, wouldn't even let him see a lawyer," Fred Panforte said, shaking his head in dismay.

The DA bolted to his feet, "I move to strike this self-serving hearsay. It's just another cheap shot attempt to try anyone other than your client! First you slander a dead girl, now you're blaming the police!" he angrily shouted.

Loeb, trembling with rage, barked, "They outta be tried for the way they treated this man and his son…" Panforte, his neck veins bulging with anger, burst into the debate yelling, "It's the truth! For chrissake, they wouldn't even let him see his mother!"

"Wait a minute! Gentlemen, knock it off!" Judge Grant sternly interceded. To the witness she said, "Mr. Panforte, you're not to speak unless spoken to by the lawyers or me. As for counsel, you will address your remarks to the Court and not argue with each other! One more outburst like this and you'll both cool your heals in the Sheriff's custody. While you're at it, let's lower the volume at bit."

In a soft tone dictated by Judge Grant, Loeb asked: "Did you harbor any animus toward Paula Brady or feel that she was in any way forcing your son into marriage?"

"No way! She was a lovely girl. She was like my own daughter! We were all very close, her mom and dad. We're good families. I don't know how all this could happen..." his voice trailed off and his chest heaved. His wife dabbed her eyes with a satin hanky while Eileen Brady's tearless eyes maintained their harsh vigil on the witness stand. "When was the last time you saw your daughter-in-law alive, Mr. Panforte?" Loeb asked softly.

"The Sunday before...before she disappeared. Sunday evening I dropped in at their place to see my grandson..." as Panforte ran his thick hand through his thinning hair he blinked his eyes and grimaced, choking back tears. "Please continue, Fred," Loeb gently urged.

"I got to their place around nine. I was on my way to our ranch in Petaluma. I wanted to tell Bob that I'd be working at Petaluma that week and he'd take my place at The Market. Bob went into the kitchen and fixed us drinks. He said somethin' about the baby doin' somethin' for the first time..." Panforte's hands covered his face, but failed to conceal tears that slid down to the corners of his mouth. He tried to continue but his voice was drowned in sobs. In her front row seat his wife sobbed convulsively, the comforting grip of the priest unable to stem her misery. Across the aisle next to Terry Kelley the dead girl's mother sat tight-lipped, her face cold, her eyes mercilessly on Panforte. Judge Grant, in an emotionless tone, said: "We'll take our recess now." The Defendant, who always remained at counsel table until the jury had vacated the room, signaled the bailiff to take him away. His lips were trembling, his face ashen and his breath coming in short, rapid takes.

27

For the first time in the trial of Robert Panforte, Pat Kelley felt the need to get the hell out of his beloved courthouse. He needed to be alone, to purge himself of the emotions that had started boiling within him from the moment he had sworn Fred Panforte to his God to tell the truth. Once outside he crossed Kearny Street to Portsmouth Square. Among old Chinamen smoking on park benches and mothers monitoring their toddles, his stomach churned and the back of his neck dampened as he reflected the generational journey from Lucca to Francisco Street. Danny Loeb's examination of Fred Panforte had stimulated unexpected and conflicting reactions in Pat. Panforte's story of his chance meeting with his future wife in a Genoa cathedral and his vivid expression of his last moments in Italy had a quality that Pat never considered. Panforte had conveyed the stark solitude of his voyage across seas and the emotional isolation he'd experienced as a foreigner in a strange new land. His description of his first view of San Francisco as he sailed through the Golden Gate illustrated the city's resurrection from the rubble of 1906. He had testified: "I was stunned by how it looked like Genoa. The hills of the City plunging right down to the water, and the Bay forming a huge natural harbor, only taller than Genoa's, and buildings all the way up the hills, just like Genoa. Only they were bigger and the whole city looked brand new, like it had just been built. I remember pretending it had been built for me – a brand new city for a brand new American."

But it was Panforte's emphasis on his feelings moments before he departed Italy that most impressed Pat. He couldn't help but sense a young man's feeling that he'd reached a point of no return, and in that courtroom moment he seemed almost heroic. Pat realized that this was so of each and all of America's immigrants, even his own grandfather, who had boarded a death ship in Cork City before the turn of the century. He'd often thought of those who had fled the countries of their birth for America as desperate, driven souls breaking out of their prisons of poverty. But Panforte's story – and it was the story of all who came before and after him – revealed the fundamental courage required of one who chooses to be re-born an American. While most believed that bravery was the child of desperation, Pat had learned from the journey of the *Precious Ones* that faith is the parent of inestimable valor. Pat was startled by the irony that Fred Panforte's testimony had reminded him of this truth and profoundly grateful that his wife was absent from the courtroom to hear it.

Pat thought back on Joe Desmond's account of his breakfast meeting with Danny Loeb at the Oregon Café when he'd confided the dominant role Panforte played in his only child's life and the vital role he'd play at his son's trial. Loeb had told Desmond that old man Panforte had to demonstrate his constant and complete approval of his son. Surely his acknowledgment of his son's mastery of the terrain of Mt. Tamalpais as a boy and his ratification of marriage to a *girl in trouble* were unabashed paternal endorsements. His angry outburst at the Chief Inspector's refusal of legal assistance for his son was a heated example of Panforte's defiance of powerful authority. But it was his emotional breakdown on the stand when recounting celebratory cocktails just a day before a doomed young mother met her death that Pat felt was most instructive to his son. Pat was certain the jury viewed his emotional collapse as a sincere expression of grief for his daughter-in-law and the natural parental catharsis of a suddenly splintered family.

Pat thought it more significant, however, that his emotional turmoil precipitated a different visible response of passion from his son. In all the long days he'd spent studying Robert Panforte or during his interviews with relatives, through all his hours in the custody of the homicide detail, he had seemed a confused young man, uncertain of the appropriateness of his own emotions. It was as though he felt he needed guidance as to what he should be feeling. But when his father surrendered to the tragedy of a June evening in the Marina his son's seemingly cool exterior wilted in the heat from the witness stand, and his athletic body shuddered with spasms of emotions, at once conflicting and too long suppressed. In the courtroom his father was teaching him that to confront the contest over his life as a phlegmatic Stanford man was a lethal prescription more deadly than the patient interrogations of homicide detectives and the relentless cross-examination of a prosecutor. Robert Panforte, like all too many sons, had never seen his father cry before. At that instant Fred Panforte taught his son the most valuable lesson of all. He taught his boy that tears of fear are unworthy, tears of loss manly. And Pat Kelley fully comprehended Loeb's brilliant strategy of using a father to teach his son how to defend himself.

Pat glanced at his watch; it was time to get back to work. As he skipped up the granite steps of the Hall of Justice another notion about Fred Panforte's testimony insinuated itself. It was a darker reflection, vaguely sinister. It was how Fred Panforte spoke of Paula. Fred had revealed the Catholic taboos of premarital sex and unplanned, unwanted pregnancy in public. It wasn't his attempt to sully the moral character of the victim that troubled Pat. Rather it was his advice to his son that someone else was probably responsible for her maternity and his conclusion that Robert would be unjustly blamed for her promiscuity. It was his implicit notion that the mischance of sexual congress was invariably the agency of a woman. There was something very troubling in the way Fred Panforte talked about women. Of course *boy-talk* and *girl-talk* have a considerable variety of themes and an infinite number of fantasies. Because Pat had been raised by and married to independent women he suffered very little of the male chauvinism of his day. But among men he'd known he'd come across a breed who, though enthusiastically heterosexual, exuded a barely shrouded contempt for the complimentary sex. Among men with such dispositions he had noted that their dialogue categorized females more by their duties than the wholeness of their being.

To these men, mothers were canonized by ignoring any consideration of the act that caused them to become mothers. Wives who tolerated the rites of the marital bed were classified as loyal, sleep-in maids. But a woman who responded to her own sensual nature was by their perverse reasoning at once desirable and detestable. Pat couldn't determine whether the revulsion these men implied was at their own sexual appetites for such women or repugnance that women had hungers of their own. It seemed to Pat that Fred Panforte, but not his son, might be of this stock of men, men who at their dark core are contemptuous of the feminine.

Pat thought of Bob Panforte's obvious devotion to his own mother and his father's complete ignorance of his mother because of her death. He recalled Eileen Brady's deep affection for her son-in-law and her gratitude that he'd given her daughter back to her. As he walked down the court corridor Pat realized that he knew very little about Fred Panforte's relationship with his wife. What was emerging in his mind was there was something quite different in both men's relations with women, and whatever that difference was the jury was unlikely to ever hear of it.

The most intriguing aspect of Fred Panforte's courtroom breakdown was it gave Pat his first insight into the weekend preceding Paula's death. Until Fred Panforte had testified about his Sunday night visit at their Marina home Pat's view of Paula and Bob was blanked out from the pleasant bridge party with the Petersens on Saturday night until that fateful and now fatal Monday night. Now Pat had Fred Panforte is his sights. He had testified that he'd dropped in on the way to Petaluma. What was Fred doing in Petaluma on a Sunday, Pat asked himself. And what was the reason for transferring Bob Panforte from the protective work environment on the Petaluma ranches to the frantic volatility of The Market, he wondered. Finally, Pat questioned if Fred Panforte's surrender to his emotions had a darker cause than the poignant scene of his grandson's accomplishments. Could it have something to do with Paula herself?

His composure restored, Panforte resumed his testimony. Loeb asked, "Fred, will you tell the jury about the your visit with your son and daughter-in-law on Sunday evening, June 4th?"

"Like I said, Bob went into the kitchen to fix us drinks. He told me the baby got up by himself in the crib for the first time and that called for a celebration." Panforte said.

"Thank you, that's all," Loeb concluded. District Attorney Moore couldn't wait to get at Panforte. He almost knocked Loeb down when he bolted from his chair. This was not the smooth Democratic candidate for Attorney General or a methodical prosecutor coolly presenting his accusations. This was a very angry man, anxious to harm another. "Mr. Panforte," Moore began, his tone dripping with sarcasm, "you've recounted a touching scene with your grandson, the Defendant and the deceased. You first learned that something was amiss in their home when he called you that Tuesday morning and said Paula had not returned from the show. In fact she was buried over at Mt. Tamalpais where he'd spent his playful boyhood days, isn't that right?"

"Objection! Calls for speculation, argumentative!" Loeb protested.

"Sustained," the judge ruled.

"You've told us that Chief Inspector O'Day wouldn't allow you to provide a lawyer for your son. If you believed your son when he told you his wife was missing, why did you think he needed a lawyer?"

"He'd been questioned all day by the cops. I just thought he needed to know his rights."

"You thought he needed a lawyer to advise him of his rights as a suspect in his wife's disappearance, is that your testimony?"

"No, no! Just his rights. That's what a lawyer's for. They tell ya if ya got any rights."

Moore modulated his voice to a gentler pitch and asked, "Now Mr. Panforte, you've told us you cooperated fully with the inspectors and provided a great deal of information about your son, his education, business, personal and family life. You also told them all you knew about your daughter-in-law." Moore pivoted, turning his back to the witness and looking directly into Eileen Brady's misty eyes, and asked: "Yet you never mentioned to Chief Inspector O'Day that your son had gotten Paula pregnant before they were married, did you?"

"I didn't tell 'em nothing about that."

"You didn't tell them she'd gone to Mexico for an abortion, did you?"

"You don't talk about these things with cops. It's too personal."

Moore spun around and confronted the witness. "Too personal? Was it too personal to discuss this purported pregnancy with the dead girl's parents?"

"I never told 'em about it, no."

"And you never mentioned it to your own wife, did you sir?"

Panforte glanced over to his wife and meekly said, "No. I never said nothin' to nobody. It was just between me and Bob."

"But it's not too personal to get up on the witness stand and defame a dead woman's memory if you think it will help your son's case, is it, Mr. Panforte?"

"Objection. It's argumentative," Loeb protested.

The D.A. said, "I'll withdraw the question. God forbid that I've offended counsel's sensibilities." Moore moved to the center of the Pit, directly in front of Kelley's desk and said, "Let's talk a little more about that luncheon conversation with your son at the Oregon Café. I gather you were counseling your son and you suggested that some other man might be responsible for Paula's pregnancy, right?"

"Yeah, that was a possibility I mentioned."

"But hadn't Paula and your son been going steady for eighteen months?"

"Well, yeah, but you never know about things like that."

"There was a war going on back then Mr. Panforte, so there was a scarcity of eligible young men. Don't you think you'd have discovered her unfaithfulness to your son?"

"Calls for speculation," Loeb moaned. Judge Grant ruled: "Gentlemen, this has gotten terribly tedious! If I allow this to go on we'll be taking testimony on Paula's junior prom date. There'll be no more speculation on the late Mrs. Panforte's personal life. Move on." But the DA returned to the Oregon Café conversation. "I believe you testified you advised your son that even if he was not responsible for Paula's pregnancy he'd be blamed. Why did you think that?"

"Well, like you said, they was going steady, so it figures people would think that. Mostly it's because people think we're really wealthy and a rich guy pays in these situations."

"But wasn't Paula Brady the heir to a considerable fortune herself?"

"I don't count other people's money, Mr. Moore."

"But you knew she was from a family of considerable means, didn't you? It's not as though your son was confiding in you that he'd just knocked up a hatcheck girl or a cocktail waitress?"

"Sustained," the judge ordered before Loeb could even mouth his objection. "Rephrase the question counsel and leave out any references to working women."

"You knew Paula Brady was a wealthy young woman. So she'd have no motive to insinuate herself into your poultry empire since she was financially secure, correct?"

"Look, Mr. Moore, this was a conversation between me and my son about a big problem. I was just trying to figure out options. I was thinking out loud when I said those things."

"Let's talk about what you were thinking at the Oregon Café. You thought Paula Brady had premarital sex with your son, right?"

"Yeah."

"Did you have any information from anyone other than your son that they'd been sexually intimate before they were married?"

"No, you usually don't do it in front of witnesses." Pat saw Angelina Panforte grimace at her husband's answer.

"Mr. Panforte, you testified that: 'She took care of the pregnancy when she went to Mexico in March.' Did you mean by that she had an abortion in Mexico?"

"Yeah."

"Did your son tell you Paula had a Mexican abortion?"

"No."

"Did the late Paula Panforte or her parents ever tell you she'd had a Mexican abortion?"

"No. Like I said before, I only talked about it that one time with Bob."

"At the time you formed the belief that Paula Brady had aborted a pregnancy caused by your son, did you have any information from physicians who treated her in Mexico?"

"No. I just knew she'd gone to Mexico, that she went to a hospital there and obviously never had a baby till my grandson was born years later. I just put two and two together."

"Sir, I submit that your two plus two came out to five! Let me ask you this: In preparing for your testimony in this case have you seen any medical records from any Mexican hospitals that treated Paula Brady in March of 1944?"

"Yeah, our investigator got a copy of her records."

"And there's absolutely nothing in those records indicating Paula Brady was pregnant in March, 1944, is there, Mr. Panforte?"

"I'm no doctor, but there's something about her ovaries."

"It doesn't take a medical degree to read these records, which clearly state that Paula Brady had surgery for a small ovarian cyst, Mr. Panforte. Did you find a single word in her medical records indicating she was pregnant?"

"I guess not."

"Is it a fair summary of your testimony that the only evidence you had that Paula was pregnant prior to her marriage was what your son told you at the Oregon Café?"

"That's about right."

"And this is the same son who lied to you when he told you his dead wife, the mother of *your* grandson, was missing, isn't that so Mr. Panforte?"

"He's my only son," Panforte sighed.

District Attorney Moore introduced Paula's hospital records from Santa Lucia Hospital in Mexico City confirming the surgical removal of a cyst on her right ovary in March of 1944. The DA glanced over to Eileen Brady. She nodded to him, acknowledging his restoration of her daughter's virtue. Her husband, however, was grim faced. He obviously wanted more blood from Panforte and doubted Moore was his equal in the art of a slashing cross-examination. "Mr. Panforte, I just have a few more questions. I'd like to talk a little bit more about the last time you saw Paula alive. I know this is very difficult for you, but we must try to get to the bottom of what happened to your daughter-in-law." Panforte nodded and was relaxed a bit by the

336 \ Phil Ryan

prosecutor's solicitous manner. Moore said, "As I understand your testimony, you dropped in on your son and daughter-in-law around nine o'clock Sunday evening. You were there about an hour, had a cocktail celebrating your grandson pulling himself up in his crib. Can you tell us anything about the conversation that evening?"

"We was in the living room, Bob and Paula on the couch near the bay window. I was in the chair with the ottoman. Bob was playing with the baby in his lap. The baby was gripping Bob's thumbs and Bob would shake 'em a little and say: 'Junior, show Nonno how strong you.' *Nonno's* Italian for grandfather, and that's what the kids call me. Paul was Grandpa. Anyway, when Bob shook his thumbs, the baby pulled himself up, sorta half sitting. So I said: 'Let me try that. How do I know you guys ain't cheating?' So Bob gives me the baby and I put him in my lap. He grabs hold of my thumbs, kicking his tiny feet and grinning, his blue eyes sparkling and pulls himself right up. 'You a strong little fella. It's that Irish/Italian blood,' I says. Then Paula laughs and says: 'You guys are nuts. Next you'll be getting him to do push-ups, and my dad will probably give him boxing gloves for his birthday.' It was real nice, just talking and playing with the baby and everything."

"Did Paula appear drunk or angry or anything to you?"

"No way! She was fine. You know, relaxed and content."

"How about your son? Was he drunk?"

"We just had one drink. Bob was drinking wine. Paula and me had a highball. I didn't notice nothin' different."

"I have nothing further, Mr. Panforte," the D.A. concluded. Panforte re-joined his wife and the priest in their family row. The priest patted him on the shoulder, but Angelina ignored him, her eyes never leaving her son, her rosary beads immobile in her gloved hand.

Judge Grant recessed the trial for the weekend. Outside her chambers' door reporters were interviewing Paul Brady. *The Examiner* reporter asked: "Mr. Brady, you were a prosecutor once. Does it seem to you the D.A.'s made no effort to find a motive for the killing? It seems to me he's content to prove that Panforte selected and prepared the gravesite in advance. Do you see it that way?" Brady, a full head taller than the reporter, looked down and said, "I believe he intended to kill Paula. I'm sure if Bob takes the stand, it will come out on cross-examination."

"Can you tell us where or when you got this information that Panforte planned to kill your daughter?" *The Chronicle* asked. Brady's voice was terse with emotion. "No. As to when I knew that he'd killed Paula, I watched him being questioned by Judge Grant. I heard him say Paula had gone to the show alone, talking about her in the past tense, then all of a sudden…I knew. I just knew. I left Judge Grant's chambers and went to a pay phone and called Paula's mother. 'Eileen,' I said, 'we won't find Paula – she's dead.'"

The Chronicle asked: "You remember talking to me out at Holy Cross Cemetery and saying you didn't think anything would be served by executing Robert Panforte, and there were no recriminations. Has this trial changed your feelings?"

"At the time I spoke to you of no recriminations I had not seen the Coroner's evidence. I didn't know that Paula lived for at least a half-hour or up to two hours after he beat her and stuffed her in the trunk of his car while she was still alive. I can't get that out of my mind." Brady shook his head slowly and continued, "I hadn't seen her grave at that time either. Anyone who saw it will never forget it. It was the perfect sepulcher, a perfect hiding place. Search parties could have hunted for days and not found anything. I can't believe Judge Grant won't take the jury out there." The lead paragraph of the morning papers had just been written: *Two fathers talked about the Panforte case in the Hall of Justice. One father was fighting to keep his thirty-year-old son Robert from the gas chamber. The other, unable to forget the battered, bloody body of his twenty-five-year-old daughter Paula, was fighting to send him there.*

"Excuse me fellas," Bailiff McCann interrupted. To Paul Brady, he said, "Counselor, the Judge will see you now." The press immediately quieted down, staring at Brady who didn't move and glared back at the bailiff. Brady wiped at his forehead as though to clear the fog from his mind and said to McCann, "I've got nothing to say to her! Not now, not ever!" He turned, pushed his way through the reporters and walked slump-shouldered down the marble corridor. The press started to follow him until Pat Kelley suddenly appeared. Pat put his hand on the chest of *The Examiner* and said, "Hold on, boys. Leave him alone. You didn't hear his last words." *The Examiner* and *The Chronicle* both nodded, and the rest of the pack followed suit. Paul Brady's denunciation of his best friend never appeared in the newspapers, although Bailiff McCann tactlessly reported his remark to Judge Lucille Grant.

Pat found his wife and son waiting for him on the Kearny Street steps. Maria had taken a cab from All Hallows School to meet them after court recessed. To Maria Pat said, "Honey, let's keep the cab. I'm beat. I can't handle a crowded streetcar." Terry jumped into the passenger front seat, his parents into the back seat. Inside the cab Pat barked directions to their home and released a long, deep sigh. Pat was usually not a man whose face or body language revealed the strains he was under. Indeed, Maria had never seen him so stressed. As the cabby pulled out into traffic she snuggled her shoulder into his side, placed her hand on his thigh and kneaded his taut muscles. Pat closed his eyes and laid his head against the backrest and surrendered to her healing touch, prayerful that her solacing tenderness would rescue him from those men drowning in the sequestered whirlpools of their paternity.

28

The Kelleys welcomed Joe Desmond and Mary Healy into their Crestlake Drive home for a Sunday dinner party. The young couple walked through a wide hallway and stepped down into a sunken, spacious living room. Pat was mixing drinks near a bay window that presented a pastoral view of an evergreen forest and the still, shadowed waters of Pine Lake. A rust colored Oriental rug framed by the dark hardwood floor drew the colors of the forest into the living room. Except for the Oriental carpet and a grand piano, the furnishings were designed for comfort rather than a display of artful taste. Two large sofas, a love seat and commodious cushioned chairs demonstrated it was a room dedicated to amiable gatherings and animated conversations. Surrounding a dramatic fireplace made of stones Pat purloined from the Russian River in Sonoma was Pat's ultimate treasure – books. From floor to ceiling, the full length of the wall, book shelves with tightly packed volumes testified to the voracious appetite of a learned man – a taste he'd bequeathed to his only son. He even had one of those oak ladders with wheels, top and bottom, that you see in libraries to climb up to the top shelves. The family story was that Pat's stepfather built it. But City Hall gossip suggested that the head Librarian of San Francisco removed it from the Library and gave it to Kelley as a house-warming gift.

At the front of the room Maria's jet-black Knabe grand piano presided. Both the Oriental rug and piano were gifts from her father and told much about his special relationship with his youngest child. Originally the carpet had graced the living room at Bertolli's ranch in Sonoma, the scene of Maria's childhood summers. When Gaetano Merola opened the maiden season at the new War Memorial Opera House his tight budget required borrowing props. Bertolli loaned his old friend his Oriental rug for the company's premier performance of *Tosca*. This carpet, on which Maria had taken her first baby steps, served briefly as the final resting place for evil Baron Scarpia, stabbed by the enraged Tosca, his fake blood staining the elegant rug.

Maria's ebony piano was another product of her father's show business career. Following The Earthquake and Fire, Bertolli took a sabbatical from the theater to devote his energies to re-building his business and the City. In 1910, the City completely restored, he and Antonietta Pompa decided to produce a celebratory, free concert at Lotta's Fountain on Market Street starring their friend Luisa Tetrazzini. Following Tetrazzini's American debut at The Tivoli Opera House she had become the world's reigning diva, selling out twenty-one consecutive performances she gave at Oscar Hammerstein's Manhattan Opera House. Grateful to San Francisco and Bertolli for catapulting her to American fame and fortune she had contributed $10,000 to the City's earthquake relief fund – the most generous individual contribution made. Bertolli wired her that he would escort her from New York to San Francisco for the Christmas Eve concert. She accepted by return wire and suggested Bertolli and Antonietta come to New York for the December world premiere of Puccini's *The Girl Of The Golden West*. Bertolli thought this an excellent way to return to his career as a producer, and an opportunity to meet with Gaetano Merola. Merola, who had urged Tetrazzini to sign with Hammerstein after the Met had rejected her, so impressed Hammerstein that he appointed him Chorus Director of his Manhattan Opera Company. Bertolli was certain his old friend would tell him the inside story of the New York opera war between Hammerstein and The Met. Most importantly, he'd decided to introduce Maria to his theatrical world by taking her to New York. His wife Renee objected to a five-year old traveling cross-country to an opera, but Bertolli was adamant that his daughter's introduction to art was timely. Along with Antonietta, Bertolli, and Antonietta's stage manger, Bernie Jacobs, little Maria set out for New York City.

The Knabe grand piano in Kelley's living room was a relic of that memorable trip. Kelley family lore had it that Puccini had advertised a black Knabe piano as the instrument on which he'd composed his *Girl Of The Golden West* in the Playbill, and Bertolli promptly purchased one for Maria in New York in 1910. But there were other mementos from Maria's maiden night at the theater that very much shaped the woman she'd become. Of course the intimacy of a cross-continental train trip with her father was bonding and unforgettable for her. She didn't have to share him with her siblings or her mom, and she woke up every day on the train trip sharing his rituals. She was fascinated and a bit frightened watching him shave with a straight razor on the rocking train, but then he'd let her rub and kiss his cheeks and confirm, "They're as soft as a baby's bottom." She watched him plan his daily wardrobe and carefully select the colors of his tie, as though in color coordination he divined the events of his day. In their Pullman she colored with her crayons while he sketched mechanical contraptions. He read or told her stories before naps and bedtime, and they dined each day with his lovely friend, Antonietta. Maria couldn't pronounce her name properly, so she called her "Auntie," which unintentionally precluded on-board gossip about the wealthy businessman and the beautiful actress.

In New York they stayed in adjoining suites at the Waldorf Astoria, and little Maria pretended to ice skate down the white and gold marble corridors of Peacock Alley. Her father took her to galleries and museums, and Antonietta and he explained Greco-Roman sculpture and ancient Egyptian and Etruscan artifacts to her. Her favorite was the *Sleeping Eros*, from Rhodes, her father told her. She didn't know Rhodes from Rhode Island, and Antonietta's explanation that the boy combined the themes of love and sleep in a classic Hellenistic exploration of the states of being was lost on her. But she happily told them "He's so pudgy and cute!"

On Manhattan nights she was bundled up and gloved in wools that were foreign to a California girl as her father and Antonietta took her to New York's full menu of performing arts venues. One night it was vaudeville, with baggy pants comedians and song and dance acts. Another it was a symphony performance. Next to Puccini's world premiere it was Antonietta Pompa's concert performance that remained vivid in Maria's memory. Antonietta had been billed as the *"Neapolitan Nightingale."* This seemed to irritate her father, but the standing room audience was thrilled by her Neapolitan songs accompanied by piano, two violins and a cello. For the second half of her program Antonietta selected arias by strong operatic woman, such as Tosca, Carmen, Norma and Aida. Before each aria she got into character with English soliloquies relating what her character was feeling moments before expressing it musically.

After Antonietta's concert her father took Maria backstage. The star's dressing room was filled with flowers and formally dressed strangers praising Antonietta's performance and beauty. When she spotted Maria holding her father's hand in the doorway her eyes brightened and she waved the girl to come to her. She swept her up into her lap and Maria gushed, "Auntie, you never told me you could sing! Are you going to sing with Signor Caruso tomorrow? He sounds nice on Papa's Victrola."

Antonietta ruffled Maria's thick black hair, "No sweetie, Caruso will sing with some other ladies. It's a different kind of show. You'll see."

The next night at the world premier Maria saw that it was a *very* different kind of show. Whereas Antonietta's audience had looked and acted like San Francisco audiences the crowd at the Met was very different. The ladies were fur coated and flagrantly bejeweled, and they all seemed to be propped up in the front rows of endless boxes like mannequins in a museum. The house was huge, larger than the Paris Opera or Covent Garden, and Bertolli shook his head at the four tiers of boxes and boxes on the orchestra level. Brooklyn- born Bernie Jacobs, escorting Antonietta, said, "This joint's just a semi-circle of boxes with an opera house built around 'em!"

"The sight lines must be dreadful," Bertolli said.

Nodding toward the Diamond Horseshoe, Jacobs said, "That's old lady Astor, let's see if she leaves after the intermission like she usually does. And that's Mrs. Vanderbilt in box four. She usually hums off key during the whole show. Check all the boxes out and you'll see J.P. Morgan's world-view. He doesn't allow Catholics, Jews or foreign-born."

The reception for Puccini at the Waldorf was a characteristic show business gathering – then or now – of money and talent. Luisa, Antonietta and Merola gravitated to the conversational conclave of the creative guests, with Bertolli and Maria tagging along. For Antonietta it was like a homecoming celebration. Performing artists live in a sort of global village that's not restricted by national boundaries. They come to know their colleagues and rivals through a worldwide network of public appearances in jewel cities and from gossip stored backstage. Bertolli was somewhat subdued in the face of so much fame. Except for Enrico Caruso and Puccini, Maria had no idea who all these fancy people were. But she liked that they didn't fuss over her, and they seemed truly interested in her reactions to the performance. When Caruso asked her what she thought of the show she said: "I think Minnie saved you from hanging 'cause it would be bad for your voice." Caruso laughed heartily and said, "Would you like my autograph, little one?"

"What's an autograph?" Maria asked.

"My signature," the great tenor said.

Maria said, "Why would I want that? I'd rather listen to Papa's records of you singing."

Caruso smiled, pulled out a small pad of paper and sketched a caricature. He handed it to Maria, who studied it for a moment and said, "The little girl you drew is wearing my dress."

"The little girl I drew is *you*," Caruso said.

"Is the man with the big tummy you?"

"*Si*," smiled the tenor.

"What am I handing you in the drawing?" she asked.

"Your autograph. See, it says *Maria*," Caruso patted her head. This priceless original caricature of Enrico Caruso receiving Maria's autograph was framed and displayed on her Knabe grand piano in her fog shrouded home on Crestlake Drive.

When they met the composer, Maria thought Puccini a handsome fellow with thick, wavy brown hair and a rich mustache under a strong nose. She expected them to talk of their childhood in Lucca, but was surprised when all they talked about was automobiles! These Lucchese boys shared a passion for cars – Puccini for recreational pleasure, Bertolli for revolutionizing his business empire.

When Bernie Jacobs realized the audience with Puccini was about to conclude he handed the maestro a libretto of *The Girl Of The Golden West*. Jacobs jerked his head in the direction of Maria. Puccini said, "Of course." He withdrew a Waterman fountain pen from his coat pocket and scribbled something on the back page advertisement where he was pictured extolling the sweetness of Knabe pianos. He handed the autographed libretto to Bertolli, who quickly read it and said softly, "*Grazie Maestro. Grazie mille.*"

Later, back at the hotel, Antonietta tucked her into bed and Maria asked, "What did Signor Puccini write on that paper for Papa? Is it about silly cars?"

Antonietta said, "It's to you Maria. It's a note from Puccini. He wrote: '*Mia piccola Maria. Practica, practica, practica! E lei saro la vera La fanciulla west.*' My little Maria. Practice, practice, practice! And you will be the true girl of the golden west.' And he signed it: Giacomo Puccini.'"

"What does it mean?" she asked.

"I think it means your father's buying you a piano."

"Really? That's neat!" Maria bolted up, saying, "Maybe I can be a composer like Signor Puccini when I grow up! But I didn't see any ladies in the orchestra. Do they only let ladies sing? Why is Papa getting me a piano if I can't play it in the show?"

"*They* don't let us do anything. *They* don't even let us vote. But your father believes women can do anything if they're smart enough to ignore what they're *allowed*."

"So Papa thinks I can play my piano anywhere I want?" Maria said.

"Your father thinks you can be anything you want if you put your whole mind and heart into it."

Maria snuggled onto her pillow and asked, "Is Papa right?"

"Yes, he's very right. Men like Maestro Puccini and your Papa are different than most men. Puccini's imagination sees secrets in the past, and his music makes us feel what he sees. Your father has a way of seeing how things will be in the future that few others can see. But it's way past your bedtime, so close your pretty eyes. *Buono notte, mia cara.*" Antonietta gently kissed her forehead.

In the dining room overlooking Pine Lake, Pat Kelley fixed Joe a martini, asking: "Where's Mary? I thought you were bringing her."

"She's upstairs with Megan looking at photos." Joe said.

Pat shook his head, "Megan thinks she's a female Ansel Adams with that cheap little camera I gave her." He handed Joe his drink, looked furtively toward the kitchen and said, "Don't say anything to Maria about the priest sitting with the Panfortes last Friday. He's a Jesuit friend of mine, and he's coming to dinner tonight."

"What the hell's a friend of yours doing with the Panfortes?"

"He's Pete Conroy. We grew up in the Mission together. He's the head of the retreat house at El Retiro. Old man Panforte's a big donor to the Jesuits."

"For chrissake Pat! You think the Church should take sides in a murder trial?"

"Look at it this way. The Jebbies figure the closer they get to the secular side of man, the more likely they'll find his soul. Besides, it's not just about cultivating the Faithful who are investing in the bull market of Heaven on margin. Father Conroy was ordered to attend during old man Panforte's testimony. The Jesuits are a spiritual paramilitary organization with an absolute vow of obedience. It's like the Army, Joe. You don't question orders."

"When it comes to Panforte, I'm not sure Maria will make such fine distinctions."

"Of course she won't. That's why I want you to keep your trap shut."

"My lips are sealed," Joe said. "How 'bout taking her a drink," Pat said, handing him a Manhattan.

In the kitchen, Joe found Maria peeking through the half-opened oven door that released the succulent scent of a roast leg of lamb. Kathleen, Kelley's fourteen-year-old, was pairing and cutting vegetables. Maria accepted her drink and kissed Joe warmly on the cheek. Kathleen interrupted her cuttings and gave him a strong hug, her firm, fully developed breasts pressing against him a bit longer than her father's friend should have allowed. Maria, wiping her hands on a red/gold apron shielding her beige, short-sleeved dress, said: "I'm so glad you and Mary could come! Your weekend's been good, yes?"

"Terrific Maria, just terrific! We're just hanging around the apartment, but it's great."

"You sound like a real homebody. It's not so bad after all, is it Joe?"

Kathleen said, "Mom, why don't you get some use out of Joe? He should help you clear out the junk in Terry's room."

"Where's Terry?" Joe asked.

"Where he always is when there's work to do out playing basketball," Kathleen said.

"Could you give me a hand?" Maria said.

"Brainless brawn at your disposal," Joe said. Maria slipped out of her apron, patted her dress and led him to the basement. Desmond followed her pleated skirt through a narrow corridor bordered on the right by a sub-basement and on the left by Maria's workroom. It was a modest room of knotty pine, including a desk with a teacher's pile of school papers, a Singer sewing machine and a half dozen cardboard cartons. It had a compact but full bathroom, and a couple of windows looking out to the side pedestrian alley and Kelley's backyard. Pat's stepfather had added the room for Maria to have her own private place to correct papers, sew or retreat from the endless demands of her kids and husband. "What's the plan?" Joe asked.

"We're moving Terry in here for his teens, so I'm moving my stuff out. Could you take those cartons to the sub-basement? But be careful, Joe. They're heavier than they look."

"What's Terry think of the move?" Joe asked.

"He loves it. He says privacy will be great for his studies. He's such a con artist. What really excites him is he has his own private entrance through the side-door. He thinks he can beat our curfew."

"Looks like a good bet to me."

"Not a chance. Our bedroom window is directly above, on the top floor. Pat's got his reading chair parked next to it, and he never sleeps until his cubs are all safely tucked in. He thinks it's important for

Terry to have privacy in his high school years. If not for his studies, at least for his hormonal battle."

When Joe returned for the next carton to store, Maria was shaking her head. "God, I'm such a pack rat! I can't believe all the stuff I've saved over the years. I even found my big sister's report cards for grades K through 8. I've no idea how I got them or why I've kept them. I guess I'm incapable of discarding anything about my family. Terry says I'm weird," she laughed, thinking that perhaps her boy was right.

After disposing of the last carton Joe said, "So Terry gets a private pad as the price of puberty. What about you? No private hideaway to perform brain surgery on scurvy kids with a marking pencil?"

"I'll move upstairs to the housekeeper's room. We'll never be able to afford one. I'll be okay." She picked up a scrapbook whose yellowing pages peeked out from the cover, loosely held together by a thin, shoelace-like binding. When she hugged it to her chest, something looking like a postcard fluttered to the floor. Joe bent down on one knee to retrieve it. It was an old photograph of a young woman. She was seated on a small round stool in front of a dressing table. She wore a white blouse with padded shoulders and puffy sleeves that tapered tightly around her wrists. Her fingers rested in affable elegance on her dressing table. Her dark waistband accented her trim waist and flaring hips. Her abundant hair cascaded in rivulets of curl, waved over her shoulders and down her erect back. Joe saw the delicate silhouette of her face, her head slightly bowed, her eyes fixed on the dressing table. It was as though the woman was studying some tiny object on the dressing table, visible only to her serene gaze. Her cheekbones were quietly decisive, and the smoothness of her cheek invited a faint touch. Her lips were slightly parted in a pose of natural suspension between sadness and joy. At the summit of her exquisite neck, below the shadow of her ear, a solitary birthmark proclaimed flawless beauty in grainy still life.

"Who is she?" his hoarse voice cracked.

"Antonietta Pompa," Maria replied magisterially.

"Antonietta… she's incredibly beautiful!" Joe muttered more to the lifeless photo than to Maria. Maria was studying Joe's reactions to the photo and the name. She seemed amused at his bewilderment. He handed her the photo and she clamped it against her scrapbook, which she pressed to her breasts, like a resting lover. As though they shared a special secret, she said: "You must know Antonietta by now. You've been typing Pat's translations of my father's correspondence.

Surely you've been introduced to the lovely Neapolitan actress."

"Oh sure," Joe fumbled. "I've read about her. It's mostly bits and pieces. I don't know where Pat's going with this stuff. Of course, I know the story about you going to New York as a kid. But everybody knows that story."

"Oh, really? Are you sure, Joe? Or does everybody just know Pat's or my father's version? You've never heard my story of the trip. Can you be sure you'll understand Antonietta's story without seeing her through my eyes?"

"I don't know that I'm supposed to understand anybody's story, Maria. I'm just typing it for Pat. I mean, a secretary doesn't have to understand the boss' dictation to type his letters." Joe was growing uncomfortable in his friends' cellar, alone with Maria and her memories.

"Come on, Joe! Who are you trying to kid? You've been fascinated by Pat's stories since you got back from the war. You're his best audience." She was smiling and trying not to be threatening, and that made Joe even more nervous. She knelt down on the floor, the scrapbook in front of her. She placed Antonietta's photo on top of her scrapbook. She looked up at Joe with that imploring look that males are powerless to ignore. She said, "It's just a girl's scrapbook. It's unlikely to contain any shocking family secrets. But it has some mementos of our trip to New York and pictures also. So you'll be able to put faces with names, and places with events. Come on. Let me take you on a little girl's journey." She arranged Antonietta's photo so it faced Joe as she showed him the time- tattered relics of her childhood.

"The photo you see of Antonietta was taken in 1910," she began. "It was in New York City and I was there when they took it. She was twenty-nine and my father was forty-four. I was five.

"This is the best likeness of Antonietta I've ever seen," she began, like the teacher she was. "It was really an accident more than a union of subject and light. It was my first day in New York, and Dad and Antonietta took me to her photo session. She was giving a concert later in the week, and they needed pictures of her for posters and programs.

She was studying herself in the mirror when the photographer's flash exploded inadvertently. You see, Joe, she never wore her hair down and free in public like you see in this photo. She never just let her hair hang naturally, her waves and curls free to fashion their own course. She was always doing something dramatic with her hair. Sometimes she'd form a bun or create a layering affect or exotic braiding. One night in the hotel she taught me

*how to braid and let me do her hair. My fingers felt like they were weav-
ing satin. She had a hairstyle for every occasion and an appearance theme
for any moment. It was a though she arranged her hair to form a mask of
the character she was playing, or present the person she chose to be at any
moment. Once she made her hair into a flowing ponytail. I don't know if
they called it that in those days. I told her that it reminded me of my horse's
tail. I guess she took offense at the comparison 'cause she never wore it that
way again. I didn't mean to hurt her feelings. I meant it as a compliment.
My pinto had the prettiest tail of any horse in the world. I was too young
to appreciate the symbolism of a horse's posterior and Antonietta too vain
to consider my naiveté.*

*It's strange. A mishap produced the only picture of Antonietta Pompa
when she wasn't play-acting. Of thousands of photos, it's the only one where
she's just herself.*

*Anyway, back at the hotel before the opera, my Dad said: "Non pissalino,
non grande teatro. No little sleep, no big theater."*

*Antonietta invited me to nap in her room while she took her bath. She
said we'd have some ladies' time. So we went down the hall to her room
and she put me on her bed and covered me with the spread. I guess I was
as tired as my dad thought 'cause I fell asleep before she'd even undressed
for her bath.*

*I don't know how long I napped, but I had this scary dream. I dreamt
we were back on the train on the first night of our trip. I was in my sleeping
berth, and my dad was telling me a bedtime story. In my dream, I couldn't
really make out the words of his story but I was soothed by his deep, gentle
voice. He finished the story and kissed me goodnight. I wrapped my arms
around his neck and hugged him as tight as I could. I tried to cling to him,
but he easily unwrapped my arms and tucked them under my blanket. He
stood next to my bed for a moment, just looking at me. Then he took out his
gold timepiece and nodded. He whispered: "Maria, when you sleep tonight,
you'll be sleeping for the first time outside California. We just crossed the
border into Nevada. So you're the first American-born family member to
journey outside the state. Sweet dreams, Maria."*

*Then he went into the sitting room of our suite. He left my door slightly
ajar so the light from the sitting room glowed into my room. I closed my
eyes and listened to the clickty-clack of steel wheels on rails and was comforted by the sway of the rolling train. In my dream the train must have
gone around a sharp curve because it listed dramatically to one side, causing the door to my room to fly all the way open. But the light in the sitting
room wasn't on anymore and I couldn't see my father in the dark. Then a*

ray of light streaked into our suite as the hallway door opened, and I saw my father step into the hallway of the Pullman car. Across the hallway another door opened and I saw a woman's form appear. She was shadowy, silhouetted in the light. All I could make out was her rich cascading hair, and she seemed clothed in veils draping her lush form all the way to her slippers. They just stood in their respective doorways, looking at each other. They were motionless save her trembling veils. Then my father reached back and closed our door and the light from the woman's suite disappeared and my father with it.

When I awoke from my nap, I was curled up in a little ball, fetal-like, and I was sucking my thumb. That was really odd, since I'd never sucked my thumb as a baby. I heard Antonietta humming in her bath. She had a pretty voice. Everything about her was pretty, like the shadowy lady in my dream.

Then I remembered her accidental snapshot. I rolled off her bed and tip-toed over to her dressing table and found her picture. I ran and jumped back on her bed with the photo. I put it on a pillow and just stared at it while she was making splashing sounds in the bathroom. I guess my mind started to play games with me. I couldn't make out the face of the lady in my dream, but I'd transposed Antonietta's face from the photo onto her veiled, richly sculpted body. I just stared at her picture, sucking my thumb.

I sensed Antonietta coming from her bath, wisps of steam in her wake. I didn't turn to face her. I just kept looking at her picture. When she reached her dressing table she started to say something, but stopped. A quizzical look appeared on her face, and she adjusted the white towel in which she'd wrapped her freshly shampooed hair. I thought she looked like an Egyptian princess in her powder blue peignoir and her towel for a crown. Her eyes darted from me to the photo on the pillow and back to me. Her smile evaporated and her pearly front teeth clamped down on her lower lip. She closed her eyes and inhaled deeply, her beautifully proportioned breasts rising. She exhaled a slow sigh and opened her eyes. Her lips were pressed tightly together, her mouth a straight line of unwelcome resolution. She sat on the edge of the bed across from me. Only her photo was between us.

Joe Desmond was spellbound by Maria's recreation of this hotel scene with the singing actress. She rearranged Antonietta's photo so that it wasn't upside down to her view. It was as though she felt a need to include Antonietta in the impending dialogue. "You know, Joe, my two oldest kids say I have too many memories. The other day during a trial recess Terry said: 'Mom, it's not healthy for a woman your age to think so much about the past. You're not even officially middle-aged.'

"But I think it's things from our childhood that we can't remember, or are so confusing we try to ignore them, that haunt us the most. I've never told anyone what happened in Antonietta's hotel room, not even Pat. I guess I haven't told Pat because I don't want to burden him with more of my life in my father's house. Sometimes it's awkward for him, what with his father dying when he was just a kid and my father so central to our family. But I think about it a lot, particularly when I feel emotionally troubled. Joe, is it wrong to talk to you about something I haven't told my husband? Maybe I shouldn't burden you with my ghosts."

"If it helps you to talk about it, who better than me? After all, I'm a professional listener by trade. The best part about talking to a court reporter is we don't talk back," He said, trying to lighten her mood. She squeezed his folded hands and said, "You're sweet, Joe. But that indifferent attitude you affect doesn't fool your friends one bit.

"I guess it's pretty obvious I'm having a hard time with this trial. It's just not what I expected. Oh, I know you all think I wanted a touching little play entitled *Maria's Revenge*, where the evil *Precious One* is banished from social paradise for dishonoring Bertolli's noble name. And it's true, I've thought of that scenario. But I'm not so hopelessly romantic that I believe Panforte's betrayal of the most important man in his life would somehow be exposed in the trial of his son.

"But I did feel that some truth about him would emerge and that's really what I wanted to witness. Truth seems a stranger in the court-room, and I don't know why. I've been taught to believe that truth – even when it's ugly or damnable – must find expression. Even truths that hurt us ought not be silenced. I feel an unspoken truth is a lie waiting for elaboration. Maybe it's what happened to a little girl in a New York hotel that's made me feel this way."

After all these years my memory of that moment with Antonietta is so vivid. She picked up her picture and looked at it for a moment. Her eyes watered and she put it back on the pillow. She removed her towel from her head and shook her head vigorously, brushing her hair back with her fingers. Her hair was still wet and her waves were kinky, the dampness constricting the fullness so evident in her photo. Her warm bath had given her skin a refined flush, and there was a dew-like moisture in the valley of her breasts when she leaned toward me and gently asked: "What's troubling you, bambina?"

I just sucked my thumb. "Can you tell me why you're sucking your thumb?" I shook my head again. "Maria, do you know why little babies suck their thumbs? It's because they remember feeling so wonderful when they're nursing at their momma's breasts. A baby at her mother's breast experiences perfect human love – softness, nourishing, complete peace. When an infant discovers that her little brain can direct the movements of her hands, she tries to recapture those sweet feelings by sucking her thumb. But because the baby's not touching and being touched by another person, she can't recreate the wonderful intimacy of first love. When she grows to understand that those feelings can't come from herself, but only from and with another, she stops fooling herself with thumb-sucking."

I didn't then understand Antonietta's homily on ego and id, but I was sufficiently vain to be embarrassed at the comparison to a baby. So I pulled my thumb from my mouth and dried it on my blouse. "Has something frightened you, Maria? Is that why you're sucking your thumb?" I remained mute but my eyes looked over to her photo on the pillow. "Sometimes when we feel afraid inside we can make our fear go away by talking about our feelings. Can you find the words, mia cara? Can you tell Antonietta what's frightened you?"

"A bad dream. A bad dream came into my nap," I replied reluctantly.

"Can you remember your bad dream?" I nodded. "Maybe if you tell me about your dream I can make the bad feelings go away. Was your father in your dream?"

At the mention of my father, I noticed her voice was lower, like someone talking secretly in church, and I felt I could tell her my dream like adults told bad things in the confessional box. So I told her about it, just like I've told you. When I told her the part about my father closing the door and the light and he were gone, I started to cry. I sobbed, "Why did Papa leave me on the train all alone?"

Antonietta shook her head and spread her arms out and said: "Veini, bella ragazza. Come here pretty girl. Come to Antonietta." I jumped desperately into her arms. I nestled my cheek against her breasts while she held me tightly, rocking to the rhythm of my sobs. I felt enveloped in her softness. Her skin on my cheek felt like the silk of her peignoir – only warmer – and the scent of her freshly bathed body like a bubbling mountain spring. My fingers played with a lock of her hair and I felt her breath breezing through my hair when she whispered: "Oh, such big girl tears for such a little girl. Don't fret. Your Papa hasn't left you, and he never will."

"He did in my dream. What if that bad dream comes back again?"

"I won't let it!" she said adamantly, assuming jurisdiction of my nightmare.

"Maria, I want to tell you some things I've never told anyone else. If you can understand what I tell you, you'll never have that bad dream again. If anything I say frightens you or makes you feel bad, just tug on that lock of my hair you're fingering, and I'll stop talking and you can tell me what you're feeling. Okay? Anything that bothers you or you don't understand, just pull gently on my hair, like the man in the puppet show with his strings. Okay?"
I whispered okay and felt her breasts quiver from her uneven breathing when she said: "You told me you couldn't make out the face of the woman in your dream, only that she had long, billowing hair and a nice shape. When you woke up, you felt scared because your father had left you. Being alone is a terrifying feeling, even for grown-ups. I think you felt another bad feeling. You felt your father had abandoned you for the woman with the invisible face and that hurt even more.

"Then you remembered that accidental photograph of my long hair and you wondered if I was the lady in your dream. And your heart was telling you that Antonietta, who seemed to love you so, was betraying you and taking your Papa away from you." I pulled on her hair and she immediately stopped talking. Then she said: "What is it, Maria? What are you feeling?"

"I just wanted to see if pulling your hair would work. It worked good! But I want to look at you when you talk. Okay?" Antonietta unwrapped me from her arms and lifted me onto a pillow. She lay on her side at the end of the bed. She placed her index finger to her lips in the universal sign of silence and said: "Now, if you want me to stop talking, just put your finger to your lips like this. Okay?" I nodded and she said: "The secret to keeping a bad dream from coming back is to fix it with a good memory. You've confused a memory with a dream. You see, darling, your father did tell you we'd entered Nevada that night on the train. And you did see him in the hallway with a woman. I was that woman, and he did come to my suite that night and that's what you saw. So it wasn't a dream at all. It's a memory, because it really happened.

"But you've forgotten the most important part of what happened on your first day outside California. Your father didn't abandon you, he didn't leave you for me. He was there to wake you up to a desert morning, to pinch your bottom after you washed your teeth. Every moment on this trip, he's been with you, his pride in you so fierce, and his love for you so open. He no more abandoned you when he came to my suite than he does when he reads his books or sketches his inventions after tucking you in."

When I saw a thin trail of tears slipping down her cheeks, I put my finger to my lips and said, "Why are you crying? Did Papa do something bad to you that night?"

"Oh, goodness no, child! Your father's incapable of being bad to those he cares for. He's not much better at harming those he dislikes." She shook her head and ran her fingers through her hair. "How do I say this to a child?" she cried, as though there was someone in the room who might give her counsel. Then she said: "Do you know the story of Adam and Eve? About how Eve tempted Adam with the forbidden fruit, and Adam succumbed and they lost paradise?"

"Yeah, I know the story. I don't like that one. How come the girl always gets blamed for everything? Papa says Adam was a big boy, he knew what he was doing."

She smiled faintly, brushed away a tear and said: "You're both right, it is a lousy storyline." She paused and then cried: "What I'm trying to tell you is…oh, God help me! I can't help it! I love your father, Maria!" She put her hands over her face and dissolved into wracking sobs. I put my index finger to my lips, hoping our signal would stop her tears with the same effectiveness it had interrupted her dialogue. But it didn't work this time. And my own tears seemed so tiny, so transient.

She got a box of tissues from the dressing table and placed them on the bed within our easy reach. She dabbed her eyes and said: "I'm sorry Maria but grown-ups don't get to pick their lovers anymore than children pick their parents. It just happens, and hopefully God keeps a worried eye on all of us. I can't apologize for how I feel about your father, and I can't do anything to stop my feelings for him. Can you understand how I feel?"

"What's gonna happen to Momma? Is Papa going away from her?"

She closed her eyes and shook her head almost angrily: "Never! He would never do that! I would never let him. But what about you, Maria? Do you feel he's done something bad? Do you think I'm bad for feeling the way I do?"

"I don't know. I don't think it's supposed to be like this, and I don't know how to fix everybody."

"You only have to fix yourself, Maria. Do you know the story about Mary Magdalene?"

I told her I didn't know that one, so she told it to me. I didn't really get the meaning of the story then, except I told her I liked the part when Mary washed Jesus' feet with her long hair. And she cried: "Can you forgive me, Maria? Can you understand I love your father and I love you? And I always will."

I didn't answer her right away. I wasn't sure she needed my absolution, and I doubted a kid was empowered with the forgiveness of sins. But her stark honesty and the way she looked when she spoke of my father made me *feel that she understood him the way I did. I thought of her marvelous hair and it made me ask, "Did you ever wash Papa's feet with your hair?"*

"No," a smile burst upon her face. "But I would. Any time he asks me to."

"Don't you think it would tickle him?" I couldn't help but ask. She laughed that deep, shoulder-shaking laugh of hers and then we were in each others arms again, laughing and crying in unity, cozy and safe in the elaborate grain of our gender.

29

Joe Desmond didn't know what Maria saw in his look when she completed the revelation of her father's adultery beyond California's border and the boundaries of his own moral center. He wanted to convey sympathy and understanding. He was deeply moved by a tender child's discovery of the dark passages of adult love. He prayed that his face didn't reveal the scattered questions and conflicting speculations that were scurrying around in his brain, searching for words to give meaning to what he'd just learned. He'd discovered so much of Bertolli's rich history from Pat that he'd begun to idealize him, to attribute a philosopher-like stoicism in the face of every beguiling temptation that might corrupt his lucid though lofty ethics. To Joe he seemed a man of extraordinary balance, riding out the storms of an utterly engaged life like a confident sea captain navigating over cresting waves, steady above unseen, treacherous currents. When Fred Panforte crucified him on a cross of gold, his tranquil dignity remained inviolate to the calculated machinations of his faithless protégé. Desmond had come to believe that the sacredness he invested in his word was so solemnly ingrained in his soul that even the liberating passion of Antonietta Pompa could not – and probably should not – shatter the chain that bound him to the core of his being.

From his daughter, Joe had just learned the verity that ruled his life did not survive Stateline. He'd shot craps in Nevada, gambling all that he was on a single roll of the dice. A man of reason, playing at passion, the ultimate game of chance. But, in games of chance, the house inevitably wins. Bertolli's vision of self tolerated no moral limbo. Typing his son-in-law's translations of his struggle to honor his marital word from breach in Antonietta's arms, Joe had come to see him as almost saintly, like his pious mentor Father Agnello. Now his daughter had just told him that on a winter night, on a train steaming through Nevada, he was just a man.

But it was Maria's part in her father's fall from ethical grace that intrigued and troubled Desmond most. There seemed no evidence of lasting trauma one would expect upon learning her father was sleeping with a woman other than her mother. Her ready acceptance of Antonietta as her father's mistress seemed to make her a co-conspirator to his faithlessness and an accessory to her mother's deception.

Yet, in her maturity, she manifested none of the insecurities or neuroses one would expect the wound her father's amorous triangle would cause. Finally, there was her obvious loyalty to and love for Antonietta that survived to this moment. It was her relationship to her father's lover that drove Joe's curiosity. He had no right to probe further, and his sensitivity to her cautioned against extending the conversation. But her story was so remarkable, and the snarl of intimate and explosive human emotions so absorbing, that he wanted her to tell more of the singer and the salesman and yes, to expose more of herself in the telling.

He broke their silence. "Jeezus, Maria! That's a lot to dump on a kid. What was your father's reaction to Antonietta telling you about their affair?"

"We never spoke of it," she said. She opened her scrapbook and removed some frayed papers. "This is the libretto Puccini signed with his little note to me." She handed Joe her memento of her first night at the opera. As he scanned Puccini's Italian scribbling, she said softly, "No more words were necessary. Antonietta's honesty with me freed my father from any explanations – then or now. They loved each other and they both loved me. What's left to say?"

"I don't know, but it's not every day a father's mistress tells his kid her old man's having an affair. Seems some paternal comment's in order."

"She wasn't that and it wasn't that way." Maria rubbed her chiseled cheekbones and patiently said: "She wasn't his mistress, Joe. A mistress is a man's possession, like a loyal pet or something recreationally useful like a set of golf clubs. Have you ever wondered why the woman's called a *mistress* and the man her *lover*? It's because mistress sounds like domestic help, servile and always pleasing, and man is the lover, dashing and powerful. That's not what they were. They were lovers, Joe. It's as simple as that. When you think about it, a loveless marriage is really an affair. It persists because it's sanctioned and convenient. But the *affairs* of true love are never convenient and always beyond third party approval."

"What about your mom? I know you're closer to your dad, but did it bother you how she felt?"

"Not really. I didn't feel we were keeping a secret from her. She was very satisfied with her life as the wife of a wealthy man with whom she shared few common interests. She was never comfortable in his world. Challenging ideas and movements were beyond her grasp, so she constructed a world she was comfortable in. Our world would have threatened her. To expose her to it would have been cruel."

"What about your teenage years? Did your relationship with Antonietta bother her?"

"Some, but I'm not sure it was much more than the normal adolescent mother/daughter conflict. But there was some resentment because I looked up to Antonietta and adopted many of her notions of what a woman was and could become. She also resents Pat's enlightened rearing of her grandchildren. She thinks Pat's making the same mistakes with our kids that Dad made with me. Although she confides his Irish charm prevents her from pointing out his paternal deficiencies."

"Was her resentment toward you the reason she didn't go to the first ever performance of our opera company?"

"Not at all. Pat's told you about that historic night, hasn't he?" Joe nodded.

"Well, Mom's failure to attend had nothing to do with resentment. Remember, she excluded herself from our theatrical world. Besides, the first performance of the San Francisco Opera Company was the culmination of Dad's dream from the time he talked Antonietta into staying in The City. Merola gave Dad four tickets to the opening of *La Boheme*, and they decided Bernie Jacobs and I should join them. It was like a reunion of our New York trip thirteen years earlier. The symmetry was irresistible. The four of us and Merola had all attended the world premier of a Puccini opera in Manhattan and now we'd all be together for a Puccini opera ushering in the City's own opera company! It was perfect! My dad bought me a formal gown and corsage. When he escorted me into the lobby, I discovered the athletic flexibility of male necks when so many heads turned to follow me. I told Antonietta, who was escorted by Bernie as the *beard*, that the men were staring at us. She laughed, 'From now on, love, you've got nothing to worry about until they stop looking at you.'"

"The beard? I though Bernie was bald," Joe interrupted. She laughed. "Oh, Joe, you think you're so worldly, but you don't even no what a *beard* is. In show business, celebrities attend functions without their spouses. In the absence of my mother, Antonietta required a male escort. So Bernie was picked for the job, as had been the case on our New York trip. A single woman in my father's company was beyond gossip if she had the services of a *beard*. Of course everybody in the business knew good old Bernie was just a prop."

"So what was it like that night?"

Maria's expression was dreamy and distant. She said, "It was different from New York. I was a lot older so I appreciated much more. We all commented on the size of the Civic Auditorium and that it was even bigger than the Met. My father was worried about the acoustics, but Antonietta told him not to be silly, Gaetano would take care of it. We were delighted there were no boxes and that it was a full house of opera lovers. And everybody knew my father and Antonietta, so they all seemed to know me. In the lobby and even when we got to our seats – which were clearly the best in the house – it was like one of my Dad's receptions or parties, where everyone knew everyone and we were all delighted to be together. In New York we didn't know anybody except Luisa and Gaetano."

"How does Merola get in the San Francisco picture?" Joe asked. "There's nothing about Merola in Pat's translations of your father correspondence after they met at Fiore d'Italia. Maria's eyes clouded. "No, I don't suppose there is. You'll find, Joe, that there are no more letters between my dad and Father Agnello after our New York trip. You see, when we returned home my father got a letter, sometime after New Year's Day. It was postmarked Lucca, from the bishop's office. It told my father that Father Agnello had died in his sleep, in the rectory of San Lorenzo in Farneta.

"The bishop wrote that his death was painless as his life had not been. He explained that Father Agnello had written a will and left all he had to my father, as trustee for his American sons. At Father Agnello's request, his remains were shipped to Genoa and interred in his family plot.

"I remember. I'd gone to my father's study to kiss him goodnight. He was sitting at his rolltop desk, the letter in his hand in his lap. He was crying. I'd never seen him cry before. I ran to him and jumped onto his lap, into his arms. He held me tightly and I wrapped my arms around his neck, but I couldn't stop his sobbing, and that made me cry. He whispered in my ear, his breathing ragged, uneven. He said: 'My little Maria, do you remember our trip to New York? Remember, I told you when we left California and entered Nevada, and how excited I was that we were the first of our family to cross new borders?'

"I couldn't' confirm that I remembered that moment because I'd not yet learned to talk through tears – his or mine. Then he said – and I can still hear his cracking voice – he said, 'About the time our train slid down the Sierra into the Nevada desert, my father died in Italy. And he never knew you except through my letters. Oh, how my father would have loved you!'

"It would be years before I learned the father for whom my dad grieved was a celibate priest. It was Pat who told me how Father Agnello had shaped my father and all the *Precious Ones* that followed."

Joe thought of that old priest dying alone in a peasant church. He'd read his writings, been witness to his designs for his boys who shaped the city and state of Desmond's birth. Joe hadn't considered his mortality. His story had been like a great novel that you want to never end. But literature and lives are limited to the pages granted by the ultimate publisher of every story. Pat Kelley never mentioned Father Agnello's death, and Joe never thought to inquire. Of course, Bertolli was eighty-three years old at the time of the Panforte trial and his teacher would have qualified for *Ripley's Believe It Or Not* to be still alive. All Pat had related to Desmond was in Bertolli's distant past, and Father Agnello seemed to Joe like a guardian angel, guiding his *Precious Ones* through the shoals of the New World out to her open seas, freed to sail toward limitless horizons. He hadn't envisioned that the sun would one day inevitably set on both the teacher and his student. Joe wanted so much at that moment to provide Maria with an appropriate comment on Father Agnello, to give her a fitting epitaph for the invisible force from a distant and ancient land who had sired so much from so little. But he said nothing to her about that. He just thought of a train destined for New York with its priceless cargo, snorting white steam into the Nevada night, and an ancient church with its incense-scarred walls beyond an even more ancient city wall. Desmond chose to believe that Father Agnello never capitulated to the perpetual grip of death until he sensed that his eldest son had surrendered to the blessed embrace of a girl from Naples. And he was certain, when they found him in the morning, that had they looked closely they would have detected the outline of a smile on his frozen lips.

"You were saying how Merola got on the podium that night," Joe nudged Maria away from memories of her first confrontation with death and his own sense of loss for someone he'd only known through the words of others. "I thought he went with Hammerstein to build an opera house in London," he said.

"He did, but Hammerstein's house failed after only a year. So Gaetano came back to America. For a while, he conducted operetta in New York. Then he signed on with Fortune Gallo's San Carlo Opera Company as a conductor. He knew Gallo from Naples. Anyway, he toured with Gallo's company all over America, presenting operas at bargain prices. Aside from needing the work, touring gave him the opportunity to visit San Francisco frequently. He'd been in love with the City since Tetrazzini's debut at the Tivoli and his dinner with Antonietta and my dad. He used to call San Francisco: *my little Italy.*

"After a while his stays in the City got longer. He worked with Antonietta's artists and got active in our musical community. When he felt there was a solid artistic pool, he moved here, taught music to survive and plotted with Antonietta and my father to start an opera company.

"He produced his first operas in 1922 outdoors at Stanford football stadium and they drew 30,000. So he knew Tom Maguire and my dad were right – the Bay Area was a great opera market!"

"So you knew Merola well?"

Maria laughed. "Of course! He was often at our house for dinner, and he spent some weekends at our Sonoma ranch. He was briefly my piano teacher."

"Jeezus, Maria! You got Puccini writing you inspirational notes, Caruso drawing cartoons for you, and the Founder and General Director of the San Francisco Opera Company giving you piano lessons! With that background you should be traveling the world today as a concert performer instead of teaching recalcitrant brats how to spell."

She grinned. "If my father had his way, I would be. That was his plan all along. It's the real reason he took me to New York. He won't admit it, but I'm sure he wanted me to be like Antonietta, so worldly and independent. But the trip to New York exposed me to more than culture. The music of Tin Pan Alley and dance music infected me. I quickly discovered that by mastering basic chords, their progressions and relations, I could play music everyone was listening to on the radio and at dances. Unfortunately for my dad, Bach and Chopin didn't lend their compositions to such facile devices.

"Desperate to get my career as a pianist back on track, dad got Gaetano to take over my piano lessons in my freshmen year in high school. Gaetano taught me what it takes to be an artist – namely talent and obsession. I had neither. So he taught me to play Neapolitan folk music that Dad could sing along to. Accompanying my dad singing, *Torna a surriento* or *O sole mio* was Merola's way of deflating dad's silly dream.

"It's funny, though. If my father lives long enough, he may see our Kathleen on stage. She clearly has the talent, even Merola thinks so. I just don't know if she has the obsession or if I want her to."

"Getting back to opening night at the Civic, it must have been a real triumph for them," Joe guided her back to her story.

"It seemed like it then, but when the curtain rose my dad seemed quieter than usual and Antonietta wasn't as vivacious as she usually was. I figured they were anxious about the audience. The auditorium was built for three-ring circuses, not theater, and they both worried about the staging. My dad had designed the lighting, using an incredibly complex overhead system to set the mood on stage. Antonietta had designed the stage from her experiences in outdoor amphitheaters in Italy. No one knew what to expect from an audience conditioned to proscenium theaters. When Merola stepped into the pit, Antonietta took hold of my dad's hand. He seemed under enormous strain. When Merola's baton drew the first note of *La Boheme* from the orchestra, I took his other hand. He trembled slightly, then squeezed my hand gently and the quiver disappeared. The three of us held hands through the entire performance, until the audience leapt its feet in wild approval as Mimi died in her lover's arms!

"I was cheering wildly. Of more than 5,000 people in the hall that night, only my dad and Antonietta weren't screaming madly. They just stood there, ramrod straight, watching the performers taking endless curtain calls, applause rolling over them in waves. I figured they weren't clapping because they'd worked so long and hard for this moment. They were so vital in bringing grand opera to the City, I figured they wouldn't dream of applauding themselves.

"Finally, Merola took center stage, the principals at his sides, the San Francisco Opera Chorus, peopled with so many of Antonietta's students, behind him. In the orchestra pit the musicians tapped their instruments in artistic homage to their leader. And *Bravos* rang out from the crowd. Merola raised his arms full length, spread them wide as if to embrace every cheering voice in the hall. Then he dropped his arms to his side and bowed from the waist, his black clad body emotionally spent. When he raised his eyes for a final look at the screaming mob, his eyes came to rest on my father and Antonietta. An infectious grin spread across his face and he nodded to them, as if to say: 'We did it! By God, we really did it!' My father nodded back to him and I saw a tear slide down his cheek. Tears of joy and triumph, I was sure," Maria concluded, her eyes downcast on her scrapbook.

She opened it and turned the yellowing pages, looking for a memento. "Here it is," she said. "This is the program for our opera company's first performance." She handed it to Joe, remarking, "It's autographed by everybody, even my dad and Antonietta. By that time I knew the value of autographs."

Joe thumbed through the program and asked: "Do you have the program for the opening of the War Memorial Opera House in 1932? That must have been another great night for your dad. But I was wondering, how come Antonietta wasn't with you in your box that night?"

Maria fingered her wedding band and mumbled, "She wasn't in the City then."

"But you had four seats in Box N and only you, your father and Pat went to the opening. You could've scalped your fourth ticket for a fortune," Joe pressed, concealing his curiosity about a vacant seat in the center box with his casual manner.

"My father wanted it that way," she said sadly. "He felt that opera in San Francisco wouldn't have gotten off the ground if it hadn't been for Antonietta. She'd earned a seat in that box by keeping an art form alive, until Merola was ready. If she couldn't be there for the opening of the first publicly financed opera house, he felt no one should take her place in their box. And that's how he thought of it – as *their* box." Joe sensed emerging anger in Maria's voice and he tried to tap into it, saying: "It's too bad she was outta town. She missed a helluva show. But what the hell, that box has seen plenty of memorable moments since then."

"Antonietta Pompa never, ever set foot in the War Memorial Opera House!" Maria said, her lips taut with rage, her eyes squinting despair. "She left for New York City the day after opening night at the Civic Auditorium. She never returned, and we never saw her again," Maria cried softly.

"But why? Why jump town when everything she's worked for has finally paid off big time?"

She dabbed her eyes with her hanky and said, "That's what I asked myself as a seventeen-year-old. How could we all be so happy together and the next day she's gone? Completely out of our lives."

"What about her theater?"

"She sold it to Bernie Jacobs. At first it didn't sink in that she wasn't coming back. It was my senior year in high school, so I was all involved in proms and graduation and stuff, so I didn't think that much about her. It's amazing how self-absorbed a teenager is.

"When I started college at Cal, I began thinking about her again. Maybe it was because I was away from home for the first time, or because Pat was playing baseball in the South and later working for the Matson Lines, away at sea in the Far East, but I realized I was pretty much on my own. So it was natural to think about her, since she'd been out earning a living when she was my age. It wasn't just that she'd been so important to me growing up or that I felt like I'd lost a family member. I'd learned to deal with family loss when my brother was killed in the war. When Michael died, at least I understood why. But Antonietta's leaving made no sense.

"So after a U.S.C. football game, I took the ferry from Berkeley to the City. I went to see Bernie Jacobs at the Washington Square Theater. I wanted to talk to him, to find out what went wrong. He welcomed me with a big hug and took me upstairs to his office. It used to be Antonietta's office, but none of her stuff was there anymore. I was stunned. There was no sign she'd ever been in that theater, even though she'd created it. I mentioned this to Bernie and he said they wanted it that way. I asked him who *they* were and he told me, my dad and Antonietta. He sat me down and helped me put the pieces together." Maria interrupted her narration and reached for her autographed program of the first opera produced by the San Francisco Opera Company. She handed it to Joe and said, "You see the date, Joe? September 26, 1923, the first performance of the San Francisco Opera Company and Antonietta's last day in the City. It was the key to the mystery of her flight from us.

"Bernie told me that September 26, 1923 was the first anniversary of the settlement between my father and Fred Panforte by which Panforte took over my father's poultry business. I didn't know about the proxy and legal battles that raged in 1922. My Dad never discussed business at home. I wasn't even aware Panforte had taken over all our ranches, even our Sonoma ranch. I should have figured something was wrong when we didn't spend the summer there. It was the first summer I stayed in the City, but dad kept it all to himself.

"Bernie told me he'd warned my dad about Panforte. And others, like Giannini, also had. 'But your father's a stubborn man,' Bernie had said: 'It's his stubborn adherence to his vision for the theater that was the key to our success. But his belief that no one who he brought here from the Old Country and gave a livelihood to, would dishonor him was fatal for a businessman in the 20th Century. After all, it was capitalist fighting over markets and resources that plunged the world into a war that cost him his son, your brother. He should've known his kind of loyalty died in the trenches of Europe along with your brother.' Then Bernie told me something that has haunted me ever since. He told me that my father was badly shaken by Michael's death. In a way, he sort of adopted Fabrizio as his son. 'Not as a replacement son, but as a boy he could father for the boy he had lost,' Bernie had said. He told me that's why my father used his influence at the State Department to bring Angelina over from Italy to marry Fabrizio and why he urged Antonietta to help her with her singing career.

"Bernie also told me Antonietta blamed herself for my father's defeat at the hands of Panforte and Loeb. She believed Panforte could never have out-thought and out-fought my father. But she was equally certain that he was so wrapped up in their show business dreams he neglected to pay attention to the details of running his company. She was sure he'd found such stimulating peace in her love of him that he was incapable of considering the perfidy and avaricious opportunism of American business.

"'If it hadn't been for me,' Antonietta had told Bernie, 'Bartolomeo would still own the largest poultry business in the West. If he hadn't loved me and joined me in our pursuit of the tender part of our souls, he'd have crushed Panforte!'

"At last, I understood their mood that night at the Civic Auditorium. They knew this was their last moment together. My dad's tears at the end of the opera weren't for the tragedy on the stage, they were for the tragedy he and Antonietta would live for the rest of their lives.

"Don't you see, Joe? Antonietta was convinced that her love for my father made him impotent in the face of his enemies, and she couldn't live here with that. She hated to think of herself as Eve. That's why she left us! She's gone from my life because of Fred Panforte! We can't ever touch her again or be touched by her because of him! That vicious bastard took more than a business from my father. He took Antonietta and left us nothing of her but that accidental snapshot!" Maria sobbed and her hands shuddered as she pointed at the 1910 photograph of Antonietta Pompa.

At last Joe Desmond was beginning to comprehend the true source and fathomless depth of Maria Kelley's hatred of Fred Panforte. In her dark penetrating eyes, she saw that Panforte had killed the love of her father and the woman she admired even more than her own mother, with the same apparent cruelty with which his son had slain his own wife. But it was not the product of evil seed that inflamed her wrath, it was lost love. If the jury took Panforte's son from him, if they exiled him to the gallows, the ignoble *Precious One* would be required to live out his years as Maria and her father had lived theirs, from that apocalyptic night at the opera a quarter century earlier. In Maria's emotionally scarred heart, Fred Panforte would lose his only son as her father had. Only there would be no bright young man for Panforte's paternal surrogacy. He would be forced to accept, as Maria and her dad had, that beyond the pain of loss lurks the deadliest of killers – limitless emptiness.

Maria's tears subsided and she composed herself to conclude her explanation of a vacant seat in Box N on the opening of the War Memorial Opera House. "But Panforte didn't stop there. It wasn't enough for him that my father capitulated and turned over his business to him. The miserable sonofabitch wasn't satisfied he'd destroyed my father's relationship with Antonietta. He wanted to strip my dad of every vestige of respect he'd spent his whole life earning. So he took dead aim on my father's place in the world of arts, and the new War Memorial Opera House gave him his chance."

"Jeezus, Maria! Your dad's like an icon in the City's opera history! I understand it was his idea to divide the World War I memorial project into two parts - the veterans' room and art museum in one building, opera, and symphony hall in another. From what I've heard, he got all the warring factions together or they'd never have gotten the damn thing built. Surely his old buddy, Merola, wouldn't turn on him."

"You have to understand how building the opera house altered the economics of opera in the City. Remember, Dad's theory was to build a *theatrical* audience to support opera. By building a new opera house, a *social* audience was attracted. With movies so popular and radio and everything, competition was fierce. Merola had to attract wealthy guarantors and corporations, which he did with subscriptions for boxes and grand tier seats. And all of these subscribers had to pledge money over and above the price of the ticket.

"Panforte didn't know a damn thing about culture, but he was a master of financial figures. That's how he got control of dad's business, playing with the numbers, cooking the books. He figured Merola needed big money for the boxes. We were far from destitute, but there was no way my dad could afford a generous contribution for the luxury of a box. Panforte made a five-figure contribution to get the center box. He told everybody he wanted it as a gift for his wife, whom he'd met when he heard her sing in a church in Genoa just before he came to America. It's true Angelina loves music. She sang for Antonietta briefly before she married. But he wasn't fooling anyone who knew him or his tactics. It wasn't a seat for his wife he was spending all that money for. He was after my father. He was trying to buy dad's place in the history of San Francisco opera.

"Gaetano was in a terrible position. He had to keep his board happy and the social crowd satisfied their money was appreciated. That's why he played it safe with the repertory the first few years at the War Memorial. He knew that money didn't mean taste, but he remembered Hammerstein's house failing in London.

"It grated on him that his friend of almost thirty years, the visionary who'd conceived San Francisco's opera company, couldn't compete in a rich man's game of buying boxes of culture they barely understood. He knew the Pacific Heights crowd would compare who got what and for how much. But, as the founder and General Director he had absolute power to determine all privileges of seating.

"For months, he kept his seating decisions secret. Not even his trusted assistant saw the list of box holders and preferred seating that Merola composed in his own hand. A week before he announced the results of this crass lottery, he consulted with a lawyer. When the seating was announced, the press published the names of the box holders. But the feature story was what Merola did with the center box – Box N." Maria fetched a paper from her scrapbook and handed it to Joe. "Read it and see what Panforte's money got him. Read it out loud!" she demanded.

Oh shit, Joe thought. Not Merola too, not more betrayal and loss.

Desmond read the document to Maria: *"Pursuant to the powers vested in me under the Charter of the San Francisco Opera Company, as General Director and, in recognition of the historic and inestimable contributions he has made to the culture of San Francisco, the San Francisco Opera Company grants to Bartolomeo Bertolli and his heirs, in perpetuity, the rights to Box N of the War Memorial Opera House. Said rights herein granted shall accrue to Mr. Bertolli at no financial cost to him. Upon his death his heirs shall succeed to the rights to Box N upon the purchase of opera season tickets for the face value of any such tickets. No further contribution, pledge, indemnification or any other payment shall be required of Mr. Bertolli's heirs. Signed, Gaetano Merola."*

Joe looked up from his reading to Maria. Her arms where folded across her chest, her small smile defiant. "All right!" he shouted, pumping his fist in the air. "He shoved that baton of his right up Panforte's tight ass!"

"I hadn't thought of it quite that way," Maria laughed, color returning to her cheeks. "I can't stand the way lawyers write, but, when that's read to me, it's sheer poetry! Now I can tell you why dad left Antonietta's seat vacant on opening night? Are you interested?"

"Don't tease me, Maria."

"Well, Gaetano could get away with shutting Panforte out of a box, but with all the money he'd donated, he had to give him some seats. So he gave Panforte seats in the center orchestra. Merola picked these because, as a conductor, he knew they were the least desirable acoustically. But it had the added benefit of allowing us to look down on Panforte and requiring him to look up at our palatial box, flanked by the cream of high society. It was absolutely delicious and I had no idea Gaetano was such a devil!"

"My father wasn't as catty as I. He wanted the seat vacant because he knew Panforte would attend opening night. He wanted Panforte to see it empty. 3,200 seats and only Antonietta's vacant! It was a message to Panforte from my father. He was telling him that his loyalty to Antonietta's love was unbreakable and priceless and there was no fortune great enough to purchase this seat of honor for Panforte's wife. Places of honor, the vacant seat proclaimed, are reserved for those who earn them!"

Maria shook her head, rubbed a tear from the corners of her eyes with her fingertips and sighed deeply. Then she reached for her scrapbook and removed old newspapers and magazines, including the October 17, 1932 edition of *Time* magazine. She had saved the reviews of the dedication and opening of San Francisco's War Memorial Opera House. She pulled out *The Chronicle's* review and then quoted from it: 'Paris has its Louvre, Rome the Sistine Chapel, Athens the Acropolis and San Francisco its glorious Opera House!' But not a word about my Dad and what he'd done to make this dream come true.

"But Gaetano knew, and in his moment of greatest triumph he acknowledged my father. The entire audience was on its feet applauding the cast and orchestra and then Gaetano finally took his bow. His outstretched arms, in the traditional gesture of a conductor acknowledging the crowd's plaudits, accepted the cheers for the entire company. Then he dropped his arms to his sides and bowed from his waist. When he straightened up, he looked up to the highest balcony and his eyes scanned the entire house until they came to rest on Box N. Pat and my dad and I were all standing, applauding like the rest of the crowd.

"Then Gaetano raised his right arm, palm up and pointed to my dad as though his conductor's arm could guide the applause to our box as facilely as he had guided the orchestra and cast. He smiled broadly and held his pose, sharing the moment fully. My dad smiled back and nodded twice. Then he half-turned to the only empty seat in the house. Antonietta's seat in Box N. With his left arm outstretched, palm up, his eyes on her chair, he passed the applause on to her vacant seat. Then he turned his eyes back to the stage, his arm still outstretched, his lips pressed tightly, fighting back tears and nodded to Gaetano. Gaetano nodded once and mouthed the words: 'Si! Brava Antonietta! Brava!'

"Did you ever hear from her again?" Joe asked gently.

"Just once. I got a letter from her when I graduated from Cal. I still have it. It's in my scrapbook. It was wonderful to hear from her after so long. And she was so proud of me for being the first of our family to graduate from college. Of course, she had all kinds of advice for my life after college. But I never forgot what she wrote about my father," Maria said softly.

Joe hesitated to ask what Maria's father's lover confided in the girl who'd discovered their adulteress affair. She ran her fingers through her black hair, her Latin lips formed a sensuous pout and she said, "Antonietta wrote: 'A good man's heart is awkward and delicate. It's clumsy because it doesn't use artifice to protect itself and precarious because it's unwilling to hide.'

"When I read her words, I knew instinctively that she understood and loved my father more truly than my own mother. Somewhere in my soul, I vowed to search for a man with an awkward and delicate heart. And I found him in Pat."

30

On Monday morning the corridor was packed with excited spectators jostling for position. Their expectant buzz was louder than usual as they waited impatiently for Robert Panforte to take the stand. All eyes were on the former football star as he stepped with athletic grace to be sworn by the Chief Clerk. Young Panforte towered over Pat, who fixed him with a reassuring stare. Loeb began his examination at the corner of the jury box closest to the audience. He remained stationary, forgoing his usual courtroom roving. His positioning forced his client to speak directly to the jurors. They in turn looked only at Panforte. Loeb favored expensive, perfectly tailored three-piece suits, jeweled or gold cuff links adorning French cuffs, and a variety of ties that implied a sense of color of a man who'd spent much time in the Museum of Modern Art. But on the day his client was in the dock, he wore a bland two-piece suit from the racks of the Emporium or, at best, Macy's. The French cuffs were gone and his tie so nondescript as to defy recollection. It was as though he'd created a spotlight for the jury on his client.

Pat Kelley had spent many weeks observing Panforte, studying his background and rearing, but it wasn't until he took the stand that Pat realized how handsome he was. He was, Pat thought, movie star gorgeous. He had the firm body and broad shoulders of a collegiate athlete, gold Tuscan skin, accented by straight, thick black hair. But it was his eyes – those aqua ovals, a mother's gift – which seemed the fluent witness to his soul. He gazed about the courtroom and then caught his mother's eyes. Loeb reminded his client that no power on earth could compel him to testify and that it was likely that everything he said from the witness stand, no matter how humiliating, would make the morning papers. Panforte nodded and said, "I just want to answer everybody's questions about what happened."

He testified that he'd met Paula at a Stanford sorority party after the Big Game in November, 1942. They started dating after his graduation when she came home to her father's Broadway apartment in the summer of 1943. Loeb directed his attention to his February 1944 conversation with his father when he related their marriage plans and Paula's pregnancy. When Loeb asked him about his father's testimony about an abortion, Panforte said, "That got all mixed up. Can I explain?"

"By all means," Judge Grant said. Panforte leaned forward and said, "My dad and me did have the conversation he described. But we had a subsequent conversation after Paula had gone to Mexico. I think my father figured from what I told him that she'd had a Mexican abortion. But she never said that and so I didn't say it to him. I think he just misinterpreted what I was saying. See, Paula planned for sometime to join her dad someplace in Mexico on an art trip or something. Then she was going to visit with her mom and aunt Lil in Mexico City. She called me from a hospital in Mexico City and said she'd had surgery. The connection was real bad, I could barely hear her. I figured it was a miscarriage or something. I guess my Dad figured that's where wealthy women go to get abortions. I never said anything about any abortion. I guess he just assumed it."

Pat Kelley commented to himself: "*More likely your frigging old man wanted to get the Catholic taboos in front of the jury.*"

Loeb asked, "Did you feel in anyway pressured to marry Paula Brady because you believed her pregnant with your child?"

"Absolutely not! When we got married, she wasn't pregnant, so where's the pressure?" he said, palms outstretched.

"All right," Loeb said, signaling our return from Mexico. "Now, you reported your wife missing on Tuesday morning, June 6, 1949. Please tell the jury what you did over the weekend before you made your fateful call to the police?"

Turning to the jury, Panforte said: "Well, like Marjorie said, we had a bridge party at our place, and we talked about house hunting in Marin with them on Sunday. But I called it off on Sunday. I decided to put up some shelves in the laundry room for my wife. I'd built a kinda back seat thing for the baby on Saturday so we could take him on drives with us in the car."

"Did you at anytime on Sunday, June 4, 1949, drive alone or with anyone else over the Golden Gate Bridge to anywhere in Marin County?"

"No, I didn't."

"At anytime on Sunday, June 4, 1949, did you leave the city limits of San Francisco?"

"The city limits? Yes. Like I said, I built this car seat thing for Bobbie. We could rearrange it into a crib. We took him with us that Sunday down the Peninsula. We got a bite to eat at Rickey's. It was the first time we took him for a drive with us..." Panforte sighed, his voice trailing off. "Then we went to a drive-in movie. It was a John Wayne movie. *The Sands of Iwo Jima*, I think. But Bobbie, Jr. and me slept through most of it."

Pat thought, a happy family outing down the Peninsula. The defense had Panforte, his wife and baby driving south on Sunday, the opposite direction of Marin. If the jury believed him, Panforte couldn't have prepared her grave the day before the killing as the D.A. had charged.

"Bob, did anything at all unusual happen on the weekend before you reported Paula missing?" Loeb asked.

"Not really. Well, maybe. Paula got an obscene phone call Sunday morning. She'd been getting them for a while."

"Tell us about these calls," Loeb said.

"All I know is what Paula told me. She had no idea who he was, except he talked real filthy and had an accent. When I picked up the phone, he wouldn't say anything. He'd just breathe into the phone. It bothered us, but something about the call that weekend really got to her. She was really upset."

"Anything else?" Loeb coaxed.

"Other than my dad dropping in and telling us about reshuffling our management assignments, I don't remember anything unusual. Paula was real pleased that I'd be working at The Market. It meant more time with her and the baby."

Loeb asked softly, "Bob, I want you to think about Monday, June 5, 1949, the day after your Dad changed your job duties to The Market. I want you to tell the jury everything you can remember about that day?"

"Well, I finished work around twelve-thirty, one o'clock in the afternoon. I went to the Oregon Café and had a few drinks, and I remember rolling bar dice for a couple of rounds with the owner, Frank Caverretta and a produce broker from John DeMartini Co. I was drinking bourbon and seven for maybe an hour, hour and a half. I went back to my office to get my car and then headed home. I picked up some lamb chops on Chestnut Street and decided to stop in at The Paragon Bar for a cocktail. I must've been drinkin' there a couple of hours, 'cause I got home a little after four.

"Do you recall how many drinks you had at the Paragon?" Loeb asked.

"Five, six rounds maybe. It's a neighborhood joint off Chestnut where everybody knows everybody else. We rolled dice for drinks. I seem to remember losing most of the time, so it was a pretty expensive day. Then I went home.

"Paula and me had cocktails together. The baby was sleeping. I went into the kitchen and prepared the chops to barbecue. I do most of the cooking at home. Paula came into the kitchen and we had another drink, and we heard Bobby, Jr. in his room. He wasn't crying or anything. It was like baby noises, like he was happy or giggling or something. So we went to get him and I picked him up and carried him into the living room to play with him." Panforte's mesmerizing crystal eyes brightened and his voice mellowed as he talked of his son. He continued: "While I was playing with Bobby, I thought of my dad. It's funny how proud fathers get when their kids do the smallest things. When my dad was playing with Bobbie the night before, I realized he couldn't be happier if Bobbie had just scored the winning touchdown against Cal. As a kid I didn't really understand how my dad felt when I did something good. I used to think he was awkward, kinda Old World. But when Bobbie pulled himself up in his crib, I understood it's a sense of wonder a father experiences that gets you. You realize the little guy kicking his chubby legs, his blue eyes laughing up at you, is part of you. And always will be."

Loeb paused to allow a young father's marvel to echo in the quiet courtroom. Panforte broke off eye contact with the jury, looked at his lawyer and said, "I'm sorry, Danny. I got a little sidetracked. What's the question again?"

"You've answered it, Bob." Loeb hoarsely. Then he sternly asked: "You've just told the jury you'd been drinking whiskey from early Monday afternoon into the evening. By my count, you've had as many as a dozen highballs. Bob, do you have a drinking problem?"

Panforte's brow wrinkled when he answered, "I don't think I have a drinking problem. That Monday was the first time I had any hard liquor since my son was born. He was born in November 1948. Other than wine with dinner, I hadn't been drinking at all since then. So, no, I don't consider this one-time occasion a drinking problem."

"Prior to the birth of your son, did you feel you had a drinking problem?"

"Yeah," he nodded candidly. "Like I said, I laid off hard stuff when

Bobbie was born. A few months before, I'd begun feeling I wasn't handling it very well. Something happened one night that made me realize I should lay off hard booze."

"Tell us what happened, Bob?" Loeb said.

"One night in late October or the beginning of November, I was out alone, down the Peninsula. I went to several bars, did a lot of drinking. Somehow I got into a fight with two guys. One was about my age; the other was younger. I don't remember what the fight was about, but it was quite a brawl.

"When I woke up the next morning, I was pretty sore all over. My little finger on my right hand was swollen, all black and blue. It turned out I broke it when I hit one of those guys. It's never healed right. You can see, it's kinda crooked." Panforte held up his crooked pinkie for the jury. He continued, "The worst thing about the morning after was my memory was like a black hole. I called my mother and told her about it. I was worried. I'd never blacked-out like that before, even when I took some pretty good licks to the head playing football. I told her I couldn't remember what happened, just the fight part. I was afraid I'd beaten the younger guy pretty badly. I told her I was going to check out the newspapers to see if they had anything about it. That's when I realized hard liquor was affecting me wrong. It made me real combative. It's one thing when you're a college kid. I realized then that I couldn't hold it, so I gave it up. Also I decided to start playing semi-pro football. When I played in school I never drank during the season. I wanted to get back in shape. Then Bobbie was born and he was the best reason to get off the stuff."

"Is it fair to say that, on Monday, June 5, 1949, you fell off the wagon after seven months of abstinence from hard liquor?"

"Yeah," Panforte shook his head at the depth of his fall. Loeb persisted: "Bob did anything happen at The Market that caused you to fall off the wagon?"

"Not really. I was real pleased that I'd be working in the City from now on. I guess that's why I had a couple of belts," his eyes dropped in dismay.

"Now going back to Monday night at your home, what if anything happened after you played with your baby?"

"Paula fed him, then put him down for the night. I barbecued in the backyard. Then we had dinner in the dinning room. Just the two of us."

"Did you have any more drinks?"

"We had wine with our dinner."

"What if anything happened after you finished dinner?"

"My memory's kinda hazy from the time I barbecued the lamb chops. I'd had too much to drink. I remember Paula saying something to the effect I'd had enough to drink. My answer was to go into the kitchen and fix another drink. I felt kinda fuzzy. When I came back from the kitchen, Paula was lying on the living room sofa. We started necking and petting. I think I suggested we go into the bedroom. I don't recall much after that."

"Well, do you recall the two of you actually going into the bedroom?"

"I don't recall actually going there, but we ended up in the bedroom."

"What happened in your bedroom, Bob?" Loeb sharply. Both Fred Panforte and Paul Brady leaned forward, their eyes fixed on the witness. Eileen Brady wore a mask of ice. Angelina held a tiny hanky over her mouth, her hand trembling, her breathing uneven. Every courtroom face was painted with tension; even the cynical press corps put down their pencils, waiting for Robert Panforte's answer. Almost bemused, he said: "I'm really unclear about the bedroom. It's all bits and pieces. I remember I wanted to go out. I didn't have any particular place in mind. I just wanted to go out with her. When I told her that, she said if I loved her I wouldn't ask her to go out in the condition I was in. I told her if she loved me she'd go anywhere I asked. I was getting angry at her. I felt like she was mocking me, saying I was a sloppy drunk. I went back in the kitchen and poured myself a double shot of straight whiskey. I guess that was my answer to how drunk she said I was.

"I came back to our bedroom. I remember Paula was at the foot of the bed. She'd taken off her dress and was standing there just in her panties. I started up about going out again and we argued. I can't remember what was said, only it got pretty hot and heavy. I was woozy, my sense of balance wobbly. Like when you've taken a shot to the head in a football game. Maybe I lunged at her, I'm not sure. Maybe I just keeled over. I don't recall actually making any impact. I remember her saying something about going to the show. But I can't even be sure it was that Monday night. After that, I don't remember anything. The next thing I knew, it was five o'clock in the morning and she wasn't there. I didn't know what to make of it. I was scared, confused."

When Robert Panforte speculated that he might have angrily lunged at his wife, the aqua blue disappeared from his mother's eyes.

Her eyelids fluttered and her eyes turned into tiny, blinking pearls. She pitched forward from her chair and crumbled to the floor in a dead faint. Before her shoulder hit the floor, Pat Kelley was on his feet. He leapt from behind his desk with cat-like quickness and was at her side even before her husband could kneel to tend to her limp body. Bailiff McCann moved with surprising quickness for a man of such abundant bulk to join Kelley and old man Panforte. The courtroom was frozen by the stricken woman. Pat tenderly waved smelling salts under her delicate nose. Her face twitched and she turned her head to escape the pungent fumes. Pat spoke to her softly in Italian, rousing her consciousness. McCann eased her shoulders from the floor, supporting her in a sitting position.

Then Pat fiercely shouted: "Remain seated until we get Mrs. Panforte out of the courtroom!" Had the Chief Clerk not acted so quickly and decisively, the confusion and creeping panic of the spectators at Mrs. Panforte's collapse might well have created a mob scene.

The bailiff and Pat lifted Angelina to her unsteady feet. Her husband babbled at her in Italian until Pat said something sharply. Pat must have used Italian for, "Shut the fuck up!" because old man Panforte was startled into silence. In Italian, Pat ordered Fred Panforte to go to his son's aid. Still speaking Italian, Pat whispered to Angelina and she nodded as he helped her down the aisle toward the door. Most of the crowd was on its collective feet, but substantially complied with the Chief Clerk's order by remaining at their seats. From the witness stand, Robert Panforte watched confusedly as the short clerk and the burly bailiff escorted his mother. Danny Loeb remained at the corner of the jury box, his eyes following the halting procession his questions had provoked. District Attorney Moore eyed the jury, searching for any affect this exceptional moment may have had on them.

As Angelina and her escorts passed the Brady family row, Paul Brady ignored her, his bitter stare fixed on the witness stand, his right hand a white knuckled fist grinding into his left palm. His wife glanced at Mrs. Panforte as she passed, her taut lips thin lines of sheer contempt. Maria and Terry Kelley stood by their seats. Pat didn't even look at them, intent on helping Angelina out of her courtroom misery. A look of horror formed on Maria's face at the sight of her husband's hands soothingly holding Angelina up, his lips moving at her ear, leniently urging her on, step by unsure step, his hands calming her quivering body. At that moment Maria felt that her husband and Angelina Panforte were sharing intimacies that were exclusive to her.

Her neck veins coursed with blood as she fought to keep her scream trapped in her throat.

Terry saw his mother's struggle. He began talking to her with soft intensity, but her eyes followed her husband and Angelina. Terry kept talking to her, trying to illuminate the darkness that had overcome her. He took her chin in his thumb and forefinger and gently turned her face to him. "Mom, look at me!" And she did. She studied her boy's face, and saw the angles of adolescence that had recently arrived. She looked deeply into his hazel eyes, so much like his father's. She bowed her forehead against his shoulder, and he wrapped his arm around her. He held her for a moment and firmly said, "Come on, Mom. Let's go. Let's show the bastards what we're made of." She pulled away from him, took a deep breath, threw her shoulders back and Maria Bertolli Kelley and her son led all but the court reporter out of the tumultuous courtroom.

Pat took Mrs. Panforte to a vacant jury room across the hall and husbanded her. Her son locked himself with his father in the holding tank. The spectators milled around in the corridors, muttering conjectures on what they'd just witnessed. The press guys ran to the phones and called in their stories of a mother's collapse in the Hall of Justice. As is often the case, the press didn't see what truly had occurred and therefore reported only the appearance of reality, missing its essence. They would write that Angelina's collapse was a result of the terrible pressure imposed on a mother witnessing her only child on trial for his life. But they didn't know what Pat Kelley did. Nor did Maria or her son know what Pat had learned after dinner at their home the previous night. Maria was oblivious to Angelina's wound, but Pat didn't have the luxury of oblivion.

He knew too much. He carried, in the pouch of his memory too many of other people's secrets, too much of others' pain. In the hush of the vacant jury room, all that Pat had learned outside its sacred confines seemed to rush at him, torrent-like, as though an imaginary dam in his conscience had burst. The profane and profound that had begun visiting him since the day he'd read the Grand Jury transcript of Panforte murder case clashed in his mind with a wild violence that made his temples throb. Yet as he closed the door to the jury room, sealing off the gawking audience to a mother's agony, Pat realized that, at last, he was alone with Angelina Panforte. From her first moments in the Hall of Justice, Pat had treated her with respect and compassion because he believed she was entitled to both. But he also hoped that there would come a time when neither her husband nor her son would be present so that he could gently probe her about them both. This was Pat's moment, made even more compelling by what he had learned over cognacs and cigars after Sunday night dinner at his Crestlake Drive home.

Maria Kelley had chased the kids off to bed, reminding them it was a school night and bribing their cooperation by assuming their dishwashing job for Mary Healy and herself. Pat, his boyhood friend Father Peter Conroy, S.J., and Joe Desmond adjourned to the living room for the inevitable cognac, cigars and men-only hour. Pat poked the embers of the fire, added a couple of logs that hissed and crackled sparks up the chimney. Father Conroy and Joe sat at each end of the sofa with Pat on the love seat across from them, their snifters resting on coasters atop a large mahogany coffee table. Pat blew a stream of cigar smoke toward the ceiling and softly remarked, "Pete, I hope you know I wasn't being critical of you when I joked about you always rescuing stray dogs, and being afraid to take out the shortstop on a double play ball when we were kids."

"Don't be silly, Pat. Besides, it's true. I never could bring myself to slide spikes high." Pat flicked a long gray ash into the ashtray and said, "I've been mulling over your comments about Confession. It's hard for me to think of you in a confessional box. I suppose when you grow up with a guy and do all the crazy kid things we did, it's strange to think of you forgiving sins."

"I'm not the one forgiving sins, Pat. I'm more like a long distance operator placing an urgent phone call. I just try to make the right connections," Conroy said.

"But why do you call Confession an Act of Reconciliation? All the priests I've heard classify it as an *act of penance*," Pat said, refilling their cognacs and placing the bottle in the middle of the coffee table within easy reach.

"It's our training. We were trained by a Retreat Master at El Retiro, Father Antonio Roberti. He used a case method, like they do at Harvard Law School. He'd have us read cases of actual confessions and require us to analyze the confessor's handling of them. Of course, he didn't use real names, but the fact patterns were real. I remember one confession he discussed with us that stood out. It was that case that taught me about reconciliation. To this day, I measure my own ability as a confessor against the standards Father Roberti established with his story."

"Can you share it with us?" Pat gently asked. "Keep it anonymous, of course. I don't want any trouble breaking the seal of Confession."

"I suppose there's no harm if we just consider it a hypothetical discussion," Conroy agreed. Pat noticed a slight thickness had crept into his diction and suspected the generosity of the cognac was illuminating Father Conroy's memory even as it loosened his tongue.

"It was our final class on The Sacrament of Confession," the Jesuit began. "Father Roberti told us to write down what we each considered the three worst sins we could imagine. 'Sins,' I remember him saying, 'that reek with such depravity they stir revulsion in you!' After we'd completed our lists he told us to put our papers aside, put down our pens and just listen. He told us not to take notes of what he was about to say.

"He said the incident took place in the last summer of the First World War. It was just after dawn on a Sunday morning and he was deep in meditation. There was a knock on his door and he heard Brother Sullivan, the sexton, calling him. He knew immediately something unusual had happened, for he was not to be disturbed during his meditations, and Brother Sullivan guarded his solitude completely. Brother Sullivan apologized for his imposition and said, 'There's a man. I heard him pounding on the chapel door, crying for a priest. I don't know how he got on the grounds, but he's driving an expensive car. I tried to calm him down. I explained this is a retreat house and he should see his parish priest. He told me his parish is in San Francisco and he needs a priest right away. He wants a priest who speaks Italian and asked me if I speak Italian. I told him no, that I was a Jesuit brother and he begged me to get him a Father. He said he'd done something terrible.'

"Father Roberti instructed Brother Sullivan to take the man to chapel and show him his confessional box and tell him an Italian-speaking priest would be there shortly.

"Once inside the confessional, Father Roberti slid open the panel and blessed the penitent through the screen. 'It is in the silhouette of the sacrament where we find the soul,' Father Roberti taught us. In Italian, Father Roberti encouraged the young man to share his troubles. 'I don't know where to begin,' the man whispered. 'Everything's so confusing. How could this happen to me?'

" ' Begin where it hurts,' Father Roberti counseled. 'It's your pain that has brought you here. Tell me how you found us.'

" 'You don't want to know what I've done?' the man asked.

" 'I already know what you've done, my son. What I need to understand

is how and why you've come to us.'

" *The man leaned closer to the screen and whispered so that only his confessor could hear, 'It's a woman, Father.'*

" *'A woman not your wife?' Father Roberti asked.*

" *'Yes...I mean no,' the man stammered. 'She is my wife. We were married yesterday in San Francisco. That's when it happened, when everything went wrong, on our wedding night.'*

" *'Before you tell me what happened last night, can you tell me a little about your wife? How you met and decided to marry?' Father Roberti suggested. The young man told him they'd met at a church service in Genoa before he set sail for San Francisco. They were both teenagers and they corresponded for eight or nine years. When war in Europe broke out, he wrote her and proposed marriage. By then he was an American citizen and held a responsible business position in the city. His employer was an influential man and was able to arrange her passage to San Francisco through the State Department, since she was engaged to an American citizen. Arranged marriages were not uncommon during the war years, Father Roberti told us. Anyway, she got over here and worked for about a year as a singer in a theatrical group in the City.*

"*Father Roberti asked, 'How did you find us, my son. What brought you to the Society of Jesus?' The man told Father Roberti he didn't know they were Jesuits until that moment. He said, 'We drove from the City to Santa Cruz for our honeymoon. My boss let us use his car. Last night I...I ran from the bridal suite. I just started driving. I had no place to go, I just wanted to get away from her. I drove up a mountain. At the summit, I turned off the highway and drove on a dirt road into a forest. When I couldn't go any further, I turned around and went back to the highway. On the way down the mountain, I saw a road on my left. It looked like it led to a forest, so I took it. Somehow, I felt safer in the darkness. I drove around a bend in the road and the forest opened up and the sun came up and I saw the cross on a chapel roof. I figured God must have guided me in my madness to this place. He must want me to seek His forgiveness. So I pounded on the chapel door until Brother came and then you came,' the man sobbed.*

"*Father Roberti told us this was the crucial moment in the sacramental process. 'I'd managed to get him to talk about himself. It's vital to allow a penitent the chance to introduce himself to his confessor, to reveal his self-image before he articulates the secret guilt that afflicts him. I gently urged him to find the words that would describe what drove him from his bride's bed. I told him his marital bed was blessed through the Holy Sacrament of Marriage and asked him what went wrong with his union blessed by*

Almighty God.

" *'He struggled to ask, 'When does a sacrament become a sacrilege, Father?'*

" *'Let God be the judge of that, my son. Just try to tell me what happened. Tell it like a story, as though it was about someone else.'*

"*The young bridegroom told Father Roberti about his wedding night. He said that, when they arrived at their hotel room they found a basket of fruit and a bottle of wine, compliments of his employer. While his bride was in the bathroom changing, he poured them each a glass of wine and munched happily on a pear. When she returned from the bathroom, she hadn't changed her clothes. She'd only removed her jacket and shoes. She sat on the edge of the bed, her hands folded in her lap, her eyes downcast. He asked her what was wrong, why she wasn't dressed for bed. She began to cry softly. He thought she must be nervous about her first night with a man, so he went to her and tried to comfort her.*

"*But she was inconsolable. He gave her his handkerchief and she dabbed at her eyes. With his handkerchief over her mouth as though she wanted to shroud her words, she told him, 'I've done something terrible, something unspeakable.'*

"*Her young husband laughed and told her that she was foolish to think she was capable of great evil. 'After all,' he reminded her, 'you've spent most of your life in convent schools and singing in church. You've had neither the disposition or opportunity to be a bad girl.'*

" *'She shook her head and said, 'If you only knew. The opportunity for sin is everywhere. Even in church. For me, especially in church. When I took my vows this morning, I committed the gravest sin of my life.'*

"*Her husband was mystified and said, 'How can you say such a thing? Our marriage is a Holy Sacrament!'*

" *'Yes,' she replied unevenly. 'And we're taught we must be in a state of grace to receive Blessed Sacraments. When we're not in a state of sanctifying grace – as I was not this morning – then to receive the sacraments is worse than a sin!'*

" *'You're not making any sense! We went to Confession Friday night, before our wedding. We were both in a state of grace,' he told her.*

" *'No my husband. The priest refused me absolution!'*

" *'I've never heard of such a thing,' he protested. 'Besides, it's God, not the priest who forgives our sins. You made a sincere act of contrition, that's enough for me and for God.'*

" *'Not if you knew the sin,' she sobbed. She tried to calm herself, 'I'll tell you what I told the priest and we'll see if you're any more forgiving. I told the priest that, when I was thirteen years-old, Sister Superior took me to* monsignor's room. I thought she brought me to him for my Confirmation lessons, since I was to be confirmed the following Sunday.

" 'I guess it was a confirmation of something. Maybe a confirmation that I was now a woman. Sister left me alone with monsignor after telling me I was to do exactly as he instructed. He talked to me for a while, mostly telling me the difficulties of doing Christ's work. He told me to kneel before him to receive his blessing. I did so and he waved the Sign of the Cross. As I knelt before him, head bowed, I saw that he'd exposed himself to me. I'd never seen a man before, and I think that's why I didn't quickly turn away. He saw that I was staring at him and told me to touch him there. He instructed me how he wanted to be touched. After a while, he told me to take him in my mouth, like a sweet candy treat, I remember him saying. And I did as I was told. After a while, he trembled and I heard him groan and thought perhaps I'd hurt him, so I became very still. Then I felt something slide down my throat. But it wasn't sweet like candy. It was tasteless, but my memory of that moment is so bitter!

" 'Then he took me to his bed and undressed me. He told me he would pleasure my body as I'd pleasured his. But there was only pain when he took my innocence. From that night on, Sister Superior took me to monsignor's room twice a month until you proposed to me in your letter. I told Sister Superior I was going to America to marry you and I'd kill myself rather than go to him again. She relented, and besides, there were other convent girls to take care of him.

" 'When I told all of this to the priest in confession the night before we wed, he told me he couldn't absolve me of such sins. I didn't know what to do. I'd come all the way from Italy to marry you. You were my escape from the torture of the convent. I was being told there was no cleansing of my impurities. I decided that I must go through with our wedding. It was my only hope for a decent life, my only chance to heal the wounds of my childhood!

" 'I felt like a fraud at the altar when you slipped the wedding band on my finger. When you gently kissed me in church, I felt somehow you could erase my past with your love. In the bathroom moments ago, the mirror told me I was living a lie. The girl you met in Genoa never existed. The woman you've married is a deceit, and our life together could only be sustained if I secreted from you my tainted touch.

"'But I truly love you, and I don't know how to love you with a lie! I'm certain you can't love me now that you know my truth.'

"I remember," Father Conroy told us wistfully, "how insignificant the three sins that I'd written on my list prior to Father Roberti's lecture were. As I've told you, he was a masterful orator, and every scholastic in the room *hung on every word. As he related what he'd heard in the confessional, it seemed that his voice conveyed the emotional panic of the young man and the strained recitation of his bride. He told us that at this point in his confession the man's dialogue became fractured and he was disoriented. He taught us that when a penitent reaches the point where they're trying to express their sin we must listen to every stammer, every sigh. He insisted we memorize every expression, be it a shaking head, a timorous voice or slumped shoulders. 'Your mind must be like a film with sound. Only when you replay the scene over and over again will you comprehend what they've told you and what you must do,' he told us.*

"Father Roberti asked the young man what happened after his wife's revelations to him. He answered: 'Father, I don't know what happened. I...I suddenly was angry. More angry than I'd ever been. I remember looking at her. She's a small woman with delicate features. Her skin is the white of a pearl and her hair black as a moonless night, her eyes the colors of the Mediterranean Sea. When she told me she wasn't a virgin, her complexion seemed to get darker and her eyes too. She looked like a Sicilian girl, everything about her dark and filthy.

"'I...I couldn't help myself. I struck her. I hit her with my fist and knocked her off the bed onto the floor. She just lay there. She didn't protest or even shed a tear. And then I tore her clothes off and took her. I don't remember hitting her anymore, but when I finished with her, her lip was bleeding and her face and body were bruised. She got up off the floor, said nothing and went into the bathroom. I poured myself more wine.

"'When she came out of the bathroom, she was wearing a robe and piece of cotton on her lip to stop the bleeding. I think the robe was pink. She lay down on the bed. Still she said nothing, and her silence made me ever more furious.

"'I went to the bed and grabbed her roughly by her hair. I told her to get on her hands and knees, like a dog in heat. Then I told her I wanted the only virgin orifice she had to offer. Oh God, Father! I sodomized my own wife! On my wedding night!'

"Father Roberti told us the man was sobbing, almost hysterical. He made no effort to lower his voice to the whispered confidentiality of the confessional box. Father Roberti told us, 'I knew at that moment, he was alone with his Savior.'

"Father Roberti whispered to the man, 'You feel that when you consummated your marriage, you sinned?'

"'What I did was unnatural, Father. I don't know why I did it. But I know it was bad. It's...it's what queer men do to each other. I beg your *forgiveness.'*

"'My son, it is not my forgiveness you need. It's God's and your wife's. Let me tell you how to achieve God's infinite blessings. I want you to go back to your hotel and bring your wife to us. She is spiritually wounded, as are you. We can heal you both, but only if you each seek our ministrations,' Father Roberti told him.

"'After what I've done? You want me to go back? What can I say to her?'

"Father Roberti answered, 'Yes, I want you to go back to her. My son, you have no idea what you've done. You think you've done something unnatural and that this is your sin. Your sin is that you've done something natural. With God's grace, I can help you. But I cannot help you if you will not help yourself. If you do not go to her, God will not come to you.

"'And your wife thinks she's a sinner. Tell her she's wrong. Tell her that her faith awaits her at El Retiro. Tell her that, like Christ on His Cross, her God has not forsaken her. It only seems that way. I can heal her, and if I heal her, you will be cured.'

"So the man drove back to their honeymoon hotel in Santa Cruz to get his wife. Father Roberti remained in the confessional box and prayed for the hour and a half it took for them to reach El Retiro. When the man was back in the confessional, Father Roberti instructed him to have his wife enter the other side of the booth. He slid open both sound-panels so that both could hear all that would be said.

"He spoke to the bride first. He told her he understood she'd gone to Confession the night before her marriage and she believed the priest had refused her absolution. He asked her if the priest was a Jesuit. She told him that he wasn't, he was a parish priest, not a member of a religious order. Father Roberti explained to her that there were certain sins considered by the Holy Father as corruptive of the Church itself. He told her that breaking the seal of confession, assaulting The Pope, desecration of the Holy Eucharist, abortion and absolution for an ordained priest's concubine so seriously struck at the moral authority of the Church, that only members of the Society of Jesus were authorized to grant absolution. Not even a bishop can absolve these five sins 'Because we Jesuits take a vow of absolute loyalty to the Pope, only we are allowed to grant absolution for these sins,' he explained to her.

"Then he told her, 'Of course, you are not expected to know this bit of Canon Law. You misunderstood the priest's lack of authority and believed he was refusing to forgive you. The good father also misunderstood what you confessed to him about the monsignor in Genoa. He thought he'd heard the confession of a priest's concubine and thus had no authority to address your problem.

"*He was mistaken. You were not and never have been a priest's mistress. Indeed, what happened to you in the rectory in Genoa was not your sin. Surely you understand that a woman who is raped has not sinned against chastity. She is the victim of sin. That monsignor raped you, my child. He forced your submission with the power of the Cross. His abuse of the moral authority of his office was more terrifying than an upraised dagger! He blasphemed his God and degraded God's child! He, not you, is the sinner! He, not you, needs forgiveness!'*

"*Father Roberti turned to her husband and said, 'My son, you have come seeking forgiveness. But God's forgiveness requires that you understand the true nature of your failing. You feel guilty because you think you did something unnatural to your wife on your wedding night. But a sin of the flesh is not committed by touching some forbidden part of the body. God created our bodies to respond to a loving touch. A sin of the flesh occurs when the spirit of love does not compel the touching.*

"*'You've just heard me tell your wife that a priest raped her when she was but a girl. I'm telling you that you raped your wife on your wedding night! Monsignor forced himself on her with the superior power of her Church. You forced yourself on her with the superior power of a man. Both of you touched her body, the very vessel of life itself, without the spirit of love. This is the sin you two men have committed. It doesn't matter that monsignor was motivated by perverse lust and you, driven by mistaken rage. Both of you defiled her spirit.*

"*Do you understand, my son? Is this the sin for which you seek God's forgiveness? Is this the sin His son died on The Cross for?'*

"*Yes Father,' the man cried. 'This is my sin.'*

"*One of my fellow scholastics asked our teacher what kind of penance he gave the guy. Father Roberti shook his head in dismay, suggesting this was the dumbest question he'd ever heard from a potential Jesuit. He told us, 'You think requiring a penitent to say five rosaries is a healthy spiritual punishment? How can ordering someone to pray be considered a prayer at all? Compelled prayer is but a word formula that speaks of God, not to Him. It is the confessing itself, the expiation of guilt that cleanses the soul. If I had my way, we'd never refer to the sacrament of penance. It's the sacrament of reconciliation!*

"*'That's your mission as a confessor. It's to bring about reconciliation of the penitent with self so they can reconcile themselves with God.'*

"*He told us to turn over our papers and look at the three sins we'd each written down at the beginning of class. Not one of us had listed a procuring nun or a molesting priest. Not one of us had thought of a violent husband, all of whom had terrorized a young woman. Then he lectured us on his reconciliation of the young couple. He explained to the man that the act of physical love had, for his wife, become an ordeal of horror. Because the two men in whom she'd entrusted her vulnerability had dishonored her trust, she was deeply scarred. It was likely, he advised, that sexual union would fill her with fear and loathing for many years to come. Possibly for the rest of her life. Father Roberti sought the man's agreement that he would refrain from the rites of the marital bed, and their marriage would be one of celibate love. He told the bridegroom, 'If you can do this, she will experience the spirit of a man's love and discover the healing power of such love. One day she may come to you, desiring your embrace. If she does, you may respond because she's come to you by her own spirit. But you must understand she may never sufficiently heal to freely make such a decision. If you're sincerely contrite you will accept this with the same equanimity that Christ accepted His Cross.'*

"'The young groom agreed,' Father Roberti told us. 'Then I requested that he return to El Retiro every year for his Easter Duty. I invited him to partake in the Spiritual Exercises of St. Ignatius to renew his strength to keep his vow of purely spiritual love. He agreed to do so and has come back every Easter since.'

"I asked Father Roberti: 'What about that convent school and the monsignor in Genoa? What reconciliation can there be for what they did to that poor girl?'

"He smiled mischievously at me and said, 'Well, Mister, it's reassuring to an old teacher that at least one of you is still awake. That situation required assistance abroad, so I sent word to our Father General in Rome of unholy activities in Genoa.'"

"The black Pope?" Kelley asked, referring to the supreme leader of the Society of Jesus, who some critics considered more powerful than the Pope himself.

"Yep," Conroy confirmed. "Father Roberti told us that Father General ordered the Pope's personal confessor, a fellow Jesuit, to Genoa. He said, 'Once there, our brother in Christ excommunicated Sister Superior and purged those nuns who had aided her.

"'As for monsignor, the Jesuit paid him a brotherly visit. He suggested monsignor might find the Pope's confessor more forgiving than a papal discovery of what he diplomatically described as certain irregularities in monsignor's liturgical practices.

"'Monsignor was many things, but a fool he was not. He confessed completely. He was advised that absolution was possible if he demonstrated

sincere contrition. This required resigning his Church office and entering into the cloister of the Chartreuse Monastery near Lucca. Once accepted by the followers of San Bruno, monsignor would spend the remainder of his life in silence. He private cell would be lit 24 hours a day and his door always kept open so he could be constantly observed, even when he used his bed pan. His forgiveness would occur if he lived out his life in comprehensive mortification,' Father Roberti announced. And every one of us in that classroom sensed the swift, searing power of the Society of Jesus, and the unflinching will to apply to any priest who dishonored the call of God!

"Then he instructed us to take our lists of what we'd considered our three worst sins to our rooms. He told us to pray for Our Lord's guidance. We were then to write an essay reconciling our imaginary sinners to themselves and God. If we were unable to compose reconciliation, then God was telling us we didn't have a vocation. Father Roberti concluded our lesson on forgiveness by saying, 'I must tell you that the troubled young man fully honored his confessional promises. He returned the following year to El Retiro for his Easter Duty and told me his wife had given birth to a son. God had truly blessed them by allowing conception on the only occasion during their marriage in which they consummated physical union. He has returned every Easter since. They are still married and still as celibate as we are. The husband has become a man of considerable means and generously donates to our Jesuit mission, and their only son has grown healthy in our Faith.

"'So you see, gentlemen, to live in the Ignatian mold, you must become men for others. If the day ever comes when there's no reconciliation, it is your failure, not the sinner's. When that day arrives, you should bolt from the confessional box, rip off your Roman collar and accept you're not a brother in Christ!'" Pete Conroy concluded his teacher's lesson.

When Angelina Panforte had fainted as her son testified to lunging at his scantily clad wife in their bedroom, Pat Kelley knew that it was the burden of waking from a nightmare that sent her to her knees. Her son's witness stand words had given expression to her deepest foreboding. From the moment of his birth she'd feared that, in some inexplicable way, the violence of his conception might have stained his soul. So she mothered him in an intensely protective fashion, monitoring his maturation for any signs of simmering anger, the sire of aggression. Liberated by Father Roberti's absolution of her husband from the demands of the marital bed, she made Robert her prime love object, lavishing him with concern. Accepting that he was being raised in the home of a powerful, possibly driven man, she tried to shield him from her husband's ambition. She banned the speaking of Italian at home in an effort to equalize the inarticulateness of father and son. She convinced her husband they were raising an American boy and that the language and customs of the Old Country would make him feel strange when he went off to school.

But her hidden purpose was to exploit Fred Panforte's artless English while her son developed the verbal skills to resist or amend his father's competitive vision of life. Her husband argued that her constant attention to the details of their boy's life would turn him into a *momma's boy*. Though she dreaded the sport of football and anguished that he might be badly injured in this odd American game that exalted violence and rewarded pain, she allowed him to play. She felt it might provide an outlet to expel remnants of aggression that seemed to her innate to the masculine soul. Through his high school years she was always there to tuck him in and listen to the minutia of his day. He playfully called these nightly sessions, "Mom Time." As an adult, it was his mother to whom he turned when troubled. It was not surprising, therefore, that it was his mother, not his father, whom he called to confess a drunken Peninsula brawl. It was his mother, not his father, to whom he first admitted that he might have lunged at his wife.

It was not his public inference from the witness stand that he'd lunged at his bride that felled Angelina Panforte. Pat was certain that Paula's mother-in-law, more than her own mother, felt the resigned terror when a bedroom is transformed into a combat zone. Angelina could feel Paula's initial astonishment that her husband had turned on her. Memory had taught her that Paula's shock would turn into excruciating pain – the ache of love's implosion. But there was no Father Roberti for Paula and her husband, no gentle, caring man to tend to the bruises of love, to mend the lacerations of hearts. Pat was certain that it was Angelina's emotional affinity with her daughter-in-law that drove her to her knees. They were bonded in their lovers' tormenting rage.

From Angelina's first court appearance at her son's arraignment Kelley had prayed that he would get an opportunity to be alone with her, that his gentle probing without the overbearing presence of husband or her son's wary lawyer might reveal something about these families in conflict that would shed light on the obscurity of their sudden and brutal fracture. Daily, Pat had graciously attended to her every courtroom need. When her delicate face had become strained at the war of words between the lawyers over her child, Pat had counseled her that all facts are not created equal, and that in American courts, District Attorney Moore's words bore the heavy burden of proving his homicidal theory to a moral certainty, while Danny Loeb's phrases only had to raise doubt in the jury's mind. At a corridor drinking fountain during a recess of Inspector Mike Murphy's testimony, Pat had reminded Angelina that there was a silent witness that stood alongside her son each day of the trial and this witness – the presumption of innocence – was the eloquent guardian angel of the criminal justice system. Angelina remembered Pat's kindness on her son's initial day in the dock when he had first mentioned to her and her husband that the terrible Indictment of her son and the awful newspaper accounts in no way stripped Robert of his garment of innocence. Understandably, she had assumed that Kelley was expressing his opinion of her boy's lack of guilt because of the obvious sincerity he had conveyed. She had not understood that Pat's passionate faith in this uniquely American judicial principle was the source of his earnestness.

At last, sheltered with her in the jury room, he had his opportunity to insinuate his inquiry further into the secret intimacies of Panforte family life. But Kelley's opportunity for interrogation was now burdened by the terrible trauma of Angelina Panforte's wedding night that he'd learned the previous evening from his boyhood pal, Pete Conroy, S.J. It had been Father Conroy's purpose in relating his teacher's lesson on the Sacrament of Confession to convey that the essence of this Catholic rite was reconciliation rather than penance. But Pat was more intrigued by the attitudes on sex and love that whispered in a confessional box three decades earlier. This abused young bride was now a grandmother, and the trial of her son had painted dark circles under her eyes, made more dramatic and grievous by her blanch skin. Yet it was the bride and not the bridegroom who was overwhelmed by guilt on their wedding night. Angelina had blamed herself for the monsignor's molestation of her. She had condemned herself as a fraud when she had exchanged wedding vows and sought to purge deceit from their marriage by telling her husband what she felt was her sordid youth. It troubled Pat that Angelina, so cruelly victimized by a perverse priest, had constructed the notion that she was a co-perpetrator in her abuse.

Although it had been Angelina's misconceived guilt that had compelled her to confess the sexual abuse of her youth to her husband on their wedding night, it was shame that drove her husband to a confessional box. But Fred Panforte had confessed the wrong sin. Or worse, he'd confessed a non-sin. Pat recalled that Panforte had told Father Roberti that his evil was an act of anal intercourse. He hadn't confessed to wantonly beating his wife, and he didn't even consider that he'd forced himself on her. After all, his confession inferred, she was his wife now, and he had a husband's right to punish her for wasting her virginity on one other than himself. Nor was her failure to consent to his use of her body at all problematical to the bridegroom. After all, her marriage vows required complete submission to her husband's desires. What Fred had sought priestly relief from was his belief that he'd done something unmanly. He believed that sodomy was an unnatural sin and that he was guilty of acting like a *finocchio*, a queer, in taking his wife as he did.

What struck Pat as heroic about Father Roberti's treatment of this troubled couple was his ability to liberate himself from the ancient mores of his church and era. He had noted that Fred expressed marital union as *taking* rather than jointly giving and receiving. He had told Fred and Angelina Panforte that she had been raped, first by her pastor, then by her husband. Clearly, the sexual victimization by her monsignor was beyond question. At the time of this confession and even at the time of the Panforte murder trial, nothing in Church-made law or man-made law accepted that a man could rape his own wife. In the very ceremony of marriage, both the Church and State vitiated the need for any further consent by a wife to any desire of her husband. It was her sacred duty to submit and, therefore, her husband was incapable of coercion. Yet Father Roberti had called it rape. And to Pat Kelley it was. Father Roberti's words that Fred Panforte's sin was touching his wife without the spirit of love and, in so doing, he had defiled her very being, resonated with Pat. It was the ineffable initiative of spirit between lovers that Father Roberti had been teaching and which Pat and Maria Kelley pursued so intently. And within the embrace of this *theology*, Pat thought, Bartolemeo Bertolli and Antonietta Pompa were not sinful adulterers at all, but tender and blessed searchers for that unity of souls which enriches beyond all measure.

Pat's unintended piercing of the *Seal of Confession* had added what he thought was a crucial piece of biography to the last of the *Precious Ones*. Just as Fred Panforte's seizure of Bertolli's business had been technically legal, so also had his crude sexual violation of his wife on their wedding night. Fred undoubtedly had categorized

Father Roberti's characterization of rape as a moral rather than legal pronouncement which, for his promise of marital celibacy, was completely forgiven. But it was the moral implications of Fred Panforte's relations with his loved ones that arrested Pat's searching mind. As a boy, Fabrizio had taken advantage of his older siblings to monopolize his father's affections. As a teenager, he'd ignored his teacher's most important lesson of personal loyalty. As a bridegroom, he'd violently turned on his bride in a disgusting display of male vehemence for which his only shame was the orifice he'd chosen to penetrate. As an ambitious executive, he'd employed cunning to abuse his benefactor's trust and his knowledge of Bertolli's passion for Antonietta to steal the man's life work. To Pat, Panforte's story was reading like the tale of a recidivist offender against those closest to him, those blinded by their loving trust in him. What, Pat asked himself, does this tell me about his relationship with his son and his daughter-in-law? He was not certain that he had gained Angelina's confidence, but realized this was his only chance to question her.

31

Angelina's hands trembled as she sipped from her Dixie cup. She looked down to the tabletop, and before Pat Kelley could begin his questioning said: "I'm so sorry for being so weak. Do you think they'll think ill of my son because of me?" Pat shook his head emphatically and said in Italian, "Not at all, Signora Panforte! Everyone in our courtroom understands what you're going through."

"*Do they really?*" she thought, but did not say. Nonetheless, Angelina was grateful that this kind court clerk spoke Italian and she thought he was quite fluent, although his accent indicated it was not his native tongue. She asked him how he had come to speak such fine Italian and Pat, not wanting to expose his relationship to Maria, claimed that his love of Dante's works had compelled his language study. She nodded approvingly and Pat said, "Signora, I've spent many years in court and I've come to believe that, for loved ones, it's a most unnatural experience. Particularly parents. The human intimacies that are revealed are only those that the advocates' questions elicit. Because they are partisans, we only hear what they want us to hear. I fear that you realized this moments ago and suspect that it was your feelings for your daughter-in-law that felled you in court."

Angelina brushed a tear from her eye and sighed, "Paula was a darling girl. She was so good for my Robert and so kind to me. I've always felt so awkward in America and...and she's always been so accepting of my shyness and language difficulty. She was more like a little sister than a daughter, so free and unmindful of the rigors of maturity..."

"More water?" Pat asked. She shook her head. Then Pat asked the question that no one had asked Angelina Panforte: "What do you remember about your last time together?"

She stammered, "It was Sunday...the Sunday before..." Pat urged her on with his eyes. "She came to our house shortly before twelve-fifteen Mass. My husband greeted her at the door. I was a few steps behind him. She was carrying the baby and her eyes were glazed. She seemed terribly upset. Suddenly, she thrust the baby at me. She did it so carelessly, I almost dropped him. She didn't even greet me. All she said was: 'Nonno' – that's what the kids called my husband – 'I want to show you something!'

"She told my husband to come to their car. It was almost like an order. I was shocked by her tone of voice and even more so by my husband's immediate acquiescence. He's not a man given to taking orders from anyone. I figured she was having car trouble or something. She'd just gotten her driver's license, so I thought she might be frustrated by something mechanical. The baby was fussy, so I took him to our garden. He loves to touch the rose pedals with his chubby little fingers, and he tries to suck in the morning fog like it's his breakfast milk.

"I don't remember how long they were out at the car. After a while, my husband called down to me to bring Bobbie back upstairs. When I arrived at the front door, Paula was standing next to the driver's side of their Chevy. My husband took the baby and I asked him what was going on. He told me he'd tell me later and then carried Bobbie to the car and placed him in a little back seat contraption Robert had rigged up to take my grandson for rides.

"I remember that Paula waved to me as she drove away. But she wasn't smiling, and I thought that she looked strange. Maybe I just imagined that. Maybe it's just this was the last I ever saw her..." Sobbing, Angelina buried her face in her frilly handkerchief. "I'm sorry," Pat said. "I've got no right to trouble you this way."

"It's not you, Signor Kelley," she said dabbing her eyes. "It's that I've never had a chance talk about Paula since....since they found her. The police had my son and I couldn't see him alone, and I didn't know what I could say to Eileen. The inspectors never talked to me. And my husband and Signor Loeb insist that nothing I could say to the jury would help Robert. They've told me my presence in court – whatever that means – is the best I can do for him. It's so awful. I feel so...so useless!"

Pat interpreted Angelina's admission of maternal impotence as her invitation for a dialogue on what she'd been unable to express to family members and the homicide detail. It was probably true that the cops felt Panforte's mother could offer no relevant evidence on the crime and that Loeb sought to sway the jury with her silent suffering. But it was equally likely that Paula's sudden and troubled appearance at her in-laws' home the day before her disappearance implied the first note of discord in the young couple's marital home. Pat carefully asked, "After Paula drove away from your place, did your husband tell you what her problem was?"

"He said that Paula was very upset about Robert's working hours running the company's Petaluma operations. With the baby's arrival and all the time Robert was spending at the ranches, she felt they had no life together anymore." Pat calculated Bob Panforte's weekly work schedule. He worked Monday through Thursday at their Petaluma chicken ranch. On Fridays, he worked at The Market. Angelina explained that Monday and Wednesday nights her son remained in Sonoma County to minimize his commute, spending the night at the Panforte Sonoma turkey ranch. Since Bob had to be at work at The Market by three in the morning on Fridays, a social life with Paula was prohibitive during the work week. It was these career demands on his evenings that had precipitated Paula's night movie excursions with friends or alone, Pat thought.

"Why do you suppose Paula left your grandson with you and invited your husband out to their car?" Pat asked.

"I'm sure she was trying to protect me. She wouldn't want me to hear anything critical of my son," Angelina said flatly. "That makes sense," Pat nodded. "So how did you leave it?"

"My husband told me he'd work everything out. I guess he told Paula he'd drive up to Petaluma and fix everything. He suggested that they take the baby for a ride down the Peninsula. Maybe get a bite to eat or take in a movie. He told me she was okay and not to worry."

Angelina told Pat that her husband decided to drive immediately to Petaluma. He would spend the night at their Sonoma ranch and assume Robert's ranch duties Monday and Bob would replace him at The Market until he sorted out a new management structure. Pat asked if her husband had invited her to join him on his Sunday ride to Sonoma County. "No, there was no need to," she replied. Pat's nod urged her to elaborate. Angelina breathed deeply, "I've never been involved in my husband's business, and he made it clear that he could solve Paula's problems alone. Besides, I never go to the Sonoma ranch. I haven't been there since he took it over. It's a working ranch now, and it's just not the same as it was when ..." Maria Bertolli's presence at her son's trial flashed in Angelina's mind. But she couldn't bring herself to say to this stranger – as considerate and gentle as he had been to her – that her first comfortable moments in America had been her summer visits to her fiancée's boss's ranch. She simply finished her sentence by saying: "I spend my summers at our place at Lake Tahoe."

Finally, he asked Angelina how her husband had mended their son's marital spat. "He called me Monday from Sonoma," Angelina replied. "He told me that he'd spent the night and would be home Tuesday. He said that he'd transferred Robert to The Market indefinitely and that he was arranging a new manager for the ranches. I told him I thought that was wonderful and that Paula would be pleased. Just before hanging up I told him that I'd spoken to our son on the phone earlier, and it sounded like he'd been drinking. When Robert told me Paula had gone to the show, he'd slurred the name of the movie. I was concerned because he hadn't been drinking for quite some time. My husband said he'd talk to him first thing in the morning."

"Do you remember what movie Robert said she'd gone to see?"

"*Home of the Brave*," she replied.

"If you're up to it, Signora, we really should be getting back," Pat said.

"I'll be all right. Just give me a few moments in the Ladies' Room," she said. Pat nodded. As she opened the door to the Ladies' Room, she turned back to Pat and said in English, "Oh, Mr. Kelley! My Robert could never do that to her. Those awful photos of poor Paula…he could never do that. Please believe me!" Pat nodded, "I'm afraid what I believe doesn't much matter, Mrs. Panforte."

Pat played with the puzzle pieces in his mind while Mrs. Fred Panforte prepared herself for her return to the courtroom. His conversation with her had taken him outside the borders of the Coroner's metaphorical window of death. Pat thought of Maria's dinner table observation that something might have happened between Bob and Paula after the bridge party with the Petersens and before Paula's Monday night disappearance that could provide the motive for her murder. Maria had also argued that she believed motive was an indication of character while she accused Pat of accepting motive as a cause of behavior. Adopting Maria's notion of motive's relation to character, Pat analyzed Paula's unexpected Sunday visit to Fred and Angelina Panforte's Sea Cliff mansion. According to what Fred had told his wife, Paula was upset at their son because he was spending too much time at his job in Petaluma thereby neglecting her and presumably their child. But why would Paula confide in her father-in-law to the exclusion of Angelina? Angelina had assumed that Paula would be reluctant to be critical of her husband to his mother. But career demands affecting marital life was a common wifely complaint, and Angelina herself had chosen to give up her singing career to accommodate her husband. There had to be something more insidious to Paula's Sunday morning troubles for her to keep it from her husband's mother. And why had Paula insisted that her father-in-law come out to their '47 Chevy to have their confidential chat? Was there something in or about that vehicle that was the true source of Paula's angst? Pat thought about Fred Panforte's emotional breakdown on the witness stand recounting a touching scene with his grandson that Sunday night in his kid's Marina home. Could this moment, this memory be related to whatever Paula had confided in her father-in-law, Pat wondered. What was Pat to make of the new facts Angelina had given him? On the night of Paula's disappearance, Fred Panforte knew that she had gone out alone to the Fox and that his son had fallen off the wagon, because Angelina had told him so. Since Danny Loeb had not presented this evidence corroborating Bob Panforte's story, it had to mean the defense lawyer wasn't aware of it. It also meant that Loeb was unaware of the fact that Fred Panforte was out and about at the very same time his daughter-in-law was – Monday, June 5th. For Pat Kelley, the answer to the mystery of Paula Brady Panforte's death would be discovered by answering the questions of who was where and when, doing what?

32

When Robert Panforte returned to the witness stand he didn't scan each member of the jury as Danny Loeb had trained him to do. He looked to his mother. She smiled meekly at him, as if to assure him that she was fine. His complexion seemed paler than usual and his eyes a bit glazed as though he had or was about to shed tears. Judge Grant reminded young Panforte that he was still under oath and his defense counsel asked: "Bob, when you woke up at five o'clock on Tuesday morning, June 6, 1949, what did you do?"

"I woke up on the sofa and called out for my wife. She didn't answer, so I took a quick trip around the house, calling for her. Then I noticed blood on our bedspread, and I couldn't figure out what happened," Panforte's lips trembled. "I knew we'd argued and I must be implicated in some way, but I didn't know in what. I was scared." Panforte shook his head.

"Did you tell anyone prior to the discovery of Paula's body at Mt. Tamalpais that you felt you might be implicated in something?"

"After I'd reported Paula missing, I called my mother. I told her I'd washed the bedspread because I'd thought of a lot of things, but couldn't put anything together. I told her if anything happened to Paula they'd probably blame me."

"From the time you reported Paula missing to Thursday morning when her body was discovered, what did you do?"

"Well, Tuesday I talked to our relatives, Judge Grant and the homicide guys. Aunt Lil was caring for our son. Most of Wednesday, I was with the inspectors either at my place or the Hall of Justice. Then on Thursday, before dawn, we drove over to Marin."

"When you left your home for Marin before dawn on Thursday, did you have any recollection where your wife's body was?"

"She was never a body to me. She was Paula and she had to be alive."

"That means you'd been awake, with no rest, for twenty-four straight hours and that for seventeen of those twenty-four hours you were in the custody of the police, right?"

"It seems so."

"Other than what you told the inspectors and this jury, has your memory revealed anything that would shed new light on what happened to your wife?"

Scanning the eyes of each juror, Panforte said, "Just what I've told you."

"On Monday June 5th did you kill your wife and bury her remains on Mt. Tamalpais?"

"I couldn't do it! I've told you what I remember. I must've been so damn drunk. No wonder she didn't want to be seen with me. I wouldn't do that…beat her so badly like that…" His lips were taut, his aqua eyes whispered of incredulity. He bowed his head and studied his folded hands. Loeb froze the image with a moment of silence, then returned to his counsel table. In a resigned voice he said, "Your witness, counsel."

The trial had reached the moment of dread for Daniel David Loeb. He had surrendered control and would be required to sit passively, masking his panic with a look of tired indifference, while Moore fixed his cross-examiner's sights on his client. Panforte looked over to Moore, and the D.A.'s eyes locked on his. Pat thought it was doubtful that young Panforte truly appreciated how alone he was at this moment. Loeb could no longer protect him, his father couldn't manipulate his environment to make it ally to his son's success and his mother's obsessive nurturing had been buried in her courtroom collapse. At last, District Attorney Michael Moore had Robert Panforte where he wanted him - alone in the courtroom, armed only with his dubious memory.

District Attorney Moore, lanky, Lincoln-like, roamed easily throughout the Pit during his cross-examination. His movements severed Panforte's eye contact with the jurors. The D.A. began, "Mr. Panforte, you seem to be having trouble with your memory. As I understand your testimony, your memory blackout that you claim on the night of June 5th wasn't the first time you'd blacked out. I understand you suffered a blackout after drinking heavily and getting into a street brawl with two men down the Peninsula. Was that the first time you'd experienced a blackout?" Moore asked.

"Yes."

"On both occasions you were drinking heavily, feeling intense emotions and behaving angrily, correct?"

"Yeah."

"But your memory of the fight with the two strangers down the Peninsula is considerably more detailed than your memory of your wife that night in your bedroom, isn't it Mr. Panforte?"

"Whadda ya mean? I blacked-out both times. I'm not following you."

"Let's see if I can help you. You remember a terrific struggle with a couple of strangers, during which many blows were exchanged?"

"Yeah, but I was luckier landing more effective blows."

"Don't be so modest, Mr. Panforte. I've seen you play football against my alma mater in the Big Game. As I recall, you played blocking quarterback on offense and backed up the line on defense. And you played those positions, by one press account, 'with great skill and fearless aggressiveness,' didn't you?"

"That's the way you play football, Mr. Moore. It's not a game for the faint-hearted." Panforte implied Moore was a wimp, who'd cringe in a contact sport. The young man couldn't have been more wrong, Pat thought. Moore asked, "I'll wager your experience backing up the line, taking on huge linemen trying to block you and tackling speedy ball carriers, came in handy in your street fight with those two men, didn't it?"

"That's for sure. I'd have gotten my butt kicked if I hadn't played so much football!"

"But you remember that one of these strangers was about your age, and the other was younger and that you won that street brawl, right?"

"I guess so. I was glad just to get outta there in one piece."

"And you remember enough of the details of the battle that you feared you might have seriously injured the younger man, so you wanted to see if the newspapers carried the story, isn't that true?"

"Yeah."

"Mr. Panforte, doesn't it strike you as odd that you remember more details about a fight with two absolute strangers than you do about what you did to your own wife, the mother of your son, on her last night alive, in your own bedroom?" Moore's voice dripped with sarcasm.

"Everything that's happened seems odd to me," Panforte answered.

"Mr. Panforte, look at those photos of your wife in front of you again! Look at the cuts and bruises on her face and body. Sir, is there any doubt in your mind that a great collegiate football player, who'd successfully beaten up two men in a drunken Peninsula street brawl, was easily capable of inflicting those wounds on her?"

Loeb was on his feet, "Objection! That's enough rhetoric!"

"Sustained," Judge Grant announced, adding, "Counsel, let's get off the gridiron. You've made your point. Redundancy diminishes it."

The D.A. asked: "Did you say that you'd stopped drinking hard liquor because it made you combative?"

"That was part of it, but the blackout was the biggest reason. It's very scary when your memory's blotted out."

"Let's talk about Monday, June 5th. You had a few drinks after work at the Oregon Café, Had anything unusual happened at work that caused you to go off the wagon?"

"Not really. I mean I was glad that I didn't have to drive up to Petaluma anymore. But I was waiting for my dad to return to figure out my new role."

"How 'bout your operations in Petaluma? Anything unusual happen there?"

"You'd have to ask my father. I was in the City that Monday."

"So nothing happened at work that caused you to fall off the wagon?"

"Not really. Like I said, I guess I was celebrating being back in the City. I'd planned just to have a beer, but we rolled dice for the round. When I lost, the guy from John DeMartini needled me about getting off cheap with a beer instead of a highball. I figured, what the hell, one drink's not gonna kill me," Shaking his head in disbelief and adopting a slightly more amiable tone, the D.A. asked: "In your numerous statements that Tuesday, you were consistent on one matter. You told your parents, the Bradys, Judge Grant and the police that your wife went downtown to the movies, didn't you?"

"I told 'em I thought that's where she went. All I was thinking about then was figuring out where she was. We were trying to find her, we all believed she was still alive."

"I see. Did you contact any local emergency rooms to see if she'd been treated?"

"No."

"How about S.F. General Hospital or any other hospitals? Did you check with them to see if she'd been in an accident and received medical treatment?"

"No."

"What about her friends? Did you survey her social circle to locate her?"

"I called Marjorie, our friend Marjorie Peterson."

"What about her other friends?"

"I was spending so much time with the homicide guys I forgot all about making calls."

"You have a summer place up at Lake Tahoe, Mr. Panforte. Did you call your Tahoe place or any of her friends up there or the places she frequented at North Shore?"

Shaking his head, "No, I didn't."

"In your efforts to find your wife, you made absolutely no inquiries at places where she might be *alive*, did you?" Startled, a frown appeared above the bridge of his aquiline nose. Panforte said: "The uppermost thing in my mind was to find out where she'd gone that night."

"In other words, you were trying to find the place where you'd buried her?"

"I was trying to get my memory back."

"Speaking of your memory, sir, you claimed that you drove your 47' Chevy out of your garage to pick your wife up at the Fox. You told the homicide inspectors that you almost hit a Muni bus because you were so drunk. Is it your paternal custom to leave your infant son home alone while you go downtown?"

"That's when I realized how loaded I was. The next day when I talked to the cops, I was mortified that I'd left him in the house and didn't have enough sense to have Aunt Lil watch him. That's why I didn't tell 'em about going for Paula right away. What would they think about a guy who forgets his own kid?"

The D.A. smiled faintly. "Let's talk about what you did remember, Mr. Panforte." Moore then whispered to the Chief Clerk, "Pat, may I have Cragen's I.R.?" Kelley handed him Patrolman Cragen's Incident Report. Looking up from the report Moore asked: "Mr. Panforte, on the morning of Tuesday, June 6, 1949 you told Patrolman Cragen your wife was wearing a green coat and scarf." As the D.A. intoned the clothing items, Murphy pulled them from an evidence container and placed them neatly on counsel table. "Silk stockings," Moore recited. Inspector Murphy dangled the stockings for a moment and gravity unfolded them. He released them and they crumbled in a leg-less lump on counsel table. "Green and brown skirt with white waist-band and a gold wedding band," Moore recited. Waving Cragen's report at Panforte, the DA asked: "Did you tell Patrolman Cragen that these were the clothes your wife was wearing when she went downtown to the show?

"Whatever he wrote in the report is what I told him," Panforte conceded.

"After Inspector Murphy removed your wife from her grave on Mt Tamalpais, was she clothed in these very garments on counsel table and described by you to Patrolman Cragen?"

"It appears so."

"Mr. Panforte, the reason that you were so unerringly accurate about every item of your wife's attire when they pulled her out of the grave is because you'd dressed her in those clothes after beating her unconscious while she was clad only in her pink silk panties!" Moore's accusing finger shot through the air at the Defendant.

"I don't recall anything like that, no." Pat Kelley scribbled a note to himself about Paula's burial wardrobe. Panic blinked spastically from Angelina Panforte's darkening blue eyes. Pat thought she might collapse again, but from some reserve in her elfin frame she summoned the strength to keep her seat. Her husband was grim-faced, staring at the back of Loeb's head, mutely demanding that he do something to stop Moore. Paul Brady was on the edge of his chair, his legs ready to spring into the fray, his misty, reddened eyes on the D.A. silently importuning Moore to go for the jugular and put the sorry sonofabitch out of his misery. But District Attorney Michael Moore didn't need his old friend to know what he would to do Robert Panforte. He'd waited so long for this moment. Moore's squinting eyes announced it was killing time in the courtroom. "Just a few more questions, sir," he informed the witness, softening his resistance with the promise of brevity. Pat Kelley removed a photo from an evidence envelope, handed it to Moore and the D.A. passed it to Panforte. In a non-threatening tone, Moore said, "This is a photograph of your wife in her grave. It was taken immediately after they uncovered her, before she was moved and before you came down the hill to identify her. What side is your wife lying on, Mr. Panforte?"

He took a deep breath and exhaled his answer, "Her right side."

"In what direction is her head pointing, Mr. Panforte?"

"In a westerly direction," he sighed.

"What about her legs, sir? What position are they in?"

"They're jackknifed, her knees touching her chest." When Bob Panforte described the fetal-like position of his wife's silk-stocking clad legs, Eileen Brady wept. Her black-gloved hands clasped and unclasped her handbag. Jurors followed the D.A. with their eyes. He raised his black eyebrows and plunged a stare into the darkening blue of Panforte's eyes. Breaching the courtroom silence, he demanded: "You arranged Paula's body in that mountain grave you had dug for her, didn't you?"

"No, I didn't."

The two men stared at each other for a few tense seconds. Moore reached down to the tabletop, amid Paula Panforte's final wardrobe. He picked up a tiny evidence envelope and removed her wedding band. He fingered it gently. As though speaking to the ring itself, he said, "That's all." He dropped the gold band onto the tabletop and it clanked loudly, echoing as it vibrated on the clean wood surface. When the finger-less wedding band stopped trembling and it was again deathly still in the courtroom, Moore looked up at Panforte and whispered, "That's all."

33

After Robert Panforte had completed his testimony, Judge Lucille Grant declared a two- day recess. She directed the attorneys to prepare final jury instructions for her review and determine whether they would be presenting any rebuttal evidence. If they were not, she planned to give the case to the jury for decision. Joe Desmond invited Pat Kelley to join him at Molinari's Delicatessen for lunch. As they walked up Kearny Street, Pat asked, "You wanna take a ride with me?"

"Ride? I thought we'd just walk up to Coit Tower and eat our sandwiches."

"We could do that, but I was thinking a ride in the country would be a nice change of pace," Pat said, implying he had more than a picnic on his restless mind.

"What about the judge?" Desmond said.

"No problem, she's at the Women's Athletic Club taking a steam bath. I sent Carl Stephens back to court to see that no one steals the seats," Pat said, as they entered Molinari's and inhaled a symphony of fragrances in the packed Italian delicatessen. They both ordered salami, made on the premises, on sourdough rolls baked a couple of doors away. Back outside in the noonday heat Pat said, "Besides, you haven't experienced the wonder of fluid drive yet. My new DeSoto's incredible! You don't have to use the gearshift anymore. You just fiddle with the gas pedal and the damn thing shifts for itself."

"Pat, you've got as much interest in advanced auto mechanics as I've got enthusiasm for celibacy. Why don't you just tell me what's on your mind? I got nothing better to do the rest of the afternoon. But a picnic and the clutchless gears of your car don't compare with the certain ecstasy of a couple of crossword puzzles."

"I wanna drive up that mountain, Joe! I wanna see what the Lucy wouldn't let the jury see," his lips pressed in resolve. As they waited for the signal to change at Broadway and Columbus, Joe said, "I'm game, but what do you figure we'll find?"

"Maybe nothing we don't already know. But I've got more questions about this case then when we started it. I've got three days to get some answers. Once it goes to the jury all that we've discovered is nothing but unmentioned history," he said. They entered the bowels of the Hall of Justice and found Kelley's car. They drove from the garage to 2322 Francisco Street and parked for a few minutes in front of Panforte's duplex. Pat checked his watch and pulled out from the curb on our way to the bridge approach. As garrulous an Irishman as he was, his wife insisted the only times Pat had nothing to say was when he was sleeping or driving an automobile. He paid a two-bit toll and nosed his car through the toll plaza into the center lane of the Golden Gate Bridge. He cursed under his breath as cars repeatedly passed on his right. Of course, it was a traffic violation to pass on the right, but Pat drove at a snail's pace, effectively blocking the fast lane. To say that he was an overly cautious driver was kind. On the Marin side of the bridge, he pulled into Vista Point and parked for lunch. "You wanna beer?" he asked.

"Sure," Joe said. "Whadda ya figure checking the grave will tell us?" Pat munched on his sandwich. "Time and terrain. What I wanna know is *when* Paula's grave was dug. That may tell us who's in the suspect pool," he said, wiping his lips with the back of his hand.

"You think seeing her grave will tell us that?"

"Let's find out," he said, switching on the ignition. They drove in silence to the base of Mt. Tamalpais and then laboriously climbed the mountain's face. Just short of the summit, Pat pulled off to the side of a gravel, tire-track path and said softly, "We're here." For a moment they stood on the edge of the road, looking down the mountainside into a shadowy forest where the ghost of a beautiful young woman seemed to whisper with the mountain breeze. "Let's go," Pat said and they began their descent down the steep slope toward Paula Panforte's still unsighted grave. The prosecution's photographs had failed to capture the precipitous grade of loose dirt and gravel that dropped from the road. Their shoes sunk into dust and grainy pebbles, and they struggled to keep their balance, their steps tentative. Joe had marched down slopes like this with a full field-pack strapped to his back, so he appreciated how difficult it must have been to negotiate this slippery grade carrying a hundred and twenty-five pound woman. Fifty yards downhill they arrived at the tree line of the evergreen forest. The grade became less pronounced, and an endless mat of pine needles, fallen leaves and jigsaw-puzzle pieces of Ponderosa pine bark crackled beneath their cautious steps. Pat slipped a couple of times and almost fell, his shoes skating on brittle pine needles. The shade and elevation cooled the temperature a good ten degrees, and the vaporous mountain air played games with their lungs. They crossed the tree line and entered the forest. The powder blue sky disappeared, sparse rays of sun knifed though swaying pine branches, spotlighting a wild fern or a squirrel secreting acorns. Pat broke the stillness of the forest. "There they are. Those must be the fallen pines where they found her."

He climbed onto the trunk of one of the downed pines, and Joe stepped onto the other. They walked, as though on a fragile footbridge to the approximate center of the trees' trunks. There was roughly six feet of air space between them, and when they looked down, the forsaken tomb of Paula Panforte yawned up at them. Pat crouched on bended knee to get a better look. Then he sat on the pine log, his short legs dangling above the heel of her grave. Joe followed suit. They sat for a moment of respectful silence. A chorus of birds chirped in the distance, their song carried by the breeze filtering through dancing conifers. The tranquility of this place couldn't be captured by a camera's lens. They examined the shallow grave and were impressed by the precision of the rectangle and the uniformity of its four dirt walls. It had an almost sculpted affect. "What's wrong with this picture?" Pat said.

"I don't know. He picked a beautiful spot. It's so peaceful, and that sword fern at the head of the grave's a nice touch. It's like Nature planted her a headstone."

"Not Nature! That fern doesn't belong here."

"Whadda ya mean? This forest is full of all kinds of ferns," Joe replied.

"Sword ferns can't tolerate afternoon sun. Look how it's completely exposed." They were in a small patch of forest that opened up to the unfiltered rays of mid-afternoon sun. Kelley slid off the fallen pine into the grave. He grasped the tips of the fern's leaves and said, "Come on down and have a look for yourself. These leaves are browning; they can't take direct exposure. This fern won't see another spring." Joe joined Kelley at the graceful plant whose shadow had once guarded Paula's bashed skull and saw that it was dying from ultra-violet poisoning. Pat said, "My guess is it's been transplanted. Let's see if we can find its natural home." They set out in a westerly direction, keeping about ten yards distance between them, tracking cautiously as though on infantry patrol. Joe's steps were wary, his feet touching the ground gingerly, a foot soldier's reflexive gait to avoid detonating hidden antipersonnel mines. Twigs and leaves crackled under Pat's brown dress shoes, while Joe's lighter steps barely disturbed the terrain. Suddenly the ground under Desmond's right foot caved in, and the bitter Ardennes forest flashed, snapshot-like, in his mind as his right shoulder thudded against the ground. "Shit!" He yelled as Kelley ran to his aid.

"You all right? What happened?" Pat asked.

"I tripped, that's all. I must've stepped in a fuckin' gopher hole or something." Joe got up and brushed pine needles off his suit jacket. "Let's have a look," Pat said, crouching on one knee over the indentation of Joe's footprint. He began pawing leaves from the spot where Joe had tripped and discovered that shrubbery concealed a hole in the ground that hadn't been excavated by any forest creatures. His fingers probed the soil. He pulled at a severed root and held its veins up to his eyes. He said, "This looks like a sword fern root. Notice how shady it is here. My guess is this is the fern's true home. Let's go back to the grave. I wanna study it through the window of death." Back at the gravesite they sat on the fallen pines above Paula's resting place, Pat deep in thought. Joe was anxious to learn his theory of the dying sword fern. "You think the attempt to camouflage the grave with that fern is the key?" Joe asked. Pat shook his head. "The fern's a key, but its present location has nothing to do with camouflage. It's *when* it was transplanted that's important."

"I'm all ears."

"It couldn't have been transplanted the night Paula was buried."

"You mean he wouldn't have had enough time to drive over here, dig the grave, transplant the fern, bury her and still get back to Francisco Street in time for the horny teenager to hear his garage door opening."

"Its not about time and distance, Joe. You don't have to rely on a pimple-faced kid with raging hormones to figure out when this pastoral scene was tampered with. Obviously it was the best Moore could come up with. But look with me through the window of death. It's the first Monday in June. The sun's already set. You saw how dark it is in that grove where that fern grew, and this is midday! No one could've found that plant in the dark, much less dig it up and re-plant it here! It could have only done during daylight hours."

Desmond noticed that Pat Kelley had deleted the personal pronoun *he* from his speculations. "Pat, I'm not sure I'm following you," he said. Pat fiddled a pine needle with his fingers and said, "We're talking about planning. Whoever killed Paula planned it days before the fatal blow. This grave was excavated on either Sunday or Monday before Paula met her killer. The prosecution's theory is that her killer is her husband. He was the last person to see her alive, he described flawlessly her burial wardrobe and he knows this area like the back of his hand. Since he worked at The Market on that fatal Monday and went on a drinking binge after work, he couldn't have dug this grave on Monday, June 5th. As for Sunday, he drove his wife and kid down the Peninsula in the exact opposite direction."

"Yeah, but Pat, ya gotta take his word for the Sunday family drive," Joe countered.

"That's true, but let's examine other possibilities," Pat said. He did not then tell Joe of his conversation with Angelina Panforte and her confirmation of the Sunday drive. For Pat there was no question about this mother's credulity. Kelley resumed his analysis: "Now, this fella Hill was also familiar with this place. We know he's a bitter sonofabitch because of what Paula's dad to him, an ex-con with an appetite for perversity. He's hanging around her home and at the Fox. We don't know where he was on Sunday or Monday, but we can be pretty sure he'd lie about it. We've conceded his motive and it appears he had the opportunity." Pat tossed the pine needle into the grave and said, "There's one other guy who knows this place and knows Paula. That's old man Panforte…"

"Jesus Christ, Pat! You must be looking in a different window than I am!".

"Joe, I'm only talking about grave digging and plant transplants," Pat said resolutely. "Old man Panforte says he drove to Petaluma on Sunday to change the ranch management. He told his wife he'd be back in town on Tuesday. Usually, he stays overnight at their Sonoma ranch…"

"Where the hell did you get that?" Desmond asked.

"From Angelina Panforte," Pat replied evenly. "So that means Fred Panforte was in the North Bay on Sunday!"

"I thought he testified that he dropped by his kid's place Sunday night on his way to Petaluma," Joe argued.

"That he did," Pat conceded. "But his wife told me he'd left for Petaluma around noon. And he did so because his daughter-in-law had come to their Sea Cliff home terribly upset about her husband!" Pointing to the sword fern, Pat said, "Look at that fern. We know where it came from. If it was planted here when Paula's grave was dug, you'd see the fern's roots sticking out from the grave wall. You don't see any roots because it was transplanted *after* her grave was dug." Desmond was having a hard time grasping what Pat meant, and he seemed to be talking to the sword fern, not to Joe. He'd never seen his friend like this before. He seemed entranced by his peculiar vision through the window of death. "You're losing me, pal," Joe said.

"All right, let's go over Paula's burial again. Remember the photos of her when Murphy uncovered her grave? Transpose those pictures of her in this grave and what do you see in the window of death now?"

"She's laying on her side in a fetal position."

"What's she laying on?"

"Her green coat. It was spread out on the floor of her grave, like a bed sheet."

"Precisely! That means her green coat was placed in the bottom of the grave before bringing her body down here. Okay?" Joe nodded. Kelley continued, "When the homicide boys found her on her side, her gaping, fatal head wound was resting on her coat. But remember, Joe! The Coroner's photographs of her head wound showed that it was clean. There was no dirt or twigs, pine needles or vegetation – nothing! Being dragged down this hill, with a cracked, bleeding skull, there'd be particles from the terrain in or around her head wound. Because her wound was clean, it means she was struck with an instrument of some kind *after* she'd been placed in this grave! She was killed right here, Joe. What you see in the window of death is *where* she died, and now you know *when* she died!"

Pat Kelley was right. All the words, photographs, exhibits, experts and earnest witnesses hadn't been able to clear the mist from the pane of Paula Panforte's death. Throughout the trial it had been like peering through a window at night, the evidence, like interior lights reflecting off a glass pane, illuminating their own likeness, distorting the view outside. But studying her grave, recalling the cleanliness of the fatal wound, the sword fern trembling in the mountain breeze, its shadow dancing on the clay floor of Paula's sepulcher finally revealed to Pat the shattering clarity of a young woman's desecration. But Pat Kelley's vision could not make out the killer's face. It was her killer's gesture that captured his visualization. He had rearranged her dead body in the grave, positioning her womb-like, so peaceful, as though to avoid shoveling a pile of mountain dirt on her lovely face and her battered breasts. Her killer knew her. Perhaps even cared for her, Kelley concluded.

"You okay, Pat?" Desmond's voice broke their mountain silence.

"I'm all right. How about you?"

"I'm fine. I just can't figure out why the DA didn't pick on the absence of debris in her cracked skull. I mean, he had photos and everything."

"The Coroner's photos and the gravesite shots don't have the impact you just experienced. Photos engage a single sense, and the significance of her antiseptic wound can't be appreciated unless all our sense are engaged. And remember, Dr. Rosenberg never came over here, so he never saw what we've seen. Face it, Joe, none of us noticed the anomaly of her head injuries from the pictures. That's why Moore wanted the jury out here."

"Jeezus, Pat! You're saying the judge fucked up the DA's case by keeping the jury from seeing Paula's grave!"

"She had her reasons and they were damn good ones," Pat replied. Then, turning his gaze back to Paula's grave, he said, "What's the gender of this scene?"

"Gender? It's a fucking hole in the ground, its got no gender," Joe said.

"It's feminine to me," Pat said, that distant look back in his eyes. "Womb and tomb not only rhyme, they have corresponding utility. Life begins in our mother's womb, and we're taught eternal life begins in Mother Earth's womb. Think about Paula's position when they uncovered her. She was in a perfect fetal position. Everything about this scene is feminine. It's enclosed, secret, intimate, interior, protected, a state of sheer peace. The only place we know this kind of serenity is in our mother's womb at life's beginning and the earth's womb at life's end."

"You're getting allegorical on me," Joe said. Suddenly Pat bolted to his feet and said, "Wait here, this picture's incomplete!" He jumped off the fallen pine and scrambled up hill to his car. He was breathing hard when he returned and was carrying what looked like a shoebox. He said, "I wanna try a little experiment. I want you to close your eyes and visualize Paula when they uncovered her grave. Try to see this as a feminine environment." Joe closed his eyes and heard Kelley slide off the pine trunk. From the grave Pat said, "Think about her clothes. Get your mind's eye to see her delicate feet with silk stockings and her gold anklet. And remember, the white loafers weren't on her feet when they found her. They were neatly placed at the foot of her grave. You got it?" Joe shrugged, "I guess."

"Now open your eyes and tell me if you see gender." Joe opened his eyes and the residue of an image of Paula curled up in her grave lingered. But his image of this reposing woman was jarred by a pair of white loafers that Pat had placed in the grave. "Those loafers don't fit. They're just not right in this picture," Joe said.

"Exactly! And the loafers they found in her grave didn't fit her feet either. I figure she wore size six, seven at the most. These are Terry's loafers, and he wears size ten. I borrowed 'em for this experiment."

"Terry's wearing white loafers? Have we got a problem here I don't know about?" Joe asked, incredulous at the possible path of puberty upon which Pat's kid might be embarking.

Kelley laughed, "Nothing like that, Joe." Pat pulled a small jar from his coat pocket and tossed it Joe, saying, "I dyed 'em with Maria's shoe dye, so they'd look like the loafers they found in the grave." Joe was relieved that *his nephew* hadn't become a cross-dresser, but mystified by his father's bizarre experimentation. Pat said, "You're right, the shoes don't belong in the picture. The reason you had that reaction when you opened your eyes was you saw a pair of man's shoes. The loafers they found in the grave with Paula weren't hers. They were a sign of maleness in a feminine universe. That's what you find discordant."

"So whose shoes were they? They sure as hell don't fit Panforte's big football feet!"

"Terry turns thirteen Saturday. He's big for a new teenager. I think the loafers they found in Paula's grave belong to that Mexican kid up in Petaluma. Although he's five years older than my kid, being Mexican suggests they'd be about the same shoe size."

"Wait a minute! We got a pair of shoes too big to be Paula's and too small to be her husband's. And you're saying a fucking farm boy's Sunday dress shoes get buried with her? Pat, you're the smartest s.o.b. I've ever known, but frankly, I think the altitude's getting to ya. You're getting kinda weird, pal."

"One thinks weird thoughts when one discovers weird things. Let's go." They drove back to the City in silence. Crossing the Golden Gate Bridge, the flaming sun slid into the Pacific and the sea darkened under the vigilant eyes of hungry, squawking gulls.

34

Pat Kelley's characterization of Paula's mountaintop tomb as feminine intruded upon by signs of masculinity focused him on Jack Hill. He suspected Hill might be the defense's source of the Fox ticket stub, and he needed to either include or exclude him as a suspect before the case went to the jury. Pat had arranged with Rocco Casselli to bring Jack Hill to the Original Joe's restaurant, and Joe Desmond had been instructed to resume his role as Sunset Strip muscle for Kelley's racket connected talent agency. Pat's selection of the Tenderloin restaurant as the meeting place was a clever bit of staging. The restaurant's clientele was an eclectic mix of bookies, bankers, politicians, cops, criminal lawyers, judges and manual laborers supping on hearty Italian food. It was situated on Taylor Street in the heart of the seedy Tenderloin District, populated with pool sharks, hookers – male and female - dope pushers and flop-house residents. He assumed the Houston ex-con would feel right at home in Original Joe's. Pat and Joe took the corner booth, where the conversation would not be overheard. Before Rocco and Hill arrived, Pat mentally reviewed his investigation, and at every point, it appeared to have sexual inferences of an equivocal nature. None was more bizarre than Jack Hill with his history of underage girls and boys who would be girls. "Somewhere in this montage of sexuality is the key to Paula's murder. Maybe we can rattle Mr. Hill's cage a bit," he told Desmond as Rocco Casselli and the homely Texan approached their booth. They didn't rise or shake hands as Hill slid into the booth across the table from them. Rocco, by pre-arrangement with Kelley, excused himself and told Hill he'd pick him up in an hour. Hill ordered a beer and said, "Rocco says ya might have a gig for my act."

Pat shrugged, "Maybe. But first we're gonna have a chat about your legal problems."

"I ain't got no legal problems. Vice dropped the charges," Hill's yellow teeth smirked.

"I'm not talking about Vice, Hill. I'm talking murder!" Kelley said roughly.

"What the fuck!" Hill started to rise, but Kelley's hand shot across the table and seized his wrist. Hill grimaced from Pat's vise-like grip. Desmond unbuttoned his sports jacket to emphasize that he was packing. "Sit down!" Pat ordered, and Hill slumped into his seat. "I'll tell you when you can leave. First, I'm gonna tell ya how things work in this town. This isn't Texas, boy!" Pat's ferocity wasn't feigned; he was furious and Hill's weasel eyes were terrified.

"I'm gonna tell ya some things I know about you, and if you've got half a brain in that cracker head of yours, you'll get the picture," Pat said. "You and your Contessa get busted by the Vice boys and they find photos and newspaper stories of the murdered girl. They don't think nothing of it, they're just morals cops with their palms out to be greased. But you're smarter than them. So you get word to Danny Loeb that you want him to represent you and whatever the hell *she* is. He sends his investigator, a guy named London, to see you in City Prison. Ya tell 'em you can help Loeb out with Panforte's defense if the little lawyer can get you out of a pimping collar. Now, Loeb's no fool, he doesn't want his own fingerprints on your information, so he sends one of his lawyer pals who works out of another office to see you. He gets old man Panforte to take care of your lawyer in cash. They probably slip you some change from time to time…"

Hill started to protest, but Pat said vehemently, "Shut the fuck up! I tell ya when ya can talk! So you tell *your* lawyer you remember Panforte from the Army and that Brady convicted your ass for dickin' a farmer's daughter. Ya tell him about hanging out on Francisco Street and the horny neighbor kid who takes pictures of his sexy neighbor. Ya buy a photo or two from the kid. Then you tell your lawyer that you saw *Home of the Brave* at the Fox the same night that Panforte said his wife was there. Since old man Panforte's feeding your shyster's meter, he runs and tells Loeb's investigator everything you told him.

"London comes up with a sweetheart deal that gets both you and young Panforte off the hook. You hate old man Brady for sending you to the joint, and you've been stalking his daughter. You've told London about the snapshot-taking teenager and you're at the Fox Theater the night she disappears! So you're a better suspect than Loeb's guy. You got motive and he doesn't. And you got opportunity by putting your sorry-ass self at the movies with the murdered girl! And it's all outta your drawling, ignorant Texas mouth! So London really gets cute and tells ya to take the Fifth. That way you don't incriminate yourself, but the jury has another, maybe a better, suspect than Panforte. But you guys didn't figure the lady judge wouldn't let them put you on the stand unless you and your lawyer give up your Fifth Amendment rights. She's a smart dame and figures not even a scummy lawyer on the take is gonna implicate his own client in a capital case. So they gotta come up with an option."

Kelley reached into his inside coat pocket and pulled out a small envelope and put it on the table. Hill had a quizzical look on his face. Pat opened the envelope with a butter knife. He held it up by the corner and waved it slightly, saying, "This is the option. Ya remember when London first came to interview you in the slammer? He told you he needed physical evidence to back up your story. That's how they got the photos of Paula sunbathing in her backyard. And that's how they got this!" Pat pulled the ticket stub from the envelope. Hill's jaw dropped and he gasped. "How the fuck did you get that?"

"You don't wanna know," Pat said cruelly. "What you need to know is what this scrap of pasteboard means to you. It's your one-way ticket to the gas chamber! You can take the Fifth until Hell freezes over, but all Loeb has to do is ask London where he got this stub."

"I didn't kill the bitch! I swear!" Hill frantically.

"I know you didn't. You come clean with me and this stub disappears," Pat said, putting the stub back in the envelope. "I wanna know everything you know about Panforte and his wife."

"Okay, okay," Hill said, his lips trembling, his left eye twitching. "Like you said, I know him from the Army. He was our training guide over at Mt. Tam. I wasn't gonna get my ass shot off by slant-eyed gooks, so I was a big fuck up. I figured to wash out. The fuckin' stockade's better than getting it on a lousy beach. So Panforte's teaching us how to make it through the woods, and he says all you gotta figure is where's north. We got no maps, no compasses, nothing. He says you tell north from the moss growing on the trees where it's real shady. He tells us the lay of the land and halfway up the summit we should veer northwest. He says Stinson Beach is southwest, so I figure that's where I'll go. I can beat an AWOL beef just saying I got lost. But I'm outta the training cycle, so what the fuck? I'd a made it too, if it wasn't for that bitch!"

"You're not telling me anything I don't already know. I don't give a shit about your soldiering," Pat said impatiently. Hill started breathing heavily. "Okay, okay. So I does my time, but I don't know that Brady's got a daughter. I don't know shit about the man 'cept he's an ornery prick! I didn't know the girl was his daughter till I read it in the papers when they dug her up. Honest man, I didn't know!"

"So what are you doing following her, buying photos of her?" Pat pressed.

"It's not what you think," Hill said, gesturing vigorously with his hands. "See, after I get outta the joint, I hook up with Contessa. She's got a lotta talent, but she can't get outta the chorus line for the big bucks. So I'm managing her, and 'bout six months ago Panforte shows up at Finocchio's with his wife. I remember him from the Army. They were with a society crowd, ya know, black tie, and her big tits showing. But I got no idea she's old man Brady's kid. She's just a gorgeous broad, and I figure we can make up Contessa to look and act like her, we'll be a headliner. Ya know show business, Jake. We had to study how she dresses, makes herself up, even how she walks and moves. That's what a female impersonator's all about. And it worked, man! I made Contessa a star by borrowing her looks. I got no motive to harm her."

Pat waved at the waiter for the check and said to Hill, "You know anything about a Palo Alto joint called The Jade Room?"

"Yeah, it's a queer bar with a pool table. It's where Frisco gentlemen go to suck off college boys. They don't do their stuff in the City."

Rocco Casselli showed up and Pat dismissed Hill, saying of the ticket stub, "It's taken care of."

As Kelley and Desmond crossed Taylor Street to the parking lot, Joe asked, "How'd you come up with that ticket trick?" Pat explained that London had planted the Fox stub in Paula's green coat while they were in chambers with Judge Grant and the lawyers. He also told Joe that he had unilaterally foiled the plan to get the ticket to the jury by concealing its existence. He said, "I figured it might be useful loosening Mr. Hill's tongue."

Pat unlocked the door to his DeSoto sedan and said, "Joe, do you mind catching a streetcar? I've got some errands to run." Joe said, "No sweat." Kelley drove up Taylor Street to Pine Street, took a left onto Pine and headed for Van Ness Avenue and the Golden Gate Bridge approach. He realized he was in a race against time. If he couldn't solve the mystery of Paula's death, both lawyers would present unwittingly false jury arguments and the jury, no matter if it reached a just result, would never know the truth. He mentally summarized what he'd learned beyond the courtroom walls. Paula had been sufficiently upset with her husband to seek out, perhaps confront his father. Fred had responded by traveling to his Petaluma chicken ranch and changing his son's job assignment. Pat had confirmed that Jack Hill was the source of the ticket stub and he believed that London and Fred Panforte had conspired to plant it. Repeatedly, Pat was seeing the hand of Fred Panforte either manipulating or dispensing special treatment to players beyond the courthouse borders who were affecting the courtroom story. The male intrusion of loafers in Paula's grave stimulated Pat's desire to meet and question Panforte's Mexican truck driver. Pat had learned from Isador Poplack that this Great Western employee was the object of special job treatment, and he was in Petaluma where Fred Panforte had gone immediately after Paula's troubled visit on Sunday morning.

After his hour drive to Petaluma, Pat Kelley met Isador Poplack in his office at Golden Rooster Milling Co. The two men shook hands and Pat apologized for interrupting Poplack's Sabbath. Izzy laughed, "I haven't been to *shul* since I was a kid fighting Cossacks back in our *shtetl*." Poplack puffed on a Havana at an oak paper-strewn desk and Kelley slumped onto a faded brown leather couch. "Izzy, I really appreciate what you're doing for me," he said.

"No big deal," Poplack shrugged. "I did a little snooping after we talked. No doubt about it, the Mexican kid's getting special treatment from Panforte. I don't know, but it's fishy. You're onto something. Just watch your step, Pat. With the Bridges trial on, Petaluma's crawling with feds and finks."

"Maybe you outta stay out of the picture," Pat suggested earnestly.

"Naw. If a surveillance sees him here, they won't figure it's outta the ordinary for a ranch driver picking up some feed on a Saturday." Pat nodded, "What can you tell me about him?"

"He's eighteen, maybe nineteen, good looking kid. Kinda quiet. Maybe a little slow upstairs," Poplack said, tapping his index finger against his forehead. "Panforte's paying off the Teamsters' business agent so he doesn't need a union card. My guess is they slip him cash under the table, 'cause he's a flashy dresser for a ranch hand. Zoot suits, that kinda shit. I hear he supports his mom and a couple of younger sisters. His father never made it outta Mexico. Don't know if he deserted 'em or if he's even alive. Here's the rub, Pat. He's a wetback, his papers are phony, but whoever did 'em is a pro. And ya can't tie it to old man Panforte or his kid."

Pat rubbed his chin, "Interesting. What did you tell him about me?"

"Nuthin'. No names, just that you're an important guy from the

City. He's scared shitless! Pat, be careful!" There was a knock on the frosted glass office door, and Izzy's foreman announced that Manual Abascal had arrived. He ushered the boy in, and Poplack offered him a seat. Abascal was a trim five-nine, clad in Levi's and a rust colored leather jacket that confirmed Izzy's speculation that Panforte supplemented his wages for a wardrobe beyond a truck driver's budget. Pat was struck by his handsome caramel-colored face, framed by straight, thin jet-black hair and large oval inky eyes. He was almost pretty, Pat thought. The boy's wide-eyed stare was doe-like, furtive and apprehensive. Izzy explained that he'd act as interpreter and urged Abascal to speak slowly since his Lincoln Brigade-learned Spanish was rusty. Through Izzy, Pat implied that he had something to do with the Longshoremen Union's defense of their leader, Harry Bridges. He told Abascal that the government was attempting to imprison Bridges because he was an Australian immigrant who had lied on his American admission papers. Pat said he was facing five years in prison and deportation back to Australia.

The boy's lips trembled and he ran his fingers through his hair. Izzy explained that the Bridges defense team was looking for non-union illegal alien laborers. They wanted to show the court that the F.B.I. looks the other way when it comes to undocumented workers who are non-union, management flunkies. Pat used the words *Mexican scabs* and Abascal didn't need Izzy's translation to know what Kelley meant. Kelley was threatening to expose his illegal alien status to Bridges' lawyers. Izzy told the boy that the minute the government got wind of it, they'd bust him and deport his ass back to Mexico to prove that they treat all federal law-breakers equally!

Abascal shook his head, started to sob and in halting English said: "What about my mamma? My sisters? Senior Panforte say not worry. He take care of us. Mamma's sick! She no go back. She die!" Izzy told him that Panforte couldn't help him now. This was too big. "Nobody gives a shit about a wetback and his mother!" he said in English. Izzy pressed Abascal to tell them what was wrong with his mother. He was stammering and sobbing and it was difficult to follow him. He told them that she had chest problems. He was drumming his fingers on his own chest and they figured he was referring to her lungs, perhaps tuberculosis. He said she needed Petaluma's dry heat rather than the humid climate of their village outside Tijuana.

Pat tried to calm the boy down. In his most soothing voice he said, "Maybe I can keep your secret if you give me a better one, one about your boss." Abascal was puzzled but trapped as he encouraged Pat with his tearful eyes. Kelley said, "I wanna know how a pair of your shoes, brown loafers to be exact, got in a murdered girl's grave!" Abascal's eyes blinked spastically and it looked like he was about to faint. Izzy said paternally, "Better level with him, kid. It's your momma's only chance" Abascal shook his head slowly and confessed to Pat Kelley. When he finished, he buried his head in his hands and dissolved into wracking sobs. Kelley patted his shoulder and said, "It's okay kid. Your secret's safe with me."

Pat motioned Izzy Poplack over to the office door. He whispered to Izzy, "Is the kid saying *signor* or *senior*?" Poplack shrugged, "I dunno. I'll ask him." Izzy did and then told Pat that Manual Abascal had said *senior*. Poplack summoned his foreman to take Abascal back to his truck. When they were alone, Izzy said, "Whadda ya gonna do now? That's some weird shit!"

"That it is, Izzy. That it is," Pat said sardonically. Izzy Poplack was certain that Bertolli's son-in-law was now armed with the weapon to destroy Fred Panforte and had the steely will to use it. He felt that Kelley's promise to the anonymous farm worker to guard his sins from revelation and protect his ailing mother had been nothing more than a clever investigator's ruse.

On his drive back to the City on Highway 101, Pat let his mind wander among the rolling hills of Sonoma and Marin Counties. It was in this fecund land that Italian, Swiss, French and German immigrants planted the vineyards that now surpassed France and Italy in quantity and quality. In Marin, the Texas-size ranches of Freitas and the Portuguese had created the diary industry, and Italian and Jewish immigrants the poultry industry. Japanese, Mexican, and Oakie escapees from the Dust Bowl harvested the fruits and vegetables in what was replacing New York as the greatest state in the Union. San Francisco's Chinese had performed surgery on the glacial granite of the Sierra to meet up with bearded Irishmen who had conquered the Great Plains, stitching a continental nation with rails. What was unique about the Bay Area, Pat reflected, was that these migrants from distant places and foreign lands had continued colonizing the Golden State throughout its first century of existence. Even now it was an unending process, a continual transfusion of new and vibrant blood into California's body politic. Yet at this moment, a great labor leader faced prison and deportation for his crime of militancy, and a migrant Mexican teenager bore the sordid debasement of a cruelly exploiting employer.

Pat was struck by the troubling irony that his unauthorized private investigation had positioned him as a virtual cross-examiner of testimonial proclamations of innocence and guilt in the Panforte murder trial. There was what the jury had heard and what Pat now knew. And there was an irreversible ticking clock, a time bomb of injustice that compelled Pat to act before the jury had the case. If the case were decided on the state of the courtroom record, it would be devoid of verisimilitude. While Pat believed that justice was sometimes attainable without truth, what he had just learned mocked the very justice system to which he had devoted his career. As he drove he couldn't help but think of Maria. Her partisan desire for young Panforte's conviction had nothing to do with his guilt or innocence or even, for that matter, truth. She wanted a conviction because in her moral universe she needed to stain Fred Panforte's paternity, to take from him through the law a loved one as he had taken her father's lover through the law's abuse. Now Pat Kelley, anonymous court attaché, was armed with a truth that revealed Paula's killer's compelling motive and would sear old man Panforte's soul more than the conviction and execution of his own son. If the trial remained uncontested by Kelley's truth, Paula's murder would remain a mystery, a tattered, unresolved tale of misguided passions and detoured love. What is my truth, Pat asked himself. It's Izzy Poplack's translation of a troubled boy, a hopelessly exploited laborer, he answered himself.

He visualized what the Mexican ranch hand had told him like a film director editing his film. Pat mentally spliced in scenes from his rogue out-of-court investigation from his interview of the Principal of St. Ignatius High months earlier, to Angelina Panforte confiding in him her daughter-in-law's unexpected Sunday visit with Fred Panforte. The movie playing in Kelley's mind was an uncensored picture of the Panforte family.

Pat had suspected Bob Panforte's homosexual experiences started when he was at S.I. He figured that the cops and the Jesuits covered up for him by saying he was busted for drinking at the Polo Grounds, when in fact, some old pervert probably sucked him off in a public restroom. Then there was the Jade Room in Palo Alto, and Jack Hill's description that it was a joint where older guys could find Stanford boys for some action. That's what the Palo Alto street brawl that Panforte testified to was all about. It was between Panforte and a guy his age, fighting over a Stanford undergrad. After Panforte beat the shit out of his competitive suitor, he turned on the kid for having the poor taste to select another guy for an assignation. That's why he called his mother the morning after. He wasn't worried about a couple of battered fags. He was worried he'd be identified with the Jade Room and that his father would be aware of its reputation. Pat thought of Angelina and her devotion to her son and that she had been cruelly schooled in male aberrance. As a child she'd been brutally subjected to male perversity, and as a bride her son was conceived in his father's contempt for her body. It was Angelina who had convinced her son to get off hard booze because it brought out his aggression. It was her son's admission that he'd badly fallen off the wagon that brought her to her knees.

Now the terrified admissions of a teenage ranch hand made sense to Pat. Izzy Poplack had said that Abascal was adamant he wasn't a faggot, but Panforte was his boss, so what could he do? It was a good job, and he wanted to stay in the country. And there was his sick mom. They did their stuff, that was between them, he'd claimed. Then Panforte wanted Abascal's fourteen year-old sister to play with 'em. Abascal didn't know what to say, but it bothered him. "It's wrong, man," he'd told Izzy. The Mexican kid who was the sole support of his ailing mother and siblings justly felt he was in a desperate situation.

On the Sunday morning before Paula's disappearance, Abascal panics and phones Paula at her home. The kid figures Panforte's wife could do something that would allow him to keep his job and his sister's virtue. He's babbling incoherently, so Paula tells him to speak Spanish. She can't figure out if the guy's a nut cake or her husband's a fruitcake. So she asks Abascal how she can tell if he's telling the truth. He tells her he was with Panforte that week in Petaluma, and they did it in his Chevy behind a grain bin. He tells her he left his shoes in the back seat of the car, on the floor. They're brown loafers he'd ordered from a catalog. He tells her his shoe size, which is smaller than Panforte's. He says he left 'em so he could prove he was telling the truth.

Pat thought of Maria's comment that something had happened after the Saturday bridge party with the Peterson's. Maria's intuition was right, he realized. She had sensed, with that unerring feminine instinct, those orisons that Hamlet spoke of, that the weekend before Paula's disappearance was the homicidal moment. At the bridge party with the Petersons, everything was lovey-dovey, and they were talking about a new baby and house hunting the next day in Marin. But Sunday morning Paula gets Abascal's phone call. She immediately goes down to the garage to see if the Mexican's

420 \ PHIL RYAN

loafers are in the Chevy. Sure enough, she finds them.

She grabs the baby and drives in furious bafflement to her father-in-law's Sea Cliff mansion. She thrusts her baby onto Angelina to exclude her from the conversation she must have with her father-in-law. She directs him to the Chevy, shows him the Mexican's shoes and tells him about Abascal's morning phone call. Almost screaming, Paula says she wants a divorce, and if Bob won't stipulate to mental cruelty she'll have her lawyers expose his homosexuality in court. Fred tells her to calm down, the Mexican's lying and it's just a greaser's scheme to extort money. He says he can prove it, but he has to go up to Petaluma and confront "that dirty wetback!" He tells Paula that he's surprised she actually took the punk seriously. He assures her that within twenty-four hours he'll prove to her that the Mexican is a complete phony. He asks her to give him the brown loafers so he can confront the Mexican with them. He tells Paula all he needs is for her to act like nothing has happened. "And for chrissake, don't say anything to Bob! If he gets wind of this bullshit, he'll go up there and kill the sonofabitch with his bare hands," Fred tells her. Then he pats her shoulder and tells her that she has honored him by bringing this unpleasantness to him. He suggests they take the baby for a ride down the Peninsula, maybe get a bite to eat at Rickey's, where they'd often dined when they were courting. He seals her compliance by telling her, "You are the daughter I always wanted."

Mollified and fervently wanting to believe her father-in-law, she takes the baby and drives back to their Marina home. Fred tells his wife his cover story that Paula was upset about their son's absences from their home due to his Petaluma work schedule. He says he's transferring Bob back to The Market full-time, but he must go immediately to the Petaluma ranch and make the necessary arrangements. Fred phones his son and tells him he's driving up to Petaluma right away to arrange new ranch management, so Bob needs to take his place at Great Western Poultry until he returns. Bob Panforte is thrilled at what he thinks is his father's confidence that he's now ready to be a full fledged "Marketman." Bob immediately calls the Petersens, and cancels their house hunting date.

The deciphering clue in Pat Kelley's movie in his mind was Manual Abascal's use of the word "senior." As he had related through Izzy Poplack his life on the Panforte chicken ranch, he'd always referred to Bob Panforte respectfully as Signor Panforte. Yet when he'd told Izzy that Panforte had confronted him the Sunday that he'd phoned Paula Panforte, he'd said, "Panforte Senior." So it was Fred Panforte who had confronted Manuel Abascal with his evidentiary loafers! And it was Fred Panforte who had told Abascal that he was keeping his loafers, and if he ever mentioned Bob

Panforte's name again, he'd end up with his wetback feet in his shoes in a hole in the ground.

On Fred's way back from Petaluma he stops at his hunting cabin, picks up an entrenching tool and drives up Mt. Tamalpais. For about an hour, he digs Paula's future grave. When he's finished he transplants the sword fern and then he places the entrenching tool in the trunk of his Cadillac along with Abascal's loafers, drives down the mountain to his hunting lodge and washes up. An hour and a half after sunset, he pays his two-bit toll at the toll gate of the Golden Gate Bridge and drives to Francisco Street to tell his daughter-in-law the good news: the wetback had made the story of her husband's bisexuality up, and as soon as the Mexican had confessed to his priest he would personally confirm his deceit to Paula.

Pat pulled out of the mouth of the Waldo Tunnel and banked his DeSoto sedan against the gentle curve of the grade. His windshield framed the majestic Golden Gate Bridge shortly before sunset, presiding over the swelling aqua orifice to the Bay, its orange spires reaching to the darkening heavens, its black roadbed like outstretched arms welcoming him back to the City. Whitecaps danced with the western wind as the sun hovered over the Pacific, preparing for its Asian morning. He paid the toll and then pulled off the bridge approach and drove down a windy hill to Fort Point in the Presidio. He parked behind the breakwater that was San Francisco's anchor for the golden span, directly under the steel-girded southernmost point of the bridge. The turbulent tides threw foaming waves at the concrete barrier that crashed with a hollow thud and sprayed salt water on Kelley's car. He had a panoramic view of the City from the Presidio Forest out over the flatlands of the Marina and up to the peaks of Nob and Russian Hills. He picked out his father-in-law's five-story apartment building topping Russian Hill on Larkin Street. Darkness had not yet given streetlights their full effect, so they seemed to be mischievously winking at Pat, as though in their humble incandesce was the first revelation of the night.

He got out of his car and walked past Fort Point's cannon emplacements. The old Spanish garrison, guarding the ocean entrance to the City, had never fired its antique artillery in anger, but all along the Presidio coastline pill boxes, bunkers and heavy weapons had nervously awaited the Japanese invasion that never came. At Land's End he rested his thick hands on the damp, black wrought iron chain guardrail and watched the setting sun bid farewell to the San Francisco day.

Salt spray freckled his face. The fiery sun-ball seemed soft to him, misshapen by unseen, distant clouds. It was like a fire-orange pastry, perhaps a lumpy éclair, he thought.

When the last flames of the sun dipped into the Pacific waters, the pale blue sky flushed pink. Pat's eyes scanned over to Sea Cliff's jagged seaside cliffs, and he tried to locate Fred Panforte's mansion, but dusk hid it from his view. He watched a gull make his final dinner dive and then glide off north, toward Fort Cronkite in Marin. He thought of his wife and Fred Panforte and he accepted that shame is stronger than love or hate. It was the humiliation of her father that compelled Maria's rage. And it was Fred Panforte's homophobic shame that drove him to slay the mother of his grandson. Maria Kelley and Robert Panforte, two grown children with powerful fathers, products of the seed of ancient enmity, and now Pat were empowered to bring their generational and moral conflict to a shattering climax. From a common laborer he'd acquired the evidence of Fred Panforte's motive for and design of Paula's death. But Fred Panforte wasn't on trial for murder, his son was. If Pat disclosed this evidence of sexual unorthodoxy, he had to be certain that a truthful outcome would result. While he was confident in his conclusion that old man Panforte was Paula's killer, he wasn't the lawyer who would present the case.

Indeed, the rationale inferences that he'd drawn had come from sources whose testimony was probably inadmissible or, like Angelina Panforte on her husband's Sunday activities, not incriminatory of him without Pat's theorizing. If all that could be presented to the jury was Bob Panforte's homosexual relationship with his employee and Abascal's phone call to Paula disclosing it, what would Moore and Loeb do with this evidence, Pat wondered. For the District Attorney it would provide the motive for Paula's murder. But that motive would be ascribed to the Defendant and other than by Pat's reasoning, be in no way attributable to his father. From the moment Danny Loeb had come to Bob Panforte's defense, his vital mission was to save his client from the gallows. And he was confident that he could do so because he was certain the prosecution could never come up with a credible answer to his *why* question. If he won an outright acquittal, that would be just the cherry on the *charlotte rouge*. But an illegal immigrant's evidence of deviant infidelity by a husband screamed the motive for his glamorous wife's death. Most importantly to Pat, Maria would be vindicated, at last she'd have her revenge. In a very real sense, Pat would have stolen Fred Panforte's son from him with the same ruthlessness that Maria felt Fred had stolen Antonietta from her and her father. But she would not know the truth. And that truth was that Fred Panforte's most heinous sin was not his betrayal of her father. It was his betrayal of his son. He had killed his boy's wife and caused him to stand trial and face the gallows for her murder. It all seemed so operatic, and he felt that he'd had become the composer. His pen would write the finale and whether the loving, beautiful soprano sang a closing aria of triumph or tragedy depended upon the major or minor keys that he would compose.

It was so ironically simple, he thought. After months of lawyers, judges, cops, investigators and the press speculating and contesting over the life of young Panforte, an anonymous civil servant had solved the murderous riddle. All he had to do was tip off Harry Bridges' lead defense counsel, Vincent Hallinan, to the scab labor practices at Panforte's Petaluma chicken ranches. Kelley and Hallinan were good friends, and their kids spent their summers together in Marin, so Pat knew that his anonymity was safe with Hallinan. By exposing the federal government's discriminatory treatment of corrupt unions over militant ones, the sordid story of Bob Panforte and his migrant ranch hand would come out. And the fallout of that front-page story would engulf the Panforte murder trial. And nowhere could Pat's fingerprints be found. But what about the teenage peasant who'd supplied Pat with the resolving story line? Pat had given his word that the boy's secret was safe with him. He'd promised to do nothing with the information that would endanger the boy's ill mother. If Pat concealed Abascal's evidence, as he'd promised, the boy and his family were safe. But Maria wasn't. Was there really any choice between the wife he adored and a kid he barely knew? If he kept his word to Abascal, was he not replicating his father-in-law's character flaw of excessive honor? After all, the jury might still convict without evidence of Panforte's twisted relationships. If so, Pat's fidelity to Maria and his promise to the Mexican kid would be moot. But he knew that justice – Maria's and society's – would have sacrificed the truth.

And there was his son, so dutiful to his mother's pain. There was no real choice between Terry and a stranger's mom, he thought. Pat had chosen to involve his son in this family struggle, and now he seriously contemplated muzzling the *coupe de grace* that his brilliant detective work had made available to him. How could he not expose Panforte's son and conceal from his own son the failed manhood of the Panforte men?

424 \ PHIL RYAN

But what of his own manhood? What about revealing only partial truth and, by its frugal expression a hapless young man paid for the sins of his father? Pat walked back to his parked car and took in the dancing lights of his city. Aloud, he whispered, "For chrissake, he's just another wetback." Then his brown, misty eyes roamed up Russian Hill, seeking Bertolli's home. He opened his car door, reached in and pulled a bronze St. Christopher medallion off the dashboard. He took the small envelope with the ticket stub out of his coat pocket. He placed St. Christopher in the envelope with the stub. He licked and sealed the envelope. He read the words he'd written on the face of the envelope when he'd decided to conceal the Fox stub's existence. "Truth and justice are lovers," he'd written. Then he threw the weighted envelope into the Bay and St. Christopher bore Panforte truth to the bottom of the bay.

35

Before court reconvened, Pat Kelley typed an amended Indictment. District Attorney Moore had previously moved to add two additional counts to the murder count the Grand Jury had returned. Pat typed in a charge of violating Penal Code Section 275(d), alleging assault as infliction of corporal injury on Paula Panforte and another count alleging a violation of Penal Code Section 245, alleging wife beating that resulted in the death of the wife. Defense counsel Loeb had not objected to these additional charges because he recognized that the prosecution was uneasy about having met its burden of proving first-degree murder. If the jury concluded that young Panforte had assaulted his wife in their bedroom, it would raise the level of his culpability from manslaughter to second-degree murder. Pat was somewhat relieved that the D.A. had doubts about the capital punishment value of his case. Although he had decided to keep his weekend discovery of Panforte's Mexican ranch hand secret, he realized that if Bob Panforte was convicted of first-degree murder and sentenced to the gas chamber he'd be morally compelled to reveal the bizarre Panforte relationships in Petaluma. While Fred Panforte was apparently willing to place his son's life in jeopardy for his crime, Pat was repelled by the notion that his self-suppression of damning evidence would contribute to a death sentence. If the jury acquitted or found Robert Panforte guilty of less than murder one, Manual Abascal's confidence in Kelley would be honored. But Pat could not keep his word in the face of a death sentence for the wrong man.

Somehow, he would have to stage "newly discovered evidence" for Bob Panforte's post-conviction relief. He dreaded the implications to his career and family, and for the first time, deeply regretted the results of his rogue investigation. Even with his thorough knowledge of Fred Panforte's personal history, Pat had not suspected the man was capable of such depravity as causing his son to ride his murder beef for him. Reflecting on Fred Panforte caused Pat to alter the case caption on the Amended Indictment. He typed: THE PEOPLE OF

THE STATE OF CALIFORNIA VS. ROBERT A. PANFORTE. He had deleted the Defendant's middle name, "Agnello," replacing it with the initial A. He couldn't bear the thought of Father Agnello's saintly name being associated with this sordid trial.

After Robert A. Panforte was re-arraigned on the Amended Indictment, both the prosecution and defense rested. Judge Grant dismissed the jury, directing them to return to court on Wednesday for closing arguments. She predicted that the lawyers' summations and her jury instructions would take two days, and the case would be submitted to them by Friday at the latest. Monday and Tuesday were housekeeping days as the lawyers and judge worked on jury instructions, and Pat Kelley reorganized the evidence exhibits for the jury.

The lawyers' final summations were unlike anything Pat Kelley had ever experienced in his court career. What had always been the climax of any murder trial – the closing argument – was surrealistic for Pat. As masterful as both lawyers were, Pat knew that they were both wrong and that the jury decision was likely to be a choice between error and catastrophic human injustice. For his part, Danny Loeb savaged the prosecution's time-line. It was predictable that he'd attack Paula's prurient teenage neighbor, but he made an even more telling point with Paula Panforte's wardrobe. He reminded the jury that the prosecution claimed that Paula was clad only in her silk panties when her husband allegedly attacked her in their bedroom. "That means," Loeb argued, "That Bob had to dress her in the clothes she was wearing in her grave while she was unconscious!" Holding up items of Paula's burial wardrobe, Loeb argued, "Look at this coat, her skirt with waistband, scarf and imported silk stockings! They're perfectly color-coordinated. Even Paula's garter belt matches her under garments. Do you really think an intoxicated husband would have such discriminating taste in apparel and colors?

"Ladies and gentlemen, use your common sense! Try to imagine the prosecution's dressing scene. Paula is unconscious on the bedroom floor wearing only her panties. Understandably, we take getting dressed for granted. But think about how time consuming and difficult it would be for a husband to dress the limp, unconscious body of his wife! First there's her bra and the garter." Loeb held Paula's imported silk stockings up, and they dangled in the breeze from the floor fan. "I want you gentlemen of the jury to reflect on the difficulty you'd have putting these stockings on your wife while she's in a deep sleep. Perhaps you ladies could enlighten the gentlemen jurors on the techniques employed to get silk or nylon stockings over toes, heals, ankles, calves, half way up thighs and attached to a garter without running or tearing such fragile fabrics! The prosecution insists that Paula's killer could not have dug her grave and returned to Francisco street when the Busby boy claimed he heard a garage door opening. Guess what? The time it would have taken to dress Paula in her burial wardrobe would have also prevented her killer from arriving at Francisco Street at the time the neighbor boy claimed!"

Loeb laid Paula's stockings on the jury rail. In amodulated tone, he concluded: "There is only one certainty that has emerged from this terrible tragedy and that is that Bob and Paula were a happily married couple. There was deep love and manifest affection between them. All the evidence tells us this. It is the story that comes from both sides of the family. It's uncontradicted. This brings us to the most puzzling issue in this case. Here you have this loving couple, with a thriving business, a new baby and dreams for another child. A girl, Bob's hoping. There's not a splinter of disharmony or friction in their marital life. Then, in an instant of time, everything is shattered. A beautiful young woman's life is lost, dreams are destroyed, a child made motherless. It is at this terrible moment that the prosecution's failure is most obvious. It is bad enough that the prosecution can't tell you when she died or where or how she died, but it's inexcusable that they can't tell you *why* she died! No trace of a motive has been shown.

"True, the prosecution isn't required to prove motive, but the law also says that you, the judges of facts, have the right to take the absence of motive into consideration." Loeb picked up a piece of chalk and stepped over to a blackboard, saying, "The prosecution's murder charge can be resolved with a simple three-letter word, and I challenge the prosecution to respond to this word." In huge capital letters on the blackboard, Loeb wrote his three-letter word: "**WHY?**" Pointing to the word on the blackboard, Loeb urged the jury, "As you listen to District Attorney Moore, keep this three-letter word in your sight, keep its implications firmly in your mind. If he fails to tell you why Bob Panforte killed his wife, it's because he didn't kill her! Why would he kill the love of his life? Why, Mr. Prosecutor, why?" Loeb silently eyed each juror and sighed as he returned to counsel table. He placed his hand on his client's shoulder and squeezed paternally. Then he slumped into his chair and tendered the stage to his lanky adversary, surrendering the crushing burden of Robert Panforte's life to twelve strangers.

District Attorney Michael Moore craned his neck to study the defense lawyer's one-word question. He shrugged, furrowed his brow and admitted to the jury, "I don't know if I can answer Mr. Loeb's dramatic question. Why, he asks. Why would one love bird attack his mate? I guess I just don't know. I don't know why a quarter of all homicides in this nation are committed by one family member against another family member. I don't know why a half of all homicides are committed by people when they're drinking. I don't know why Cain murdered Abel. I don't know why, since the first moments man scribbled letters in the sand and carved symbols on cave walls, husbands have murdered wives, wives slain husbands and both have killed their children.

"I know why men steal. They're hungry or greedy. I know why the burglar enters your house in the dead of the night. It's because he's a sneak and a cowardly thief. I know why the con man lies and cheats. He does so because he's weak and must find vulnerable prey. What unites all criminals, ladies and gentlemen, is their victims are strangers to them. They don't steal from their wives, they don't burglarize their mother's jewel box and they don't cheat their brothers and sisters. Anonymity is their universe. What most often distinguishes homicide from all other criminals and murder from all other crimes is the familiarity of it all. Killer and victim invariably know each other – often most intimately. Because of this familiarity, because the slain if often a loved one, we are fascinated with motive, with the why of it all. Why Hamlet? Why Macbeth? Oh, noble Othello, why Desdemona? Why your loving princess? But this is not literature, this is life. This is not theater, it's a court of law. In this court and by your oath, you need not determine the Defendant's motive for killing his wife. His motive may be as inscrutable as Hamlet's, as shocking as Macbeth's, as tragically apparent as Othello's or so perverse as to exceed the limits of our imaginations."

The DA flipped the revolving blackboard over and said, "But Mr. Loeb was right about one thing. This case can be resolved by a three-letter word." On the blank slate, in large capitals, Moore wrote: "WHO?" Pointing to his word, the DA argued: "This is the question you are here to decide. Who killed Paula Brady Panforte? Who was the only person with the opportunity? Who bloodied her nose? Who knew the Mt. Tamalpais terrain like the back of his hand? Who had an Army entrenching tool with Mt. Tam residue on it in his garage? Who became enraged at Paula because she had mocked his drunkenness?

The Defendant, Robert Panforte, that's who!"

The DA moved behind his counsel table and the jurors followed him with their eyes. "Mr. Loeb has correctly told you that the People bear a heavy burden of proof. But you as jurors have a heavier burden. You have the burden of judgment, the pressing weight of deciding the facts of Paula's death and the obligation to judge the worth of her husband's life. The People of the State of California have asked that you punish this Defendant for his crime by taking his life. As a man, I have had to struggle mightily with so grave a decision. Murder by its very nature touches so many more lives than the life taken. Months before you were sworn as jurors, Mr. Loeb made a legal argument in this court, and his words are the purest expression of first-degree murder I have ever heard. This legendary defense lawyer said: "…the killer is thoughtful, deliberate, his intent sculpted by thorough premeditation. It is precisely the coldness that is manifest, the frigid deliberation to terminate human life which is revealed that is said to justify the state, with comparable aloofness, imposing the ultimate penalty. So offended is society at the icy indifference to human life displayed by such a killer, that the law declares: 'An eye for an eye. A life for a life.' In the name of the People, I ask you to find Robert A. Panforte guilty of the murder of Paula Brady Panforte. I urge you to recommend that he pay for his crime with his own life. His death will not bring Paula back. It will not restore a lovely daughter to her mother and father. It will not bring his mother back into the life of their son. And it will not reconcile the Defendant with his God. But your verdict will proclaim The People's outrage, and this is all I am empowered to ask."

Pat Kelley felt nausea creeping in his gut. Unlike the DA and defense counsel, he had no blackboard on which to scribble his three-letter question: "**HOW?**" In the answer to Pat's *how* question – which the jury would never be asked – an even more profound issue would be found. How could a father allow, indeed cause his son to stand trial for his sin? This was the trial moment when all silently acknowledged the transfer of sovereign power to common people. Without fanfare or a single ordaining word, the Panforte jury, as history would name the anonymous twelve, had been invested with the powers of kings, prime ministers, presidents and generals. Like countless juries before and after them, history had just endowed them with the wisdom to declare what was evil and what was not. They possessed the absolute power to condemn or pardon and the transcendent judgment to decide the duration and quality of another man's life. All in the courtroom genuflected to the power of their peers. Pat Kelley was now powerless to aid this jury. A hush descended on the courtroom as silence saluted democracy's seizure of the court of justice. The only thing in was sight a pair of silk stockings from Lucca, hanging from the jury rail, barely shivering in the still breeze of the floor fan.

Saturday morning at the Hall of Justice passed with no word from the jury. They'd been deliberating a day and a half. A few minutes after noon there was a flurry of speculation in the sparsely populated courtroom when a request came from the jury room. It turned out to be a request for two packs of cigarettes and the score of the Big Game. Judge Grant approved the smokes and denied the sports update. Ten minutes later Bailiff McCann returned and said, "They've got a verdict, judge." Judge Grant reached for her robe and ordered the jury brought in. Both lawyers appeared at their counsel tables, as though the jury's decision had permeated the marble walls of the courthouse, summoning them to triumph or defeat. Moore's expression was unrevealing, as was Loeb's. The Bailiff brought Robert Panforte from the holding tank and the young man shook hands with his lawyer. He was outwardly composed but it seemed that he gripped Loeb's hand longer than a normal handshake. Inspector Murphy rumbled up the side aisle brushing off reporters' questions, and took his seat alongside Moore. Only the families, press and court personnel were present to receive the jury's judgment. Maria and Terry Kelley, celebrating his 13th birthday, had taken a Cal alumni train to Palo Alto to cheer on Cal's Golden Bears in the Big Game. Bailiff McCann, like a confident maitre d', led the jurors to their box. Judge Grant said, "I understand you've reached a verdict?"

"We have, Your Honor," the jury foreman, a Persian rug salesman with a jet-black toupee, announced.

"Mr. Bailiff, collect the verdict," the judge instructed. The foreman handed the jury form to McCann, who presented it to Judge Grant. Expressionless, the judge read it to herself and then handed it to the Chief Clerk. Pat Kelley said, "Will the Defendant please rise and face the jury?" Robert Panforte rose and faced the twelve. In a resolute voice, Kelley announced: "We the jury, find the Defendant, Robert A. Panforte, guilty of murder!" Angelina Panforte gasped and fell back against her chair's backrest. Her husband's mouth dropped open, but Paul Brady leaned forward in his chair, knowing there was more to come. Kelley looked down at the paper verdict and then directly into Panforte's aquamarine eyes and said: "We the jury, fix the degree of guilt as murder in the second degree. Signed: Allen Kent, Foreman." Paul Brady's fist smashed into his thigh. Fred Panforte was confused, his eyes darting between Loeb and his wounded wife. The lawyers and Inspector Murphy were impassive. Robert Panforte rubbed his lower lip confusedly as he took his seat. "Do counsel wish the jury polled?" Judge Grant asked. Both lawyers nodded and the clerk asked each juror if this was his or her individual decision. It was unanimous. "All right," Judge Grant said. "Ladies and gentlemen, you are excused with the thanks of the Court. Bailiff McCann will check you out of your hotel."

McCann led the jurors out of the courtroom and the judge said, "Gentlemen, if there's nothing further, we'll adjourn until Monday morning. We'll discuss any motions as well as pre-sentence matters." She banged her gavel authoritatively and left the bench. The prosecution team quickly left the courtroom, ignoring the shouted questions of the press. Loeb huddled with Mr. and Mrs. Panforte. He was attempting to explain what the verdict meant to Angelina. She listened, doubt and suspicion on her face. She sluggishly raised her hand to halt Loeb's torrent of words. "You mean they won't take him from me and kill him like a wounded animal," she asked her son's defender.

"That's right, Mrs. Panforte. There's no death penalty in this case any longer."

"You saved my son's life, then?" she murmured.

"No, Mrs. Panforte. Those twelve strangers did," Danny Loeb confessed with sincere humility and an unconcealed sigh of enormous personal relief.

Pat Kelley met his wife and son at John's Grill after they had returned from the Big Game in Palo Alto. The Kelley's were seated at author Dashiel Hammett's favorite table, another headwaiter's testimony to Pat's restaurant clout. Over drinks, Maria and Terry replayed Cal's crushing victory over Stanford, made even more delightful by taking place before 90,000 fans at Stanford Stadium. During dinner Pat steered the conversation to Maria's coed days at Berkeley, telling a story about her leading Cal women's tennis team to victory, breaking a decade of Stanford dominance. It seemed like Pat was avoiding the Panforte verdict by engaging in the small talk of athletics. But when the waiter cleared the entrée plates he said, "While you guys were yelling yourself hoarse at the game, the jury came in with a guilty verdict." Maria's smile evaporated. "Guilty? They found Panforte guilty of murder?" she asked softly. Pat said, "That they did,"

"One or two?" Terry sharply.

"Second degree murder," Pat said, not taking his eyes off his wife. Maria's eyes darkened. "That means…" her voice trailed off and her husband finished her sentence, "Five to life, but no gas chamber." Maria lit a cigarette. Her hand trembled when she dropped the match into the ashtray. Her face was pale. She stamped out her cigarette after only one drag. She was struggling to frame more questions for Pat but felt her words drowning in conflicting emotions. Her husband was even more conflicted because he knew who was guilty and who was not and he dared not tell her. As a progressive woman, Maria did not believe in the death penalty because she doubted its deterrence value. But Pat was certain that Maria was confounded because she was so invested in young Panforte's conviction. She couldn't truly see the young man because her vision was blinded by his father's presence. She believed that Fred Panforte had taken Antonietta Pompa from their lives as surely as if he'd slain her. So unless Fred Panforte's loss was as terminal as hers and her father's had been, the scales of justice were unbalanced. Fred Panforte would be separated from his son for a while, perhaps even for a long while. But he would one day get him back. It was this thought that stabbed at Maria's heart. Once again Fabrizio had used the law to defeat Bertolli's heirs, and even Maria's husband couldn't prevent his triumph. Terry, sensing his mother's defeat, reached across the table, grasped her hand and said, "It wasn't our fight, Mom. Don't worry. Like the Irish rebels say: *Our day will come!*"

On Monday morning the courthouse mob that had deserted the Panforte verdict for the Big Game had returned. An ocean overcast hooded the City in gray, signaling the end of Indian summer and promising a temperate Thanksgiving weekend. All of the family regulars were present, but a new spectator had joined the sentencing vigil. Maria Kelley was seated in her first row seat, flanked on one side by her son and on the other by her father, Bartolomeo Bertolli! In a handsome three-piece charcoal suit he sat ramrod straight, his arms folded across his chest, his gray eyes riveted on the vacant Bench behind his son-in-law's courtroom desk. Fred Panforte was slumped down in his seat, clutching his wife's black-gloved hand like a terrified child awakening from a dreadful nightmare. An apprehensive Danny

Loeb caught Joe Desmond's eye as though to ask: "What the hell's *he* doing here?" Joe shrugged, indicating that he had nothing to do with his presence, but was secretly delighted that Bertolli's quiet dignity so greatly disturbed old man Panforte and his forensic gun. Judge Grant took her seat on the bench. A white lace collar overlapping her black robe brightened her face. She'd clearly spent some time working on her hair and her modest make-up displayed more careful application than was her habit. She looked fresh, actually pretty. Outside the presence of the jury she called court to order. "Gentlemen, any motions?" she inquired.

Loeb replied, "No Judge, we're prepared to face sentencing."

"Do you wish a pre-sentence report?" she said.

"That's not necessary, Your Honor. My client's life has been exhaustively examined during the trial. It's an open book. We're ready for sentencing right now."

"Mr. Moore?" the judge asked.

"That's fine with the People."

"Very well." Judge Grant nodded to the Defendant and Robert Panforte rose to face his fate. Judge Grant needed no notes to pronounce her sentence, and as she spoke her eyes never left Panforte's: "The jury, having found you guilty of murder in the second degree, it is the judgment and sentence of this Court that you, Robert A. Panforte, be delivered by the Sheriff of the City and County of San Francisco to the custody of the California Department of Corrections. You will serve the term of imprisonment in the state penitentiary prescribed by law, for the murder of Paula Brady Panforte, your wife." Judge Grant paused, then added, "The mother of your son. The term of your imprisonment is five years to the remainder of your life."

Paul Brady slowly pulled himself up from his front row seat. At the border of the Pit, he laid his boxer's hands on the rail. He was erect, his dignified bearing commanding respect. In the authoritative voice that had swayed so many juries and judges, he said, "Judge, don't give him five to life. Give him just five minutes with me in your chambers. Alone!"

Judge Lucille Grant allowed silence to capture the courtroom. She leaned forward on her elbows and peered deeply into Brady's bloodshot eyes. In this moment he was again the daring man she'd come to respect and love so many years ago. He was right, she thought. She had devoted her career to justice. She felt that its pursuit was more noble and tangible than even the search for God. She felt that the justice she had just dispensed was somehow lacking the clarity that fairness proclaims. The implausible image of these two men alone in her chambers, free to give expression to the intrinsic violence of their natures, locked in mortal combat, seemed to Lucy at that moment the purest manifestation of human justice conceivable. It didn't matter which man walked away alive. For, in their grunting, sweating, bloodletting congress both men would spend themselves; both would release their torrents of bewildering or grieving rage. And men, when spent, at last know peace. For a brief moment, Judge Lucille Grant believed that trial by combat was more civilized than the trial by jury. But she knew that her office, not her feelings, must determine their fates. She spoke directly to Brady: "Paul, you have been my mentor for as long as I've known you. At this moment, you've taught me my final lesson. You've taught me about the claustrophobic limits of my judicial power. I cannot give you my chambers, and I know that you're repelled by my heartfelt sympathy."

At this moment that Bartolemeo Bertolli rose from his aisle seat and joined Paul Brady at the rail of the Pit. He was eighty-three-years-old, but on this day, his bent body and fragile limbs seemed infused with vigor. His gait was steady, his broad shoulders back. Bertolli grasped Brady's arm just above his elbow. Brady, thinking that a bailiff had intervened, turned his head and saw Bertolli's calm, gray eyes. "Mr. B?" Brady whispered hoarsely. Bertolli said softly, "Come, Paul. Finito! It's finished." The two men turned and took two steps down the center aisle, and then Bertolli stopped them. He pivoted to face Fred Panforte. In Italian he said to him, "Fabrizio! It is you, not your son, who has dishonored our father!"

Pat Kelley thought, *"Oh, Nonno! If you only knew how right you are!"*

Fabrizio Panforte bowed his head to his hands and his shoulders trembled. Bartolemeo Bertolli's mere presence had terrified him. But it was Bertolli's mention of their teacher's sacred name that pierced his crusted soul. His wife looked at him, and then turned away. In disgust, it seemed to Pat. Bartolemeo Bertolli led Paul Brady out of the courtroom, and forever out of Lucille Grant's life.

Ten years after the electronic iron bars of San Quentin Prison whined shut on Robert Panforte only a few San Franciscans retained any memory of his celebrated trial. It is one of the curious aspects of front-page murder trials that journalism never writes the final act of the play. For Pat Kelley, however, the Panforte murder trial lived on. As the years flew by, the players in the drama in which he had played a invisible part visited him frequently, like a champagne hangover, throbbing and remorseless.

Chronologically, the first casualty of Bob Panforte's conviction was Judge Lucille Grant. The trial judge whom Pat had gerrymandered to the bench and whom both trial lawyers had wanted to preside resigned, sold her Ashbury-Heights home and moved to the north coast town of Mendocino where she opened up a small art gallery. In the aftermath of Panforte's sentence to state prison, Paul Brady had instituted a court battle for the custody of his grandson. Fred Panforte had joined issue, but Daniel David Loeb had refused to take the case. At last, Pat reflected, brilliant Danny Loeb had had enough of Fred Panforte. As for the paternal combatants' wives, Eileen Brady and Angelina Panforte, they maintained a dignified and silent passivity, both no doubt contemptuous of their blustering spouses. With appalling insensitivity the Presiding Judge had assigned the custody case of Robert Panforte, Jr. to Judge Grant, who promptly quit the bench on which she had served with such distinction. Neither the Bradys nor the Panfortes won custody. Instead, Bobby, Jr. was given new parents. A domestic relations judge charged the little boy's rearing to a Sicilian fisherman and his barren Irish wife. With the tacit approval of the judge, the Chief Clerk created a new birth certificate for the boy with a new date of birth and new name. It has never been clear what happened to Bobby Panforte's original birth certificate, but there is no existing record of it.

After losing his custody battle, Brady dove headlong into the bottle. He was kicked out of the prestigious law firm he had founded, disbarred for blowing too many statutes of limitations on his clients' claims, and on his son-in-law's fifth anniversary in prison was found dead in a Tenderloin flop house. His old friend, Dr. Ernie Rosenberg, performed the autopsy, as he had on Brady's daughter. Dr. Rosenberg listed the cause of death as "cirrhosis of the liver."

Angelina Panforte had vacated their Sea Cliff home and moved permanently to their north shore Lake Tahoe home. She returned to the City monthly for visits with her son at San Quentin. Other than the winter months, her husband commuted on weekends to Lake Tahoe. District Attorney Michael Moore had graduated to the Attorney General's office. As the head of the Department of Justice he had blocked Bob Panforte's parole efforts.

As for Bartolomeo Bertolli, on a foggy summer of 1953 he was present at a performance of "*Madama Butterfly*" conducted by his friend Gaetano Merola at the Sigmund Stern Grove. As the final chords of Act I shimmered in the leaves of the forest amphitheater, Merola collapsed on the podium. Prone beneath Puccini's masterful score, Maestro handed his baton to his concertmaster to complete the performance and died. Bertolli never again attended a performance of the San Francisco Opera Company that he, his lover and Merola had founded. Two years later, the first *Precious One* died peacefully in his sleep. His daughter had recently founded and was the principal of a Sunset District elementary school for Chinese immigrant children. She added Mandarin to her fluent English, Italian and French, and sent a generation of Asian children onto her beloved University of California. From the commencement of Panforte's prison term, the subject of the Panfortes was never again brought up in the Kelley household.

Pat had maintained his position as the Chief Clerk, and the Kelley's three children rewarded their parents by winning full scholarships to college. Kathleen, the oldest, had graduated from Julliard School of Music, and by 1960 was on her first European piano concert tour. In homage to her grandfather, she performed as Kathleen Bertolli. Their youngest, Megan, was a Berkeley undergraduate pursuing her teaching credential, destined to follow her mother's footsteps as an early childhood educator. As for precocious Terry Kelley, he had sped through Berkeley with a double major in philosophy and English and the Boalt Hall School of Law in a mere six years, with the highest academic honors. In August of 1960, he had taken the California

Bar Examination and would be admitted to practice in November. While waiting for his bar results, he was being heavily recruited by prestigious downtown law firms. He had taken a law clerk position with the Montgomery Street law firm of Buchanan & Polk. Terry had no intention of joining a downtown law firm or, as he and his father called them, "those white-shoe boys," but the money was good and he wanted a taste of how "the respectable side lived." From the Panforte trial on, he was destined for the courtroom. It was during this hiatus between Terry's legal education and his first courtroom appearance as an advocate that his father made decisions that had profound implications for the two families that had for so long been locked in bitter, unresolved hostility. Pat decided to take an early retirement from the Superior Court. He explained to the Presiding Judge that, with his son about to become a San Francisco trial lawyer, he believed it was inappropriate for him to remain the court's chief administrative officer. He also had put in place a new court management system by dividing the civil and criminal courts and employing different administrators for each. This, of course, significantly diluted the Chief Clerk's powers, to which his wife laughingly commented, "That's lovely, darling. Now you'll be the last of the imperial Chief Clerks." Their son corrected, "First and last." Pat was confident that Maria's inheritance from her father's estate assured her financial security should anything happen to him.

But Pat Kelley rarely did anything in which all of his motives were apparent. He'd never really let go of the Panforte case, nor was he able to rationalize his role in its terribly flawed outcome. He'd taken inordinate, indeed unwise risks as a court attaché during the trial. While he had gotten away undetected, the risks he now planned to take must leave no possible trail. After a theater evening at the Curran, father and son adjourned to Tosca's North Beach saloon where Pat told his son the unadorned truth about Paula Panforte's murder. What they would do together about this truth might jeopardize his son's legal career before it even began.

In the ten years since his son's conviction, old man Panforte had utilized every avenue available for his son's release from imprisonment. Repeatedly blocked by Attorney General Moore, Fred Panforte decided that a pardon from the Governor was the only way to get around the parole authority of the California Adult Authority. In 1958, right-wing U.S. Senator William Knowland ran for Governor of California and Fred Panforte became one of his principle fundraisers. It was an easy alliance, as Knowland ran on a reactionary "right to work" plank, and Panforte's business had always been anti-union. California, like the rest of the nation, was mired in the witch-hunt mentality of the McCarthy era, but Senator Knowland's unabashed attack on organized labor galvanized the trade union movement behind Democrat Pat Brown. This gubernatorial campaign was Terry's maiden entry into California politics, and he was a key organizer of graduate and undergraduate students that ultimately parented Berkeley student activism. Pat Brown's landslide election ended Knowland's political career and swept Democrats into office, controlling both houses of the legislature for the first time in years. Fred Panforte's efforts to secure political clemency for his son seemed dashed.

Terry listened calmly as his father related the full scope and awful discoveries of his investigation. When Pat concluded his narrative he asked his son what his legal options were. Terry studied his father's face and noticed for the first time lines across his brow indicating aging and the stress of the secrets he'd born alone for years. Terry said evenly, "You only need legal options when you're compelled to make choices. You made your choices ten years ago." Pat nodded as Terry sipped his drink. Then his son said, "I think you're really asking me about moral options, and they aren't covered on the Bar exam. So why don't we cool it with the Socratic bit and try to talk through this." Pat smiled at his son, at last relieved of the burden to be his teacher. "Is it keeping all this from mom that's bugging you?" Terry asked.

Pat rubbed his chin and said, "It's not so much that. I mean, what the hell good is what I learned if all I can tell her is that old man Panforte screwed over his own kid like he screwed everyone else. What really gets to me is I figured out what really happened to Paula, and I can't do squat about it. I should have let that damn planted ticket stub get to the jury and just butted out."

"Dad, had you done that, old man Panforte would have pitched a perfect game. His kid walks and he gets away with murder."

"So I'm a saint because his kid's in the pen and he *still* gets away with murder," Pat bitterly. Terry reached across the table, affectionately squeezed Pat's wrist, "Dad, you don't wear guilt well. You haven't told me all this shit because you're seeking absolution. I'm a big boy, so drop the subtleties." Finally Pat asked, "What can we do about it legally?"

"We?" Terry smiled. "We can start by accepting the limits of law. There's only three reasons to go to court: to get money, to keep money or to stay out of jail. Mom never understood that revenge or moral vindications aren't among them." Pat nodded, urging his son on. Terry said, "A courtroom's a place where we either do something *for* someone or do something to someone. You've got to decide which preposition you want to pursue. If you want to do something for Bob Panforte, you're talking about a habeas corpus petition based on 'newly discovered evidence.' That's problematical for a number of reasons, not the least of which is the Fox ticket stub that you threw in the Bay. You're looking at a felony obstruction of justice beef, so as of this moment and forever, there was no ticket stub!"

Pat sighed, "Okay."

Terry said coldly, "You've got to decide who you want to do something to." His father didn't hesitate, "I wanna get old man Panforte!" Terry smiled. "It's about time. But, Dad, we'll only get one chance. What impresses me about old man Panforte is his precision. He uses the law but never directly participates in the legal process. He stole Nonno's business by manipulating corporation laws, but he refused to confront him man-to-man. Same thing with his kid's murder trial. He stays on the periphery and uses Loeb to do his dirty work. That's old man Panforte's strength – he uses the letter of the law to avoid its spirit, which is open, hostile conflict. We've got to take his strength and transform it to weakness. By the way, what ever happened to the Mexican kid?" Pat explained that Abascal's mother had died a few of years after the trial, and that Izzy Poplack had hired him and straightened out his immigration status. To Terry that meant that Fred Panforte could no longer control Abascal. But he explained to his father that, even if Abascal testified to his homosexual relationship with Bob Panforte and his admission of it to Fred, the inference that old man Panforte was Paula's killer was not inescapable. Therefore such newly discovered evidence was simply not material.

Sipping Irish coffee, Terry said, "Dad, your investigation was unconventional to say the least. So we've got to use it unconventionally." Pat realized that an extraordinary transformation was taking place. The poet's line: "The child is father to the man" had come alive in his son. Terry related to his dad that Fred Panforte's cozy political alliance with the "right to work" movement had introduced him to Arkansas speculators who were eyeing California's lucrative poultry industry. He explained that the law firm for whom he worked represented an Arkansas syndicate, and their prime target was Panforte's operation. "That's the real reason I accepted the Buchanan & Polk job offer," Terry said. "I wanted to get as close to old man Panforte's business as I could." Delighted, Pat nodded and Terry continued: "The firm's client is Little Rock Enterprises, and they're negotiating a deal to buy-out Panforte and move the business to Arkansas. Actually, Buchanan & Polk is representing both sides in the deal. Montgomery Street law firms don't see conflicts of interest when there are so many zeroes, and this is a huge deal. I've managed to get myself assigned to the partner in charge, so I've done most of the due diligence for the Arkansas guys and a good portion of document drafting. These southern boys realize Panforte owns the biggest poultry operation in the state and they figure if Panforte makes the deal, they can cherry pick the other poultry outfits.

"I've got to admit, these guys are shrewd. They realize that labor costs are the key to profit margins. Arkansas is a Jim Crow, "right to work" state that keeps unions out by pitting black workers against whites, effectively exploiting both. California's unionized, so these cracker capitalists are coming after our poultry businesses." Pat smiled proudly at his son's infiltration into Panforte's poultry empire. He said, "You wouldn't have suffered the boredom of Montgomery Street lawyers if you didn't have a plan in mind. Since I appear to be your first legal client, how about clueing me in?"

Terry replied, "I've arranged to deliver the legal documents for the sale of Great Western Poultry Co. to Panforte at his Lake Tahoe residence. I explained to my boss that I knew Mr. and Mrs. Panforte personally, and that Mr. Panforte had once worked for my grandfather. Since this is a community property state, Mrs. Panforte's signature is essential for the deal to close. I mentioned that I was fluent in Italian and therefore could explain the intricacies of the deal to Panforte's wife. Since I'd drafted most of the documents, I was fully aware of the deal points. I was most convincing when I pointed out to him that I wasn't yet admitted to the California Bar, and if any ethical questions came up later about the firm representing both sides in the deal, I'd be the harmless non-licenses fall guy." Pat shook his head in happy amazement at his son's manipulation of his employers. As they left Tosca's, Terry said, "How about driving up to Tahoe with me? Now that you're off cigars, you could use some of that mountain air in your old lungs."

"Ah, the Sierra! Terry, do you know what's engraved on the façade of the Supreme Court building in our capitol?" Pat asked playfully. Terry replied with mock seriousness: "*Give me men to match your mountains.*"

Pat Kelley grinned. "Amen."

Their four-hour drive to Panforte's North Shore lakeside chalet was a dialogue as intense as that of a theatrical director and playwright preparing for opening night. It was also the dress rehearsal for what father and son were about to do. For Terry this was his maiden trial, and during their journey to the Sierra he was composing his closing argument. The final summation, his father had taught him, was the literature of a lawsuit, and in its telling was the resolution of conflict. For Pat, collaborating with his son on the staging of a play that they had jointly authored was the most thrilling moment of his career. At last, through his son, his anonymity and compelled muteness would be ended.

Terry's law firm had arranged for him to meet with Angelina Panforte for an hour before her husband would arrive to discuss the closing documents of the sale of Great Western Poultry. She had been informed that Terry would be accompanied by a notary public. A Mexican maid led them into the living room of the Panforte chalet where Angelina Panforte was sitting on a large beige sofa sipping coffee from a demitasse cup. She had aged terribly since the trial. Her hair was snow white, and black circles emphasized the Tahoe blue of her eyes. She instantly recognized Signor Kelley as the kindly clerk who had been so sympathetic to her and her son during his trial. The young lawyer, a bit over six feet tall, had an athletic build like her son once had, but he moved with an almost feline-like grace. Angelina felt there was something familiar about this young lawyer's passionate hazel eyes and almost golden skin. Pat introduced Terry as the lawyer who would explain the terms of the legal documents necessary to complete the transaction. He told her that he would notarize their signatures. Then he told her that Terry was his son and that he had attended her son's trial, escorting his mother, Maria Bertolli Kelley. Wide-eyed, Angelina cupped her open mouth with a trembling hand. Pat said gently, "Signora Panforte, you needn't be frightened. Remember when we first spoke at your son's trial, I told you that he was presumed innocent?" She nodded meekly and Pat continued, "Well, we still think he's innocent and Terry can prove it, if only you will let him!"

"But how…after all these years…the lawyers and politicians?" she cried.

In Italian, Terence Kelley replied: "Signora, my father has devoted his career to our justice system. It almost always works the way it's supposed to. But it's a system of humans, so sometimes it errs. With your help we think we can correct the mistake in your son's case." Angelina noted that Terry's Italian, in contrast to his father's, was the flawless Tuscan dialect no doubt inherited from his mother. To Pat she said softly, "So what do you want of me?"

"All I ask is that you listen carefully to what your husband and Terry talk about. Then just do what's right," Pat said. Her eyelids dropped in assent.

When Fred Panforte arrived the three men shook hands and went into the dining room where Terry spread out the documents on the table. "You lawyers must hate trees, with all that paper," Panforte smirked.

"Mr. Panforte, I'm going to explain all these documents, but I will do so in Italian so it will be easier for both of you to follow my advice," Terry said. Fred Panforte shrugged indifferently. In Italian, Terry said, "My name is Terence Bertolli Kelley. I am the grandson of Bartolemeo Bertolli, the son of Maria and Pat Kelley..."

Panforte, wild-eyed, said, "Jesus, what the..." Terry held up his hand and said, "Just listen for a moment. There's more at stake here than a business deal. These sale documents bind Little Rock Enterprises to pay into escrow the sum of nine million dollars, payable to Fred and Angelina Panforte, as the sole owners of Great Western Poultry Company. Since California is a community property state, Mrs. Panforte's signature is required. Although your son has been eligible for parole for some time, Attorney General Moore has blocked his release. Even though your son has been a model prisoner, the man who prosecuted him is still convinced he should have been gassed!" Angelina shuddered at Terry's words. Terry continued, "You figured this out long ago. That's when you started playing politics to buy your son a gubernatorial pardon. Only you backed the wrong horse, so you've got no juice with Pat Brown's office. But I do!

"This brings us to the second batch of documents. These papers are for my signature. It's a petition to the Governor's clemency secretary for a pardon or parole for Bob Panforte to Placer County to live with his mother. The basis of the petition is that newly discovered evidence proves that Bob was wrongly convicted of a murder committed by someone else!" Fred pounded the table. "Jesus! That's great news!" he said.

"Shut up, Fred! He's not finished," Angelina said angrily, using his American name for the first time in their marriage. In Italian, Pat said,

"Excellent advice, Signora!"

Terry resumed: "What we do or don't do with this evidence of innocence will be decided in this room. We're going to have sort of a trial. I'll be the prosecutor of Paula's real killer and, therefore, in effect, I'll be your son's defender. You and your wife will be the jury. You will not be deciding your son's innocence, but you will determine the true murderer's guilt. Just like a criminal trial, your verdict must be unanimous. If either of you vote not guilty, our little trial never took place."

Terry arranged the papers in neat piles on the table before the Panfortes. He walked to the other side of the table, as though the dining room table was the jury rail. He paced as he spoke, transforming the Panforte dining room into the Pit. He said: "Think of what I'm about to say as a closing argument. All that I will tell you is contained in the petition that will assure your son's freedom. Before summarizing this newly discovered evidence, I must tell you its source. The evidence of your daughter-in-law's killer was discovered by the Chief Clerk of the Superior Court!" Both Panfortes glanced at Pat who was expressionless and relaxed. Terry remarked, "No doubt you're wondering why a mere court clerk would undertake a homicide investigation. But it would be a mistake to think of Patrick Kelley as a mere court attaché." Angelina nodded at Pat, but her husband was puzzled.

Terry continued, "You see, during the trial the Chief Clerk discovered a Fox ticket stub in the pocket of Paula's green coat – the coat that shielded her in her tomb! This ticket stub had been planted by your investigator under your direction, Fabrizio! Had the Chief Clerk allowed the stub to reach the jury room, your son would have been acquitted! But his acquittal would have been the product of your prostitution of American justice, just as your theft of Bartolemeo Bertolli's business had been! So the Chief Clerk suppressed that ticket stub and the jury never learned of it. But my father felt compelled to find the truth about Paula's death, and his search led him to Petaluma.

"Once there, Isador Poplack introduced him to a Great Western Poultry Company truck driver named Manuel Abascal. Abascal was an illegal alien in your employ with a terribly sick mother. Out of fear or guilt or both, he told the clerk the truth about his relationship with his bosses – both you and your son!"

"What the fuck is going on here?" Fred Panforte yelled in English. In English, Pat said menacingly, "This isn't Farneta, Fabrizio, and Terry's not Bertolli! He's an American boy, and playing hardball is his national pastime. You better get a hold on yourself. Do you really think those Southern Elmer Gantry's will go through with this deal when they read about what really went on at your chicken ranch?" Panforte slumped back in his chair.

"Let my words take you back to the first week in June 1949," Terry's mellifluous baritone promised. "It's Sunday morning, June 4th. Unexpectedly, your daughter-in-law and grandson show up on your doorstep. Paula's almost hysterical, and demands that you come out to their car where she has something to show you. She shows you a pair of brown loafers and tells you they belong to a Mexican ranch hand. She says he called her at home earlier and claimed he was having a homosexual relationship with your son! She's hurt and livid and tells you she wants a divorce. At your soothing Lucchesi best you assure her it's a lie, a cheap extortion by a greaser. You tell her not to mention it to anyone and that you'll go immediately to Petaluma and get the truth. You tell her you need his loafers to confront him. Mollified by your evident sincerity, she agrees. Then you tell your wife a phony story that Paula's upset about Bob's Petaluma work schedule, so you're going to Petaluma to straighten everything out.

"In your Caddy, you drive to Petaluma, confront the poor Mexican kid with his shoes and threaten to kill him and ship his sick mother and sister back to Tijuana if he ever mentions your son's name again! Satisfied that you've petrified him, you drive to your Mt. Tamalpais hunting cabin, pick up an Army entrenching tool and drive up the summit and excavate a grave for your daughter-in-law. When you finish your grave digging you transplant a sword fern to the head of her grave. It's a nice touch, you think, sort of a natural tombstone. Back at your cabin you dye Abascal's loafers white, wash up and drive to Francisco Street for that touching scene with your grandson. While your son's mixing you and Paula drinks in his kitchen you tell her that the Mexican has admitted that he made up his story to get money for his mother. You tell her that you've arranged for her to meet with him and his priest so that he can confess what he's done.

"You spend the night at your Sonoma ranch waiting for that certain moment when Paula's alone. Monday evening you call your wife and she tells you that Paula's gone to the movies and your son is home with the baby, but he's been drinking again. You drive to the Marina, only this time you park your Caddy across from the Palace of Fine Arts, around the block from their home. You let yourself in with your key and find your son passed out on the couch with a *True Detective* magazine sprawled on his chest. Perfect, you think, everything's just perfect. You go down to the garage and drive the '47 Chevy to the Fox to pick up Paula. After the movie's out she sees the Chevy and thinks her husband's come to pick her up. She's happy, then surprised when she sees you're the driver. You quickly explain that the Mexican kid is over at your hunting cabin with his priest waiting to confess to her. She tells you you're such a dear for doing this for them and jumps into the passenger seat. She's still quite tipsy from too much booze. She removes her white pumps and falls asleep before you reach the Golden Gate Bridge tollgate. She will never awake from her sleep. Once at your Mt. Tam cabin, you brutally beat your slumbering daughter-in-law, stuff her in the trunk of the Chevy and toss in the Army entrenching tool.

"When you reach the grave you'd prepared the previous day there's just a sliver of a moon. But you don't need a full moon. You knew the pile of loose dirt you'd previously dug rests, pyramid-like, on the right edge of the grave where you had shoveled it. You unwrap her from her green coat and pull it from the Chevy's trunk. Was that a groan, you ask yourself. No matter, you think, as you reach for the jack handle next to the spare tire. You slide down the slope, your steps sure. You cover the floor of her grave with her green coat, sealing off the dampness, cushioning her eternal bed from pebbles and subterranean roots that might disturb her soft body. You lay the jack handle on the edge of the grave, then climb back up the hill for her. You carry and drag her down to the fallen pines. It had been more of a struggle than you'd anticipated, but at last you lay her on her back, on her green coat, in her own grave. You see the outline of her bounteous breasts stretching her blouse and then, pulling it back, the tides of breath and life still ebbing in her.

"A glitter of silver hovers above her in the black of the forest night and comet-like descends upon her, an icy jet stream of unimaginable malice in its wake, and cracks against her skull! Jack handle kisses auburn hair. The mountain echoes to the sound of steel and bone, silencing the crickets' nighttime symphony, and Paula's breasts slump in resignation for the final time. You're frozen for a moment, your muscles taut. Then a reservoir of perverse madness bursts from your soul and you begin beating on her breasts with your fists, tattooing them with the ball-like imprints of your shame. As suddenly as your desecration of her began, you stop to catch your breath. You gently rearrange her body, rolling her onto her side. You turn her lovely face so that her familiar green coat will console the schism you'd carved in her skull with steel. You push her knees to her chest so she can cuddle herself through eternity." Terence Bertolli Kelley allowed a moment of memorial silence and then breathlessly quoted Hamlet: "*Murder though it have no tongue, will speak with most miraculous organ.*"

Angelina Panforte stared, but not in disbelief, at her husband. Fred Panforte calmly glared at his accusers, and in English, said: "Very impressive! But I think you've missed your calling. You should be a novelist. The Mexican punk's bullshit is what real lawyers call hearsay, so it ain't admissible." Terry smiled sardonically. "Fabrizio, what a real lawyer will tell you is that parole or clemency proceedings are functions of the executive branch. As such, they are administrative hearings where the rules of courtroom evidence don't apply. More often than not they are banquets of hearsay! So your objection is overruled, although your ignorance is duly noted."

In English, Angelina said: "He's not finished." Terry resumed: "Your daughter-in-law secure in the mountain grave, you drive back to the City. You drive to Fort Point, tie Paula's white pumps to the Chevy jack handle and toss them into the Bay. You drive to Francisco Street and park the Chevy in your son's garage. You take the Army entrenching tool out of the trunk and set it next to the garbage can. It doesn't occur to you that placing this tool with Mt. Tam soil on it in your son's garage will link him to Paula's grave. You lock up and walk to your Cadillac for the drive to your Sonoma ranch that you'd told your wife you'd be staying at."

Terry switched back to Italian, saying: "Fabrizio, you disappoint me. From Farneta until this moment, you've studied men greater than yourself and learned or pilfered their secrets so you could anticipate their actions. You read Bertolli's confidential correspondence, and he trusted you to place his business in your hands to pursue his dreams of opera in San Francisco. Your flaw is your inability to appreciate those you consider lesser men than yourself. So you foisted phony evidence on a silent court clerk, certain that a mere bureaucrat would not discover it or if he did, would do nothing about it. But it was this ticket stub that revealed your culpability to him and spirited his quest for the truth. The only other mistake in your perfect crime was underestimating your own son. When you talked to him on the phone after he'd reported Paula missing, you told him to stick to his story and not to volunteer anything. You didn't think the entrenching tool you'd left in his garage would puzzle him and stimulate thoughts of Marin as a locale for Paula. Worst of all, you failed to realize your son's desperate faith that his wife was still alive!

"I'm shocked that at this moment you seem to have lost your analytical abilities. You don't realize that you have only two choices. You can either privately admit your guilt to your wife and us, in which case the sale of Great Western Poultry will go through and we will privately intervene with the Governor to secure your son's release. Or you can continue living your lie, and I will file *a friend of the court* petition on your son's behalf with suitable copies to the press and your Arkansas buyers. Once your shame is public, you're finished, Fabrizio!"

Panforte's eyes darted to his wife, but she ignored him. Pat intervened, "Counsel, perhaps you should explain the third set of documents that you've prepared for signature. I think that Signor Panforte should be fully informed on the gravity of his decision." Terry slid the documents across the table to the Panfortes. "Your signature on these documents effectively confirms your private admission of guilt to everyone in this room. These papers direct the disbursement of the $9 million purchase price of Great Western Poultry. Under the terms, you get one-third, Mrs. Panforte gets a third and the remaining third goes to your son upon his release from prison. You will place one-half of your proceeds into a trust for a ten year-old boy. Your son will do likewise with his share. This trust fund is for a boy named Billy Bonfiglio. He's your biological grandson, and we can only hope that your genes are recessive. He was adopted by a caring couple. The trust fund is a modest acknowledgement of the kid's terrible losses. You've got a choice. Don't sign these papers, and I sign my papers and you can kiss your millions goodbye. Sign the papers and I tear up my petition of truth."

Fred Panforte's head collapsed into his hands, and his chest heaved with his sobs. He looked up at his wife, "What do I do?" he pleaded. Angelina rose from her chair and said, "Sign the papers, Fred!" She picked up a three-page document from the third stack. She placed her signature on it and flung it across the table at her husband. "Sign this one first. It's our property settlement and divorce papers! You keep the Sea Cliff house and I'll have this place for Robert and me. I'd greatly appreciate your leaving now. I'll pack your things and send them to you." Panforte started to protest, but she silenced him: *"Basta! Firma!"*

And he did. Terry Kelley tore up his petition and gave it to Fabrizio as a tattered memento of his shame. After he'd left, Angelina showed the Kelley men to the door. She took Pat's hand and said, "Will I be able to see my grandson?"

"I'm afraid not, Angelina. The boy's been given a completely new identity by the court," Pat said. He removed a photo from his briefcase and handed it to her. "Here's a picture of him on his tenth birthday. I'm sorry it's black and white. You should know he has your lovely blue eyes."

"You are a good man, and you have a fine son. My words can never thank you enough. Please tell Maria I...I...didn't..." Pat cut her off: "She knows you had nothing to do with her father's troubles. Goodbye, Angelina, and good luck."

On the drive back to the City, father and son were uncharacteristically quiet until they were out of the mountains east of Sacramento. Pat broke their silence, suggesting that Terry ought to be the one to break the news to his mother. Terry shook his head, "No way. I'll sit in with you, but she's your wife, and you're the one who's vindicated her. I just gave you a narrative voice." Pat rubbed his chin as his son drove onto the freeway. "You know, Dad, I've never forgotten that night you whipped that Marine on the steps of the Italian Church. You taught me a lot that night." Pat dreaded his boy's recollection of his homicidal moment. Pat just shook his head. "You feel guilty that I saw the darkness you were capable of, don't you? Dad, get over it! You and mom tried to make me a renaissance man. I think you did a damn good job. When you attacked that Marine you taught me that ruthlessness in defense of love is no vice. That's what we taught old man Panforte tonight."

When they arrived at Crestlake Drive they found Maria dozing on the living room sofa, Kathleen's tape of her Julliard performance of Beethoven's final sonata playing. Pat gently roused her. Through sleepy eyes, she saw her two men standing over her. Pleasantly surprised that they were back so soon from what they'd told her was a weekend gambling trip, she dreamily asked, "Did you guys win?" Pouring them each a glass of port, Pat said, "That's one way of putting it." Maria sat up and straightened her baby blue robe. She intuited that there was more than a gaming sojourn to be told. Her son explained that they'd indeed gambled at North Shore, that they had pitted their characters against another man's and that to understand the stakes they'd played for she must listen to Pat's story. With that introduction, Pat told his wife the full narrative of his investigation of the Panforte murder case, including Angelina's wedding night. Maria, her eyes wide, covered her mouth with her palm. She was mortified that she had prayed for

Bob Panforte's execution as the penance for his father's sins. Her husband concluded: "All these years I've been haunted that I've kept this from you. But I couldn't tolerate the tale's apparent ending. Darling, I couldn't bear to inflict more pain on you. Until Terry came up with a decent final chapter, I didn't know what else to do."

Maria turned to her son and he told her of the plan they had jointly hatched at Tosca's. He replicated their mock two-person jury trial, and in a voice as steely as she had ever heard, told her the starkly brutal choice they had given the last *Precious One*. She looked to her husband for the verdict, and with assassin-like coldness he told her: "As Fabrizio always has, he chose a coward's way to hide his shame." Maria took a final sip of port. She studied her husband and son and marveled at their composure. She had prayed her entire adult life for this moment, but she had never imagined that her husband and son would be the agency of Fabrizio's destruction. But it was not triumph that she felt. It was as though her precious men had exorcised her soul, liberating her to love without memories' scars, healing a little girl's wounds. Pat said gently, "Maria, Fabrizio tried to rob your father's dignity to make it his own. He failed, but he kidnapped Antoinette's love from both of you. We simply took from him the only decencies in his life – his wife, his son, his grandson." Father and son rose from the loveseat and embraced. Terry lifted his mother into his arms and kissed her goodnight.

Alone in their bed, Pat rested his head on his wife's breasts, her breathing rocking him to sleep. She ran her fingers through his hair and gently petted his cheek. She closed her dark, watering eyes and held him close, at last secure that this man with his awkward and delicate heart was hers. And always would be.

THE END

ABOUT THE AUTHOR

Phil Ryan is a native San Franciscan whose interest in trial law began as a young boy when he sat through a front-page murder trial with his court-reporter father. After discharge from the Army, he entered into public service in 1962 as the youngest legislative aide in the California legislature, and worked as a civil rights organizer during the Mississippi Freedom Summer. It was his experience battling Jim Crow politics that he considers the seminal moment in his life.

Ryan attended Santa Clara University and graduated *cum laude* from Howard University Law School in 1969. That same year he served as Project Director of the New Mobilization to End the Vietnam War, organizing a demonstration that attracted 250,000 people to Golden Gate Park.

Crafting a high-profile, 37-year career as a trial lawyer, Ryan specialized in criminal defense and entertainment law. His celebrity clients included Academy Award winning movie stars, all-star professional atheletes, elected public officials, sitting judges, authors and rock stars. The *San Francisco Chronicle* featured him as "San Francisco's Rock n' Roll Lawyer."

Ryan retired from law in 2006 and has since spent his time writing books, essays, news stories and poetry. *All Sins Remembered* is his first novel in a trilogy. His second novel, *Bella Cora*, is set in Gold Rush San Francisco. He lives with his wife, Dr. Dina Bitton, on Russian Hill in San Francisco.